Elizabeth Elgin served in the WRNS during the Second World War, and met her husband on board a submarine depot ship. A keen gardener, she has two daughters and five grandsons and lives in a lovely Roman village near York.

ELIZABETH ELGIN

All the Sweet Promises

GRAFTON BOOKS
A Division of the Collins Publishing Group

LONDON GLASGOW
TORONTO SYDNEY AUCKLAND

Grafton Books
A Division of the Collins Publishing Group
8 Grafton Street, London W1X 3LA

A Grafton Paperback Original 1990

ISBN 0-586-20804-6

Printed and bound in Great Britain by
Collins, Glasgow

Set in Times

To
the Wren ratings
of the 3rd & 7th submarine flotillas
Holy Loch & Rothesay
1939–1945

1

Vi looked again at the letter half-hidden behind the sepia vase on the kitchen mantel and wondered bitterly whose fault it had been. Some seaman pissed out of his mind in a dock-road pub, like as not. Ale talk for listening ears. Careless talk, that cost lives.

'Taking ammo to the Middle East. Danger money this trip, so fill yer boots, lads. Sup up.' Somewhere, someone had opened his mouth and Gerry had paid; him, and fifty others.

The letter was addressed to Mrs Violet Theresa McKeown and she took it down, holding it between finger and thumb. She didn't take out the folded sheet. There was no need. Since it arrived four days ago, every last word was beaten into her brain.

'. . . and it is with regret we must inform you that your husband Gerald Patrick McKeown has been reported missing, believed lost at sea as a result of enemy action on the night of 23rd/24th April, 1941 . . .'

There was more, of course, about sympathy and sorrow and about writing again when they had anything more to tell her. She hadn't been able to read the signature at the bottom of the page, and that seemed wrong, somehow. A man from the shipping line tells you your husband has been lost at sea and you don't even know his name. There were the initials GWE/BW typed at the top of the letter but they hadn't helped. Dead is dead, no matter who signs the warrant, though it might have been nice to think that BW had felt compassion when she typed that letter and a

7

bit of respect, maybe, for Stoker Gerry McKeown of the Mercantile Marine.

Vi slipped the envelope into the attaché case packed ready for the shelter. All her important things were in that case: her marriage certificate and wedding snaps; her Post Office bank book, rent book and ration book. And Gerry's last letter.

'. . . Thanks for a fine leave. You are the best there is and I love you, Vi. Take care of yourself . . .'

She closed her eyes tightly. Gerry didn't often use her name. *Girl*, he called her, but this last time he'd called her *Vi* and written that he loved her, and he'd never done that before. Not ever. But he'd known, hadn't he, that this trip was his last.

'Come home to me,' she'd whispered when he left. 'Promise you'll take care. *Promise*, Gerry.'

But it hadn't been up to him. The SS *Emma Bates*'s name was on that torpedo, so he hadn't had much of a choice.

She reached for her mother's photograph and laid it in the case with the rest of the things. She was glad Mam hadn't lived to see another war. The last one had brought her trouble enough. Four kids to rear and a husband coughing away his lungs from mustard gas. Da had died a year after the armistice, so they hadn't needed to give Mam a pension.

Vi looked around the kitchen and wondered why she had scrubbed the floor and cleaned the window. Tonight there would be another raid, sure as hell there would, and everything would be covered with muck and dust again. Tonight, if the bombers came, it would be for the seventh night in a row; a whole week without sleep. London was almost at a standstill, said the man in the cigarette queue, and now it was Liverpool's turn. The Germans, he reckoned, were trying to wipe out the docks, yet somehow

8

the city centre seemed to be getting the worst of it – and all the shops and offices and streets of little houses.

Vi closed her eyes. *Mother of God, don't let them get my house. They've taken my man and my job; let me keep my home.*

The gate handle clicked sharply and she drew aside the lace curtain. A man crossed the yard and rattled the door knob.

'Are y'there, Vi?'

'Richie. Come in.'

Richie Daly had sailed down the Mersey in the same convoy as Gerry and now he was home. Vi's heart contracted painfully then settled into a dull ache.

'All right, then? Bearing up, are you?'

'Just about.' She didn't like Richie Daly. A shifty-eyed little devil, and his wife always expecting.

'I see they got Lewis's, Vi.'

'Yes. Two nights back.' No need to remind her. She'd worked there, hadn't she?

'So how are you making out?'

'I'll manage. There'll be other jobs. But what brought you, Richie?'

She knew why he had come and what he would tell her, and she didn't want to hear it. Yet still she asked for news of the *Emma Bates*.

'Well, bein' as how I was there, like.' He drew out a chair and settled his elbows on the table. 'Bein' as how I saw what happened that night . . .'

'Yes?' She sucked in her breath, angrily, noisily.

'Well, old Gerry didn't suffer, Vi. Be sure of that. The *Emma* was just astern of us in the convoy and keepin' station fine, even though she was a coal-burner.'

'She'd keep station all right, with Gerry shovellin'.'

'Yes.' He stared fixedly down. 'Well, one minute the old tub was there and the next – ' He slammed a fist into

9

the palm of his hand. 'They was carryin' ammunition, see. They wouldn't know a thing, any of them. Commodore didn't even stop to look for survivors, so don't worry yourself none.'

But she did worry and she needed to know every last detail.

'Where did it happen?'

'Two days out from Halifax. Canadian destroyer escort had just left us.'

'But I thought he was going to Alexandria.'

'Naw. The *Emma* left Liverpool without cargo; took RAF bods to Canada then loaded up with cordite and shells for the return trip. It was a clear night. We was all sittin' targets. Always at night those bastards do it. It's a dirty way of fightin', but it was quick for old Gerry.'

'Yes,' she said dully. 'Quick.'

'Ah, well.' He got to his feet, pushing the chair legs against the floor tiles with a grating that set her teeth on edge. 'I'll be goin'.'

'It was good of you to come, Richie.'

Liar. You hate him for coming because he's told you that Gerry isn't just missing, but dead.

''s all right. Just thought you'd rest a bit easier if you knew he didn't suffer none. Well – I suppose I'd better get goin' . . .'

That's right. Shove off. I don't want you here. It's Gerry I want. It's him should've been coming home tonight.

'Hey, listen.' He turned, foot in door. 'What about a drink, eh?' He reached out, placing a hand on either shoulder, pulling her nearer. 'I'll be in the Tarleton about nine; will I see you, Vi?'

'No, you'll not.' She shrugged away his hands with an exaggerated gesture. 'At nine o'clock we'll all be in the shelter, like as not. And won't your wife be needing a

10

hand when the sirens go? Getting near her time again, isn't she?'

'Aw, don't worry about Lil. It's you I'm thinking about, Vi. A well-set-up woman like yourself must be – you know . . .' He was grinning. A dirty little grin.

'No, I don't know. Must be *what*?'

He was too stupid to catch the contempt in her voice or heed the warning that narrowed her eyes.

'Well, missin' it, like. Y'know. A bit of the other.'

'Oh, I see. And you're offerin' . . .?'

'That's right.' His eyes brightened and he reached for her again, a hand trailing her breasts. 'I've been at sea a long time. Come on upstairs, Vi.'

He pressed nearer and she felt the hardening in his loins. There were small ginger hairs on his chin and his groping mouth stank of beer. Disgust shivered through her, and stepping out of the reach of his hands she hissed, 'Get out of my house, you mucky little sod! Bloody get out, or I'll swing for yer!'

The sepia vase hurtled across the room and she heard the crash as it shattered against the tiles, heard the slamming of the door and running footsteps. Then the red mists cleared and she sank to her knees, picking up the pieces, moaning softly. Gerry's mam, God rest her, had given her that vase. '*Maybe you can find a use for it, girl.*'

The tears came then; great gasping sobs she had been unwilling and unable to cry since the day of the letter. They came from the deeps of her heart and rose to a wail of anguish.

'Gerry lad, why, *why*? You said you'd come home. You *promised*.'

She knelt there long after the sobs were spent, hugging herself tightly, eyes closed. The floor was hard and cold and her knees throbbed with pain, but still she crouched

11

there. Gerry was dead and she was alive. Sore knees were a small part of her penance.

Stiffly, reluctantly, she rose to her feet and began to sweep up the litter of broken china. She had never liked that vase. Probably Ma McKeown hadn't liked it either.

'Thanks, Ma.' A small, sad smile lifted the corners of Vi's mouth. 'I found a use for it.'

The smile flickered and faded. Since the arrival of the letter a coldness had grown inside her, and a pain in her throat that wasn't really a pain but a hard, tight ball of anger. It got in the way when she had tried to cry yet it allowed no room for self-pity. All her feelings had been for Gerry, with the coal-pitted hands, who had never harmed a soul. Gerry, with the bitty hair, whose right foot turned in when he walked. Gerry, who had loved her.

Sighing, she lifted the dustbin lid and watched the brown china pieces slip from the shovel, then raised her eyes to the May sky. It was hard to believe that very soon that innocent sky could throb with the sounds of death. Liverpool was taking a beating, and rumours were free for the asking on every street corner and in every food queue. There had been rioting down by the docks, some said, but no one knew exactly where; and Mrs Norris swore they were throwing the dead into mass graves, and half of them good Catholics without the last rites.

Vi wished she could fire a gun and shoot down those bombers if only for what they had done to Gerry, but it was easy to be brave in this small, precious house when the sun still shone in the evening sky and a west wind blew away the stench of bombing and burning and broken bodies. It was a different matter when the sirens wailed and she hurried, dry-mouthed, into the clammy cold of St Joseph's crypt. Fear came easily then, even though it was the deepest and safest shelter for streets around. And when the all clear sounded, even though the realization that she had survived yet another night sent relief singing through her, there was the agony of wondering what she would find when she returned to Lyra Street. Mary had told her not to be a fool, to come to her house and get a decent night's sleep. Mary lived in Ormskirk, and so far they had been lucky there. But Vi needed to be in her own little home. It was all she had left now, so she had thanked her sister and left it at that.

Breathing deeply, fighting sudden fresh tears, she stared at the whitewashed walls of the tiny, tidy yard. Gerry was gone, but his rose still grew there. Last autumn he had planted it.

'A red rose for Lancashire, girl.'

'But Gerry, it'll never grow.' Not here, she had thought. Not in this airless back yard with its cat-fouled alley, yet now it bore shining green leaves and four fat flower buds – and Gerry would never see them.

The fingers on the clock of St Joseph's church pointed to eight, though it had long since ceased to chime the hours. Chiming clocks and the ringing of church bells were forbidden for the duration of hostilities, or until the invasion came. They'd ring out loud and clear then.

But maybe there wouldn't be an invasion. It was nearly a year since Dunkirk, and if they'd been going to come, surely they'd not have waited this long.

The potman at the Tarleton had it all worked out, though. The Germans would invade, he said. The air raids on London and Liverpool and Birmingham and Clydeside were to knock out communications and close roads and railways and make everybody so pig-sick that they'd welcome Hitler with open arms. He'd gone on saying it until people complained and the landlord was forced to tell him that such talk amounted to the spreading of gloom and despondency; it was almost as bad as careless talk and

13

would land him in the Bridewell if the police got to hear about it.

Eight o'clock. Soon it would begin to grow dark, and she hadn't seen to the house yet.

Since the bombing had started, the ritual checking of number seven Lyra Street had given Vi comfort. It was all she had left of Gerry, now. The ugly little terrace house was her husband, her lover and the child she had never conceived. It was, she supposed, her last link with sanity.

Almost without thinking she reached down to turn off the gas and water taps, then climbed the narrow stairs and pushed open the door to her right, smiling at the riot of roses that covered the walls. Her bedroom wallpaper never failed to give her pleasure. It was like awakening each morning in a garden in the country, though Gerry had cursed something awful, matching up the roses and rosebuds on the uneven walls. They had ignored the seriousness of the news bulletins that night and taken a trip down the Mersey on the *Royal Iris* to celebrate the finishing of their bedroom, though Mr Chamberlain had told them next day that they were at war with Germany. So Vi called them her last-day-of-peace roses and vowed they would remain there until the war was over, even if it lasted four years, like the last one had done. Now those roses reminded her of Gerry, who had pasted them there, and she wondered if she would ever find the courage to scrape them off.

Sighing, she began to fill a carrier bag with essentials; an insurance, she supposed, in case the worst happened. Shoes first, then a towel, soap and toothbrush; and stockings and knickers, of course, and room enough left for her handbag, gas mask and a warm woolly scarf.

There was nothing to check in the front parlour; hardly anything to say goodbye to, for the room was empty of furniture and must remain that way until the shops would

14

once again have chairs and sofas and rugs and curtains to sell.

Vi walked across the echoing emptiness to gaze at the mantel shelf and the reminders it held of Gerry. A vase from Shanghai; a pair of plates, hand-painted with gold dragons, from Hong Kong and, on his last trip but one, the two goblets. They were heavy and sparkled when she held them to the light, and she thought they were the most beautiful things she would ever own.

'But whatever'll we do with crystal glasses, Gerry?'

'We'll drink out of 'em, thick 'ead,' he assured her solemnly. 'When this old war's over we'll have wine every Christmas, and that's a promise, girl.'

So she had placed them on the mantel with the vase and the dragon plates, and Gerry had promised her two more, next time he docked in Cape Town. Now, not knowing why, she lifted them down. Usually she never took anything but essentials to the shelter, but tonight, after Richie Daly had blundered into her kitchen, she needed the comfort of those glasses. Gently she placed them in the carrier bag.

'That's it, then.' She drew the thick blackout curtains and the nightly ritual was finished. Carrier bag and coat lay on the kitchen table beside the attaché case. Everything was ready and she returned to the yard to sit on the bench beside the rose tree, to sit and wait, eyes closed, and will her clenched fingers one by one into relaxation.

The bombers were late tonight, but there was still time, she supposed. Double British Summer Time added two hours of daylight and the Luftwaffe needed the cover of darkness. But soon the light would begin to fade; then fire watchers would take up positions on rooftops and each air-raid warden and ambulance driver would feel a churning in his stomach. At fire stations and first-aid posts and rest centres, men and women would look up at the sky just as she, Vi McKeown, was doing now.

She closed her eyes, concentrating once again on her tightening fingers, trying not to think of Richie Daly and the *Emma Bates*; trying not to weep when she thought about the waste of a good life, of fifty good lives.

She was still sitting there when the silence began, those few moments of suspended time that came before the sounding of the air-raid sirens. She had come to recognize that silence, to smell it, almost. It was a void so strange and complete that there was no mistaking it. They were coming again; coming to kill and maim and blast and burn.

Reluctantly she rose to her feet, her breathing loud and harsh, the weariness she had been fighting since the air raids started overpowering her senses. God, but she was so afraid. Afraid of tonight and tomorrow and all the empty tomorrows. It was as if the bombing was draining her of all feeling, leaving her so spent that all she wanted to do was to close her eyes and not open them again until it was all over.

The first of the sirens sounded distantly and she ran to the kitchen, gathering up her belongings with hands that shook. Her mouth had gone dry again, fear writhed through her. Turning the back-door key, she looked longingly at the lavatory door. Why did that awful wailing always make her want to pee?

Now another siren had taken up the warning. Nearer, this one, its strident undulation beating inside her head. For just a few seconds she stood petrified; then, taking a deep, shuddering breath, she ran down the entry and into Lyra Street.

The ARP warden, out of work since 1930 and now a man of standing with his steel helmet, army-style respirator and dangling whistle, banged on the door of number five pleading through the letterbox with its occupant.

16

'You'll be safer in the shelter, Mrs Norris.' Grumbling, he turned to Vi. 'She does this every blasted night, the stubborn old biddy.'

'Best leave her,' Vi offered. 'She says it's more comfortable under the kitchen table. Reckons that if her name is on a bomb it'll find her, wherever she is.'

'And who are you, then?' The warden had no time for niceties.

'Mrs McKeown from number seven, and you'll not get Mrs Norris out of there, not if you rattle that letterbox all night.'

Poor, silly Ma Norris, who had never been quite right since her three sons were killed on the Somme in the last war. Three telegrams, all in the same week. Enough to drive a saint round the bend.

'And what about number nine?'

'Gone to Preston, to relations,' Vi called over her shoulder, hurrying to the gate of St Joseph's, where Father O'Flaherty would be checking in his flock. Then, against all her better instincts, she stopped and slowly turned to look back down Lyra Street. Amazed, she shook her head. Never look back, Gerry always said. Just four weeks ago, as they stood at the dockyard gate he had said, 'Ta-ra well, girl.' Then he'd kissed her and walked away; and though she waited until he was out of sight, he had never once looked back to where she stood.

All right, so sailors considered it unlucky, she thought defiantly, but women were different. Women did silly things all the time; that's why they were women. Gently, sadly, she smiled at her house; her house and Gerry's.

'I'll not be long,' she whispered, then turning abruptly, walked quickly towards the church.

'And when,' demanded the Countess of Donnington of her daughter, 'are you going to give me a date? I mean, I feel so foolish, don't I?'

17

The Countess was annoyed. Only that morning she had suffered humiliation at the hands of a shop assistant in Harrods, and anger still raged through her. 'And please take that towel off your head and have the goodness to look at me when I'm speaking to you!'

'Sorry.' Lucinda Bainbridge ran her fingers through her half-dry hair. 'I was listening, truly I was, and I'm sorry you feel foolish.'

'Don't be pert. Just give me one good reason why you and Charles cannot be married at once.'

'Well, I – I'd like to wait a little while, I suppose.'

'I see. And had you forgotten you will be twenty in November? Has it ever occurred to you that I was wedded and bedded and well pregnant by the time I was your age? Most of the girls who came out with you are married, so why must you be different?'

'Perhaps because I've always thought it might be nice to have a honeymoon in Venice.'

'Well, you can't. No one can go to Venice – or anywhere else, for that matter – until this dreary war is over, so please stop prevaricating.'

'Yes, Mama.' Once more Lucinda took refuge beneath the towel and began to rub furiously. Mama was on her pet hobbyhorse again and it was too foolish, really it was, to have a hurried wedding in London, where she hardly knew a soul, when it could all be so lovely at Lady Mead. When the government let them live there again, of course.

'I mean, Charles won't always be at the War Office. They could post him to a regiment and send him abroad just like that!' Elegantly, dramatically, the Countess snapped her fingers. 'And where would you be if he got killed? You should get married now and get that baby started. That's all I ask, Lucinda. At least try to see my point of view.'

'I do. Oh, I do.' Lucinda accepted her mother's need

18

for a Bainbridge heir and she understood her feelings of guilt, too, even though no one ever blamed her for the accident. But there had been no more children, and now Cousin Charlie would inherit. But please, Mama, Lucinda pleaded silently, don't treat me like a complete idiot. I realized a long time ago why you were so set on Charlie and me marrying, and I'm very fond of him, and I'd like to go on living at Lady Mead for the rest of my life. But let me do it in my own time, and *don't* make me feel like a brood mare.

'I mean, don't you think I've got worries enough, Lucinda, what with this terrible war and the bombing? And if those Germans ever get here, we'll lose everything. They don't like the aristocracy.'

'I rather think that's the Communists.'

'And what about all the shortages? It's enough to turn one grey.'

Only that morning she had stood, she, Kitty Bainbridge, had *actually stood* in a queue for nail polish, and when it came to her turn there was no more left. 'I'm sorry, modom, don't blame me for the shortages. There *is* a war on, you know,' the common little bitch had said with relish. And soon there would be a shortage of clothing and wouldn't those shop girls have a field day, then!

'Worries enough, I said. And when did you last see Charles? You spend too much time with those wounded soldiers.'

'Airmen, Mama.'

'You're running after them morning, noon and night. I suppose you'll be off with them to the theatre again, when you ought to be with Charles.'

'Charlie's fire watching tonight, and I saw him a couple of days ago.'

Two days ago, in this very room, Mama. Charlie got annoyed with me because I wouldn't let him. Called me

19

frigid and said all the other chaps' girls were willing enough, and would it matter all that much if he put a bun in the oven for me? So I let him, Mama, right there on the sofa, and it wasn't a bit nice, and in the end Charlie went off in a huff . . .

'A couple of days ago? And what did he say? That boy will go off with someone else, mark my words.'

'No he won't. We'll be married, I promise we will.'

And she hoped she would feel better about getting the baby everyone seemed to want so much. She wanted it too, and maybe when she and Charlie were married and in bed and they'd had a few drinks and she was wearing a black nightie, then maybe it wouldn't be so bad.

'Married! I wish I could be sure of that.' Lady Kitty looked obliquely at her daughter. Lucinda was tall and beautiful, and most times obedient and biddable. It was a pity she was an only child; the fault of the riding accident, of course. Secretly, she had been grateful to the farmer who had strung barbed wire across that particular gate.

Kitty Bainbridge had not enjoyed her pregnancy, though she accepted that her family record had been taken into account when Donnington proposed. The Cravens were a prolific lot, wretchedly poor but very fertile. There had been eight of them, four girls and four boys, and only ten years between first and last. So Kitty Craven had been welcomed to Lady Mead, and the Dowager died happy in the knowledge that her daughter-in-law of six months was five months pregnant.

But the getting of that child was not the pleasurable romp she had been led to believe, and her pregnancy was a sick one. As for Lucinda's birth – she still shuddered just to think of it, and she had prayed that the next one would produce the son she so desperately needed to enable her to call a halt to the whole disagreeable business. But fate intervened and the young Countess of

Donnington was thrown from her horse and, badly cut and bruised, lay concussed for two days and nights.

Poor Kitty, everyone said, when she did not conceive again; thank goodness there's a lesser Bainbridge to carry on the line.

Thank goodness indeed, poor Kitty agreed, and from then on Lady Lucinda, smiling in her pram, and her three-year-old cousin Charles, featured hugely in her future plans. And when they married, thought the Countess happily, the Bainbridge comforts would still be hers to manipulate, provided the Earl popped off first and, as he was fifteen years older, it was almost certain that he would.

'Well,' said the Countess, '*are* you to be out on the town again with your wounded soldiers?'

'Well, they do rather want to take in a show, but we'll have to see what's open. Don't worry, though. If there's another raid and it gets bad, we'll go to the nearest tube station. It's safe enough down there.'

Kitty Bainbridge closed her eyes and shuddered. She had had enough of the blackout and the bombing and the shortages, and if she let herself think too much about the invasion she would become quite ill. It was all too much, waiting for that upstart Hitler to make up his mind; to envisage the Germans strutting down the Mall as they'd strutted down the Champs Élysées. And all because of Poland!

'Oh, and could I please have the hot-water ration today, Mama? You did have it yesterday and Thursday too, and I must have a bath.'

'Then you'll have to take it standing up in cook's enamel bowl.' If they'd had a cook! If the wretched woman hadn't taken herself off to war work in a factory canteen for three times the money, or so she had said. 'They hit the mains last night with a land mine. No electricity for two

21

days, the gas turned off too, and now no water. It's beyond belief, it really is. I wonder sometimes what the world is coming to.'

Our world, Mama, Lucinda brooded. Yours and mine. It's changing, but you won't accept it. There are no servants now, no seasons in London or Monte, and our lovely, stubborn, precious little island might be invaded any day. France has gone, and Belgium and Holland, and the German army is only a few miles away across the Channel. I know why you are so jumpy, Mama, but you mustn't think you are the only one who is being put out. This is everybody's war; we are *all* suffering and we are *all* afraid . . .

'Look, don't get upset. It doesn't matter about the bath.' It was selfish even to think of one when the fire service needed every drop of water to douse the bombed, blazing buildings. She laid an arm around her mother's shoulders. 'You're tired – everyone is. Why don't you pack a bag and go to Cromlech? You'd be able to get some sleep up there and – '

'Scotland? How can I go there? McNair's living in Cromlech, or had you forgotten?'

McNair, the elderly gillie who had agreed to live as caretaker in the Earl's shooting lodge. Lady Kitty had been furious, declaring that the man was arrogant enough without giving him licence to sleep in his employer's bed and sit upon his lavatory.

'It's either the McNairs or a dozen bombed-outs from Clydeside, m'dear. Take your pick,' came the bland retort. The Countess had settled for McNair.

'Then how about Lady Mead? We've still got the Dower House, and Lincolnshire is lovely in May.' So very lovely, Lucinda remembered.

'My dear good girl, the Dower House is bursting at the seams with furniture, not to mention Nanny. Besides,

22

there's no petrol left till the next coupons are due, and I won't go by train.'

'Then mightn't it help keep your mind off things if you took up war work? The WVS ladies are in the tube every night making tea when the sirens go. Or you could drive an ambulance.'

The Countess could *not* drive an ambulance. For one thing, she couldn't see a thing in the blackout without her glasses; and for another, the uniform wasn't half attractive enough. War work? Oh dear, no. It was enough with Donnington's preoccupation with his Home Guarding and a daughter who thought more of wounded soldiers than she did of family duty.

'No thank you! No need for us all to go in at the deep end.'

'Oh, Mama, don't make it more difficult than it already is. Do please try.'

But Mama would never budge. She had been completely against the war, right from the start. She was, dare her daughter think it, extremely selfish.

'Look, darling, I got a hunting-pink lipstick yesterday and some rose-geranium soap. I'd hidden them away for your birthday.' Not strictly true. She had intended using them herself. 'But if you like you can have them now.'

'Can I? Oh, Lucinda, what a poppet you are!'

Lucinda sighed. Poppet? Oh, no. She was a fool, that's what. But at least for a little while Mama would be happy, and keeping Mama happy had become a way of life, almost.

'I'll run upstairs and get them,' she smiled.

Last night too she had waited. She had waited at the beech tree until the sky began to darken and the sudden, distant roar of aircraft engines told her that soon the bombers would be flying again.

She had hugged herself tightly then against the nausea she always felt when Rob was flying and begun her desperate bargaining with God.

It's Jane, God – Jane Kendal. Rob's on ops again, so please take care of him and S-Sugar. Don't let anything happen. Let him come back, oh, please *let him come back!*

Cold with fear, she had waited for take-off, willing it not to happen, knowing it would.

Take off. To leave the ground. Birds did it all the time with ease and grace, but for the crews of the bombers that flew from Fenton Bishop aerodrome she knew that to take off meant dry-mouthed apprehension and an ice-cold hand that twisted your guts and made you want to throw up the supper you had neither tasted nor enjoyed. In those fearful few moments hands clutched good-luck charms and lips moved in unashamed prayer, until the clunk of the undercarriage as it folded into the belly of the aircraft told them they had made it. Then to each of the heavily loaded bombers that roared over her head Jane had whispered, 'Good luck. Come back safely,' and when they were all specks in the distant twilight and the savage pandemonium of their leaving no more than a muted throbbing, she had sent her love high and wide so it would find her lover in that vast, uncaring sky.

'Take care, Rob. Please take care . . .'

Eleven bombers had taken off from Fenton Bishop last night, and in the early hours of the morning eleven had come home. Rob was safe. Tonight he would be with her.

The trees were green now with the tender leaves of May, yet when first she knew Rob those trees had been silvered by February frosts. They had met just three months ago, yet now it seemed that the whole of her life had been crammed into those few fleeting weeks; as if her living had had no meaning before they met and her future would have no substance if ever he left her.

Now she stood at the gate of Ten-acre Pasture, staring across the hedgetops to the control tower that jutted into the gentle landscape with angular obscenity, begging silently that when she turned the corner he would be there.

The early evening sun was warm on her face and the sky so clear and calm that it seemed impossible so beautiful a world could be at war; that small, beautiful world that was Yeoman's Lane, and Tingle's Wood, through which it ran. The beech tree was a part of it too, and the stile beneath it where they always met, at seven.

She sucked in a steadying gulp of air, letting it go with little huffing sounds before she walked on and turned into the lane.

Rob wasn't there. It was seven o'clock, and he hadn't come. Her suddenly cold hands clenched tightly as she walked on, past the stile and the beech tree, into the green cool of the wood. The path was narrow and rough with tussocky grass and she trod carefully, eyes straining ahead to where the path ended abruptly at the outer limits of the aerodrome, blocked by a high steel-mesh fence – a cruel fence to keep lovers apart – and no one else had discovered the break in it through which Rob always came.

She saw him then, running swiftly towards her, and she pulled aside the fence, squeezing through the gap. He had come! For another night at least, he was safe.

She didn't run to meet him but stood there loving him, stretching out the seconds. Then he held out his arms and she went into them, laughing, wiping out the days they had been apart in that one eager meeting.

'Rob, oh Rob.' She spoke his name softly, her lips

gentling his cheek. Then, pulling a little way from him, she closed her eyes, lifting her lips to his.

But he did not kiss her. Instead he took her face in his hands, forcing her eyes to his.

'Jenny, I can't stay.'

'Darling, no! Why not?'

'They've just told us we're on standby.'

'Which means you'll be flying,' she whispered dully.

She traced the outline of his face with her eyes, loving the dear, untidy hair, the mouth that smiled widely and often, the eyes that were old in a young man's face.

She reached out for him again, and his arms felt lean and hard through the sleeves of his tunic. He was too thin. Flying was feeding off him, draining him, leaving him taut as an overwound spring.

'You'll be flying,' she whispered again. 'That'll be three nights out of five. It's madness.'

She disliked herself for what she was saying, for she knew the risk he had taken to be with her. When the bombers at Fenton Bishop were under orders, a blanket of security covered the aerodrome and to breach that security was the most serious thing. If there should be a call to briefing and Rob wasn't there . . .

'Have you been briefed yet?'

'No, but there's a call out for pilots and navigators in – ' He glanced at his watch. 'In fifteen minutes.'

'That makes it pretty certain then, doesn't it? And if anyone finds you here, you'll be in terrible trouble. I love you for coming, darling,' she whispered, 'but you mustn't stay.'

'I'm all right for a couple of minutes.' He shook two cigarettes from a paper packet, lit them, and placed one gently between her lips.

She pressed closer. Last night, perhaps, the bombs that fell from Rob's plane had killed women and children and old, helpless men, but for all that he was a tender lover. She wished the dead ones could have known that.

'Any news, Jenny?'

'No.' She smiled up at him, knowing what he meant. 'I had a fright this morning, though. There was a long buff envelope in the post with OHMS on it and I thought, "Oh, my God." But it was only something for Dad.'

'They've forgotten you. How long is it now since your medical?'

'Oh, ages.' She didn't want to talk about it or even think about it. Before they met she had accepted her call-up into the armed forces because it was one of the things that happened in wartime; accepted it because it was a moral necessity. There was a war on, so you didn't question anything; and if she was completely honest, there had even been times when she had looked forward to leaving home with a kind of guilty relief. But not any longer. Now there was Rob, and even to think of being parted from him left her sick inside.

She turned to him and closed her eyes, reaching for the back of his head, pulling his face closer.

'Forget it.' She shivered, without knowing why, and he took off his tunic and wrapped it around her shoulders. Longing flamed in her again at the smell and feel of it.

She was not ashamed of the need that screamed inside her. Sometimes she wanted to shout, 'Listen, world, Rob and I are lovers!' But their loving was a secret thing and their meetings furtive because of her parents.

'How was it, last night?'

'Like it always is,' he said quietly.

She felt the shrugging of his shoulders as if he were trying to forget for a little while the fear that never seemed quite to leave him. Fear of a bad take-off, of night fighters, of flak and searchlights. Fear of cracking up; fear of fear itself. Rob did not subscribe to the popular image of a

27

bomber pilot, didn't talk about wizard prangs or pieces of cake, or sport a handlebar moustache. Rob flew with calculated care, mindful of the lives of his crew and the need to get them back to the safety of the debriefing room and steaming mugs of rum-laced tea.

'Rob, let's go to York on Saturday and stay the night.'

The words came out in a rush and she felt her face flame. But she had no pride now where Rob was concerned, and what had pride to do with loving?

'The night?' He asked it quietly but she felt a tensing of his body. 'Could you make it?'

'I know I could.' She nodded confidently. 'My cousin will say I was with her. You want us to, don't you?'

'I love you, Jenny.' His voice was rough and his arms tightened around her. 'Remember that, always.'

Always. She recalled the time of their first coupling. It had been gentle, a sweet, surprised discovering, and they had looked at each other shyly afterwards, unable to speak. But now her need of him was desperate and unashamed, and their clandestine meetings were not enough. She wanted something to keep secret inside her; something to balance the loneliness of life without him if one night he shouldn't come back.

'If I start a baby, will you marry me?'

'You won't.' He kissed her harshly, as if to add strength to his denial.

'But I might. I could easily – '

'You *won't*, Jenny.' He drew deeply on his cigarette then sent it spinning away with a flick of his fingers. 'And we'll talk about York tomorrow, sweetheart.'

'All right, then.' She shivered again. 'If you're flying tonight, Rob, what time will take-off be?'

'I don't know. They haven't told us anything, but if something doesn't happen by nine, I reckon they'll stand

28

us down.' He was looking at his watch, again. 'Sorry, Jenny. You'll be all right?'

'I'll be fine. Just fine.'

She wasn't fine. She was angry they had wasted the precious minutes on stupid small talk. Then she took off his tunic and gave it back, helping him into it, fastening the buttons possessively. 'Take care, Rob. Promise to be careful.'

'I will.'

'And promise never to stop loving me.'

'Never. I promise.'

The same dear words, each time they parted. The same sweet promises, part of the ritual of their loving.

'Goodnight, Rob MacDonald,' she whispered, and he reached for her and kissed her gently, the sadness in his eyes making her suddenly afraid.

'Goodnight, Jenny.'

He went abruptly and she stood there, eyes on his back, willing him to turn, knowing he would not.

She watched as he broke into a run along the perimeter track; the same track his bomber would lumber round tonight if standby became reality.

Despair shook her, her body screaming silently at the pain of leaving him, choosing not to think of the risk he had taken to be with her.

Damn this war, she thought. Damn it, *damn it*!

She turned then, tugging at the wire-mesh fence, squeezing through. Head down, she ran through the wood, past the beech tree and the stile, not stopping until she came to Dormer Cottage.

'Hi!' she called to no one in particular. 'I'm home.'

She took the stairs at a run, up and up to the attic she slept in. Breathlessly she flung herself down on the window seat.

She liked this large, low room at the top of the house.

From its windows she could see for miles, across fields and trees to the aerodrome beyond. From here she could watch and wait for take-off, count the bombers out, bless them on their way.

There was nothing to see, yet. Toy trucks moved between hangars; a minute tractor drove slowly down the main runway. Maybe they wouldn't go tonight. Maybe it would be all right.

She pulled her knees up to her chin, hugging them for comfort, thinking about Saturday and York, and Julia, who had reluctantly agreed to alibi her.

She closed her eyes. On Saturday night she would be Jenny MacDonald. No one else called her Jenny. She was Jane, except to Rob, and now no one else would ever be allowed to use that diminutive. Jenny and Rob. Mrs Robert MacDonald, of Glasgow, though where in Glasgow she wasn't at all sure. What she did know was that he lived with his mother and two brothers, and that after the war he would go back to work in an insurance office.

Frowning, she made a mental note to ask his address, though where a man lived was not important. What really mattered was that he loved you and that tomorrow he would be waiting by the beech tree, at seven. Everything else was a triviality.

She rested her chin on her knees, preparing herself for the long wait. Her parents were down there in the garden, Missy, her labrador bitch, at their heels.

She was sorry about the tension between them. It had started when they discovered she was meeting Rob, and they had asked for her promise that she would never see him again. It was the start of the lies and deceit, but she didn't care. Only Rob mattered now.

She closed her eyes, easing into her favourite fantasy. She did it all the time when Rob was not with her, recalling words they had spoken, hearing music and shared laughter.

Tonight the air was gentle and the earth green with tender things growing, but when first she met Rob a bitter wind blew from the north-east and the bombers were grounded, standing shrouded against the frost and snow like great wounded birds. Candlemas, and there was a dance in the sergeants' mess. Often, now, she thought with wonder that she almost hadn't gone . . .

Her mother was against it. Aerodromes were dangerous places, she fretted, the recent air raid and the death of two young Waafs still fresh in her mind. Her parents didn't want her to become involved with Fenton Bishop's aircrews. They were a wild lot, her mother said. They had rowdy parties at the Black Bull and sang dubious songs. She only gave in when she learned that the vicar's niece would be going to the dance and that the Air Force would be providing transport.

Jane had never been to the aerodrome before – not actually past the guardroom and through the gates – and she hadn't known what to expect that night. All she was able to see from the back of the truck was the rounded outlines of scattered Nissen huts and, on the dark horizon, tall, wedge-shaped buildings hung with dim blue lights.

A corporal wearing an SP's armband helped her down, and from the distance she sensed the clunk and slap of a double bass and drums that tapped out a rumba beat.

On either side, white-painted kerb stones glowed faintly through the blackness as she walked with the rest towards the sound of the dancing, for ears were of more use than eyes in the blackout.

The aircrew mess was a drab building, erected in the haste of war, with a brown polished floor and girders that criss-crossed to support a low tin roof. Thick blackout curtains covered the too-small windows and cigarette

31

smoke hung in a blue haze, drifting lazily, trapped in the roof space above.

The room was noisy and hot. She laid her coat across a table then stood, not knowing what to do, wondering irritably why she had made such a fuss about coming . . .

But thank heaven she had, she thought now. Oh, Rob, imagine. We might never have met.

Her foot began to tingle and she shifted her position. Her father was still in the garden. He was wearing his blue police shirt and the strap of his truncheon hung from his left trouser pocket. The war had brought extra responsibilities to the village constable and now they were beginning to show in the tired lines on his face.

She wished her father and mother were like other parents and not so narrow-minded. But they were old. Her mother must be nearly sixty.

'We waited so long for you, Jane. We had given up hope, then suddenly there you were, a little stranger . . .'

A little stranger. God, how *awful*. And how awful to imagine people of their age doing *that*. It made her glad she was disobeying them; gladder still that she and Rob were lovers.

All seemed normal and quiet at the aerodrome and the sun was beginning to set. She lifted her left hand. Almost nine o'clock.

'. . . if something doesn't happen by nine . . .'

The cough and splutter of an aircraft engine came to her clearly on the still evening air. Fear sliced through her and she tried to close her ears to the sound, but as if to mock her it was joined by another and another until the air was filled with a shaking roar. The pilots were revving up the aircraft engines; there would be no stand-down. Soon, Rob would take S-Sugar on to the runway and wait for clearance from the control tower. Then a green light would stab through the gloom and he'd be roaring down

32

—

the narrow concrete strip, faster and faster, holding Sugar back until it seemed the boundary fence was hurtling to meet them. Then slowly, reluctantly almost, they would rise into the air and Rob would let go his breath, and his flight engineer would say, 'Bloody lovely,' as he always did.

That was when she'd wish them luck, as they roared over the village, and she would watch them all until they were silhouetted against the dying sun, small and graceful in an apricot sky.

She counted twelve green lights, blessed twelve Halifax bombers on their way. In less than half an hour they were all airborne and Rob was flying on his seventeenth raid over occupied Europe.

Take care, my love. Come home safely.

God, but she was so afraid.

2

At the door of St Joseph's church, Father O'Flaherty waited impatiently and importantly.

'Down ye go, Theresa.' He always used Vi's second name, declaring that the name of a flower, however sweet and modest, must give precedence to that of a saint.

'Thanks, Father.'

Vi walked carefully, eyes on the trailing habit of Sister Cecilia, who negotiated the twisting downward steps with a child beneath each arm.

The crypt was damp and smelled of the occupation of the past six nights. Benches and chairs had been placed around the walls, and biscuit mattresses, still folded, were stacked in the corner nearest the stone steps. Not for sleeping on, it was stressed, but for direst emergencies only, such as dying, birthing or suspected heart attack. Opposite, alongside a loudly dripping tap, Sister Annunciata topped up the already bubbling tea urn, switched on, Vi suspected, without the priest's permission.

Vi took a corner seat farthest away from the door. Tonight she didn't want to talk. Tonight Gerry had died, really died. After the letter came she had hoped for a miracle and prayed for one, too, but Richie Daly's visit had snuffed out that hope in one short sentence. Gerry was dead, because no seaman, not even a little toerag like Richie Daly, would lie about a thing like that.

She closed her eyes. No more tears, Vi, she told herself. You and Gerry had four good years. Just be thankful you didn't get the baby you wanted so much. No fun for a kid, is it, growing up without a da. Better face it, Vi, you're

34

on your own, now. There's only Mary and the sisters you haven't seen for ten years, if you can count them. Margaret and Geraldine had gone to Canada as domestics in the early thirties and married Canadian husbands, and wouldn't come back to Liverpool, they wrote, for a big clock.

They'd been good to Mam, though, sending her money when they could. Neither had been able to get home for her funeral, but they had telegraphed a big wreath and paid their fair share of the undertaker's bill, after which the letters and dollars stopped and Vi and Mary had grown even closer.

A child cried and was silenced with a bottle of orange-coloured liquid. Lips moved without words, fingers counted rosary beads. Tonight, everyone seemed to be waiting. Two hours gone and still nothing had happened. Weren't they coming, then, and if they weren't, why didn't the all clear sound?

Sister Annunciata caught the priest's eye and held up a packet of tea, but he shook his head and pulled aside the blackout curtain at the foot of the circular staircase. Vi jumped to her feet and followed him to the door of the church, wincing in the sweet, cold air.

'Father, can you spare a minute?'

'What's to do, Theresa? Go back down, where it's safe.'

'Just a word, Father.'

She followed his upward gaze. The sky was dark, with only the outlines of dockside warehouses standing sharp on the skyline. Long, straight fingers of light searched the sky in sweeping arcs, meeting, touching briefly as if in greeting, then sweeping away again to circle the brooding night.

'Almost beautiful, isn't it?'

'It is, Father.'

35

'And what's on your conscience, Theresa?' The priest's eyes followed the wandering searchlights.

'It's Gerry. He – he's dead, it seems certain now. Someone who was there came to tell me tonight.'

'Dead - is - it - God - rest - his - soul.' Father O'Flaherty's thumb traced a blessing.

'Will you say a Mass for him?' Two half-crowns, warm from her fingers, changed hands. 'Tomorrow, Father?'

'I'll do that, Theresa, and I'll pray for you, child. Now go back down and tell the Sisters to make tea. It's too quiet up here. Too bloody quiet by half, so it is . . .'

She said, 'Thank you, Father,' and began the uneasy descent. It was always worse going down, and spiral stairs were the very devil in the dark if you had big feet. It meant you had to walk sideways, almost, like a crab. Vi wished the good Lord had endowed her with size fours, but it wasn't anybody's fault, really. Her feet were big because she hadn't worn shoes till her third birthday, or so Mam had said.

She stood for a moment behind the thick black curtain, unwilling to pull it aside. Added to the musty crypt smell there would be the stink of sweat and unchanged babies, all mingling with the stench of fear, because tonight everyone was more on edge than usual. Maybe because tonight the warning had been a long time sounding, had started its tormented wailing just when everyone began to think the bombers weren't coming. And now it seemed they weren't, because nothing was happening.

Perhaps, though, it was all part of a war of nerves. Perhaps those bombers had flown up the river as they always did, just so the sirens would send Liverpudlians hurrying to the shelters for yet another night, then per-versely they had turned inland and dropped their bomb loads on Manchester instead.

But they couldn't be that stupid, Vi reasoned derisively

36

as she nodded to Sister Annunciata and called, 'Father says you're to make the tea.'

Backs straightened, nodding heads shot up. Tea was a soother, a healer. It had been the blackest day of the war when the government announced the rationing of tea. Oh, yes, capture India, cut off the tea supply, and Britain would capitulate within a week, said the potman at the Tarleton.

'Won't be long now!' The nun's call coincided with the first of the bombs. It was a fair way off, but those who sensed it rather than heard it, those whose eyes became suddenly afraid, knew that two more would follow. Bombs came in threes, to those who counted.

There was a strained, listening silence, broken only by Father O'Flaherty's startled feet as they took the stairs in record time. Then the briefest pause before he drew aside the curtain to enter with dignity and calm.

'Well now, and just in time for tea,' he beamed as a second and third bomb fell sickeningly nearer.

It wasn't the noise so much. Vi pulled a dry tongue around dry lips. She had always imagined that an exploding bomb would have made an infernal, ear-splitting racket, but it didn't. It *crunched*. You felt a bomb as much as you heard it. It shocked the earth it slammed into, and those shock waves slammed into the soles of your feet and raged through your body and paralysed your mind.

More bombs fell, and more, until the air was full of a strange continuous roaring and the earth shook as if it were afraid.

Vi sucked in her breath. They were nearer tonight than they had ever been. Any closer and they'd hit St Joseph's. *Mother of God, be with us*.

Babies stopped crying, hushed by the fear around them. Eyes were wide in white faces; fingers and lips moved in silent, age-old prayer. Someone laughed hysterically.

The bombs stopped as suddenly as they started but the hollow screams of anti-aircraft shells continued without pause.

That's it, lads. Let 'em have it. Shoot the bastards down. Make 'em wish they hadn't come.

Was that to be it, then? Short and sharp tonight. Eyes turned again to the tea urn.

The big one dropped just as they began to relax. One bomb, not three, and a tearing, screaming explosion that set the lights swaying on their wires and filled the air with choking dust. Eyes swivelled upward, bodies tensed again. The roof would cave in. It would.

'Jaysus, Mary and Joseph,' roared the priest.

The roof disgorged another shower of dust and rubble, and held fast. There was a ten-foot crack in it, wide enough to take a man's fist, but it held.

The lights swayed more slowly. One of them flickered, then died with a ping.

'Don't any of yez dare to sneeze,' ordered Father O'Flaherty, but no one laughed.

The all clear came with the morning light, high-pitched and steady, the sweetest sound in the world.

'That's it, then. Away to your homes the lot of you, and God go with you,' called Father O'Flaherty.

Wearily, fearfully, they filed out to face the day. Vi smelled the desolation before she saw it: a mingling of dust and rubble and burning, water-doused timber. Somewhere, the bell of a fire engine clanged and men's voices called urgently.

Then she was standing at the church gates and looking down Lyra Street; looking, but not understanding. She took several steps nearer, counting as she walked.

One and three, they were all right, but number five had gone, and number seven. And opposite, number four and number six. There was nothing there but a terrible, yawning gap. That last bomb had taken out those houses as if it had come with a great grasping fist and scooped them up and crunched them into rubble as easily as if they'd been made of matchsticks.

Number five. Mrs Norris. She'd still be in there, under the kitchen table, and number seven – Mother of God, that was *hers*!

Only then did she comprehend the implications of that great, obscene gap. They had hit her house, destroyed her home – hers and Gerry's. A vicious pain slashed through her. She closed her eyes and opened her lips to a terrible moan.

'No. Oh, *no*!'

She stood there, fighting for breath. There wasn't a thing left. Not one thing. Just beams and brick rubble. Chairs and pots and pans all gone, and her lovely dusty-pink eiderdown. And four years of scrimping and saving and sweeping and polishing and loving that little house; the house Gerry came home to. If he could see it now . . .

But Gerry wasn't coming home. He didn't need this house any more. If she had polished and dusted till the crack of doom, it would have made no difference. Her husband was dead, her job had gone and now she had no home.

Hot, bitter tears rolled down her cheeks, and with them came back the noise of the street. A stranger's arm encircled her shoulders.

'Come away, pet, an' I'll make you a cup of tea. It's only an 'ouse.'

'Thanks,' Vi whispered, 'but leave me a minute.'

She took a step nearer, staring at the drunken heap of rubble. There was nothing there she recognized. Not one familiar chair or table top. And where was her gas stove and the red rose bush from the yard?

There wasn't a yard. It probably wasn't even her rubble,

either. Hers from across the street, most likely. It was like that with bomb-blast. Sometimes it just rushed round things; other times it flattened all in its path then picked up the debris and flung it away. You could never tell.

She stood there retching. She needed to be sick. She wanted to go down on her knees in all the muck and dust and cry and cry until she was sick. But she wouldn't. She couldn't, because this wasn't Vi McKeown standing here shaking, and it wasn't Vi's house that bomb had taken. All this was happening to someone else, so it was no use getting upset over what didn't concern her.

A policeman with red-rimmed eyes and a stubble-covered chin was saying something.

'You what?' She looked at him vacantly.

'I said, was you all right and do you know who lives here?'

'Why?'

'Because there might be people in there, that's why.'

'Her in number seven's all right, but there's an old woman in there, I think. Under the kitchen table.' She nodded vaguely in the direction of number five.

'Christ Almighty! Over here, lads! There's a woman under that bloody lot!'

He took the arm of the girl who stared at him with shock-darkened eyes. 'There's the WVS women at the bottom of the street. Go and get yourself a cup of tea and tell 'em you need some sugar in it.'

But Vi didn't move except to turn her back on the men with the picks and shovels. She didn't want to look when they found Ma Norris. *If* they found her, that was. If there was anything left to find. She hoped the poor old thing had gone. It'd be a release for her. No more hiding from the post office boy who brought telegrams from the Somme each day.

Vi supposed she had better be going. Go where? But

40

did it matter? She raised her eyes to the sky. It was a beautiful sky. Very blue, even through the smoke haze. The early-morning sun was there, too, as if last night had never happened.

Then she saw the wall – her bedroom wall. It stood out, jagged and broken like a decaying tooth, and it was covered with pale pink roses. Roses Gerry had pasted there.

For a moment she gazed at her beautiful bedroom wallpaper then anger took her, shook her, slapped her into life again.

The bastards! The rotten, evil bastards!

Well, they weren't getting away with it this time. They couldn't take your man and your job and your home and not answer for it! She made her silent vow to the piece of wallpaper that flapped in the breeze.

I'll have 'em for this, Gerry. On our mam's grave, I'll have 'em!

The piece of paper tore loose. She watched it slip and slide this way and that to fall at her feet. Tenderly she picked it up. It was all she had left of four years of happiness, and it was very precious. Special too, because it bore witness to her vow.

'You all right, luv?' the policeman asked again.

'I'm fine,' Vi said. And she was. And fighting mad, too.

'Got somewhere to go, have you?'

'Yes. To town – to London Road.' To the recruiting office, that's where.

'Town? You'll never make it. No trams, no buses, and the roads blocked with rubble. And two unexploded bombs in the Mile End Road. It'll take all day.'

'That's all right.' She'd got all day. All the time in the world, in fact.

'Please yourself.' He had better things to do than argue the toss.

Oh, she would please herself, all right. She would get down to the city centre somehow. Vi McKeown knew every back street and jigger north of the Liver Building, and she would get there. Things had gone too far. They had taken all she had, and nobody did that to a woman of Liverpool and got away with it. She was joining the fight. She wanted in, right in the thick of it. She was joining the Navy and she would go wherever they sent her. What she could do she had no idea; but she would stand on the cliff top at Dover and heave rocks at the arrogant sods, if that was what it took.

She sniffed away the last of her tears and slipped the piece of dirty, rose-covered wallpaper into her carrier bag. Her city was battered and burning. She was alone in the world and owned nothing but the clothes in which she stood, a small attaché case filled with important things and a brown paper carrier bag containing shoes, stockings, and two crystal goblets carefully wrapped in a pair of white cotton knickers.

It wasn't a lot to show for twenty-five years of living and breathing, but at least she was alive. Now it was time to move on. Pulling back her shoulders, she walked, head high, out of Lyra Street.

This time, she did not look back.

The Countess of Donnington stood at the window of the first-floor sitting room, intent on the street below. She had spent a fear-filled night beneath a stone slab in the meat cellar and, what was more, completely alone. Now the air raid was over and still her husband and daughter had not come home.

Last night's bombing had caught her unawares in the West End. Normally, to go out alone would have been unthinkable, but unoccupied men were thin on the ground now and invitations almost non-existent. She had gazed petulantly at a mantelpiece empty of deckle-edged cards, remembering the time when she had never wanted for an escort or a party. But most men of her acquaintance were in uniform now, and having the time of their lives, she shouldn't wonder, with girls young enough to be their own daughters.

The alert last night had sounded just as Londoners were beginning to think that just for once there would be no air raid, and the first bombs fell as the last notes of the sirens gave way to an uneasy, brooding silence. Panic-stricken, she had made her way back to Bruton Street, her feet rubbed into blisters in flimsy evening slippers, wondering how taxis could disappear so completely whenever she needed one.

She could have found shelter, of course. Hotels and restaurants and clubs always opened their doors to anyone caught above ground when the bombing started. But if she was going to be killed, she had tearfully decided, it would be at her home in Mayfair. No one, but no one, would dig Kitty Bainbridge out of a communal shelter in Soho. For Soho was where she had been last evening, wondering what to do and where to go to fill the time; there, in Shaftesbury Avenue, she had seen Lucinda and the airmen. And it was then she had decided that war work or not, her daughter's excursions with convalescent wounded must stop at once. She had felt quite peculiar and quite, quite shocked; how Lucinda could bring herself to do it was a complete mystery.

So she had made her fear-filled way home to spend another night in the cellar, her moods alternating between terror and self-pity, until the high, sweet sound of the all clear brought relief and anger. When Donnington got home in that ridiculous Home Guard uniform of his and her daughter had torn herself away from those men, then all hell would break loose. The Countess guaranteed it.

Lighting the last of her cigarettes, she inhaled deeply. The world had gone mad, with every capital city in Europe occupied by strutting Nazis. How soon before they were in London, too?

'At last!' She espied her daughter rounding the corner from Berkeley Square. Running quickly downstairs, she was waiting in the black and white tiled entrance hall long before the doorbell rang.

'Sorry about this.' Lucinda was pale and dust-stained, her eyes dark-ringed. 'Are you all right, Mama?'

'No, I am *not* all right!' Pent-up emotions broke loose. 'I have been alone all night! And might I ask where you have been until now?'

'I'm sorry, truly I am, but I had to look after the boys. They're still a bit wobbly, you know, and when the bombing got rough I thought I'd better find us all somewhere to go. We were fine in the tube, but it – '

'Lucinda! Listen to me! I saw you last night, though you chose not to see me, and I cannot understand your casual attitude to life. You imagine this war gives you the excuse to disobey me and do exactly as you wish. You stay out all night. You think more of those creatures, it seems, than your fiancé. You – '

'*Creatures*, Mama?'

'Well, what else is one to call them? I was ashamed last night, deeply ashamed that my daughter should be seen in such company, such – '

'Such *what*?' Lucinda's eyes flew wide with disbelief. 'Sorry, but I don't understand you.'

'Well, they're such a terrible sight, aren't they? Their faces, I mean; so – so *grotesque*. You'd think they wouldn't want to be seen in public; but no, there they are, living it up, and my own daughter aiding and abetting them as if she were doing something clever. That tall one, the one with his hands all over you – '

44

'Mama, you don't know what you're saying.' Bright red spots flushed Lucinda's cheeks. 'I'm not hearing this; I'm *not*!'

'Stop playing the innocent with me, child. Sufficient to say I was deeply embarrassed, and the time has come to put an end to this absurdity. You will give up this so-called nursing immediately and you will give me a date for your wedding – '

'Be quiet, Mama! Shut up and just for once listen to *me*!'

'I – I . . .' The older woman's mouth sagged open and remained open. Lucinda, who had always been so obedient, speaking to her mother as if good manners had gone out of fashion?

'You are without doubt, Mama, the most unreasonable, the most selfish woman I have ever met, and I am not in the least ashamed to be seen with those boys. I'm proud of them, in fact. Yes, they *are* a terrible sight. They were all fighter pilots and they got hit, you see. Oh, they managed to bale out, but not before their faces and hands had burned. No eyelashes, no eyebrows, no hair, no features any more. That was their reward for trying to keep the bombers away from London, away from people like you, Mama!' She shook with outrage, her voice thick with unshed tears. 'The tall one, mind, the one with his hands all over me – on my *shoulders*, actually, so I could lead him – well, he's a bit luckier. He'll never have to see himself day after day in a mirror and wonder if it was worth it because he's blind, you see. His eyes burned, too!'

She was weeping now. Tears of anger and pity and pride ran down her face, making rivulets in the grime.

'So don't moan to me about your unhappy lot, Mama. You think this war was started just to inconvenience you. You whine and whinge and think of no one but yourself.

You are a bitch, Mama; a selfish, bad-minded bitch, and it is I who am ashamed of *you*! I'm going out before I say something I'm sorry for.'

'Lucinda! Come back and apologize *at once*. You can't speak to me like that. I can't believe my own ears!'

'Then you'd better, because I meant every word of it.'

The front door slammed shut and the Countess collapsed on to the bottom step of the staircase, her legs useless. Her daughter had taken leave of her senses and her husband was never at home when he was needed. The world had gone completely mad.

Hubert James Bainbridge, tenth earl of Donnington, called out to his daughter as she passed him on the opposite side of the street, but she did not hear him. He'd have sworn she was crying, poor child. It was a terrible world for the young ones to grow up in. Not a lot for them to look forward to.

He watched her disappear round the corner of the street then, shrugging his shoulders, walked on, thinking again of that incredible whispered conversation at company HQ.

Such news, and so completely unbelievable. He would have to telephone around and see if anyone else had any titbits to add to the mystery. Better not tell Kitty, though. Kitty was totally preoccupied with the threatened invasion, and to tell her this would be asking for trouble. And the rumour might not be true, though it had come from Freddie Elton, who didn't often get it wrong. But *Hess*, flying here in a Messerschmitt. Hitler's deputy, no less, baling out over Scotland then surrendering amiably to a farmer and demanding to be taken to the Duke of Hamilton. It was a real kettle of fish and no mistake. The man must be a raving bloody lunatic even to think of coming to this bomb-happy island. Rudolf Hess, eh? Who next but the whole German army?

Carefully he opened the front door of his house, quietly he crossed the hall to the library and closed the door behind him. Then taking off his tunic and loosening his tie, he picked up the telephone.

The elderly admiral sighed and penned his name to yet another scrap of printed paper. It was all he did, these days; signing chits was all he seemed good for. Too old to be in uniform, really, so he supposed he should be grateful for the desk job in a small dark room at Admiralty House. He rose to his feet, genuinely pleased to see the pretty girl who smiled at him from the doorway.

'Goddy, darling!' Her kiss was warm. 'It's good of you to see me.'

'Good of you to come, Lucinda.' He held her at arm's length. 'But what on earth have you been up to, eh?'

Her face was tear-stained, her clothes creased and her pale blonde curls dull with dust.

'It was the air raid, I suppose. Spent last night in the tube and it was, oh, *awful* getting here.'

'What's it like out there? Afraid I didn't get home last night. Slept here, in the basement. Is it as bad as they say?'

'It's unbelievable, Goddy. Everything is at a standstill and so many people in the underground, just sitting there with nowhere to go. I walked here from Bruton Street and it was like a nightmare.'

'A lot of casualties, I shouldn't wonder.'

'Over a thousand, I heard, and heaven knows how many more injured and homeless. What's happening to us, Goddy?'

'I don't know for sure, girlie, but we'll sort it all out in the end, just see if we don't. They say the British lose every battle they ever fight, except the last one.'

The last battle. And how far away would that be? But

47

there had been a full moon last night, a bomber's moon, with all London laid out clearly for the Luftwaffe pilots. And this morning the devastation and burning had been terrible to see. Unexploded bombs everywhere; water for fire hoses almost non-existent; the acrid air thick with smoke and tiny pieces of charred paper swirling on the breeze. Poor, proud old London.

'It's wrong of me, but I wish I could be at Lady Mead, Goddy. It must be beautiful now, in Lincolnshire.'

'Ah, yes.' He clamped an empty pipe between his teeth. 'I remember your christening. It was a May day just like now, and warm and sunny. The chapel at Lady Mead was full of flowers, and how you screamed and yelled. Nanny was pleased, I seem to recall. Said you'd cried the devil out of you, and that was good.'

'Dear Nanny. She's at Lady Mead, you know. The Air Force was very good. They didn't throw us out entirely. Pa had all the good stuff stored in the Dower House when we had to leave, and Nanny's there now, looking after it. She writes every week. But you must be very busy and I came here to ask a favour, a big favour. I hope you don't mind?'

'Of course I don't. Just tell your old godfather, and if I can I'll help. But what about a cup of tea, eh? My writer is a little wonder. Never seems to run out of rations, bless her. And last night she went to a do at the American Embassy and came back with a packet of chocolate cookies – er – biscuits, no less.' He thumbed a bell-push on his desk, and a woman in naval uniform opened the door. 'Leading Wren, this is Lucinda Bainbridge, and she's in desperate need of a mug of tea. And do we – er – have a biscuit?'

'Sir, you know we do, though how you got to know about them I can't imagine.'

'I want to be a Wren,' Lucinda whispered when they

48

were alone again. 'That's why I came – to ask you to help me. I ought to be doing more than I am. I – I had a terrible row at home this morning. I'll have to go back and say I'm sorry, but I want to join up, truly I do. And not because of Mama,' she finished breathlessly. 'I really want to do something useful.'

'I'm sure you do, but Kitty mustn't ever know that I'd had a hand in it.'

'Are you afraid of her? All right then, I'll join the Waafs or the ATS. I don't mind which, but I've got to do something, Goddy. Sometimes I feel so ashamed.'

A knock on the door announced the arrival of two white mugs of tea and an anchor-decorated plate on which lay, unbelievably, two large thickly coated chocolate biscuits.

'Leading Wren, you're an absolute marvel,' the Admiral said.

'Oh no, sir,' she smiled, eyes bright with mischief. 'It's because I'm feeling so pleased about my leave chit.'

'Your leave chit? Did I sign it?'

'No sir, not yet. But you're going to, aren't you?'

'Hussy,' barked the Admiral to her retreating back. 'She's a good girl,' he confided, offering the plate to Lucinda. 'Her young man was taken prisoner at Dunkirk and not so long ago her father was badly hurt in the Clydeside blitz, but you'd never know it.'

'There you are, Goddy. That's what I mean. That's why you've got to help. This war is affecting everybody but me, it seems. You *will* try to get me in quickly, won't you? I can't type or do anything useful that I can think of, but I learn quickly. There's got to be something.'

'Want a job here in the Admiralty, do you? Somewhere in London, near Charlie?'

'Anything will do, though I'd rather go away, if you could manage it.'

'Hmm. We'll have to see. I don't carry a lot of weight now, in spite of all my gold braid. Now a few years ago . . .' His mind flew back with ease to the last war and an up-and-coming young officer on a smoke-belching dread-nought at Jutland. Now that had been one hell of a scrap. 'Still, I'll do my best for you, girlie.'

He discussed the matter later with his writer.

'I'm afraid I'm not entirely au fait with the women's side of things. Do we know anyone in Recruiting, Leading Wren?'

'Is your goddaughter serious about joining up, sir?'

'Very serious, it would seem.'

'Then I think I know who'll be able to help her. Oh, and sir, you'll never believe this – it's quite peculiar, really. It's Rudolf Hess. There's a strong buzz that he's in Scotland. Have you heard anything?'

'Hess? *Here*? Piffle and tommyrot, Leading Wren!'

Hitler's right-hand man in Scotland? Whatever next? The Admiral dismissed the rumour without a second thought and concentrated on more important matters: his goddaughter's immediate entry into the Women's Royal Naval Service, no less.

Poor child. Her mother wasn't the easiest person to live with, but joining up! Surely she'd have done better to marry young Charlie Bainbridge and settle down to start-ing a family. Been on the cards for ages, that wedding. Strange that Lucinda should not want to stay in London. It was a rum do, and no mistake.

He regarded his in-tray with a weary eye, then, sighing, picked up his pen again.

Jane awoke without effort, Missy's cold nose on her cheek.

'What is it, girl?' Her eyes were wide in an instant. The bombers were coming back. Missy had heard their engines

50

long before a human ear could pick up the first faint sound and had come to tell her.

'Can you hear them, then?' She pulled back the curtains and opened the windows wide, patting the seat beside her.

The sky was light to the east, streaks of red and gold piercing the grey. Birds were starting their morning singing, roused by the missel thrush in the pear tree. Below her, in the orchard, apple and pear and plum frothed pink and white with blossom, and over in Tingle's Wood a sea of bluebells rose out of the morning mist.

It was all so normal, this May-morning canvas, but soon the bombers would return, stark silhouettes against a pale sky, reminding her that the war was real, setting the frightened pulse in her throat beating again.

She saw them before she heard them. Two Halifax bombers, wheels already down; two black nightbirds coming home to roost. She held her breath, listening. They had taken off with ordered precision; they would straggle home in ones and twos, their engines making a different sound in the thin morning air.

'That's the first of them, Missy.'

She reached into her pyjama jacket and hooked out the chain that hung around her neck. On it were her confirmation cross and the farthing Rob had given her soon after they met. It was bright and new, with the King's head on one side and on the other a wren and the date, 1941. Rob said it was appropriate, since that was what she was going to be. 'Keep it for luck, Jenny-love.'

She had done better than that and taken it to a jeweller to be plated and put into a mount so it could hang on her chain. He had been obliged to tell her, of course, that it was an offence to deface a coin of the realm, but he had done as she asked because women brought sentimental tokens to him every day of the week and, anyway, it was

51

only a farthing. To Jane, though, it was precious and priceless and she wore it always. Now she held it in her hand with the cross, a silent pleading for Rob's return.

The ninth bomber came out of a lightening sky at six o'clock exactly, and though she sat there for another hour, it was the last.

'. . . *and three of our aircraft have failed to return*,' the man who read the news would intone on the midday bulletin. Were they just words he was reading, or did he realize that three aircraft meant twenty-one crew, and countless women waiting anxiously for the phone call that would tell them their man was safe – or the letter that would tell them he was not?

She began to dress, cold clumsy fingers fumbling with buttons. How soon before she could phone the aerodrome? Not quite yet. Crews had to be debriefed and they would have to eat, too. Yesterday morning it had been all right. Eleven bombers had taken off; eleven came home. But three crews not back yet – *oh, please not Rob*!

Long before the sun was making shadows, she was standing beside the phone box at the crossroads outside the village, willing the minutes away. Soon it would be half-past seven, and exactly at half-past seven she would ring the aerodrome.

She always used the public box when she phoned Rob. Police telephones were not to be used for private calls, said her mother. It was better that way, she supposed, though if things had been normal at home Rob could have phoned her there. Just a quick 'Hullo, Jenny. Everything's fine.' And perhaps a whispered 'I love you.'

But things weren't normal at home because her parents had said she must not meet Rob. Her parents were old and had forgotten, if ever they had known, what it was like to love someone as she loved Rob. And she wasn't waiting any longer, damn it.

Impatiently she wrenched open the door and, taking the pennies from her pocket, picked up the receiver with a hand that shook.

'Number, please?' The switchboard answered quickly and it seemed like a good omen.

'Can I have 220, please?' She arranged her pennies in front of her.

'Just a minute, Jane.' This morning it must be Ruth on duty. Ruth knew everybody's voice, even when they had a cold. 'Have two pennies ready.' The coins clinked into the slot. 'Press button A. There you are, now . . .'

Jane pressed hard, the pennies fell with a clatter and a voice said, 'Fenton Bishop 220.' It was a Scottish voice and it gave her comfort.

'Can I have the aircrew mess?' she whispered, stiff-lipped. Her hand was wet and she gripped the receiver tightly, thinking back to the night of the February dance and how the telephone was fixed to the wall beside the door.

She took a deep breath. In just a few seconds Rob would be talking to her and it would be all right. It *would*.

When she asked for Sergeant MacDonald there was a pause, then the man on the other end of the line told her to wait. She had thought she would hear him calling Rob's name but instead he hissed, 'It's Mac's girl.'

The background noises stopped and she knew he had put his hand over the mouthpiece. She closed her eyes tightly. She felt very sick. She wanted to put the phone down and pretend it wasn't happening but the noises came back and a different voice said, 'Sergeant MacDonald isn't here at the moment. Could you phone back later?'

'Has he gone out?' Panic had her now; ice-cold, screaming panic. 'Has he left the camp?'

'Well – no.'

'Then where is he?'

53

'I'm not sure.' He was prevaricating but his voice was kind; too kind. She took another breath then let it go before she asked, 'When shall I phone?' She was shaking and her mouth had filled with saliva.

'Look, do you think you could leave it until tomorrow? Or maybe you could get in touch with the Adjutant's office, or the padre?'

She knew what he was trying to tell her, and tomorrow wouldn't do. 'He was flying last night, wasn't he?' she made herself ask it.

'Yes, love, he was.'

He seemed reluctant to talk to her, but probably this man was aircrew, too. Perhaps talking to her about Rob made him feel that someone was dancing on his own grave. She whispered, 'Please tell me.'

'Sergeant MacDonald isn't back yet.' The words came in a rush. 'He's – he's overdue, but don't get upset. He could have ditched or landed down south somewhere. Try not to worry.'

A sudden hatred came over her; a cold, bitter hating of everything that lived and breathed. She wanted to hurt the man who had told her Rob hadn't come back, but he had tried to be kind and anyway she couldn't think clearly. There was a noise in her head that was making her dizzy so she whispered, 'Thank you,' and put the receiver down. Imagine, she'd thanked him for telling her Rob was missing! Clasping her arms over her stomach, she tried to stop the writhing inside her. O God, God, God! Why did you let this happen?

She did not remember going home. She'd pushed her bicycle most of the way before she collected enough sense to get on and ride it.

When she walked into the kitchen her mother looked up and said, 'Where on earth have you been at this hour?'

Jane looked at her and at her father and hated them,

54

too. They were old. They had been married for more years than she and Rob had lived. Why weren't they dead, like Rob? He wasn't coming back; she knew it.

Her father put down his paper. 'Is anything wrong, Jane?'

Wrong? Something had just kicked the breath out of her body but no, nothing was wrong.

She needed to weep, but there was a pain in her throat and it was stopping the tears, so she laughed instead. She stood there and laughed until she shook. There wasn't anything else to do but laugh.

She heard her mother say, 'Stop her, Richard. She's hysterical,' and her father shouted 'Jane!' and took hold of her shoulders, but she went on laughing.

His hand on her cheek hurt. He slapped her hard and it made her head jerk back. She stopped in the middle of a scream and the breath left her body with a groan. It was the first time her father had hit her and he looked upset, but suddenly she was very calm and her voice was steady as she said, 'I'm sorry. I shouldn't have done that, but the man I've been going out with is missing. He was on ops last night and he hasn't come back.'

It didn't sound like her voice. It was as if the words were coming from inside her and someone else was speaking them.

Her mother covered her mouth with her hand and her face went pale. Jane was glad about that. She wanted her to be hurt, and her father too. If only because they were alive, she wanted it.

'You used to pretend he didn't exist, didn't you?' came the voice from inside her. 'Well, he probably doesn't now. Are you satisfied?'

She wouldn't cry. Not in front of them. She closed the door behind her and walked upstairs to her room. Her face was chalk-white in the mirror and her eyes were large and wild. She said, 'He's dead. Overdue means missing and missing means dead. They don't come back.'

She took his photograph from beneath the lining paper in her drawer and looked at it and tried again to cry. She would have given anything to weep until she was sick, but the pain was still there to stop her. She slumped down on to the bed. She didn't know if she was rocking or if it was the room.

The door latch clicked and her father stood there. He looked so utterly miserable that she tried to feel sorry for him but she could not. She needed the whole world to be miserable.

'Would it help to talk about it?' he said.

When she was little, she always talked to him. Once, she had loved her father very much.

'His name was Rob.' The real Jane was speaking now and every word was a stab of pain. 'I never told you that, did I? I don't know a lot about him either, but it doesn't matter now, does it? He lived in Glasgow but I'm not sure where. His father's been dead a long time and he has – had – two brothers.' Her father put out his hand but she pulled away. 'I loved him very much. He was so young and it wasn't his war. It's your fault, yours and Mother's. It's your generation should be getting killed, not ours!'

Richard Kendal nodded, his eyes bright with pain. 'Perhaps you're right. We saw it coming and we did nothing.' He walked over to the window. 'Are you all right?' he asked without looking at her. 'Mother said she thought you haven't been looking too good lately – a bit peaky.'

She knew what he was trying to say. They thought she might be having a baby, and if she really wanted to hurt them she could tell them she might be. But all the fight had gone out of her and she was afraid. Not of having

56

Rob's child, but of having it without him. But Rob had said it wouldn't happen.

'I'm all right, Dad. Don't worry.' She saw kindness in his face and compassion, and she whispered, 'I did love him so. Don't blame us. There was so little time.'

He held out his arms then, and because she hurt so much, because she wanted to be a little girl again, she went to him and the tears came.

It was good to weep. She wept until there was nothing inside her but low, gasping sobs and her body was limp.

Her father rocked her in his arms, just as he had done when she was little, and when her mother came in with a cup of hot milk and one of her soothing tablets, she swallowed it obediently, a child again.

'There now. It's going to be all right.' Her father held her tightly until her eyes began to close and from far away she heard her mother pick up the cup and saucer.

'I think she's asleep now. When she wakes, don't tell her the letter has come. Leave it for a while.'

So it was here, the OHMS envelope she had dreaded. Her call-up papers had come and she must go away.

Oh, Rob, I have to leave you . . .

57

3

'*Flamin' Norah! Don't tell me it's gone!*'

'Sorry, lassie.' The ticket collector picked up his coat and bag. 'You've missed it by ten minutes. The next train to Garvie leaves at midnight.'

'That's it, then. I'm adrift.' ETA Ardneavie 2200/22/6, her travel instructions stated precisely – which really meant that Wren Violet T. McKeown was expected to arrive at her destination by 10 P.M. on the twenty-second day of June. 'And that train left on time!' she flung accusingly.

'Aye. They sometimes do. Last week one arrived on time too. But you'd better away to the Naval RTO and get your warrant seen to. You'll no' get into trouble, then, if you're late arriving.'

The railway transport officer. She would find one, they had told her at the training depot, at most main-line stations. Get into difficulties, travelwise, and the RTO would sort it out.

'Over yonder, by the pile of mailbags.' The ticket collector had seen it many times and would see it many times more before the railways returned to normal. If they ever did.

Vi picked up her cases. She had travelled from Rosyth to Glasgow, hardly any distance at all, yet still she had missed her connection. Slamming her feet down angrily, she made for the mailbags.

Mother of God, what a place to be stranded in. But didn't all railway stations look the same, turned by the war into dismal places? Dimly lit, permanently blacked

58

out, they had become dirty and dingy and smelled of neglect. When the war was over, in a million years, and little Marie asked, 'What was your war like, Auntie Vi?' she would tell her, 'Drab, queen. Very drab.'

But it wasn't only the stations, she frowned. Passenger trains never ran on time now. Indeed, men and women not in uniform were asked most pointedly not to use them. *Is your journey really necessary?* the posters demanded accusingly, making it downright unpatriotic for a civilian to even think of occupying a seat on a passenger train.

Vi nodded and smiled at the young soldier and the pale-faced young girl who stood beside him. You smiled at everyone now. You cared about other people and tried to be kind to them, even though they were strangers you would probably never meet again. It had taken a war to do that, Vi realized; though she wouldn't mind betting that on the day peace came, all the caring would end and people would go back to minding their own business again, just as they had before it started. And it would be the same with railway stations. Once the war was over, they would be clean and bright, with everything freshly painted and flowers planted in the tubs. And people going on seaside holidays would have forgotten how stations had once been larger than life, almost; places of meeting and parting, from which dusty, crowded trains had borne servicemen and women to who knew where.

The young soldier and his girl were soon to part. Now, they smiled, standing with fingers entwined, bodies touching, and even when he left her the smile would remain and she would save her tears until his train was out of sight, trying not to think of the brave goodbye that might be their last.

Vi jerked back her shoulders. She had whispered her own last goodbye at a Liverpool dockyard gate, though she had not known it. Two months ago on an innocent

April afternoon, yet already she had lived through a lifetime of sorrow. Now another life was about to begin, one in which she was no more than a surname and number, a woman who had lifted her hand in salute and sworn allegiance to King and country. For as long as the war lasted, she would be a part of the Royal Navy and there could be no remembered yesterdays, no thoughts of tomorrow. One day at a time was how it now must be, and this one day she was adrift, tired and hungry, with new flat-heeled shoes that hurt like hell.

Briefly she closed her eyes, mentally peeling off the scratchy black stockings, lowering her feet inch by beautiful inch into a bowl of cool water. It made her think of bath night at Lyra Street; of the ritual carrying-in of the tub and filling it from pans and kettles set to boil on bright red coals. Then the joys of Vinolia soap and towels hung to warm on the fireguard and flames dancing on her nakedness. Seven Lyra Street. All she had loved, wiped out in a second. It was the reason she was here now, standing bemused in this ill-fitting uniform, black and white all over, like a penguin grown tall and lanky. It was as if she stood in a noisy limbo; all the yesterdays had gone as if they had never been and all the tomorrows were no more than a tantalizing promise. It was why she was adrift with a travel warrant the RTO must stamp. It was the cause of her sore toes and blistered heel and empty, aching stomach. One vicious second, that was all it had taken. Funny, really.

The RTO's office was a small prefabricated hut with a sign on the door that instructed her to knock and walk in. Inside, it was lit by a single bulb wrapped round with a brown-paper shade and furnished with three wooden chairs and a counter on which stood two telephones and a litter of timetables and pads. Its walls were almost covered by official posters urging all who read them to *Dig For Victory*, *Save For Victory*, *Resist The Squanderbug*, *Join The Wrens And Free A Man For The Fleet* and remember that *Careless Talk Costs Lives* and *Walls Have Ears*. From every small uncovered space, Mr Chad poked down his long nose to demand, *Wot, no leave? Wot, no fags?* – or beer or trains or anything else in short supply which, Vi supposed, was just about everything.

'Just what do you mean, the London to Glasgow train terminated at Crewe?' asked the leading hand of the two Wrens who stood at the counter. 'Trains don't do that.'

'This one did. They told me to get off and try to get on the next train going north,' protested the younger of the two, flushing pink.

'Which happened to be my train,' the tall blonde offered uneasily, 'already two hours late from Plymouth.'

'Which doubtless made you miss the Garvie Ferry connection,' their inquisitor barked. 'You're trying to pull a fast one, aren't you? You've been skylarking somewhere!'

'We haven't! It was the train, truly it was!'

'All right then, your train was delayed. So what do you expect me to do about it? Lay on a destroyer and escort?'

'N-no. We just thought you might okay our travel warrants. We should have been at Ardneavie ages ago.'

'So you should.' He read the green documents with pleasure. 'And you'll both be in the rattle when you get there, won't you?'

Vi studied the bright red anchor on the man's left sleeve. A *hook* in naval slang, his badge of rank. A very new hook and most probably the reason for his arrogance. He had a mean little mouth, she thought dispassionately. If she wasn't mistaken, someone above had just kicked his backside and, true to naval tradition, he was passing the reprimand down. But nobody had the right to be that

61

nasty; not even if his backside was black and blue. He should pick on someone his own size, not two young kids who were near to tears.

'But we couldn't help our trains being late. I thought you'd be able to put it right for us.'

'Did you now? And you know what *thought* did, don't you? Mind, if you were to say *please* very nicely, I just might decide to stamp your warrants . . .'

'Might you just! Then you'd better decide to stamp mine while you're on with it!' Vi had heard enough. Elbowing her way to the counter, she slammed down her own piece of paper. 'And be sharp about it!'

'Hey! Hold on there!' The leading hand flushed dark red. 'You wait your turn and speak when you're spoken to. I'm dealing with these two at the moment.'

'Well, from now on you're dealin' with me as well, so get stampin' or we'll miss the next train an' all,' Vi hissed, meeting his gaze, preparing to stare him out. 'Come on, mate. Shift yourself. There's a war on, or hasn't anybody told you? And while you're about it, where can I get something to eat?'

'There's a Church of Scotland canteen a couple of blocks down.' Tight-lipped, the man stamped and initialled the three warrants, his eyes not leaving hers.

'Thanks,' she glared back. 'Next train to Garvie leaves at midnight, doesn't it?'

'Correct. Get off at Garvie Quay. The ferry'll be tied up alongside. Overnight sailings are suspended for the duration but they'll let you go aboard. Depart Garvie tomorrow morning, 0600 hours. ETA Craigiebur Pier 0800 hours.' He said it reluctantly, repeating it parrot-fashion. 'All right? Understood?'

'Fine. That's all we wanted, thanks. Sorry to have put you out.' Vi picked up the three warrants, her mouth pursing with disapproval.

'No need to take it like that. I was only having a bit of fun.'

'There now. Fun, was it? Well, you could have fooled me, mate!'

With a final warning glare, Vi wished him goodnight, then threw open the door and marched out, head high. Only then did she allow herself a smile.

'Well, fancy 'im with the 'ook, pulling rank like that then? Nasty little twerp.' Her smile widened into a grin. 'But how about you two? All right, are you?'

'Just about.' The tall, fair girl smiled back. 'He was giving us a bad time, though, till you came in. I get the feeling he doesn't like Wrens.'

'You could be right, queen. Some sailors don't. They think that women in the Navy are Jonahs – bad luck. Or maybe he doesn't want freeing for the Fleet, eh? But forget about little Hitler in there. We've seen the last of him.' Vi studied the warrants closely. 'Now then, which one of you is Bainbridge, L. V.?'

'That's me – Lucinda.'

'And I'm Jane Kendal.'

'Well, now.' Vi handed back the warrants. 'And I'm Vi'let, well, *Vi*. And since it looks as if we're all goin' to the same place, why don't we take our kit to the left luggage then see if we can't find that canteen?'

'Could we? I'm *starving*,' Lucinda gasped. 'They gave me sandwiches for the journey, but I left them on my bunk.'

'And I shared mine with an ATS girl,' Jane sighed. 'I'm so hungry I feel dizzy.'

'Right, then!' Vi swung her respirator on to her left shoulder and pulled on her navy-blue woollen gloves. 'There's nothin' wrong with any of us that a cup of hot tea and a ciggie won't put right.' She smiled happily, her delight genuine. Life had taken a turn for the better. She

63

had found friends, and food and drink were only a couple of blocks away. All in all, it wasn't such a bad old war.

The canteen was like a thousand others, run by unpaid volunteers and makeshift and bare, but the smile of the elderly helper was as bright as her flowered pinafore.

'Three teas, please.' Cautiously Vi eyed a plate of paste sandwiches. 'And have you any – er, food?'

'It's getting a bit late, but I think I can find you something a wee bit more filling. How does hot pie and beans sound?'

It sounded nothing short of miraculous, and Vi ordered three.

'That'll be one and sixpence, and sorry there's no sugar. Our ration is used up and there's no more till Tuesday. There's saccharin on the tables, though.'

Vi dug deep into the pocket of her broad canvas belt and placed three sixpenny pieces on the counter. That was something else she would have to get used to, she supposed. No purse. No handbag either.

She smiled her thanks, and placing cups and plates on a large tin tray, bore them triumphantly to the table.

'Aaah,' breathed Lucinda.

'Food,' Jane murmured.

Vi sniffed appreciatively, her neglected stomach churning noisily. The pies were round and flat, the pastry pale, their concave lids filled with beans in bright red sauce.

'Aaah,' Lucinda said again, impatiently sinking her knife into the pie crust, watching fascinated as hot brown gravy oozed out. Blissfully she closed her eyes. Nothing had ever tasted so good. Not even after-theatre suppers at the Ritz with Charlie. Eyes downcast, she ate without speaking, pausing only to smile at Vi. How lucky she had been to meet Violet, but wasn't that the story of her life? Hadn't there always been someone to make decisions for

64

her, smooth her path? But she was on her own now. Henceforth she must carry on from where she had started that momentous morning in Goddy's office. Heady stuff, it had been. That act of defiance warmed her even now, just thinking of it. Triumphantly, she forked a straying bean.

Jane ate without pausing. Hunger was an unknown experience; she had never imagined it could actually hurt. And wasn't it wonderful to be here, actually *here*, in Rob's city. Out there in the gathering darkness was the tenement where Rob had once lived with his mother and brothers. How strange that from all the many places to which she might have been drafted, chance had come up with Ardneavie. Two days ago she had stood in line in the drafting office at the training depot, wondering where she would be sent. The Wren immediately before her was assigned to Appledore, in Devon; the one behind her to Aultbea, in the far north-west; but for Wren Kendal it had been HMS *Omega* and the Wrens' quarters at Ardneavie. In Argyll, they told her. Across the Firth of Clyde from Glasgow. It was Fate. It had to be.

Vi ate steadily, rhythmically, savouring every bite, looking around her at yet another facet of this, her strange new life.

Take this place, now – this green-walled, text-hung church hall where servicemen and women could sit out their loneliness for the price of a cup of tea. A place where men snatched from those they cared for could write cheerful, loving letters with no word of their secret worries. How would the rent be paid? How would the children be fed and clothed, on Army pay? Yet she, thought Vi, was as free as the air, with no home to worry about, no children to rear on a pittance as Mam had done. From now on the windows she polished, the floors she swept, the cups and saucers and plates she washed would

65

not be her own. It would have been too sad to think about had she not met two apprehensive Wrens: Lucinda and Jane, kids hardly out of their gymslips who would need a bit of looking after. Count your blessings, Mam had always said, and she must never, ever forget it.

'Hey, but that wasn't half good.' She rubbed the last of her bread around her plate. 'Better than a Sunday dinner, that was.'

'Mm. I feel almost human again.' Lucinda took cigarettes and a lighter from the depths of her khaki drill respirator bag, and flicking open the expensive-looking case, handed them round. 'I say, do you suppose they charged us enough? Sixpence seems so little . . .'

'I don't think they want to make a profit.' Vi shrugged. 'They open these canteens to help the war along.'

They were run by the women of a bombed city, most of whom had already lived through one war. Women who had been forced, in the name of Victory, to return to work in shops and factories, yet still found time at the end of the day to brew tea and serve hot meat pies, and smile. It made you proud, really, to belong to this daft, defiant little island.

'Hullo there, girls!' A soldier with the badge of the Gordon Highlanders shining on his cap leaned over, an unlit cigarette between his fingers. 'Got a light, blondie?' He winked broadly at Lucinda, who flicked her lighter and winked back.

'Thanks, hen.'

'My pleasure.' The corners of Lucinda's mouth quirked up into a beaming smile as Vi watched, fascinated. It was amazing, that quick, dancing smile of hers. A sudden dart of sunlight ending in deep dimples, one on either cheek. Lucinda was pretty, Vi acknowledged – chocolate-box pretty. Not at all like sad-eyed Jane, whose hair glinted

66

auburn and who, one day, would be nothing less than beautiful.

'Now then, tell me about yourselves.' Vi wasn't nosey, she just liked people. 'We're all goin' to Ardneavie, aren't we? HMS *Omega*? I wonder what it's like.'

'A shore station, I shouldn't wonder,' Lucinda hazarded. 'Well, I'm a sparker – a wireless telegraphist – and Jane's a coder, so it's got to be something to do with signals. What's your category, Vi?'

'General duties.' Vi smiled. 'I'm a steward. Not a mess steward, though; more on the cleanin' side, I think it's goin' to be. Where did you two meet up? Trainin' depot, was it?'

'No. I did my training in London.'

'And I,' Lucinda offered, 'learned the mysteries of the Morse code and the iniquities of squad drill at Plymouth signal school. We met up at Crewe station. Funny world, isn't it?'

'Funny?' Vi dropped a saccharin tablet into her tea, watching it rise, fizzing pale green, to the surface.

'Y-yes, but I can't explain.' She could have, Lucinda realized, but they would think her a little mad if she did. How did you say you felt free for the first time in your life? A strange freedom, though; one a barrage balloon would know if someone severed its cable and set it at liberty to wallow and wander at will. Or until some high-flying fighter pilot fired a cannon shell into it and it fell, deflated, back to earth. 'I suppose it's because joining up was something I *had* to do. My family – my mother, especially – were totally against it. Oh, I'd registered when I was eighteen, like everyone else. But that was in Lincolnshire, where we were living at the time. Then suddenly we had to leave for London, so I suppose the call-up people didn't know where I was. I waited and waited, and my mother told me to leave well alone, that

67

the war would get on very nicely without my efforts. W-e-ell . . .'

She paused. No need to tell them about Charlie and getting married or the unholy row with Mama or the hell that was let loose when she told them she'd had her medical for the WRNS and if anyone tried to stop her going . . .

'Well, I felt dreadful about it, and one morning I went to see my godfather at the Admiralty and begged him to get me into the Navy. And so far, I haven't regretted a minute of it, not even today. I shouldn't be grateful to the war,' she said softly, cheeks flushing pink, 'but I am. Do you think me quite mad?'

'No, queen, I know just how you feel.' Vi nodded. 'I came out of the shelter one mornin' and all I had was gone. At first I couldn't believe it. It was never goin' to happen to me. To her across the street, perhaps, but not to me. Then I got mad. I cursed and blinded and I swore to get even . . .'

No need to tell them about Gerry. Not yet. Not ever, maybe.

'. . . get even with big fat Hermann. I went to the recruitin' office in a right old temper and I joined up there and then. "I'll do anything," I told them, and it wasn't till afterwards that I realized I'd done the right thing 'cos where else was I to go? Only to our Mary's, and she didn't really have the room. So I do know what you mean.'

Jane flicked cigarette ash into the upturned tin lid. 'I – I suppose I'm glad to be here too. I'm an only child, you see, and it gets a bit stifling sometimes. I registered just after my eighteenth birthday and had my medical almost at once. Then nothing happened.' Not Rob. Don't tell them about Rob. They wouldn't understand. They couldn't.

'I really thought they'd forgotten me, lost my records

68

or something. But my call-up papers came eventually. Report to Mill Hill, London on the twenty-fifth of May, they said. It was a relief, I suppose. Fenton Bishop – that's where I live – is a one-street village where nothing happens.'

Not until the machines moved in to throw a great concrete runway across the fields, and buildings grew like mushrooms overnight and were camouflaged brown and black and green, and the bombers roared in, and Rob came . . .

'I suppose,' Jane whispered, 'that I was glad, too.'

'There now.' Vi beamed. 'Takes all sorts to make a world, dunnit? Shall we have another cup of tea? There's loads of time.'

'I'll get them.' Lucinda jumped to her feet, collecting cups, plates and cutlery together and placing them on the tray. 'Anyone want anything else?'

'No, ta.' Vi wiggled her toes, wondering if she dared take off her shoes just for five minutes, to ease the throbbing, shooting pain. But do that and she'd never get them on again, and she would arrive at Ardneavie not only late, but shoeless!

Jane ran her finger round her collar. It was far too tight and chafing her neck. How would she ever get used to wearing a tie? And oh, the panic this morning when she lost a collar stud. She must remember to buy a spare set. Searching on hands and knees at the crack of dawn was not the best start to a day, especially a day like this one!

'Tea up!' Lucinda set down the cups, then, unbuttoning her jacket, sat down at the table, chin on hands.

'Do you suppose we're ever going to feel comfortable in these uniforms? I mean, one feels so *awkward*.'

'Don't we all, queen? It isn't as if they fit, either.'

'And they're so *fluffy*,' Jane mourned. 'I wonder how long it's going to take us to wear them smooth.'

69

'Well, I wouldn't have minded, but they just threw mine at me when we were kitted out. Look at this. Miles too big.' Lucinda rose dramatically to her feet, holding out her arms. 'The length of these sleeves! It looks as if I've got no hands.'

'My skirt is miles too long. Fourteen inches from the floor it's supposed to be, yet it's nearly tripping me. What am I expected to do – grow into it?'

'Oh, it'll be all right. This get-up'll be quite smart, once we've had a go at it.' Vi looked at her double-breasted, six-buttoned jacket. Black buttons, anchor decorated. Clever, that: no polishing. A tuck here and there, perhaps, and a couple of inches off the length, and their skirts would be quite presentable. And white shirts were very smart, really, and would look quite good when they had learned to cope with the board-stiff collars and not to knot their ties so tightly. No, there was nothing wrong with their uniforms that couldn't be put right, as far as Vi was concerned. The shoes, though, were altogether a different matter.

'I think,' she said sadly, 'that I'm goin' to have trouble with me feet, though. I should have been kitted out a week earlier but they'd got no shoes to fit me. It's a terrible trial havin' big feet.'

'I suppose it must be.' Lucinda frowned. 'Does it – er – run in the family, Vi?'

'Nah. It's because I never had no shoes till I was three. Me feet just spread. Y'know, I can remember the first time I wore them. Mam got 'em from the nuns – you could get all sorts of things from the convent in them days. Free, they were, and I can remember one of the Sisters putting them socks and shoes on me, and me yellin' and screamin' like mad and tryin' to take them off. Then the weather got cold and I must've realized it was nice

70

havin' warm feet 'cos Mam said she never had no trouble with me after that. But that's why I've got big feet.'

'I don't like these woollen stockings,' Jane pouted. 'I've done nothing but itch since I got mine.'

'And the underwear is a bit much,' Lucinda added. 'Pink cotton bras and suspender belts!' She gave an exaggerated shudder. 'And the *knickers*!' Directoire knickers in navy-blue rayon with long, knee-reaching legs. 'I thought they went out with Queen Victoria. No wonder they're called *blackouts*.'

'Or passion-killers.' Jane giggled.

'You're right.' Vi grinned. 'Imagine gettin' knocked down by a tram in the middle of Lime Street wearin' *them* things. You'd never be able to look the ambulance men in the face, would you? We're goin' to have to cut about six inches off them knicker legs.'

'I suppose we'll get used to everything, in time,' Lucinda shrugged. 'We feel awkward in uniform at the moment and a bit self-conscious. And white shirts are hardly the thing for long train journeys. All those black smuts from the engine, and the door handles covered in grime, and the dusty seats . . .'

'You're right, queen. We're fed-up and tired and we've missed our train, but it'll all come right, just see if it doesn't. And at least we don't have to worry any more about what to wear. What about the poor civilians, then? They get the sticky end of the golden sceptre every time, don't they?'

'Clothes rationing, you mean?'

'Clothes rationin',' Vi affirmed solemnly. 'Imagine the Government doin' a thing like that, eh?'

It had happened suddenly, just three weeks ago. The British public had opened its morning papers to the stark announcement that clothing and footwear were rationed. Coupon values had been placed upon every conceivable article, and henceforth it would be illegal to buy anything without surrendering the appropriate number of clothing coupons. Briefly, it stated that sixty-six coupons had been considered adequate for normal use. The bomb-shell exploded when it added that those sixty-six coupons must last for a whole year.

'*It is outrageous*,' the Countess had written to her daughter. '*How is one to be decently clothed when one must hand over sixteen coupons for a coat and five for a pair of shoes? We shall all be in rags . . .*'

'It's fair, I suppose,' Jane argued. 'Clothes were getting very expensive and in short supply too. Now everyone will at least get a fair share.'

'But three whole coupons for a pair of silk stockings,' Lucinda wailed. 'My mother was always catching hers on her rings. She went through any amount of stockings in a week. She won't be able to do that now.'

'She'll have to go without, then – or paint her legs, as it suggested in the magazine. Gravy-browning is supposed to be good.'

'Good grief!' Mama bare-legged! Lucinda shook with silent joy. Gravy-browning? But it really wasn't funny, come to think of it, since poor Pa would be the whipping boy for the silk stocking shortage. One thing was certain, though. Worrying about clothing coupons would at least make Mama forget the invasion for a while.

'What's so funny?' Vi demanded.

'My mother. Having to paint her legs.' Lucinda's smile gave way to a throaty laugh. 'But she'll find a way round it.'

She would, too. Lady Kitty's wardrobes were crammed with clothes, and she would give those for which she had no further use to someone with little money – in exchange for some of their coupons, of course. That it was against the law would not worry milady in the least. The Countess of Donnington upheld only those laws with which she agreed, and the rationing of footwear and clothing and the issuing of clothing coupons were not among them.

'It'll be hard on my sister,' Vi considered. 'Got two kids, Mary has. Just imagine – *eight* coupons for a pair of pyjamas and five for a blouse and seven for a skirt. And you've even got to give up a coupon for two ounces of knitting wool as well. I don't know how she'll manage. Go without, herself, I shouldn't wonder.'

'I suppose we're lucky, missing all that.' Jane remembered the three pairs of London-tan stockings she had left behind her. It was useless to try to hoard silk stockings, stated the women's magazines. They deteriorated with time, and the only way to prolong their life was to store them carefully in airtight containers and only wear them on special occasions. It was patriotic to go bare-legged, insisted fashion editors, whereupon almost the entire female population of the United Kingdom had wrapped their precious stockings in cellophane and placed them, sighing, in screw-topped jars in dark cupboards.

Furtively Jane scratched an itching calf. Some women had all the luck. To be stockingless at this moment, she thought fervently, would be nothing short of bliss.

The canteen began to empty. The Gordon Highlanders had already left, the airmen from the corner table had hoisted kitbags to shoulders and gone their separate ways, and the soldier who had spent the entire evening writing letters called a goodnight and walked out into the darkness. At the counter the elderly lady took off her pinafore and put on her coat.

'I'm away to catch the last tram,' she smiled. 'The front door is locked now but the caretaker will let you out at the back, so you'll be welcome to stay for a wee while longer. Good night, girls. Take care of yourselves.'

'I suppose we'd better all be making tracks,' Vi murmured reluctantly. 'All got our respirators?'

Lose a respirator and the cost was deductible from pay. Respirators were a nuisance; it was a punishable offence for any member of the armed forces to be caught without one. Respirators had to go *everywhere* with them, like the Ancient Mariner and his albatross.

'Are you wanting away, ladies?' A white-haired man limped ahead of them and opened a door at the rear of the room. 'You'll take care in the blackout, now.'

'We will. We'll be fine, ta.' Vi looked at the medal ribbons, proudly worn on the shabby jacket. Earned in the last war, no doubt, and that stiff, awkward leg too.

They wished him good night, then stood a while, blinking in the darkness, listening to the slam of the door bolts. The dense blackness lifted a little and they were able to pick out the skyline and the dim glow of white-edged pavements and white-ringed lampposts. The blackout was complete. Even torches had to be covered with paper and car headlights painted over, except for a small cross of light at their centres. They would all be troglodytes before the war was over, thought Lucinda, with eyes that stood out on little stalks.

Ahead of them a match flared and a lighted cigarette glowed briefly like a small bright beacon, reminding them of streetlamps and bonfires and shop windows blazing with light. One day those lights would go on again, but not just yet, Lucinda thought sadly.

'It's very quiet, isn't it?' Jane felt with the toe of her shoe for the kerb edge. 'Was it this quiet when we came, Vi?'

'Well, no, but it's late now, innit? Past eleven, I shouldn't wonder. Don't worry. We'll soon be at the station, and it'll be noisy enough there.'

They walked carefully, staring ahead into the night.

'Did we pass a row of dustbins on the way here?'

'Don't know. Don't remember any,' Vi admitted dubiously.

'No more did I. I hope I'm wrong but I – I think we're going the wrong way.'

'What makes you say that?' True, it had been reasonably light when they left the station, and Glasgow, its war scars softened by the approaching night, had seemed like Liverpool to Vi. Here, too, were boarded-up shopfronts and sandbagged doorways. Here, as in her own city, bomb-ravaged buildings stood stark against the glow of a sinking sun, strangely, tragically beautiful. But now the sameness was gone. These were not the streets and alleys Vi knew and felt easy in. Here were unexpected turnings she could not recognize; and there was something else, she thought, suddenly apprehensive.

'When we left the station, do you remember any trams?'

'Yes, one.' Lucinda frowned. 'Going in the opposite direction, but I haven't heard any lately.'

'Well, you wouldn't. Not now. Don't you remember the canteen lady leaving to get the last tram?'

'Yes, queen, I do. But take a look at that road. No tramlines there.'

'Then we're lost,' Lucinda said flatly. 'It's because we left by the back door. We went the wrong way, I suppose. It's easy enough in the blackout. I suppose now we've either got to cut through the next side street we come to and try to get to the main road, or turn round and find the canteen and start again.'

It would be better, they decided, to retrace their steps and find the door by which they had left. That way, they would know exactly where they were, and this time, if they turned right, then right again, they would be on course for the station. They *must* be.

75

'Stupid, innit, the way you can lose your way in the dark, 'specially in a strange place?'

'Hmm. I wonder what travellers did hundreds of years ago when there were no proper roads and no streetlights or signposts?'

'They spent the night at an inn, if they'd any sense.' Lucinda laughed. A nervous laugh, because she was beginning to feel uneasy. And everything was too quiet, though it was an accepted fact that if one stood very still in the blackout and listened intently, there were always footsteps out there, somewhere. Or the intimate glow of two cigarettes and the soft, low laughter of unseen lovers.

'Well we,' said Vi firmly, 'are goin' to spend the night on the Craigiebur ferry, all nice and comfortable, and we'll be at Ardneavie in time for breakfast. So let's get it right this time, eh?'

They did not find the canteen, nor any building like it, nor any doorway that even vaguely resembled the one through which they had left.

'We've got ourselves lost,' Vi said. 'That's what we've gone and done.'

Around them the darkness was absolute, the silence oppressive. It pressed in on them from all sides, menacing, frightening.

'What do we do now?' Jane whispered, her mouth suddenly dry.

'Do you suppose that if we stood still and listened, we might hear someone? Well,' Lucinda shrugged, 'they say you're never alone in the blackout, even though you can't actually see anyone.'

'Ar, hey,' Vi said uneasily, 'don't be saying that, queen. It's a pity we can't see the street names, though I don't suppose it would do us a lot of good if we could – well, not without a street map.'

'Then let's stand still for a little while and listen. Someone is bound to come this way eventually.'

'Or we could try keeping going. Maybe that way we'll hit civilization.'

'I think we should stand here,' Vi decided. 'Stay still and listen and try not to panic.'

'Quiet!' It was Jane who heard the footsteps first, and they stood unmoving, ears straining, hardly breathing.

'Yes!' gasped Lucinda. Heavy footsteps, coming nearer, slow and measured.

'I think it's a man,' Vi whispered, 'but don't worry. There's three of us and only one of him.'

'Shall I call out?' Lucinda asked.

'Okay. Or maybe a whistle would be better.'

'Right.' Lucinda ran her tongue round her suddenly dry lips and let out a long, slow whistle. 'Hullo? Anybody there?'

They waited, breath indrawn, but there was no answering whistle, no reassuring call. And now the footsteps had stopped.

'Where is he?' Jane demanded.

'Probably surrounding us.'

'Now listen, don't be worryin'. I don't know what he's doin', but if the worst comes to the worst, scream for all you're worth. It puts 'em off, does screamin'.'

'Never mind about *him*,' Jane choked. 'What about the time!'

'Oh, Lord!' Lucinda flicked her lighter. 'The train!'

'Get that light out!' The voice was deep and masculine.

'It's him!' Vi gasped. 'Try again.'

Lucinda held the lighter above her head and flicked it again. 'Help us! We're lost!'

'Okay. Stay there.' The voice was nearer now, the footfalls heavier, quicker. 'And *put that light out*!'

77

He came suddenly out of the blackness, looming large above them.

'Who is it?' Vi demanded.

'Police.' Briefly he shone a torch on his face and they glimpsed a uniform and the black and white chequered band around his cap. Then he shone the light on them, laughing softly. 'Well now, if it isn't three wee Wrens.'

'Thank goodness you've come, officer. We're lost and we've *got* to get back to the station.' Lucinda's relief was obvious.

'Now which station would that be?'

'Central. And our train leaves at midnight. Can you tell us how we get there? A short cut, perhaps.'

'Short cuts, is it? Are you no lost enough already? No, no. Best you stay with me till we get to Argyle Street – you'll no be able to miss the station then.'

'Is it far?' Vi was anxious.

'Och, no. You'll soon be there. Just follow me and mind your step.'

They followed him blindly, hands clasped, until he called to them to stop.

'There now, this is where I leave you. Here's the Queen Street corner, and you just turn right and keep going full steam ahead. The station's no far.'

He stood listening to their uncertain footsteps, shaking his head as the night closed in around them.

What was this war coming to and where would it all end when they were taking on lassies to help fight it? Aye, and lassies who couldn't walk a few hundred yards without getting themselves lost. And as for that train – he shone his torch on the watch at his wrist. Well, they'd missed that, and no mistake. Dearie me, he chuckled out loud, where *would* it all end?

* * *

The policeman was right, Vi brooded. It hadn't taken them long, but she knew instinctively as they hurried into the hollow gloom of the station that they had missed yet another train.

'Flippin' heck,' she hissed. 'Twenty past twelve!'

'Maybe it's still there,' Lucinda panted as they retrieved their kit and heaved it, gasping, to platform 8.

'An' maybe pigs'll start flyin',' Vi snapped. 'I mean, miss one train – that's fair enough; but *two*?'

'Bordering on carelessness, I'd say.' Lucinda nodded soberly. 'Not to mention what's going to happen when we get there. If ever we do, that is.'

'That's it, then.' Morosely they regarded the deserted platform. 'The next train leaves at six for the eight o'clock ferry. Six in the mornin', that is.'

'Then I suppose it's the RTO again,' Lucinda ventured.

'You *what*?' Vi exploded. 'Face 'im with the 'ook again? Tell 'im we got lost in the blackout? Oh, that'd make 'is day, that would. "Been to the ale house, 'ave yer?" that's what he'd say. We'd be in the rattle before you could say wet Nelly!'

'You're right. I suppose they only okay your warrant if you're late through no fault of your own.' Jane shrugged. 'Getting lost isn't exactly an act of God, is it?'

'No it isn't. It's plain bloody stupid.'

'Then we're in trouble.'

'We are. Up to the ear-'oles in it. We'd better think up an excuse. It'll 'ave to be good, so don't come up with something like us all bein' knocked down by a herd of stampedin' giraffes.'

'Or attacked by a plague of locusts?'

'Hey, Jane. Tell yer funny friend that locusts isn't valid neither,' Vi retorted, pan-faced. 'Come on, queen. Get thinkin'.'

'Then seriously, how about an air raid? No bombs, of

course – they could easily check up on bombs – just an alert, so we'd all be forced to find a shelter.'

'Sounds good. About eleven o'clock, would you say?'

'That's it.' Vi nodded. 'That's just about right. And by the time the all clear went, the train had gone. Okay?'

'But would a train be allowed to leave during an alert?' Lucinda frowned. 'Wouldn't it have to stay in the station?'

'Ar, hey, Lucinda, whose side are you on?' Vi demanded.

'Sorry. Just a thought.'

'Well, like 'im with the 'ook said, you know what *thought* did, don't you? No, it's got to be an alert, and if we all keep to the same story we might just get away with it. We'll get it all worked out and one of us'll do the talkin', all right? Stick together, eh?'

'Like the Three Musketeers, you mean?'

'The three *wot*? Who the 'ell are they, when they're at 'ome?'

'*Were*. Three soldiers; figments of fiction.'

'Imaginary, sort of?'

'That's it. Three inseparable friends.' Lucinda smiled. 'They stuck together through thick and thin. One for all and all for one. Rather like us, I'd say.'

'Mmm. Like us.' The idea pleased Vi and she smiled broadly. 'Well then, since it was my fault we missed the train again, it'd better be me who does the talkin' when we get there. You two'll just have to stand behind me and nod your 'eads.'

'But Vi –'

'No buts. I'm the biggest and the oldest. No more to be said. Now, let's grab that bench. If we stay there all night we can't miss the next train, can we?'

'Want to bet?' Lucinda liked Vi McKeown. Vi had what Goddy would call a defiant set to her jib. It would be really rather nice, she thought as she picked up her cases

80

for the fiftieth time that day, if they could all stay together, though it was hardly likely. *They* didn't do nice things like that. *They*. The faceless ones who spoke with the omnipotent voice of authority and who, for the duration of hostilities, would be obeyed without question.

It would be all right, Jane thought without conviction. Surely it would all come right. It wasn't that she doubted that the Allies would win – of course they would. But where and *when* would it all end? Years and years and years it would take.

'Now then, young Kendal. Don't look so miserable!'

'Sorry, Vi. I didn't mean to. I was just wondering how long it's going to be before it's all over and we can go home.'

'Not long.' Vi beamed. 'Now that us three's in the Navy it'll be over by Christmas!'

'Bless you, Vi. I shouldn't have said that, should I?'

'You say what you like, queen. It's still a free country, innit? We're all a bit fed up, but it'll pass. It's like Mam used to tell me. "Nothing lasts, our Vi. Good times nor bad times nothing lasts." An' she was right. Tomorrow night we'll be laughin' our 'eads off about all this.'

'Of course we will,' Lucinda whispered. 'And let's all try like mad to stay together, shall we?'

'Like them Musketeers, you mean?'

'Like them.'

'Right, then. All for one! Let's grab that bench. We'll soon be on our way. Not long to wait. Five hours'll soon pass.'

But contrary to Vi McKeown's shining optimism, that night was the most uncomfortable any of them could remember. Not only were they the longest hours they had ever been called upon to endure, but the coldest.

'You wouldn't think it was June.' Jane shrugged into

her greatcoat then spread her raincoat over her knees. 'I'd give anything for a cup of tea. *Anything*.'

'Then let's all close our eyes and wish like mad for the WVS lady and her trolley to materialize right here in front of us like a dear little fat fairy.'

But of fat fairies bearing hot sweet tea there was never a sign and the fingers of the station clock jerked away the minutes with maddening languor, the tedium of their watch being broken only by the intermittent arrivals and departure of trains.

'I wonder,' Vi frowned, 'where that lot'll end up, poor sods.'

They were watching the departure of a troop train from an adjoining platform. The soldiers, laden with packs, had arrived in trucks, and at-the-double feet quickly formed into orderly ranks before disappearing into the unlit interiors of a dozen carriages. Sergeants rapped out indecipherable commands, corporals checked kitbags and wooden crates and boxes into the luggage vans, stamped their feet and saluted their officers smartly. Then the engine belched smoke and steam and pulled reluctantly away from the platform.

'Ships that pass,' Jane murmured.

'Think they're going abroad?'

'Suppose so. Going down river to Greenock, I shouldn't wonder. Probably to a troopship . . .'

'Where d'you imagine they'll end up?'

'Middle East, perhaps. Or maybe the Far East: Hong Kong, Shanghai, Burma . . . Would you ever volunteer for overseas, Vi?'

'Dunno.' Mentally, as was her considered duty, Vi blessed the receding train, commending its occupants to the care of St Christopher. 'Ask me tomorrow when I've got some food inside me. Now you two try to get some sleep and I'll keep me eyes on that platform. We don't

82

want that train creepin' in and creepin' out again while nobody's lookin'.'

She reached out and pulled them to her in a protective motherly gesture. 'Close your eyes, now. God bless. And don't worry. It'll all come right, just see if it doesn't.'

It was 5.30 A.M. and a new day had begun. Vi stretched her cold legs and rotated her ankles. Her feet still hurt and she felt the tingle of cramp in her right arm where Jane's head rested heavily. Poor kids. They'd fallen asleep, a head on each shoulder and she was determined to leave them like that for as long as she could.

Not for a long time had Vi felt so uncomfortable. She was cold and unwashed and hunger pangs were beginning to gnaw again. But the train would soon be arriving and then they'd –

'Paper!' A sudden commotion behind her caused her to start as a voice called urgently, stridently, 'Special edition. Paper!'

Vi twisted her head then stared, eyes wide, at the newsboy's billboard.

'Mother of God!' Sleepers forgotten, she jumped to her feet and read the word again. It was written large and thick in bright red ink and it sent a shock of fear slicing through her. 'Will you look at *that*!'

'Sorry.' Jane rose unsteadily to her feet. 'Been asleep. Didn't mean to. . .'

'Never mind about sorry.' Impatiently Vi shook Lucinda's arm. 'Look at that, for Pete's sake!'

There was no mistaking the word. Even in their befuddled state its meaning was frighteningly explicit.

'*Invasion*.' Jane's lips formed the word but no sound came.

'Dear God, *no*.' This was it, then. Just when everyone was beginning to believe it would never come.

83

'I'm goin' for a paper.' Vi ran to the paper-seller, digging into her pocket for a penny, shaking open the newspaper with agitated hands.

'RUSSIA ATTACKED ON 1,800 MILE FRONT', screamed the headlines. 'SOVIET TOWNS AND PORTS BOMBED'.

'Listen, you two.' Vi began to read, her voice strained with disbelief. ' "At dawn on Sunday, 22 June, between 3 and 3.30 in the morning, three million German troops marched into Russia . . ." '

'Russia?' Jane gasped. 'They've invaded *Russia*?'

'That's what it says, queen.'

'But didn't they sign a pact, or something?'

'Since when have pacts meant anything to Hitler?'

Instantly they were wide awake. Suddenly, discomfort forgotten, relief sang through them. Hitler had taken on the mysterious Soviets, but why had he chosen to invade Russia and not the British Isles?

'I suppose that lets us off the hook,' Lucinda offered. 'Well, for the time being.'

'And maybe just this once Hitler won't get it all his own way. Remember what happened to Napoleon.'

'Those Russians probably don't know yet what's hit them. But how much do we know about them, anyway?' Lucinda frowned. 'How many troops do they have and how many tanks and guns? I mean, it's not all that long since they threw out the Tsar, is it. It's dreadful for them, and it might just as easily have been us. I suppose they'll be on our side now.'

'Suppose they will,' Vi agreed. Then her lips broke into a beaming smile. 'Just take a look at *that*.'

The 6 A.M. Glasgow to Garvie train approached platform 8 gently, apologetically almost, then came to a stop with a squealing of brakes and a hiss of escaping steam, and they looked at it with wide-eyed wonder.

'It's come,' breathed Vi and so disbelieving was she that

she checked its very existence with the engine driver and his black-faced fireman.

'This *is* the Craigiebur Ferry train?'

It was indeed, said the driver, and it would arrive at Garvie at 7.40 for the eight o'clock ferry.

'I don't believe it,' Jane gasped as they piled cases, coats and respirators on to the luggage rack. 'I do *not* believe it.'

'You know what's going to happen?' The corners of Lucinda's mouth tilted mischievously. 'This train won't leave on time as the last two did, and we'll miss the ferry.'

'Ar, hey, Lucinda. You've got a funny sense of humour,' Vi wailed. 'If we miss that ferry again I'll shoot myself, honest to God I will!'

'Me too. I feel awful,' Jane sniffed. 'I'm hungry and tired and my collar's choking me. And my shirt is filthy and I'm filthy, and if I don't get a bath soon I'll start to smell!'

'Then we'd all better close our eyes and think not of Victory but of hot water and soap and bathsalts and soft warm towels.'

'And mugs of tea,' Vi croaked, 'and a plate of bacon butties.'

A woman guard slammed the door of their compartment, blew hard on her whistle and waved her green flag. Slowly the train began to move and bumper met bumper, clink-clanking the length of the train. Then the 6 A.M. Garvie connection drew slowly away, carrying with it Wrens Bainbridge, Kendal and McKeown.

It seemed like a small, sweet miracle. Leaning back, they closed their eyes and thought of hot water and soap and bacon sandwiches and mugs of tea. What might happen when eventually they arrived at Wrens' Quarters, Ardneavie, mattered little. They had caught the train at last, and beyond that not one of them was able to think.

* * *

'You're adrift! You should've been here yesterday fore-noon,' rapped an irate Chief Wren. 'And you're dirty and sloppy and you look as if you've been dragged backwards through a hedge, the lot of you! Where in heaven's name have you been until now?'

'We've been comin', Chief. As fast as we could.' Vi took a step forward, assuming command. 'I met up with these two on Glasgow station. They'd missed the connec-tion, too. Sorry, Chief. The trains were shockin'.'

As if she had no part in the conversation, Jane gazed around her. This regulating office was small, and unlike its bare, efficient counterpart at the training depot, was homely and almost feminine. On either side of the Victor-ian fireplace with its flower-filled hearth stood an easy chair. There were even pictures of ships and groups of Wrens on the walls.

'*How* shocking?'

'Well, take Kendal 'ere.' Vi jabbed a thumb. 'Now her train just stopped at Crewe. Goin' no further, they said.'

Lucinda glanced from Vi to Chief Wren Pillmoor, wondering who would be the victor. Vi had the situation under control but the chief could, and probably would, pull rank. She looked like a lady who was used to getting her own way, Lucinda considered. And those eyelashes! They were longer than Mama's and Mama's were false. Chief Pillmoor's eyelashes were nothing short of magnifi-cent, and thick and spiky as a stableyard brush.

'I see. And Bainbridge?'

'Bainbridge's train was late, an' all. Four hours late into Glasgow. It's the bombin', see?'

'And you missed not only the 8 P.M. train but the next one, too?' Chief Pillmoor's eyebrows winged upwards questioningly.

'Ah, well. Yes. We were all starvin', Chief, so we went to this canteen. That's when the sirens went and we had

86

to go to the shelter. And by the time we got the all clear, the midnight train had gone, too. We waited on the station all night and it was perishin'. But it's the war,' she added without guile, and because the chief had taken a liking to the woman with the thick Liverpool accent who met her gaze without flinching, she told them to cut along to the galley; if they were lucky they might just make standeasy.

Never had three Wren ratings moved with such swiftness, drawn by the tantalizing promise of hot tea. They had made it. They had arrived at their given destination, had ridden out the Chief Wren's wrath, and tea – and toast, too, if their noses were to be believed – were within blessed reach. Hopes high again, they tapped on the galley door.

'Well, what d'you know, girls? We did it.' Gently Vi eased off her shoes, wriggled her toes, then stood for a blissful moment, eyes closed. 'An' we're stayin' together, too. Smashin', innit?'

Around them lay the litter of kit they had carried to the very top of the big old house; to cabin 9, their strange bare room. They gazed without emotion at three black-painted iron bedsteads piled with folded blankets and sheets, at the familiar blue and white anchor-decorated bedcovers and the essential thick black curtains at the window. This, then, was their home for as long as the war lasted. For the duration.

'At least we've got beds and not bunks.'

'Yes, and it's nice and quiet up here.'

'It's luv'ly. Let's get our beds made up and do our unpackin'. Who wants which bed, or doesn't it matter?'

It did not matter, nor which chest of drawers belonged to whom. Midday meal would be at 1230 hours, and they had been told they were excused duties for the remainder

87

of the day. What lay beyond they had no inclination to contemplate.

'Cheer up. The worst's over. This billet's goin' to be all right,' Vi urged. Already she had inspected the house that stood on the edge of the sea loch. 'I was talkin' to a girl in the galley. Seems they leave you alone here to get on with it. No more polishin' or drillin' or kit inspection – well, only once a month. And two late passes a week and when you've had those you can get in through the pantry window if the front door's been locked.' Although Chief Pillmoor wasn't everybody's cup of tea, Vi had discovered, at least the lady was fair and had no favourites.

She gazed with compassion at the two dejected figures. Their eyes were dark-ringed, their faces pale and their hair lay dull and uncurled. Kids, that's all they were and in need of a bit of looking-after. Neither was wearing a ring, but that was nothing to go by. Hadn't she taken off her own wedding ring and hung it around her neck with her red identity tag and the St Christopher medal Father O'Flaherty had given her? No rings, no questions, Vi had decided.

'It'll be fine here,' she beamed. 'Just see if it isn't. And we'll all feel better when we've had a bath and a decent night's sleep.'

Vi had a roof over her head again, bed and board and two shillings a day pay, and, better than that, she had found someone to mother. The woman from Liverpool was happy. Well, near-as-damn-it happy.

'They've arrived, Ma'am.' Chief Wren Pillmoor placed three sets of official documents on the officer's desk. 'Railways still in a mess after the air raids – they were so delayed they missed the last ferry connection. Spent the night on Glasgow station, it would seem.'

'Oh dear, I hope they're none the worse?' Third Officer Suzie St John was genuinely concerned.

'A bit travel weary but otherwise okay, Ma'am. Bainbridge, Kendal and McKeown. Two C of E and a Roman Catholic. I've put them in cabin 9, next door to the boat's-crew lot. McKeown is the steward we've been expecting and the other two will be working on the ship. They're all three going to see Sister this afternoon. No problems, that I can see.'

Suzie St John sighed her relief. She was charming and gentle and life had not fitted her to cope with the forty assorted females now in her care. Thus she was constantly grateful for the unfailing vigilance and support of her Chief Wren. 'Time for a drink before lunch, Pat?'

'Thanks, love. Sherry, please.' Formalities over, Patricia Pillmoor drew out a chair, pulled off her hat and settled down for a chat. About Russia, of course. Indeed, there could be no other topic of conversation since it had hit them like a bomb-blast on the early-morning news bulletin. A hundred divisions pouring across the frontier. Russia invaded by Germany, the non-aggression pact between them counting for nothing.

Amazing, when you thought about it, but it was turning out to be an amazing war. And one thing was certain. There would be no invasion of the British Isles, now. Chief Pillmoor raised her glass.

'Cheers.' She smiled. 'Anything new on the wireless about Russia?'

4

The dying sun turned the hills that ringed Loch Ardneavie from green to misty grey, and trees cast long purple shadows. The new occupants of cabin 9 were tired, yet sleep did not come. Lucinda lay, gazing upward, thinking about her mother so far away in London and about last night's misfortune, which would have pleased the Countess greatly: three miserable women spending the night on a hard station bench.

'There you are, I said no good would come of it. Sneaking off and joining up as if this war were some marvellous crusade,' Mama would have said. 'It would seem that you can't even get yourself from A to B without making a mess of it. But if you'd listened to me, you'd be married to Charles now and doing your duty as a good wife should!'

Poor Charlie. He had protested strongly when her call-up papers came. Clever old Goddy, she thought, but Charlie was quite put out.

'The *Wrens*, Lucinda? But the Bainbridges always go into the Army,' but he had forgiven her, eventually, when she promised to try to take her leave when he took his.

'They usually let you do it,' he'd told her, 'if you're engaged or married. Tell them it's on compassionate grounds, and you'll get away with it all right. You really ought to be wearing a ring, Lucinda. Surely there's something, somewhere, to fit you.'

Indeed there was. Lying in the bank in a strongbox; several Bainbridge rings, in fact. There was even the ruby the first earl gave his wife to celebrate the title bestowed by James Stuart in 1604, but she would have liked a ring, Lucinda brooded, of her very own; a dainty diamond cluster she and Charlie had chosen together. Something new, and hers alone. That, probably, was why her left hand remained bare and the date of their wedding still uncertain. A little romance, she sighed, might just have tipped the scales. But she really must send Charlie her new address and tell him how peculiar it all was; about the strange customs, still revered because Nelson had established them; about rooms which were now cabins, walls which had become bulkheads and a kitchen she must now call a galley. And the saluting was beyond belief. One saluted everyone and everything, even the quarter-deck, the moment one set foot on it. She supposed she would have to salute Charlie now. And one didn't go to work, one went on watch; pulling the blackout curtains was called darkening ship; and no one went to the lavatory, they went to the *heads*! Yes, she must write a long loving letter to Charlie. Tomorrow.

Vi said her rosary then prayed for Gerry's soul. It still bothered her that she should feel so contented with her new life when Gerry was dead.

I miss you, lad. I need to tell you about yesterday, meeting Jane and Lucinda, and about Ardneavie House. It's smashing here, Gerry. No sirens or bombs, and a lovely garden, full of flowers. Ardneavie House is big – at least ten bedrooms – and Lucinda and Jane and me are on the top floor with the boat's-crew Wrens. Just them and us, up here in the roof, and a storeroom and a bathroom.

The bathroom's lovely, Gerry. Hot water in the taps, lots of it. No boiling kettles and lugging the bath in from the yard. This house belonged to a shipyard owner, but the Navy took it from him for the duration and now it's a hostel for Wrens. I suppose that man had servants. They'd sleep up here on the top floor, I shouldn't wonder, because there's a little back staircase that goes down to the kitchens – sorry, lad, galley! *And all the rooms have big windows. You can look out and see hills and trees and not another house in sight. There's this big depot ship in the loch and it's got a flotilla of submarines . . .*

Submarines. It had shocked Vi to realize that her own side fought every bit as dirty as the Germans and that German seamen were torpedoed, too. Her first sight of a submarine had brought back the pain of Gerry's death and she'd had to tell herself that those in the loch were *ours*, so they couldn't be all that bad.

Strange, how easy it had been to accept the harshness of the training depot and the lessons she had learned. Never to volunteer for anything, for instance; to keep her bedspace clean and tidy; never, ever, to forget the eleventh commandment, *Thou shall not get found out*; and if you were prepared to agree that every word of King's Regulations was Holy Writ and accepted that leave was a privilege and not a right, then life in the Navy needn't be all that bad. The time to start worrying, she supposed, was when the war was over and they were all sent home – for where was home, now?

. . . I miss you, Gerry. I think about you always and I pray for you. I won't ever forget you, lad; not while I live and breathe, I won't. And I'm sorry about my ring, but it's best I don't wear it. I can't have people ask me where my husband is. It would hurt too much. I've never been able to say I'm a widow. I know it inside me but I can't say it out loud; not yet, Gerry.

Goodnight, lad. I'm fine, honest to God I am. Don't worry about me . . .

Vi punched her pillow and stuck her face into it. Oh, damn all this killing. Why did men have to do it? *Why?*

* * *

Almost dark now, and the bombers would be taking off from Fenton Bishop, heaving and thrashing into the air, into the same sun that had reddened Loch Ardneavie. How long would it be, Jane demanded silently of the darkness, before she was able to speak of Rob or think of Rob and not weep inside her? It was nearly two months since her call-up papers had come; two months since S-Sugar had not come back. She had been angry at first, then disbelieving, but finally she had gone to the aerodrome to see the padre, begging him for news of Rob.

'I'm not his next of kin, you see, and I never knew exactly where he lived. I want to write to his mother. Can you get her address for me?'

But such things were confidential, said the padre. He was evasive about Rob too; almost as if he hadn't wanted to talk about him.

'Try to forget, my dear,' he had said. 'Accept that it must end.'

That was when she first realized that to lose someone you love is not to feel instant separation. Rather it is first like a hopeless drifting, a little apart from the world, afraid and unwilling to reach out and ask for help. That day, in the padre's little room, she accepted it was best she should be leaving Fenton Bishop, best she should be away from the sight of the uniform Rob had worn and the constant sound of aircraft. She wanted to be a number, to dress exactly as the other numbers dressed, to be nothing and no one.

That same night she had gone to Yeoman's Lane for the last time, accepting without pain that she had thought their love was untouchable, yet now it was as if it had never been. Now, that loving counted for nothing and all the sweet promises they had made were empty words that floated like echoes in a great grey void. Tomorrow's promises they had been, and tomorrow never came.

'I can't come here again, Rob,' she had whispered, dry-eyed. 'Tomorrow I am going away . . .'

'You awake, Lucinda?' Midnight, and sleep still evaded Vi.

'Afraid so. I must be too tired, I suppose. I was thinking about home, actually.'

'Where's home?'

'Lincolnshire, really, though we live in London now,' she whispered into the darkness. 'But I love Lincolnshire and Lady Mead – that's the house I grew up in. We lived near Donnington on Bain, right in the country. Too beautiful. I wish I could go back there.'

'You shouldn't have left it, queen.'

'Had to, Vi. The Air Force requisitioned it. Lincoln-shire is a flat county, you see, exactly right for aero-dromes, and they took our house for the airmen, I suppose. I'd love to see it again, though I think Mama won't ever go back there. But Lady Mead will be Charlie's one day, so I'll make it, eventually.'

'Charlie's your brother, is he?'

'My cousin. I don't have a brother, that's why Charlie will inherit.'

'Inherit?' Vi was instantly alert. 'You rich or somethin'?'

'Not really. We've got plenty of *things* – goods and chattels and land – but very little money because we can't sell anything. Something to do with entail, you see.'

Vi did not see, but people who inherited things intrigued her.

'If you like that house so much,' she demanded bluntly, 'won't it make you mad to see your cousin get it?'

'Oh, no. I'm going to marry him, you see.'

'Just to get an 'ouse? But you love him, don't you?'

'Of course I love him.' Of course she did. She always

94

had. Well, almost always. She hadn't liked him very much that night on the sofa. 'But what about you, Vi? Who do you love?'

'I – I don't have nobody.' *Sorry, Gerry.* 'Free as the air, I am. Got no things, neither. They was all bombed in the May blitz.' Just two crystal goblets in a drawer in Mary's sideboard.

'But you *do* want to get married, Vi? Every woman wants her own home, and babies.'

'Homes get bombed and babies need shoes and clothes and food. You can't rear a baby on love and fair words.' Why had she started this conversation? She didn't want to talk about her other life. Her wound had gone deep and she wasn't ready, yet, for the knife to be turned. 'What about you, Jane? You got a boyfriend, eh?'

'She's asleep,' Lucinda whispered. 'Lucky so and so.'

Jane Kendal was not asleep. It was seven o'clock and she was in Tingle's Wood, waiting for Rob. And it was all a mistake about his being missing because he was there now, at the perimeter fence, smiling his lovely smile, saying 'Hullo, Jenny.' It was her favourite fantasy. It sustained her when the pain inside her became near-unbearable, and it was not for sharing.

Morning came, silver and gold, with sunlight that skimmed the surface of the loch and gilded the poppies and roses in the garden at Ardneavie. On either side of the lane that led to the jetty, creamy-white elderflowers scented the morning air and pale pink clover and forget-me-nots grew thickly, scorning the war, denying its existence.

'Did you remember,' Jane asked, 'that this is Midsummer Day?'

'Damn! And I should have remembered to dance barefoot through the dew and bow to the rising sun.'

'Be serious. Aren't you feeling scared? I know I am.'

They were standing on the jetty with a score of chattering women, waiting for the launch that would take them to the depot ship *Omega*.

'Nervous? I feel sick, Jane. Positively *sick*. I mean, what if I miss a signal? What if the man on the other end transmits too quickly and I can't keep up with him? They do, you know. Some of those operators are stingo. Oh, it was fine at wireless school. Mistakes didn't matter so much, but now – well, it's for real, isn't it, and maybe lives depending on me. Wish I didn't have to go on watch.'

'You'll be all right. We both will. We can only do our best. They can't put us against a wall and shoot us if – '

'Hullo. You're the new girls, aren't you? They said you'd be coming. Bainbridge and Kendal, isn't it? I'm Molly Malone, *Mary*, really, but with a name like Malone . . .' The Wren who introduced herself was slim and smart in a uniform which fitted her perfectly. She had a wide smile, a freckle-dusted nose and a distinctly Irish accent. 'I work in the teleprinter room in the CCO. Like to come on board with me?'

'Please. We feel very strange.' Lucinda forced a smile. 'CCO – that's central communications office, isn't it?'

'It is, and it all goes on there: wireless, coding, decoding, signal distribution. We like to think we're indispensable, that the flotilla couldn't manage without us. Our submarines are all operational, you see, except for a couple of recent arrivals that are working up; new boats getting a crew together, that is, doing sea trials and dummy runs with torpedoes. The CCO looks after submarines at sea and keeps – '

'Don't!' Lucinda had gone visibly pale. 'I'm so nervous I can't think straight.'

'Then don't be. You'll be working with a great crowd. Have either of you ever been on an HM ship before?'

They shook their heads forlornly.

'Then you'll not know about saluting the quarterdeck?'

'We'd heard, but where is the quarterdeck, and how will we know when we're on it?'

'You'll know. It's aft, always. At the back end, that is, and as soon as you step on to it, you salute. It'll get to be second nature, don't worry. And you're both wearing your blackouts, aren't you?'

'Yes.' Jane frowned. 'But what's so important about knickers?'

'You'll see, when we get on board. Look! There's the launch now. That's Lilith's lot bringing it in. They're the only Wren crew in the flotilla, so they've got to be good.'

'Why?' Jane demanded blankly.

'Because they're women in a man's world. We all are. Wrens rarely get a *real* ship, you see, and some of the old hands look on us as intruders, to say the least. A few openly resent us; that's why we've got to try to be as good as they are.'

'Resent us?' Lucinda's stomach turned a somersault. It was going to be worse even than she had feared. Pictures formed in her mind of bloody-minded leading hands and a frowning chief telegraphist, all of them men and all of them waiting, grim-faced, for Bainbridge, L. V. to make her first mistake; a mistake so terrible that talk of its consequences would reverberate around the Home Fleet for years to come. 'Isn't that a bit unfair?'

'Well, they don't actually resent us, I suppose. Not really. But we've got to live by *their* rules and not expect privileges because we happen to be women.' Molly shrugged. 'But will you look at that boat's crew? Aren't they as good as any men?'

The all-woman crew were bringing the launch in, leaping with fearless agility to the jetty and tying up efficiently, as though they had been born on boats and lived on them all their life.

'Let's have you then!' the coxswain called. 'All aboard. Chop chop!'

They followed Molly on to the launch, hitching up their skirts as she did as they swung over the side, taking their places beside her, feeling strange and excited and apprehensive.

'There'll be a high gangway to climb when we get alongside *Omega*,' she told them. 'Well, more of a ladder, really. First time you go up it can be a bit frightening, but hang on with both hands and *don't* look down. Okay?'

They nodded mutely.

'And when you get to the top you'll be on the quarter-deck, so don't forget to –'

'Salute,' they chorused.

'Let go for'ard! Let go aft!'

A boathook pushed the launch from the jetty, a wheel spun in capable hands, the engine coughed them on their way. Then a half-turn astern, and they were heading confidently to the depot ship *Omega*.

'Makes you feel proud, so it does,' Molly beamed. 'Men won't ever be able to sit on us women again, when this war's over. Lilith's as good as any man. I never worry when we're out in a force-eight gale; not if she's in charge.'

Force-eight gales? High ladders from which she must not look down? And, when she reached the wireless office, men who might resent her being there and fiends who transmitted Morse at devilish speeds . . .

'I feel sick,' Lucinda whispered. '*Very* sick, and it's got nothing at all to do with the sea.'

The shore receded, the depot ship and its clinging submarines drew closer. Now *Omega* was not dull grey as distance had suggested, but a mottle of khaki and black and olive-green, the colours of camouflage. Now the ship

98

appeared ungainly and broad-beamed. Not for *Omega* the greyhound outline of a frigate but rather that of a clumsy old sow with submarine piglets suckling beside her.

'It's bigger than you'd think.' Jane gazed up at the towering bulk. And Molly Malone was right: the gangway was little better than a ladder that clung to the ship's side with fragile tenacity. Up and up. How many steps? Twenty? Thirty?

'Don't be looking so worried.' Molly Malone's smile was altogether too smug, Lucinda considered bleakly. And how was anyone to make even the bottom step of that wretched ladder thing when the launch was rising and falling like a demented yo-yo?

The engine slowed and died. A boathook reached out and latched on to the ship's side, and a small, dark-haired crewgirl pulled them in until they touched with a gentle bump. Then, one foot on the launch, one on the gangway, she held them steady.

'Carry on!' At once the gangway came alive, trembling and shaking and bucking as forty feet slammed up it.

Jane held on with both hands, gazing ahead at Molly's legs, counting every step, praying she would reach the top before the whole thing collapsed beneath their weight and they all fell, helpless, into the water below. Twenty-one, twenty-two, twenty-three, and she was there. Ahead of her, Molly stepped on to the deck, lifting her right hand in salute. Bemused, Jane did the same. Now she knew why sailors saluted the quarterdeck. It was not that Nelson had died there, nor was it because many years ago the crucifix that hung there demanded obeisance. Oh, no. It was because everyone was so desperately grateful to get off the shifting, jerking, swaying ladders the Navy called gangways.

'All right?' she croaked.

'Think so,' Lucinda muttered.

'Right, then.' Like virgins to the sacrificial altar, they followed Molly Malone to the place where it all happened; where Wrens must learn to live in a men's world because now the war was nearer to them than it had ever been. And frighteningly real.

The central communications office of HMS *Omega* was large and surprisingly light, with white-painted bulkheads and an excess of highly polished copper and brass. At the far end, eight wireless receivers stood in line abreast; doors marked *Teleprinters*, *Coding* and *Signals* opened off the main office space, while in its centre men sat at typewriters, index fingers jabbing furiously.

It was odd, Lucinda thought, that men should be doing a job more suited to women, but this was a *real* ship, wasn't it, on which, if Molly was to be believed, women had yet to establish themselves.

'All right, you two! Over here!'

They knew without being told that this was the chief telegraphist, whose word was law on starboard watch; knew it without seeing the three brass buttons on either sleeve cuff which pronounced his rank or the lightning-flashed wings on his right arm that told them he was the telegraphist they sought.

'Er – Chief – er.'

'Wetherby. And you're adrift, the pair of you. Should've been here yesterday forenoon!'

'Yes, Chief.'

'Sorry, Chief.'

'All right, all right. Cut out the chat! Which one of you is Kendal?'

Eyes wide, Jane stepped forward.

'Right, Kendal. Over there.' A finger indicated the door marked *Coding*. 'Jock Menzies is your leading hand. He'll put you right. And you, Bainbridge, over there!'

100

The finger jabbed again, pointing to the only unmanned receiver in the line. 'That's yours.'

For just a few seconds, Lucinda hesitated; for just long enough to take in the shock of white hair, the lined, weather-worn face and the tremendous size of him. Then, taking a shuddering breath, she walked in a daze to her position.

The set, she considered, was a new one or maybe one which was less used. Either way, though, there was a belligerency about it, with dials that gazed at her like eyes; mean, shifty eyes, warning her to beware.

'All right, Bainbridge. Get your jacket off and get stuck in!'

Reluctantly Lucinda did as she was ordered, then with cold, clumsy fingers she began to roll up her sleeves.

It was all too awful. The morning she had slammed out of the house and walked through the blitzed London streets to Goddy's office she had been out of her mind; shell-shocked, or something. An act of defiance it had been, and look where it had got her. Mama had been right. She should be married to Charlie now, and safely pregnant at Lady Mead with Nanny, and if Charlie were to phone her tonight and ask her to marry him tomorrow she would cry, 'Darling! Yes!' and slap in a request for marriage leave without more ado. Near-frantic with apprehension, she gazed up, eyes wide. 'Chief?'

'What is it, girl? You sick, or something? Got a bellyache?'

'N-no, thanks. It – it's just that I'm so nervous.'

'Nervous? What of?'

'Of getting it wrong, Chief. Or not getting it at all.' Fear forced the words. He'd think she was an imbecile, anyway, so why not tell him and prove him right. 'I'm scared I'll miss a signal or not be able to read it. And I

101

worry what will happen to those men at sea if I do. I'm afraid. Really afraid.'

'Afraid, girl? That there'll be one of the boats at sea and you'll miss . . .' He threw back his head and roared with laughter. 'Afraid you'll miss the transmission? Oh, dear.'

'What did I say? What's so funny?'

'*You* are, Bainbridge. Oh, for Gawd's sake, didn't they teach you anything at wireless school? Didn't they tell you that no ship at sea, *no ship at all*, would be daft enough to send out a signal – well, not in wartime, they wouldn't! Gawd Almighty, Jerry'd have a fix on 'em before they could say "tot time". Break radio silence? Only in the direst emergency. Never, almost. All they do when they're at sea is take down the messages *we* send to *them*, so don't worry about not picking up a signal, 'cause nobody'll be sending you any.'

'Oh, Chief.' Lucinda flashed him a smile of pure joy. 'I've got a lot to learn, it seems.'

'Seems you have, girl, but learn it you will. So get yourself settled. There's one of the submarines – *boats*, we say – up in the Gareloch doing trials. *Sparta*, she's called, pendant number P.268, and that'll be her call sign. Now she'll transmit in code every hour, on the hour, and you'll read those signals and write them down then give a receipt. That's all there is to it; nothing to be scared about in that, is there, Bainbridge?'

'No, Chief,' she frowned. 'But didn't you just say that a ship at sea doesn't transmit?'

'It doesn't, girl. It doesn't. But *Sparta* isn't at sea. She's all safe and snug in the Gareloch where Jerry can't reach her. Safe as houses, she is.'

'And she'll transmit on the hour?'

'*Exactly* on the hour, and if she's only a couple of

102

minutes late, you sing out, Bainbridge, because I shall
want to know.'

'Why, Chief?'

'Because on the hour means just that and failure to
transmit at the given time usually means one thing.
Trouble.'

'I see.' She fixed him with anxious eyes. 'But something
like that isn't likely to happen, is it?' Not when I'm on
watch? Oh, *please*, not when it's on my wavelength.

'No, Bainbridge, it isn't. As a matter of fact, I've only
known it happen once when a new submarine was doing
trials. In '38, in Liverpool Bay. Boat called the *Thetis*.
Bad job, that was. Terrible loss of life. But it isn't going
to happen this morning.' He dug his hands into the
pockets of his jacket and, because sailors are the most
superstitious of men, he crossed his fingers. Just to be
sure. 'So get yourself settled. *Sparta*'ll be coming up in
five minutes exactly.' He leaned over and adjusted the
dials. 'There now, that's just about it. She'll make regular
transmissions till eleven hundred hours then she'll be
doing a deep dive, so you'll hear no more from her till she
surfaces at fifteen hundred hours. All right? Got it?'

'Yes, but why will *Sparta* stop sending out signals during
the dive? I mean, you'd think it would be the one time
she would – '

'A good question, girl, and one to which there is a very
simple answer. A submarine *can't* transmit when it's
underwater. It's an absolute impossibility.'

'As I said,' Lucinda smiled ruefully, 'I do have a lot to
learn.'

'And as *I* said,' Chief Wetherby returned the smile,
'learn it you will, girl. Learn it you *will*!' He nodded in
the direction of the brass-banded bulkhead clock. 'Nearly
time. And you know *Omega*'s call sign, don't you? GXU3.

That's what you'll be listening for,' he said as he walked away.

Questions, questions, but not a bad kid, that Bainbridge. Not like some they sent him; six weeks in wireless school and they thought they knew it all. Bainbridge would make a good sparker, given time. In spite of that plummy voice, she'd make it all right, or his name wasn't Walter Wetherby!

GXU3, Lucinda thought feverishly, eyes on the clock. GXU3. The fingers of her right hand clutched tightly at her pencil; those of her left hand were crossed, firmly, desperately.

Oh, Goddy! She sent a silent message winging to the small room at the Admiralty. Why didn't you tell me it would be like this? Why didn't you warn me?

She closed her eyes and swallowed hard, adjusting her headphones, moving the dials a fraction with fingers that were stiff and cold. She would die. She really would. Before this watch was over she would be a nervous, screaming wreck.

It came up out of nowhere, GXU3 demanding her attention. This was it! Oh, my God!

Panic slapped her hard and for the splitting of a second she hesitated. Then, collecting her thoughts, shutting out all sound save that in her headset, she began to take down the message. The persistent pinging assaulted her ears and she forced it into her head. On and on. One page of the signal pad already filled; got to turn over. Careful. Don't lose any. For God's sake, don't!

Dit-da, dit-da-dit. A. R. They came at last. The letters that signified the end of the message. It was over and she had done it. She had got it all! Ripping the sheets from her pad, she held them triumphantly high.

'Ta, love,' said the messenger, taking them from her as

if they were any old signal, carrying them to the coders who would make the groups of figures into words.

Only then did Lucinda glance to her right. Only then was she aware of the telegraphist who sat beside her, who smiled and gave her the thumbs-up sign.

Elated, she grinned back. Bainbridge L. V., had done it, and nothing that happened now – absolutely *nothing* – would be half as bad as that first terrifying signal.

Someone tapped her on the shoulder then placed a mug as big as a chamber pot beside her. The tea was strong and sweet and laced with tinned milk, and she drank it gratefully. She was calmer now; confident, almost. For the first time in her life she was doing something for herself; doing it without help from anyone, and what was more, she was getting it right. It was heady stuff. Raising her mug, she turned again to the telegraphist at her side, giving him her most brilliant smile.

'Bainbridge,' she said. 'Lucinda.'

'Lofty.' He raised his mug in turn. 'Everything all right?'

'Fine, thanks,' she breathed. Absolutely fine. Wonderful, in fact.

Sorry, Charlie, she exulted. Afraid I've changed my mind. No wedding, old thing. Well, not just yet, anyway . . .

Vi stared into the mirror, tweaking her tie straight.

'Mother of God, worra face.' Funny eyes, funny nose, mouth too big and teeth too crooked. A face, she sighed, that only a mother could have loved.

'Happy birthday, face.'

Twenty-six today. She had almost forgotten. Twenty flaming six. She could be thirty before this war was over. It was frightening, if she let herself think about it, how much could happen in a year. Last birthday there had

105

been a card from Gerry, written on shore leave and left with Mary for posting, yet now she was a woman alone. Now, just one year later, she was 44455 Wren McKeown, V. T., a steward who would spend the remainder of the war cleaning and polishing whatever the Navy told her to clean and polish.

But at least she was alive, which was something to be glad about, so she winked at Vi-in-the-mirror then turned to the window and the almost unbelievable beauty outside. She would never tire of that view, never get used to hills that changed colour at the whim of the sun, or the trees and flowers and a sky free of rooftops and chimney stacks. And out there in the loch lay the depot ship, with only five submarines tied up alongside now because one had left. She had seen it that morning, black and sleek, leaving hardly a ripple behind it, slipping silently away on the morning tide. And farther down the loch had waited the frigate that would escort it out to sea and stay with it, someone had told her, until it reached the safety of deep water.

Vi had never imagined she could think kindly of any submarine again, but if it was one of your own then surely it was right and proper to wish it well, and raising her hand she had traced a blessing on the early morning air.

She wondered where that submarine was now and what it was called. Perhaps Jane or Lucinda would know. They were there now, on that depot ship. She had watched from the window as they walked down the jetty, anxious as a mother sending her children off on their first day at school. She thought about them a lot, wondering how it was going for them on their first real day on active service; the first day, she supposed, of the rest of their lives – of the duration, at least.

The duration. For as long as the war lasted. And how many days and weeks and years made up a duration was anybody's guess. It had all happened one Sunday morning when an old man in London decided that that was how it would be. She remembered it clearly. Gerry's ship had been in the Albert Dock and they had just finished papering the front bedroom. At eleven o'clock she had turned on the wireless to hear the old man tell them they were at war with Germany. Again.

But today she wouldn't think about it. Today was her birthday and Jane and Lucinda would soon be coming ashore, bursting with news. The thought pleased her, and she smiled.

Jane Kendal's introduction to the war at sea was far less traumatic than that of her cabinmate. She had, in fact, enjoyed her day.

'Lucky for me,' she said that night at supper, 'that coders often work in pairs so there was someone to help me along. My oppo was very patient – oppo means opposite number, by the way – and he's very nice.'

'Young, was he?' It was important that Vi should know.

'Oh, no. About forty, I'd say. He's got a daughter almost my age, but I shall like working with him.' She could not help but like him. From their first hullo the rapport was there, for Jock Menzies spoke with Rob's accent.

'There, now.' Vi was well pleased. She need not, she conceded, have worried about either of them. The young ones had done very well. 'Anyone want more pudding? There's plenty left over.'

'Please.' The baptism of fire behind her, Lucinda had found her lost appetite, and bread-and-butter pudding was one of her favourites. 'Just a little.' She held out her dish and Vi spooned it full.

'Remember I was telling you how nervous I was?' Lucinda confided, spoon poised. 'Well, I didn't know it at the time, but the telegraphist on the next set to mine – Lofty, he's called – was on my wavelength too. I was really afraid I'd not get it all down, and all the time he was listening out for me. He'll be doing that for a day or two, till I can take over my own wavelength completely. But I wish I'd known. It would've saved a lot of agonizing.' She smiled suddenly, and the smile set her eyes dancing and brought the dimples back to her cheeks. 'Look – why don't we celebrate? Let's go out tonight.'

'Well, I was wonderin' – I've been thinkin' . . .' Vi was remembering that today was her birthday and there was the ten-shilling note in her money belt and wondering if she should ask them if they would like to see the film in Craigiebur. *Love on the Dole.* One of the stewards had cried all the way through it, she said, so it must be good. But Vi did not ask them because someone said, 'Hullo. You'll be the new lot in cabin 9.' Someone who was tall and black-haired, with milkmaid cheeks and deep, dark eyes; eyes so deep and dark it was impossible not to notice them.

'Who's askin'?' Vi demanded with Liverpool directness.

'Lilith. From cabin 10. Lilith Penrose.'

'Vi McKeown.' Vi took the extended hand. 'And these two's Lucinda and Jane.'

'Yes.' Lilith nodded briefly. 'I noticed them on the launch this morning.'

'Well then, that's fine, innit? Anythin' else?'

'No. Just wanted to say hi, and tell you about the message.'

'Message? Who for?'

'That's just it. I'm not quite sure. It's all a bit vague, you see. Look, when you've finished eating I think you'd better come up to cabin 10 and get it sorted out. In about five minutes – all right?'

It was not all right. Vi did not like mysteries. Nor did

108

she like being summoned to the cabin next door, but Penrose *was* a leading Wren. 'What about it?' she asked.

'Okay by me.' Jane nodded.

'Me too,' said Lucinda.

'Right, then. We'll see you in five minutes.'

'And what did you make of that?' Lucinda demanded when they were alone. 'A message for one of us but she's not sure which. Peculiar, wouldn't you say?'

Peculiar, they all agreed, but they knew they would go to cabin 10 none the less, for the deep, dark eyes held a mystery. And secrets.

The door of cabin 10 was stuck and Vi thumped it hard.

'Hang on.' Lilith Penrose removed the wedge that held it. 'Glad you've come. Soon have it sorted out.'

Vi looked around her. The room was spacious, with two large windows and a cast-iron fireplace which was obviously used, for log baskets stood either side of it and an airer hung with bell-bottomed trousers and thick navy-blue sweaters swung above it. But it was the table in the centre of the room that aroused Vi's curiosity because it belonged, she'd have sworn, on the landing outside. She was certain, in fact, because only that morning she had dusted and polished it. Shrugging, she gazed pointedly at two Wrens she had not met before.

'Sorry,' Lilith smiled. 'Meet Constance Dean and Fiona Cole – Connie and Fenny – my deck hand and stoker.'

Vi nodded briefly. 'What's this message, then?' Her gaze had returned to the circular table, and she was uneasy.

'The message?' Lilith closed the door and slid back the wedge. 'You must try to understand that it isn't a message, as such. It just came to me and I knew it must be for one of you.'

'Came to you?' Now Lucinda had noticed the table. She

109

had seen one like it before – well, almost like it. Letters and numbers set at random around its perimeter and an upended wine glass in the centre. A planchette, they had called it at school. It had started as a game but had taken over their lives, almost. They'd been in terrible trouble when Matron discovered their secret, and each of them had promised never to do anything so wicked again.

'Came to me,' Lilith asserted calmly. 'I get messages all the time.'

'From the planchette?' Lucinda's eyes were fixed on the glass.

'That's not what it's called and the message has nothing to do with – *that*.'

'It's a ouija board, innit?' Vi had heard about such things. Mention a ouija board at Confession and it would be three Hail Marys and an extra Mass from Father O'Flaherty, soon as look at you it would.

'It's nothing to do with ouija, either. That,' Lilith nodded towards the table, 'is my own thing. If you believe, it will tell you what you want to know. It's a part of my religion, of the *old* religion.'

'It flamin' isn't, and I should know,' Vi countered. '*I'm* a Catholic.'

'The *old* religion, Vi, has been with us as long as time and has nothing to do with the Church of Rome. My mentor is the earth mother and my conscience is ruled by karma.'

'And what's karma, when it's at home?' demanded Vi, who knew that consciences were ruled by parish priests.

'It's a Buddhist belief,' Lucinda whispered. 'Sort of take what you want – and pay. I'm right, aren't I, Lilith?'

'Vaguely. But karma isn't entirely Buddhist dogma. Everyone pays, or is rewarded eventually, usually in another life on earth.'

'Sorry.' Vi had heard enough. 'We've changed our

110

minds.' She was having nothing more to do with such heathen talk, message or no message. 'Come on, you two.' Pushing away the wedge she opened the door with a flourish and, part relieved, part disappointed, Jane and Lucinda followed her. 'Sorry,' Vi said again over her shoulder.

'So am I,' Lilith spoke quietly. 'Because I was just about to wish you a happy birthday.'

'You *what*?' Vi flung round to face her. 'Who said it was my birthday? Who told you?'

'The message told me, Vi. I had a feeling it was for you.'

'Message my foot! You've seen my record sheet, haven't you?' It was the only way she could have known, unless Mary had phoned. But Mary wouldn't know where to phone until tomorrow when she got the letter. 'Haven't you?'

'All record sheets are confidential, kept locked in Patsy Pill's office; you should know that. No one sees them but her and Ma'am.'

'Then how did you find out?'

'I don't know. I never ask. He just said, "Happy twenty-sixth birthday, girl."'

'*He* said?'

'It seemed like a message from a man.'

'*Girl*, did he say? You're sure it was *girl*?'

'Quite sure. Does it mean something?'

'It means nothin'. Nothin' at all.' Vi tilted her head defiantly. 'Come on, you two. We're not soddin' about no more with rubbish like that!'

She closed the door with a firmness she did not feel then sank gratefully on to her bed, dry-mouthed and suddenly cold.

'Vi!' Jane gasped. 'You're as white as a sheet and you're shaking. Get her some water, Lucinda.'

'I'm all right, honest I am.'

'No you're not.' Lucinda offered the glass. 'And it *is* your birthday, isn't it?'

'What if it is? There's dozens of ways she could have known.'

'There aren't, Vi.'

'She guessed, then.'

'I don't think she did, but happy birthday all the same. Are you really twenty-six? Did she get it right?' Jane smiled.

'I suppose so.'

'And have you any idea who sent the message?'

'No, queen.' Vi honestly had not. It could only have come from Gerry, and Gerry was dead. 'That Lilith's a good guesser and we're goin' to keep away from her and her funny religion, aren't we?'

They said they were, though they knew it was not true. They would be drawn back to that table and its shining glass, nothing was more certain. Vi knew it too, for how she could prevent it she was too shaken, at the moment, even to contemplate.

'Load of old nonsense, that's what. Forget Lilith Penrose, eh? Even her name's funny, innit?'

'Lilith?' Lucinda shrugged. 'It was the first name in creation, some say.'

Vi gathered her forehead into a frown. 'Who says?' Everybody knew that Eve was the first woman. It said so in the Bible, plain as the nose on your face.

'I-I don't know. Someone must have said it, I suppose – that Lilith was Adam's first wife, I mean.'

'Well, that someone was *wrong*,' Vi said grimly. 'Just you forget such things, Lucinda. Like I said, we'd all better keep away from cabin 10 and all that carrying on. She's been nosing around in the regulating office, bet you anything you like she has, and she doesn't fool me!'

112

The smile was back on Vi's lips again. Leading Wren Lilith Penrose would have to get up very early in the morning to catch Vi McKeown on the hop.

'An' it's still me birthday, innit, and if we're not too late for the transport into Craigiebur, I've got a spare ten bob I feel like spendin'. My treat. Anybody interested?'

5

Jane fidgeted with the signal pads on her desk, plucked a thread from the sleeve of her jacket then stared blankly at the chewed end of her Admiralty-issue pencil. What was this phenomenon? Why did everyone sit, breath indrawn, like figures in a tableau? Why this silence, a silence so unexpected and inexplicable that it screamed '*Listen to me*!' Through the half-open door of the coding office she could see Lofty's back; beside him Lucinda sat unmoving, her left hand relaxed on a dial.

'Quiet, isn't it?' The sudden dense hush was so uncanny that Jane felt compelled to whisper. 'Has the war stopped, or something?'

'It happens.' Jock shrugged. 'Sometimes, it's as if it takes a breathing space.' Sometimes, he said, no hand depressed a Morse key or lifted a telephone or received a signal, and even the teleprinters, tired of their own unending chack-chacking, switched themselves off. It was only minutes, the duration of that fleeting armistice, but such a stillness was so unaccustomed, embraced a silence so complete that it was always noticed, and wondered at. Such moments happened mostly during the ungodly first hours of a new day, those breathless hours when a soul sighs away from a dying body. They were to be expected in that, the middle watch, when eyes were gritty with tiredness and the air stale and limbs cold, but it was less usual in a busy forenoon watch as this.

'It's as if everyone is waiting for something, isn't it?'

'I know what you mean.' Jock blew out rings of cigarette smoke then watched them widen and disappear. 'It's just one of those things, so try to remember what it's like next time there's a panic on, eh? And there's no' a thing you can do about it, lassie, so why don't you sit back and enjoy it? Or maybe you'd like to watch the boat coming alongside?'

'Which boat? Is *Sparta* back from trials?'

'No. This one's *Taureg*, a T-boat. A big one, home from patrol. She's had a bad time, so the buzz has it. Landed herself in big trouble in the Bay, but managed to get out of it. The skipper and commander are going to be there, so it'll be caps in the air and three cheers and all that. You might find it interesting. Away with you, now. I'll let you know when things get going again. Just nip up the steps outside the navigator's sea cabin. You'll get a good view from there.'

Reluctantly Jane pushed back her chair. In truth she wasn't really interested in *Taureg*'s arrival, but anything that broke the self-imposed purdah of her existence was welcome, she supposed, for she still stood outside the real world, looking in; a part of her still waited in Yeoman's Lane and none of this strangeness around her was really happening. She wished it were not so. She wanted to come alive again and fall in love again; but that was not possible, for no one but Rob MacDonald would do – and Rob was gone.

'Okay, Jock. Thanks.' Smiling, she pulled on her hat. 'Won't be long.'

The navigator's sea cabin was small, wedged between the CCO and the signal deck, and one he seldom used since the depot ship rarely went to sea. Indeed, the whole total of *Omega*'s movement was a half-swing around her mooring buoy with the incoming tide and a half-swing back again on the ebb. But the view from the coding-office

115

portholes was varied and interesting, a slowly changing panorama for those with time to gaze.

She lifted her face to the sun, half closing her eyes against the silver dazzle that bounced across the water, breathing deeply on the tangle-scented air. The two submarines which had lain alongside *Omega* at the start of her watch now stood off in the loch, still as two sentries, awaiting *Taureg*'s arrival, and she wondered how any man could volunteer to serve in such a craft; how he could live in quarters so cramped, with no privacy at all. And that was apart from the danger. So small a boat in so vast a sea. She tried to imagine what it would be like to sink to the sea bed and stay there, calmly, with only a steel hull between a man and the enormous, pressing waters.

I would panic, she thought. My mind would go numb. She who loved the fields and trees and the wideness of the North Riding could not have endured so claustrophobic an existence. She wondered which of the escort vessels would bring *Taureg* in. She still found it hard to believe that any British ship could be in danger so near to home; even when Jock had explained that unless a submarine was in water deep enough in which to dive, an escort was essential.

'It's the Brylcreem boys. Those Coastal Command laddies are inclined to bomb first and ask questions later.'

She hadn't really believed him, but so much of her new life had still to make sense to her that she had not challenged his statement.

Her eyes swept the broad waters of the loch. *Capricious* and *Lothian*, two of the flotilla's escort frigates, swung at their buoys, which could only mean that the *Jan Mayen* had gone out to bring the submarine in. She felt a moment of sorrow for the *Jan Mayen*'s crew: Dutchmen who had brought their little ship to Portsmouth when Holland was overrun by the Nazi armies, choosing to leave their country and fight on with the British Navy rather than give their ship into enemy hands. How sad for those sailors never to receive a letter from home; never to know if the families they had left behind were safe and well and managing to get enough to eat; not even daring to wonder if they were still alive. Yet those people, the fellow countrymen of *Jan Mayen*'s crew, would put their lives at risk to give help and shelter to British airmen. Foolish, wonderful people.

Tears of pride stung her eyes and she brushed them away with an impatient hand. *God, when it's my turn, please let me be brave, too . . .*

'Penny for them, Jenny.'

'Uh? Sorry?' Startled, Jane's head jerked up.

'Tell me what's making you so miserable. Bad, is it?'

The man at her side wore sea boots and a thick white sweater, and he looked at her with one eyebrow raised, a small, teasing smile lifting the corners of his mouth. And he had called her Jenny.

'Nothing's making me miserable.'

'That's all right, then. Thought you might be feeling a bit strange. New here, aren't you. Where do you work?'

'In the communications office, actually.' She said it primly, nose tilted.

'And are you going to like it on *Omega*, Jenny?'

'Don't call me that. My name is *not* Jenny.'

'I'm sure it isn't.'

'Then *why*?'

'Because all Wrens are Jennies. Got to be, haven't they? My name's Tom, by the way. Tom Tavey. What's yours?'

Grudgingly she told him.

'Then can we start again? Hullo, Jane Kendal.'

'Hullo.' She wished *Taureg* would come and she wished the sailor would go away. He was trying to pick her up, of course, but any Wren new to the flotilla must expect to be fair game, she acknowledged, especially in a base so isolated, where women were outnumbered by fifty to one.

'Ever seen a submarine get the full treatment when it's done a patrol?'

'Afraid not.' Until a few days ago she hadn't even seen a submarine. 'Is there something special about it?'

'When a submarine's had a spectacular patrol, yes. *Taureg* got depth-charged in the Bay of Biscay. A whole pack of German destroyers were after them. They had it pretty rough, by all accounts.'

'But they obviously made it.'

'They deserved to. They'd dived, you see, but eventually they had to surface – the air must've been getting bad – and up they came, damn nearly alongside a German destroyer the pack had left behind when they called off the hunt, waiting there, just in case *Taureg* surfaced. And surface she did; too near for the German to train his guns on her but near enough to get her own gun on *them*. Pumped one straight into the destroyer's magazine, then took off, the cheeky sods! Laughing like drains, I shouldn't wonder.' He grinned. 'Bet they couldn't believe their luck.'

'It isn't funny, all that killing.'

'No, Jane.' The smile was gone in an instant. 'Necessary, though. It's them or us, isn't it? You don't hang around to say "Sorry, mate." That's what war is all about. Anyway, *Taureg* survived thirty-eight depth charges so she deserves a bit of a cheer. But we'll know exactly what she's been up to when we get a look at her Jolly Roger.'

'*Jolly Roger*?' Jane's eyebrows shot upward. 'On one of His Majesty's ships?'

'That's right. The pirate flag. All returning submarines fly one if they've had a good patrol.'

'You're pulling my leg!' Did he really expect her to

believe such Peter Pan and Wendy nonsense. In the Royal Navy?

'All right, then. Wait till they come alongside.'

She shrugged and stared unspeaking down the loch, and wished again that he would go away.

'That's the skipper arriving, and the submarine commander,' he said, pointing to the well deck below them. '*Taureg* can't be long now.'

His Majesty's submarine *Taureg* came home to base smoothly and smartly, escorted by a frigate of the Free Netherlands Navy. On her fore and after casing, seamen submariners in bell-bottomed trousers and white sweaters stood comfortably at ease; on the bridge stood three officers, smartly dressed.

Jan Mayen gave a salute on her siren, then slipped away to her mooring buoy, leaving the submarine and her crew to savour their homecoming.

The bosun's pipe whistled shrilly over the Tannoy. '*Attention on the upper deck*,' commanded the disembodied voice. '*Face to port.*'

Omega's captain and the submarine commander beside him lifted their hands in salute; heads high, *Taureg*'s officers returned it as the at-ease submariners snapped as one man to attention.

'Three cheers for *Taureg*!' came the order and once, twice, three times, hats and caps rose in the air and once, twice, three times the assembled well-wishers roared their approval.

So this was how a submarine came back from a successful patrol! And how very understated and very British, with every man of its crew trying not to show how pleased he was or how embarrassed, and quietly thanking the good Lord for getting them out of the mess in the Bay, and if He wouldn't mind, could some other perishing submarine have the next thirty-eight? And whilst He was on their wavelength, how about a spot of leave . . .?

'It *isn't*!' Only then did Jane see the flag. 'Not the skull and crossbones!'

Tom Tavey laughed. 'It *is*.'

'But you wouldn't think it would be allowed.' Grown men on a killer submarine, flying a Jolly Roger! 'Do they all do it?'

'All of them.' He nodded. 'Every submarine takes one on patrol and someone sews on the bits as they happen. Take a look.'

The youngest of *Taureg*'s officers was holding out the flag for all to see, proudly proclaiming the success of their patrol and the reason for this, their special homecoming.

'See the white bars in the top right-hand corner, Jane? They represent enemy ships sunk by torpedoes, and the crossed guns on the left means they've been in a surface action – that'd be when they got the German destroyer – and the dagger below is a special operation.'

Unbelieving still, Jane counted the white bars. Three ships sunk on this patrol; three merchantmen sent to the bottom, and thank God Vi wasn't here to see this! 'Special operation?' she murmured.

'Cloak-and-dagger stuff. Usually picking up an agent from one of the occupied countries, or taking one out. A couple of weeks back there was a strong buzz that *Saffron* landed one by dinghy into France. A young woman, I believe it was.' He said it matter of factly, as if it happened all the time.

'Then let's just hope that *Taureg* has brought her back again,' Jane whispered. What next would be asked of women and what would women do, when at last peace came? Would they, could they, after the sudden heady freedom thrust upon them by war, ever go back to what they had been?

'You're doing it again, Jane Kendal. Frowning. Looking chokka.'

'I'm not. Really I'm not. It – it's just the way my face is arranged, I suppose.' Adroitly, she changed the subject. 'What's happening now?'

The returning submarine had nosed in to the depot ship's side, and willing hands on the well-deck rails pulled on her stern lines, easing her closer, making her fast. Now the sentinel submarines were under way again, gently manoeuvring to take up positions alongside *Taureg*.

'They've stopped engines. That's the skipper and commander going on board her now. The pink gin'll be flowing in the wardroom and there'll be an extra tot for the lower decks, I shouldn't wonder.' He glanced down at his wrist. 'Almost eleven o'clock. You'll hear the pipe soon, over the Tannoy.'

'Forgive me, but what's so special about eleven hundred hours?'

'What's so special?' His face registered disbelief, then his lips parted in a smile. 'Eleven o'clock is tot time; time for spirit that oils wheels and greases palms and sometimes even settles debts. *The rum ration*, Jane. Oh, I can see I'll have to teach you a thing or two about the Royal Navy.'

'Oh, I know all about *that*,' she returned airily, 'but it's only a drink of rum, after all . . .'

'Lesson one, Wren Kendal. Rum is never drunk. It is sipped or it is gulped; sippers and gulpers, that is. And make no mistake, the rum ration is very important to a matelot; not only to be sipped or gulped, but something to be used for bargaining or the repayment of a favour, or even bottled and taken home on leave. It would be a sad and sorry day for the Navy if ever they stopped it. There'd be mutiny, I shouldn't wonder.'

'But what about sailors who don't like rum?'

'*Don't like* . . .?' Tom Tavey's face registered blank

disbelief. 'Well, there might be the odd one or two who've signed the pledge,' he acknowledged, 'and they get threepence a day on their pay if they don't draw, as we call it. I've never met one, though,' he added hastily. 'There now!' His face brightened as the bosun's pipe shrilled over the Tannoy: '*Up spirits! Up spirits!*'

'That's it, Jane. Tot time. That's the call for the leading hands to collect the rations from the rum bosun. Best pipe of the day,' he grinned. 'See what I mean? Soon cleared the well deck.'

And so it had. *Taureg* had done well and had received her just and sincere due, but this was tot time, and on board the depot ship *Omega*, first things came first.

'Well, thanks for explaining it all to me, but I'll have to be going too, I'm afraid.' She turned to walk away, but he stopped her, a hand on her arm.

'Come out with me tonight, Jane. There's a good hop on, down in Craigiebur. Or would you rather see a flick?'

'If it's *Love on the Dole*, I've seen it, but thanks all the same.' She'd been right, he *was* trying to pick her up, which was a pity, really, because she liked to dance. But dancing made her remember a cold Candlemas Eve, and every sentimentally crooned love song reminded her of something that was best not remembered, and she wasn't ready, yet, to stick out her chin and smile.

'The dance, then? The band is very good.'

'Sorry,' she said, over her shoulder. Tom Tavey was nice, but no, not just yet. And besides, he was altogether too attractive, too sure of his masculinity, and it unnerved her. 'Sorry,' she said again.

'So am I, Jenny Wren.'

Eyes narrowed, he watched her walk away. Maybe she went in for officers, or maybe, he realized, she already had a boyfriend. A good-looker like her probably had half a dozen in tow. And she *was* good-looking, and intriguing too. Something to do with her eyes and the way they looked at you, yet saw nothing. And as for that red hair! Weren't redheads all ice on the thatch but with a red-hot fire burning in the hearth? With luck, this one would run true to form. Then, remembering it was five minutes past tot time, he ran down the ladder to the well deck, and away to the spare-crew mess.

She was a little darling, though. Might be interesting to have another try. A girl who looked like Wren Jane Kendal would be worth it. Well worth it . . .

She turned to watch him disappear down the ladder. He did it nimbly, his feet scarcely touching the narrow steel treads. His shoulders, she tried not to remember, were broad, his skin attractively tanned. Ought she have said yes to his offer of a date, accepted the challenge in those probing blue eyes?

Shrugging, she walked slowly down the ladder. Accept? Of course not. How could she have? He'd called her Jenny, hadn't he, and no one did that.

She blinked as she stepped back into the office, closing her eyes against the sudden change of light. Jock looked up briefly, then motioned for her to hurry.

'Come on now, lassie. There's a rush-immediate to be seen to. K-tables we'll be needing. You call, I'll subtract. Chop chop!'

The war had started again, but wouldn't it be wonderful, Jane thought, if during those brief moments of stillness, no one had been wounded or blinded or burned. And no aircrews reported missing.

The launch headed for Ardneavie jetty and Lucinda sighed contentment. Another watch over, another day of getting it right. To be enjoying the war was very wrong, but her new-found feeling of achievement was akin to joy. She should, she supposed, feel thoroughly ashamed.

123

'Got any money?' she asked Jane, fishing deep into the pocket of her broad canvas belt and pulling out a shilling and three pennies.

'Not a sausage. Flat broke till payday,' Jane sighed. 'Which means we'll be staying in tonight. Or we could go to cabin 10.'

'To Lilith's? Why not? But what about Vi? Think she'll come?'

'I don't know. She was a bit shaken up last night. She thinks Lilith is guessing, and maybe she's right. But I want to go, Lucinda. There's something I've got to know.'

'About a man?'

'Maybe. By the way, you should ask Chief Wetherby to let you watch next time a submarine comes back from patrol. D'you know they actually fly a Jolly Roger? It was *fascinating*.'

There now, she had admitted it. In spite of her affected disinterest, *Taureg*'s return *had* been well worth watching. Which was, she decided, the whole trouble with Ardneavie and *Omega* and the strangeness of life in the Royal Navy, pitched into it feet first as she had been. Part of her embraced it gratefully whilst the other, the sad, secret part, rejected and resented it, all the while clinging blindly to what had been. Yet this morning, a part of her had been guiltily glad that *Taureg* had sunk three enemy ships, not to mention the destroyer. Four up for S-Sugar, she had thought with bitter satisfaction.

'And there was a sailor there – submariner, I think he was – and he asked me for a date, but I said no.'

'Why?' Lucinda demanded, eyebrows arched. 'Bad breath and big ears, or something?'

'No. He was nice; *very* nice and rather good-looking, I suppose.' He would probably have been good to dance with, too. He had only one fault, in fact. He was not Rob MacDonald. 'But he wasn't my type, not really.'

The launch bumped gently against the jetty, and the Wren ratings of starboard watch hurried ashore.

'Oooh. I can smell it from here.' Lucinda closed her eyes and sniffed the air ecstatically. 'Liver, with onion gravy. Do hurry, Kendal dear. I'm *ravenous*!'

They went to cabin 10 that night; Jane because nothing would have kept her away; Lucinda because she had nothing better to do; and Vi reluctantly, because someone had to keep an eye on Lilith and her peculiar ways and maybe, though the eldest of the trio would never have admitted it, because she was more than a little curious about the birthday message. Half of her wanted to believe it; the other half clung to the dogma of her church and rejected it out of hand. One thing, though, was certain. Leading Wren Lilith Penrose would have to be watched, or Lucinda and Jane would be in it, right up to their earholes.

'I thought you'd come,' Lilith smiled, answering their knock. 'It works better if you believe.'

'Believe? Who said anythin' about believin'?' Vi demanded bluntly, wanting things straight, right from the start. 'You know the way it is with me. I'm not messin' about with no glasses. All I've come for is to see fair play.'

'Then that's a great pity, Vi, because you're a true medium, I'm sure of it.'

'Yer wot? *Me*? I'm a good Cath'lic, that's what I am.'

'And a natural medium in spite of it. But not to worry, we're going to get somewhere tonight, so let's make a start, shall we?'

'Not me. I'm going into Craigiebur.' To emphasize her words, Connie Dean pulled on her hat.

'With him?'

'Yes, Lilith. With him. *Again*.'

'Then you're a fool. When will you get it into your head

125

he's no good for you? How many times must I say it before it sinks in?'

'Johnny loves me!' Connie's cheeks flamed. 'And I told him you said he was married and he says it isn't true.'

'Then he won't mind letting you look at his paybook, will he? Paybooks don't lie.'

'Oh, shut up, Penrose! You're bad-minded. You might be boss of the launch, but what I do in my own time is none of your bloody business!'

The door slammed. Angry feet slapped against the stone stairs.

'Silly little fool. And you can't blame the men, not entirely. Away from their wives, and girls like Connie handing it out on a plate.' Shrugging, Lilith slid home the door wedge. 'But I'm right, I know it. She'll find out too late, but that'll be her funeral.'

'Right about what?' Vi demanded.

'That Connie Dean's going to land herself in big trouble if she doesn't finish with that man. Apart from being married, he's got a nasty reputation where the Wrens in this flotilla are concerned. But Connie's a good-time girl. That's all she joined up for. Men, and to get away from her parents.'

'This feller – a submariner, is he?'

'No, he's on one of the escort frigates. Johnny Jones. There's quite a few fancy their chances around here, and I know about them all; but our Johnny's a real lecher, so be warned.' Picking up the glass, she began to polish it slowly and carefully, breathing deeply until her anger was gone. Then, smiling, she asked, 'Sure you won't join us, Vi?'

Settling herself on the window seat, Vi shook her head. 'No. Ta, all the same.'

'Right, then.' Lilith returned the glass, rim down, to

the centre of the table. 'Pull up your chairs and let's make a start. Fenny next to me, please.'

'Will it tell us,' Jane asked uneasily, 'or must we ask it?'

'We'll see if there are any messages first. If not, we'll try a question. Now, put your index finger *very lightly* on the glass, left finger if you're left-handed. Gently,' Lilith breathed. 'Think of the person you want to contact.'

'Dead or alive?' Lucinda wasn't sure.

'Either, though those who have passed on make better contacts. Concentrate, now. Clear your mind of all negative thoughts and believe. Believe in it with all your heart. Charge it with positive vibrations.'

'How will we know who the message is for?' Jane's cheeks were flushed, her eyes large.

'The glass will move to the letters and spell out the words, and whoever the message is for will recognize it. Concentrate. Think of your contact. Think hard.'

Jane closed her eyes and made her mind a blank; Lucinda sighed tremulously, and from her seat in the window Vi coughed nervously, yet the glass remained stubbornly still.

'No messages tonight.' Lilith removed her finger. 'We'll have to ask it. Anyone got a question?'

'Me! Well – if it's all right, that is. I don't know what to do, though.' Excitement churned inside her and every small pulse in Jane's body beat dully. Not that anything would happen. It was just an ordinary glass on an ordinary table. Of course it wouldn't work, but she must try. She must try everything.

'Take the glass – carefully,' Lilith warned. 'Hold it in your hands. Make contact. Talk into it. Believe in it.'

Dry-mouthed, Jane cupped the glass in her palms, lifting it until her lips were level with its rim and her breath filled it.

'Glass, beautiful glass, what has happened to Rob? If

127

you know, please tell me. And if you can't tell me, please give me a sign. *Please*.' She raised her eyes to Lilith's.

'That's right, Jane. Put it back on the table and everybody try again.'

Four fingers made contact and the glass became a part of them, a living, shining thing. Slowly, it slid across the table.

'Oh, my God!' Lucinda gasped.

The glass moved more smoothly, more quickly, then came to rest at the figure zero. Then, without pausing, it moved anti-clockwise around the table, circling the letters again and again, stopping nowhere.

'It's charged,' Lilith breathed, 'but it isn't enough. Vi, we need you, too.'

'Please,' Jane begged. 'For me.'

Vi crossed over to the table. Maybe just this once. And she did owe Lilith something for the birthday message.

'All right, then.' She closed her mind against Father O'Flaherty's disapproval. 'But only for you, Jane.'

Five fingers reached out and the glass began to move again, surer, stronger. S-E-V-E-N. It came to rest precisely beside each letter before coming to a halt in the centre of the table.

'Well, Jane?' Lilith asked, nose wrinkled. 'Does *seven* mean anything?'

'It does, oh, it does! Only Rob could have known seven.' Tears shone in her eyes then spilled down her cheeks. 'Oh, Lilith . . .'

'Now look what you've gone and done!' Vi was on her feet in an instant. 'You've made her cry with your messin' about. There, now, queen.' Her arm encircled the shaking shoulders protectively. 'It's all right. Dry your eyes, pet. We're not doin' it no more.'

'But Vi, I'm *not* upset. I'm not crying, not really.' Jane

128

raised her face, eyes blissfully bright. 'It's all right. The message was from Rob. It *was*.'

'Good,' Lilith sighed. 'Anyone else got a question?' She challenged Vi with her eyes, demanding she should stay at the table. 'What about you, Vi? There's something you want to know, isn't there? Something you're not sure about?'

'Well, I'm not sayin' I believe it, mind, but I want to know about that happy-birthday message. There's only one person could've sent it and he – he's dead. Where did it come from? Was it from the glass, Lilith?'

'No, Vi. The message was between me and him. He sent it, I picked it up. It came through very clearly. He was very insistent.'

'He's dead,' Vi repeated dully.

'Dead or not, he wanted to say happy birthday.' Lilith spoke gently, her eyes kind. 'A lot of love came over, but I sensed that he was restless, and anxious too. Why don't you try to put his mind at rest, Vi?'

'I – *no*!' She wouldn't touch that glass again, not if Gerry were trapped in Purgatory for the rest of time, she wouldn't.

'Leave it.' Fenny Cole pushed back her chair. 'You know what happens if we try to force it, Lilith. We've done well enough for one night, and it'll be standeasy soon. Let's all try again tomorrow.'

'Shall we?' Lilith looked directly at Vi. 'Tomorrow night, after supper?'

'I don't know.' Vi let go a shuddering breath. 'I'll have to think about it.'

'Well, whatever you decide, you mustn't talk about this. No one else must ever know,' Lilith warned. 'Patsy Pill would have a fit if she found out, and we'd all be at defaulters'.'

No one, they all said. Not a single word to anyone. Not

even to the padre next time he came to Ardneavie to hear Confession, Vi thought grimly. What happened in cabin ten must be a matter of conscience.

'We'd better be goin',' she whispered. 'Ta-ra, well.'

'Goodnight.' Smiling, Lilith held open the door. 'Blessed be.'

'It's cocoa tonight.' Vi set down the standeasy tray. 'And I've brought up some bread and jam, in case anybody's hungry.'

They said they weren't, but they jammed the bread and ate it without speaking.

'I know you're both a bit sceptical.' Lucinda broke the silence. 'But sometimes it's uncanny the way those things get at the truth. We used to do something quite like it at school. After lights-out we'd all get up and play with this planchette thing. And it got a hold on us, too. We'd be there for hours, then wake up bog-eyed and fit for nothing next morning. It didn't take Matron long to realize that something was going on and put a stop to it.'

'*If* they work,' Vi frowned. '*If* what happened tonight wasn't somebody's finger pushin' that glass.'

'I was the only one who knew about *seven*, and I didn't push it, I swear I didn't,' Jane said quietly. 'It was as if it knew exactly where to go.'

'All right. Maybe it works,' Vi acknowledged. 'So if you was me, what would you think about that happy-birthday message I got?'

'If I were you, Vi, I'd believe what I wanted to believe. If the message could have been from someone you care for, then where's the harm in it? It's only if you let it take over your life that it's wrong.'

'That's all right, then.' Vi's eyes were clouded and sad. 'Because I wanted Gerry to remember my birthday. I was so lonely for him I could almost have believed that he did, though I know I mustn't.'

'Your church? Eternal damnation, and all that?' Lucinda smiled. 'Oh, I think love is stronger than such things. You must care for him a lot, Vi. Gerry – is that his name?'

'Was. He's dead. Got killed at sea. Torpedoed.'

'Oh, I'm sorry, truly I am.' Lucinda's eyes begged forgiveness. 'I shouldn't have asked. Too stupid of me. I didn't know.'

'Of course you didn't. How could you know? Don't worry, queen. I've been bottling it up inside me far too long. Best I should talk about it.'

'Does talking about it help, do you think?' Jane's heart still thudded uneasily. 'Would talking help take away the pain?'

'Maybe. They say the pain goes in time, and then you can remember things and be glad. I'm a – a widow, you see. It's the first time I've said that word since Gerry died, but I've said it now. *Widow*.'

'Vi, I'm so very sorry. I'd no idea. No ring, you see.'

'I took it off.' Vi pulled out the chain on which her wedding ring hung. 'Thought it was better that way. Daft of me, wasn't it?'

'No, I can understand.' Jane's voice was gentle. 'There are things you can't talk about; things you keep inside you – memories, mostly.'

'Rob? You've lost someone, too?'

'On the eighth of May. Missing from a raid over Germany. We weren't married, but we were – close.'

'Poor kid.' Vi smiled softly. 'This is a bugger of a war, innit? Why the 'ell did they let it happen? Why didn't us women get together and tell 'em it wasn't on? Them that caused this war and them that's getting fat on it should be made to fight it out between them, not our fellers.'

131

'But isn't there any hope at all for Gerry?'

'Don't think so. There was this bloke came to see me. Sailed in the same convoy as Gerry. Told me the *Emma Bates* got a direct hit. Not a lot of hope. They was carryin' ammunition, see.'

'Will it hurt too much to tell us about him?'

'Hurt? No. All the hurt inside me is for Gerry, really. Never had a crack of the whip, he didn't. The eldest of thirteen kids. Ma McKeown said thirteen must've been her lucky number because she never had no more after that one. But Gerry was never a child. Had to grow up fast, him being the eldest. When he was twelve he lied about his age and went to sea as a cabin boy.' Vi's eyes were clouded, her gaze distant, seeing the gates of the Albert Dock, and Gerry walking away from her.

'Then later he remustered as a stoker, and a right swine of a job that was. On the old coal-burning boats he ended up, shovellin' coal into red-hot boilers. Always got the shitty end of the stick, Gerry did. That's why I made a fuss of him when we got married. Nobody had ever made a fuss of Gerry before and he was real chuffed. "You're a lady," he'd say. "That's what you are." And he treated me like a lady, too, not a shop-girl. Didn't even mind about me great big feet.' She smiled. '"Only the best for you, girl," Gerry'd say. *Girl.* That's what he called me. That's why I can half believe what Lilith said. Only me and Gerry knew about that.'

'So you've nothing left now, Vi? Your home – you said it was bombed.'

'That's right. Nothing left now, but dreams. Ar hey, lovely, it was. Me an' Gerry'd build up the kitchen fire and we'd sit there and talk about what we'd do if we won the Irish Sweepstake. "First thing we buy is an 'ouse for you, girl, near your Mary's," Gerry'd say, "with a garden and a bathroom." He wanted a bathroom real bad. Well, dreams are cheap, aren't they? Like promises. Gerry promised he'd take care, promised to come back to me, but . . .'

'Rob promised, too, always to love me,' Jane whispered. 'And I'll always love him. I'll never forget him. Never.'

'Oh, dear, I feel quite full up.' Lucinda felt guilty. Nothing half so terrible had happened to her; no one she loved had been killed or even hurt. Indeed, had it not been for the blazing row with Mama she would still be living with her parents, seeing Charlie twice a week and helping the wounded airmen get back their confidence. And she would still be listening to Mama's complaining and thinking up excuses for not having the wedding just yet, which hadn't been fair of her, really, because she did want to marry Charlie. Later, though. She and Charlie had made no promises. He had always been there, like a brother, their relationship easy. He hadn't proposed to her, either, not actually asked her to marry him. Like everyone else, he had assumed she would. Even Nanny took it for granted. 'Once you and Captain Charles are married I shall look after your babies, Lucinda, as I looked after you.' Babies and Charlie. The two seemed inseparable. She and Charlie weren't in love, not really in love. Their relationship was civilized and uncomplicated, and she wished it could have been that way too for Vi and Jane. 'Shall we go again to Lilith's?' she ventured.

'Yes!' Jane's reply was instant. 'Oh, I know it's wrong to believe in such things, but Lilith couldn't have known about *seven*, could she?'

'Is it a special number?'

'I suppose it is. Seven was the time we used to meet. My mother didn't like my seeing Rob, so it wasn't easy for him to get in touch with me. He never knew when

133

he'd be flying, you see, so I'd wait for him every night at seven and hope he'd be there.'

'Did you know him long, queen?'

'Not really, though I felt I'd always known him. Thirteen weeks and four days, that was all. Then he went missing.'

'Three months. It isn't a lot,' Vi sympathized. 'I was luckier than you. Me and Gerry had four years. But missing isn't – well, there's a chance for your Rob, isn't there? One day there'll be a letter tellin' you he's all right, just you see if there isn't.'

'There won't, Vi. I'm not his next of kin. The Air Force will write to his mother if there's anything to tell, and the awful part of it is that I don't know where she lives. Somehow, Rob didn't get around to telling me where. He meant to, but addresses didn't seem important – well, not until it was too late. All I know is that he lived in Glasgow. Funny, isn't it, loving someone the way I loved Rob yet knowing so little about him.'

'No clues? Did he mention where he went to school?' Lucinda jammed a second slice of bread.

'No. Only that he got a scholarship to the local academy. And I know he worked in insurance, but there must be hundreds of insurance offices, and dozens of schools.'

'And he never mentioned the street he lived in – even casually?'

'Never, though he did say his local picture house was the Pavilion and I know his mother took her loaves to be baked at a place called Jimmy McFadden's bakery, but they're not in the phone book, either of them. I've looked.'

'Then you'll have to be patient, won't you; wait till he gets in touch with you. And one day there'll be a letter, I'll bet you anything you like there will.'

'Or a message,' Jane said softly, 'like tonight. We *will*

134

go to Lilith's again, Vi. You won't try to persuade me not to?'

'No, queen, I'll not do that. But it won't be tomorrow nor Friday because I'm on late duty those nights. But we'll go, all of us, just as soon as we can make it.'

And get to the bottom of that Lilith woman and her tricks – if tricks they were . . .

6

Monday evening, warm and bright. Eight days since the invasion of Russia, with the German divisions thrusting far and deep, said the announcer who read the six o'clock news, trapping thousands of Soviets west of Minsk.

It was terrible to imagine, Jane brooded, what might have happened had Hitler chosen to invade the British Isles instead of the Soviet Union. What had influenced that choice? Fate, had it been, or the flippant tossing of a coin? Or was it something more deep and sinister? Hitler believed in the occult, it was said; could the stars, then, have been responsible for so tremendous a decision? Was it possible for a man who had goose-stepped his hordes over half the world, almost, to be so naïve?

And when he was done with Russia, what then? Would London be his next prize or would he rest content with all he had taken and let the war settle into an uneasy stalemate?

But this must stop! It was unpatriotic even to *think* such things. Hitler would *never* take London. For the time being, the possibility of invasion had lessened. The German war machine was wholly occupied with the total subjugation of Russia, giving the shattered British Army time to heal its Dunkirk wounds and start thirsting for revenge. We *would* win. Alone and battered as we were, of course we would. Somehow, we always did. But how long, she mourned, would it take and how many shining young lives would be snuffed out before the price was finally settled?

'What's to do, queen? Lost a shillin' and found a meg?'

136

'No, Vi. I was thinking about – about going to Lilith's. We *will* go,' she said as they got up from the supper table. 'You said you would,' she urged, when doubt showed at once on Vi's face. 'You did, Vi, and it's only fun, isn't it?'

'Well, just as long as that's all it is.' Vi hesitated. Only yesterday she had attended Confession and Mass in Craigiebur and was reluctant to blot her clean copybook so soon after. 'As long as we're all agreed it's only for laughs.' She was wavering. She wanted to talk to Lilith again. She would have dismissed that message without another thought had it not been for one word. *Girl.* No one could have known about that. 'What about you, Lucinda?'

'I'm afraid you'll have to count me out.' Lucinda's cheeks flushed crimson. 'I've – er – got something on tonight. And before anybody says anything, I couldn't get out of it.'

'Nothin' to do with us.' Vi's face showed very plainly that even though she didn't wear a ring, a girl who was engaged and who might well be getting married on her next leave should not have anything on, so to speak.

'Well, I'm telling you, Vi, so you can stop looking like Nanny. It's Molly's date, really – Molly from the teleprinter room – but she's in sick bay so I said I'd sort it out for her.'

'I see.'

'No you don't.' Vi even sounded like Nanny, Lucinda thought. 'Molly had a vaccination and she looked awful. Her arm was red and swollen and she was obviously running a temperature. So the signal bosun said she'd better see the MO and he asked Lofty to listen out for me so I could go with her.'

That much made sense, Jane agreed. Another peculiar naval custom. *Wren ratings shall not attend the ship's doctor without a female chaperone.*

137

'Well, she saw the surgeon-lieutenant and he sent her to sick bay ashore until her temperature is down. But she had a date – a blind date, actually. Some man who'd come up on her teleprinter the other night and asked her to meet him. Name of Nick, she said, and she was to meet him at Craigiebur jetty at half-past seven. She asked me to go along and explain. She was quite bothered about it. I couldn't refuse, could I?'

'No,' Vi agreed. 'I don't suppose you could. A sailor, is he?'

'Think so. From Roseneath, Molly said, so it's quite a way to come. I don't think she knew a lot more. Well, it *is* a blind date and I shan't make a habit of it, so you needn't look so disapproving, Vi McKeown.'

'Sorry, queen. Didn't mean to.' Vi grinned. 'So that leaves you and me, Jane, unless you're goin' somewhere.'

'Me? Oh, no.' The reply was instant. 'I'm going to cabin 10. There's so much I need to ask.'

'Hey! For fun, we said,' Vi warned.

'All right. I give you my word I won't take it seriously. It's just that it was a bit much, that *seven* coming up like that. I've got to try again. You do understand?'

Vi understood. Like the word *girl*, it was too much of a coincidence to go unchallenged. And Lilith Penrose wasn't a bad sort. There was something decent about her, in spite of her peculiar beliefs, Vi conceded. And what Lilith believed was her own business. It was a free country, after all, and wasn't free countries what this war was all about?

'What about you, Lucinda? What time will you be back?'

'About eight, I suppose. I've only to explain about Molly. Shouldn't take long.'

* * *

Craigiebur, thought Lucinda, must once have been a pleasant place. Small, with hills on three sides, it was easy to imagine the summer holidaymakers arriving from Clydeside on the peacetime ferries. Now, the beach was desolate, criss-crossed with coils of barbed wire, and most of the seafront hotels and boarding houses had been requisitioned for Army and Navy personnel or for government offices evacuated from Glasgow.

She looked at her watch. The evening ferry was approaching, and right on time too; the ferry they had missed last Sunday. Was it really only a week ago they had missed it; just a week since Vi had refused to be put out about it and had kept their spirits up during that cold, uncomfortable night?

Vi. It was as if they had always known her. Vi of the ready smile, who had lost everything. Motherly Vi, who called everybody *queen* and who said *gale* for girl and had a sister *Murry* in *Ormscake*. Dear, lovely Vi, who would give short shrift to any of Mama's moods. Lucinda laughed inside.

And what about poor Jane, who had looked so pale and ill last Sunday night? Surely there must be a way to help her find Rob's mother. Why, even now she might have heard that her son had made it home again. Aircrews who bailed out over occupied Europe did get back, though little about it was released by the censors. Charlie said there was a lot going on in the occupied countries that the ordinary British public knew nothing about. Charlie said that – *Charlie*. Oh, dear. Here she was, waiting for a sailor called Nick who was already fifteen minutes late. Whatever would Charlie make of that, if he knew? Smiling just to think of it, she concentrated on the ferry, which was now making a half-turn, slowing and swinging to come in port side on to the jetty.

It occurred to her that Nick could be on that ferry. She

should wait a little longer. There were plenty of reasons for his lateness. She would wait until eight o'clock. Nick had quite a distance to come; she owed him that much.

By eight o'clock the ferry had come alongside and all the passengers disembarked. Soldiers and sailors and ATS girls and Wrens returning from leave, a few civilians and a kilted Scot with a goat trotting amiably behind him on a lead. Now the jetty was empty save for a Post Office van collecting sacks of mail, and of Nick there was no sign – unless he was the man in RAF uniform looking at his watch as if he just might be waiting for someone. Should she ask him? Dare she? Did she really have a choice? Straightening her shoulders and clearing her throat, she walked up to him.

'Excuse me, sir' – well he *was* an officer – 'are you Nick?' The colour flamed in her cheeks. 'Nick who's meeting Molly at half-past seven?'

'Well, if I am I'm unforgivably late, honey. And I'm not Nick, though I sure wish I was. You're Molly, uh?'

'No, I'm Lucinda. It's a bit complicated. I'm here because Molly is ill. I think I'll have to give up and go.'

'Me too. Er, Mavis – that's my date – isn't going to show, it seems. Guess we've both been stood up.'

'Guess we have. Aren't you a Canadian?'

'Getting near. American. Michael Johnson Farrow, from Vermont, New England.'

'Lucinda Bainbridge, from Lincolnshire, old England.' Smiling, she took the extended hand. And that, really, was when she should have said it was nice meeting him and wished him goodbye and run to catch the Ardneavie transport which was just now pulling away. But she didn't, because she was curious about him and, besides, he was still holding her hand.

'Forgive me,' she smiled, 'but what is an American

doing in the RAF? This isn't your war. Why did you come?'

'Now that,' he smiled, 'is best related over a couple of drinks.'

'Drinks, sir? On a Scottish Sunday?'

'They'll serve us at my hotel, no bother. And it does seem like Nick and Mavis aren't going to show . . .'

'Seems like it. And I'd be glad to have a drink with you – if you can get one.'

Sorry, Charlie, but he's a long way from home. And tomorrow, just to make up for her fall from grace, she silently promised, she would write to Charlie again, even though he hadn't replied to the letter she sent him a week ago. And wasn't there a war on and wasn't life far too short to worry about a couple of drinks? Seemed mean, actually, to refuse. She smiled into Michael Farrow's eyes. 'Very glad,' she said.

Lilith was waiting as if she had known they would come. Fenny, setting out the table, smiled a welcome. Connie, chin on knees, sat on the window seat, staring out over the loch.

'Want to join us, Con?'

'No, thanks. You know I'm no good at it.'

'That's because you don't believe; it makes you a disruptive influence. Or is it that you're afraid of what the glass might tell you?' Lilith chided softly.

'Oh, leave me alone, can't you! You're always on at me. You've got your knife into Johnny and you won't let it rest. Why can't you take my word for it that he's all right?'

'Because I'm older and wiser than you are, Connie Dean, and I feel responsible for you, though heaven knows why I should. And why aren't you seeing him tonight?'

141

'Because he's watch aboard, that's why. And while you're playing your silly game, why don't you ask it why you're such an interfering old bat?' She jumped to her feet, tears trembling in her voice. 'I'm going downstairs to listen to the wireless, and if you don't mind your own business I'll tell Ma'am what goes on up here, just see if I don't!'

Choking on her sobs, she slammed out, leaving behind her a disbelieving silence.

'Ar, hey, Lilith.' Vi found her voice. 'Weren't you a bit hard on the kid?'

'I don't think so. And Johnny Jones isn't on watch tonight. He came ashore on the early liberty boat. I saw him. It's my belief he's avoiding her and it's got her worried. And don't get me wrong, Vi. I get no satisfaction seeing her so miserable.'

'Don't upset yourself,' Fenny soothed. 'You aren't Connie's keeper.'

'You're right. Connie's a big girl but it doesn't stop me worrying, especially as I know there's trouble ahead for her. And tears.'

'Yes, and deep down she knows it too, Lilith. But isn't there something you want to ask Vi?'

'There is,' Lilith smiled. 'I want to know about the man who sent you the birthday message. He was close, I know that much. I think you are married to him.'

Unspeaking, Vi nodded.

'Tell me his name. It's better if I know.' Lilith's voice was gentle.

'His name is Gerry and when he – when he died he was on the SS *Emma Bates*. Torpedoed.'

'And do you have anything belonging to him? Something I could hold?'

'No, queen. All we ever had between us was blown to

142

smithereens in the bombin'. I've got some pictures and his last letter, but they're at my sister's. Sorry.'

'It doesn't matter, but if I can hold an object I get better vibrations, you see. Often I can tell if that person is alive or not. It might have been worth a try.'

'Gerry was lost at sea at the end of April. I don't think there's much hope, now. I'd like to think there was, but I'll have to be like our mam and learn to accept what I can't do nothin' about. It's better that way, in the end.'

'But won't you try? I get such strong feelings about you, Vi. You won't believe it, but you *are* a medium,' Lilith urged. 'He'd come through so easily to you if you'd only let him.'

'You owe it to him,' Fenny urged.

She did, Vi brooded. If Gerry were crying out in Purgatory then it was her duty to help him, and be blowed to Father O'Flaherty's wrath.

'I don't know what to do, Lilith. Your religion's new to me. I can't believe that the dead ever come back to us – well, only Our Lord, that is. But I'll try. Just this once.'

'Good. You won't regret it. Shall we sit down? Lucinda's not here, I see. Not that she's any great help. Her vibrations are minus! She hasn't come alive yet, though she'll be quite a girl when she does. But it's Gerry who's important now. I feel he's got something to say.' Lilith handed the glass to Vi. 'Speak into it. Ask it whatever you want to know.'

Hesitantly, Vi took the wine glass, cupping it in her hands as Jane had done, her heart thudding dully, embarrassment staining her cheeks. And then it was as if the glass suddenly shone and sparkled, just as the Cape Town goblets shone and sparkled; it seemed she was holding a telephone receiver and all she had to do was speak into it, to Gerry. Sighing gently, she closed her eyes.

'Glass, please tell me about my husband. Tell me he

143

didn't suffer none and tell me he's at peace. And if you can, tell him thanks for remembering my birthday and tell him that I love him. Be sure and tell him that, won't you?'

Gently Lilith took the glass, upending it on the table and four fingers reached out to touch it. Slowly, it began to move; firmly and surely it spelled out a word.

'No!' Vi snatched back her hand. 'What does it mean?' Tears filled her eyes. She had felt so close to Gerry yet now the glass mocked her.

'Hush. Be still, Vi.' Lilith's arms circled her shoulders.

'How can I be? I wanted to know that he died gently. I wanted him to be at peace. I needed him to tell me so, yet all I get is *letter*. What's it playing at? How do you send a letter to a man what's dead?'

She covered her face with her hands, stifling her sobs, sucking in gulps of air. Loudly she blew her nose then brushed away the tears that wet her cheeks. 'Sorry,' she whispered. 'I shouldn't have done that. Suppose that thing doesn't work for Cath'lics, eh? Why don't you have a go, Jane? See if you can get some sense out of it.'

'Vi, I'm so sorry. I wanted to try again but I won't, not if it upsets you.' Though mingled with disappointment, Jane's compassion was real.

'It won't upset me, queen.' Vi's cockeyed grin was back. 'But that's my lot. I'm not doin' it no more but I'll sit in for you, if you want me to.'

'You don't mind? Honestly?'

''Course I don't. Go on. Give the old glass a rub.' Wipe my tears off it, Jane, and my hopes, she thought. Only St Jude can help me now. Poor, hard-worked St Jude, who gets landed with the hopeless cases. 'Go on, luv. Get goin'.'

Tenderly Jane polished the glass with her handkerchief then lifted it to her lips. 'Rob, my darling, send me hope. I'll wait for ever for you, but say we'll meet again, soon.'

Carefully, reverently almost, she placed the glass in the centre of the table. Slowly, reluctantly, it moved from letter to letter. *Jenny. Forget.*

Frowning, Lilith spelled out the letters. 'Who's Jenny?'

'I am. Rob called me Jenny, but it's all wrong. He wouldn't say that. The padre at the aerodrome said it but Rob wouldn't. He *wouldn't.*'

'Now listen, both of you. You've been upset tonight and I'm sorry. But please trust me.' Lilith reached across the table, taking a hand from each, holding them tightly as if to pass on something of herself. 'Please, I beg you, have faith. Don't give up. I wouldn't ask it of you if there wasn't hope.'

'I know, queen, an' I'm sorry I made a fool of meself. I'm a daft ha'p'orth and I know you mean well, Lilith. No hard feelings,' Vi whispered, 'but that's me finished.'

'Well, I'm not giving up. Rob *is* alive, I know it,' Jane choked. 'He's somewhere in Europe, trying to get home, and I won't take *forget* for an answer. I won't.'

'And you won't be upset, either of you? This is only a setback, remember.'

'Don't worry. We're goin' downstairs to listen to Tommy Handley and the nine o'clock news.' Vi was herself again, already accepting that which she had no power to change. It was Jane she grieved for; Jane who so fiercely resisted Fate, who would never accept that anything could touch her first, precious love. 'And d'you know what? One of these days we're goin' to switch on that wireless and the man's goin' to tell us it's all over, just you see if he isn't.' One of these days.

Lucinda took off her hat, placed it with her respirator beneath her chair then gave her full, unblinking attention to the American pilot who stood at the bar. Michael Johnson Farrow was tall and good-looking. Devastatingly

145

good-looking. Even the scar that ran from eye to jaw on his left cheek only added to his attractiveness. His eyes were blue, shaded by thick dark lashes and as sharp as his film-star features. Michael Farrow, she decided, was not a man to tangle with; the jut of his jaw told her that. Michael Farrow was a man who would get what he wanted – if he wanted it badly enough. He limped a little, too, though like most of the war's wounded, he went to great pains to hide those injuries, received in another country's war.

Lucinda smiled serenely. It was good that she could look at this man so dispassionately yet find him so exciting. Strange that belonging to Charlie gave her protection in a peculiar sort of way; an immunity kind of, against falling in love. Thus protected, she could admire, desire, even wonder what it would be like to be loved, *really* loved by him, yet feel no guilt for her wanton thoughts. Being engaged to Charlie protected her from herself, too, and it was rather nice, she acknowledged, to have such unfaithful, unladylike fancies, yet not feel one iota of guilt. She'd like to bet he was a good dancer, too; the build of him guaranteed it. And when he danced, his hold would be firm and intimate, and when he kissed it would be hard and gentle, both at the same time. And dry, she shouldn't wonder. Not like the way Charlie did it. Charlie sometimes slobbered when he kissed her. She really must speak to him about it, once they were married. Surely there was something he could take for it.

'Say, honey.' Michael Farrow turned, smiling. 'No gin. No bourbon. No wine.'

'Oh!' She blushed bright red and rid her head at once of such wanton thoughts. Whatever next! She'd be wondering what he'd look like undressed, or something equally delightful. 'Beer, then?'

'Tepid or warm?'

'Do I have a choice?'

'Tepid bitter, coming up.' He placed two glasses on the table then sat down opposite. 'Now, Lucinda Bainbridge, tell me all about yourself.'

'I was about to ask the same of you, sir.'

'Well, for a start you can cut out the "sir" and call me Mike like most guys do, and I'll call you Lucy. Lucinda's a bit stiff – upper class, sort of – though you *are* upper class, aren't you? I can tell by the way you speak.'

'I – I don't think I'm any class, really. I'm a Wren and I wear the same uniform and get exactly the same pay as all the other Wrens. And as for the way I speak – '

'Kind of clipped, and brittle. I'm getting real good at picking out accents now. Mind, the further north I get the harder it is.'

'You'd have fun with Vi, then. She's from Liverpool. "Ar, hey, Loocinda, yer don't arf talk luv'ly. Just like a frewt." Fruit, you know. She's a darling. But tell me about you? Just what is an American doing in our air force? How did you manage it? And *why*?'

'How is easy. I crossed the border into Canada, walked into a recruiting office, told them I wanted in on their war and they said, "Okay, buster, sign here!" Then I did my training in Canada, got my wings, got a commission and came over here. They posted me to a fighter squadron in Digby.'

'But that's in Lincolnshire!'

'Sure is.'

'You make it sound very simple. Now tell me why, Mike. You didn't have to come. This is our war, not America's.'

'I came, I guess' – embarrassed, he looked down at his glass – 'because I don't like people being pushed around. That, and because I have an English granny. And because I'm a bloody fool . . .'

147

'But a very nice bloody fool. It makes me feel all warm inside when someone cares about us.' Her fingertips traced the length of his scar. 'How did you get that?'

'I got posted south with the squadron last June after Dunkirk. Me and my Hurricane had a tangle with a Messerschmitt. He won, I bailed out. Haven't flown since, though I reckon they'll pass me fit again before long. Y'know, Lucy, I felt real bad about this scar. I'd take a look at myself and think, "Jesus. What a mess!" I thought everyone must be looking at it. But then you touch it and talk about it like it's not all that important. Sure it doesn't turn you off?'

'Why should it? I've seen a whole lot worse.' No need to tell him about her airmen and their poor, burned faces. 'But we were talking about this crazy American who flies a fighter for the British.'

'I'd rather talk about you, Lucy.' He picked up her left hand. 'No rings?'

'No rings, Mike.' Sorry, Charlie, but I don't have a ring, do I, though that isn't strictly what he means.

'Tell me, Lucy Bainbridge, why didn't we meet when I was stationed at Digby?'

'Because Lincolnshire's a big county and anyway, my family left to live in London.'

'Where, in London?'

'Bruton Street. It's near Berkeley Square.'

'Say, that's where the nightingales sing!'

'Do they? Well, I suppose they *might*, sometimes,' she teased.

'Ever heard them, Lucy?'

'Never. Only sparrows.'

'Okay. Tell you what, why don't we give it a try? Next time I've got some leave, you and me can meet in London and we'll sit real quiet in the blackout and listen for those nightingales, uh?'

148

'Idiot! And I don't have leave due until September.'

'Okay. I'll take mine in September, too. I'm only stooging around at training bases till they pass me fit for flying again. I'll be able to fix it.'

'September's a long time away. We live day to day in this war, but I don't have to tell you that, do I? You're wearing a medal ribbon so you probably know more about it than I do. Let's just talk about now.'

'Suits me.' He took her other hand. 'We'll talk about a guy called Nick who didn't show and who has my heartfelt thanks. And we'll talk about you and me, honey, who were meant to meet.'

'Ships meet, Mike, and pass . . .'

'Not you and me, Lucy.' Hell, but it couldn't end here, tonight. There was so much to say, so much he needed to know about her. He'd always figured he'd take the war in his stride, stay heart-whole till it was over, then go home and find himself a good New England girl like everyone expected he would. But this Lucy Bainbridge was different. Right now he wanted more than anything to dance with her, feel her closeness. And as they danced, he reckoned, those ridiculous blonde curls would be just about level with his chin. 'Say, is there any place we can dance tonight?'

'In Scotland? On a *Sunday*?'

'But you do like dancing?' Hell, she'd just got to!

'I love it.' She always had, but now she accepted that one of the crosses she must for ever bear was the problem of Charlie's feet, both of which gave him trouble the instant he placed them upon a dance floor. Charlie danced in beelines and did a marching turn whenever it was necessary to change direction. Nor did the turns and beelines ever vary. Quicksteps, rumbas and waltzes were all alike. Poor, dear Charlie. She should be feeling guilty sitting here like this, holding hands with a stranger, but she didn't, because having a drink with a man who had come from America to fight for us and got himself wounded for his pains and been given a Distinguished Flying Cross was no more than her bounden duty.

'You do, Lucy? Then what say we make a date right now? How about tomorrow? There's a dance hall here in Craigiebur, isn't there? Half-past seven suit you?'

'Half-past seven will be fine.'

'At the jetty – same place.'

He was still holding her hands and she didn't care. She didn't give a damn, in fact. One, just *one* night spent dancing with an American from Vermont, New England, was little to ask in return for a lifetime of beelines and marching turns.

'Lovely. I'll look forward to it, Mike. But what about your date? What if you were to meet Mavis at the dance, I mean?'

'We-e-ll.' He rubbed his chin ruefully and his smile, she thought, was sheer bliss. 'Truth is, there isn't a Mavis – not here, that is.'

'She's your girl, back home?'

'My *girl*?' He threw back his head and laughed. 'Y'see, Lucy, it's like this. When you said about Nick not turning up, I came out with the first name that came into my head. I wasn't waiting for anyone. I'd been killing time watching a submarine go out – and watching you waiting there. When you came up to me I couldn't believe my luck.'

'Then *who* is Mavis?'

'Mavis,' the smile widened, 'is my aunt Adeline's parrot.'

'A parrot! Called *Mavis*? Oh, Mike!' Laughing with him, she held up her glass. 'Here's to Mavis.'

'And to Nick. God bless 'em both!'

* * *

150

'You awake, Vi?' Wren Bainbridge, shoes in hand and two hours adrift, pushed open the door of cabin 9.

'Lucinda! Where the 'ell have you been?'

'Sorry, Vi. I tried not to waken you.'

'Waken my flamin' foot! D'you know what time it is?'

'Actually – er – yes. Is the blackout all right? Can I switch the light on?'

'Go ahead.' Jane's bedsprings creaked. 'We weren't asleep, either of us. Vi was certain you'd suffered a fate worse than death. You're lucky the pier patrol didn't catch you. What happened?'

'Nothing happened. We talked and talked and I missed the last transport.' Lucinda hung up her jacket then unknotted her tie. 'Lord, my feet! We walked all the way back. I suppose I'm in trouble?'

'Not unless anybody saw you coming in. We told the duty Wren you were in the bathroom when she did last rounds. How did you get in, by the way?'

'I remembered what you said about the pantry window, then came up the back stairs. And bless you both for fixing it for me. Mike was really concerned.'

'Mike?' Vi frowned. 'I thought his name was Nick.'

'Sorry. Must have got it wrong. His name is Michael Farrow, actually, and he's in the Air Force.' Best not explain too much. Blind dates were one thing; being picked up by an American was altogether another. Or had she picked *him* up? 'He – he's stationed at Machrihanish and he's very nice, Vi. Truly he is.'

'No business of mine who you go out with,' Vi grumbled, 'and for Pete's sake get yourself into bed or we'll all be in the rattle. Y'know, I seem to remember you said eight o'clock. What really kept you, Lucinda?'

'Nothing, honestly. I just felt sorry for him, that's all. Wounded, and all that way from home. Actually, he's an American.'

'A Yank? What the 'eck's he doin' in our war?'

'I really don't know. I suppose he has his reasons. Said he didn't like seeing people pushed around.' Lucinda pulled on her pyjamas. 'Anyway, I think it's extremely noble of him to join in the scrap with us and that's why I said I'd go out with him again.'

'Again?' Vi cocked an eyebrow. 'And what would your Charlie say to that, if he knew?'

'He won't know. Mike is in Craigiebur on a seventy-two-hour leave pass. He'll be going back to Machrihanish early Tuesday and that'll be the end of it.'

'Ar, hey, come off it, queen. Machrihanish isn't the other end of the world. A feller that's come all the way from America can find his way back to Ardneavie, no bother at all!'

'Vi! I said I won't be seeing him again after tomorrow night and I won't.'

'That's all right then, isn't it? I bet you didn't tell him you were engaged, though.'

'No, I didn't.' Why ever should she? What a fuss Vi was making. After tomorrow night it would be all over, wouldn't it? And was she expected to live like a nun when the war might go on for years and years? 'And I didn't ask if he was engaged, either. Oh, Vi, it's all right. I promise you it is.'

'Look, queen, you don't have to answer to me. What you do is your own business. But be careful, eh?'

'I will. I really will. And thanks for getting me off the hook. It was awfully sweet of you both.'

Parts of this war, thought Lucinda as she snapped off the light and got into bed, were really rather nice. Since leaving home she had met such lovely girls: Vi, Jane, Molly, cabin ten and the lovely duty Wren who had turned a blind eye to the unlocked pantry window. She really was most grateful to Goddy for getting her into the Wrens. In years to come she would look back on it all with affection, and surely just a little freedom before she settled down wasn't all that much to ask. Tonight had been fun, and tomorrow night would be even better.

Her toes wriggled in anticipation of a night spent dancing with Michael Johnson Farrow, the second of his names given for Alice Johnson, his beloved English grandmother who had gone to America as a governess when Queen Victoria was on the throne, and though she had married a citizen of the United States and never returned to the country of her birth, even to visit, she had steadfastly clung to her Englishness. A very stubborn lady, it would seem, and Mike was a chip off the old block, Lucinda smiled, one who liked having his own way. Like tonight, for instance, when he had flatly refused to let her hitch a lift back to Ardneavie and insisted on walking the whole three miles with her.

'But Mike, your leg . . .'

'Aw, to hell with my leg. The MO said it needed exercise and, anyway, you're not supposed to notice it, honey.'

So she had left him at the pantry window and begged him to take it easy on the walk back, but he had laughed and told her not to be late tomorrow night.

Tomorrow. Seven-thirty, at the jetty and, oh dear, what *would* Charlie say to that, if he knew? Vi had implied he might not like it and probably she was right, but she wouldn't mind betting, Lucinda pondered sleepily, that Charlie had the odd date or two. Charlie had fun, and he'd probably go on having fun long after they were married – which would be all right, she supposed, as long as he did it discreetly.

And tomorrow night she too would be discreet and thoroughly well-behaved, and when it was over she would

153

offer her hand to Mike and wish him luck and she wouldn't even kiss him goodbye.

She sighed and closed her eyes, and her lips tilted into a smile of pure contentment.

A parrot called Mavis, indeed . . .

7

When she awoke that morning, there had been nothing, Jane considered, to indicate that the coming day was to be so completely unforgettable. It had started with an early call, as it always did, and progressed by bleary-eyed stages to the breakfast queue and the realization that this was Monday; tomatoes on toast was always Monday.

Jane glared at her plate. 'When this war is over, I will never, ever, eat another tinned tomato.'

'Nor me. It'd do a whole lot more for the war effort,' Fenny Cole sighed, 'if they were to leave them in their tins and drop them on Berlin!'

'If there is anything more revolting than tinned tomatoes on toast,' Lucinda fervently agreed, 'it is tinned tomatoes on toast gone cold and soggy. What a way to start the day. Ah, well, it can only get better, can't it?'

So they had called a goodbye to Vi, who was scraping the uneaten breakfasts into the pig-swill-for-victory bucket, and hurried down the jetty, as they always did, to the launch that always waited there.

'It's going to be hot again.' Lucinda lifted her face to the sun. Indeed, there had never, the locals said, been a June like it. For the entire month the sun had shone from a near-cloudless sky. The good weather had come with the new moon and would last, they predicted, until the next one.

Jane eased a finger round the neck of her shirt. This was not a day for the wearing of starched collars and ties and itchy wool stockings, and she thought with envy of the off-duty Wrens who would roll bathing costumes in

155

towels and make for the head of the loch and the cool, shallow water that lapped the shore.

'We're in for another scorcher,' she said to Jock. That was all she had said, but it had been the start of something wonderful, something unbelievable, almost; the day on which despair vanished and the pain and hopelessness that had wrapped her round since that May night dropped from her in the speaking of a word.

'You could be right, lassie. I was talking to an old body in the pub last night and he told me it was the hottest summer in his remembering; in eighty-three years, he said.'

'I'd agree with every word.' Jane used a signal pad as a fan. 'But don't you think the old ones remember only what they want to remember? My mother does it all the time. The summers were different when *she* was a girl. They could always be sure of a good haytime and corn harvest, and summer began on the first day of June and ended when the apples were picked and stored safely in the loft and not one day before. Or so she said.'

'I mind fine just what your mother means. I do it myself all the time. Nostalgia, I suppose.' Jock smiled. 'Now when Flora and I were married there was nothing so certain but that we were on our way up in the world. The Glasgow tenements we'd both been reared in weren't half good enough and we found ourselves a little house in a better district and thought we were doing just fine.

'Yet now we often think back to our courting days. Happy days, Jane, spent mostly in the picture house. All red plush seats and red silk curtains, it was. It seemed like a palace, though, to us. And I think fondly of the room and kitchen I was brought up in and the street-corner gangs, yet I suppose that tenement is a slum now, and the old Pavilion little better than a flea-pit. I – '

'Jock! The Pavilion, you said?'

156

'Aye. The local picture house. Flora and me saw our first talkie there. Now, *that* was something to remember.'

'And are there many Pavilions in Glasgow?' Her heart thudded dully, her mouth was suddenly dry.

'Aye. It's a popular name for picture houses and dance halls. But why d'you ask?'

'Oh, it's just that someone I knew – I *know* – had a Pavilion near where he lived. You see' – she took a deep, steadying breath – 'it was someone I was close to, but I never knew where he lived – well, not his actual address.'

'But he mentioned the Pavilion?'

'Yes, Jock, and he lived in a tenement, too.'

'So do a lot of bodies in Glasgow. If there's one thing that place is no' short of, it's tenements.'

'I know,' Jane shrugged. 'It was just a thought. I do so want to find where he lives, though. I want desperately to see his mother.'

'Sounds important, lassie.'

'It is. He flew from the aerodrome near our village and he went missing, you see, and it'll be his mother they write to when there's news of him.'

'And was he special, this young man?'

'*Is*, Jock. Very special. I'd give anything to know he was safe.'

'But shouldn't you have heard something by now? A letter, maybe?'

'I don't think so. My parents didn't approve of him. Sometimes I think they'd even hold back a letter if they thought it had come from him. It's terrible of me to think my own mother and father would do such a thing, but I'm an only child and we've never seen eye to eye over Rob.

'Oh, I don't mean there was something wrong with him. They didn't really have anything against him. But he was a pilot, you see, and they thought no good would come of my seeing him. Aircrews don't have an easy time. So

157

many of them get killed or go missing. They were only thinking of me, I suppose.'

'Poor wee Jane.' Jock thought with sadness of his own daughter, very little younger, and wondered for how much longer they could protect her from the taint of war. 'Did this laddie no' mention anything at all that might have helped? His school, or his church, perhaps?'

'No, Jock. I've thought and thought but there's only one other thing, though you'll not have heard of it. Glasgow's a big place, after all . . .'

'Try me.'

'If I said Jimmy McFadden's, would it mean anything to you?'

'The bakery on the corner?'

'Oh, Jock! It *does*! You know where it is!'

'Whisht now, will ye?' Jock had whispered as heads turned. 'Don't let Chiefie hear ye! Try to look busy, hen, even if we aren't.'

'But I can't believe it,' Jane hissed, picking up a pad and writing in the date. 'The Pavilion and Jimmy McFadden's bakery. It's got to be where Rob lived. You don't know him, or his mother? Rob MacDonald? His mother is a widow and he's got two brothers in the army.'

'No, I don't know the family, but there's an awful lot o' they MacDonalds about, remember.'

'I suppose there must be, but it seems you might well have grown up in the same tenement.'

'I doubt it. That area is all tenement blocks. Finding someone among that lot is like looking for a needle in a haystack, though some of the buildings have been knocked about in the bombing and there's bound to be a lot of them boarded up now. That might narrow down the field a wee bit, but you'd still have one hell of a job finding where he lived. I'll give you that for nothing.'

'I'll find it.' She was light-headed with joy. One minute

they had been talking about the weather, the next she had discovered the picture house and the bakery, the only places Rob had ever mentioned. 'It all seemed so hopeless, but now – well, I've at least found the haystack.'

'You're no' intending looking? That area's no place for a young girl like yourself.'

'It was good enough for Rob.'

There was no answer to that, Jock Menzies conceded, but even so, he felt obliged to warn the silly wee thing of the hopelessness of it all. 'Maybe it was, but they'll no' let you go to Glasgow. No' without a pass.'

'Then I'll stick in a request for one.'

'An' you'll no' get it. Glasgow's out of bounds unless you live by there or need to travel through it. There's been a lot of trouble in some parts.'

'What sort of trouble?'

'Well, like razor fights and beatings-up and sailors getting their pockets dipped. And there's the street women, Jane.'

'Jock! I wouldn't be looking for a prostitute, would I? But if I can't get a pass then I'll have to think of some other way, won't I? I'll get there, though. I *will*.'

'. . . *and away round the corner to Jimmy McFadden's with the loaves for baking*,' Rob had said. Find that baker's shop and she had pinpointed the tenement block. Oh, glory be! Just as she had been giving up it had happened. This morning the outlook had been bleak, then with one small word it had changed. For the first time since that awful May morning she was free to hope again. An ordinary conversation had yielded the words she most wanted to hear and had become special and was meant to be. Somewhere in Europe, Rob was alive. It was as certain as day following night.

'Oh, Jock,' she whispered. 'Isn't everything *wonderful*?'

For the rest of the watch her head was full of cotton

wool, her thoughts far away across the Clyde, and Jock said thank goodness he wasn't young and in love or there'd be no work done at all, and didn't she know there was a war on and couldn't she at least try to get *one* subtraction right?

'And just what,' Lucinda demanded as they waited on the quarterdeck for the Ardneavie-bound launch, 'has got into you? You've had a silly look on your face all day, you knocked over a mug of tea and called Chiefie Wetherby *ducky*, and now you look as if you're going to go off pop at any minute. You haven't been at Jock's rum, have you?'

'No, but I do have something to tell you,' Jane exulted, 'though it's going to have to wait till everybody's here.'

'Meanie. Not just a tiny hint?'

'Well, it's about Rob, but I'm not saying any more till Vi and Lilith's lot are all here. You'll never believe it, though. I can hardly believe it myself!'

She was first off the launch and first up the jetty, with Lucinda almost running to keep pace with her.

'Kendal dear, do slow down.'

But such news could wait no longer. Good news was for sharing. And when she told them, they would help her to get to Glasgow, with or without a pass.

'Oh, Lucinda, do hurry,' she laughed.

Life was good again and nothing was so certain but that all would go well for her. Of course it would.

'. . . so you see, that's how it happened.' Jane laughed, as they sat at supper. 'Now all I've got to do is get there. The rest will be a piece of cake.'

'But Glasgow's a big city and Jock was right,' Lilith cautioned. 'One or two parts are a bit rough.'

'I'll be all right. You're worse than my mother, Lilith.

160

And I'll find my way easily. Jock used to live there and he told me exactly where McFadden's shop is and how to get there – even the number of the tram and the stop I'm to get off at.'

'I suppose you know how Ma'am feels about it?' Fenny added her doubts to the rest. 'And *if* you got there, where would you sleep, Jane. You can't get to Glasgow and back in a day.'

'I'd get a bed at the YWCA. Or why shouldn't I stay with Rob's mother? Who's to say she won't put me up?'

'I still think you shouldn't go alone,' Vi insisted. 'Glasgow has been bombed the same as Liverpool has. I know what it'll be like. There could be whole streets without a soul in them. You'd be scared rotten on your own after dark.'

'Why should I be? And it's light until ten o'clock, now.' What harm could come to her? Hadn't Rob lived there, tenements, bomb damage and all. What then could be so wrong with it? 'Please don't spoil it,' she pleaded. 'Please be glad for me.'

'We *are* glad for you, queen; all of us. We're all real chuffed. But promise you'll be careful. And don't expect too much,' Vi begged. What could she say? How was she to tell her that the news could be bad, that all Rob's mother might be able to tell her could be exactly what Jane didn't want to hear. 'Promise you'll not build your hopes too high.'

Mother of God, don't let her be hurt any more. She's so excited, so happy. Don't take it away from her.

'Of course I'll take care.' Jane jumped to her feet. 'Look, I'm sorry but I'm just not hungry. See you all later, uh?'

'Oh, dear.' Lilith shook her head. 'What's it going to do to her if she hears something that isn't good? What if

161

she finds he's not just missing but dead? It would destroy her.'

'D'you suppose I haven't been thinking that?' Vi retorted. 'But I'll bet you anything you like she won't get a pass, and then what'll we do? There'll be no living with her if that happens.'

'Then we'll have to find another way,' Fenny said quietly. 'We've got to help her. It'd be too cruel if we didn't.'

'And I agree.' Lucinda spoke up clearly. 'Jane could do it without a pass. Once she was off duty she could catch the late-afternoon ferry and be in Glasgow before it got too dark. Surely between us we could cover for her.'

'And what about when she's adrift in the morning, when she doesn't turn up for her watch?'

'Then she'll have to fix it first with her opposite number. If nothing went wrong she could be back here in time to go on late duty.'

Lilith frowned. '*If* nothing went wrong.'

'Well, I say we leave it,' Fenny insisted. 'After all, we don't need to worry until Ma'am says no to the pass. We don't have to think of anything till then, do we?'

They agreed, all of them, that they did not. Only when Jane's request was refused need they puzzle over ways and means, they said. And after all, there was a chance that Miss St John just might give Jane a pass.

'Do you think it would do any good to set up the table?' Lilith asked.

'I don't think so.' Vi remembered that not so very long ago the glass had given Jane the answer she had least wanted to hear. 'The way things have turned out, it might be best to leave well alone.'

'You could be right. The state she's in at the moment wouldn't help any. She's so charged up, the glass would

162

take off like a rocket. I've never seen anyone so excited. The change in her is amazing. Kendal's a different girl.'

And let's all hope, Vi brooded, that nothing happens to spoil that sudden singing happiness, though one thing above all was certain. If recent events were anything to go by, life at Ardneavie House would never be dull.

From the top of the street that ran down to the jetty, Mike Farrow saw Lucinda waiting and quickened his step.

'Hi, honey! Sorry I'm late.'

'You're not. The transport was early.'

She was glad he had come. There had been times when she had expected him not to, and to see him hurrying down the hill made her suddenly happy.

'Everything all right last night, Lucy? You didn't get caught, or anything?'

'No. Everything was fine. I crept up the back stairs and straight into a telling-off from Vi. But it was all right. They'd fixed the duty Wren for me.' Lucinda laughed. 'I'm not in the rattle, or anything. But how about you, Mike? I worried about your leg.'

He shouldn't have walked her home to Ardneavie, but he'd insisted, choosing to ignore the three miles back.

'Then you needn't have. I managed just great. It was a lovely night and every so often I stopped and stood and stared a bit. Y'know, Lucy, everything was so beautiful in the half-light. My granny once stayed in Craigiebur, would you believe? She worked for a family who always packed the kids off to Craigiebur for the summer. That's why I decided to spend a weekend here. Must remember to take a couple of snaps before I go back and send them to her.

'Snaps? Where on earth did you get a film?' Such things had become non-existent from almost the first day of the war. Nowadays the few available went immediately under

163

the counter and only the lucky few ever managed to get one. 'They're like gold dust here.'

'Oh, parcels from home; comforts for the troops, I guess,' he grinned. 'But let's walk a way, first. It's such a swell night.'

It seemed natural that he should take her hand, and because it felt rather nice, she entwined her fingers in his and smiled happily up at him.

'Why don't we walk down to the mouth of the loch, Mike? Someone told me there's a boom net right across it, to keep the Germans out. I'd like to know how it works.'

'I've seen it. As a matter of fact it's two huge nets made of steel links and there's a couple of tugs that drag them backward and forward when something wants to get in or out of the loch. Nothing could get through it or under it. Reckon you're all pretty safe in there, honey.'

'I suppose we are.' Until now, though, she had never thought what sitting ducks those ships could have been. 'And how do you know all this?'

'Because I watched a submarine and a frigate go through last night, while I was waiting for Mavis,' he laughed, his eyes teasing her. 'C'mon, Lucy Bainbridge. Let's go.'

Lucinda's answering smile radiated pure joy. She felt so easy with Mike and not in the least bit guilty about having dates with a man she hardly knew, though Vi had half-implied that she should. Serve Charlie right, in fact. She had sent him her new address a week ago and this morning there really should have been a letter from him. But Nanny had written, bless her, even though it had mostly been a discourse upon the treacherous Scottish climate and the need to wear her warm knickers when the nights began to draw in – and was she remembering to take her syrup of figs every Friday night as she had promised?

'Penny for them.'

'I was thinking about Nanny's letter.'

'You had a nurse?'

'A nanny. There's a difference. She's in Lincolnshire now, at Lady Mead.'

'Looking after your brothers and sisters?'

'No. I'm afraid I don't have either. But when I went to boarding school she stayed on with us. She'll look after my children, I suppose.'

'I see. So you're going to have kids, Lucy?'

'Of course.'

'And have you figured how many?'

'Three or four, I suppose.'

'All planned out, eh? You got a father for them in mind?' He needed to know. For no reason at all it was suddenly important that he should.

'A father? No.' She was amazed how easily the lie fell from her lips. 'But all women want babies, don't they?'

'Guess they do. A lot of guys want them as well. Take me, for instance. Reckon I'd like three or four, too.' He tucked her arm in his and they took the tree-lined path to the mouth of the loch. Three or four kids? It was a new one on him but it sure would please the folks back home. It would please Granny too, especially if those kids had an English mother. 'C'mon, honey. Let's take a look at this boom thing.'

She smiled again and the corners of her mouth darted upward into the sudden, sunny grin that so intrigued him, and her dimples deepened into fascinating little hollows.

Lucy Bainbridge was a real doll. She was, come to think of it, exactly the mother he would choose for the children that up until two minutes ago he hadn't realized he wanted.

Lucinda took off her hat and ran her fingers through her hair. The night was warm and balmy and the sheltering

165

trees screened out any sights of war, and where the path ended abruptly at the meeting of loch and river there was neither ship nor submarine nor coil of rusting barbed wire within their vision. A still bright sun rested on deep purple hilltops, and below them, seabirds, clean, brilliantly white seabirds, dipped and drifted and called.

'Isn't it peaceful?' Lucinda murmured. 'It's as if the war hasn't found this little corner yet.'

'Probably once the whole of Craigiebur was like this; maybe it was a swell little place and that's why Granny remembers it. I'm glad she can't see it now. It's a pity that war kind of cheapens things, if you get my meaning.'

'I do. Not cheapens, exactly, but *demeans*. I saw it at Lady Mead. When we left it, the old house had a pained expression. I know it sounds silly, but it looked so lost, as if it was never meant to be a billet and barrack room, and was hurting inside.'

'You said the RAF had taken it. You've seen it since?'

'Only once. But we are allowed access if we ask them first and give them plenty of notice. They left us a few rooms to store things in so we're entitled, occasionally, to take a look at them. It's all in a terrible jumble because Pa had to get everything out of the attics as well – war regulations, you know. No one must have things in attics now, because of the risk of fire bombs. But all in all, the Air Force has been pretty good. The lawns get cut – after a fashion – though Nanny says that the roses and clematis on the south wall have got out of hand and Pa would have a fit if he saw the rose beds. We were able to keep the kitchen garden because it's a good way from the house and we've a gardener there, still, though he's very old and can't do a lot.'

'And how come your nanny is still there, too? Did she sit tight and refuse to budge?'

'Oh, no! One simply couldn't do that, Mike. When

Authority wants a house, Authority takes it, and no arguing. But they realized our predicament. After all, the family has been there since 1605 and they've accumulated an awful lot of rubbish – it all had to be put somewhere. So, as I said, they let us keep three rooms and the Dower House, too. That's where Nanny is now. The more valuable things are there, and the paintings. Nanny has two bedrooms and the big kitchen and the rest of the Dower is all storage. Pa's agent goes there twice a year to check it over, and for the rest, Nanny sits guardian over it as if it was her own. I wish I could spend one of my leaves there, just to see the old place and let it know it isn't forgotten. And to see Nanny too,' she added.

'You love that old Lady Mead, don't you?'

'Yes, Mike. Too much, I think. But Lady Mead seemed always to be there, unchanging. All the time I was away at school I'd long for it; and when we went to London for the season I couldn't wait to get back to it.

'Christmases there were unbelievable. The great hall goes up through two storeys and we'd have an enormous tree. And there were log fires everywhere so no one noticed the cold and damp – well, not at Christmas, anyway. Christmas was the only time it was really warm. And – oh, Mike, I'm sorry for going on and on. Terrible bore, aren't I? It's just that I do miss it so.'

'You're not boring me, honey.' He liked to listen to her talking with that crazy English accent. 'But how come you could ever give it up? Well, an Englishman's home is his castle, they say. Why didn't your old man tell them to push off when they said they wanted the house?'

'But he *couldn't* have! There *is* a war on. It would've been unpatriotic even to think of refusing. And they'd have taken it, anyway. So Pa co-operated fully and got a few concessions out of it. At least Nanny is still around there.'

'Gee, you Brits.' Mike shook his head in bewilderment. They sure took some understanding. They could take over half the globe without as much as a by-your-leave, yet surrender their homes without a whimper. 'Seems you'd endure anything for King and Country.'

'Don't be so sure about *that*! Mama played merry old hell, even though she'd rather be in London, and Pa kept on and on about the game rights and managed to get a couple of weeks' shooting out of them. Mind, he's always careful to invite the RAF commanding officer when a shoot is on, the cunning old devil. But don't get us wrong, Mike. We Bainbridges don't give up without a bit of a scrap.'

'Reckon you don't,' Mike acknowledged, 'else how have you managed to hang on there all that time – four and a half centuries, almost?'

Had those four hundred-odd years made Lucy what she was, frank and uncomplicated and so very polite? Mike liked her politeness and the way she smiled a lot. That smile made a guy feel good, just being with her.

'How indeed? But what about you, Mike? Tell me about Vermont, New England, and about your family. And what do you do, in civvy street?'

'I'm an engineer. And you know about my granny who's eighty-six and about my aunt who has a parrot. The rest will keep.'

Keep? For when? Lucinda demanded silently. Certainly not until next time because there wouldn't be one, there really wouldn't.

'Look. It seems we aren't going to see the boom nets working and it isn't any use waiting because there isn't a ship in sight. Hadn't we better be making our way to the dance? And Mike, tonight I *must* catch the last transport back.'

'Okay, honey. But just one thing. I don't suppose

168

you've got a photo on you? Or maybe you could send me one?'

'Now why would you want a picture of me?' she asked him, surprised and pleased.

'To remind me of the classy English girl I met in Craigiebur, I guess.' His face was solemn now, and his eyes no longer teased her. They still walked arm in arm and so close that she had only to move her face a little to her right and her lips would be very easy to kiss. But not yet, he decided. Later, maybe, when they said goodnight. 'Do I have to have a reason, Lucy?'

'No. Not really. And as it happens I do have a snap with me.' One with Charlie on it. One she had placed inside her paybook to remind her, dutifully, of the man she was to marry and of Lady Mead and of Nanny, who had taken it; a photograph that would give her the opportunity to say, 'Who's the man? Oh, that's my fiancé. He's in the Army and we'll probably be married on his next leave.' That would put the record straight, wouldn't it? Mike would have to know about Charlie, and giving him the snapshot would be the best way to do it. 'At least, I think I have.' She thrust her hand into the right-hand inside pocket of her jacket; a pocket specifically sized and situated for the safekeeping of paybooks. 'Yes, here it is.'

It was a good likeness of them both. Charlie's shirt was open almost to his waist, his sleeves rolled up beyond his elbows. His hair was slightly untidy and his smile made his teeth look nicer than they really were.

'Say, Lucy, your hair was long, then.'

'Yes. Afraid I had to have it all chopped off when I joined the Wrens. Regulations. Hair mustn't touch the collar.'

'Hmm. Think I'd rather have it the way it is now. And what's that place in the background?'

'That's Lady Mead. Part of the south wing and the

169

orangery. It was taken last year when we were all down there, helping clear everything out.'

'Looks a swell old place. What are you wearing, Lucy?'

'What d'you mean, what am I wearing?' For God's sake, why didn't he ask about Charlie?

'Your clothes. I want to know *exactly*.'

'Okay, then. I'm wearing an old pair of jodhpurs and a pale blue Aertex shirt – my school hockey shirt, actually.' Now ask about the man beside me with his arm on my shoulders. Go on, Mike. *Ask*.

'Y'know, Lucy, I don't think you should ever let your hair get that long again.' He was studying the snapshot intently, as if it were a valuable painting, hung, well-lighted, in some exhibition. 'Short hair, like you've got it now, frames your face, shows your bones better. Who's the guy, by the way?'

'Him? Oh, that's Charlie, my cousin. He's Pa's younger brother's boy. Charlie's older than me because Pa married late, you see. Late, and somewhat unproductively.'

Dear Lord! Did she have to go on like this? All she had to do was say, 'That's the man I'm engaged to.' Simple enough, so why was it such an effort?

'In the Navy, is he?'

'The Army.' Her reply was brief because she was angry; angry with herself for not being straight and honest, and angrier still because suddenly and inexplicably she did not want to be straight and honest, and had never, she realized, had the slightest intention of being so. At least, not where Charlie was concerned.

'*Oh, Lucinda, how could you?*'

'*Ar, hey, queen. It's nothin' to do with me, but wasn't that a bit naughty, eh?*'

Nanny and Vi were sitting like prim little consciences, one on either shoulder, and they could both mind their own business because tonight Lucy Bainbridge was out dancing with an American. And after tonight their ships would have passed and sailed in opposite directions, so what the hell?

She watched him place the snapshot in his wallet, then taking her arm again he said, 'Right, honey, let's get weaving. We'll be there in time for the first dance, if we get a move on.'

When they reached the Rialto dance hall there was already a queue outside. Dammit, Mike frowned, everybody formed queues these days. Queues for food, for cigarettes, for beer, even. They did it automatically and without a murmur of complaint; most unlike the usual run of Brits. One thing was certain, though. Granny Farrow wouldn't stand in a queue for anybody, bet your bottom dollar she wouldn't!

But maybe, he thought, the British were still a bit bemused after Dunkirk, still licking their wounds and wondering how it had happened to them, the lords of empire. And maybe soon they'd jerk themselves out of their beleaguered apathy and start snapping back at the Krauts and be their old, arrogant British selves again. Didn't they always land on their feet, in the end?

The queue began to move. At the cashier's window Mike asked, 'How much, honey?'

'Two shillings.' She smiled broadly. 'And if the young lady is with you, that'll be four.'

He handed her a ten-shilling note and received change of three florins.

They parted company at the cloakrooms, and Lucinda handed in her hat, respirator and jacket, placing the receipt carefully in her belt pocket. Then, running her fingers through her hair and placing a threepenny-piece in the attendant's saucer, she walked to the dance floor and Mike, who waited beside the open glass doors.

Her heart raced with excitement. She would dance every dance, if Mike's leg stood up to it, of course. She would slide and glide and twirl with never a hint of a beeline or marching turn.

They chose seats halfway down the hall, not too near the band, having mind to their eardrums.

Lucinda looked around. The hall was large, with a well-polished floor. It was airy, too, but only because the heavy blackout curtains did not need to be drawn yet and the windows were open wide to the summer night.

At the end of the hall, on a dais decorated with dusty potted plants, members of the dance band sorted their music.

The drummer was young, his short hair obviously cut by an Army barber. To his left sat a middle-aged civilian lady saxophonist and an accordion player wearing naval uniform. They chatted easily, that strange assortment of musicians, handing round cigarettes, checking the beer glasses beneath their chairs.

To the far left of the group, the pianist in RAF uniform sat at the ready, his hands relaxed on his knees, taking occasional sips from the nearest of the three pints of beer standing in readiness on the piano top, smiling at a giggle of young girls who sat beside the dais.

'I wonder what they're going to be like.' Mike nodded in the direction of the band.

'Don't know. They're a bit of a hotchpotch, aren't they? But some of them might have been musicians in civvy street, so they might be quite good.'

The hotchpotch dance band was very good, swinging into the first quickstep with style and in perfect dancing rhythm.

'Care to dance, lady?' Mike rose to his feet, holding open his arms.

Unspeaking, Lucinda went to him, and before they had

172

covered a circuit of the floor she knew she had been right. Mike *was* a good dancer, his hand, light on her back, exacted just the right pressure to make following him easy.

'This is going to be good, Mike.'

He squeezed her hand in reply. Good? It would be better than he had ever imagined. And hadn't he been right? Didn't those ridiculous curls of hers reach exactly to his chin?

The floor was uncrowded and they glided and turned and slid and spun. Mike sang softly in tune to the music.

Lucinda pushed a little way from him, smiling up into his eyes. Strange, how his touch pleased her, how right his nearness felt. Mike Farrow was a very attractive man and it was just as well, she thought, half in sorrow, half with relief, that this meeting was destined to be their last. A girl could fall heavily for a man like Mike; a girl who wasn't engaged, that was.

'Why didn't you tell me,' she laughed when the quickstep came to an end, 'that you were a marvellous dancer?'

'Modesty forbids,' he teased, lifting an eyebrow. 'And anyway, you never asked.'

Lucy was easy to dance with and so light in his arms that he had felt she would float from him should he move his hand from her. Her hair smelled sweet and newly washed and it had been a distinct effort not to pull her closer and rest his cheek on her head.

Lucinda gazed around her with rapt interest. This was the first 'hop' she had ever attended. Every other dance had been a formal gold-printed invitation affair, usually with Charlie and always amongst acquaintances of long standing. Now, one of the delights of leaving home would be going to informal hops and dancing with whomever she pleased. And, what was more, there would be no need to hold an inquest at the end of hops, no Mama wanting to know who had been there, who danced with someone he or she shouldn't have danced with and was that dreadful Maudie Thingummy there again hawking around that unmarriageable daughter of hers? Ah yes, from this night on, dances would be fun!

The hall was beginning to fill now; the seats around the perimeter of the floor were all occupied. Land girls and ATS girls in Army uniform and Wrens stood around in groups. There were even a few men in civilian dress, though not so many, for civvies were completely out of favour. Men in the armed forces now had the pick of the unattached female population, all of whom turned up pert noses at civilians, wondering why they were not in uniform, wondering, even, if they were conchies, for to speak to a conscientious objector, let alone dance with one, was completely unthinkable.

From the far corner of the floor a group of sailors eyed girls who sat alone, whilst from another, soldiers did the same, doubtless determined to beat the Navy to the best of the pickings. The civilian girls, Lucinda thought, looked pretty and cool in cotton dresses; last year's, without a doubt, for since the strict rationing of all clothing, coupons had to be spent frugally and hoarded against the cold of winter and used for thick coats and shoes. Not one of them wore stockings, she noticed, though not so long ago it would have been unthinkable. But now there was a war on, wasn't there, and the unnecessary wearing of silk stockings had become a sinful luxury.

The pianist announced a waltz, and without speaking, Lucinda went into Mike's arms. When he rested his cheek on her head, she moved closer, unprotesting.

> If I should fall in love again
> I'd fall in love with you, again . . .

174

He moved his head so that his lips touched her cheek, and whispered the words of the song in her ear.

> With your hand in mine,
> I'd whisper, 'I love you.'

This was all wrong, Lucinda thought, eyes closed blissfully. Here she was, unfaithful in thought if not in deed, and glad, glad, *glad* she had not told Mike about Charlie.

> If I should lose my heart again,
> I'd choose you from the start again,
> I'd be just the same if I loved again
> I would still fall in love with you . . .

Sweet, sentimental words. Evocative words to pull at the heart-strings of lovers parted by war or to fuel the needs of those who were not.

At the end of the waltz, Mike released her abruptly and they walked back to their seats without speaking. Lucinda sat down diffidently, aware of the change of mood and the unaccountable silence between them. It was almost a relief when a quickstep was called, the drummer reminding the dancers that those who wished to jitterbug should keep to the centre of the floor.

'Can you jitterbug, Lucy?' The band had crashed into action.

'No, but I've a feeling I'm about to learn.'

The strangeness had gone and whatever had so briefly happened was forgotten.

'Okay, then. Just relax. And anything goes just as long as you keep your feet moving to the beat of the music. And try to relax your shoulders, too – okay?'

The jitterbug had not been a part of the dancing curriculum at Lucinda's finishing school in Lucerne nor was it like anything she had ever experienced. In this wild,

175

New World dance, partners did not dance close; only hands touched, and after the heady suffocation of the previous dance it was good to have time to get things back on an even footing again, to be twisted and twirled, to be pulled and pushed, to kick her feet and stamp and sway.

'Mike!' she gasped when the music ended. 'That was like nothing I've ever known!'

'Sure it was, but did you like it?'

'You bet I did,' she choked, quickly checking the laugh that rose in her throat because she had had a vivid picture image of Charlie dancing the jitterbug – and she couldn't tell Mike why it was so very funny.

Near-exhausted, they sat out the silly dances that followed; the Lambeth walk, the palais glide and the chestnut tree, laughing at the antics of those who risked dancing the boomps-a-daisy, without doubt the silliest dance of them all.

Hands, knees and boomps-a-daisy,
I like a bustle that bends.
Hands, knees and boomps-a-daisy,
What is a boomp between friends?

And with every *boomps*! bottoms were banged together, not at all daintily, and everybody roared with delight.

Only in this summer of 1941, Lucinda thought fondly, could a man ask a perfect stranger to dance with him, then proceed to bump her bottom with his own until she cried for mercy. But in the strange state of siege in which they had all been compelled to live, people were losing their stuffiness and becoming more relaxed. Well, almost everyone.

'Oh, my goodness!' Lucinda burst into peals of laughter.

'What's so funny?' Mike grinned. 'Come on. Give.'

'Too stupid, really. Actually, I was imagining McNair

176

in his kilt and sporran, boomps-a-daisying with my mother.'

'And who, for Pete's sake, is McNair?'

'He's Pa's gillie from Cromlech, further north. He's caretaking there at the moment, but he's so dour you'd have to know both him and Mama to realize how really funny it is.'

'Cromlech? Another house? Listen, honey, how many places can one family live in at the same time?'

'Cromlech is very tiny, Mike, and I'm afraid that three houses is just about all we do have.'

She really must be more careful. Tonight was to be just for the two of them and no one must be allowed to intrude, certainly not Mama. And Mike must never know about her title. Some Americans, she had found, were over-impressed by such things, though most went quite Bolshie if one was even mentioned, and she wanted Mike to like her for herself and not dislike her because Pa was an earl. She wondered fleetingly about Mike's family in Vermont and what they were like. But that, she sighed, she could probably never know.

The girls who had sat alone were beginning to pair off with soldiers and sailors, sitting close now, shoulders touching, talking earnestly, for war allowed no one the luxury of time. Women, Lucinda realized, came to public dance halls for many reasons. Some came simply to dance, some to revel in odds stacked in their favour by the heady influx of uniformed men into Craigiebur and to flirt and tease and enjoy what little was certain in an uncertain world. And some came here because they were lonely; because they ached for the feel and touch of a man. Women too young to be brides, thrown into brief, unnatural marriages in the haste of war, had learned that the pitifully few nights of wifehood were little recompense for the enforced celibacy that stretched unending ahead of

177

them, the occasional censored letter their only comfort. Embarkation-leave wives they were called, the women who tonight stood a little apart, trying not to be noticed yet hoping to be asked to dance, to be held, however briefly, in the arms of a man.

It was a sad state of affairs but it simply did not do, Nanny had counselled, to love too well, for passion that flamed hotly died in the flames of its own creating. Fine words indeed, though how Nanny had become an authority on flaming passion, Lucinda had never dared enquire. But she was probably right. Passion, Lucinda had recently realized, could be embarrassing and thoroughly uncomfortable. Charlie's attempt to put paid to her virginity had convinced her of that, though the three-minute episode on the sofa at Bruton Street had been Charlie's only fall from grace. Most times he was charming and friendly and fun to be with, which was a firmer foundation on which to build a marriage – or so Nanny had said – than the doubtful emotion that invariably followed love at first sight.

'Hey, Lucy!' Mike's fingers snapped an inch from her nose. 'Where were you?'

'Oh! Miles away. Sorry, Mike.'

'You looked troubled. Want to talk about it?'

'No, thanks. It wasn't all that important. Just something someone once said about – er – hasty marriages.'

'And repenting at leisure?'

'Something like that. But what about you, Mike? When will you be leaving Craigiebur?'

'Tomorrow morning, first ferry out. Which reminds me that I've no way of getting in touch with you. Guess you'd better give me your phone number – if you're allowed calls, that is.'

She should have told him she was not, but 'Ardneavie 358,' she said at once, 'and if I'm not there, ask for Vi.

She'll take a message. She works in quarters, you see, so she's usually around. Three-five-eight, Mike. Write it down.'

'Don't need to. It's easy to remember.'

Like you, Lucy Bainbridge. But then, he could never forget her because he didn't intend to. Last night had been the start of it, and how far it would go between them or where it might end, he had no way of knowing. Only one thing was certain. Right now he wanted her as he'd never wanted any woman. 'Ardneavie 358,' he repeated. No, sir. He wouldn't forget it.

The silly dances were over now, and newly met couples were more relaxed and easy in each other's company. The pianist looked at his empty beer mugs then announced the last dance before the interval.

Lucinda jumped eagerly to her feet. Mike gathered her to him. They fitted so well, moved as a whole; it was as if they had always danced together.

Lucinda sighed and moved a little so their cheeks could touch; Mike's hand pressed her back and she moved still nearer.

The sound of applause caused her to open her eyes briefly. An ATS girl stood at the microphone and, tilting it towards her, began to sing.

> . . . magic abroad in the air,
> There were angels dining at the Ritz,
> And a nightingale sang in Berkeley Square.

She was a tall, slender girl, and not even the khaki masculinity of her uniform could take away from her striking beauty.

> I may be right, I may be wrong,
> But I'm perfectly willing to swear

That when you turned and smiled at me,
A nightingale sang in Berkeley Square.

Lucinda tilted her head and smiled up at Mike. 'Only sparrows,' she teased softly. 'Honestly, it's all I've ever heard.'

He pulled her against him again, settling his chin on her head. 'Wait until we're there together, honey. I'll guarantee nightingales.'

The moon that lingered over London town,
Poor puzzled moon, he wore a frown.
How could he know we were so much in love.

The singer's eyes were focused on a spot high at the back of the hall; a spot that was Alexandria, maybe, or Iceland or Hong Kong, but only she who sang for a faraway lover could know.

The streets of town
Were paved with stars,
It was such a romantic affair.
And as we kissed and said goodnight,
A nightingale sang in Berkeley Square.

'The girl who's singing has heard nightingales,' Lucinda whispered, 'I can tell . . .'

'Sure, honey, I know. Love songs are best sung by people in love. Wonder when she last saw her guy.'

Suddenly Lucinda felt wretched. But wasn't that what this war was good at: drawing people together then tearing them apart again? Wasn't it happening to her and Mike? Last night had been a whim of Fate, the great puppet-master. Fate had caused them to meet, manipulated them closer. Yet in so short a time he would tire of his game and let the slender strings slacken and sag, and it would all be over for them.

180

'Mike, I know all dances have a last waltz,' she whispered, 'but I'm afraid the very next one will have to be ours. I couldn't get a late pass so I'll have to get the ten o'clock transport back to Ardneavie. Late passes take twenty-four hours, so I couldn't manage one for tonight. I'm sorry.'

'Don't be. I suppose it'd be pushing your luck to try the pantry window again?'

'I'd better not . . .'

'What time do you normally have to report in?'

'Ten thirty, but we are allowed two late passes till eleven.'

'Ten thirty? Holy cow! That Ardneavie House must be worse'n a convent!'

'It isn't, Mike. Not a bit like one,' Lucinda giggled. 'It's very nice, really. And I've got two lovely friends. That's why, I suppose, I don't want them to have to stick their necks out for me again. You do understand?'

'Sure I do.' He tweaked her nose playfully then gathered her into his arms as the waltz began – and they couldn't, Lucinda thought vehemently, have played anything more unsuitable had they searched through their music all night.

> I'll be loving you, always,
> With a love that's true, always

sang the sad-eyed ATS girl, and Mike sang softly with her, his lips murmuring against Lucinda's ear.

> When the things you planned
> Need a helping hand,
> I shall understand, always,
> Always . . .

This was not right, Lucinda fretted. Mike was not playing fair, and thank goodness that after tonight he'd be

181

out of her life. Pushing him away she choked, 'Mike! Don't do that, *please*. Singing in my ear gives me a very peculiar feeling.'

'Sorry, honey.' He drew her close again. 'Won't happen again,' he said comfortably, returning his lips to exactly the same position, breathing slowly and deeply so that with luck the peculiar feeling would return.

'Mike,' Lucinda warned, but she did not push him away again because, what the hell, this was their last dance and, anyway, it was a rather pleasant peculiar feeling.

> Not for just an hour
> Not for just a day
> Not for just a year
> But always . . .

How disturbing songs seemed to be, these days; how evocative and suggestive and sensuous, Lucinda thought from the safety of Mike's arms. And wasn't it nice how everybody now seemed to sing as they danced, as if it were possible to sing the war away.

The waltz ended, the pianist called a twenty-minute interval and the musicians picked up their empty glasses and left for the nearest public house.

Immediately a replacement band took the stage. An army sergeant carrying a violin case took the lady saxophonist's seat, a Wren draped her jacket over a chair, then, rolling up her sleeves, sat down at the piano; a flaxen-haired soldier wearing trews of the Black Watch tartan claimed the drum kit.

'What a free-for-all it's going to be,' Mike grinned. 'Sure wish we could stay behind and listen.'

They left, reluctantly, by the door at which a small elderly man with an indelible purple ink pad and a rubber stamp marked the back of each outstretched hand with a star.

Lucinda received her stamp. 'Thanks, but what's it for?'

'That's your pass-out, Jenny. You'll no' get back in here without it, unless you want to pay again, that is.'

The dancers were hurrying to favourite pubs, hoping for a glass or two of best Scottish mild before the night's ration ran out and the landlord was forced to call that the beer was finished, and that was all till tomorrow. The deprived drinkers would mutter then, and grumble and ill-wish the cause of their privation. Being conscripted into the armed forces most men reluctantly accepted; having their children evacuated to the countryside even made some kind of sense; putting up with food rationing and clothes rationing and shortages of absolutely everything could be endured in the name of Victory, but to tamper with a man's rightful supply of ale was altogether a different matter and one for which Hitler could never be forgiven.

'Want to try and grab a quick glass?' Mike was developing a shuddering affection for British beer.

'Don't think we'll have time.' Lucinda was enjoying the cool night air and the beauty of the sunset. 'Look, Mike, it won't be long till blackout time. Keep your eyes on the bay; it's fascinating to watch . . .'

Arms linked, they leaned on the rusting promenade rail. There were no street lights, but to their left and right, strung out along the sweep of the bay like low, bright stars, house lights shone bravely. Then, almost as if an alarm bell had been rung, the lights disappeared one by one as blackouts were placed in position and curtains reluctantly drawn. In less than three minutes the bay was totally dark, the houses barely discernible against the wooded hills.

'There now. Wasn't it amazing? It always gives me a strange feeling to see the lights go out so completely. I think the blackout is the most unnatural thing about this war. Oh, Mike, won't it be lovely having lights again!' But when, when, *when*?

Duty steward Vi McKeown also had reason to resent the blackout. It was her responsibility to darken ship, and tonight there had been complications. The exact cause of her discomfort was the pantry window, which was left, by unspoken consent, until all latecomers were safely accounted for. Only then, its purpose served, could the catch be slipped and the wooden shutters folded over. And there would have been no bother at all had not Leading Cook Kathy MacAlister gone in search of a tin of marmalade and switched on the pantry light.

That one unthinking act brought the pier patrol to Ardneavie House with uncanny speed, and banging on the front door they ordered, 'Get that bloody light out!'

Anyone would have thought, Vi grumbled, that it was a searchlight MacAlister had switched on and not the insignificant glow a sixty-watt bulb gave to a window measuring two feet by three.

'Watch it,' the leader of the naval patrol warned, 'or somebody here'll get slapped in the rattle!'

Whereupon Chief Wren Pillmoor, attracted to the scene by the noise and upset, quickly ascertained that her own rank was superior to that of the aggressive petty officer and archly advised him that if anybody at Ardneavie House was going in the rattle, she would put them there, thank you very much, and wouldn't the pier patrol be better employed getting the drunks back on board *Omega* and leaving the Wrennery blackout to someone more suited to deal with it?

'Damn that window!' she hissed. 'I'm sick and tired of it, McKeown! But any more nonsense and I'll have it nailed up, so help me, and that'll be the end of it,' she added darkly, leaving Vi in no doubt at all that the pantry window and its after-hours use was no mystery to Chief Wren Pillmoor.

That was when Vi walked down the path, looking up and back towards the house, making sure that not one pinpoint of light showed. And that was when the camouflaged Army truck pulled up at the gate and an officer, pushing down the window, demanded her attention with a snapping of his fingers.

'You, there! Over here, at the double!'

'Me?' Vi gazed at the blackened face and the slightly comic wilting greenery stuck in the webbing of his steel helmet.

'Of course *you*! Is this Ardneavie?'

'Who's askin'?' She had to be sure. They could be a truckload of Germans, for all she knew, come down by parachute. 'I mean, how do I know where you've come from?'

She gazed up at him, unblinking. His hair was cut short, his face inclined to roundness and his mouth she disliked at once, as it was too much on the big side and drooped at the corners. Gormless-looking, Vi would have called him, had it not been for his undoubted arrogance and the unspoken proclamation of birth and breeding and his divine right to be heard and obeyed.

'Where we've come from, *sir*!' He reminded her of the three pips at his shoulder. 'And if this is the Wrens' quarters at Ardneavie, please find Lady Lucinda Bainbridge for me and be sharp about it. I haven't got all night.'

Shocked, Vi stood very still. *Lady* Lucinda? Jesus, Mary and Joseph, Lucinda had a handle, and her never saying a word about it!

'Sorry, but she's not in. She – she's watch aboard and she'll not be ashore till past midnight.' Instinct put the lie on Vi's lips. 'Who shall I tell her was askin'?'

'Tell her Captain Charles Bainbridge called. *Bainbridge.*' He said the name slowly, mouthing it as if she were deaf or stupid, or both. 'Tell her I was passing on manoeuvres – got it?'

'Sir.' The corporal at the driving wheel coughed loudly, looking pointedly at his watch. 'With respect, sir, we *are* overdue. We're going to be in lumber if we don't make it back to HQ by 2300 hours and – '

'All right, all right.' Testily Charles Bainbridge returned his attention to Vi. 'Be sure Lady Lucinda gets my message.'

Vi looked him straight in the eye. Malevolently, defiantly. She had perfected it at the training depot, that non-speaking and-the-same-to-you-mate stare. Its official name was dumb insolence.

'Did you hear what I said?'

'I heard, *sir*,' Vi ground. And three bags full, *sir*!

She stood as the truck reversed awkwardly in the narrow lane then watched until it disappeared into the darkness of the Craigiebur road.

Flamin' Norah, but what was she supposed to make of that? Lucinda a lady! Lovely, scatty Lucinda, who was always as broke as the rest of them, one of the upper crust!

But she should have guessed, Vi acknowledged. What with Lady Mead and Nanny and that lovely, plummy accent, it should have been there for anyone to see. Yet Lucinda hadn't told a soul, and what was worse, the snotty so and so with three pips up was Charlie, Lucinda's intended. Mother of God, it didn't bear thinking about.

In that instant Vi was filled with overwhelming satisfaction that Lucinda was out with her American. Instantly all opposition to Lucinda's infidelity was completely withdrawn, because Charlie Bainbridge was pig-ignorant, and nasty with it, too.

Good on yer, Lucinda – Vi sent her new-found thoughts winging – I don't know what you're doin' right now, queen, but do it a bit more, eh?

Charlie was a toe rag, Vi brooded darkly. He was worse than a toe rag, in fact. Charlie, she was forced to admit it, was a right little twerp!

With difficulty, she returned her attention to the blackout, brooding on the unjustness of life, wondering what a girl as nice as Lucinda could be thinking about.

She glanced down at her watch. Ten o'clock and time to riddle the ashes from the boiler then fill it to the brim with coke. And after that she would sit at the table outside the regulating office and tick off the late passes as they came in. Would Lucinda, she wondered, be adrift again and come in by way of the pantry window? Oh, but she hoped so!

That's my girl. Vi, grinned, making a mental note to check the pantry-window catch. You're goin' to be a long time married to that Charlie. Have fun while you can, queen!

Lucinda came in through the front door at 2228 hours.

'You're early, love.' Vi smiled. 'Had a good time then?'

'Oh, *yes*, Vi. Mike's a marvellous dancer and he can jitterbug, too. But you needn't worry. He didn't ask me for another date.'

'Worry? Listen, queen, you're a big girl now. What you do is your own affair. What really bothers me is' – she dropped her voice dramatically – 'well, I wonder why you never told us you'd got a title?'

'Me? You mean – oh, Vi, who told you? Did Charlie phone?'

'No, Charlie didn't phone.' Vi waited pointedly for an explanation.

'Look, Vi, I'm sorry, but why should I tell anyone?'

Lucinda's face flushed bright red. 'I mean, I like it better being just me. I don't suppose you'd keep it to yourself? Having a title can be a bit of an embarrassment, actually, especially when it's just about all one has. We aren't rich, you know, or eccentric. It just so happens that in my case my father's an earl. Nothing at all to do with me, really. But how did you find out, Vi? Who phoned?'

'Nobody *phoned*. Someone told me, though.' The bad news could wait no longer. 'Your Charlie's been.'

'*Charlie! Here?* Oh, my God, and I was out! What was he doing at Ardneavie? What did he say?' Lucinda seemed near to tears.

'Not a lot. He was on manoeuvres, he said. He was only here a couple of minutes. Time was a bit short, I think.'

'Vi! I've just thought!' Lucinda's cheeks flushed scarlet. 'Where did you say I was?'

'Out with an American, of course.' Vi grinned. 'What did you think I'd tell him – that you were watch aboard and wouldn't be ashore till midnight?'

'You told him I was on watch? Oh, Vi, what a darling you are. I suppose that's why I haven't heard from him. He hates it, but every so often he has to go on manoeuvres. Poor Charlie. And I was thinking awful things because he hadn't written. Now I know you're angry with me, and you've every reason to be, but don't go on about it, there's a dear. I'll write him a letter before I go to sleep. I promise I will.'

'Me, angry? Away with your bother! And I wouldn't write that letter tonight. Leave it till tomorrow. You won't feel half so guilty about things in the mornin'. Now off you go upstairs, queen. I've just got to make a hot drink for Ma'am, then I'll be up. Fancy a cup, do you?'

'Yes, please. That would be lovely.' For a moment Lucinda hesitated, her eyes troubled, then brushing Vi's cheek with her lips she whispered, 'You *are* an old love, Vi. Thanks.'

Eyebrows raised, Vi watched Lucinda's retreating back. No more dates, eh? My word, but she wouldn't like to bet on it.

She shook her head dolefully. Mike Farrow wasn't going to fade into the sunset, Vi knew it for sure, for when Lucinda Bainbridge walked in her eyes had borne the dazed, delighted expression of someone who had just been kissed goodnight, very thoroughly kissed goodnight. Oh, not even with somebody else's money would Vi be betting on it. Sighing, she placed the kettle to boil.

Lucinda lay wide awake, staring up into the darkness until it broke into shifting, swimming shapes, thinking about Mike, remembering their goodbye . . .

She had not expected him to kiss her and was pleased when he placed a forefinger beneath her chin and, tilting it gently, placed his lips on hers. She was glad of the blackout because she knew she was blushing furiously, yet she felt cheated too, because she had wanted it to last just a little bit longer.

'Goodbye,' she whispered, the palms of her hands flat on his jacket lapels. 'Tonight was fun and it's been great knowing you. Good luck, Mike. Take care of yourself, won't you?' On tiptoe she returned his kiss, this time without embarrassment. 'And I hope it won't be too long before you see Vermont again.'

She stood quite still, making no effort to pull away, to walk towards the waiting transport.

'Darling,' he whispered. His arms tightened around her and their lips met again. And because she didn't want that kiss to end she moved closer so that she felt the unyielding hardness of his body against hers and she lifted her arms and clasped them tightly around his neck. Then she closed her eyes, and the peculiar feeling she had felt on the dance floor returned to shiver and shake through her. When his hands slid down to her thighs and pulled her still closer, she was too bemused to think of anything but the sofa in the sitting room at Bruton Street and wonder how it would have been with Mike.

Shocked into mobility, she shook her head clear of such thoughts. 'Mike!' she gasped, pushing him away.

For a moment she stood, seeing only his outline against the darkness, then she turned from him.

'Goodnight, Lucy,' she heard him whisper as she ran towards the transport.

'Goodbye, Mike,' she called. Oh, God, goodbye . . .

Petulantly she thumped and turned her pillow, throwing off her blanket. It was hot tonight; far too hot. This heatwave had gone on long enough.

She directed her thoughts to Charlie. Poor old love, where was he now? Bivouacking beneath an army lorry, maybe not too many miles away and hating every minute of it, she shouldn't wonder. But she would make it up to him, she really would.

And what was Mike doing? Was he asleep yet or packing his bag, maybe? Would he remember that earth-shattering clinch or did he kiss all his girlfriends that way? She wished she could be a fly on the wall of his hotel room, watch him undress, stretch and yawn then tumble into bed. She knew intuitively that he slept in the nude.

Damn! She closed her eyes tightly. Whatever Mike Farrow was doing now was no business of hers; not even if he had the chambermaid in his bed. They'd had a date, that was all, and in the morning all that remained would be a purple star on the back of her right hand. Funny that she hadn't wanted to wash it completely away . . .

* * *

190

Flight Lieutenant Michael Farrow was not making love to the chambermaid, though he was feeling extremely contented and pleased to have got things clear in his mind now.

The feeling of wellbeing had been with him since he had kissed Lucinda goodnight and noted her reactions, and it had continued when the desk clerk had nodded in the direction of the residents' lounge then presented him with a glass of whisky. Not firewater whisky, but treasured malt from under the counter, hoarded jealously since the outbreak of war and rarely offered to Sassenachs or foreigners.

Now he sat with the precious glass beside him, writing to his English grandmother so far away in New England. He told her that he had found the house her long-ago employers once rented for the month of July and that the honeysuckle and pale pink roses still climbed its walls, though in truth they did not. And he declined to mention that its windows were criss-crossed with tapes of brown paper, that it was now a billet for soldiers and that an anti-aircraft gun stood in its neglected garden.

Then he looked at the snapshot Lucinda had given him, and taking his nail scissors, cut it into two.

'Sorry, chum,' he smiled, dropping Charlie into the waste-paper basket and, turning over the remaining half, he wrote a message on the back. He was loathe to part with Lucinda's picture, but right now his grandmother's need was the greater.

Folding the sheet of notepaper he placed Lucinda's photograph inside and stuck down the envelope.

'Here's to you, Gran,' he whispered, lifting his glass. 'Hope you approve!'

But of course she would. No one could help but approve of Lucy Bainbridge. And when the old lady turned the photograph over and read the words he had written there, then that would surely make her happy.

This is Lucy, the girl I intend to marry.

Real happy it would make her.

8

The mess hall at Ardneavie House stood splendidly transformed, shining from the ministrations of mops and dusters, tables folded and carried away, chairs arranged around the walls; for this was the occasion of the monthly dance, which would, with a little luck and effort, degenerate into an abandoned romp enjoyed by all. All save Chief Pillmoor, that was, who was known to dislike the event intensely and sigh with relief when it was over.

The dance was always held in the mess hall, the largest room in the house, a room spacious enough to hold forty couples in reasonable comfort and still leave space for the refreshments table and, in the window recess opposite, a smaller table that housed the gramophone and a stack of strict-tempo records.

'It all looks very nice,' Pat Pillmoor offered reluctantly as Vi arranged flowers and ferns in white enamel jugs borrowed from the galley shelves. 'I wonder if you would do duty steward here when the dance starts, and keep an eye on the beer barrel and refreshments?'

'Sure, Chief, no bother, though I don't think anybody's goin' to get very drunk on *that*.' It was a very small barrel. 'I was thinkin' that a pot of tea might be a good idea. Can I ask the galley for one?'

'Why not? I suppose the tea ration will stretch to it? Is there anything to eat, by the way?'

'Sandwiches and rock buns, I think.'

Pat Pillmoor nodded her approval. Leading Cook MacAlister always rose to the occasion, even though the sandwiches were almost always of boiled beetroot and the

192

currants in the rock buns finely-chopped prunes that deceived no one.

'Good. And don't forget to keep an eye on the stairs. Cabins are strictly out of bounds to – er – *visitors*, understood?'

'Yes, Chief.' Though why the fuss Vi could not imagine. After all, there was nothing new about goings-on – they'd started the day Adam tasted his first apple – but why bother with upstairs? No Wren could be that stupid when the cycle shed was available, and the wood shed, and the warm and cosy boilerhouse, to say nothing of the unused stables and the endless possibilities of the hayloft above. 'I'll keep an eye open, don't worry,' she said.

'And you won't forget the blackout, McKeown? Leave it as long as you can, but no later than ten o'clock. I don't want another complaint from the pier patrol.'

The pier patrol. Naval policemen who patrolled the environs of the jetty each night. Heavy-booted and gaitered, they were the terror of the 15th Flotilla. Nor was the pier patrol over-popular with the Ardneavie Wrens, who disliked having torches shone on them while in the throes of an ardent goodnight. But the crushers, as they were called, were hefty lads, and few argued with them. They wouldn't find cause to complain about the Wrennery blackout again, Vi resolved. Tonight, the pantry window would be bolted and shuttered, and hard luck to anyone trying to get in after-hours. Tonight, she would have the ship darkened long before sundown; bet your life she would!

She looked around the empty room, for the helpers had left now to powder noses and paint lips and change into clean white shirts, the luckier ones dabbing earlobes with forbidden perfume from the bottle they knew would be their last until the war was over. It was a great pity, most women mourned, that lipstick and scent and face creams

193

should be among the first casualties of war and disappear from the shops almost completely, when it would have been better to have allowed a more reasonable supply to be made. Why couldn't the faceless ones, the *They* people who made such decisions, realize that a bottle of scent or a bright red lipstick in a shiny new case could have done more for the uplifting of female morale than an extra sixpence on the meat ration? Now even men were being called upon to suffer, for shaving soap and razor blades had gone 'under the counter', too.

Vi dismissed the problem of shortages from her thoughts. Tonight, even though she would be on duty, there was the dance to look forward to and, counting her blessings further, she thought with pleasure of yesterday's fortnightly pay muster and the wealth lying snugly in the pocket of her belt. She had looked forward to the experience of her first real pay parade, not to mention the pleasurable anticipation of monies due.

'Come on, Vi!' Jane and Lucinda, each with hat correctly angled, stocking seams straight and shoes shining – pay parade demanded full and correct dress, even to the wearing of woollen gloves on a brilliant July morning – had hurried her downstairs.

The paymaster's table had been set up in the recreation room with a writer at the ready and pound notes, ten-shilling notes and half-crowns in precise piles in front of him.

Lined up at the table were leading Wrens and ranks below, petty officers and chief petty officers having already been paid. Now it was the turn of other ranks, who waited comfortably at ease, feet twelve inches apart, hands behind backs, waiting for the command that would announce the arrival of the paymaster and Third Officer St John, and snap them all to attention.

Fascinated, Vi watched the writer count the coins into

piles of eight. And why, she frowned, was a clerk in the Royal Navy called a writer? Why wasn't he a pay clerk like anywhere else?

'Hey, Jane, why is that feller called a writer?'

'Because that's what clerks were called in Nelson's day,' Jane hissed, 'and if it was good enough for Nelson . . .'

'I shouldn't have asked.' Vi sighed, taking her place in the line with the rest of starboard watch.

'Atten – *shun*!'

As one, feet stamped together, arms slammed to sides, chins jutted. Pay parade had begun and Vi took careful notice of each small detail, determined when her turn came that nothing should go wrong.

'Next!' At Pat Pillmoor's terse command, the Wren at the head of the queue stepped smartly forward and saluted; then, offering number and surname, held out her paybook. Then she saluted again, took a backward step, turned to her left and walked quickly away.

Vi swallowed hard. Two more to go, then it was her own turn. She ran her tongue round her lips, her paybook at the ready at her side, a finger between the centre pages.

'Next!'

Vi stamped forward and lifted her right hand in a smart salute.

'44455 McKeown, V.T., *sir*!'

Her left hand shot out, paybook open. *God, don't let me drop it*.

'One pound, twelve shillings and sixpence.' The writer placed two notes and a half-crown upon the book.

Vi saluted again, took the required backward step then swivelled on toe and heel to her left.

She had done it! She had got it right! Tucking the money in her belt, she returned her paybook to its special pocket. Thirty-two and six, nearly a pound a week, and all her own. No rent man to come calling, no coalman, no paying through the nose for unrationed food to eke out the weekly allowance of butter, sugar, meat and milk. Now, all was found; bed, board – even laundry.

Vi shook her head sadly. Who'd be a civvy? Poor things. An awful time they were having, and nobody seemed to give a damn.

'Vi! How about a run into Craigiebur tonight?' Lucinda pocketed her pay. 'We're rich again! What do you say to fish and chips and a couple of beers?'

'You're on, queen.' Vi grinned. And Lucinda was right. She, Vi, was especially rich – and in something far more precious than shillings and pence, she thought fondly as she stood at her favourite window, watching Lilith's launch tie up at the jetty. Her old life was contained in a pile of rubble in a bomb-gutted street; her new one held friends and flowers and tree-covered hills, and she spent each night in her bed, for Ardneavie's sirens never wailed out a warning with the coming of the night. That other life was behind her; no need to think about it until she had to, until the war was over and they thanked her kindly, then threw her out. That was when she would become a seaman's widow again, and homeless and job-less and unwanted. But until that day came, she wouldn't even think of it – well, hardly ever.

Reluctantly she turned from the window, and taking off her jacket and skirt and stiffly starched shirt, replaced them with a blue and white mandarin-collared overall. Rolling up her sleeves, she began the mopping and dusting of cabin 9. Soon, when the paymaster had left, she could begin the routine cleaning of quarters, all safe and secure and in accordance with King's Regulations – and the exacting requirements of Chief Wren Pillmoor. It was good to know exactly where she stood, Vi thought, to know exactly how far she could push those in authority before they pulled rank and pushed back. In this ordered

196

new life they would even think for her – if she let them. Taking the least line of resistance, some might have called it. Vi shrugged. Since the morning she had stood, bemused, in Lyra Street gazing at the wreckage of her home – hers, and Gerry's – Vi would have called it a matter of survival. And survive she would!

'No complaints, Gerry,' she had whispered to the empty room. 'No complaints at all, lad . . .'

Vi rearranged a wilting blue lupin and checked that the sandwiches and rock cakes were properly covered with a clean white cloth. Then, taking the polishing mop, she gave a final rub to the floor.

Yes indeed, the room looked very nice, she admitted, taking up a position in the doorway from which she could view both dance floor and the stairs upon which she was to keep an eye.

Ar, hey, Chief, Vi thought shaking her head in disbelief. There'll be nobody sneakin' up them stairs for a bit of canoodling; nobody here is *that* stupid, honest to God they're not.

The Ardneavie dance came alive with the arrival of the eight o'clock liberty boat, and soon the floor was filled with couples. From the doorway, Vi smiled across at Lucinda, who had taken charge of the music and the winding-up of the gramophone and the insertion, when necessary, of the sharp steel needles.

Lucinda smiled back, her cheeks dimpling. There had been a change in her these last few days. Vi frowned. A change hardly noticeable; more, perhaps, a preoccupation with the telephone.

'Anyone rung?' Lucinda had taken to asking as she hung up her respirator and took off her hat; a casually meant enquiry that deceived no one. Was she, Vi wondered, feeling guilty about Charlie, or was her sudden interest in phone calls connected with Mike Farrow?

'Don't be worryin' yourself, queen. If there's a call for you I'll make sure you know about it.' Even, Vi had silently added, if it was from that Charlie of hers.

Charlie. Captain Charles Bainbridge. Even on so short an acquaintance, Vi disliked him. Lucinda would have to learn to stand up for herself once she was married to that one. Fellers like Charlie rode roughshod over a woman, given half a chance. Whatever did Lucinda see in him? Or were Lucinda's lot like that? Did they still have arranged marriages? Did they still marry for money or did they learn to love where money lay? Had that happened to Lucinda? Well, common she and Gerry might be, Vi brooded, but theirs had been a love match.

She smiled down at her left hand and the ring once more in its rightful place. She felt better now that everyone knew. Being able to talk about Gerry had given her an amazing peace, and with it had come the wisdom to accept what she was powerless to change. Tonight, Vi acknowledged, she was as happy as she would ever be.

She smiled again at Lucinda. Then, like a wise old chaperon, searched the room with her eyes for Jane, pleased to see her dancing with a tall, fair-headed sailor and smiling up at him as if she was enjoying his company; chatting and laughing, an altogether different Jane; a girl who was happy again, even though her request for permission to visit Glasgow had been refused. Now she laughed a lot, her eyes happy with dreams. Even the refusal of the pass had not upset her.

'It doesn't matter. There'll be a way. I'll get there, even if I have to wait until I go on leave,' she had said. But leave was eight weeks away and Vi knew with certainty that Jane could not, would not wait that long.

Don't do anything silly, Vi silently beseeched. If it's meant to be, then it'll work out for you and Rob. But be patient, eh?

Patience, though, was a word Jane Kendal did not acknowledge. By an almost unbelievable coincidence she was near to finding Rob's mother, and soon they would get to know each other and talk about Rob to her heart's content. For Rob was alive, Jane knew it, and wanting her and missing her every bit as much as she missed and wanted him. She smiled up at Tom Tavey again, knowing he was attracted to her and sorry for him because of it. He had asked her to dance immediately he came into the room and now he held her a little too close, asking too many questions.

'Tell me about yourself, Jane?'

'Tell you what?'

'Oh, where you come from and what your family is like, and how old you are and what your favourite colour is . . .'

'Jane Elizabeth Kendal. Nearly nineteen. Only child. Father in the North Riding Constabulary – Yorkshire, that is,' she supplied, smiling. 'And I dislike green and I come from a tiny village called Fenton Bishop.'

'A nice little village, is it?'

'Beautiful, I suppose.'

'Farming country, I shouldn't wonder?'

'Yes.'

Hell, but he was making heavy going of it, he chided himself silently. Acting like a tongue-tied goon.

Fenton Bishop. A tightly knit little place, he thought, eyes half closed, with anyone living more than five miles distant a foreigner, just as it was in Devon.

He looked down at her glinting auburn hair. No more than a couple of lads in Fenton Bishop, he supposed, and if the war hadn't come she would probably have married one of them.

'Farming country? Well, now, I'm a farmer myself. Me and my brother got a place in Devon.'

'Then why are you in the Navy, Tom? I thought farmers were exempt from call-up?'

'So they are, mostly. But the farm isn't all that big. Couldn't carry the two of us, the man from the Ministry said. So I tossed Dan for it – Dan's my brother – and I won. Always wanted to see a bit of the world, so the Navy suited me fine. And Dan has taken on a nice little land girl so I reckon he's well suited, too.'

Jane smiled again. She was beginning to like Tom Tavey. A man's man, this submariner; one who would be fiercely protective of his woman. He would expect and receive her total devotion, and her fidelity would be absolute; an adoring woman who would give him several children, conceived in passionate haste. Viewed with total disinterest, Jane conceded that he was attractive yet possessed of one all-condemning fault. He was not Rob MacDonald.

'Settling down at Ardneavie, Jane? Going to like it in the 15th? Got a boyfriend back home in Yorkshire, have you?'

'Yes, yes and no, in that order,' she laughed, her eyes teasing.

'Got a boyfriend Somewhere in England, then? I want to know, Jane,' he said quietly, suddenly serious. 'It's important.'

'Why?' His unexpected intensity startled her. 'Look, I don't think I want to talk about me any more, Tom. But you did ask about a boyfriend and – well, I do have one, though I don't know where he is. I'm waiting to hear, you see. He's been missing since May but there'll be good news of him soon, I know it. Sorry,' she whispered, 'but it's only fair you should know. We can be friends if you'd like, but – '

'But I'd be wasting my time if I got any wrong ideas.'

Hell! The only girl he'd seen in months who did

anything for him, and wasn't she carrying the torch for a missing boyfriend! Oh, he was sorry for the bloke. You couldn't be glad about anybody going missing when any day it could be your own turn. But he wished he didn't find her so bloody attractive. He'd thought of little else but Jane Kendal since the morning *Taureg* came back from patrol and he had come here tonight only to see her again. Yet now all she was offering was crumbs.

'Wrong ideas? Tom, I didn't mean that I think you – ' She stopped, her cheeks burning red.

'Of course you didn't. And it was my fault, nosing into things that don't concern me.' Stupid fool, that's what he was. He should have known a girl like her would be spoken for. 'I'd like us to be friends, though. Just the odd date, no strings attached.' That was it, then. He *was* settling for crumbs.

'Then that's fine, Tom.' Because of her new-found happiness and because Tom Tavey had understood about Rob she said, 'Of course we can be friends. I'd like that.'

Vi saw them together, and smiled. The good-looking sailor seemed to be getting on well with Jane. Maybe a date or two would be good for the kid, help take her mind off Glasgow and Rob MacDonald's mother. Vi hoped it would turn out all right but sometimes she had her doubts, for something about the whole thing didn't ring true. It was nothing she could put a finger on; just something she could not explain.

It was then that Vi felt her first rasp of apprehension; a feeling that started beneath her tongue and tingled through her to the ends of her toes. As Jane and her sailor linked hands and walked off the dance floor a small voice whispered, 'Good-looking? Of course he is, but look again, Vi, girl. Hadn't you noticed how broad his back is? Hadn't you thought that maybe one day she might be glad of a shoulder like his to cry on?'

Mother of God, stop it! she told herself. Jane's going to be all right. *All right*. Okay?

Lucinda, tired of winding the gramophone handle and eager to be asked to dance, called over to the girl who sat moodily alone by the open window.

'Give me a break for half an hour, Connie, there's a dear girl.'

'Oh, all right.' Reluctantly Connie Dean rose to her feet. 'But I'm expecting Johnny on the next boat ashore, so it'll only be until he comes.'

'Bless you. Give me a call when you've had enough.' Lucinda smiled. 'But someone has just come in who promised me a couple of dances. Hey there! Lofty!'

Lofty? Lucinda frowned, making for the telegraphist who worked at her side and who had gentled her through her first frightening days in *Omega*'s wireless office. What was his real name? She had known him three weeks, yet still he was Lofty Bates; tall, gangling Lofty, who never panicked and who read the Morse code at speed as easily as most other people read the printed word. Was he Bill, or Fred, or John, or George? How odd that it was possible to like someone so much yet still not know his name. 'Now don't forget, Lofty,' she smiled, linking her arm in his, 'you promised to dance with me.'

Together, amiably, they walked to the refreshment table, where Vi poured tea into mugs and Kathy Mac-Alister filled beer glasses from a large white jug.

'Now then, you lot. Stop yer grabbin'!' Vi ordered as the carefully arranged trays of food were quickly emptied. 'And only one spoon of sugar, remember!'

Vi was enjoying herself. Serving people was what she was good at, helping them as she had done in the hardware department where once she worked. Nor did the meniality of scrubbing and sweeping and polishing worry her either, because she was good at that, too.

'I'm goin' to the galley,' she called over the noise. The tea leaves in the cream enamelled pot would stand a drop more water on them, she considered. Waste not, want not, and there *was* a war on, and didn't every ounce of the tea ration have to be brought here on ships in convoy? 'Shift over you lot.' Holding the two-handled pot high she pushed through the crowd.

My, but the dance was going well. Getting a bit noisy, maybe, but the supper interval would calm things down a bit. And she had been right, Vi thought as she placed a kettle to boil. Chief Pillmoor had been too anxious about upstairs. She had kept a careful watch and there had been no *visitors*.

'Just as if . . .' she whispered, then stopped, the satisfied smile leaving her lips the instant she saw the sailor through the open door of the galley.

She had first noticed him earlier, standing apart, not speaking or dancing. Now she saw him again, leaning too carelessly on the wall by the staircase, his eyes moving right and left. Then suddenly he was mobile and taking the stairs two at a time.

'Oh, no!' Vi reached the foot of the stairs in time to see him disappear to the left of the landing, though she was unable to see where he went. She only heard the loud creaking of a door as it was opened and the gentle click of its closing. But only the door of cabin 2 creaked so loudly; Vi knew it could be no other.

For a moment she stood quite still, shocked beyond belief. Stupid, that's what it was. A girl who risked taking a man to her cabin deserved all she got, but reporting it to Chief Pillmoor was something Vi found not a little distasteful. Yet, for all that, she found herself running quickly downstairs because maybe it wasn't like that at all. The sailor could be there for a different reason, like thieving, perhaps, and thieving was a different kettle of fish.

Without another thought, Vi knocked firmly on the regulating office door. 'Chief! You'd better come. There's a sailor just gone into cabin 2!'

'You're sure?' Pat Pillmoor's head shot up.

Vi felt bad, now that she had done it. A Judas, that's what she was; snitching on her own. 'I'm sure, Chief.'

'Right!' Pat Pillmoor slammed on her hat, eyelashes fluttering in agitation. When things became official she always felt the better for her hat. 'Come with me, McKeown, but don't say anything unless I speak to you first.' When things became official, a witness was not a bad idea, either.

At cabin 2 they hesitated, then, taking a deep breath, Pat Pillmoor threw open the door.

'And what,' she rapped, 'do you think you are doing?'

The sailor who stood at the chest of drawers spun round, white-faced, wide-eyed.

'Answer me, man! What are you doing here? Stealing, are you?'

Vi sighed with relief. The sailor was alone. There had been no assignation; the open drawer spoke for itself.

'No, Chief. Sorry, Chief,' he muttered. He was young, Vi thought. A bit of a kid in a Navy of grown men. 'I – I didn't mean any harm. I wasn't doing anything.'

'I'll be the judge of that,' Pat Pillmoor snapped. 'You'd better come downstairs to my office. I've got words to say to you, sailor. Come on – chop, chop!'

Shoulders sagging, he offered no resistance. One step ahead of them he walked slowly down the stairs.

'That will be all for now. McKeown.' Pat Pillmoor paused at the regulating office door. 'Don't say a word about this to anyone, is that understood?'

204

'Yes, Chief.'

Soberly Vi returned to the galley and turned off the gas tap. The dancing had started again; they wouldn't want the teapot now.

She side-stepped quickly as a conga chain left the dance floor and snaked into the recreation room. Feet stamped, bodies swayed. Only she, Vi, had seen the sailor go up the stairs and no one, it would seem, had seen him come down.

Boom, boom, boom-boom. *Hi, yi, conga*! A kid, that's all he'd been.

The front door slammed open, the conga chain lurched noisily down the path. A kid, Chief, that's all he is. Go easy on him, eh?

Chief Petty Officer Pillmoor closed the regulating office door, took off her hat and sat down at her desk.

'Name and rank?' she demanded, longing for a cigarette.

'Thompson. Ordinary seaman.' Frozen-faced, the sailor stared ahead.

'You were stealing, Thompson!'

'No, Chief. Just looking for – '

'Going through drawers is *just looking*? You were stealing. I shall call the pier patrol and have you searched.'

A thief, she thought regretfully. Baby-faced, eyes wide with misery, little older, surely, than her own son. But a thief.

'Don't do that, Chief. I'll turn my pockets out, if you want. There's nothing in them.'

'Maybe not, but there might have been. You went into that cabin looking for money, didn't you? Don't lie to me. I want the truth, Thompson. That, or the pier patrol!'

'I didn't go there to steal – well, not money.' His eyes met hers, pleadingly. 'I swear to you, not money.'

205

'Then *why*?' This did not make sense. The lad didn't look the thieving sort nor had he tried to brazen it out. He just appeared desperately afraid, truth known; a small, cornered animal.

'Smoke?' She reached for her cigarettes and, taking one out, threw the packet to him. It fell on the floor and he swiftly retrieved it, placing it carefully on the desk.

'No thanks.'

Pat Pillmoor flicked her lighter and inhaled deeply. 'If you weren't after money,' she asked softly, 'what were you doing in that cabin? What were you looking for?'

'I wanted – I wanted a pair of – ' He stopped, red-faced. 'I was looking for some underwear, Wrens' underwear,' he finished, eyes to the floor.

'Wrens' underwear! Good God, man, what's the matter with you?'

'Nothing, Chief. Nothing, honestly. But it was the only way, see? My time's nearly up. A month, that's all they gave me . . .'

'A month? *Who* gave you a month?'

'The blokes in the mess, Chief.'

'I think, Thompson,' she said, leaning back in her chair, 'that you'd better begin at the beginning; only this time I want the truth.'

She fixed him with an unblinking stare, wondering what it was all about and why it was making less and less sense.

'I'll tell you,' he whispered. 'I went into that cabin to try to find a pair of – of knickers, or something that Wrens wear underneath. I had to. They wanted proof, in the mess. "Give you a month to prove yourself, Tommo," they said. "Bring back a scalp, or else." They wouldn't leave me alone. But it was my own fault. I shouldn't have admitted that I'd never – never – '

206

'Never gone the whole way with a woman,' she supplied. 'How old are you, Thompson?'

'Nearly eighteen, Chief.'

'God Almighty!' Hardly two years older than Peter, the son she would fight like a vixen to defend. And if this war went on for very much longer, she brooded, there could stand her own son, tormented by men who should have known better, mocked because he'd never slept with a woman.

'I'm sorry, Chief. I know now I shouldn't have done it. And you'd better get the pier patrol in and charge me with thieving. I'd rather it was that. If they found out the truth, they'd never let it rest. "Can't get your hands on a pair of Wren's knickers like a normal bloke. Got to pinch 'em," they'd say.'

'And are you a normal bloke, Thompson?' She was not very proud of herself for asking.

'Course I am. I like girls. I've got one of my own, back home, only I've never . . .'

'Yes. I see.'

'I've tried, though. I tried twice this week but it didn't come to anything. One of them screamed and the other slapped my face.'

'So it would seem that if you can't provide proof of your – er, virility, things aren't going to get any better for you in the seamen's mess?'

'Better!' His voice shook with despair. 'It's going to be unbearable, that's what.'

'Now listen, Thompson, because I'm going to talk to you like a mother. And I'm old enough, don't worry. I have a son back home in Shropshire not a lot younger than you are, so I know what I'm talking about.' She smiled, and she was talking to Peter, the boy she had reared alone.

'It isn't clever to take a woman, you know; not unless

207

you care for her, that is. Oh, they've got big mouths, those men in your mess, Thompson, shouting the odds like the idiots they are, though they'd be the first to whinge if someone got their own sisters into trouble. But I'm afraid you'll just have to stick it out, that's all. You'll be more of a man than they are, if you can.'

'Yes, Chief,' he said, without conviction.

'Or you could,' she smiled, 'beat them at their own game. Now, see here, Thompson, I won't call the pier patrol; I won't put you on a charge, even. You're free to go, but before you do . . .'

She rose slowly to her feet, then opened a cupboard and took out a large cardboard box marked *Lost Property*. In it was a pair of black gym shoes, several odd stockings, two pairs of navy-blue knickers, a vest, two white collars and a pale pink brassiere. All legitimately lost; left in the drying room and forgotten. Now they lay unclaimed in the bottom of a cupboard and, until now, unwanted.

'Right, lad.' Pat Pillmoor offered the box. 'Take what you want.'

'You mean I can' – he plunged his hand into the box, pulling out a pair of knickers, dropping them, blushing, as if they were red-hot – 'I can have something? I can tell them I . . .?'

'Take the lot, if you like. Tell them you rampaged through the Wrennery like a man possessed, but if I were in your shoes I'd settle for one stocking and maybe *this*. One of these is far harder to – er – come by.'

She held up the brassiere, examining it carefully. It bore no indication of ownership; no Wren's good name would be lost in the seamen's mess tonight. 'Here you are. Put the blasted thing in your pocket and get out of here before I change my mind!'

The sailor's face registered disbelief and relief and joy, and his hand was on the doorknob in no time at all. Then he stopped and slowly turned. 'Thanks, Chief,' he choked. 'Thanks a lot. You're a real lady, that's what.'

He had reached the front door before she called him back.

'Thompson! Your name – what is it?'

'David,' he told her, frowning.

'That's all right, lad. On your way!'

She watched him go, proof of his prowess stuffed in his pocket, watched him run down the jetty and join the knot of sailors who waited for the launch that would take them back to *Omega*.

David, who could so easily have been Peter. But she had done the right thing; of that she was *very* sure.

The dance thrashed on. Couples slipped out into the gathering twilight, the better to say their goodnights. Beside the front door, Connie Dean waited, still, for her Johnny, and Vi began the routine of darkening ship, closing windows, drawing the heavy black curtains. At the pantry window she paused. Best not shut it fast. Not tonight. Reaching up, she removed the bulb from its socket and laid it carefully on the shelf.

Chief Pillmoor stubbed out her cigarette and looked at her watch, then walking purposefully to the door of the mess hall, she called, 'Last waltz, you lot!' She sighed with pure pleasure. Ten more minutes and with luck they'd all be gone. Another dance almost over, thank God. At the door of the regulating office she met the duty steward.

'Just come to do your blackout, Chief.'

'Thanks, McKeown. I'll see to it.'

'Okay, Chief. Everything all right, is it?'

'Everything's fine.' Smiling, she tapped her nose with her forefinger. 'The lad was dared to pinch a pair of

209

blackouts. No harm in him, so keep it under your hat, eh?'

'Not a word.' Relief showed plainly on Vi's face. 'Goodnight, Chief.'

Pat Pillmoor stood for a moment at the window, staring out into the deepening darkness, seeing nothing now but the red port-side light of the launch as it pulled away from the jetty. Then she drew the curtains across the window.

'And goodnight to you too, young Thompson.' She grinned, placing the lost-property box back in the cupboard. 'And the very best of British!'

'It was a smashin' night, wasn't it?' Vi rolled up and fastened the last of her curlers. 'I think everybody had a good time – well, everybody but Connie. That Johnny of hers has stood her up again.'

'Well, *I* enjoyed it. Do you know, in fifty years from now when my grandchildren are being taught their history,' Lucinda laughed, 'they'll say, "What was your war really like, Grandmama?" and because I shall have forgotten all the awful things I shall say, "My war? We danced, my darlings. Oh, how we danced!"'

'Hmm. And you got yourself a belting feller, didn't you, young Jane?' Vi remarked. 'Where did you find him, then?'

'He found me, the morning *Taureg* came back from patrol. I told you about him – the spare-crew submariner.'

'And what, when it's at home, is a spare-crew submariner?'

'Well, it would seem there's a nucleus of submariners they can call on if there's an emergency, and Tom is one of those. He could be sent on patrol at a minute's notice or he could get a permanent draft. There's a new submarine joining the flotilla very soon, he told me, a V-class boat. He'd like a berth on that one, he said.'

210

'So until that happens, you've got yourself an admirer,' Lucinda teased.

'No. Tom Tavey knows the way things are. I told him about Rob. And talking about Rob – '

'Which you do all the time!'

'Talking about Rob, how am I to get to Glasgow without a pass?'

'You can't.' Vi frowned. 'You know it's just not on. The crushers would be sure to stop you somewhere along the way. You'll just have to wait till your leave comes up.'

'Nearly two months! Oh, no! There's got to be another way.'

'I thought you were going to be sensible about it,' Vi admonished, 'but it seems you're not.'

Mother of God, she fretted silently, would the kid never learn? Surely, if Rob MacDonald were in enemy hands he'd have written by now. Surely her parents wouldn't hold back a letter from a prisoner of war. No one could be that rotten.

'Sense has nothing to do with what I feel about Rob,' Jane said quietly. 'Try to understand. Isn't it natural I should want to find his mother?'

'And beg her for comfort that maybe she can't give you?'

'No, Vi. But it was a million-to-one chance I'd ever meet anyone who could tell me where I could find the Pavilion and McFadden's bakery; and with odds like that on my side, I know things are going to turn out right. They've *got* to.'

'All right, queen, they will. But shouldn't you be prepared to accept that it might be a long time – years and years, maybe – till you meet your Rob again?'

'It could be, but it won't be, Vi. I shall meet him soon. I want him now, you see. I couldn't wait years and years. I couldn't do it!'

'You could if you had to,' Vi whispered. 'I know I'd settle for that. If I knew there was that kind of a chance for me I'd wait for ever.'

'Oh, Vi, I'm sorry. I didn't think. Forgive me.' She gathered Vi in her arms and hugged her close. 'I didn't mean to hurt you, honest I didn't.'

'Away with your bother, young Jane. I know you didn't. Now move yourselves, the pair of you, and get your heads down. Past midnight it is and the bleedin' light still on!'

She watched as they bounced into bed, then switching off the light she smiled. 'Goodnight,' she whispered fondly. 'God bless.'

Pat Pillmoor tapped on the wardroom door and walked in without ceremony.

'Just to let you know that everything is all right. No one adrift, Ma'am. Everything quiet.'

'Good.' Suzie St John lifted the teapot at her side, an eyebrow raised. 'Want a cup? It's still hot.'

'Not for me, thanks. I'll get off to bed, if you don't mind. It's been a long day.'

'Well, it's a great relief to me when dance night is over, Pat. I always expect something awful to happen, but it never does.'

'Of course it doesn't. Everything went like clockwork tonight. No incidents.'

'Good. And by the way, which duty will Wren McKeown be on tomorrow? The letter from her sister should be arriving in the morning and I shall want to see her as soon after that as I can.'

'McKeown's on late watch all week, but I'll check the post first, then send her to you after breakfast.'

'Fine, Pat. I shall have to take it gently, shan't I? It's going to be a shock, you know.'

'Yes, but she'll be all right.' Pat Pillmoor rose to her

feet, hand over her mouth. 'Salt of the earth, McKeown is. There'll be no upset. Goodnight, Ma'am. Sleep well.'

She closed the door quietly then walked slowly up the stairs.

'Like clockwork?' she whispered. 'No incidents?'

God, but who would be a chiefie in charge of a hostel full of women! They should give her a medal when this lot was over; a damn great medal!

'You know, I thought I wouldn't like late watches, but I have to confess' – Lucinda stretched luxuriously, plumped up her pillow then bit into her second slice of bread and marmalade – 'that late watches do have certain advantages, one of them being breakfast in bed. You're such a love, Vi, to bring it up to us.'

'An' I'm a fool, too. You know we're not supposed to have food in cabins. One day we're goin' to get caught and then where will we all be?'

'In big trouble, along with the rest of starboard watch.' Jane grinned. 'But it is good of you, Vi. You spoil us, you know.'

'Ar, hey, it's only marmalade butties and tea, and everybody does it on lates, I suppose.' Pink-cheeked, Vi shrugged away the compliment. 'And you're not bad kids.' Not bad? She clucked after them like a mother hen, she readily admitted it, and loved them as if they'd been her own. 'And you'd better make the most of it, because soon we'll be startin' a week of earlies and up at the crack of dawn. Now then, are you goin' to shurrup and let me tell you what was on the news?'

Vi McKeown was a lovable, loving, uncomplicated woman whose only addiction, as far as they could tell, was listening to news bulletins. She tuned in the wireless and listened to them all, duties permitting. She listened avidly,

213

missing not a word, as if the whole course of the war depended upon it.

'All right, Vi. Are we winning?'

'Winnin'?' Vi cleared her throat. 'Not winnin', exactly. More holdin' our own, just about. The man said that the Americans have landed soldiers in Iceland; something about relieving our own troops there for active service. Think them Yanks should have come 'ere, instead. Lord knows, we could do with 'em.'

'Come here? But don't you think the Americans are already taking risks, helping us? Look at all the food they're sending – dried milk, dried eggs – '

'And Spam,' Lucinda offered. 'Oh, I love Spam.'

'Well, enjoy yerself,' Vi grinned, 'because if this war goes on for four years like the last one did, we might all be sick to death of Spam. But I suppose the poor civvies are glad enough of a tin or two. D'you know, before I joined up my meat ration was one shillin' and tuppence worth a *week*? Mother of God, I was beginnin' to forget what meat tasted like.'

'But you've got to admit the Americans are sticking their necks out,' Jane persisted. 'They're doing everything they can for us, short of declaring war on Germany.'

'Then it's a pity they don't.' Vi shrugged. 'According to me da, it made an 'ell of a difference when they came in on our side last time. Wish they'd make up their minds and get themselves here.'

'But this isn't their war,' Lucinda argued. 'Why should they fight?'

'Because sooner or later they're goin' to have to,' Vi pronounced. 'Stands to reason, dunnit? After Russia, where else is left for Hitler's lot to go?'

'Was there anything about Russia on the news, Vi? How are they doing?'

'Terrible, poor sods. The news man said that Minsk has

fallen now. Them Germans have taken Lord knows how many prisoners and thousands of tanks and guns. It'll be Leningrad next. Is there no stoppin' them?'

'Churchill doesn't like the Communists.' Lucinda stirred her tea thoughtfully. 'But the last time he spoke on the wireless he said that anybody who fights Hitler is our ally.'

'So we'll have to get to like them,' Vi retorted complacently.

'Even though they murdered their Tsar?'

'Well, we did it to one of ours, didn't we? And anyway, them upper-crust lot deserved to be shot, beggin' your pardon, Lucinda,' Vi countered sternly. 'Me da said our troops should've packed it in and shoved off back 'ome in the last war, just like the Russians did. He said some of his officers were right swines. Said they should've been put up against a wall and shot.'

'Was your – cr – *da* a bit Bolshie, Vi?'

'Can't remember him, but according to our mam he was. But can you blame him. A slow death from mustard gas, he had. Died after the war was over. Mam always said a sniper's bullet would've been kinder. She tried to get a war pension but they wouldn't give her one. Said Da should have been wearing his gas mask. And he would have, if they'd ever given him one.'

'I suppose, Vi, that makes you a bit of a Communist too?' Lucinda ventured. 'Not that I'd blame you, of course.'

'*Me*, Bolshie? Oh, no, queen. Always had this ambition, see? Always wanted our own house, Gerry and me did, and Communists don't believe in that, do they? "Get a house of our own," Gerry used to say, "and there'll be something behind us, girl; something to leave to our kids." Only we never had kids and anyway, Gerry is – ' She stopped abruptly, reluctant, even yet, to say so final a word. 'But I'm sorry for them poor Russians. Imagine

215

trying to get away from the Germans; imagine havin' to pack what you can get on to a cart or somethin', then setting fire to the rest. Just think of it, having to burn your home down, because that's what they've got to do. Burn everything, Stalin has told them; houses and factories and even the crops in the fields. The Germans must get nothing, he says, but scorched earth. Well, that's what it said on the news this morning. Terrible, innit? Scorched earth.'

'And it might just as easily have been us,' Jane whispered uneasily. 'It still could happen.'

'Well, if they take it into their heads to land at Liverpool, they'll not get a lot. Only rubble. You wouldn't believe what them bombers did to the old town. Street after street wiped out and it was a smashin' place, once. I'm glad Gerry never saw what they did to it. Just ten nights, it took. Every night they came, till the docks and the city centre was nearly all gone.'

'There was nothing like that at Fenton Bishop,' Jane said quietly. 'Oh, there were the nuisance raids – dive bombers strafing the aerodrome – but no blitz. How did you stick it, Vi? I'd have got out.'

'Well, there was this joke goin' round Liverpool, see. People used to say that as long as the liver birds stayed, then they would stay, too. Said that if they came out of the shelters one morning and found them birds had flown away, well, that'd be it, folks said. Liverpool would be finished then.'

'What sort of birds are they, Vi? Real ones?'

'Ha!' Vi shrieked with laughter. 'Ornaments, they are. Two of them, great big things, stuck on top of the Liver Buildings, down on the Pier Head. Don't know what they're supposed to be, but Liverpudlians call them the liver birds. Ships coming up the Mersey can see them miles away; and when they do, the seamen know they're nearly home. Anyway, them birds is still perched up there, so I reckon Liverpool is going to struggle through.' Vi grinned. 'They'll be all right, which is more than we'll be if we don't stir ourselves. Patsy Pill will be doin' morning rounds soon, and this cabin looks like a tip.'

'Okay, Vi. Jane and I will tidy round and make the beds if you'll clean the shoes.'

'Fine. Suits me, though one of you had better bring up a mop and floor polish,' Vi ordered comfortably, spreading a newspaper on the floor. Vi liked cleaning shoes. It was something else she was good at. The rubbing in of the blacking and the rhythmic swish of the polishing brush never failed to soothe her, and the end product, three pairs of brilliantly shining shoes, was reward enough.

'I'll go.' Lucinda threw back her bedclothes. 'And I'll check on the letter rack while I'm down there.'

'Bet you anything you like she's hoping there'll be something from Mike Farrow,' Jane said as the sound of Lucinda's slippered feet receded. 'I think she likes him a lot. She tries not to show it, but she does.'

'Now, don't you be sayin' things like that, especially to Lucinda. Don't be putting ideas into her head. She's goin' to marry Charlie, isn't she?'

'I know she is, but you said you didn't like him, didn't you, Vi? You said yourself he was a right little sh – '

'Maybe I did,' Vi hastily interrupted, 'and maybe I shouldn't have, but don't you ever tell Lucinda I said that, because maybe Lucinda likes him. Maybe she wants to marry him.'

'And maybe Lucinda wants Lady Mead, though I don't suppose she'd admit it. It was her home as a child. She was happy there until they parted her from her nanny and packed her off to boarding school. It's a back-to-the-womb situation, if you ask me. I don't think it'll be a love match. She doesn't talk like a girl in love, does she? And

217

another thing – Charlie won't learn to dance, and you know how Lucinda loves dancing.'

''ere, hang on a bit. It's a husband she's after, not a dancin' partner.'

'Of course it is, but why – ' Jane stopped short as Lucinda returned, breathless, with mop, polish and three letters.

'Here you are.' She passed round the envelopes. 'One for me from London – looks as if it's from Goddy; one for you, Jane, and one for Vi.'

'Ar, just look.' Fondly Vi gazed at the childish print. 'This'll be from Paul, me little nephew, bless him.' She pushed it into her overall pocket. 'Now come on, you two. No reading letters till this room is finished. Don't want a blast from Patsy Pill, do we?'

There was no blast from Chief Pillmoor when she did her daily inspection of sleeping quarters. With only a hasty glance around the cabin and without the usual forefinger search for dust she murmured, 'Fine. Oh, McKeown, Ma'am wants to see you at once – all right?'

'But Chief, I'm not on duty until noon!'

'*Now*, McKeown!'

'Flamin' Norah!' Vi exploded as the door closed quietly. 'Hope it isn't going to take long. And we were going into Craigiebur this mornin' to queue at the chemist's for a lipstick. Well, it looks as if you'll have to go without me, girls.' She shook her head dolefully. 'Something tells me this isn't goin' to be my day . . .'

Vi rubbed her shoe toes on the backs of her stockings, checked that her hair was well above her collar, then knocked diffidently on the wardroom door.

'Come in, McKeown.' Third Officer St John looked up, smiling. 'Sit down, won't you?'

'It's all right, Ma'am.' Sitting in the presence of an officer, even when asked, was not on.

'Very well.' Suzie St John took a deep, slow breath. Carefully, now, she thought. Just as she had rehearsed it.

'Your sister has sent me a letter, one she wants you to see. She phoned me two nights ago.' The Wren officer cleared her throat. 'There is something you must know, and she thought it would be best if I told you.'

She paused, searching for exactly the right words, gazing as she did so into the chalk-white face, the wide, apprehensive eyes.

'Our Mary?'

'That's right. Mrs Mary Reilly, from Ormskirk.'

'But why? What's wrong? The children – '

'Nothing is wrong and the children are fine. It isn't bad news, McKeown, but I think you really must sit down.'

Suzie St John sighed. McKeown had gone so pale. 'It really is good news,' she urged, 'but even good news can sometimes come as a shock.' She glanced at the glass she had placed in readiness beside the brandy flask. 'Mrs Reilly has asked me to break it to you – and I entirely agree with her – that two days ago she received *this*.' She held up a folded piece of paper. 'She said she thought that to telephone you or send it without warning might be upsetting for you, so I asked her to send it to me first.'

Vi swallowed hard and it hurt her throat. She had seen such things before – air-mail letter cards – only the one in the officer's hand was white and not the usual pale blue. And this one, Vi could see, bore the words *Censored* and *Stalag* and a word that looked like *Absender* McKeown, G.

'Ma'am. It's got Gerry's name on it.' Her voice sounded strange and far away.

'Yes, and his number; his *prisoner of war* number.'

'My husband is dead. Lost at sea.' She had gone dizzy.

The desk top was tilting. Blindly she groped for the chair and sat down heavily.

'No! Your husband is *alive*! He's in a prisoner-of-war camp in Austria. This letter was sent to your sister, asking for news of you. Your husband has written to you, he says, but has had no reply. He's very worried. They seem aware in his camp that Liverpool has been badly bombed.'

'But if he's written to Lyra Street, the house isn't there any more. His letters will be – '

'In a dead-letter box, in some post office.'

'Ma'am, you wouldn't . . .? It *is* true? I'm not goin' to wake up and – '

'And find you dreamed it? No, McKeown, you are not. Your husband is alive.' Suzie St John was smiling, holding out a glass. 'But I think you'd better try to swallow some of this. As I said, even good shocks . . .'

Shakily, Vi lifted the glass to her lips. She had never tasted brandy before and it tore at her throat and made her draw in her breath.

'Drink it all, McKeown.'

Obediently Vi tilted the glass again. More carefully, she trickled the liquid down her throat then set down the glass with hands that still trembled. And it was not only her hands. She was trembling all over and she couldn't stop. She felt sick, too. Oh, God, not sick. Not here, in Ma'am's office!

'Tell me again,' she pleaded.

'I will, and gladly.' The quarters officer knew the worst was over. It was going to be all right. 'Your husband is a prisoner of war, McKeown, and I want you to take this letter and read it again and again. Read it until it registers, then come back to me and we'll have a talk about getting a letter back to him. It will have to be censored, but censors are flesh and blood like the rest of us. And your sister told me that she has already written to your husband

220

telling him you are safe and well. I'm so very happy for you, McKeown. Just give yourself time to get used to it.'

'Yes, Ma'am.' The garden, that's where she would go. The garden, beside the red rose bush. 'Thank you, Ma'am, and oh, God bless you!'

Slowly, uncertainly, she rose to her feet, gripping the desk top, reaching for the letter. She must tell Jane and Lucinda. She must tell everybody. But not just yet; not until she was certain, absolutely certain.

Alive. *Alive*. The words beat loudly and gloriously in her head and she stumbled, dazed, to the bench that stood beside the climbing rose. She had so often sat beside it. When first she came to Ardneavie House it had borne one red bloom to remind her of Gerry and the bush he planted in the yard at Lyra Street. And she was sad because Gerry's rose had been so wantonly destroyed, though it shouldn't have mattered because he would never see it flower – or so she had thought.

Now the rose beside her was a riot of blossom, throwing its fragrance over her like a blessing, promising that one day she and Gerry would plant again together. Where, she did not know; when, she dare not begin to guess. But Ma'am had told her Gerry was alive and the letter in her hand had been written by Gerry. It was all she needed to know.

She unfolded the page, her heart thudding. It *was* Gerry's writing; spindly, sprawling writing, the words brief and to the point.

Dear Mary,

I am writing to you because I am desperate and worried. I keep writing to Vi but she does not write back. The guards here say that Liverpool has been burned to the ground. Is Vi with you? Is she safe? Write to me soon. I must know. God bless you all,

Gerry

'*Alive,*' she whispered to the nodding red roses. '*Alive,*' she told the hills, the trees, the clump of blue lupins.

The tears came then; tears that scalded her eyes and tasted salt on her lips. She wept with great, jerking sobs. She had so wept for his death; now she wept for his life.

Sweet Jesus, thank you. Our Lady and St Anthony and St Jude, thank you, thank you.

Even though he was a captive, ringed round by guards and guns and high fences, even though he might sometimes go hungry, Gerry was not dead. Oh, she could well imagine his worry and the guards taunting their prisoners: 'We are bombing your cities and your ports. London and Plymouth and Liverpool all burn. Your homes are gone . . .'

But soon Gerry would know she was safe. And wasn't it better for him to be out of the war? Merchant seamen were dying daily in their hundreds. The Atlantic was a fearsome battleground; even Winston Churchill acknowledged that the battle of the Atlantic must be won before Hitler could be defeated. As a prisoner, Gerry was out of the reach of the U-boat packs, his war over. One day he could come home, and until then she could wait.

She blew her nose loudly and raised pink and puffy eyes to the sun. This, she had complained, was not going to be her day; yet now it had become the loveliest, weepiest, most wonderful day she would ever know. 'Gerry love,' she whispered, 'you promised you'd come back to me and you will. Oh, lad, I'm so happy I could die.'

Only then did she remember. The commodore of Gerry's convoy did not stop to search for survivors, Richie Daly had said. Well, she had thanked the Virgin and all the saints, but now it was obvious that the devil, too, deserved his due; the German U-boat commander who must surely have plucked her husband from the sea.

222

'Thanks, Fritz,' she sniffed. 'You lot are rotten bastards, but thanks, mate. Thanks a lot.'

Looking up, she saw a face at the window of cabin 9. 'Hey, Jane,' she yelled. 'He's alive! Gerry's alive!' Then, jumping to her feet, she began to run.

9

From her seat beside the window, Vi set aside the stocking she was darning. The light was getting worse, the sky darkening to an eerie yellow-brown, tinting to sulphur the clouds that hung low over the hilltops. All day the sun, that same sun which for weeks had shone so brilliantly, had been blotted out by haze, and though the window was wide open, the cabin was hot and airless.

The storm was about to break. The heatwave, which had begun on their first day at Ardneavie, would soon be over. A whole month it had lasted, Vi reflected; four and a bit not-to-have-been-missed, never-to-be-forgotten weeks since she had walked into the RTO's office on Glasgow station and her life as a Wren had really started. They were hungry and tired that night, with Jane near to tears, Vi recalled, and all of them wondering what the whole bewildering business was about and where it would end.

Vi allowed herself a smile. How comic they must have looked: jackets too big, skirts too long and oh, those shoes. It made her wince, even now, to remember her throbbing feet and the way the thick black stockings made her legs itch. But a month had seen a difference. Now, their uniforms were altered to fit, their skirts the regulation fourteen inches from the floor. Now, Vi's shoes no longer tortured her, for the cobbler in Ardneavie village had come to her aid, soaking her shoes with rainwater then setting them to dry on his patent stretcher. Now, the length of their knicker legs had been shortened by several inches, though Lucinda had voiced her doubts at the time.

'Ma'am's going to notice at kit inspection,' she warned as the scissors came out.

'No she's not. Three pairs of knickers, that's all she'll want to see. She's not going to take a tape measure to them.'

Now, Vi knew every rating in Ardneavie House. It was as if, she thought, she had always been a steward in the WRNS, so easily had she adapted to the life.

Such a month it had been. She had thrown off her widowhood with incredulous joy. Life was so good that just to think of that morning in Ma'am's office made her ache all over. Gerry was alive. Soon, now, he would receive her first letter; a letter filled with I-love-yous.

'But what shall I say to him?' she had demanded, pen poised, of Lucinda and Jane. 'I can tell him I've joined the Wrens, but I can't say where I am. I can't tell him about the terrible bombing, either; they'd censor that, too.'

'So tell him you are safe and well and a Wren. Ask him to send his letters to Mary's address – he'll understand why – then tell him you love him. If I were a man and a prisoner of war that's all I'd want to know,' Jane had said with the wisdom of the very young. And that was what that letter card had been about, Vi smiled: a single sheet of I-love-yous, folded into four.

'A penny for them.' Lucinda's offer cut into her thoughts.

'Oh, I was thinkin' about all sorts of things; about Gerry and about it bein' just a month since we all came here.'

'Seems like a year!' Jane fanned herself with the note-pad on which she had been writing. 'God! It's so *hot*!'

A month, Jane thought. A good month, for together she and Jock had accidentally discovered the whereabouts of McFadden's bread shop. It wouldn't be long, now, before she found Rob's mother. At first, she had considered the possibility of going to Glasgow without pass or permission with trepidation; but since Vi's wonderful news about Gerry, it had seemed that the gods were smiling on the Wrens of cabin 9 and that nothing could go wrong for any of them. And who was to say she would be caught? Jane reasoned complacently. Why shouldn't she get away with it?

She gazed out at the threatening storm. She was glad, now, that Tom had broken their date for tonight. Since the night of the Wrennery dance she and Tom had met often. He was fun to be with, a good friend who kissed her without passion. Tonight they had decided to go to the pictures, but no matter. Tom's face had appeared at the coding office porthole. 'Sorry, Jane, but it'll have to be some other time.' He was leaving at once for Barrow, he had told her, with the crew that was to sail a newly built submarine to Loch Ardneavie. HM Submarine *Viper*, the latest addition to the 15th Flotilla.

She would miss Tom while he was away, and if he joined *Viper*'s company, as he hoped to do, she would worry about him when he was out on patrol. Not as she had worried about Rob, of course. The hours Rob had been away in S-Sugar were a torment, her relief on his return almost indescribable. But Tom was what Jane would have called nice, had she been asked to categorize him; someone who had understood the way things were, and for that alone she was grateful.

'There's going to be one hell of a storm,' she murmured, returning to the letter she was writing. 'And not before time!'

Lucinda lay on her bed, legs relaxed, arms hanging limp, feeling like a thrown-away rag doll. Like other fair-skinned, fair-haired women, prolonged heat drained her of energy and she silently agreed with her cabinmate, glad now that the ending of the sweltering heat was in sight.

Dit, dit, dit-da. The sound had pinged intermittently inside her head since morning. *Dit, dit, dit-da* . . . Now it was back again, the letter V for Victory. Victory in Europe, the news announcer had read: the mark of the unseen army of resistance. It had drummed out over the air; a sound, it was said, to remind the alien occupiers of Europe that the British would be back – and until they were, the vigilant eyes of patriots in France and Belgium and Norway and Holland and Denmark would watch from the maquis, from scrub and undergrowth. And they would silently wait for any chance to hit at the conquerors. From now on, the V-sign would be seen and heard and daubed on walls all over occupied Europe. V for Victory! Take heart, Europe! We will return! Fine, brave words, but *when*? Lucinda sighed, shaking the sound from her head.

'I ought to write to my mother,' she said to no one in particular. The last letter from Bruton Street had been one long complaint. Her mother had already used up all her clothing coupons and there would be no more until December! Just *what* was the government about? And there had been another air raid on London, she had written, the first for ten weeks, and just as everyone was thinking they were over. The first, Lucinda realized, since that awful morning she had picked her way to the Admiralty through the horror of the London streets and begged her godfather to pull rank on her behalf and speed her entry into the Wrens. She and her mother had quarrelled violently that morning, Lucinda recalled, and though she had apologized, not one single word of it had she regretted. And Mama was still complaining. Poor Pa. Small wonder he spent most of his time with his Home Guard platoon.

Dit dit dit-da. There it was again. She wondered what

the Russians of Smolensk would have thought about that stirring V-for-Victory broadcast as they set light to their homes and possessions. Smolensk was overrun now, and proud Leningrad only eighty miles from the German armies. So much had happened to the Russian people in a month. So much had happened here at Ardneavie, too. The past thirty days, Lucinda reluctantly admitted, had been some of the happiest of her life, in spite of the war. Or maybe because of it. Now, she was a free agent – or as free as any member of the armed forces could be. Hers was a different kind of freedom, really. Lady Lucinda was forgotten. Now she was truly Bainbridge, L. V. Even the discovery of her title had caused little comment. Now she was the same as thirty-nine other women, and it was good.

She turned her head, wondering how Jane could find the energy even to lift a pen, wishing she could write to Mike and thank him for the letter she had received four days ago, which had left her pink-cheeked with delight. But Mike had given her no address, telling her only that he was in London to attend a medical board and would then be travelling on to RAF Cranwell.

So he had done it. He'd applied for flying duties again, and the board in London was to assess his fitness. Why was it so important that he should fly? Couldn't he do more for the war effort by helping in the training of pilots? Being shot down must have been a dreadful experience; couldn't he have left it at that?

. . . *Saw a show – Lupino Lane in* Me and My Girl *– and wished my girl had been there with me*.

Mike! I am not your girl! she had protested silently, though she wished she could have been with him, sitting shoulder-to-shoulder in the intimate darkness, fingers entwined. But it would never be. Now Mike would be posted to a fighter station, Somewhere in England, and they would never meet again. Knowing him had been great, but –

The urgent knocking caused heads to lift.

'Bainbridge,' said the Wren who poked her face round the door. 'Phone call for you.'

'Me?' Lucinda frowned. 'Now who . . .?'

But probably it would be from Charlie, bored with duty behind his War Office desk. Charlie hated writing letters.

Quickly she ran downstairs to the telephone which stood beneath the letter board. 'Bainbridge,' she murmured into the receiver.

'Lucy, honey . . .'

'Mike!' She laughed, relieved. 'Mike, how lovely! Where are you?'

'Back at Machrihanish, sweetheart. The idiot medics have said I'm still not fit for flying, so I need a shoulder to cry on. Are you on late duty tomorrow night?'

'No, but. . .'

'Fine, then. See you at seven thirty at the jetty, okay?'

'Well, yes, but – '

'Swell! See you, honey,' Mike called as the line went dead.

Ooosh! Lucinda let go of her breath. Mike Farrow was back with a vengeance. Seven thirty at the jetty – oh, damn, damn, damn! Tomorrow was Sunday and the dance hall would be closed. But did it really matter? Mike was fun to be with. Just to see him again, to walk with him and talk with him would be good.

I've missed you, Mike, she thought soberly. I know I shouldn't have, but there it is, I have. And I'm glad you'll not be flying just yet.

'That was Mike,' she said, closing the cabin door behind her. 'He's back at Machrihanish and I'm meeting him tomorrow night,' she added, almost defiantly.

229

'Well, now,' Vi said comfortably. 'That'll be nice for you, won't it?'

'You – you've nothing to say about it, Vi?'

'Me? No business of mine, queen. But put the record straight. Tell him about Charlie.'

'Yes. Yes, I will,' Lucinda said absently. Of course she would. Mike was a dear person and it was only right and proper that she should tell him. And when she did, he would probably tell her about his girl in Vermont – or maybe his wife. He *could* be married. And maybe he would say that that made it okay for them to go on meeting. But it wouldn't, she thought vehemently. Mike Farrow was altogether too attractive, and when she was with him it was only too easy to be unfaithful to Charlie – *mentally* unfaithful, that was. The other form, the wonderfully abandoned, all-the-way infidelity was not even to be considered. 'Anyway, I doubt if I'll be seeing him again after tomorrow.'

'I wouldn't take bets on it, girl,' said Vi. 'But be straight with the bloke, eh? And hasn't it gone dark?' she remarked, changing the subject, Lucinda thought, as adroitly as Nanny ever could. 'Do you think we could put the light on – without blacking out the window, I mean?'

'I don't know,' Jane frowned. 'It isn't blackout time for nearly two hours yet, but I don't think a light would be a good idea.'

She was remembering hit-and-run raids on Fenton Bishop aerodrome. Dive bombers coming out of a darkening sky, guided by the dim gooseneck flares either side of the runway; strafing, bombing, then away into the gloom again as quickly as they had come. Last time, though the attack had lasted barely two minutes, two young WAAFs had been killed.

She walked over to the window, and a draught of cool air met her face.

230

'Ouch! See that?' She started as the first flash of lightning darted over the hilltops and, closing her eyes, she began to count. *One, two, three*. The thunder crashed then rumbled sulkily, its echoes trapped in the ring of hills. 'Three seconds between flash and crash. That makes the centre of the storm three miles away – well, that's what my dad always says.'

'Good,' Lucinda breathed. 'Now all we need is rain; lovely, lovely rain . . .'

On cue, the storm clouds opened and Vi leaned out to close the window. 'There now,' she beamed. 'Raindrops as big as penny pieces. Do the garden good.' Lightning forked again, briefly illuminating the loch. 'Time for standeasy,' she remarked as thunder crashed directly overhead. 'Are we going downstairs, or is somebody goin' to bring it up?'

'I'll go.' Lucinda jumped to her feet. 'Just think of it. Won't it be lovely and cool tonight! I shall sleep stark naked on top of the bedclothes!'

'It's that phone call from her American,' said Vi as Lucinda clattered downstairs. 'Sleep naked, indeed! That Mike is giving her ideas!'

'I think you could be right, Vi, but don't tell her, eh?' Jane grinned. 'Finding out for herself is going to be quite an experience for her – and a *whole* lot more fun!'

Lucinda smiled at the bell-bottomed Wren driver as she left the transport, then inhaled deeply, enjoying the scent of rain on soil. How different this former holiday town was now from the Craigiebur Mike's grandmother had known. How strange to her now would be its unpainted hotels and boarding houses requisitioned for the war effort, its beach shut off and deserted, save for seabirds. But strangest of all to her would be the empty flower beds which in gentler days must have delighted the eye with

231

displays of brilliant geraniums and soothed the senses with the scent of stocks and carnations and lavender. Now those beds grew cabbages and carrots and long rows of peas and beans. With the coming of war, even the smallest area of soil grew food. A lawn was a needless, time-consuming luxury. Dig it up in the name of Victory, and plant food! Tear out your herbaceous borders, demanded the propaganda posters, and grow potatoes. Even gardens must make a contribution to the war effort, and only the minimum of flowers should be allowed. Dig for Victory!

The cabbages stood drenched and dripping, the earth was black again and the air sweet to Lucinda's nostrils. She walked slowly towards the jetty, an unaccustomed awareness pulsating through her. She was early – ten more minutes to the half-hour – yet she needed to turn the corner and see Mike standing there; and when they met she would smile and say, 'Hullo. Lovely to see you again,' and he would say, 'Hi, Lucy. Glad you could make it.' Nice and easy it would be, and friendly and fun.

He was waiting there when she reached the top of the jetty, his elbows on the topmost guard rail, gazing up the firth, watching the distant gathering of merchant ships soon to sail in convoy west to America, where the bright lights still shone; or north to Archangel and Murmansk with ill-afforded tanks and guns and fuel for the Russians, who were now our allies.

He did not see her until she stood beside him, and when he turned he only smiled briefly. Her relaxed greeting died on her lips and she could only look into his face and know that this meeting was not between friends.

Without speaking, he cupped her face in his hands and kissed her gently. Eyes closed, she let her mouth linger on his.

'Hullo, Lucy.'

'Hullo, yourself.' She wanted him to kiss her again, but he did not.

'I've missed you, honey.' He took her hand, then tucked her arm in his.

'You can't have. It's only been – '

'I said I've missed you, woman. Don't argue!'

'Sorry.' She was surprised how apprehensive she had felt at their meeting; shy, almost. But now the intimate moment had passed she would soon feel easy again.

'What have you been doing with yourself, sweetheart?'

'I was about to ask the same of you.'

'Your news first, Lucy. I know you're just bursting to tell me something.'

'Oh, I *am*, Mike! It's about Vi. Her husband wasn't lost at sea. He's in a POW camp in Austria. Isn't it marvellous? D'you know, we laughed and cried and danced all over the place when she told us. And it made everyone at Ardneavie so happy. People kept coming up to Vi and hugging her and telling her how glad they were. I felt as if it happened to me, I was so thrilled for her.'

'I'm glad about it, too. You care for Vi a lot, don't you?'

'Oh, I *do*. She's so straight and wise, somehow. And she treats us like a couple of kids even though she's only a few years older. I hope they won't ever split us up – any of us. Jane's a sweetie, too.'

'Any news of her boyfriend?'

'No – and yes. She's almost certain now that she can find his mother. Jock Menzies – he's the coder she works with – once lived in that area, so now she's trying to get to Glasgow without a pass. Pity she never knew the exact address. She could have written there ages ago, if she had.'

'You don't know where I live, honey.'

'I do, Mike. Vermont, New England. You told me.'

233

'But not *where* in Vermont.'

'Well – no. But then,' she smiled, 'our circumstances are different, aren't they? Jane and Rob were in love.'

'And we aren't, of course.'

'Don't be an idiot, Mike! How could we be?' *Tell him now. Tell him about Charlie! There'll never be a better moment!* 'I mean, we can be friends, you and I – good friends, like Tom Tavey and Jane. Tom understands about Rob – no strings attached – and you must . . .' She stopped, her cheeks burning.

'And I must understand about *who*, Lucy?'

'N-no one, Mike!' *Tell him!* 'But people can be good friends, dear friends, without – '

'Okay, my good, dear friend.' He bent and kissed the tip of her nose. 'Pax!' *Okay, Lucy Bainbridge, a truce, but only for now. This thing between us is fact. It isn't going to go away!* 'What are we going to do?'

'Well, it's Sunday, so we can't dance or drink.'

'We could maybe get something at my hotel. The barman half hinted he'd got a couple of bottles under the counter.'

'Can't we just talk, Mike? It's so lovely and cool, now. And you haven't told me what you got up to in London. Was the air raid bad?'

'Bad enough, but I didn't get up when the sirens went. I thought "What the hell?" and I put my head under the bedclothes and let them get on with it. I was browned off, I guess, with the medics. No joy, they said, when I told them I was fit. I'm to see them again in September for another check-up. Meantime, I was told to exercise my leg.'

'Fine. We walk, then.'

'Aw, the heck to it! Like I told them, you don't fly a fighter with your legs. What about Duggie Bader? I wanted to know. But they put me in my place all right. "Bader is Bader," they said; end of conversation!'

'Poor love. You *are* sorry for yourself, aren't you?'

'Well, wouldn't you be, Lucy? We're short of pilots yet I'm stooging about at Machrihanish, which is a *naval* air station, I'll have you know, trying to look like I'm busy.'

'Then why send you there?'

'We-e-ll, I suppose it's an open secret that Spitfires and Hurricanes are being adapted for use on aircraft carriers, and I'm there, I reckon, because I've flown both and can help the Navy pilots get the feel of them. But half the time they don't know where I am. That's why I'm here now. They think I'm in London till tomorrow night.'

'Mike! That's awful of you, going absent without leave. Don't you know there's a war on?'

'You bet your life I do, honey, and I sure as hell want to get back into it!'

'Well, you can't just yet, so where shall we walk?'

'How about back to Ardneavie? We can take it easy, and talk. Or not talk. What time do you have to be in?'

'Eleven. But remember, you'll have to walk all the way back.'

'So? Didn't the quack say my leg needed exercise?' Amiably he took her hand in his again. 'Now tell me what you've been doing with yourself, Lucy. Everything.'

'Why, Mike?' She glanced up sharply, anxious again. 'Can't we just talk about – oh, anything but me?'

'Ships and shoes and sealing-wax?'

'If you like.' But not about us, her eyes begged him. Please, not about us.

So they walked, hardly speaking. And they sat at the roadside beside Loch Ardneavie, watching from a distance the ships at their buoys, and the launch bringing liberty-men ashore, and the little planing dinghy that bounced between ships, carrying messages, doing the bidding of

235

Omega's officer of the watch. And sometimes, when they were very still, they could hear the bosun's pipe, shrill and high, carrying across the water. But always they held hands, bodies touching, not wanting to be apart, and Mike Farrow frowned, knowing it was the same for Lucinda, too. He could sense it in every nervous movement, in the downcast eyes that suddenly would not meet his.

'You know we've fallen in love?'

They stood in the garden, saying goodnight in the gathering dusk. She was cradled gently in his arms and the suddenness of his words shocked her.

'Mike, *no!*' He felt her start, felt the stiffening of her body as she tried to pull away from him. But he held her tightly, making little hushing sounds, his lips against her cheek.

'Yes, Lucy, *yes!* Say it! Say "I love you too, Mike."'

She shook her head fiercely. She wouldn't say it; couldn't say it. She wouldn't even let herself think it. 'It's nearly eleven. I've got to go.' Her words were clipped and shrill with tension. 'It's been fun. Thank you so much for a lovely evening.'

'Oh, cut out the niceties, for God's sake! We've got things to talk about, you and me. I'll see you tomorrow night, same time.'

'No, Mike. Not any more. Anyway, I can't – '

He silenced her protests with his lips. He kissed her long and hard, kissed her until her head sang with the delight of it. And because her legs would no longer support her she clung desperately to him, eyes closed.

'Tomorrow night,' he said again.

'No! I can't. Tomorrow I start late watches for a week.'

'What time do you go on board?'

'Noon, but – '

'What time shall I be here, then?'

'I don't know. There'll be the cabin to clean and the floor to – '

'Ten o'clock? That'll give us a couple of hours. Okay?'

She nodded, unspeaking. She had no choice but to meet him and tell him about Charlie. 'This is the last time,' she would tell him. 'You mustn't love me, Mike. I'm going to be married, you see – probably on my next leave. I should have told you about him – Charlie, my cousin, the man on the snapshot I gave you.' It would hurt him, but it would hurt her, she thought bitterly, much, much more.

'Okay, I said?' Mike demanded harshly.

'Yes,' she whispered. 'Ten o'clock – here, at the back of the Wrennery.'

He didn't speak again. Taking her jaw in his hand, he turned her face to his. Then he kissed her gently and walked abruptly away.

'Goodnight,' she murmured, but already he was gone.

Lucinda nodded to the duty Wren who sat outside the regulating office.

'Bainbridge. Late pass,' she jerked, walking to the mess hall, not wanting just yet to face Vi and Jane. But nothing remained on the standeasy table; no bread, no margarine or jam, and the tea in the pot was cold.

'Damn!' But she wasn't hungry; merely seeking a few minutes alone before going upstairs, a few minutes in which to pull herself together, to breathe in deep, calming gulps of air and slow down her pounding heart.

Mike must not love her, and after tomorrow she must never see him again or phone him or write to him. She was going to marry Charlie; she *wanted* to marry him. Dear Charlie, whom she had known since she could remember. Perhaps her mother had been right all along. It was time she stopped prevaricating and fixed a date for their wedding. She would write home tomorrow and tell

237

them what she had decided. She placed her hands on her burning cheeks, then lifting her chin she opened the cabin door.

'And where the 'ell have you been?' Vi flung.

'Been? You know where I've been.'

'Oh, of course I do, but I didn't know you were on a late pass. The duty Wren'll be doin' last rounds soon, and Jane isn't in!'

'Okay, then. I'll go down and check the pantry window. She'll be with Tom. It'll be all right, Vi. We can say she's in the bathroom or somewhere.'

'Can we heck as like! And it isn't just tonight. What are you goin' to tell the Chiefie on board when she doesn't show for late watch, eh?'

'Oh, no! She hasn't . . .?'

'She flippin' has! She's gone AWOL, that's what. She must've caught the four o'clock ferry. And you'd better read this.' Vi thrust a sheet of notepaper at Lucinda. 'She's gone looking for Rob's mother, that's what!'

Dear V & L,

Have gone to Glasgow. Don't stick your necks out for me. I don't know when I'll be back, so report me AWOL tonight.

Wish me luck!

J.

'Oh, Lord!' Lucinda folded the note and handed it back. 'What's going to happen to her if she can't find her way there? She'll get herself lost in the blackout, most likely, and all alone, too.'

'Well, if that turns out to be the case, let's hope she'll have the sense to try to get back to the station. At least she'll be all right there and she'll be able to catch the first boat train back.'

'Yes, but she'll still be too late to go on watch, even if

she does. And that's if she's lucky and the crushers don't pick her up somewhere along the way and ask for her leave pass. We're going to have to do as she asks, Vi.'

'I don't want to,' Vi said stubbornly.

'And do you think I do? But we don't have a choice, do we? I'll do it, if you like.'

'No you won't. We'll both go. It's still one for all, isn't it? But we won't tell Chiefie about this letter, eh? Let's just say that she's late in – all right?'

Lucinda nodded and opened the door. 'Come on, then.'

'She'll be up to the ear 'oles in trouble when she gets back.'

'Yes, but she won't care; it will all have been worth it.'

'Worth it? By the heck,' Vi muttered, 'I hope you're right, queen. Ar, well, let's get downstairs and get it over with!'

Chief Wren Pillmoor was listening to the wireless, humming softly with the dance band, feeling soothed and almost at peace with her world when the knock came; an urgent, purposeful knock that made her whisper, *'Now* what?'

Clicking off the set, she looked up at the mantel clock. Eleven twenty. Someone not in who should have been, most likely. 'Right, then, what is it?' she demanded, opening the door.

'Won't keep you, Chief, but can we come in?' Vi asked, stepping inside without invitation, to be closely followed by Lucinda. 'It's Kendal, see. She's adrift.'

'And did she have a late pass?'

'No, Chief.'

'Then she's nearly an hour adrift, and since there are means of entry to this house other than by the front door, I take it there's more to it than that? Well, you wouldn't be here if there weren't, would you, McKeown?'

239

By the heck, Vi thought with grudging admiration, Patsy Pill hadn't come down with the last fall of soot, and that was for sure.

'You're right, Chief,' she admitted.

'Where is Kendal?' Pat Pillmoor gazed at each Wren in turn; a gimlet gaze that demanded an answer.

'We don't know, exactly,' Lucinda offered. Well, they didn't; not *exactly*.

'Then where approximately? Glasgow?'

Eyes gazed at shoe toes. Neither Wren spoke.

'Glasgow it is, then. And I suppose you both knew she intended going, even though Ma'am had refused her a pass?'

The silence grew. Lucinda shuffled her feet. Vi coughed.

'All right. If you are both determined not to help your friend, you leave me no choice. I must get a patrol to pick her up.'

'Chief! There's no need for that! She's only goin' – ' Vi stopped abruptly.

'Going *where*, McKeown?'

'That's it, you see. We really don't know, Chief.' Lucinda took a step nearer to Vi, an instinctive closing of ranks.

'Pipe down, Bainbridge, and don't speak until you're spoken to! *Where*? I asked!'

'Ar, hey, Chief. Kendal's all right. She won't get into any trouble,' Vi pleaded.

'Won't she just! Well, she's in trouble already!' the Chief Wren snapped. 'Kendal's not just adrift, she's absent without leave, and that, in the Women's Royal Naval Service, spells trouble, I'll have you know. So the sooner you both come clean, the better. Now, let's start again. Kendal *has* gone to Glasgow, hasn't she?'

'We think maybe she has, Chief, but we don't know

where, honestly we don't,' Lucinda whispered. 'Even Jane doesn't know.'

'*What*! You mean she's gone off on some wild-goose chase? The stupid little idiot! What time did she leave?'

'We're not sure, Chief. We think she'd get the late-afternoon ferry. She told us nothin', see? Suppose she didn't want to land either of us in it.' Vi was anxious now. 'And Lu – Bainbridge is telling the truth. We don't know where she's making for, only that it's near a bread shop.'

'She's looking for a man, isn't she? She's got to be.'

'No, Chief. The man was reported missing two months ago. Kendal's looking for his mother, and that's all we know,' Lucinda offered reluctantly, the tilting of her chin confirming that no more information would be forthcoming.

'Looking for a bread shop in Glasgow? Lord preserve us!' Pat Pillmoor's eyelashes swept beseechingly upward. Well, there was nothing else for it. Much as she disliked doing it.

'Right, you two, cut along, and if either of you is keeping anything back that might have been of help, then you're both in it with Kendal. *Deep!*'

'There's nothin', except that the woman she's lookin' for is called MacDonald,' Vi offered.

'Thanks a lot, but there are more MacDonalds in Glasgow than bread shops!' Chief Pillmoor was clearly not impressed. 'Oh, get off to bed, the pair of you!'

The door closed softly. Patricia Pillmoor lit a cigarette, inhaled deeply then lifted the telephone. It was connected to the regulating office on board HMS *Omega* and it was answered at once.

'Ah, Chief! Pat Pillmoor here. Do me a favour. I've got a Wren gone AWOL and she's heading for Glasgow. Man trouble, I think, so I want her picked up, if possible

241

– for her own good, naturally. Anything you can do to help?'

'I wonder where she is.'

'Thought you were asleep, Lucinda.'

'No chance. It's those creaking bedsprings of hers. I miss them.'

'What time is it?' Vi punched her pillows then arranged her hands behind her head.

'Nearly two, I think. Wonder what she's up to.'

'Lord only knows,' Vi whispered, 'and He'll not tell. I mean, she wouldn't get there till late, so surely she wouldn't go looking for McFadden's tonight – not with the blackout coming on. Maybe she's hanging around the station till morning.'

'Well, I hope not, because if she does she'll get stopped and asked for her pass. Central station is swarming with crushers. No,' Lucinda frowned, 'if I were in Jane's shoes I'd get a bed for the night; not the YWCA – she'd be too easy to find there. But there are plenty of places around the station. She should be able to get something for a couple of bob.'

'Don't!' Vi pleaded. 'Now you're really gettin' me worried.'

'Then don't be, Vi. Jane was meant to find Rob's mother, so what can go wrong?'

'Nothin', I suppose, except that when she does get back she'll be up at defaulter's so quick her feet won't touch the floor.'

'And do you think that's going to worry Jane? It will all have been worth it, in the end.'

'But will it?' There was a strange crawling sensation at the back of Vi's neck whenever Glasgow was mentioned. 'Oh, don't get me wrong; I want the poor kid to be lucky, but what's it goin' to do to her if Rob's mother has heard

242

the worst, and tells her? What if the Air Force has said he's dead, now? Jane's nuts about the feller. It would finish her.'

'But Vi, you once thought Gerry had been lost at sea, didn't you?'

'Ar, well . . .' Vi sighed, and surrendered. There was no answer to such burning optimism. No answer at all.

10

When they awoke the sight of Jane's empty bed brought them face to face with reality again.

'Terrible, innit?' Vi's eyes met Lucinda's. 'It's as if a part of us has gone missing.'

'It has,' Lucinda said soberly. 'I wonder where she is and what she's doing.'

Now it was Lucinda's turn to have doubts and Vi's to be the comforter.

'She'll be all right, queen. She'll be back here tonight, right as ninepence and twice as cheeky. Just see if she isn't.'

They turned as the door opened without ceremony.

'Nothing?' Chief Pillmoor asked briefly.

'No, Chief.' Vi shook her head. 'Sorry.'

Strangely apprehensive, they went down to breakfast; no tea and toast in the cabin this morning. Unspeaking they jammed bread and ate it without tasting it.

'You've heard nothing, I suppose?' Lilith set her plate on the table and sat down beside them.

'By the heck, but bad news travels fast,' Vi muttered. 'And no, there's nothin' to tell. She's gone to Glasgow looking for Rob's mam, we *think*.' No need to mention the note. 'Who told you, Lilith? Didn't think anybody would know about it yet.'

'I was down in Craigiebur yesterday afternoon. I saw her at the jetty, waiting for the ferry, and I guessed what she was up to.'

'And what do you think about it?' Vi asked. 'Got any *feelings*, like?'

'None at all.' Lilith shrugged. 'But we could get the glass out later.'

'No, ta. Best we don't meddle.' Vi sighed. 'Let's just leave it and hope for the best.'

They were making their beds when Lucinda told Vi.

'Look, I'll be popping out soon,' she murmured. 'I'm meeting Mike at ten – '

'Oh, yes.' Vi concentrated on enveloping the bed corners.

'Vi, I've *got* to see him. Things seem to be getting out of hand, sort of. Mike's got it into his head that he's – well, attracted to me, so there's nothing for it but to – '

'So you still haven't told him about Charlie?'

'No, but I will. I'll tell him this morning. I'll have to, Vi. But when I do he'll understand. We'll be able to say goodbye then, like civilized people.'

'And are you attracted to Mike?' Vi demanded with true Liverpool directness. 'Isn't that what it's really all about?'

Lucinda gazed at the anchor on her bedcover for several seconds. 'Yes, I'm afraid I am. I don't think I'm in love with him,' she frowned, 'but when I'm with him I'm as jumpy as a kitten, and when he kisses me – oh, he does it so beautifully . . .'

'Hmmm. So now you're goin' to send him back to Machrihanish and that'll be the end of it – is that what you think?'

'That's right. And I'm going to marry Charlie, so you can stop looking at me like that!'

'I'm not lookin' at you like anythin' at all.' Vi drew in a deep, steadying breath. God give her patience! If only she had a silver shilling for every time Lucinda had said she was going to marry that Charlie, she'd be rich! 'But you're too near the problem to see things straight. And it isn't

245

any business of mine, queen, but do something for me, eh? Before you say anything at all to Mike, think about it, will you?'

'Sorry, Vi, but there's nothing to think about. I don't have a choice, really.' Lucinda wielded the floor mop with unnecessary ferocity. 'I don't even *want* a choice. I shall marry Charlie.'

'I know. Lord knows, you've said it often enough. And you'll have your babies and bring them up at Lady Mead – with Nanny's help, of course. You've got it all cut and dried, haven't you?'

'Yes, I have,' she flung with unaccustomed stubbornness.

'Well then, you'd better get yourself washed and changed. Leave the cabin to me,' Vi ordered. 'Go on. Chop, chop!'

Without speaking, Lucinda gathered up towels and sponge bag. Eyes downcast, she left the room, closing the door quietly behind her.

'Aaah!' Letting go her breath, Vi sat down heavily on the bed. What a mess it all was. A right load of trouble she'd landed herself with that night at the RTO's office. Pleadingly she raised her eyes to the ceiling.

Listen, Lord. Will you tell me what I'm to do with the pair of them? The end of it, eh? Going to marry Charlie, was she? And Mike Farrow would understand? A pig's ear he would! And as for Jane and her love life! *Will you just tell me, eh?*

Lucinda closed the garden gate behind her, sighing with relief that Chief Pillmoor had not called her into the regulating office for another inquisition. She was early. Mike wouldn't be here yet, which gave her time to compose herself and think out exactly what she would say to him.

She walked past the greenhouse, where already tomatoes were ripening, and on to the vegetable plot, where the Wren gardener was pricking out lettuces. Lucinda had only recently got to know the gardener, a quiet, elderly woman called Miriam who kept herself to herself. A little old to be in the women's forces, she considered. She must be at least forty, and women of her age group would not be called on to register for ages yet. Molly Malone said Miriam had worked for a professor at Oxford, and Lilith had told her that the small, grey-haired woman had had a sweetheart in the Flying Corps in the last war who was killed the day before the Armistice.

The gardener straightened her back and smiled.

'Hullo. Lovely drop of rain we had, wasn't it? Oh, and he's waiting for you . . .' She inclined her head towards the woodland garden, an up-sloping tangle of silver birch trees and rhododendrons and foxgloves and lush green grass; an area too wild ever to fear the invasion of peas and beans and cabbages.

Lucinda smiled her thanks, wishing her heart would behave, repeating in her mind the words she would say.

. . . *so you see, Mike, that's the way it is – I should have told you and I'm truly sorry I didn't – but you do understand . . .?*

She climbed the stone-slab steps, counting them as she went, telling herself to be calm, wondering whether the turmoil inside her was apprehension or joy or a mixing of both.

He was sitting on the grass, knees raised, his back against a tree. He smiled and patted the grass beside him, and she took off her hat and laid it with her respirator beside his.

'Hullo, Mike.'

'Hi, honey.' He shifted his position so that their shoulders touched. Taking two cigarettes from his case, he lit them and passed one to her, an intimate gesture which gave her pleasure.

'You were early, Mike.'

'Guess so. Couldn't sleep.'

'Nor me.'

'Hey! Will you look at that?' Gently he traced the dark rings beneath her eyes. 'What kept you awake, Lucy? Something's worrying you. Tell me.'

'It's Jane. I spent most of the night thinking about her. She's gone AWOL; off to Glasgow, looking for Rob's mother. Chiefie was livid. She looked in this morning with a face like thunder. I suppose she was on her way to tell Ma'am about it.'

'Don't worry. Everything seems worse after a bad night. At least I'm not to blame for those shadows, though I did rush it a bit last night, I reckon. Sorry.'

'That's all right.' So he was sorry, now. He hadn't meant what he'd said. He didn't love her. 'It really doesn't matter. In fact it makes it easier for me to tell you about – well, that I'm – I'm going to be married.' The words came in a rush, spoken to the grass at her feet.

'About – to – be – *what*?' Each syllable hissed out like a bullet. 'Say that again!'

'Married. To Charlie.' Slowly she raised her eyes. His face was white, his mouth set traplike, the scar on his cheek a livid red weal. 'I should have told you right at the start, Mike, but I thought it didn't matter. After that first time, I didn't think we'd be meeting again.'

'But we did meet; it was inevitable. Like us falling in love was inevitable.'

'But I'm *not* in love with you! I never once said –'

'No, you didn't. You didn't have to say anything because I know when we're together that you *are*. You want me, Lucy, every bit as much as I want you, so don't make with your high-society manners! Admit it, woman!

248

You want me to undress you, don't you? You want me to touch you, kiss you – '

'Stop it! I won't listen, I *won't*.' She turned from him, eyes closed.

'Okay. Stick your head in the sand, then. Pretend that none of this has happened. Anyway, who is he? The guy on the snap is it?'

'Yes. That's my – my fiancé.'

'So why didn't you tell me then, all nice and easy? "My fiancé", you could have said, not "my cousin". Well, I'll tell you why you didn't say it. It was because even then you knew about us.'

'All right!' Savagely she crushed out her cigarette. 'I like you, Mike, and yes, I think I'm attracted to you, but – '

'*Think*! Hell, *think* doesn't come into it. You should be sure. You should be so sure that even the thought of spending another night without me tears your guts out! Do you know what it's really about? Have you ever been loved, *properly* loved, Lucy?'

'Yes, of course I have.' She could not look at him. 'Charlie and I, we . . .' She pulled in a steadying breath. 'Once, on the sofa we – '

'I see. And it was good, was it, you and him on the sofa? Really got you going, did it?'

'Please! I'd rather not talk about it, if you don't mind. It's best forgotten.'

'Is it, now? Well, that's something to be thankful for, I guess. But take notice, Lucy. When *I* make love to you, you'll never forget it, that I will guarantee!'

He reached for her roughly, pulling her close, and she closed her eyes and lifted her mouth to his. This was the last time they would meet, so what did it matter? Raising her arms, she clasped them behind his neck; and when he leaned heavily against her she sank without resistance into the grass.

'Darling.' He reached for her knees, straightening them gently so that she lay supine beneath him. 'I want you.'

His mouth found hers, and it was back again – just like the night he whispered in her ear as they danced, and lovely and peculiar feelings shivered through her. Only now those feelings thrashed and crashed inside her and made her want to strain closer so that every part of them touched and loved and sent off sparks. *You want me to undress you.* Yes, she did. She damn well did! Undress her slowly, his hands touching every part of her and his lips and his tongue –

'No!' God in heaven, what was she thinking about? 'Mike, please, *no*!'

With all her strength she pushed him away, then pulling her knees to her chin she hugged herself into a tight, impenetrable ball.

'Why, darling, *why*?' Another minute, just one more minute! 'What's with you? Admit it, honey. Say it! Say, "I love you, Mike. I want you." Go on, Lucy.'

'All right, I do love you, and yes, yes, *yes*! I want you, too. But I'm going to marry Charlie. I am, Mike.' She was shaking violently now. 'It's all settled and there's no getting out of it.'

'There's got to be! Now hear this good!' Taking her face in his hands, he turned her eyes to his. 'Look at me, Lucy! I love you, I want you and I sure as hell will have you. And I give you fair warning, lady, that I shall not fight fair!'

'Oh, be quiet! You don't know what you're saying.' Her voice rose shrilly. 'There's so much you don't know about me.' She had to make him understand, convince him that it simply wasn't done like this. There was an order of things she had been brought up to accept and

250

respect. She was going to be married. All right, so they had never got around to announcing it in *The Times* or the *Tatler*, but their engagement was fact. Everyone knew it.

'Know about you? That your father's an earl, for instance? You didn't intend mentioning that either, I suppose?'

'How did you know?' Her head jerked up. 'It really isn't any of your business, but who told you?'

'The postman in Bruton Street told me, as a matter of fact.'

'Bruton Street? Just what were you doing there?'

'It's a free country, isn't it? As a matter of fact I'd been to the Haymarket to pick up some kit, and it suddenly hit me that your place couldn't be all that far away . . .'

'The morning after a raid, you went shopping then calmly strolled down Bruton Street?' This was bordering on the ridiculous, she thought wildly, but at least it gave her a chance to pull herself together.

'Why not? As good a time as any, I'd say. And the bombs didn't stop the postman. "Hey, pal," I said to him, "which is the Bainbridge house?" And he told me I was standing right next to it and that I'd just missed the Earl. "He went out not a minute ago – you'd pass him at the top of the street – the gentleman in Home Guard uniform," he said.'

'So?'

'So I put two and two together, but there's still a couple of things I'm not sure about. Want to tell me?'

'Well, it's true, I suppose. My father really is an earl – oh, light us a cigarette, will you?' She handed him her packet.

'Say, "Please, darling."'

'Please, darling.' The endearment came easily, naturally.

'That's better. Didn't hurt, did it?' He smiled, giving her the lighted cigarette.

'Well, Pa being the Earl of Donnington is really what my marriage to Charlie is all about.' She settled herself against him, her free hand searching for his. 'If I'm really truthful I've got to admit that it tidies things up, keeps everything in the family, sort of. I'm not just an only child, you see, but a *female* only child, and when Pa dies everything will pass to his brother, my uncle Guy. And one day, Charlie will inherit. It's the way things are, Mike. It's what I always wanted.'

'You've got it all worked out, haven't you? Everything just as it always was, and you the lady of the manor.'

'I'm Lady Lucinda already, Mike. I've grown up with it. It's a part of what I am, because of where and to whom I happened to be born. Oh, I know Americans think titles obscene and obsolete.'

'Doesn't bother me one way or the other, though it'll please the old lady, come to think of it. Still likes her aristocracy, Grandma does. But what the heck? We've only got an hour and we're wasting time on trivialities. Let's start again. Let's start with "I love you, Lucy Bainbridge, and I'm asking you to marry me."'

'And I – I'm afraid I love you, but I'm going to marry Charlie. I am, Mike. There's no changing it.'

'There's got to be, because there's no way I intend losing you. I'm a real stubborn guy when my mind's made up, so hear this good. I love you, I want you and I'll get you.' He drew her to him. 'Close your eyes and let me kiss you.'

'No. You'll get me all het up again.'

'Okay, okay. Point taken. But don't say you don't want me!'

'Hell, of course I want you, Mike Farrow. I want to

252

know that loving is good, not like it was – ' She stopped, red-faced.

'Not like it was with Charlie on the sofa? My darling girl, it'll be nothing like that.'

Slowly he unfastened the buttons on her jacket and she closed her eyes and he kissed her again, his tongue forcing her lips apart, relaxing her mouth. Nor did she stop him when he undid the small buttons on her shirt. She wanted him to. She wanted him to kiss her breasts, kiss every part of her. She wanted him to –

'No! *Don't*!' She shook her head despairingly. 'Please don't. We mustn't. We *can't*!'

'We *can*, Lucy, we can.' He was kissing her lips, her eyelids, the little pulsating hollow at her throat.

'Mike! Listen to me. We can't, I tell you. Not at half-past ten in the morning. It isn't decent!'

For just a moment longer he held her, then he pushed her a little way from him as the tension inside him snapped and slowly left him.

'Darling,' he whispered. 'My lovely, lovely darling.' She was so innocent, this Lucy of his. *Not at half-past ten in the morning!* He threw back his head and laughed. 'Hell, how I love you!'

And she loved him, God help her. 'Mike, what am I to do?'

'Do? If I had my way you'd write the guy a dear-John letter right now then marry me.'

'Don't be an idiot. And anyway, I'm not twenty-one yet. Can you imagine Pa giving me his permission?'

'But you don't need permission. A woman is of age at seventeen according to Scottish law.'

'But I'm English.'

'Doesn't matter. You've been living in Scotland for more than three weeks, haven't you, so you qualify, Scottish or not. I know. I've been making enquiries.'

'Don't say any more.' It was *not* possible, Scottish law or not. Imagine the scandal, to say nothing of the gossip. Her mother would hit the roof and there'd be nobody on her side, not even Goddy. 'I just won't listen.'

'All right, sweetheart. I know how you must be feeling right now so I'll not push it for the time being.' Come to think of it, this was neither the time nor the place. 'But think about what I've said – about what we've *both* said – and promise me you won't let them talk you into changing your mind.'

'I promise. But I can't tell Charlie yet. I just don't know how.'

'Okay – so you love us both, but you love me more?'

'I – I – yes. At this moment I do.'

'Fine. That'll do for a start. Now tell me you do.'

'I love you, Mike Farrow,' she choked, her lips close to his cheek. 'Oh, when we're like this, I love you so very much. But give me time.'

Bending down, he picked up their respirators and hats. 'We've got half an hour yet. Let's go to the top of the brae.'

He took her arm in his and they walked close, thighs touching. He did not tell her again that he loved her, nor she him. For a little while longer they were in a world of their own creating, so there was no need, when reality belonged in the other, faraway world.

'Here, put this inside you – it's all I could manage to get.' Vi pushed pudding plate and spoon at Lucinda. 'And hurry up. The launch'll be at the jetty in a couple of minutes. You cut it fine, didn't you?' she demanded, eyes on the window.

'We went walking up the brae and we didn't notice the time.'

'And you still haven't told him, I'll bet.'

'I have. He knows.'

The sudden bright smile quickly vanished. Yes, he knew about Charlie, but what difference would it make? Close to Mike, nothing had mattered, but here, alone again, she was forced to admit that nothing had been resolved. She was in a worse mess than ever, in fact; promised to one man, in love with another.

'Vi, there's something I've got to tell you, something – '

'Not now. The launch is coming. You'll have to go.' Vi retrieved discarded hat and gloves. 'Where's your respirator? And look at your shoes. They're a disgrace!'

'Hell!' Quickly Lucinda rubbed shoe toes against stocking legs. 'Look, we'll talk later, okay? See you then.'

It was not until she was running down the jetty that she really missed Jane. Going on board alone seemed strange, and what Chief Wetherby would say about being a coder short, heaven only knew. Oh, please, *please* let everything have gone right for Jane and let her be on her way back, this very minute, she prayed silently.

'Get a move on, Bainbridge!' Connie Dean called, boathook at the ready. 'We haven't got all day!'

Lucinda scrambled aboard, her eyes meeting Lilith's, shaking her head in answer to the unspoken question.

Oh, Jane, be lucky – wherever you are.

So far, Jane Kendal had been very lucky. She had caught the ferry without mishap, though it had made a slow crossing against the wind and the delayed Glasgow-bound train had had to give way to a goods train carrying tanks and ammunition in steel boxes. The passenger train had been halted, shunted into a siding and there it had stood until the ammunition train thundered past.

No one waiting there had complained; there was a war on and dissent of any kind was unpatriotic. And who knew but that the ammunition and tanks were bound for

255

Russia, and please God they would not arrive there too late.

The ferry connection pulled into Central station two hours and ten minutes late, and Jane had long ago decided to find a bed for the night and begin her search in the morning.

So far her luck had held; she had not even seen a naval patrol much less been stopped and asked to show her leave pass. What would happen when she returned to Ardneavie she had no way of knowing, but nothing they might do to her could take away from the pleasure of finding Rob's mother. The bad dream she had lived through for so long was over, and if the news of Rob would perhaps not be all she craved, at least it would not be wholly bad, of that she was sure. Rob was not dead; she knew it with absolute certainty. At this moment he could be on his way home to her, being hidden by day, travelling in the company of the maquis by night, making for the Spanish border and freedom.

Jane's luck continued to hold. She found a room in the first small hotel at which she enquired.

'Alone, are you?' the receptionist asked pointedly.

Nodding, Jane met her eyes. She signed the register, giving her home address, thinking about the night in York that had never been. 'Quite alone,' she smiled.

'Breakfast at eight sharp.' The receptionist held out a key and Jane smiled again, too happy to be in the least put out by the middle-aged, disapproving stare.

She slept well, and was delighted to find the luxury of hot water in which to wash, then breakfasted on dried eggs, cleverly scrambled, toast and bright red jam, and a large mug of saccharin-sweetened tea.

It was half-past eight when she boarded the Maryhill tram. Excitement pulsed through her. She knew exactly where to alight, thanks to Jock's precise instructions, and from there on all that remained would be to find Jimmy McFadden's corner bakehouse. It could be in any one of six apartment blocks standing in close proximity, Jock had told her, at the same time warning her to keep to the streets and not even to think of taking a short cut down a close, no matter how safe it might appear.

She remembered all he had told her, yet she was not prepared for the desolation of the area when she left the tram and stood to watch its clanking, swaying rear end as it rounded a bend and disappeared from her view. The destruction was terrible to see: huge buildings sliced cleanly into two, doors opening on to yawning voids, shattered windows that stared back at her like dead eyes. What had prompted Rob to volunteer to fight for this? she silently demanded with shuddering distaste. Had it been her, she wouldn't have lifted a finger to save these streets from Hitler's bombs. Yet they were Rob's home and he had thought them worth fighting for, she thought to her shame. And maybe when the war was over, he would do as Jock had done and make his home elsewhere. Move on and move up.

She completely encircled the first of the blocks – what the German bombers had left standing. There was no bakery there, no picture palace with *Pavilion* above its doors. Boys stood in groups on each corner, some of them making clicking noises as she passed or long-drawn-out wolf whistles, but she walked on without turning. Women were beginning their daily shopping, knowing instinctively where to find the tomato queue, the one-orange-per-child queue and the queue for ration-free offal, and which butcher had found enough meat scraps to make into sausages and would be selling them, one to each ration book, at ten o'clock. Such news circulated the tenements and was rarely found to be inaccurate. And after two or three hours spent waiting, a housewife might even be able

257

to provide an off-the-ration meal for her family; if the queuing had gone well, of course.

Jane smiled as she passed, wondering if one of them might be the woman for whom she searched. Only then did it occur to her that having found the bakehouse and by some small miracle the apartment she sought, who was to say that its occupant had not gone out to join the queues or left to do her war work or even gone away to visit a friend on the far side of the city?

But that could not be, for in that first moment of doubt, Jane's nostrils had picked up the aroma of baking bread and she set out towards it.

She found the Pavilion picture palace first, then there it stood, exactly as Jock had described, *J. McFadden & Sons. Bakers and Confectioners*. Jimmy McFadden, who placed his neighbours' loaves to bake when the last of his own bread had been set to cool. Here, at last, was the tenement in which Rob's mother lived.

'Aye,' said the lady behind the bread shop counter, 'I mind Mrs MacDonald fine. She's no' left any baking the day; well, with her three boys away, she doesn't call so much. But you'll find her on the second landing, second door on your left, hen. Visiting, are you?'

'Yes, I am.' Jane's smile reflected her complete happiness. 'And – thanks.' How many, many thanks, dear nice lady with the flour-smudged pinafore, you can't begin to know.

The bell tinkled as she closed the door, a happy, homely sound that compensated in part for the boarded-up doors and windows of almost half the apartments she passed. But the one she sought had bright, shining windows, a green-painted door and a well-scrubbed doorstep. And to the left of the door, polished to an amazing brightness, a

258

brass nameplate announced that here lived M. J. MacDonald. Margaret Jean, Rob had once told her. Heart thudding, Jane lifted the knocker. *Don't be out, Mrs MacDonald. Please, don't be out.*

The door was quickly answered.

'Aye?' said Margaret MacDonald, for the woman who stood there could be no other.

'Are you Rob's mother?' Jane whispered, tears pricking her eyes. 'I'm Jane,' she smiled.

'Jane?' Brown eyes – Rob's eyes – regarded her questioningly. 'You know my son?'

'Yes. He must have told you about me. I lived at Fenton Bishop.'

'Ah, then you'd best come away in.'

The eyes were apprehensive now and for the first time Jane felt fear.

'I'm here to ask for news of him. He never gave me your address, you see. I've been a long time finding you. Can you tell me anything? Is he still missing? They haven't written to tell you that he's – he's – '

'Come in and I'll set the kettle to boil. Will you take a cup of tea?'

'No, it's all right, truly.' A woman living alone had a tea ration of two ounces a week; it wasn't fair to expect her to share it.

'Well, I'm making just a wee pot – you're very welcome to a cup.'

'If you're sure.' Jane stepped into the little lobby, off which opened two doors. Its red-tiled floor was scrubbed clean, the brass knob on each door shone. Rob had called their apartment a room and kitchen; was this it, then?

'Come away in. I'll soon have the kettle boiled.' She lit a single gas ring, which stood on a small table beside the brown sinkstone. 'Sit down, will you.'

Jane watched as she opened the window and, reaching

out, lifted a milk jug from a meat safe which hung there. Why hadn't she thought to bring some small present along, a packet of cigarettes or a bar of the chocolate that lay uneaten in her drawer?

She looked around her, at the black-polished cooking range, unlit – because of the rationing of coal she shouldn't wonder – and the clipped rug in front of it. Then she smiled, for there on the mantel above stood three photographs: two of kilted soldiers, the other of the man she loved so well.

'Oh,' she gasped. 'I have that photograph, too. It was taken in Canada, wasn't it, when Rob got his wings?'

'Aye. That's so.' Margaret MacDonald seemed strangely reticent to talk about her son. Jane frowned, watching as Rob's mother polished two china cups and saucers and laid spoons beside each, and she felt an anxiety she could not explain. It seemed that she was too taken up with the teamaking; as if she occupied herself with trifles to give her time to collect her thoughts, search her mind for some recollection of a girl it seemed Rob had not mentioned.

'I like your bed.' Jane hesitated. 'I should think it's lovely and snug in the winter.'

'It's what we in Scotland call a hole-in-the-wall bed,' the older woman supplied. 'Built into the wall, you see, with curtains to draw over for privacy. The boys sleep – *slept* – in the other room, the three of them. I'm sorry I have no sugar to give you.'

'I don't take it.' Jane accepted the cup, then, as their eyes met she whispered, 'Mrs MacDonald, you do know who I am, don't you? Jenny, Rob called me. He did talk to you about me?'

'No. I'm sorry, but I can't bring you to mind. He didn't talk a lot about anything on his last leave. Have you been friends for long?'

'Not long.' Friends? Dear, sweet heaven, *friends*? 'But we cared deeply for each other. We met at a dance at the aerodrome; I was with him the night he went missing – the eighth of May. I tried talking to the camp padre but he wouldn't give me your address. It was pure chance I found you. Please tell me you've heard that he's all right.'

'I'd like to be able to, but I can't. I got a letter from the Air Ministry telling me he was missing, but I've heard nothing else.'

'Then that's good, isn't it? It's more than two months since it happened; they'd have known by now if – '

'I don't know. I don't know how they do things. I'll show you the letter I got, if you'd like.'

She opened a drawer, then passed a long buff envelope to Jane, who took it apprehensively. Suddenly, she didn't want to read what was inside it.

'Thank you,' she murmured.

'There's a telegram inside the envelope. It came first. You can read that, too.'

Jane withdrew the small yellow envelope. The printed telegram inside it was marked *Priority* and bore Mrs MacDonald's name and address. '"Deeply regret to inform you,"' Jane whispered, '"that your son Flt/Sgt R. MacDonald is reported missing from operations over German territory Stop Pending receipt of written notification from the Air Ministry, no information should be given to the press. Letter follows . . ." Dear God, how awful. How *bald*.'

The letter dropped to the floor and Margaret MacDonald stooped to retrieve it. 'There's no' a lot more news in this. It just tells me where he was when it happened and that they hope that his aircraft landed, even that he might be a prisoner. And they said nice things about him and reminded me again I was not to speak to the press as it might prejudice his chances of being got out of Europe *if* he had managed to land safely, that is . . .'

'Oh, I'm so sorry for you.' Impulsively Jane took the older woman's hand in her own. 'But I do know how you must be feeling. I love him so much, you see. I felt so awful when they wouldn't tell me anything, and I didn't know where you lived so I couldn't write to you. But they seem hopeful, don't they?'

'Aye, that's what I thought. Then I read the last bit. About his kit, it is. They said his kit and personal effects had been carefully checked and were being sent some-where to a central depository, from whom I'd hear in due course. Sounded pretty final, that did, but they still haven't sent his things back to me.'

'And they won't, because they probably suspect he's on the run in France, or somewhere in Europe. Oh, are you sure he didn't talk to you about me? We were so close.'

'How close, child?' The question was blunt, its implication unmistakable.

Jane lifted her eyes and gazed unspeaking into those beside her.

'I see.' Margaret MacDonald shrugged. 'Then Rob had no right.'

'He had *every* right,' Jane protested. 'We both did. We were in love.'

'No right, I said,' the other woman repeated stubbornly, her eyes on the photographs on the mantel shelf. 'I brought my boys up without help, but I brought them up to be straight, to do the decent thing. Rob had *no* right.'

'Please don't be angry,' Jane begged, her cheeks flushing red. 'It wasn't like you think. Rob was my first love and he's the only man I want. Can't you see that I lost him, too? Won't you give me just a little sympathy?'

'I'm sorry, child. I don't doubt that you cared deeply for him, but this distresses me. I think you should go.'

262

'*Go?* Please, no! I came to you for news of him, for comfort. Let me stay for a while. Promise that as soon as you hear something you'll tell me. It's not much to ask, is it?'

'No, but you must forget Rob. He's not for you. And – and you mustn't come here again. I can't be a party to this. I can't.'

'A party to what?' Fear hit Jane like a slap to her face. 'What are you trying to say? Is it too much to ask – just a note saying he's all right?'

'I can't tell you any more.' The older woman's eyes were bright with threatening tears. 'And I'm asking you to forget my son. It's best that you should.'

'But *why*? And a party to *what*? You must tell me.' She was shaking now and fear was with her again, just as it had been the morning she waited in the phone box at the crossroads; just as it had been when the disembodied voice told her that Rob had not returned. 'Try not to worry,' he'd said. And now the feeling was back, and that same crawling under her skin. 'You've obviously got a good reason for all this, but don't you think I have a right to know what it is? Rob and I were – were *lovers*, doesn't that count for anything? What is wrong, Mrs MacDonald? I want to know.'

'Then you shall, and maybe then you'll understand. I won't be a party to what's going on between you and Robert. You're not to blame – how could you be? – but you must put all thoughts of my son out of your mind and not come here again. He can give you nothing. Robert is married.'

'No! I don't believe you. I won't!' Married? Rob *married*? Oh, God, God, *God*. Her words rose to a shrill cry of anguish. 'You don't like me. You don't want me here, but don't lie to me. Tell me you didn't mean it!'

The room was spinning, and she took a step towards

the mantel shelf then grasped it for support. She wanted to scream her disbelief, but there was no breath in her body. She wanted to plead with the woman who stood white-faced before her, but her lips had gone stiff. She stood, icy cold, suspended in shock.

'Are you all right, hen?' A hand, cold as her own, grasped hers. 'I'm sorry to have been so hard on you, but there was no other way.'

'But I don't believe you. I don't! Do you hate me so much?'

'I don't hate you at all. How could I? Just half an hour ago I didn't even know you existed.'

Didn't know? Then Rob really hadn't told his mother about her and he'd had good reason not to. But *married*?

'When?' she demanded harshly.

'Early March. He was on a seventy-two hour pass.'

'Yes.' Jane remembered it. She had missed him almost unbearably and had been waiting in Yeoman's Lane at seven o'clock as she always did. And when he came he kissed her urgently, hungrily, and she had taken it to mean that he had missed her, too. That same week they became lovers for the first time.

'I'll show you.' Margaret MacDonald opened the drawer again and took out the postcard-sized photograph. 'Look at it. That's him and Phemie.'

Him and Phemie. Rob and his wife shoulder to shoulder. Rob staring ahead, his eyes a blank, and the woman beside him, a carnation in her coat lapel, gazing fixedly into the camera.

'That's *her*?' God, but she was ugly! A dull, slab face; small eyes, *piggy* eyes, lashes thick with mascara; hair bleached to straw with an untouched parting of black. Ugly? She was obscene! 'She – she's *dreadful* . . .'

'She's carrying Rob's child.'

'Pregnant? How can she be? When did it happen?'

'At Hogmanay, if my reckonings are true.' Margaret MacDonald was glad it was over now. 'The bairn's due in September.'

Hogmanay? New Year's Eve. She hadn't known Rob then. There were still thirty-two days to run before that night in the sergeants' mess when they were to come together like two halves of a perfect whole and she had fallen so desperately in love. Yet thirty-two days before, that woman had conceived his child.

'What's her name?' she demanded.

'Phemie – Euphemia.'

'He doesn't love her, you know.' She was speaking to Rob's likeness now. 'It's me he loves. What happened before – it's all a mistake. When Rob comes back, he'll tell you it was. You're his mother. Why didn't you stop it?'

'Because Phemie was two months gone. Give me a better reason than that.'

'I can't. But he doesn't have to stay married to her. Divorce isn't so – '

'Divorce is wholly unacceptable.' Margaret Mac-Donald's voice cut in harshly. 'There is no such word in this house. We are all of us Catholics. Rob's marriage must stay!'

'You mean . . .?' But of course they were. She should have noticed. The religious picture above the fireplace; the crucifix above the bed; the lighted candle beside the pictures of three absent sons. 'You mean there's no way out for him?'

'No way at all. You'll have to accept it, child. No matter what might happen in the future, no matter how good the news of Rob might be, I can never let you know. Rob's marriage was a shock to me, I'll admit it, but he was married in his own church of his own free will.' She

265

touched Jane's face gently with her fingertips. 'I'm sorry. So very sorry.'

Jane gazed around her, fixing a picture of the room in her mind, for now, each time she thought of Rob, she must bring back this room and all that had happened in it. She must remember his mother's words, *'of his own free will'*. She must at all times tell herself that another woman carried Rob's child; a woman who would never let him go.

'Are you all right, Jane?'

'I'm fine, thanks.' Of course she was; fine, but sick with a feeling in the pit of her stomach as though she had taken an almighty punch and was reeling, still, from the pain of it and the suddenness. But she was all right, of course she was. She would make it back to Ardneavie, somehow. She held out her hand for her respirator. 'Just fine,' she said.

The leading hand in charge of the naval patrol at Glasgow Central station saw the girl who sat on the bench near the barrier at platform 8. *Red hair*, the description ran; *medium height, the crossed flags of a coder on her right arm.* She was sitting there, white-faced, hugging herself as if she were cold. A kid, that's all she was. He brought out his pocket book. *Kendal, Jane*, he had written there. *WRNS Quarters, Ardneavie.* Looked as if she was going back.

'Just a minute. That Jenny over there,' he said thoughtfully. 'I think she's the one we want. Maybe I'd better have a word. You lot stay here.' Alone, he crossed the platform, and even when he stood beside her she did not see him.

'Are you Kendal, then? AWOL from Ardneavie?'

'Kendal? Y-yes. Oh, yes.'

266

The face that stared up at him was white, her eyes wide. She looked lost and afraid.

'Listen, Jenny, are you all right?' He sat down beside her, concerned. 'Has anything happened?'

'No. Nothing's happened.' Just her world crumbling into little pieces, that was all. Just that she would never see Rob again, even if he got back home. Their meeting and their loving had never been. No, nothing had happened.

'And are you going back to *Omega* now, of your own free will?'

Oh, but that was good. Of her own free will, just as Rob had married *her*, that woman.

'Yes. I'm waiting for the Garvie Ferry connection.'

'So you'll be back in quarters at . . .?'

'At about ten o'clock tonight,' she whispered. 'I suppose they're looking for me?'

'Yes, they are.' He looked at her with pity. Poor little devil. Somebody, somewhere, had given her a rough ride. 'But as far as I'm concerned I haven't seen you – all right?'

'Seen me? What do you mean?'

'I mean, just be on that train, that's all.'

'I will. And thanks.'

'Don't want any thanks.' He rose to his feet. 'I'll be watching you, Jenny. Try and do another runner and I'll pick you up so fast your feet'll not touch the ground!'

'Yes,' she said, eyes fixed on the barrier. Ten o'clock tonight. There'd be Chief Pillmoor to face, and Vi and Lucinda. She didn't care about Patsy Pill but she minded a lot about her friends. What would she tell them? How would she tell them?

'Right then, Kendal . . .'

She heard him walk away, boot nails ringing, but she didn't turn her head. She ought to be worried about

267

tonight, but she wasn't. After this, she would never worry again because nothing that happened in the future would be as awful as this day, or what she could remember of this day.

How had she got here? When or how had she boarded the correct tram and what instinct had told her where to leave it? And was this day Monday still, or had time slipped by unnoticed and it was Tuesday? She had no way of knowing. All she knew clearly was that Rob was dead. Or as good as. Hope was gone now. Phemie, ugly, pig-eyed Phemie, was carrying his child. Rob belonged to someone else.

The train slid, clanking and hissing, into platform 8. Unsteadily she rose to her feet. Her stomach churned and rumbled. She was hungry, and she'd be hungrier still by the time Chief Pillmoor had had her say. She fished in her pocket for her ticket and offered it at the barrier.

'Craigiebur,' said the collector. 'Change at Garvie Quay.'

She was on her way back, and what might happen when she arrived at Ardneavie House she neither knew nor cared. But Vi would be there and Lucinda, and she'd be safe with them. Vi and Lucinda wouldn't ask questions or tell her she'd been a fool or say she'd brought it all on herself. And perhaps, when she was back in cabin 9 again, the ache inside her would lessen and maybe she would be able to weep; weep until there were no tears left in her. And Vi and Lucinda would understand.

It was five minutes past ten o'clock when Jane knocked on the door of the regulating office.

'Kendal! You're back, then.' Momentarily, Pat Pillmoor's face registered relief. 'And what the hell have you been up to? And before you tell me some cock-and-bull story, remember you'll be better advised to tell me the truth – though why you didn't confide in me in the first place I can't imagine! If you're in some sort of trouble, Kendal, well, that's what I'm here for.'

'I'm not in trouble of *any* kind, Chief.'

'But there's a man in it, isn't there?' There usually was.

'Not any longer, Chief.'

'What d'you mean, Wren Kendal?'

'Oh, it doesn't matter. And I don't want to talk about it.'

'Well, I *do*! You skip off to Glasgow after being refused permission – didn't you think there might have been good reason for Ma'am's refusal? – then you come back here after going absent without leave and say it doesn't matter. Oh, I know I'll get no sense out of you tonight, so you'd better cut along; but don't leave quarters without my permission, Kendal, unless it's to go on watch. And consider yourself remanded. Which watch are you on?'

'Starboard, Chief. Lates.'

'Right. Tomorrow morning at ten hundred hours. Be here. You'll be at defaulter's!'

'Yes, Chief.' So what, Chief? Who the hell cares, Chief? Nothing mattered any more. Nothing at all. 'Can I go now, please?'

'You don't care, do you, Kendal?' Pat Pillmoor's face registered anger and disbelief. 'You don't give a damn, do you?'

'I don't know.' She shook her head in bewilderment. 'I honestly don't know. Please don't go on and on about it. I went AWOL; I'm admitting it and I know all this is my own fault, but please let it drop because I can't take much more, I honestly *can't*.'

'What do you mean, girl?' In an instant the older woman was on her feet, only then fully noticing the pale face, the pain-filled eyes, the obvious state of shock she should have recognized minutes before. 'Tell me what

269

went wrong. There's a man in this, there's got to be, and I want to know if anything happened.'

'Nothing happened. No one laid as much as a finger on me. I just went looking for someone, that's all.'

'And you found him – and then what?'

'I found *her*.'

'And?'

'And – nothing.'

'Very well, Kendal, but I advise you to be more open with Miss St John in the morning. Remember that she and I are responsible for your welfare here, and you'd do better to accept that and not stand there in defiance. Oh, get out and get yourself off to bed. You look all in! And Kendal,' she called to the drooping defeated back, 'if MacAlister is about, tell her I said you'd better have a hot drink.' Poor kid. She looked as if a good stiff brandy would be of more use right now. Something *had* happened, Pat Pillmoor reasoned, silently debating whether or not to get in touch with sick bay and have Sister come over. The kid was suffering; she looked as if she was in deep shock. 'And put plenty of sugar in it!' she called, but there was no reply. Ah, well. Better go and tell Ma'am the little fool was back.

Wearily Jane climbed the stairs, gently she opened the door of cabin 9. Then she said, 'Hi! I'm back.'

'Bloody 'ell! And what've you been up to?' Vi yelled. 'Mother of God, we've been worryin' ourselves silly, and you just walk in and say you're back! Well, go on, then. Tell – '

She stopped, seeing for the first time the eyes wide with misery in a white, expressionless face.

'Ar. What's to do, girl? You look as if you could do with a cup of tea, or something.'

'I've had a cup of tea.' Listlessly Jane took off her hat and threw it, with her respirator, on to her bed. 'And if

270

you don't mind, I've had all I can stomach from Chiefie, so no inquests, please.'

'It wasn't good then, queen?'

'No, Vi, it wasn't. Rob's dead, you see, and I don't want to talk about it ever again – all right?'

'Dead? God, *no*! Oh, Jane love . . .' She held out her arms but Jane turned abruptly away.

'Where's Lucinda?' she demanded sharply.

'She's on watch, queen; not ashore, yet. Listen, love – '

'I'm going for a bath.' Jane hung up her jacket then kicked off her shoes. 'I need one. I stink!'

The door closed quietly, firmly. She was having none of it, Vi brooded. Whatever had happened in Glasgow, Jane was telling them nothing. God help her, the kid needed a shoulder to cry on, needed to talk to someone, to share her grief, yet there she was bottling it up inside her. 'I hate this war,' she hissed. '*Hate* it!'

Unbuttoning her overall, she hung it behind the door; slowly she undressed, then pulling on her pyjamas she switched off the light and drew back the blackout curtains, straining her eyes for the first sight of the green starboard-side light of the homecoming launch. And there was something else. This morning Lucinda had had something on her mind, of that she was certain; something to do with Mike Farrow – she'd take bets on it.

'Eh, Gerry love,' Vi murmured. 'We're in a worse state than Russia 'ere, that's what. Both of 'em in trouble. Don't know what I'm going to do with the pair of 'em, and that's a fact, lad.'

The instant she opened the door, Lucinda saw Jane's hat and respirator.

'She's back! What news then?'

'Nuthin',' Vi sighed. 'Except that – well, Rob's dead, she said.' It was the only way to tell it.

'Oh, *no*.' Lucinda closed her eyes tightly. 'You're sure, Vi? Did Rob's mother – '

'I don't know what happened, or who told her. She'll not talk about it. She just said, "Rob's dead," then went to the bathroom. She's still in there.'

'How was she?'

'Awful, queen. Bloody awful. It's like she's not properly with us. But I knew something would go wrong; I knew it.'

'We'll have to help her, Vi; be kind to her. She'll tell us.'

'I wouldn't bank on it, girl. It's gone deep. Best we leave her alone. She'll tell us when she's good and ready. Anyway, wasn't there something you wanted to talk about, Lucinda?'

'N-no. Well, compared to this, my problems just don't exist.'

'But you were bothered enough this morning – something you had to tell me, you said.'

'I – well, it was just that Mike got a little bit passionate and I'm afraid I rather liked it.'

'Now see 'ere, Lucinda! You didn't – er?'

'No, we didn't, but it'd have been easy. I wanted to, Vi. I got myself in hand, though, and there was a lot of heavy breathing and fastening up of buttons before we both got ourselves pulled together. It would have been the easiest thing in the world, Vi, and I wasn't one bit sorry or ashamed. I'm still not. All that bothers me now is that I never felt that way about Charlie.'

'Didn't you, now? Seems you've got problems, Lucinda Bainbridge.'

'Seems I have, Vi. I've been thinking about it on and

off all afternoon. Mike's wonderful. He's like no man I've ever met, but I shall marry Charlie. I *will*, Vi.'

'All right, queen. You're goin' to marry your Charlie. Did you tell Mike that?'

'Of course I did, and he said the hell I was! God, it's such a mess! I never intended all this to happen. I thought I could handle it.'

'Famous last words. Well, now you know you can't, but what you're goin' to do about it is up to you, Lucinda.'

'That's just it. I don't – *Jane*!' she gasped, turning her back on the door. 'God, Vi, what are we to say?'

'Say?' Jane whispered from the doorway. 'When there's nothing to say, you don't say anything.'

'Jane, dearest girl.' Slowly Lucinda turned to face the sad-eyed girl who stood there; then, her own eyes bright with tears, she kissed her cheek lightly. 'I'm sorry,' she murmured. 'So very sorry.'

'Right, then.' Jane hung her towel over the end of her bed. 'I'll have to be up bright and early in the morning. It's defaulter's for me at ten o'clock. What d'you think I'll get?'

'Lord knows.' Vi shrugged, eager to steer their conversation in a less traumatic direction. 'They can't take away your pay, I'm pretty sure of that, but it's good for fourteen days' stoppages, is goin' AWOL.'

'Stoppage of privileges – that's no shore leave and confined to quarters, isn't it?'

'Except for goin' on watch – yes.' Vi nodded. 'Well, you'll be able to catch up with your mendin' and letter writin', won't you, Jane?'

'Ha! It won't interfere with my love life, that's for sure,' Jane commented. 'But I couldn't care less what they do. I'm so chokka they could send me to the glasshouse for six months and I wouldn't give a damn. Funny, isn't it?' She started to laugh. 'The nearest naval glasshouse is in

273

Glasgow, isn't it? Bloody funny, that is.' The laughing continued, high-pitched, nearing hysteria. 'Really bloody funny!'

'Jane! Stop it!' Taking her by the shoulders, Vi shook her roughly. 'Stop it, or I'll hit you.' She held her hand threateningly high. 'I will, Jane.'

'All right. Go ahead. Hit me, if it'll make you happy.'

Slowly Vi lowered her hand. The laughing stopped, though its echoes hung menacingly on the air above them.

'I could do with a hot drink,' Lucinda said hastily. 'Who's coming down? They'll just have put out standeasy for the late watch.'

'Okay,' Jane agreed, shrugging into her dressing gown. 'I might as well get it over with – after all, I'll have to face them all sooner or later, won't I?'

'Yes, you will.' Lucinda smiled gently. 'But we'll be with you, Kendal dear, so don't worry.'

By the heck, Vi thought as they walked slowly downstairs, there's more to Lucinda than meets the eye. Or was it, she sighed inside her, that Lucinda was changing for the better? What had Lilith said? Something about Lucinda not being alive yet, though she'd be quite a girl, once she was. So was she really coming to life? And was it because a prince had kissed her, at last? One thing was certain though, she thought, quickening her step. Both Lucinda and Jane were upset in their different ways and there'd be no prizes for guessing where the pair of them would end up before very much longer. Next door they'd be, with the table and the glass, and both of them lapping up every word the damn thing spelled out. And she mustn't let it happen; she had promised the good Lord it wouldn't. She had done her penance for her fall from grace. After Gerry had come back to her she had confessed to the visiting priest and vowed never to meddle again with such things. It had been Our Lady and St Jude who had given Gerry back, not Lilith's glass. And when she had said her Hail Marys and attended the extra Mass she had been given and read psalms one to ten, Vi had written to Father O'Flaherty, telling him about Gerry and enclosing a ten-shilling note for a Mass of Thanksgiving to be said in St Joseph's. She was keeping to the straight and narrow now. She was keeping away from Lilith's funny religion, and she'd do her damnedest to keep Jane and Lucinda away from it too.

'Hang on!' she called. 'Wait for me, you two!'

A proper worry, that's what they were; a proper worry, God love the pair of them.

11

'So you see, McKeown, that's all I want to know. What happened in Glasgow? What makes a girl like Kendal do what she did?' Pat Pillmoor demanded. 'I'll tell you quite honestly, the state she was in when she got back had me worried.'

'And don't you think it had me worried, too?' Vi looked down uneasily. 'It still has, but what do you want me to say, Chief? Want me to land her in worse trouble than she's in already, do you?'

'You know I don't. I asked you here because I want to help her – is there anything I can tell Ma'am, a good word I can put in?'

'It's good of you, Chief, but there's nothin' you can do.' Vi shook her head dolefully. 'She's past caring what happens to her.'

'She's not got herself into trouble?'

'Is she havin' a baby, do you mean? No, she's not. She went to Glasgow lookin' for – ' She stopped abruptly, lifting her head, staring squarely into Pat Pillmoor's eyes. 'See here, Chief, I'm not snitchin' on Kendal. I didn't know she was goin' – not for sure, I didn't – but if I had I wouldn't have tried to stop her.'

'Because she was trying to find a man?'

'No, she wasn't. She went lookin' for her boyfriend's mother. She wanted news of him, if you've really got to know, Chief. Her feller went missing and yesterday she found out he was – was – '

'Dead?' Pat Pillmoor supplied, flatly.

'Yes. That's what she said. So there's nothin' you can

276

say will help her now. And there's nothin' you can do to her that's goin' to make one scrap of difference. It's a bit of sympathy and understandin' that girl needs now, not punishin'. With respect, that is,' she added hastily, realizing she had gone too far and not giving a damn about it. 'And since you're askin', Chief, I'm worried sick about her. She's not with us, you know. There's a look in her eyes that isn't natural nor normal. A bloody good weep, that's what Kendal needs, and I know what I'm talkin' about!'

Pat Pillmoor pushed back her chair and rose to her feet. It had, she supposed, been worth a try, though summoning McKeown to her office had not been the wisest of decisions. Kendal had known exactly what she was doing; the pity of it was that the outcome appeared to have been so tragic. Poor kid. Death was hard to come to terms with, at her age.

'All right, McKeown. Leave it with me. Forget we ever had this talk – all right?'

'Right, Chief.'

Patsy wasn't a bad old stick, Vi decided, heading for the galley. At least she'd tried to help. And maybe it wouldn't do any harm to take the kids a slice of toast and a mug of tea up, though they'd both said they didn't want any breakfast. By the heck, but she'd be glad when ten o'clock had come and gone, Vi sighed. No kiddin', she would.

'Hey, Kathy,' she called to the leading cook. 'Give us three hot toasts, eh? An' you couldn't nick a bit of Ma'am's butter, could you?'

Hot buttered toast. Just the thing to make them all feel a bit better.

Chief Pillmoor accepted the cup of tea Third Officer St John poured from the naval-issue, anchor-embellished pot and drank it gratefully.

'Well?' Suzie St John demanded fretfully. She had no love of defaulters' parades and the ten o'clock appointment had her strangely on edge.

'Not a lot.' Pat Pillmoor set down her cup. 'Have you finished eating? Mind if I smoke?' The visit was an unofficial one, so she passed her packet to her superior then flicked her lighter obligingly. 'McKeown wasn't exactly forthcoming, but I did get to know that Kendal went to Glasgow to see her boyfriend's mother.'

'So she wasn't – I mean, she didn't – '

'Spend the night with a man? No, Ma'am. Far from it. She was told that her boyfriend is dead, it appears.'

'Oh, *no*! The poor girl!'

'I know. It's hard on the kid.' She hadn't been all that much older, Pat Pillmoor recalled, when they had carried her husband home on a field gate, his face covered by a coat. 'But AWOL is AWOL. There's no getting round it.'

'No, Chief. And it will have to go on her record sheet, too.'

'I doubt that'll worry her a lot, right now.' She paused, hand on the door knob. 'You'll have to give her fourteen days. At least.'

'Damn it!' Suzie St John snapped to the empty room. Most times she liked her job as quarters officer and cared deeply for all the girls in her charge, in spite of the trouble they sometimes caused her, but this morning she wished with all her fervent heart she had joined the Women's Land Army. 'Damn and *blast* it!'

His Majesty's submarine *Viper*, new from the builder's Barrow yard, sailed at half-speed into Loch Ardneavie, replying to the sonorous salutes of the boom-defence vessels that had dragged back the nets to let her in, preparing to make a smart and efficient arrival at her new base.

Petty Officer Tom Tavey stood on the fore casing beside the three-inch gun, watching crewmen in clean white jerseys and caps set at a correct angle arranging themselves fore and aft of the conning tower in readiness for their homecoming.

The early-morning sun touched her new, immaculate upper structure, her white ensign streamed out in a warm, whimsical breeze. *Viper* was all new; her bulkheads gleamed white, her undented brasses shone like gold. *Viper* was a beauty and Tom Tavey wanted to join her company. He wanted to be rid of the spare-crew monotony, needed the doubtful thrill of stalk and kill, the precarious pleasure of a deep dive, then breaking surface into a still, inky blackness – to keep watch with eyes and ears as batteries were charged, and clean, cold air replaced the stale smells of submersion, and submariners took turns on the upper casing to breathe in the sweet sea-scented night air.

Ahead of them, an Aldis lamp flashed from *Omega*'s signal deck, and the planing dinghy, carrying the flotilla's morning mail, bounced on the shining wave crests towards the quarterdeck ladder.

Tom Tavey felt good. He had enjoyed the few days of sea-time; now he could look forward to a hot bath on the depot ship, see to his dhobeying, then look in at the coding-office porthole – and Jane, if she was there, of course. If she was not working late watch. If she hadn't taken off for Glasgow, as he'd suspected all along she might. But he would always take second place in Jane's affections, he accepted; even if the missing boyfriend never turned up, that was all he'd ever be.

There had been times, mind, when he had almost been on the point of wishing the bloke's Halifax had buried itself in some German bog, or caught an ack-ack shell in one of its fuel tanks. But he had not, because sailors are the most superstitious of men and know that ill-wishes rebound, and not for anything did he want to die in a coffin called *Viper*, deep on some seabed. Not even when he had wanted her so much that his body screamed with need of her had he wished Rob MacDonald ill.

Soon, he would see her; Jane, who was happy again, whose joy shone in her eyes and pinked her cheeks and made her even more beautiful.

And he'd be content to play second fiddle, grateful just to be with her, knowing that maybe he could hope for nothing more. Yes, yes and yes. Didn't they say that everything came to he who waited? Okay then, Tavey; be prepared for a long siege, my handsome, he grinned. And one heck of a wait.

Vi gave a final spit and polish to Jane's shoes.

'There you are, queen. At least she'll not find fault with *those*.' Critically she inspected the stiff white collar and freshly laundered shirt. ''ere, pass me your hat and let's give it a bit of a brush. And don't forget your gloves. You know it's full dress, at defaulter's, don't you?'

'I do, Vi. I do.' Jane smiled thinly. 'But, quite honestly, I don't much care. All I want is to get the damn' thing over and done with.'

'And you don't care that it's all going down on your record sheet; that this terrible misdemeanour will live for ever in the annals of the 15th Flotilla?' Lucinda grinned.

'Now, turn round and let's have a look at the back of you,' Vi ordered, wielding the clothes brush and removing a small white speck from a sleeve; then, finally pronouncing herself satisfied, she dipped into the pocket of her overall.

'Right then. You'd both better have your letters now.'

Jane's letter bore her mother's handwriting and she placed it, unopened, in the pocket of her jacket. Lucinda gazed at the London postmark and Charlie's large, notice-me writing. The letter inside, she knew, would be no more than a page in length and would tell her that absolutely nothing was happening; that everyone who was anyone had left town, and roll on his next leave, which, she had already calculated, was somewhere about the same time as her own. Then he would sign it *Yrs, C.* and maybe place the sign of a kiss beside it if she was lucky, adding that he'd probably give her a ring tonight, depending of course on the mood of the War Office switchboard operators or how busy he happened to be.

But he wouldn't phone her. He never did. Lucinda frowned, wishing the letter could have been from Mike, which was too stupid, really, because it was only yesterday they had met, only yesterday that —

She shut down her thoughts, her cheeks turning pink. Only yesterday she had closed her eyes and longed for him to love her, all-the-way love her. And then she had told him 'No!' Oh, why, why, *why*?

'Hey! Listen to this!' Vi gave her full attention to the reading of yesterday's newspaper, removed from the wardroom waste-paper basket at darkening-ship time. 'Them cheeky Italians have attacked Valetta Harbour and sunk all the boats there! They've got a bloody nerve, that lot!'

'Poor little Malta,' Lucinda sympathized. 'They're having a terrible time, aren't they? I suppose that, strategically, Malta is very important. Wouldn't Hitler just love to get his hands on it!'

'Well, he can't have it. It's ours,' Vi pronounced flatly, turning the page. 'Hey up! What about this, then? Five hundred and one civilians killed so far this month in air raids. Poor old civvies. Copping it up right, left and centre, aren't they?' She glanced out of the window at the wild, safe countryside, remembering Liverpool and Lyra Street and Gerry's red rose bush. 'I mean – '

'Sorry to interrupt.' Jane pulled on her hat and picked up her gloves. 'But I'd better go downstairs. Only ten minutes to go.'

'All right, queen. They can't shoot you, remember.'

'Good luck, Kendal dear,' Lucinda called sadly.

'Thanks,' Jane murmured, without looking back. And as for the rest of them – she squared her shoulders and lifted her chin – the rest of them could go to hell! Patsy Pill, Ma'am, the whole rotten 15th Flotilla. To hell and back, for all she cared.

'Come in then! Come in!' Chief Wren Pillmoor gave a pull to her tricorn hat then glanced at the wall clock.

'Now listen, Kendal. Is there anything you want to tell me that might help? Going AWOL is a pretty serious business and if I can help you, put in a good word with Ma'am I'll – '

'There's nothing, Chief, thanks.' Jane Kendal's face was an unreadable blank, her half-closed eyes showed complete indifference. 'I went to Glasgow without a pass, that's all there is to it.'

'All there is . . .' For the first time, Pat Pillmoor saw properly the torment in the young Wren's eyes, the unhealthy paleness of her skin, the dark rings beneath her eyes. Any minute now the girl was going to pass out, if she was any judge.

'Are you all right? A drink of water, perhaps?'

Unspeaking, Jane shook her head.

'Okay, then, but as soon as this is over, you go straight to sick bay ashore – and that's an order! The sooner Sister has a look at you, the better.'

'Then she'll be wasting her time if you think I'm

pregnant, because I'm not, absolutely *not*!' Jane looked pointedly at her watch. 'It's ten o'clock, Chief.'

'Fine! If that's the way you want it!' Pat Pillmoor inclined her head towards the door. 'Let's get it over with.'

When they reached the wardroom she paused. Parrot-fashion she said, 'Stay here until you are called in. Then advance smartly to the desk and stand to attention. Do not salute. Do *not* speak unless spoken to. When ordered to dismiss, leave the room smartly – okay?'

'Yes, Chief.'

'Wren Kendal, Ma'am.' The Chief's leather-gloved hand made a smart salute. 'Defaulter.'

The officer inclined her head.

'Right, Kendal! At the double! One-two, one-two, one-two, *haaaalt*!' Pat Pillmoor rapped.

Jane stood stiffly to attention, eyes focused on the picture rail opposite, wishing she could feel something – bitterness, amusement, contempt, hatred even – but she could not.

'Please read the charge, Chief Wren,' Susie St John asked firmly.

'The charge is, Ma'am, that for forty-eight hours Wren Kendal absented herself without leave or permission from Wrens' Quarters, Ardneavie, and from her designated duties on board His Majesty's ship *Omega*.'

'Thank you, Chief. Have you anything to say, Kendal? Do you accept these charges?'

'Accept, Ma'am.' Her eyes shifted a little to the left to a bluebottle that had settled there.

'But Kendal – *why*? You're the last person I'd have expected to do anything so foolish. Is there nothing that might help to – '

'Nothing, Ma'am.' Her voice was toneless, her eyes followed the fly's stop-and-start progress along the rail.

283

'Very well, Kendal. You seem set upon defiance. Seven days' stoppage of all privileges,' she snapped. 'Seven days' extra duties. Two extra squad drills. Dismiss!'

Unspeaking, Jane took a backward step, did a smart about-turn and left the room. The wardroom door closed quietly.

'Sorry, Chief,' Suzie St John said with genuine regret. 'She looks terrible and Lord only knows how she's suffering, but – '

'AWOL is AWOL, Ma'am, as I said.'

'Yes, but – look, Pat, something is very wrong. The girl looks dreadful.'

'I agree. I even suggested she went to see Sister, but she insisted she wasn't pregnant. I don't think she is, either.'

'You don't?' Third Officer St John sighed her relief. Unwanted pregnancies she could do well without. 'All right, Chief. I'll leave it to you.'

Pat Pillmoor smiled, saluted as a matter of habit and stepped outside.

'Right, Kendal! Down to the regulating office. This little lot has to go on your sheet. And you know what it entails, don't you? Seven days' stoppages means exactly that. No leaving quarters except to go on duty; you'll do three squad drills next month, instead of the compulsory one, and extra duties means that when you are not on watch you work here in quarters. You do anything the leading steward tells you to do or you work in the galley, washing up or cleaning vegetables – understood?'

'Yes, Chief.'

'And when you are not on board *Omega* you report twice a day to the regulating office, either to me or to the duty Wren – okay?'

'Yes, Chief.' Jane did not care. She was empty of emotion. She felt nothing except the pain inside her, just where she supposed her heart should be, and the insistent, mocking whisper. Always it was there, that whisper: *Phemie, Phemie*. Ugly, pig-eyed Phemie. 'I understand, Chief.'

And I wish I were dead, Chief. Oh, God, how I wish I were dead . . .

'Well?' demanded Lucinda.

'How much?' asked Vi, as Jane closed the door of cabin 9 behind her, throwing hat and gloves on her bed, peeling off her jacket.

'Can't complain, I suppose,' Jane answered, and gave them the details.

'It could've been worse,' Vi acknowledged. 'Most thought you'd get double that.'

'Won't you be able to slip out at all – not even for a crafty half up in the village?' Lucinda suggested hopefully.

'Afraid not. I've got to keep reporting to the regulating office so they can keep tabs on me.'

'Ar, well, never mind, queen. They 'aven't put a ball and chain on you and goin' on watch'll break the monotony a bit, won't it?'

'And when it's over, we'll all have a good run ashore.' Lucinda smiled brightly. 'We'll go into Craigiebur and celebrate.'

They were trying so hard to cheer her up, Jane knew, and she appreciated it, she really did, but why couldn't they leave her alone, when all she wanted was to creep into a corner, put her head on her hands, and weep!

But tears would not come and every waking moment was spent thinking about that woman, hating her with every iota of her strength.

How could Rob have done it? How could he have given her his child? How had it been, between them? Had he whispered love-words to Phemie as he had whispered

285

them to her; those same, precious words she had thought were theirs alone?

If I get pregnant, will you marry me? she had asked him. Oh, but that was a joke! It was Phemie who had his child inside her.

'Hey! You were miles away! It's standeasy time, I said. Come on downstairs, queen. You look as if you could do with a good cup of tea.'

'No. You two go.' Jane forced a smile. 'I don't want anything, honestly.'

'Ar. Come on down, eh? Nobody's goin' to say anything to you,' Vi urged. Of course they wouldn't. Half the Wrens in quarters had been on defaulter's parade for one reason or another. Nobody cared.

'No, Vi.' Jane took her mother's letter from her pocket and slit it open with her thumb. 'Think I'll catch up with the news from home.'

Please, Vi. Please, Lucinda. You're both being good and kind and I love you both for it, but let me be just a little while longer. I'll come to terms with it in my own time and in my own way, she thought. I'll even tell you the truth, one day. But not yet. Please, not just yet.

'I could kill the bastard who got Rob,' Lucinda hissed as they walked downstairs. 'Bloody shoot him, so help me, and not turn a hair.'

'Yeh,' Vi agreed, shaken. 'Shoot 'im.'

My, but Lucinda was coming out of her shell these days, Vi realized. Going on blind dates, coming in late through the pantry window, getting herself in a twist over an American. And swearing. The ladylike Lucinda was fast becoming one of the girls. She'd be spitting next! Pity she was going to marry that little snot Charlie.

'What did they give you?' asked Jock when starboard watch took over from port watch and Jane took her place beside him.

'Seven days' stoppages; seven days' extra duties. A couple of squad drills . . .'

'Then you were lucky, hen. Och, I cringed just to think what could have happened, every time I thought about it. You were a silly wee besom!'

But he had been patient when groups of figures refused to be subtracted each from the other and told her in a gentle, fatherly voice to take her time and no' to fash herself.

'So you've come back, you soft young ha'p'orth,' was all Chief Wetherby had said gruffly, and everyone else had taken their cue from him and said nothing, not even about Rob being dead.

'I'll come down to ship's sick bay with you, Jane,' Molly Malone had urged. 'You're looking dreadful, so you are. The surgeon-lieutenant's a decent feller; why don't you ask him for something to make you sleep?'

'Thanks, Molly, but I'll sort myself out in time. It'll pass.' Or so people said.

But it wouldn't pass and she would never forget. Always it would be with her, Rob and *her* together. In bed. Naked bodies close, making a child. And she, thought Jane with self-disgust, had asked Rob to spend the night in York; she it had been, when she looked back on it, who had made all the running, right from their very first meeting. And now Phemie was seven months gone; Phemie, who must also have wept for Rob, must still be worrying and waiting and hoping for news of him. And it would be Phemie they would tell when the maquis got Rob safely over the frontier into Spain or Switzerland. Because Rob wasn't dead. He *wasn't*. One day he would come home. To *her*.

Tom Tavey walked into the galley at Ardneavie House as though he had every right to be there.

'Can I talk to Wren Kendal?' he demanded, looking directly at Leading-Cook MacAlister. 'Only ten minutes.'

'Okay by me,' she shrugged, 'but you'd best go outside to the stables. Nobody'll see you there.'

'Thanks,' Jane whispered, laying down the potato knife.

'No skin off my nose, but don't be long and watch out for Patsy,' the cook warned. 'Got eyes in her backside, that one.'

'I tried to see you last night,' Tom said softly, closing the stable door, 'but the Commander sent for me. I'm leaving spare-crew – it's official. I've got a berth on *Viper*, as I wanted.' He tilted her chin, kissing her cheek gently. 'We're off on sea trials at noon, you see, so it had to be now. I couldn't go without seeing you, saying how sorry – '

'Sorry? Sorry about what?' Her eyes warned him off. She had come here to get away from potato peeling, not to talk about Rob.

'About your man,' he said gently. 'Chief Wetherby told me he was – '

'Dead?' Jane finished, her voice harsh. 'Oh, if it could only be that simple. But you see he – he isn't dead, though it's my fault they think he is. I couldn't admit it; couldn't tell people that . . .' She took in a deep, shuddering breath. 'Couldn't tell them the truth.'

'Then will it help to tell me?' He pulled her into his arms, his voice indulgent. 'And isn't it a fact that nothing matters half so much as we think it does? Maybe just to talk about it . . .'

'Talk about it? Make myself say it, you mean. Say that Rob isn't dead, but something – worse?'

'God, Jane, not . . .' Not the things he himself feared? Hadn't he always said it: best be dead rather than burned or maimed or blinded? 'They didn't tell you he's . . .' He

288

left the words hanging in the air, unwilling to give them sound.

'They told me – his *mother* told me,' she choked into the rough serge of his jacket, 'that he's – married. Married to a woman called Phemie.' Her lips were tight with distaste at the mere mention of the name, and every word hurt. 'We were lovers and all the time he was married. Can you believe it? Can you?' Her voice was high now, and wild, her eyes bright with unshed tears. 'Oh, God, what did she do to get him? What's so wonderful about her? What has she got that I haven't, because I tried; God, how I tried. I even asked him to spend the night with me.'

'No! You mustn't talk like that.'

'*Mustn't?* Not even when it's the truth? I was so besotted that . . .' She pushed him a little away, then lifting her eyes to his she demanded, 'Do you want me, Tom? Would you like to make love to me, go away somewhere on a dirty weekend, because you can, if you want to. Any time you'd like. Or don't you want me either?'

'Want you?' He let her go, anger flushing his face. 'You know damn well I do. I've thought of not much else since the day I met you, but I don't want you like *that*. I don't want it stuck on a plate under my nose, Jane; not in cold blood. God Almighty! Who are you trying to punish – me, or yourself? All right, so a man's let you down. Is it the end of the world? What's got into you, you stupid little bitch?'

'Don't call me a bitch!' Her voice rose to a tormented wail. 'Don't you *dare*, Tom Tavey!'

'Then stop acting like a tart or you'll get treated like one!'

'Aaaah!' Lunging at him, she lifted her hand. But he

289

caught it and held it, brutally firm. 'God! How I hate you!'

'Better to hate me than hate yourself,' he said softly, feeling her body go limp, relaxing his hold on her wrist. 'Oh, Jane, my poor darling.'

He gathered her to him again and he felt her body shaking against his. 'There now,' he murmured. 'Let it come. Have a good cry.'

He held her gently, rocking her, hushing her, just as her father had done that morning they told her Rob had not come back. And now she wept again for Rob in another man's arms; wept bitterly and long because this time she had really lost him. Her sobs shook her body and tore at her throat, and all the while he held her without speaking, patting her, stroking her, loving her silently.

'And shall I tell you something else?' She tilted her head, brushing her eyes with fingers that shook. 'Did you know she was two months gone when he married her? They gave him a seventy-two-hour pass so they could make it legal, then he came back to me.' She gazed pitifully up at him, then covered her face with her hands. 'The night he came back, we made love. I'd missed him so much, you see. It seemed right. I'd not have cared if I'd got pregnant. I wouldn't!'

'Hush. Be still.' He took out a handkerchief and dried her eyes, then placing it to her nose he commanded her to blow, as if she were a small child.

Obediently she did as he asked, taking in deep gulps of air, fighting the sobs that still shook her.

'Goodness, what a mess you've made of your face,' he chided, drawing her to him again, laying his cheek on her hair. 'But thank you for telling me, sweetheart. Best you should tell Lucinda and Vi now. They'll understand.'

'Yes.' She sniffed inelegantly. 'And Tom.' She touched his face with her fingertips. 'Forgive me, please.'

'Only if you behave yourself while I'm at sea and don't say any more crazy things like – ' He stopped, his eyes on the door, and she turned, following his gaze to where Kathy MacAlister stood silhouetted against the morning sunlight.

'Look, sorry, Jane, but you'd better get inside. Chiefie's on the warpath, looking for you. Wants you at the regulating office *now*. I told her I'd sent you on an errand to Miriam.'

'Hell!' Jane began to run, calling a goodbye over her shoulder, telling Tom she would see him in a week and to take care. She was almost breathless when she knocked on the door of Chief Pillmoor's office and her eyes were still wet with tears, her cheeks flushed.

'Just where have you been, Kendal? Been out, have you, when I told you not to?'

'Yes. I've been out, Chief.' She dabbed her eyes impatiently with the handkerchief she had not given back. 'I've been in the garden, crying.'

'Yes. Yes, I can see now that you have.' Pat Pillmoor's anger was gone; compassion gentled her eyes. 'Perhaps it's as well. Maybe a good weep will help.' She smiled, then shrugging her shoulders she said, 'Oh, cut along, Kendal, and for goodness' sake wash your face and powder your nose. And Kendal,' she said softly. 'It *will* pass. It will, believe me.'

'Yes, Chief.' But it won't pass, Chief. I won't let it. And as long as I live I'll hate that woman; hate her with my last breath, too. 'Thanks, Chief.'

Kathy MacAlister was filling the standeasy teapot when Jane returned to the galley.

'All right?' she asked, over her shoulder. 'Any trouble?'

'No. I don't know what Chiefie wanted – probably just checking up on me. All she told me was to wash my face.'

'Well, then, get along and do as she says, chop, chop! Tea'll be ready when you get back – and the potatoes you haven't finished,' she added archly.

Jane took the back stairs to the cabin, striding them two by two, calling each name as she ran, slamming open the door.

'Vi! Lucinda! There's something I must tell you! I should've told you before,' she called above the noise of the running cold-water tap. 'Tom's just been and – and I've been crying.' She splashed her face vigorously, unwilling to look at them, ashamed of her deceit. Then, eyes closed, she reached for a towel, and holding it over her face she said, 'Rob isn't dead.'

Then she lowered the towel and saw the joy in their eyes replaced by apprehension as they looked at her bleak, tear-swollen face.

'What's to do, queen?' Vi asked gently.

'It's – I don't want you to tell anyone else, though, and I know you won't, but Rob's – Rob's married, you see.' The words came out clearly and calmly, with relief, almost. 'His mother told me he's still missing but she said I mustn't go there again.'

'*Jesus*!' Vi hissed.

'It *is* true?' Lucinda frowned. 'She wasn't just saying it to . . .?'

'No. I saw his wedding picture. I'll tell you about it one day soon, but just for now can we not talk about it please, and – and standeasy's ready. Coming down for a cup and a wad, are you?'

'We're coming.' Lucinda's smile was gentle. 'And we're with you all the way, Kendal dear. All for one – don't ever forget it.'

'Thanks,' Jane whispered, suddenly calm now that the truth was out. And she must soon acknowledge that the world had not ceased its spinning. She and her lost love

292

were of no consequence in the order of things. Night still followed day; nothing had changed. She had been stupid to expect that it could or would. 'Thanks a lot.'

His Majesty's submarine *Viper*, pendant number P103, stood off from the depot ship *Omega*, her Aldis lamp flashing from the conning tower. Alongside her, HMS *Lothian* waited, ready to escort the small craft to open waters and stand guard against predators.

Wrens Kendal and Bainbridge sat in the bows of the launch that carried starboard watch to duty, and though it was mid-August the sun had lost little of its warmth. Behind them the water at the head of the loch lay purple, reflecting the heather that was beginning to flower on the hills around. They saw *Lothian* and *Viper* as the launch rounded *Omega*'s stern.

'Look, Jane! There's the new boat! Any sign of Tom?'

'He'll be below.' Jane shook her head. 'The seamen will be taking her out. They're going up to the measured mile for speed trials, I think. And they'll be doing gunnery practice, too. Tom's pleased he's got a boat, though I don't know why. I'd panic, in his shoes. Couldn't bear to be shut in like that.'

'I don't suppose it worries submariners.' Lucinda shrugged. 'They're all volunteers, aren't they, though Lofty said a lot of them do it for the extra money.'

'It'd take more than danger money to get me to sea in one of those.' Mentally Jane wished *Viper* good luck and a safe return. 'I suppose they'll be on your wavelength, Lucinda.'

'Suppose they will.'

Smugly Lucinda recalled her first watch. There had been a submarine doing practice deep dives in the Gareloch that morning. *Sparta*, an S-boat, call sign P268. Of all the call signs and all the ships in the Home Fleet, she

293

would never forget those two; not ever. But the mean-eyed W/T set was her familiar friend now, and Morse code at speed had ceased to bother her.

The launch bumped gently against the quarterdeck gangway, and Connie Dean's boathook reached out.

'Carry on aboard,' Lilith Penrose called as the engine sputtered and died.

Even the gangway held no terrors for them now and their salute at the head of it was automatic. It would be a lovely, lovely world, Lucinda thought with passionate gratitude, if it wasn't for the killing and wounding and families being separated. She wished she didn't like being a Wren quite so much. She really shouldn't feel this happy. Life on active service was surely not meant to be like this. Endured, maybe, but not enjoyed.

But perhaps one day her own item of sorrow would come. She frowned. Perhaps – oh, God forbid it! – something would happen to Mike, and then what would her lovely world be worth?

'Come on then, Bainbridge!' Molly's Celtic brogue dispelled the morbid thoughts. 'Shift yourself, or we'll be late on watch!'

Lucinda quickened her step. Another day, another watch about to begin. Another mark on the calendar. One day nearer their leave.

'Coming!' she called.

They went to cabin 10 after duty that night. They checked the blackout carefully, then laid a dressing gown at the foot of the door to hide any telltale chink of light.

Vi had not wanted to go. She had promised her conscience never to go again, after the miracle of Gerry's deliverance; but Jane was upset, and though Lilith's table and glass were nothing but a nonsense in Vi's eyes, if it helped the poor kid forget her troubles for just an hour, then who was she to gainsay it?

'You can count me out,' Connie Dean fretted, 'and don't be talking half into the night, either. There's some of us want to sleep!' Defiantly she pulled the blankets over her head, wriggling into the hollow in her mattress.

'I take it Dean is not with us,' Lucinda observed.

'Dean hasn't been with us for weeks now,' Lilith retorted grimly. Then she placed her fingers to her lips and shook her head warningly, mouthing the words, 'Say nothing.'

'We'll have to be very quiet,' Fenny whispered, moving the table carefully into the middle of the room. 'There'll be all hell let loose if Chiefie catches us at this hour.'

'Chiefie *won't* catch us,' Lilith said softly, arranging figures and numbers into the now familiar sequence. 'Something will happen tonight, I feel it. Even if Bainbridge takes part,' she added without rancour.

'I hope you don't mind my coming.' Lucinda smiled apologetically. 'As a matter of fact, I'd rather like to give it a try tonight.'

'Got a question for the glass?'

'Er, no. Not exactly, but if there's anything for me – well, I'd be grateful for the information, so to speak.'

'If there's a message for you, *and you believe*, then you'll get it, Lucinda. But this isn't a game, remember. Now then, let's get started. Are you coming in on it, Vi?'

'Think I might.' She was doing it for Jane, after all. 'Not for long, though, if that's all right with you lot. It's late and we shouldn't be messin' about at this hour.'

'At midnight, you mean?' Lilith looked at her watch. 'Oh, I don't know. I often find that midnight is a good time.' She took a clean white handkerchief and began to polish the wine glass. 'Ah, yes. A *very* good time. Who's first?'

'Me, please.' Jane took the glass eagerly, cupping it in her hands, warming it, filling it with her breath. Then quietly, her voice uncertain with emotion she said, 'Is there a message for me and can I have it, please, if there is?'

She set the glass down in the centre of the table, her eyes not leaving it, her cheeks flushed to an unnatural red. Five fingers reached out. In the room there was no sound save that of shuddering indrawn breaths.

The glass moved smoothly, anti-clockwise, circling the table top. Then positively it moved from letter to letter. It made only one word, then its vibrations ceased as sluggishly it returned to the table centre.

'Forgive?' Lilith frowned. 'Does *forgive* make any sense to you, Jane?'

'Yes. I wanted a message from Rob,' Jane choked, eyes bright, 'and it makes sense.'

'Forgive? It's a strange message, though,' Fenny remarked uneasily. 'Usually the dead send – oh, Jane, I'm sorry. I shouldn't have said that.'

'It's all right,' Jane whispered, lips stiff. 'I know you didn't mean to – '

'No, it's *not* all right.' Lilith pushed back her chair noisily. 'That message didn't come from beyond, I know it!' She looked questioningly into Jane's eyes. 'Look, love, I'm sorry. I know Glasgow was bad news, but are you sure, positively sure, that Rob is officially dead?'

'I – I – Yes, Lilith.' Her eyes dropped to her fingers. 'I've lost him.'

'Then I wouldn't go along with that at all. That message came through too well, somehow. Oh, I can't explain it – call it intuition I suppose – but I want to try something else.'

'I think she should leave well alone. I think we all should.'

296

Jane looked up sharply and her eyes met Vi's. *That's enough*. The message was as clear as words. *You know he isn't dead* . . .

'I – maybe Vi is right,' Jane muttered. 'I think perhaps . . .'

'Jane, *please*.' Lilith's voice was low and urgent. 'Have you anything of Rob's – a letter, a button from his coat – *anything*? If I could hold it I would know, you see.'

'Only this.' Too quickly Jane unfastened the chain around her neck. On it hung her confirmation cross, her Admiralty-issue identity disc and the farthing Rob had given her. She had been going to destroy that wren-decorated coin. Yesterday she had removed it from the chain, ready to throw it far into the waters of Loch Ardneavie, but she had not done so. 'It's all I have. He gave it to me on our first date.'

'Thank you.' Lilith held out her hand, then placing the coin to her forehead she held it there, eyes closed.

'The third eye,' Fenny whispered in explanation.

'Good. Good.' Lilith's lips moved into a sweet and gentle smile, and opening her eyes she handed the farthing back.

'Keep it very safe, Jane. There's love on it, love between you, and whoever gave it to you is *not* dead!'

'Now see here.' Vi gave an exasperated cluck. 'We've had enough messin' about for one night. These two ought to be in bed. I reckon we should call it a day.'

'No, Vi! *Please*.' Hurriedly Lucinda picked up the glass. 'Just a few more minutes. There's something I want to know. It's important.'

'I'll bet it is,' Vi grunted. 'Well, all right then – but make it quick.'

Lilith held out the white handkerchief and Lucinda polished the glass.

'All sit down, then.'

Fenny straightened the pieces of paper which bore the letters and figures. Jane sat, cheeks burning, eyes bright, a small, sad smile lifting her lips. Vi waited, her mouth buttoned tight. This was the last time they'd come here. The very last.

'Glass, dear glass,' Lucinda whispered. 'I have a problem and you know what it is. Help me, please. Tell me what to do.'

Hesitantly she set it down, then letting go an anxious breath, she joined her forefinger with the rest.

The glass did not move. Apprehensively, Lucinda's eyes met Lilith's.

'Concentrate,' Lilith whispered. 'Believe . . .'

'*Move*, damn you!' Vi hissed.

The glass came to life. Wildly it skittered clockwise around the table, disarranging the figures and letters, sending them flying.

'Stop!' Lilith commanded.

Startled, they lifted their fingers, eyes wide with unasked questions. Lilith picked up the wine glass and wrapped it in the handkerchief. 'Why did you do that, Lucinda?'

'Do what?'

'You mocked the glass. Why?'

'Mocked it? For heaven's sake, it's just mocked *me*! I asked it in all sincerity what I should do and it went berserk!'

'It was angry, Lucinda, and you must never do that again. Never ask a question when you already know the answer. Is that clear?'

'Sorry, Lilith. You're right, I suppose. Maybe I do know.' Tears trembled in her eyes then spilled on to her cheeks. 'Maybe I do.'

'That's it! That's enough!' Vi was on her feet, enraged. 'Come on, you two. I've had a bellyful of this messin'.

298

Always ends in tears, it does.' Bending down, she removed the dressing gown from the door bottom and deftly kicked away the wedge. 'Bed!' she snorted. '*Now!*'

'Oh, Vi dear.' Lucinda laughed sniffily. 'You sounded so like Nanny.'

'Did I now?' Vi closed the door of cabin 9. 'And sometimes you act like you still need lookin' after, the pair of you! Now see here, Jane. I know we said we wouldn't talk about it, but you didn't ought to have done what you did. The girls here think Rob is dead, and as far as you're concerned, that's how it's got to be. Can't you let well alone, queen?'

'No, Vi, I can't. Lilith was right, you see. She knew Rob wasn't dead, and that makes me happy because it only bears out what I know is the truth. Rob is alive. Where he is I don't know, but he's *alive*. And there was something else Lilith said. Love on that farthing. Love between us.'

'You silly little fool!' Vi brushed her hair with unnecessary ferocity. 'Love him, do you? After what he did to you? How can you, Jane, when there's decent fellers like Tom Tavey real gone on you? Where's the sense in it?' Then, as if wound up and unable to stop, she turned her bewilderment on Lucinda. 'And you're no better, are you? Askin' questions when you know the answer! Come on, then. You'd better tell me what it was!'

Lucinda stood over the wash basin, toothbrush poised. 'Oh, it was nothing, Vi. All over and done with.'

'Over and done with, my foot! It was about your Charlie, wasn't it? Him and Mike Farrow?'

'Yes, Vi, it was actually.'

'And?'

'Well, I just wondered – I wanted to know – oh hell, I care for them both, you see,' Lucinda choked.

'Oh, I see, all right. You wanted to know which one of

them to marry – was that it? And like Lilith said, you already know the answer!'

'Yes, I do, Vi. I shall marry Charlie – of course I will – but I'm in love with Mike. I think I loved him right from the start. And he loves me – he told me so – and it's only a matter of time before he asks me to spend the night with him.'

'Good grief! But you'll tell him no, won't you, queen?'

'Sorry, Vi.' With studied concentration Lucinda measured an exact inch of toothpaste on to her brush. 'I shall tell him *yes*. It might be all we ever have, you see.'

Vi collapsed on the bed, searching for words. For a while she sat open-mouthed with amazement, then her lips moved stiffly.

'Bloody 'ell,' she croaked. 'Oh, but we're in a right mess 'ere and no kiddin'! I reckon we'd all best sleep on it, eh?'

Sighing, defeated, she turned off the light, then walked carefully to her bed. Drawing the blankets up to her chin, she closed her eyes tightly.

'Goodnight, each,' she murmured. 'God bless.'

She couldn't say her rosary tonight, she really couldn't. Opening her eyes wide she stared upward.

Goodnight, Gerry lad. Take care. And, oh, Mother of God, they're at it again, the pair of them. Will you just tell me what I'm to do with them, 'cos I'm buggered if I know – beggin' your pardon. They've got me beat this time, well and truly beat, they have.

She sighed deeply and drew the blankets over her head. Ah, well, tomorrow was another day, thanks be.

12

Tomorrow *had* been another day and a better one in every way, thought Vi, looking back on it with pleasure. It had started at breakfast – about the wearing of civilian clothes for sports and off-duty periods in quarters.

'It's true,' Fenny proclaimed. 'Molly told me, and the Captain's secretary told her. There's an AFO about it. It's real gen.'

You couldn't get better than an Admiralty Fleet Order, they conceded – and *if* it was true, wouldn't it be just marvellous to take off stiff collars and ties and thick black stockings and put on trousers or skirts with swirly pleats and pretty blouses again?

'I don't believe it,' Lilith said. 'They've had a sudden rush of blood to the brain at Admiralty House, that's what. Their lordships couldn't have thought that one up on their own. Since when have they ever – '

'It's true,' Fenny repeated defensively. '*And* we'll not need to carry our respirators everywhere either, before long. Just on leave, or when we're away from base for any length of time.'

'And I suppose there's an AFO about that too?'

'Yes, *and* about the new-style hats for Wrens!'

Everyone laughed then. Civilian clothing they might just accept, but the bit about respirators and new-style Wren hats – well, somebody had been having Fenny on, they teased. Like the occasional wearing of civilian clothes, new-style hats would be just marvellous. Any change of shape would be marvellous. That the present headgear was distinctly frumpish was accepted by one and

301

all. Any hat which looked as if it had been sired by Panama Hat out of Schoolgirl Velour could be nothing else, and it had one all-important thing in favour of its retention. A hat so unglamorous must surely have been pleasing to Nelson, and wasn't it a fact that if it was good enough for Nelson . . .?

'They've been teasing you, Cole dear,' Lucinda smiled. But wouldn't it be lovely to wear civvy clothes once in a while she thought, and wouldn't it be too wonderful to wear a ball gown again!

Briefly she closed her eyes, and there she was in a dress of rose-trimmed floaty chiffon, dancing with Mike on a lantern-lit lawn.

'Excuse me, one and all.' Jane pushed back her chair. 'But duty calls. And when you're all scoffing your spuds at supper tonight, kindly remember poor Kendal, who peeled them.'

Jane, Vi noted with relief, looked decidedly better, though whether common sense had brought about the improvement or Lilith's dratted wine glass, she was unable to decide.

And watch aboard went well, too, for with three submarines on patrol and *Viper* doing sea trials, it was a busy one which seemed to pass in no time at all – except for Molly Malone, who complained long and bitterly.

'A good watch?' she choked. 'Sure it was the divil of a time I had. Didn't one of the teleprinters go out of order and wasn't the Signal Bosun playing merry hell about it all evening and himself blaming me as if I'd done it meself on purpose? And as if I would've, with the signals piling up there and all of them rush-immediates. Jaysus, roll on my leave!'

Leave. It would not be long now. Soon Lucinda and Jane and Vi would each write out a request for leave of absence, all the time bearing in mind, of course, that leave was not a right but a privilege. If approved, that request would yield a ration card and rail warrant and the all-important pass that gave them permission to travel.

They would be real Wrens when they'd had their first leave, Lucinda decided, wishing she could spend the entire seven days at Lady Mead but knowing she could not.

Leave? Jane thought. It would be strange to sleep in her own room again, good to walk with Missy over the September fields.

It would not be good to see the bombers and hear the bombers and know she must never hope to meet Rob again. And it would not be good to walk through Tingle's Wood to the perimeter fence. But would she want to? Did she want to lay the ghost of that first love?

It was half-past eleven when they got back to Ardneavie House; 2330 hours Navy time.

'I'm shattered,' Jane sighed.

'Me too. Hope it's kye for standeasy,' Lucinda sighed.

She had acquired a fondness for ship's cocoa. Kye, it was called, made not with the usual powder but with chocolate, grated roughly from a block and melted in boiling water. Add to it then some tinned milk and two spoonfuls of brown sugar, and there you had kye, a drink rich and thick. So thick, Lofty had said, she should be able to stand her spoon in it. Like hot chocolate blancmange it was, and very fattening.

They were standing beside the duties board when the telephone rang; taking down the *On Duty* discs that hung below each name and replacing them with *In Quarters* ones.

But no one ever answered the hall telephone if she could avoid it. Such an action often meant climbing to the top of the house or taking and delivering a message in accordance with the information supplied by the duties board discs. A nuisance, in other words.

303

So the telephone continued its intermittent ringing until Vi emerged from the boiler room and took it from its hook.

'Yes, she's in now. Yes, I'll get her, *sir*.'

'It's for you, Lucinda.' She handed the receiver to her friend, and watched the smile that lighted her eyes disappear the instant she whispered, 'It's Charlie . . .'

'Oh, Charlie dear. How nice – what do you mean where have I been all night? I've been on watch.' Her tone was acid with disappointment. 'There *is* a war on, you know.'

A silence, then, 'No, I'm *not* annoyed with you, dear, but it *is* late and, as I said, we do have a very thriving war on up here.'

Another silence, and, 'Now, Charlie, I didn't mean that and I know it isn't your fault you're stuck at the War House when you'd much rather be in the thick of it like the other chaps . . . Yes, dear, it was terribly sweet of you to sit there ringing me all night and of course I'm glad to hear from you . . .'

'I take it,' said Vi, who had listened without shame to the entire conversation, 'that your Charlie was not best pleased.'

'No, he wasn't.' Lucinda shrugged. 'He was distinctly snotty, in fact. But it was my fault, I suppose. I could have been a little nicer, couldn't I, but I thought, you see – '

'You thought it was Mike ringing you,' Vi finished, sagely. 'But you've been haunting the letter board since he went back, haven't you, and looking on the telephone pad for messages and going around like a cat on hot bricks, waiting for news from him. Why don't you ring the bloke and have done with it?'

'Because I don't know his phone number, that's why. I don't really know his address either, only that it's RNAS Machrihanish. Goodness, and I could never understand

304

why Jane didn't have Rob's address. Oh, Lordy, Vi! You don't think Mike's married, do you?'

'I'd ask him next time you see him, and meantime, how about this to be going on with?' Vi dipped into her overall pocket and brought out the envelope. 'Came second post. From Mike.'

'Vi, *thanks*! I was so worried you see, not hearing.'

'Worried? For goodness' sake, girl, you only saw him a few days ago!' *Marry Charlie?* 'Off you go, then, and read it. I'll get the standeasy and bring it up.'

And maybe then she would tell them that by that same second post had come a letter from Mary, inside which was the one thing she had prayed so hard and so long for; a letter from Gerry.

Oh, yes. She closed her eyes and smiled blissfully. This particular tomorrow had been a good one, in spite of those dratted kids . . .

'Will you listen to this!' Lucinda demanded, pink-cheeked as Vi set down the supper tray. 'Have you ever heard anything like it? "Meet me Monday at Craigiebur Pier, will you? I'll be on the 2 P.M. ferry. Take care . . ."' She did not read out the *My very own Lucy* bit, nor the last line, which had pinked her cheeks. *I love you so much and want you so much. Always.*

'Meet the afternoon ferry, must I? And what would he do if I were on lates, might I ask? Oh, it's so typical!'

'No, it isn't,' Jane reasoned. 'He's perfectly able to work out your watches. He's got the brains, after all, to fly a Hurricane.'

'*Had.*' Lucinda hastened, though come September when he'd seen the doctors he'd be flying one again. It was all so unnecessary, too. Mike had come here to fight for us and got himself wounded for us; he'd done his bit. Why couldn't he let well-enough alone? 'Y'know, I don't

305

know how he manages to get so much time off, not that I'm complaining, of course.' She bit deeply into the slice of bread and jam Vi had brought upstairs. 'Well, on Monday you'll only have one more day to go in the sin bin, Jane. We'll have a real old run ashore when it's over, won't we?'

'We will.' Vi looked pointedly at her watch. 'But it's nearly midnight, and since we were up till all hours mucking about next door, I think we should get our heads down.'

Last night. Mucking about. Lucinda frowned. The glass had told her nothing because there'd been nothing to tell. *Don't ask questions when you know the answers . . .*

But that was just the trouble: she *didn't* know. When she was with Mike she loved him to distraction; but when they were apart and she could think straight, she knew that common sense would prevail and one day she would marry Charlie. It was for ever the same in wartime. Passions ran high; there was no tomorrow. But one day the war would end and they'd all go home, and there'd be street lights and church bells and everybody would be only too glad to put it all behind them. And Mike would return to Vermont, New England, and the Air Force would give back Lady Mead.

Lady Mead. That was really what she would be marrying; she could delude herself no longer. She still wanted to wrap her childhood around her and for everything to be as it was before they'd sent her away to school. Funny, but it had never rained in summer at Lady Mead, and the snow had always come just in time for Christmas, and Mama had breezed in, ordered the packing of a portmanteau, kissed her and breezed off again, and it had been just wonderful once more – fields and trees and Tilly, her pony. And Nanny. And that was how it could be again – well, as near as she could make it. Nor would she leave her own children or send them away to school; well, not until they were able to understand, that was.

So she could be a little in love with Mike, couldn't she? For just a while she could give her heart full rein, and when this war was over she would remember him with happiness and never complain again. It was easy, really, when you thought about it sanely and sensibly. Indeed, there was only one thing wrong, she accepted sadly. Come Monday, sense and sanity would go winging up the Clyde the minute their lips touched, and those lovely, unladylike feelings would tear through her and she would think things that would make Nanny blush for shame. Vi was right. She wanted it all ways, truth to tell. Mightn't be a bad idea if she tried acting like an adult for a change, she told herself. She'd be twenty in November, and most girls she knew were married and one or two of them smugly pregnant, too. But oh, Michael Johnson Farrow, I wonder if you sleep in the nude and how it would be between us in a big sinful double bed!

'I said, I think we should all eat up and get ourselves to bed.' Vi's voice broke the erotic spell. 'And would you mind telling us what you were thinking about, Lucinda, all those miles away?'

'I was thinking, actually, about Mike,' she sighed, loosening the knot in her tie and placing her collar studs in her belt pocket for safe keeping. 'And wondering if he sleeps without pyjamas, if you really want to know!'

'Then could you try thinking about Charlie for half a minute?'

'Charlie? Why?'

'Because it'd wipe the silly smile off your face, girl, that's why! And will you both please eat up and sup up and get yourselves undressed.'

*　*　*

307

Later, in the darkness, Vi could bear it no longer.

'Listen, you two – I had a letter from Gerry this afternoon. I didn't say anythin' because I thought – well . . .'

'You thought it might upset me.' Jane's bedsprings creaked as she turned over. 'Oh, no, Vi. When lovely things happen to someone else, I know that sooner or later it's going to be my turn. Now what did he say?'

'Well.' Vi smiled across the dimness. 'He said it was the best day he'd ever had. He got a letter from our Mary and one from me and a Red Cross parcel as well. And he goes out to work on a farm, so that'll be nice for him, won't it, not bein' locked up all the time.'

'Yes, and I suppose the farmer will give him some extra food, too. Farmers are luckier than most, that way. There were a couple of Italian POWs working for one of the Lady Mead tenant farmers. One of them spoke quite good English. He said it was better than getting shot at.'

'Mm. That's what I thought. The waiting's goin' to be awful, but one day, God willin', at least Gerry'll come home.' She felt beneath her pillow for his letter. He'd said he loved her, too, but that was between her and him. 'Well, I'm goin' to say me prayers now.'

'Then will you say one for Rob and me?' Jane whispered. 'I know I'm not a Catholic, but Rob is. Can you put a good word in?'

'Course I can, queen.' Though how, she frowned, you could get rid of a perfectly good Catholic marriage was beyond her.

But faith moved mountains, didn't it? Oh, well, it was worth a try. 'Goodnight,' she said softly. 'God bless.'

St Jude. Tightly she closed her eyes. *Sorry, but I've got another one here for you.* Another miracle? Pushing it a bit, wasn't she? *It's like this, see . . .*

* * *

Monday morning brought with it the first scent of autumn, with mists trailing the shores of Loch Ardneavie and the sun a dim gold sphere that struggled to break through over cloud-tipped hilltops. In the garden, cobwebs sparkled with tiny dewdrops and haws hung shiny red on the hedgerow. But by early afternoon the sun shone brightly and Lucinda waited, heart bumping joyously, as the Garvie ferry tied up. Of Mike there was no sign, though she knew that very soon he would walk down the gangway and say, 'Hi, honey,' and smile his lovely, lopsided smile and she would say, 'Hullo, Mike,' and lift her face to be kissed. And then they would link little fingers and walk to the little strip of land so surrounded by trees that it was impossible to see one iota of the war when you were there; just branches above, and long lush grass underfoot, and the sun dancing on the water ahead as if it had never been anything but peacetime in that small, secret place. Or maybe they would walk along the seafront and remark on how well the cabbages and leeks and sprouts were growing in the flowerbeds, or maybe they wouldn't talk at all once they'd said *Hi* and *Hullo*, except perhaps to decide to go to the dance at eight.

Lucinda frowned anxiously. Almost all the passengers had disembarked now and still he had not come. Surely he hadn't missed the ferry? Just suppose he was still there, on Garvie Quay, trying desperately to phone her?

Mike came ashore as she had almost decided to wait there until the next ferry arrived. He was smiling and apologetic and he didn't say 'Hi' though he bent down and kissed her mouth lingeringly.

'Sorry, darling. Just finding a safe place to leave my kit. Didn't think it was worth bringing it off.' He kissed her again so that the protest died on her lips.

'Your *kit*, Mike?' Eventually, fearfully, she asked him. 'Why have you brought your kit with you?'

'Because, my lovely Lucy, I'm en route for Hampshire – Worthy Down, to be exact. Posted there . . .'

A clenched fist hit her hard in the pit of her stomach, and her mouth was suddenly dry. 'You're not flying again?' This wasn't happening. 'You said September, maybe, when you'd been to London again.'

'No, sweetheart. Worthy Down is another naval air station, near Winchester, I believe. It'll be exactly the same as it was at Machrihanish.'

'Except that you'll be so far away, Mike.'

'Far away? It's no distance at all!' He tweaked her nose tenderly. 'Where I come from it's only a hop and a spit. It'll be all right. We'll still meet, and you'll be on leave in September, won't you? Any idea when?'

'I think about the fourth,' she murmured, 'though I'm not sure.'

'Okay. I'll fix it so I get some leave, too. Or I'll see if I can't wangle the visit to the medical board around that time. And I'll phone you, and write. I'm not going to Australia, honey.'

'I know. So how long do we have, Mike?'

'Right now? Well, I guess I'll have to go back with the ferry. About half an hour, I figure. I'm getting the overnight train to London.'

'*Half an hour?*' She had thought about what they would do tonight, yet in thirty minutes he'd go back with the ferry to Garvie. 'You didn't have to come all this far, just for half an hour. You really shouldn't have.'

'I'd come for half a minute, Lucy. I love you, remember.'

'I don't want you to go,' she choked. 'And I know Hampshire isn't the other end of the world, but it might as well be, as far as we're concerned. Oh, *why* did you let them post you?'

'Hey, I'm only a flight lieutenant – well, squadron

310

leader as from two days ago – but I gotta do as I'm told, like everybody else. And when I'm back on flying duties again, I'll try to fix me a posting to Scotland. It'll all work out, you'll see. But we're wasting time. Where can we go for twenty-odd minutes?'

'There's that little nab end that juts out into the water. It's lovely there.'

'Okay. And we'll talk about you and me, Lucy, because I want to get things straight between us.'

'We'll have to watch the time. I don't want you to get the ferry back, but – '

'It'll be okay. They usually give a blast a few minutes before they sail. I'll make it all right.'

They linked hands and walked slowly to the quiet place; the place, Lucinda realized, that now she would visit often. And he spread his raincoat on the grass and they sat, hands clasped, watching the sun make patterns on the water.

'I want you to give me your address, Mike; your Vermont address. And when I write to you at Worthy Down I'll give you all my addresses so you can find me easily. We mustn't be like Jane and Rob. Jane was a long time finding Rob's mother when he went missing, and I don't want to think it would be like that for us.'

'So what's brought this on, uh?' He took her face in his hands and kissed her gently. 'Rob was on operational flying; I'm not. We'll worry about things like that later, okay?' He fished deep in his inside pocket and took out a diary and fountain pen. 'But I'll give you my Vermont address, though I surely could find you, darling. I know where you live in London and I sure as heck could find the house in Lincolnshire. The place in Scotland's the only one I'm not certain about, though I'd find that, too, if I thought you were there. So don't go worrying yourself, okay?'

311

He tore out the page and handed it to her. 'There you are: address, phone number and all. That suit you?'

'Thanks. And I'm sorry if I seem to be worrying, but that's just it. I am.'

'Then stop it. I can think of better things to do with the time we've got, but I'll content myself with kissing you breathless and asking you for a promise.'

'Anything you want,' she murmured, her lips on his.

'I know the way it is with you, Lucy, and I know it isn't going to be easy for you to break with Charlie. But promise me one thing, sweetheart. Promise you'll not let them stampede you into marrying him.'

'I won't. I promise.' Oh, dear sweet heaven, what was she saying! Not so long ago she had convinced herself that marriage to Charlie was what she still wanted, yet now . . . 'Though how, I don't know.'

'How? If push comes to shove, you'll pick up the nearest phone and yell for reinforcements, that's how. I'm serious about us. I want you, and sure as the Lord made little green apples I'll have you!'

'Mike, it – it's not – oh, just kiss me. Kiss me and kiss me and – '

He kissed her long and hard; kissed her until the lovely, sinful feeling was back again and she pressed closer and closer and never wanted them to be apart. She wanted those last few moments to be marvellous and wonderful and so unforgettable that when she was old and alone she could remember the day the sunlight danced on the water and tall trees screened out their war. Her lips throbbed from the need in his kisses, and every small, wanton pulse beat inside her and wanted him as though there was no tomorrow.

'I love you, Mike. I'll always love you.'

'Good. That'll do just fine to be going on with. Now tell me your news.'

'Well, most important, Vi's heard from Gerry and he's fine. He's just had a parcel from the Red Cross and he goes out working on a farm nearby. Vi's glad. It's the way she wants it. He's better there than on the Murmansk run. We sent a big convoy not so long ago with stuff for the Russians, and the buzz had it that the U-boat packs were waiting for it and not a lot got through. Vi's a realist. Wish I could be more like her.'

'And Jane? How's she taking Rob's death?'

'She's – well . . .' No. She couldn't tell anyone. Not even Mike. 'She's having to get on with living her life as best she can, I suppose,' she whispered, eyes downcast. 'Oh, this war's got a lot to answer for!'

'Even though we wouldn't have met, without it?'

'Who says we wouldn't? Who's to say I wouldn't have done the Atlantic crossing on one of the Queens and met you in Times Square or Fifth Avenue? Or even Vermont?'

'Idiot.' He pulled her close again, resting his cheek on her head. 'When are you going to tell your folks about us?'

'Mike!' He'd asked it with such suddenness that she jerked away from him, startled. Tell Pa and Mama? She hadn't got around even to thinking about that. And even supposing she were considering anything so drastic, what could she tell them about Mike? His background? She knew little of that. His immediate family, then? An English grandmother, an aunt and a parrot, that was all, except for the New England address. 'Are you married, Mike?'

'Married? Me?' He laughed out loud, head back, then drew out his paybook from his inside-right pocket. 'Here. See for yourself.'

'N – no – I . . .'

'Go on, honey. Be my guest.'

'I didn't mean – there's no need.'

But she *did* mean, and after what had happened to Jane the need *was* there.

She opened the small, thin book and it was all there. His number and name with S/Ldr written over a crossed-through F/Lt; his address, too, exactly as he had written it down for her. And on the same page was his next of kin. Father. Michael Johnson Farrow.

'Why is next of kin always written in pencil, Mike? It's the same in my paybook.'

'Because *single* men and women – ' he emphasized the word single, then paused, making sure she was looking into his face – '*single* people get married, and when they do their next of kin changes. One day, they'll rub out my dad and put your name there, Lucy. In ink, then, because it'll be permanent.'

'Sorry, Mike.' She handed back the paybook. 'One day I'll tell you why I asked, though really I don't know a lot about you and I want so much to know absolutely everything.'

'Okay, then. I'm six feet and one inch tall. I weigh 154 pounds and have a scar on my left cheek. I like horses and small children, and I got a first in engineering at Yale. I like seafood and dislike cheese. I like dancing – with the right girl, of course – and swimming, and I must be the only North American who doesn't chew gum. I snore in bed – or so I'm told – and – '

'*Snore*? Who told you that?' she demanded.

'My granny.' He grinned. 'Oh, and I don't wear pyjamas, though I do keep a set under the pillow in case of air raids.'

'Mike!' She laughed with delight. 'Now just fancy that! I knew you slept in the nude, I *knew* it!'

'Hey, no kidding? And what other dark thoughts has milady entertained?'

'You'd be surprised!' She turned away, her cheeks

burning. 'Oh, Mike my darling, you would indeed. But what I want to know, too, is what you did in civvy street. And I want to know about your parents and your brothers and sisters.'

'Well, my dad's name is the same as mine, as you know now, and my mother is small and plump and very pretty. Her name is Josephine – Dad calls her Josie. I don't have a brother but my sister is called Alicia – '

'Alicia Johnson Farrow.' Lucinda smiled. 'For your grandmother.'

'Right first time, though she's married now to Redmond Fairfax. A very old family, the Fairfaxes. Red was at Yale with me. And Aunt Addy is a maiden lady – Dad's elder sister. She dotes on Mavis, of course.'

'And what will you do when the war's over, Mike?' She was being unforgivably rude but she really wanted to know.

'Me? I'll take a vacation first, I guess, then I'll go back to what I was doing before – to Dad's, er, firm.'

'And what is that?'

'Oh, a bit of this, a bit of that. Construction, engineering.'

'Building, you mean?'

'Sort of. But don't worry, honey. I'll be able to keep you, all right, and all those kids we plan to have.'

'Mike! I *never* . . .' Her cheeks were scarlet again.

'You did so, Lucy! Three or four, you said. And since I'd like a couple of each too, I reckon we should have them together.'

'Be serious, darling.' She felt restless, all at once, and *that* feeling was still there, too, and it really wasn't fair of him, getting her so hot and bothered when they'd only got a few minutes left.

'Oh, I *am* serious, Lucy Bainbridge.' The teasing smile was gone and his eyes narrowed as they met hers. 'And before I go I want this thing settled between us. Say you'll marry me, Lucy. Please.' He tilted her chin so she was forced to look at him. 'Promise me you will.'

'I – oh, darling, how can I? I don't know if I love you or if I just want you.'

'Either will do – or both. Say yes, Lucy.'

'Then yes, yes, *yes*,' she sighed. 'But don't do anything yet. Let me tell my people in my own good time. Don't say anything to anyone. No announcements.'

'Sorry, honey, but I've already told my granny. And she sure as heck'll have told the family and – '

'You've *told* her? *When*?'

'After our second date, I think it was. I haven't had a letter back yet, though I shouldn't wonder if most of Vermont knows about it by now.'

'Oh, Michael Johnson Farrow.' She laughed. 'I used to ask myself what it was about you that I liked so much and now I know. It's your cheek! You're – you're *incorrigible*!'

'Yes, but sexy with it.'

'That, too.' She laid her lips on his cheek, right where the scar ran deepest. There was no denying it. She loved Mike and she was in love with him, too. And that was exactly as it should be, because when they had made love she would be able to look at him and still like him. Three or four children! And at least a couple more passionate accidents?

'Don't go,' she whispered as the Garvie ferryboat's siren gave out two sharp blasts. 'Stay with me?'

His kiss was hard with passion. It hurt her mouth and she was glad. If kisses got babies, as she'd once believed, she'd be pregnant now.

'Come on.' He pulled her to her feet and they ran without stopping to the gangway two seamen were just beginning to pull inboard.

'I love you,' he said.

316

'And I love you,' she called, not caring if the whole of Argyll heard it.

She stood on the pier until his face became a distant blur, and she was still standing there long after the ferry was no more than a speck and the smoke from its stack had disappeared beneath the horizon.

'Take care, Mike,' she whispered with her heart, 'and write to me soon and, oh, stay away from flying for a while yet.'

She wept, then; hot tears that stung her eyes and tasted salt on her lips. Was this, then, how it had been for Jane?

Fear stabbed through her; not fear for herself, but for him. But she *would* tell them at home. She would tell them firmly and then she would tell Charlie. She'd show them all that this Lucinda was in all ways different from the one who had crept out and joined up. It made her think of Goddy and she wondered if she should tell him about it too, and ask his help. Or would it be unfair to involve him yet again?

I promise, she said to Mike. It had been easy, then, with his lips only a kiss away. But now he was gone and she was alone again, and afraid; so very afraid.

'Look after yourself, Michael Farrow,' she whispered. '*Please*.'

'You'd better,' Vi said as she placed two pairs of brilliantly polished shoes beneath two bedside chairs, 'find Jane's spare pair and I'll give them a quick once-over.'

'Tonight's her last night, isn't it? I've never known seven days drag so.' Lucinda pulled Jane's shoes from under her bed. 'I feel as if I've been on stoppages, too. Shall we all go out tomorrow night?'

'Good idea. I'm not doing anythin'.'

'Nor me.' Lucinda shrugged. 'Oh, imagine, Vi – getting himself posted down south.'

317

'You're lucky it wasn't overseas.' Vi dabbed bootblack on the end of her brush. 'There'll be letters, though, and surely he'll ring you.'

'He can try, I suppose, but he'll probably never get through from all that way away. You know how hard it is to get a trunk call; even the telephone lines are on war work now. God! I'm so fed up!'

'Ar, hey, come on, queen. You'll see him again. It isn't as if you've quarrelled, or split up, or anythin'.' Mother of God, she hadn't given him his marching orders. 'You *haven't*, Lucinda?'

'No. Far from it. As a matter of fact, he asked me again to marry him.'

'And this time you said yes?'

'I did, Vi, and I meant it then, I truly did. But now he's not with me, well – I'm not very brave, you see, not when it comes to facing up to the parents. My mother's going to hit the roof and Pa won't be best pleased, either. He does so dislike upset. And as for Nanny and Charlie . . .'

'Yes, I see what you mean.' Vi breathed heavily on the toe of Jane's shoe then polished vigorously. 'But that's your mam and dad, and Nanny and Charlie taken care of – how about Mike and Lucinda, eh? Don't they deserve a bit of consideration?'

'Me and Mike? Do we deserve any? Mike knew I was engaged to Charlie and I knew I was engaged to Charlie, so why did we both end up in this mess?'

'Being engaged – married, even – doesn't provide automatic protection, queen.'

'Then what should I have done? Sat the war out in a convent? And I'll tell you something else! Mike has already told his grandmother about us. After our second date he wrote to her that he was going to marry me. Half of Vermont probably knows about it by now! It's a mess, Vi, and that's putting it mildly. What am I going to do?'

318

'Sorry, but I can't help you and I wouldn't, not even if I could. This is something you've got to do for yourself. By yourself.' Vi's voice was gentle. 'You aren't bein' fair to Charlie nor Mike. And you certainly aren't bein' fair to yourself, either. All I can tell you is to sleep on it, girl. Get it all worked out in your mind. It won't be long before we go on leave – surely that'll be time enough. See how you feel about it then.'

'So you're not saying I should give Mike up?'

'I'm saying nothin', Lucinda. Nobody can. You're on your own in this one.'

'Yes.' On her own. Alone. 'Yes, you're right, Vi.' Think about it carefully. No rush. 'You usually are . . .'

'Okay, then.' Vi placed Jane's shoes beside her bed. 'And I think it's time for the blackout.'

'Yes,' Lucinda said again, walking over to the window and gazing out at the darkening sky. 'Vi! Come and look. Isn't that *Viper* coming back, and *Lothian*?'

'It is. And *Lothian*'s flashing.' Vi smiled. 'Can you read it, then?' Anything at all to get Lucinda's mind off her troubles. 'What's he saying?'

'It's – it's – ' Lucinda screwed up her eyes. 'I'm not very good with lamps, but it's in plain language – yes – it's only *Lothian* breaking off escort duties, handing *Viper* back to *Omega*, sort of.'

'There now.' Vi beamed. 'Nice, isn't it, bein' able to read them little flashin' lights?'

Yes, it *was* nice, Lucinda agreed silently and with pride. If anyone had told her on that eighth day of May that she would be reading the Morse code with complete ease, she'd not have believed them. Seemed she wasn't entirely devoid of brains; only when it came to her love life.

'It's very beautiful out there, isn't it, Vi?'

'And peaceful and safe.'

They watched as *Lothian* slipped astern to her mooring

buoy, leaving *Viper* small and black, silhouetted against the blaze of a bright orange moon.

'That's Tom Tavey safely back.' Vi smiled.

'Yes.' But where was Mike now? Was *he* safe? Would he be waiting at Glasgow for the London train? She looked at her watch. Nearly half-past ten. Maybe he had already left and was miles away, by now. 'I hope Tom asks Jane for a date, now he's back. He's quite gone on her, you know. Take her mind off – well, *things*. Must be sure to tell her he's just come in.'

And this, Jane thought with silent triumph, was the last night; the last coke bucket she would fill. Already she had peeled her last potato and scrubbed clean her last pan.

Just fill up the coke buckets for morning, the leading steward had told her, and check all the blackouts – and that'll be it.

She slammed shut the fuel-store door, then picked up the heavy buckets for the last time and walked slowly across the stableyard, her eyes on the sky.

The days were shortening now, and there was a chill on the night air.

She breathed in deeply, glad it was all over, gazing at the moon, which was uncannily large and strangely bright. An August moon. A harvest moon, blazing low in the sky. A bomber's moon.

Oh, Rob, wherever you are, take care.

She pulled back her shoulders and lifted her chin. She wouldn't cry! She bloody well *wouldn't*!

And not just Rob, God, but all our aircrews, tonight. Look after them. Let them all come home safely. Please.

13

It was amazing, Vi thought, looking about her with exasperated affection. Liverpool hadn't changed. The Mary-Ellens still sold flowers outside Lime Street station and the street women still touted for business inside it. And those funny, fat liver birds were still perched there at the Pier Head, saucily defiant, one facing upriver, the other facing down. They hadn't flown away, Vi grinned, and Hitler had given up and sent his bombers somewhere else.

Swinging her respirator on to her shoulder, she made for the bus terminus. There was still the stink of destruction about the place: a dusty, gritty smell that mingled with the acrid stench of burnt-out timbers and unshifted rubbish. Sandbags were piled against basement grilles and unused doorways, and the corrugated sheets fixed hurriedly over shattered shopfronts were still there, a paradise for scribblers.

'Nice flowers?' A Mary-Ellen held out a bunch of golden chrysanthemums. 'Only a silver shillin' to you, queen.'

'Ta.' Vi offered two sixpences. A bunch of flowers would please her sister.

'Come on then, Jenny. Let's be havin' you if it's Ormskirk you're wantin',' the conductor of the red bus called. 'Haven't got all day. There's a war on, in case you didn't know.'

'Less of your lip.' Vi swung her case on to the platform then took her seat at the front of the bus, gazing at pot-holed streets and broken, battered buildings. And soon their route would take them along Scotland Road and past the bottom of Lyra Street. She had never thought she could look again at the jagged gap that had once been her home – hers, and Gerry's – but things were different now. Lyra Street belonged to the past. She had left it in anger as a widow, yet now she was a wife again. And it had not caused her grief to come back to dirt and devastation and the unbowed breed who had thumbed a defiant nose at the Luftwaffe, for these were the streets to which she would return when it was all over and Gerry came safely back to her.

A feeling of pride and love and contentment washed over her. There were no pine-covered hills here, no trees and uncrowded skies and flower-filled gardens, or views that took your breath away no matter how many times you looked. But this bawdy city was where her roots were. For seven days she was home again, and it was good.

Lucinda pressed the doorbell of the house in Bruton Street, not quite believing she had arrived. She had been unable to find a taxi at King's Cross and the journey by underground to Oxford Circus seemed to take for ever. But she had returned the cheery greetings of the bombed-outs who nightly slept in the ready-made shelters, and she smiled a goodnight as she handed in her ticket.

The streets were dark. No light showed, though she knew there were people out there in the blackout. Sometimes she knew it by the half-shielded glow of a cigarette end; sometimes she heard footsteps or voices; and sometimes she almost collided with a shape that loomed suddenly at her, and she would say 'Whoops!' and laugh and go on her way into the darkness.

On the other hand, of course, there were people who had collided with lamp posts or tree trunks, and on those occasions they didn't say 'Whoops!' or any word remotely like it, and they certainly didn't laugh. The blackout was responsible for more black eyes, come to think of it, than Joe Louis.

She pressed the bell again, harder. Once there would have been a light shining outside and the door would have been opened without her ring. But there was no footman now; no servants at all. Servants were undemocratic and unpatriotic, and besides, they were all on war work.

Her father answered the door eventually, peering into the darkness, muttering, 'Lucinda! Good heavens! Home on leave already? Afraid your mama's out, and I'll be out too in five minutes. Why didn't you think to tell someone you were coming?'

'I did, Pa.' Warmly she returned his kiss. 'At least twice.'

'Ah, well, you'd better come in and take your coat off.' He closed the door then switched on the light. 'When are you going back?'

'Wednesday. Overnight train. When will Mama be in?'

'Not at all sure. Look here, you'll be all right, won't you? Got to finish dressing, y'see. Freddie Elton managed to get hold of a brace of grouse and I'd rather like to help him eat them.'

She told him she would be fine and of course he must go out, and that it would be pleasant to have the house to herself. Or did she mean it was pleasant that Mama was out and she could potter around, hanging up her uniform, having a bath, washing the smell of the train from her hair? 'Any hot water left, Pa?'

'Sorry. Afraid you'll have to boil kettles, m'dear. Well, I'll leave you to it, eh?'

'And welcome home to you too, Lucinda,' she grinned, throwing her case on the bed, kicking off her shoes. But she'd have bet anything there'd be hot water at Nanny's, in spite of fuel rationing, and she found herself wishing she could have spent her leave in Lincolnshire, imagining her welcome at the Dower House, with a kettle boiling on the stove and the teapot warming and a plate of egg sandwiches covered with a white cloth. Of course, going to Lady Mead wasn't on, not this time, but next leave she would go there – and they wouldn't even miss her at Bruton Street.

She took Charlie's photograph from her dressing table, looking at it long and hard. She wished he had been at the station when she got there. No! She didn't at all! She wished Mike had been there. Mike would have found a taxi. Mike, she shouldn't wonder, was good at everything.

She undressed slowly, then took the silk dressing gown from the wardrobe. It would be strange to wear civilian clothes again. She hoped Mama hadn't found the silk stockings she had hidden away.

Damn! The doorbell rang, and she shrugged into the dressing gown and hurried downstairs. She opened the front door, poking her head round it, aware of her near-nakedness.

'Who's there?'

'It's me, old love. What ho! The Fleet's in, eh?'

Lucinda drew in her breath sharply. Damn again! And just when she was beginning to relax and look forward to a quiet night alone.

'Hold on a minute.' She pulled the blackout curtain across the door then snapped on the light. Dutifully she lifted her face for his kiss.

'Hullo, Charlie,' she smiled, grateful at least that someone had remembered she was coming home. 'It's good of you to call, but you needn't have bothered.'

'Of course I need. Only too sorry I couldn't meet your train.'

'You'd have waited two hours if you had.'

'Bad journey, old thing?'

'Absolutely awful. Bodies everywhere, even in the corridors. And most of the lavatories were crammed with cases and kitbags. Pretty ghastly . . .'

'Shouldn't have joined, should you?' He seemed glad about the nightmare journey. 'Should've stayed here and married me.'

He reached for her again, his lips finding hers, and she pulled away, trailing the back of her hand across her mouth. She didn't want him to kiss her. She had forgotten how sloppy his kisses were. It had been different with Mike. Mike's mouth had been tender and teasing, intended to please and his kisses were gentle and passionate at the same time, and he never acted as though her lips were his exclusive property and kissing them his considered right. Not like Charlie. Charlie just grabbed. And plonked.

'Look, dear. I'd rather like to have a bath. Afraid Pa and Mama are out, so could you amuse yourself till I'm done?'

'I'd rather have a spot of passion on the sofa first.' He reached for her again, sliding a hand down her dressing gown, cupping a breast, squeezing the nipple roughly.

'Charlie, *no*! I'm dirty and sweaty and rather tired, and if you don't mind . . .' She shouldn't have told him they were alone.

'Don't worry. I'm not particular, old love.' Roughly he pulled open her robe, gazing narrow-eyed at her nakedness. 'It's months since I saw you and I'm feeling randy as hell!'

'Don't, Charlie! And behave yourself!' God, how coarse he could be. 'I'm not very good company tonight, I'm afraid, and I'm certainly not in the mood for anything on the sofa so – '

'Well, I *am*!' His mouth found hers again, and for the first time she smelled a mixing of whisky and peppermints

325

on his breath. 'Don't be a prude, Lucinda, and stop being a tease. This is me, remember, the man you're going to marry.'

Marry? She pulled the gown round her again, tying the belt tightly. Marry? Oh, no, and this was the time to tell him so.

'Now look here, Charlie. There's something – '

'No, *you* look! I'm brassed off listening to the other chaps and how much they get. Hang it all, where's the harm in it when two people have been engaged as long as we have?' His face was red now, and sullen. He pulled again at her dressing gown and she heard the ripping of silk in his hands. God! He'd had too much to drink. He was going to rape her!

'Stop it! Damn well *stop* it!' She dashed away his hands, then sent him staggering against the door. 'I told you no and I mean no, so bugger off before I catch you one where it'll hurt!'

'There is no need to swear.' His jaw sagged, his mouth opened wide with amazement.

'There are times you'd make a plaster saint swear! And please close your mouth. It makes you look very foolish, Charlie.'

'Well, well, *well*.' He recoiled from the screaming anger in her eyes. 'Nasty little habits you're learning in the Wrens, it seems.'

'Yes, I am, and you'd better watch out because I've learned how to deal with *your* nasty little habits, Charlie. So get out of here at once, and don't ring me until you're sober – and sorry!'

She stood for a time after he had gone, marvelling at her sudden courage, hugging herself, choking back the tears. Then determinedly she ran to the library, slammed the door behind her and dialled trunks, asking for Mike's number.

326

'There is a delay on Winchester calls,' the impersonal voice of the operator intoned. 'Kindly replace your receiver. I will call you back if the number is available.'

Of course it was available, and why did they always use such official language?

'Please try,' she whispered. 'It's very important.'

'Trunk calls are attended to in strict rotation, caller. Please replace your receiver.'

Damn! Oh, Mike, please be there.

Impatiently she paced the floor, picking up old, uninteresting books, wrinkling her nose at the musty leathery smell of them. All these books would be Charlie's, one day. Everything would be Charlie's – when Pa was dead, and Uncle Guy. And what was keeping them on the exchange? Why were there such delays, now, on everything? The books were in a terrible jumble. They really ought to be catalogued and rearranged. And repaired too, when the war was over.

She glared at the telephone. 'Ring, won't you?'

It rang, eventually. After thirty minutes of pacing and fuming and despairing and almost picking it up at least six times and demanding to know what on earth they were doing, it rang.

'I have the Winchester number now, caller. Do you still require it?'

'Please, oh, *please*. And thanks.'

The operators on the switchboard at RNAS Worthy Down had no knowledge of Squadron Leader Farrow's extension number but suggested trying the officers' mess.

It seemed an age before the phone was answered and she was able to ask if Mike was there.

'Yank!' called a voice, then miraculously he was saying, 'Farrow. Who is this, please?'

'It's Lucinda, Mike!'

'Lucy! Are you home? I rang there a couple of hours ago and there was no reply.'

'There wouldn't be.' No need to waste precious seconds explaining her father's dislike of answering telephones. 'I was two hours late into London. Can we meet, darling?'

'We surely can. Tomorrow?'

'Yes! When? Where?'

'How about eight o'clock, your place? I'm coming to London in the morning to see the medics again. Appointment is for two fifteen but I don't know when I'll be through. Can we go for a meal or take in a show?'

'Whatever you'd like. But don't call for me. Meet me at the top of the street, the Berkeley Square end.'

'Okay by me, honey. Maybe we'll get to listen out for those nightingales at last.'

'Anything you say.'

'*Anything?*' he said, softly, suggestively. 'By the way, got anything to tell me?'

'Only that I love you. So very much.'

'That's all I want to hear. I happen to be pretty crazy about you, too. We'll talk about it tomorrow night. 'bye, Lucy. See you.'

Reluctantly she put down the receiver. *Anything?* Yes, Mike Farrow, anything. Anything at all.

She held her hands to her burning cheeks. My, but she wished Charlie would walk in this very minute and her mother with him. She wished they could be here, now, when she was so full of love for Mike that she would say, 'And you might as well know, Mama, and you too, Charlie, that I'm in love with someone else; someone I'm going to marry – and there's nothing you can say or do that will make me change my mind!'

But Mama would not walk through the door now – maybe not even until morning – nor Charlie either, and by tomorrow the sudden surge of courageous defiance would have lessened. Tomorrow those words would not come so easily or so bravely, and Charlie would be acting as if nothing had happened and her mother would be demanding to know when they were getting married.

But tonight Mike loved her and she him and tomorrow would come, she vowed fiercely. She would make it come, and not even her ingrained fear of her mother's whiplash temper would prevent it.

'I love you, Michael Johnson Farrow.'

She said it loudly and clearly and the words gave back some of her courage.

Head high, she went in search of kettles.

Once more she stood at the beech tree but tonight the bombers at Fenton Bishop aerodrome were grounded. Earlier, almost as soon as she had got home, she had gazed across the fields from her bedroom window and known it at once, for no mechanics or armourers or fitters swarmed over them; no tankers filled them with fuel. Tonight the bombers stood deserted, save for the men who guarded them; the crews who flew them were already away in search of beer or girls or merely a bed and a night of quiet sleep.

She did not know why she had come here unless it was to prove to herself that she was learning to live without Rob MacDonald, accepting that they would never again meet in Yeomans Lane at seven. Or was it to turn back the clock to the May evening, four months ago, when he had come striding around the perimeter track, smiling when he saw her there, breaking into a run?

That night, Rob was flying and he had not come back. And he had promised never to stop loving her, yet all the while he was married to someone else.

God, it's Jane Kendal. Beseechingly, she closed her eyes. *Can you tell me what I'm doing here, wanting him,*

329

willing him to come, knowing he never will? And will you
tell me how I'm to forget him and get on with living my life
again? Will you tell me how I'm to surrender him to the
woman who is having his baby and how I'm to stop hating
her with every breath I take?

She had been eaten up with a fresh bitterness since the
moment she arrived home on leave, telling herself it was
a mistake to have come back to Fenton Bishop and lay
bare her wounds again. And because she had not spoken
about Rob, her parents thought she had forgotten him
and started talking about Colin again, asking her if she
had seen him since she came home.

They wanted her to marry Colin Clayton. They always
had, especially her mother. Nice, safe Colin, whose pedi-
gree they knew backwards; Colin, who need never leave
home because he was a farmer's son and exempt from
call-up. A civilian, that's what he was; a young man who
remained a civilian despite the taunts that all young
civilian men had to endure: 'Bloody civvy!' 'Get some in,
mate!' – the *some* meaning time in the armed forces.

And God, if you're there, I know I'm spoiled and
childish and I don't deserve to have Rob back, but I'll go
to church on Sunday and I'll wear my uniform to please
Dad and I will try to be better because I don't like being
like this and I'm truly sorry that I am. But if I asked you if
I could see Rob again, would you just let me look at him
for half a minute so I could know he was all right? I know
he's married to Phemie now, but just to see him – even if
he didn't see me there, watching him? And for that half
minute, God, you could have the rest of my life . . .

She turned abruptly, calling to Missy, hurrying away.
Never, as long as she lived, would she come here again;
as God was her witness, she would not.

'Jane! Wherever have you been?' her mother fretted as
she hung Missy's lead behind the back door. 'We've been

330

waiting supper for you since seven. Dad's just about famished.'

'Been? Oh, nowhere in particular.' Only trying to say goodbye to a ghost and bargaining with God again. Offering the rest of her life for half a minute. 'Just walking, that's all.'

14

Vi left the Liverpool-bound bus at the Scotland Road stop
and took a deep, steadying breath. The morning she left
it she had vowed never to return, yet here she was, heart
thumping, only a cock-stride away from the end of Lyra
Street.

Poor old Scotty Road, she thought, compassion washing
her. It had never been much of a place to live and maybe
it should have been knocked down, but not that way. It
hadn't deserved all those bombs and land mines and
incendiaries, and the people who lived along it and in the
stiff little streets leading off it hadn't deserved it either.

She turned into Lyra Street, looking not at the great
jagged gaps on either side but ahead of her to St Joseph's
church and the faded clock face with fingers that pointed
to eight.

The bombs had missed the church that night and all the
people sheltering there; missed it by a second in time.
Funny, the difference a second could make.

She walked on, trying not to feel strange in her uniform.
She had decided against wearing it tonight; but Mary had
said that Father O'Flaherty would like to see her in it, and
in all honesty she had little else to wear. Everything she
had, every carefully pressed blouse and skirt, even the
grey costume she had worn to her wedding and the pink
chiffon blouse and matching hat, had gone. All buried
beneath the pile of rubble that once was number 9 and
number 7 Lyra Street; rubble that sprouted grass now,
and little white daisies and wild red poppies.

Against her will, she stopped and stared at the terrible

waste of it all. That little house had been like a thousand other little Liverpool houses, ready for demolition, saved by the war. The corporation wanted them pulled down and replaced by neat new homes: two-up, two-down and a bathroom, of course. And hot and cold water in the kitchen, too, and windows that didn't rattle every time a wind blew in from the Mersey. But for all that she had been proud of her home, hers and Gerry's, and she had polished the windows and donkey-stoned the front step every day except Sunday and swilled the pavement outside every wash day with suds from the boiler.

She looked up at the sky as if those bombers were still there, skulking behind the autumn clouds.

'Bastards,' she hissed, then walked on without so much as another glance.

She saw Father O'Flaherty at the church door, looking down at his watch then looking up at the clock as if daring either to be wrong.

'Father, hullo!' she called, all at once glad to see him again. 'It's me, Vi McKeown.'

'Well, so it is, though I hardly recognized you in your sailor's uniform. And how are you, Theresa? As if I needed to ask.'

'I'm fine, thanks. No complaints at all. I was hopin' you could spare me a few minutes, Father.'

'Confession's over, Theresa.' He tapped his watch. 'Whatever it is will have to wait now till Saturday night.'

'No, Father. It's you I've come to see – if you're not too busy, that is.'

'N-no. Come on in.' He looked at his watch again. 'Now Mrs O'Keefe's away to Bootle to see their Bridie's new baby but I think I can manage a cup of tea for the pair of us – if you don't mind taking it in the kitchen. Saving the coal ration for the winter, you see. Now, tell

333

me your news. Are you happy? Are you going to Mass and Confession up there in Scotland?'

'I am, Father. The Catholic padre visits regularly.'

'He does? Thanks be. And wasn't it wonderful news about your Gerald? Ah, but it made my day when I got your letter.'

'It's Gerry I came to see you about – well, partly.' She accepted a cup of tea, refusing sugar. 'I wanted to thank you for all you've done – havin' a Mass said, and all that.'

'It was right and proper of you to want a Thanksgiving Mass, child. So many don't think to thank the Almighty for prayers answered. And how is your man, then?'

'Well, Father. Funny, though, wasn't it? Him thinkin' I'm dead in the bombing and me thinkin' he was lost at sea.'

'Ah, yes. The power of prayer.' He looked again at the clock on the kitchen mantel.

'Yes, and that's another of the reasons I'm here, Father. It's my two friends in the Wrens, see? Lovely kids they are, but they've got themselves in a shockin' mess, the both of them. I'm prayin' for them every night, but sometimes I feel like giving up and speakin' me mind instead.'

'Tell me about it.' His eyes left the clock face with a look of resignation. 'Though I suppose it's this war to blame for their troubles. It's a terrible thing that women should go to war.'

'Oh, I don't know.' Vi found her own eyes straying to the mantelpiece. 'That mornin' I stood there and looked at what they'd done to Lyra Street, well, there was nothin' else I could've done but join up. You can only take so much of their cheek and then it all boils up inside you. And what else could I have done, with nowhere to go?'

'Maybe you're right, Theresa. But your friends . . .?'

'Well, one of them ought to be gettin' on with her

334

wedding, but I don't think she's all that keen, now. Doubts, you see, Father, and I don't want her to do anythin' she'll be sorry for.'

'Like marrying the wrong man?'

'The wrong man,' Vi echoed, meaningfully.

'And could it be that you've made up your mind, then, who the wrong man is?'

'I have, Father.'

'I see. Don't you think that's a bit presumptuous of you?'

'If you mean I ought to be mindin' my own business – well, yes, I suppose it is. But I haven't interfered.' She frowned, aware she was not getting the attention she had hoped for. 'Father, am I keepin' you, or something? The clock – you keep lookin' at it.'

'Ah, so I do. But it's about this time I go to the Tarleton, Theresa. For my ciggies. The landlord rations them out to five a customer every night. Mind, he's not of our faith, that man; no respecter of the Catholic cloth, and if I'm not there handy he'll let someone else have them. I've been gasping for one all day, and that's the truth. A terrible addiction the nicotine is.'

'Well, if all you want is a swallow, Father.' Smiling broadly, Vi dug deep into her respirator case, pulling out her hand with a flourish like a conjuror pulling out a rabbit. 'Is this what you're in need of?'

'Theresa! A ciggie! The saints preserve you!' Eagerly he struck a match; blissfully he puffed and inhaled. 'Aaaah. Now then, where were we? Your friends?'

'Well, it's Jane and Lucinda, see. Lucinda's the one who can't make up her mind. She's really engaged to Charlie but it's Mike she should be marryin', if you ask me. I met that Charlie of hers and a right little – well, he was stuck-up and bossy, and Lucinda's a smashin' kid.

335

But her mother's a bit of a hard-faced one, it seems to me. She keeps pushin' it, and it isn't right, Father.'

'And your other friend?' The priest's face was relaxed and benign, the ash on the end of his cigarette an inch long. 'Boyfriend trouble, too?'

'You could call it that, but there's not a lot Jane can do about it. Her feller's married, see.'

'Been leading the poor girl on, has he? Needs a whipping.'

'You're probably right.' Vi sighed. 'But Jane won't say a word against him. I want to tell her like I want to tell Lucinda. And so far I've said nothin', but I can't stand by, can I, and see both of them ruin their lives?'

'You can, Theresa. You *must*.'

'Oh, you're right, I suppose, but it's hard trying to pretend it's none of my business, seein' them both unhappy. Mind,' she added obliquely, 'there's no hope for Jane, anyway. Her bloke's a Catholic.'

'Is he so? And your friends?'

'They're Protestants, Father. Mind, I light a candle regularly for them, but it's goin' to take more than candles to sort them two out. It's keeping my mouth shut that's so hard. One of these days I'll – '

'They aren't influencing your beliefs, Theresa, these Protestant friends of yours?'

'Course they're not! It's just that I worry about them, and trying not to stick me oar in and say somethin' I'd be sorry for isn't easy. I don't suppose you could say one for them? Coming from a priest, a prayer would add a bit more weight, like.'

'Ah, your faith is a credit to you and surely I'll pray for your friends. And that Protestant landlord'll have sold my ciggies by now so we might as well warm up the tea in this pot and have another cup. But it's a terrible thing, the cigarette craving. The very first time you feel you'd

336

commit murder for one is the time you should give them up, Theresa McKeown. Myself, I crossed the Rubicon years ago. I can't seem to do without them, and that's a fact.'

'Ar, hey, that's terrible. Me – I can take 'em or leave 'em.' As if to add substance to her words she rummaged in the depths of her respirator bag, bringing out an unopened packet of twenty. 'We get one of these every day. It's our ration, though I never smoke them all. And sixpence is all we pay for them.'

'Twenty a *day*? For *sixpence*? Jaysus, Mary and Joseph.' His eyes took on a glassy stare. Shakily he rose to his feet. 'Come along, will you. Let's be lighting those candles . . .'

'Ar, that's good of you.' Vi beamed. 'I'm real grateful. And if you like – well, you need these more than I do.'

She held out the packet, the cellophane wrapping crackling seductively in her fingers.

'For me? All of them? You're sure you can spare them?' His eyes made circles of disbelief, his hand reached out eagerly.

'Course I can. And while you're about it, can you say one for Gerry, too?'

A second virgin packet was added to the first and an expression of total joy transformed the priestly face.

'Theresa, there's good you are to a crotchety old man. Good, I said.'

Vi smiled broadly. And she didn't need the ciggies, not really.

'Now just be careful of them packets, Father,' she warned solemnly. 'They're stamped *Duty Free. HM ships only*, and the ciggies are, too. Don't flash them around or we'll both be in trouble.'

'As if I would.' He patted the cassock pocket in which they lay. 'There isn't even Mrs O'Keefe will get to know about these. And Theresa – about your friends. You were right not to have interfered. They'll have to work out their own salvation. There's none of us can presume to play God, remember.'

'I know. I knew it all along, really.' Vi picked up her respirator and gloves. 'You're right, Father.'

'Yes. Sadly I am. But there's one thing you can do for those girls. Be there, Theresa, with a shoulder to cry on and a kind and gentle word at the ready. Be there, when they need you.'

'I will. And it's good of you to pray for them, specially as they're – '

'Not of our faith, you mean? Ah, well, there's Protestants getting killed every minute of the day. It isn't only our lot fighting this war.' He closed the door behind them, taking the well-worn path to the church porch. 'Anyone else deserving of a mention while we're about it – anyone at all?'

Anyone? Vi smiled secretly. In his present state of cigarette-induced euphoria, Brendan Francis O'Flaherty would have prayed for the soul of William of Orange. Prayed for King Billy, he would, and never turned a hair!

'No thanks, Father.' Vi smiled. 'Gerry and the girls'll do fine to be goin' on with. Just fine.'

It was still not dark when Lucinda crossed into Berkeley Square. She had left the house early, unable to bear the waiting any longer, and walked the surrounding streets, killing time.

There had been no phone call from Charlie and she had been jumpy all day, expecting him to ring, disappointed when he had not. Not because she wanted him to; merely that she needed to know where he would be this evening. It would be too awful if . . .

But London was a big city and, for the duration, a very dark city, so the chances of bumping into him were slim.

338

Mike was not there, but it was not yet eight o'clock. She carried on walking around the perimeter of the gardens, thinking about her mother, who, since arising at ten complaining of a splitting headache, had asked question after question.

'What on earth do you mean, Lucinda – popping down to Brighton tonight to see a friend? What about Charles?'

'My friend *lives* in Brighton – I didn't say I was going there. And I saw Charlie last evening. He'll be on duty tonight.'

'And do I know this friend?'

'I shouldn't think so, Mama. We trained together at Plymouth and her name is – is Patricia Pillmoor.' *Sorry, Chief.* 'And I think it's rather nice that she wants us to meet.'

Lucinda ran her tongue round her lips. She didn't like telling untruths but she could be hardly expected to say, 'As a matter of fact, Mama, I'm meeting an American called Mike. He picked me up one Sunday night in Craigiebur.' Or had she picked *him* up? 'And almost from that minute on I've been in love with him. So much in love that sometimes I don't know whether to laugh or to cry . . .'

Of course she couldn't say it, so the untruths came thick and fast. She was amazed at her own deceit. And she knew she must try to remember all those untruths and deceits because liars had to have very good memories.

'I don't know why you can't spend a night at home, Lucinda. You've been hopping about the house all day. Talk about a cat on hot bricks. I'd say,' she said without looking up from her newspaper, 'that you are up to something.'

'I am not!' Her cheeks blazed red. 'I wish you wouldn't always – '

'Emily Lees-Smith is getting married on Saturday. Big

affair, I believe, at St Margaret's.' The Countess changed the subject with irritating skill. 'Why couldn't it have been you and Charles? I get so embarrassed when people keep asking when it's going to be your turn.'

'Then don't be, Mama. It hasn't got anything to do with *people*, anyway. Don't keep on about it. Please.'

She should, she knew, have told her mother then. There wouldn't be a better time.

'And perhaps you'd better tell *people* that Charlie and I won't be getting married,' she could have said. If she had been brave enough, that was. If just to think of her mother's anger didn't make her sick inside, still.

So she had said nothing and stayed by the telephone in case Mike should ring, imagining the upset if her mother got to it first.

Cat on hot bricks? Her mother had been right, she was forced to admit. She very often was.

Impatiently she flicked her lighter, glancing quickly at her watch. Still not eight o'clock. Don't be late, darling, she pleaded silently. Late? What if he couldn't come? What if he'd phoned to tell her so after she'd left?

There were footsteps; hurrying footsteps. Let this be him. *Please* let it be.

'Mike?' She called his name softly, breaking into a run at his answering whistle. 'Oh, Mike . . .'

Their lips met urgently, hungrily. It was good to feel his closeness again, the hardness of his mouth. And it was easy to recall the way she wanted him; good to know that his need was as great as her own.

'I've missed you. Oh, how I've missed you.' She drew a little away. 'Let me look at you.'

'It's almost dark.'

'It doesn't matter.'

She traced the outline of his face, touching his eyes, his

340

chin, that scar that was so much a part of his attractiveness, lingering her fingertips on his lips that he might kiss them.

'Tell me,' she whispered.

'I've missed you, too. We can't go on like this, Lucy.' It was a statement, a plea, a challenge.

'I know,' she murmured, eyes closed.

'We've got to talk about us.'

'Yes.' Her mouth searched for his again. She felt tipsy, dizzy. There was a singing in her ears and her heartbeats throbbed dully in her throat.

'*Now*, Lucy. Before I go back.'

His hands slid possessively to her buttocks, pulling her closer, and the familiar feeling was back in her again and with it her terrible, tearing need of him. But he was good at arousing her, she thought helplessly; good at kissing her, touching her, manipulating her so that coherent speech and thought became impossible.

'Mike.' She struggled to surface from the warm whirlpool of her emotions. 'What did the doctors say, this afternoon?'

'I'm fit again for flying, it seems.' He said it as casually as he knew how, yet still he felt the stiffening of her body, the sudden jerking back of her head. 'But they didn't tell me when or where. I'll not know that for a week or two yet.'

'Flying again,' she said flatly. Most of the fighter stations were on the south coast and they'd be a million miles apart. 'Oh, God.'

She strained closer as if to steady the sudden shaking in her limbs and he held her tightly, whispering in her ear.

'There'll be leave, honey. More than most guys get. Every six weeks, once I'm operational. I'll come up to you, I promise. Don't let's spoil tonight, though.'

'All right. We'll not talk about it.' He was right. Tonight

341

was *now* and there was so much to say, so many missed kisses to redeem. 'Let's walk a little. It won't be too dark tonight. There's still half a moon left. Where are you staying?'

'I've fixed an apartment. Some place no one's in need of for a while.'

'How long have you got, Mike?'

'Till morning. There's a Navy truck leaving Victoria at ten; I'll be getting that.'

'But that's only a few hours!'

'Long enough, if we make the most of it. It's up to you, Lucy.'

She knew what he meant; knew exactly what he meant.

'There'll be nobody in the Wrennery checking me in tonight,' she told him softly.

The moon came out from behind a cloud and she saw his face clearly for the first time.

'Those nightingales – can you hear them?' She smiled tenderly, loving him so much it was like an ache inside her.

'Sure I can. I remember when we first met you told me they only sing for people in love.'

'So they do. Maybe that's why they're making such a terrible noise.' She took his face in her hands, reaching on tiptoe to kiss him, suddenly sure of herself; sure of their love. Only a few hours, yet when they had lived them nothing would ever be the same again. 'I love you,' she said softly. 'Have I told you, lately?'

'Your friend must be rich,' Lucinda whispered as they unlocked the door of the Eaton Square apartment. The janitor had been most respectful, touching his cap as he handed over the keys, saying 'Good evening, sir, madam.'

'Stay there while I check the blackout.' Mike strode down the passage, then at the touch of a single switch, it

342

seemed, lights flooded the rooms on either side. 'Okay. Guess it's been done.'

'*Very* rich,' Lucinda breathed, taking in the furniture and furnishings, the profusion of flowers. 'Are you sure we're in the right place?'

'Sure I'm sure, and hey, take a look at you? You look swell, honey; just swell.'

'Oh?' She laughed with pleasure, glad she had dressed carefully for him. 'This is the first time you've seen me without my uniform, isn't it?'

She took off her coat, spinning round for his approval.

'You look a million dollars, Lucy. Didn't realize till now you had legs.' He grinned. 'Say, how about fixing us a drink while I check the rest of the place?' He nodded to a tray of decanters and glasses on a side table.

Critically, she took stock of the room. Low sofas, expensively covered; antique tables and mirrors, several good paintings.

She wandered from table to table, picking up paper-weights, a silver cigarette box, ornaments of jade. It was easy to recognize the trappings of affluence. They had surrounded her, Lucinda realized, since ever she could remember. Rare and beautiful objects, handed down through the generations to be loved and cared for, then passed on. And rare and beautiful objects were here too, in plenty.

She didn't hear him return; not until his arms wrapped her round from behind and his lips brushed the nape of her neck.

'Everything seems okay.' He looked at her empty hands. 'No drink? What'll you have?'

'Should we, Mike?' She looked anxiously at the decanters. 'Drinks are very hard to come by, these days.'

'It's okay. Relax. No one's going to burst in and throw us into the street. Gin and lime?'

343

She nodded, unspeaking, wondering how he could be so familiar with the layout of the place, so easy in his surroundings. And the janitor had known him, hadn't he? He'd handed over the keys as if they'd been expected.

'You've been here before, haven't you, Mike?' Uneasily she accepted the too-full glass.

'Sure I have. I use this place whenever I can. I like it – don't you?'

'Of course I do, but' – she walked over to the fireplace, standing with her back to him, watching him through the mirror on her left – 'but have you ever brought anyone else here? A woman, I mean?'

He hesitated for only a second.

'That isn't entirely fair,' he said quietly, looking across to where she stood, meeting her reflected gaze.

'You have, then,' she whispered dully.

'Lucy, don't look at me like that.' He took her glass gently, setting it on the mantel, making her face him. 'This is *now*, and it's you I love, you I want – for always.'

She stared stubbornly down at the floor, hurt and angry and, yes, jealous. But of course there had been others. A man so blatantly attractive couldn't *not* have had affairs. And why should she feel so awful about it? She wasn't coming to Mike exactly brand spanking new, either.

And wasn't this 1941 and wasn't there a war on and wasn't it too stupid to worry about what was past or what was to come when all that mattered was now, *tonight*?

'Sorry.' She took an uneasy breath. 'I'd no right to ask you that.'

'Forget it.' He pulled her to him, whispering in her ear, arousing her with his lips just as he had done the night they first danced together and that feeling had surged through her with such delightful wantonness. 'Happy again?'

'Yes, and I truly am sorry, but tell me just one thing. Whose apartment is this?'

'Aah. I thought we'd get around to that. Well, if you must know, this place belongs to the corporation I worked for before I joined up. But it's okay,' he added hastily. 'I can stay here whenever I want. Before the war it was used a lot for entertaining, but no one comes over now, though the janitor's wife still looks after it. So quit worrying, sweetheart. It's okay for us to be here and it's okay about the drinks.' Finger beneath her chin, he tilted her face. 'Don't go home tonight, Lucy. Stay with me?'

Panic slashed through her. She had wanted this, longed for it, yet now she was afraid.

'But I haven't packed anything,' she gasped, suddenly confused and shy. 'Not even a toothbrush.'

'You can borrow mine, if you want. They say if you can use a guy's toothbrush you must surely be in love with him.'

'Then I'll use your toothbrush, if I may,' she told him gravely, loving him, needing him. 'And yes, Mike, I'll stay, if you want me to.'

'I want you to,' he said, love etched deeply on his face. 'Oh, Lucy Bainbridge, how I want you to.'

They sat on the hearthrug, backs against a sofa, drinking wine. Only one lamp burned dimly and firelight reached out to each corner of the room, gentling it with flickering shadows.

'You hungry, honey?'

'Not really.' She couldn't even think of food; not when every nerve end jangled and every small pulse in her body beat out want for him. She was happy, yet apprehensive too, thinking about the women who had been here before, wondering if they'd been good at making love and if Mike would find her frigid by comparison. 'I'd like more wine, though. And can we dance, when the late-night music comes on?'

'Sure we can, but you haven't told me how it's been at home.'

'Not good, really.' She held out her glass. 'I haven't had a chance to talk to my parents, and as for Charlie . . .'

'He's been around, has he?'

'Last night. We ended up yelling at each other and he went off in a temper.'

'You want I should see the guy – tell him you're in love with me?'

'No, Mike – thanks.' She inched closer so that their legs and thighs and shoulders touched. 'Best I should do it, when the time is right.'

'You'll tell him good, though? Tell him before you go back to Ardneavie, uh? No pussy-footing?'

'I will. I promise. Charlie I can just about manage; it's my mother I worry about.'

'She'll be difficult?' Mike frowned.

'Difficult? She invented the word!'

'Hell! Now see here, Lucy.' He took her face in his hands, turning it gently so their eyes met. 'I love you and I'll not have you upset over this. Let me see your folks. What kind of a guy lets his girl take all the flak, anyway?'

'It'll be all right.' She laid her head on his shoulder, warmed by wine and fireglow. 'After all, they can't force me to marry Charlie.'

'I guess not. But are you going to be hurt when some other woman gets Lady Mead? You love that old place, don't you?'

'Yes. I always have.' She lifted her mouth for his kiss. 'But one night not so very long ago, I made my choice and, yes, I was sad for a while. Lady Mead was always there, you see, solid and unchanging. And all I ever thought about was living in it again, one day. With kids all over the place, and ponies, and it never rained, either. And Nanny was back in the nursery, as she'd always been, as I'd always remembered. But it was all a childish daydream,' she concluded. 'It had to be, because not once was Charlie ever a part of it.'

'I'm sorry, sweetheart. I'll make it up to you. You know that.'

'You don't have to, Mike. I grew up, though, that night. It's you I want, though I get a bit panicky when I think of the upset it's going to cause. You won't stop loving me, will you?'

'Never.' He took her free hand, kissing each fingertip. 'Not ever.'

'And you'll take care, won't you? You *will* take care?'

'I will. I promise.' He rose to his feet, taking her glass, turning on the music.

'Care to dance, lady?' He folded her in his arms, his cheek on her head. 'You're sure about us, Lucy; sure about tonight?'

She reached up, wrapping her arms around his neck, straining closer.

The music was soft and suggestive and their feet moved slowly in small circles, bodies close.

'Happy? No regrets?'

'Happy, yes,' she sighed, eyes closed. 'Regrets? How could there be?'

'I love you,' he said.

The dance band signed off at midnight, bringing their closeness to a sudden end.

'This is the BBC Home Service,' the announcer intoned in his emotionless newsreader voice. 'Here is the late-night news and this is Stuart Hibberd reading it.

'Today, a communiqué from the Russian front

347

announced that Red Army forces are falling back to Leningrad in order that its defence may be – '

'Sorry, chum.' Mike snapped up the switch. 'You didn't want the news, Lucy?'

She shook her head. Nothing must invade this moment or encroach on the magic that made up this night. For a few, charmed hours there would be no war, no other world except the small, secret one in which they stood. Tomorrow Mike would leave her and there would be Mama and Charlie to face. And there'd be sirens and bombs and the Russians digging in around Leningrad, and Australian soldiers still holding out in brave, beleaguered Tobruk.

But tonight nothing and no one existed save herself and Mike and their bright, shining love. And this night would be doubly precious because soon Mike would be flying again, and this might be all she would have.

'Hey!' He kissed the tip of her nose. 'Why the frown?'

'Sorry.' She smiled. 'I was just thinking about – us.'

'And that makes you sad?'

'No, darling. It's just that when I think there's so very little time . . .'

'Right now, there's all the time in the world.' Slowly he pulled down the zip on her frock and she moved her shoulders in a shrug so that it fell softly to her feet.

He looked down at her, eyes narrowed; at the soft slope of her shoulders, the whiteness of her skin.

'You're so very beautiful,' he said softly, reaching behind her for the clasp that held her brassiere, unfastening it, slipping the straps from her shoulders. 'So very beautiful, my Lucy.'

Unhurriedly he kissed each breast, each nipple; heard the indrawing of her breath, felt the tremor that jerked through her.

'No, Mike!' She stepped back from him, hands covering

her nakedness, cheeks blazing red. 'Sorry, but – look, could I have a bath?'

Oh, damn, damn, *damn*. What was she saying; she who wanted him so much yet all she could think about was a bath!

'Surely you can, honey.' The tension left his face and he smiled at her unworldliness, and was glad because of it. 'Come on; I'll show you where.'

The bathroom was pink and white and warm. Soft towels stood in neatly folded piles, bath salts and large tablets of pink soap were there in plenty. A bottle of Chanel perfume stood unopened on a shelf beneath a pink and gilt mirror, and beside it stood talcum powder, a swansdown puff and a jar of cold cream.

'Help yourself, honey. I'll be next door, in the shower. You want I should shave?'

'No. Don't bother. I – I won't be long.' She swallowed hard.

He closed the door but she could hear his whistling above the sound of running taps.

She shook rose-scented bath salts into the water, watching it turn to pink, wondering why she was spoiling everything.

The water was very hot and she ran more than the permitted six inches, feeling reckless and all at once determined to splash herself with the perfume, no matter who it belonged to.

She lowered herself into the water then lay back, willing herself to relax. She loved him so much. Since they had met, every erotic fantasy she had ever indulged in had centred on double beds and Mike, yet now she was afraid and unsure; not of him, but of herself.

She lathered the soap furiously, rubbing it on the sponge, making suds on the water, and when the door opened and Mike stood there, she held the sponge against herself, then lowered it again.

He was wearing pyjama trousers in pale green; in his hand he carried the matching jacket.

'Here you are, Lucy. It's all I could find.' He laid the jacket over a chair. 'Thought maybe you'd feel better in – something.'

She looked candidly at his body and the short, fair hairs on his chest and the scar, made more noticeable by the hot water.

He was lean almost to the point of thinness though his shoulders and arms were muscled. He was good to look at – beautiful – and she loved him.

'I'm getting out now,' she said softly, suddenly, inexplicably at ease. 'Pass me a towel, darling.'

She looked into his eyes and saw anxiety there. Oh, Mike, my darling, is it the same for you, too?

He held wide a bath sheet and she stepped into it, standing quite still as he patted her dry.

'Feeling better now, Lucy?'

'Just fine.'

'Me, too.' He smiled.

She shrugged into the pyjama jacket, buttoning it to the neck, rolling up the sleeves, watching as his eyes searched her body.

Taking the towel, she wiped the mirror free of condensation, looking critically at her reflection. The jacket skimmed her knees and it was baggy on her, like a smock. She looked down at her feet, pink from the hot water and wondered whatever had become of the double-bed-and-Mike fantasy and the clinging black nightdress she had always seemed to wear for him.

'Will I do?' she whispered.

'You'll do.' His voice was rough.

God, but she was good to look at. Lucy Bainbridge could wear a sack and still look seductive.

His eyes took in her long, exquisite legs. Even her feet were sexy.

He unfastened the buttons on the jacket, gently kissing the hollow at her throat, trailing his lips over her neck, her shoulders, bending to kiss her flat, tight stomach.

She lifted her arms, pulling his head closer, whispering, 'I want you, darling. *Now*.'

From the mantel the clock chimed a single, silvery note, reminding them that tomorrow was already an hour spent.

Together they sank to the bed and he leaned over her, his hands beneath her buttocks, arching her body to meet his.

There was no other sound but the beating of heart upon heart. And nightingales singing.

Jane prayed as a child prays, hands over eyes, peeping. She knelt now, gazing at the old, decaying church through fan-spread fingers; at St Crispin's, that smelled of dusty hassocks and damp walls and six hundred years of existence.

And six hundred years of prayers and supplications had gone up from these worm-pitted pews; mostly from women, she supposed. Prayers for deliverance from the Black Death and Spanish Philip's Armada; thanks for Agincourt and Drake's little ships and Waterloo and Mafeking relieved and, not so very long ago, thanks for the ending of the slaughter called the Great War – the one to end all wars, they'd said.

And now, on this first Sunday in September, the people of Fenton Bishop joined with every church and chapel in Britain, offering thanks for a victory snatched from the defeat of Dunkirk and for the fighter pilots who threw back the German bombers and halted the invasion that must surely have followed.

Mr Churchill had called for this National Day of Prayer, asking that men and women everywhere should give thanks for favours past and entreat most earnestly for victory to come. Just as the German people prayed for it, Jane thought.

So what was God to do, then? Toss a coin? But all through history the British had muddled through, so God must have had a two-headed penny, she thought, irritated by the singsong voice of the vicar. She tried to remember that she was here to pray for those who were fighting *this* war – *her* war, because now she was a part of it, caught up in a conflict she had known was coming. She had never been more sure of anything on that last of her schooldays when the entire assembly had sung, 'I vow to thee, my country', and she had almost choked on the words and cried all the way home, not because she had left school but because she loved England so much and the North Riding and the beautiful little part of it called Fenton Bishop. Colin had asked what was the matter and she'd said it was her hay fever bothering her again.

A Brownie in the row in front dropped her collection penny and retrieved it, giggling. Everyone was here today. St Crispin's had never been so full of Scouts and Guides, soldiers from the gun sites around and airmen from across the fields. And Fenton Bishop folk, of course. It took a war, though, to fill St Crispin's.

'. . . and we give thanks for those who have made the most glorious of sacrifices; those who have fallen in the course of duty. May they rest eternally in the peace of Thy –'

Fallen? Jane puked on the word. To fall was to descend, to throw oneself down. Those men and women hadn't *fallen*, they'd been killed. Bloody well killed.

Not Rob, though. Somewhere, he *was* alive. She closed her eyes and bowed her head.

God, it's Jane Kendal and I want to thank you for Rob. What happened between us was wonderful and precious . . .

Why was she doing this? It was over now, wasn't it? Really over. Rob had a wife, and a baby soon to be born.

'God, I'm sorry. I shouldn't have loved him so much, but I didn't know he was married. I know now that he can't be mine any more.

'But look after him, will you, because he *is* out there, somewhere, trying to get home. Don't let anything happen to him.

'And I'm sorry I've been so awful. Help me not to be so moody and childish and help me to be kinder to Mum and Dad . . .'

And kind to Tom, too? To good, patient Tom, who loved her? But he could never take Rob's place. No one could.

The tears came, then. They came without sobs, the silent tears of surrender. And they came from the deeps of her heart so that her body shook with the effort of trying to stifle them.

'Jane?' Her father pressed a handkerchief into her hand, looking sideways anxiously, because the prayers were over and it was time for the collection and 'Onward, Christian Soldiers'.

'I'm all right, Dad,' she whispered, rising to her feet, opening her *Hymns Ancient and Modern* at the correct page even though she knew the words backwards. Poor Dad. He looked so tired.

She gave back the handkerchief, squeezing his hand briefly as she did so, smiling up at him, glad she had worn her uniform today, as he'd asked her to.

Then she closed her eyes again as the singing soared triumphantly.

'I love him, though, God. I always will. And I'd still give you the rest of my life just to see him. Just for half a minute, God. That's all.'

She sucked in a deep, shuddering breath then joined in the last verse.

Colin Clayton was waiting at the porch when they left, smiling at her parents, wishing them a polite 'good morning', dropping back a little so that he and Jane walked alone.

'It's good to see you again.' His eyes took in her uniform and she wondered if he felt embarrassed. 'I suppose you've been really looking forward to coming home?'

'Yes, Colin. Counting the days.'

And I tell lies too, Colin, because I've dreaded coming back here, opening up the wound. And I've been trying to lay a ghost, but I don't know how . . .

The soldiers were being formed into ranks outside the church gates, ready to march back to the gun sites.

'I – I suppose you do a lot of that, Jane – marching?' He turned his back on the squad as it stamped off.

'No, Colin. Hardly any at all, once I was through training depot. I quite like squad drill, though.' And I've still to do extra drills when I get back; part of my punishment still outstanding. I wonder what you'd think, Colin, if you knew that quiet little Jane Kendal went AWOL. And I wonder what you'd say if I told you I wouldn't care if I never saw Fenton Bishop again – not until the war is over, that is, and the airmen and the bombers all gone. 'I suppose you've just about finished with the harvest?'

'Yes. I've a bit more time for myself now. I was wondering if you'd like to come out one night before you

354

go back, Jane?' He looked uneasy; not like the Colin she'd grown up with. 'There's *Dangerous Moonlight* on in York. They say it's good.'

'I – I'm . . .' She began to say no, and then she remembered the tears she had cried for a love that was over. She'd even told God it was over. 'Well, yes, I'd like that. I'll look forward to it, Colin.'

She wouldn't like it; she would endure it. And she wouldn't look forward to it but it would please her parents when she told them, and they'd glance at each other and think that the affair with the airman was over and done with.

'Can you make it Monday or Tuesday? I'm going back on Wednesday, you see.'

Back to Ardneavie House and Lucinda and Vi and to Tom, who would understand and be kind to her; back to her own war, where there were no young men with wings on their tunics to remind her. Back to being a surname and number again, because only that way could she hope to survive.

They all met at the bench beside platform 8. Jane was there first, followed by Lucinda an hour later, and by Vi, whose train pulled into the station at Glasgow at five o'clock exactly. Five in the morning, that was.

'Ar, hey. I 'aven't half missed you both.' She hugged them, her smile warm and wide. 'Hey – remember the last time we were here?'

'Don't we just! Fed up and far from home, weren't we. We've changed a bit since then.'

'Oooh. Remember him with the hook?' Lucinda laughed. 'Remember how we used to think that anyone with rank up was the Archangel Gabriel?'

'And remember how long our skirts were?'

'And me feet? Mother of God, me feet . . .'

'We aren't rookies any more, though.'

They weren't. They'd got some in and they'd had their leave and the fluff was gone from their uniforms.

'Well, now, let's be hearin' your news.' Vi settled herself on the bench. 'How was London, Lucinda? Saw your Charlie, did you?'

'London was – well, London.' Lucinda smiled. 'And Charlie was – '

'Charlie?' Vi supplied, slab-faced.

'Exactly.' No need to tell them about the awful upset when she'd got home after – after Mike. They'd been waiting for her, Charlie and Mama, demanding to know where she had been all night, refusing to accept her explanation.

'Maida Vale, Lucinda? You stayed the night in *Maida Vale* with your friend from Brighton?' her mother had shrieked. 'I can easily check up, you know!'

'You may please yourself, Mama.'

She had refused to meet Charlie's eyes, though, and he had left in a temper, eventually, telling her that he wasn't entirely without influence and that he'd have her posted down south again because the Lord only knew what she'd been getting up to in Scotland.

She had turned on him angrily then, telling him that if he did he need never speak to her again. It was the nearest she had got, come to think of it, to telling him she would never marry him.

'Exactly. Let's not talk about Charlie.'

'And talk about Mike Farrow instead?' Vi offered. 'Did he manage to get up to London, then?'

'Yes, he did.' But she couldn't tell them about Eaton Square and how unbelievably good it had been; how she'd almost wept in his arms, afterwards, from the sheer joy of it.

'He's been passed fit for flying again, but he doesn't

356

know when.' She heard the sharp intake of Jane's breath and looked up to meet eyes wide with apprehension. 'He – he says he'll get leave quite often, when he's operational.'

'Yes,' Jane whispered. 'They do.'

'Well, and how was Yorkshire?' Vi beamed, sensing the tension. 'Mam and Dad all right, were they?'

'Yorkshire was fine. Everything was fine.' Jane smiled. 'I had a marvellous time.' So marvellous that I couldn't wait to get the next train back, she added silently. So damned marvellous that, next time, the Navy can stick their leave! 'How was it with you, Vi?'

'Ar, smashin'. And the kids – well, I love the bones of them two, you know.'

And poor little Paul had given up his bed for her and slept on the floor of his parents' room on a mattress borrowed from next door. Vi had felt bad about that. She loved her sister dearly, but she didn't ought to intrude, not four times a year she didn't.

'An' I had a look at Liverpool – well, what's left of it – an' I went to see Father O'Flaherty and the Sisters and . . .' Oh, yes, she'd been glad to see them all, but it would be good to see *Omega* again, and the hills and the trees and the wide, wide sky; great to watch Lilith and Fenny and Connie bringing the launch in, and Patsy Pill's eyelashes going up and down like windscreen wipers.

Their train arrived on time, actually on time, and the ticket collector appeared with his bag and vacuum flask and called, 'Garvie Ferry connection arriving now,' trying not to look smug about it. And they smiled and wished him 'good morning', and he told them to change at Garvie for Craigiebur, just as he'd told them the time before.

They would be back at Ardneavie House in time for morning standeasy; back to chunks of Kathy MacAlister's warm-from-the-oven bread, and tea, hot and sweet, from cups as big as chamber pots; back to cabin 9 and late duty with starboard watch. Like coming home, almost.

Ah, yes, Vi sighed contentedly, there were places far worse than Ardneavie House. Far, far worse.

15

'You're back, thanks be!' Dramatically Lilith Penrose closed the door of cabin 9 behind her. 'I've got to talk to you. I was pretty certain before you went away, and this isn't going to keep any longer!'

'Yes, we all had a smashin' leave, thanks.'

'Vi! This is serious, and Fenny agrees with me. Something has got to be done about Connie.'

'And what's she been up to now?' Vi clearly resented the interruption. She had carried up a tray by way of the back stairs and was looking forward to the resumption of the forbidden late-watch breakfasts taken comfortably in the cabin. 'That Connie's gettin' to be a pain in the neck with her moods. It's time you told her about it, Penrose. You're her leading wren, after all.'

'Yes, I know.' Lilith frowned. 'She's pregnant, you see. Well, I think she is . . .'

'*Whaaat*!' At once the boat's-crew coxwain had their attention.

'Does Chiefie know?'

'How far gone is she?'

'Poor kid. When did she tell you?'

'She didn't tell me. Nobody knows yet – well, not officially, that is.' Lilith shrugged. 'And I don't know how pregnant she is, but I'm as sure about it as I can be – and it's all down to Johnny Jones, if you ask me. He'll have to be told.'

'Maybe she's told him already,' Vi offered hopefully. 'Maybe he's goin' to do the right thing by her.'

'Is he hell! He's been avoiding her like the plague lately.

But I knew he was married and it's my guess Connie knows it now. Why else has she been acting the way she has? The poor kid is probably out of her mind with worry. Okay, so it's none of our business but we can't just do nothing. One of us has got to talk to her, but who?'

'You!' they said in unison.

'Yes, Lilith. You,' Vi said quietly. 'I know I'm the only married one among us and maybe it'd be better coming from me, but like I said, you are her leading wren, and if she is pregnant it's high time she was off that launch. Heaving and tugging on them ropes could do harm to that baby. She could even lose it.'

'Maybe that's what she wants.' Lilith sighed. 'Maybe it would be for the best. But it's up to me, I suppose, though I'm not looking forward to it.'

'I'll help, if you think it would do any good,' Vi offered. 'I'll be there, when you ask her.'

'And be sure to tell her we're all behind her,' Jane urged. 'Tell her we'll help her all we can. Nobody's going to point the finger. Let's face it, there but for the grace of God go a whole lot of us.'

'*Amen*!' Lucinda agreed fervently, her brows drawn into an anxious frown; for did she know with absolute certainty that Mike wasn't married? And couldn't that wonderful, exquisitely careless night together have made her pregnant, too? And where was the woman, she silently demanded, her whole body aching for the man in whose arms she lay, who even thought for a moment to ask if he were married, much less to remind him to be careful? 'Amen to that . . .'

'Right, then. Leave it to me,' Lilith said quietly, ominously. 'But that little bastard Johnny's got it coming to him!'

The door closed behind her, and breakfast in the cabin had suddenly lost its pleasure.

'I've never seen Penrose so mad,' Jane remarked. 'Friend Johnny's in for a rough passage if Lilith gets her knife into him.' She shivered then, and her mouth went dry, and for the life of her she didn't know why.

'You could be right, queen.' Vi nodded sagely. 'I'll tell you what, though. There's never a dull moment here, and that's for sure. What flamin' next, will you tell me?'

The occupants of cabin 9 had slipped easily back into the safe and familiar routine at Ardneavie House as if the seven days of their leave had never interrupted it. But then, it was an accepted fact that the Royal Navy ran like a precise machine, each wheel and cog oiled by leading hands and NCOs, with the officers who drank pink gins in the wardroom only there to sign chits, preside at defaulters' parades and be saluted. Or so those who lived on the lower decks believed. Now the three were again a part of that machine, with starboard watch taking the late duty whilst port watch had arisen, zombie-like, at the heathen hour of five and been about their business on *Omega* just one hour later.

Early watch had much to commend it, though; its participants enjoyed a few hours to themselves in the afternoon, with evenings free for dating and dancing and picture-going.

Late watch, on the other hand, played havoc with the love life of Ardneavie Wrens but allowed the luxury of sleeping later, breakfast carried stealthily to cabins and leisurely ablutions. And those who kept late duties had the advantage of a shorter watch, for *Omega*'s captain was of the opinion that the sooner all women were off his ship the better – especially in winter, when darkness came early and a blacked-out warship was considered no fit place for females. *Omega*'s captain was a 'regular', and he and his ilk thought and acted like the peacetime sailors they were; even now, after two years of war and two years of females on several of His Majesty's ships, the sight of black-stockinged knees and disturbingly undulating bottoms still made them yearn for the good days when the only ladies on ships had been Navy women visiting the wardroom for Sunday tea or for carefully regulated dinners: sweethearts and wives who knew their place, by God, and had been off the ship by sundown.

Not that Wrens were altogether a nuisance, of course. Some of them, it was becoming increasingly hard to deny, were even possessed of a brain, though nothing would have dragged the admission from the diehard regulars. So Jane, for whom the mysteries of jumbled, coded groups of figures and letters held no mystery now, and Lucinda, who Walter Wetherby admitted was fast becoming the equal of the best telegraphist in the wireless office, smiled at their opposite numbers on port watch and took up their duties with an assurance that neither would have believed possible on that twenty-third day of June last.

'How was your leave, then?' Jock asked in his usual paternal voice, and Jane absently replied, 'Great, just great,' turning the pages of the K-code tables with dexterity, saying, 'I'll call, shall I?' which told Jock Menzies that the girl was doubtless not sorry to be back.

'Tom Tavey has been at the porthole asking after you,' he remarked obliquely. 'Told me that *Viper* is away to sea for more trials this forenoon. He's a decent lad, that Tom.'

'Yes, Jock. I like him.' She said it partly because that was what Jock wanted to hear and partly because she was beginning to accept it to be true. Tom *was* a decent sort; one with broad, protective shoulders and a gentle smile. And eyes that loved her unashamedly.

Lucinda took her seat at the receiver which was now her friend and smiled again at the telegraphist who handed over the watch; then, adjusting her headset, she moved the dials with confident fingers. But for each of them, Connie Dean was never long away from their thoughts, nor the look in the eyes of Lilith Penrose, who wanted vengeance and would have it by any means possible, Lucinda thought uneasily, whether by the sticking in of pins or by some age-old incantation. For Lilith practised a religion which demanded that Johnny Jones should pay, and pay he would. Nothing could be more certain.

'There now. That's got another wee rush over with.' Methodically Jock Menzies straightened pads and pencils then lit a cigarette. 'And you have a visitor.' He nodded in the direction of the open porthole which framed Tom Tavey's face. 'Here, away with this signal to the typists, then take a wee word with your boyfriend. *Two* minutes, mind.'

'He's not my boyfriend,' Jane defended, pink-cheeked, but she carried the decoded message to be typed then slipped unnoticed through the CCO door.

'Tom, hullo!' She was genuinely pleased to see him and was grateful for the wide smile that warmed her still-bruised ego. He was wearing a thick white sweater, his trousers tucked into knee-high sea boots; dress that made him look more like the farmer he really was than the submariner he had chosen to become. 'All dressed up for some more sea-time, I see.'

'You bet. We've been at it since daylight, loading up. We'll be gone for a couple of days, firing torpedoes.'

'Just firing them? But what *at*?'

'At nothing, my lovely. We just let them go. It's all part of working up.'

'Isn't that a terrible waste?' Jane demanded. 'And isn't it dangerous?'

'Bless you, no. *Lothian* is escorting us, and they'll

363

retrieve the torpedoes when they've run and bring them back to *Omega*. And they can't do any damage.' He laughed, her curiosity pleasing him. 'Practice torpedoes only carry dummy warheads – no explosives. Satisfied?'

'Yes, Tom.'

'Right! Now when will I see you again?'

'When you get back.' She said it without hesitation. 'I'll be on early watch by then. But I can't stay. Jock said two minutes.' She turned to leave him. 'Take care, Tom.'

'I want to kiss you.' He took her arm, his voice low with need.

'Tom! No!' Here, in broad daylight? On one of HM ships? She smiled into his eyes. 'Behave yourself and, Tom – mind how you go.'

She stood a moment, watching him run nimbly down the well-deck ladder. Don't ask for too much, Tom, she pleaded silently. Give me time.

'Two minutes – okay?' She looked pointedly at her watch as she returned to her desk.

'Aye.'

'Tom's off to do dummy runs with torpedoes this time.'

'So I heard. *Lothian*'s escorting them. They'll soon have finished working up. *Viper*'ll be operational before much longer. Er – you'll have fixed yourself a date?'

Jock had never been able to get to the bottom of the Glasgow business but he still felt in some way responsible, having pointed her in the direction of McFadden's bakery in the first place. But all young girls needed a boyfriend and it mightn't be a bad thing for Jane to take up with a laddie like Tom and forget the airman and the misery he seemed to have caused her.

'Yes, Jock, we've fixed up a date. And you can stop worrying about me.' She smiled. 'I'm a big girl now.'

'Oh, aye?' A big girl, was she? He sharpened his pencil with unnecessary concentration. A bairn not yet nineteen and her with a sheltered upbringing, he shouldn't wonder, before she was pitchforked into this lot.

Tom was kind and considerate and exactly the man she needed to help her over the pain of losing Rob, Jane decided. But soon Tom would want more than she was prepared to give; more than she was prepared to give to any man again – and then what?

Oh, Rob MacDonald, why did we have to meet? Why did you spoil me for other men, and when, when, *when* will I ever forget you?

Fenny Cole poked her head round the door of cabin 9 and looked pointedly at Vi.

'I'm going down for the breakfasts.' She hesitated. 'Lilith says will you go next door – *now*.'

So this was it. Vi frowned. Lilith intended having it out with Connie. It was a matter, really, in which Vi would rather not be involved, but something was very wrong with the girl – though not for a minute could Vi imagine her taking their interference lying down, especially if she wasn't pregnant, after all.

Uneasily she knocked on the door of cabin 10, then walked in. Lilith was standing at the window; Connie lay on her bed, arms behind her head, giving no sign of recognition as Vi closed the door quietly.

'Hullo, queen. You not up and about yet?' Vi asked with a brightness she did not feel. 'Not very well, aren't you?'

The observation was well made, for Connie Dean's face was pinched and pale.

'Very well?' She swung her legs to the floor then sat up to face them, back straight, head high. 'If you mean am I being sick as a pig every morning, yes, I am! Well, that's what you wanted to know, isn't it?'

365

She said it quietly, with relief, almost, her eyes misting over with tears.

'Con, love!' Instantly Lilith was beside her, gathering her close. 'It's all right. Vi and me want to help you. We all do, only tell us.'

'Help me? Nobody can help me! Oh, God, Lilith, what am I going to do?'

'How far on are you, queen?' Vi asked with typical practicality, for the expected defiant outburst had not happened and the time for shilly-shallying was over. 'How many periods have you missed?'

'Next week it'll be three. And there's no doubt about it. I went last week to the civilian doctor in Craigiebur. I'm having a baby, all right. "Get married as soon as you can," was all he said. I asked him to help me – was there something I could take, I asked, but he said it wasn't possible. Told me I mustn't even so much as *think* of doing anything so silly . . .'

'I should damn well think not!' Vi countered hotly. 'If you're thinking about one of them back-street biddies and their mucky knitting needles, just forget it! You're not the first to end up in trouble, girl, and you'll not be the last!'

'I know, Vi, but that's no comfort to me. You two don't understand.' She gave a small, helpless shrug, the Connie of old long gone. 'I come from a tiny village, you see, and it can be a nasty gossipy little place – and most times it is. And worse than that, my dad's an elder of the chapel. God! He's so strait-laced and holy. No Sunday papers. Chapel twice on the Sabbath and Bible class in between, and my mother not much better.

'My dad's going to kill me! Okay, so it's happened before in the village, but they usually get the girl married before she's showing too much to wear white – and that makes it all right, would you believe? But who's going to marry me?' Tears flowed freely now, sobs shook her shoulders. 'The ones at home who can't get their babies fathered go away to a relation – to work, they usually say – but they come back sooner or later, without the kid, poor little thing. Everybody knows, though. Those girls never get husbands, after that. Go into domestic service, usually. But it's not going to happen to me. I'll – '

'Connie, *listen*.' Gently Lilith stemmed the near-hysterical outburst. 'What did Johnny say when you told him? You *have* told him?'

'Oh, yes, I told him, as soon as I'd missed. But he didn't want to know and I just can't get hold of him now.'

'But the baby is his?' Lilith persisted.

'It couldn't belong to anyone else. I told him that, but he said if I tried anything on he'd get all his mates to – to swear they'd been with me, too.'

'The little *shit*! My, I'll fix him yet, that one! But it's you we've got to worry about right now, Con. First thing you must do is tell your parents.'

'She's right,' Vi said softly.

'Vi, I *can't*! You don't know them like I do and you don't know that village!'

'Oh, Connie, Connie. They can't be that bad,' Lilith comforted. 'Of course it'll be a shock to them, but they'll get used to it, in time.'

'They will, queen. They'll get ever so fond of the little thing, just you see if they don't. Where's the woman who can resist a tiny baby – especially if it's her own grandchild.'

'My mother can, and she will too. My dad'll see to that. He's a Victorian prude. You should have heard him preaching his sermons about harlots and the terrible lusts of the flesh – '

'Oh, ar. And how did he get you, then?' Vi demanded. 'A gooseberry-bush baby, was you?'

'I *can't* go home. I *won't*.'

367

'All right, then. But at least tell your folks, then we'll know where we stand. Write them a letter this morning before we go on watch, then go and see Sister in sick bay. She'll know what to do. And we're all behind you, aren't we, Vi? We'll help you all we can – you know that, don't you, Con?'

'Thanks, both of you. And thanks for not saying I told you so.' Connie sniffed and dabbed her eyes. 'And I'm sorry for all the things I said when you tried to warn me, Lilith.'

'Forget it. Just get yourself off to sick bay and after that we'll take it one day at a time – okay?'

There was a coughing and a fumbling outside the door, then Fenny came in with the breakfast tray: hot mugs of tea and thick slices of bread spread with marmalade.

'Lucinda's got yours, Vi, and letters too.'

She smiled, and things in cabins 9 and 10 returned to normal. As normal as they would ever be again, that was.

'It's true, then?'

'How did she take it?' Jane and Lucinda demanded when Vi returned.

The breakfast tray and three letters lay atop the chest of drawers, and Vi eyed the tea longingly.

'Yes, the poor kid's in trouble, all right.' She accepted the mug Lucinda offered and drank from it deeply before she continued. 'She didn't try to deny it, either, but she's goin' to need all the help we can give her because there'll be none from her mam and dad. Says she's frightened of them two at home, but Lilith said they've got to be told.

'Ar, he's a wrong 'un, that Johnny. Gettin' a girl into trouble, and him married. Away from their wives, them fellers are and out for all they can get, some of them.

368

Sorry, queen. I wasn't meanin' to be personal,' she choked, pink-cheeked. 'Not your Rob . . .'

'No, Vi.' Jane's smile was thin. Rob hadn't got her pregnant, though how often had she longed for a child to bind him to her? 'Not my Rob. By the way, who are the letters for?'

'One each.' Lucinda bit into a slice of bread. 'Ormskirk and York postmarks for you two and mine's from Charlie.'

Nothing from Mike. Never anything from Mike. Just a hurried phone call the night after Eaton Square. *I love you, Lucy. You're mine, now, and never forget it . . .* !' Then nothing.

Where are you, Mike? What's happening? Just a couple of lines on a postcard, *please*.

Vi fingered the envelope bearing her sister's handwriting. Not fat enough for it to contain a letter card from Gerry, but letters from Austria were spasmodic and she had received four, which she read and reread almost every day.

'Aren't you going to open your letter, Lucinda?'

'Already have.' Lucinda pushed the envelope into the pocket of her dressing gown. 'Read it whilst I was waiting at the tea urn, actually.'

The letter contained what for Charlie amounted to an apology; he was sorry that her leave had turned out such a disaster for them both and suggested they make plans to be married on her next one – or sooner, should he be posted to a regiment.

No, Charlie! *No*! She couldn't bear it now if he as much as touched her. Not after Eaton Square.

'I think,' she murmured thoughtfully, 'that I'll put in a call to Mike before I go on watch.'

'*You'll* be lucky!'

'I know, but it's worth a try. I just might get through.

369

And if I can't get him this morning I can always try again tonight, after I come off watch.'

'You know we can't use the Wrennery phone after lights out.'

'All right, then. I can nip out and use the call box across the road. As long as nobody closes the pantry window, I'll get back in all right.'

'Now see 'ere, Lucinda, that wouldn't work and you know it. There's no lights in phone boxes and you'd have to take a torch. At that hour the pier patrol would pick you up before you'd had time to dial the operator. Have you got to phone Mike?' Vi demanded bluntly.

'Yes, Vi, I have. I haven't heard from him since – oh, ages.'

'But there can be all sorts of reasons why he hasn't been in touch.'

'It's a week now. Even if he's on the move again, surely just a couple of lines?' Lucinda's eyes were anxious, the quicksilver smile gone. 'All right, so I'm being stupid. I keep telling myself there's a war on, but – '

'But you're set on phoning him, aren't you, queen? All right, then. Go downstairs now and put a call in. Tell the operator it's urgent and you just might be lucky. If it doesn't come through before you go on watch you'll just have to try again tonight. Book the call, then come downstairs after lights out and sit by the phone and wait.'

'Y-yes, but what if I get through and Mike's in bed?'

'Now listen 'ere.' Vi's patience was wearing thin. 'Do you want to talk to the bloke, or don't you?'

'Okay, Vi. I'll go down now.'

'And we'll worry about tonight when tonight comes – all right, Lucinda?'

'I'd say,' said Jane when she and Vi were alone, 'that our Bainbridge has got it bad. I wonder what really

370

happened on leave. She never told us, did she, only that they'd met in London.'

'No. She never said, but it's my guess we'll soon know.'

And further than that, Vi was not prepared to say.

Wren Connie Dean was already waiting at sick bay ashore when starboard watch straggled down the jetty to pick up the launch for *Omega*.

'Strange, isn't it, going on duty without Connie?' Fenny sighed.

'What will you do?' Jane demanded of Lilith, 'if Sister says she must come off boat's-crew? You can't work a boat with just the two of you.'

'I'll ask for a relief when I pick up my launch. There's sure to be a seaman they can loan me until drafting depot get a replacement here. And there's no *if* about it. Connie is pregnant, so there's no place for her now in my crew. Not three months gone, there isn't. By the way, she phoned her parents this morning. Got through to them straight away. No delay at all. But that's always the way with bad news, isn't it? Seems always to travel quicker than good.'

'And what did they say?'

'Say? Seems her father gave her a real old rocket. Hit the roof, and her mother too. Told her she was no daughter of theirs and not to even think of coming home and shaming them.'

'How *could* they? And just when she really needs them,' Lucinda protested. 'Isn't there anywhere she can go, Lilith? The Navy can't just turn her out.'

'No, and it won't. I had a talk with Patsy Pill. I had to. Connie was breaking her heart after that phone call. Patsy says Connie can probably stay on at Ardneavie House for a time, then it'll have to be the unmarried mothers' home for her. But Patsy's going to talk to Ma'am about it first and see what they can come up with.'

'And what about the baby?'

'I'm afraid Connie will have to leave it behind for adoption when she comes back here. The Wrens *will* take her back, it seems.'

'But Lilith – I think she loved Johnny. What if she wants to keep it?'

'She can't, and she knows it. Best it goes to a family who really want it. Being adopted carries no slur with it; being the child of an unmarried mother does, though God knows why. It isn't the kid's fault.'

'And Johnny Jones will go scot-free! It's still a man's world, isn't it? That joker needs someone to give him a damn good hiding,' Fenny protested.

'Forget him. Johnny's mine.' Lilith's eyes narrowed to small, vindictive slits. 'Leave that one to me, because before I'm finished with him he'll wish he'd never been born.'

She uttered the words with such certainty, such hatred, that there seemed nothing more to say and, chastened, they stared out across the loch to the launch that headed towards them, and to the escort ship *Lothian*, with the new submarine *Viper* in her wake, going out to sea to fire torpedoes.

'It's getting colder.' Fenny shivered. 'Suddenly it's autumn.'

But no one replied or even nodded assent, for each of them knew that summer was indeed gone – and with it those golden, uncomplicated weeks that could never return.

And what ahead now, but winter?

It was very dark and very still when Lucinda opened the door of cabin 9 and edged her way slowly and carefully to her bed.

'That you, queen?' Vi was awake still, and the creaking of Jane's bedsprings confirmed that she too had not slept. 'Get through all right, did you?'

'Yes. I got through. Look, would you mind if I put on the light?' Lucinda whispered. 'I need a cigarette.'

'Okay by me.' Jane sat up in bed and arranged a pillow at her back. 'Did they have to get Mike out of bed, then?'

'No, they didn't.' Lucinda drew deeply on her cigarette. 'They didn't because he wasn't there. The man I spoke to told me Mike left Worthy Down last Sunday night. That must have been just after he phoned me. He must have known he was leaving yet he didn't say a word.'

'Maybe he couldn't,' Vi reasoned. 'If he was goin' back to flying again and on the way to a new squadron, it isn't likely he'd tell you. You can't go shouting things like that down the phone, can you? Careless talk, innit?'

'He could have told me he was on the move,' Lucinda protested. 'Just a hint. I wouldn't have asked him where.'

'So what are you worrying about?' Jane soothed. 'He's been posted somewhere, that's all. You knew he would be, eventually.'

'Yes, but what I wasn't prepared for was the absolute finality of it. The man said he was sorry, but Mike had left some time ago and no, he *couldn't* tell me where he'd gone, and then he said he suggested I wait until Mike got in touch with me – as if I was some little pick-up, being a nuisance.

'But Mike's had time enough to get in touch. Even if they've sent him up to Orkney, a letter doesn't take over a week! And they do have phones there. Where is he, Vi? Why did he go off like that?'

Her eyes were dark and full of pain and already brimming with tears.

'Now see here, queen. Don't be thinkin' your feller has

done a Johnny. By what you've told us he was pretty serious about you.'

'So was Johnny serious about Connie. Serious about getting what he wanted, that was!'

'Yes, but you and Mike didn't go that far,' Jane reasoned. 'Mike wasn't – '

'Mike was – and we *did*.' Lucinda stubbed out her cigarette. 'That night we met in London, we spent it together – very much together.'

'And are you – might you . . . ?' Vi's eyes dropped to her fingers.

'Am I pregnant, too?' Lucinda whispered. 'I don't know yet.'

'Oh, flamin' Norah!' Vi threw back her bedclothes and reached for her cigarettes. 'This is a right old carry-on, innit? Didn't you tell him to be careful? Surely you both had the sense to – '

'*Sense*, Vi? When does sense come into it? I loved him, I wanted him and that's all there was to it. Making love isn't something you talk about. It just happens. I knew what I was doing – well, I thought I did.'

'She's right.' Jane sighed. 'Things seem so much more urgent when there's a war on. There's no tomorrow for people like us. *Now* is all that matters. Leastways, that's what I thought.'

'So you understand?' Lucinda asked softly.

'Oh, yes. And I used to long for Rob's child. He'd marry me then, I thought. But try not to worry, Lucinda. Not yet. Not till you know for certain. And there'll soon be a letter from Mike, just see if there isn't.'

'Of course there will. I've never met your feller, Lucinda – well, not Mike, that is – but a bloke who'll come and help us fight our war when he could be sittin' safe at home isn't the sort that does what Connie's feller did. So stop your worryin'. God, this ciggie's foul.' She shuddered. 'Me mouth tastes like the bottom of a parrot's cage! D'you think we could nip down to the galley and make a quick brew?'

'Best not,' Jane cautioned. 'Patsy Pill would hear us. Got ears like radar scanners, that one.'

'Suppose you're right.' Vi sighed. 'Reckon we'd best get our heads down again. Ar, come on, Lucinda. Get yourself undressed and into bed. You'll be all right, I'd bet a week's pay on it. It's poor old Connie we ought to be worryin' about just now.'

'I know, Vi. It isn't getting pregnant that worries me so much, it's Mike.' Lucinda tugged at the knot in her tie. 'Where is he? I mean, where *really* is he? He could have been in touch, somehow. I *know* it.'

'Oh, Lord! You can't think he's done a bunk?' Jane asked, wide-eyed.

'Well, doesn't it look like it?'

'Has he thump!' Vi's voice held a certainty she didn't wholly feel, because men were men the whole world over – well, excepting Gerry, that was. 'You'll hear from your feller, I know you will, so pick them clothes up off the deck and put them tidy over your chair and let's be hearing no more of your nonsense – all right? And get yourself into bed, for God's sake. I don't know about youse two but *I* need me beauty sleep!'

Mother of God, if this war went on for very much longer she'd have a face like a tired prune, with them two and their love lives. 'And get yourselves off to sleep,' she ordered, snapping off the light, 'and don't be lying there, tossin' and thinkin'. Things won't seem so bad in the morning; well, exceptin' for that poor kid next door, that is . . .'

But though they lay quietly in the darkness of cabin 9, sleep came only reluctantly.

Are you married too, like Rob? Lucinda thought. Is it

375

over between us, Mike? And in the mess when the talk gets bawdy, will you brag about the blonde Wren who was a pushover – a piece of cake?

And if Mike had gone, if he'd really left her and if she was pregnant, then what would happen at Bruton Street? Mama really would have something to go on and on about then, she shuddered, dry-mouthed.

But if that happened, she wouldn't go to London. She'd go home to Lady Mead and nobody would take the baby away from her. Nobody would convince her it would be better off farmed out into respectability as they'd convinced Connie. She was a Bainbridge; she'd manage, somehow. There'd be money coming to her when she was twenty-one, wouldn't there? Not a lot, but it would help. She'd get by, of course she would. If Mike had really left her, that was. If her period didn't come on Friday. And she'd try to be especially nice to Connie, she really would, and oh, Mike, where are you? Don't stop loving me? We did hear nightingales, remember? We *did*, my love.

Vi lay very still, pretending sleep. What was this war doing to people? Connie worried out of her mind, and now Lucinda. Why did babies happen so easily – well, to other people, that was? She and Gerry hadn't been so lucky. A couple of kids to worry about and fuss over would have been welcome, but they hadn't come along. Just two, of course. Not one every year like Ma McKeown had had, God rest her.

Poor Connie. She'd have to give her baby away. She'd carry it and help it to be born; she'd feed it and love it and then one day she'd leave it at the home and go back to the Wrens again.

Vi dabbed her eyes with the sheet. Poor little unwanted kid. She'd have adopted that baby; she'd have taken it and loved it and watched it grow up. If things had been normal, that was. If Gerry had still been at sea and Lyra Street hadn't been bombed; if the war hadn't happened.

But if the war hadn't happened, Connie wouldn't be pregnant, would she, and Lucinda wouldn't be worrying and counting the days.

Lucinda? By the heck, but that old mam of hers would go flaming berserk if her daughter turned up at home and told her she was in the puddin' club. And what would Charlie have to say about it? Oh, damn this war! Damn it, damn it, *damn it*!

What would have happened to me, Jane thought, hugging her pillow tightly, if *I'd* got pregnant? Could I have stayed in Fenton Bishop? Could I have taken the gossip, the side glances? Could I have borne to see my child – my child and Rob's – being treated differently from the rest? Because a child like that was always an *illegitimate* child, never a normal one. It carried the mark of its mother's stupidity for the rest of its life – or it did in Fenton Bishop. They'd never let you forget. That's how it was for Connie, now: afraid to go home with her shame. Yet Johnny Jones would get away with it – even though Lilith had vowed to get even with him, he would, because what could Lilith do that would make one scrap of difference? In a man's world – just what?

The weather was becoming colder. That morning, the first frost of autumn had sent the boat's-crew Wrens hurrying to carry up coal and fill the baskets either side of the hearth with sawn-up driftwood, collected during the summer and stacked to dry in a corner of the stables.

Before many more weeks had passed, Loch Ardneavie would be lashed by winter gales and the women who crewed the launch in need of that summer bounty to dry out sodden clothing and wet canvas pumps. And all through the winter, cabin 10 would smell of drying wool from the bell-bottomed trousers hung on the pulley rack and socks steaming and roasting on the fireguard. But their winter evenings would be warm and snug, for coal was severely rationed and the boat's-crew cabin the only one to be allowed a fire.

'I hope,' frowned Fenny, 'that the wood lasts out. They say around these parts that January takes back what July gives, and we did have a smashing summer, didn't we?'

A wonderful summer. A sunbright summer and a crew who had worked well together and been the equal of any three seamen. Now, all that was to change.

'Chiefie told me that Connie's relief is due any time,' Lilith said reluctantly. 'Coming up from HMS *Hornet*. Experienced, I believe.'

At least they wouldn't have to nurse her through the rough waters of winter. 'Oh, I could shake Dean! She'd have made a good cox'n, one day.' Strong, fearless and a good swimmer; Connie's absence was already felt.

'Where is she, by the way?'

'In the toilet, being sick, I think.'

'Damn! Not again!'

'She'll be all right,' Fenny Cole soothed. 'She's a whole lot better than she was.'

'And a whole lot thicker round the waist. What's she going to do, will you tell me, when her skirt won't button up?'

'Swop it for a bigger one?'

'I suppose so. But Ma'am's really sticking her neck out, keeping her here. King's Regulations definitely state a Wren should be discharged by the thirteenth week of pregnancy. Connie's that – and more!'

'Granted. But let's not look for trouble. Let's worry about it if it happens, uh?'

'*When* it happens, you mean.' Lilith's face took on an unaccustomed sadness, for the third eye given to all psychics had already seen nothing but pain ahead for Wren Connie Dean. 'We've got to be good to her, Fenny; all of us. We're all she's got, now. And hurry yourself, will you?' she snapped, embarrassed by her rare show of emotion. 'We should be at the end of the jetty by now. Want us to miss the boat, do you?'

Lucinda scanned the letter board, just to be sure, but the midday post had not yielded the letter for which she so desperately longed. But this morning, with shuddering relief, she had known she was not pregnant.

Thanks, Mike. Briefly she had closed her eyes. *Thanks at least, for that* . . .

'Come on, Kendal dear. Chop chop.' A pale ghost of the quicksilver smile briefly tilted the corners of her mouth. 'Last day of late watches, thank the Lord. Forward into the breach . . .'

Jane Kendal did not reply. Her friend was well aware of her silent sympathy; there was no need now for words

379

between them. Lucinda was hurting inside and to tell her that the pain would lessen wouldn't help. Not for a long time.

Jane turned up the collar of her coat as they stepped outside into a grey and cheerless forenoon.

'God, but it's cold,' was all she said.

Connie Dean stood at the window, staring out across the loch, watching the launch make fast alongside the *Jan Mayen*. They were managing well without her. Soon, when it was time to go to *that* place, they'd say goodbye then forget her in a week. Because when it was all over, when she put on her uniform again and came back to the Wrens, she wouldn't be returning to Ardneavie House. They would draft her to another crew in another place, where no one need ever know about Johnny's baby.

She had seen Johnny only two days ago; seen him from a distance, waiting for the Craigiebur transport, and a knife had sliced into the numb thing that was her heart and sent pain screaming through her.

What is she like, Johnny, your new woman? she had wanted to ask. Does she believe your lies, or is she a woman alone, her man gone to war and in need of the comfort you are only too willing to offer? It's safer with the married ones, isn't it, Johnny . . . ?

She gazed, dry-eyed, as that same transport now came to a stop at the gates of Ardneavie House, watching intently as the tail-board slammed down and a Wren jumped out; a dark-haired, dark-eyed Wren wearing a lanyard on her jacket, the lanyard only boat's-crew could wear.

'Oh, no,' she whispered. 'Not already?'

Her relief had come. Now she must leave cabin 10 and move downstairs to wherever a bed or bunk was available. One more step in the direction of the unmarried mothers' home and the misery that awaited her there. Why couldn't she have awakened this morning to realize with blazing gratitude that it had all been a bad dream; that she would pull on bell-bottoms and sweater and take her place in the launch with Lilith and Fenny? But her hands had wandered, as they did so often now, to her swelling abdomen – and the bad dream was reality; nothing had changed.

'Oh, God,' she whispered out loud to the suddenly dear, familiar room. 'I'm so miserable I wish I could die.'

When she wandered downstairs for afternoon standeasy, Connie tried not to notice the case, kitbag and respirator outside the regulating office door. The day she had refused to think about was here; her relief was fact and her arrival would set in motion the events that would take her, step by reluctant step, to *that* place.

Like a little hunted animal, she made for the warmth of the galley where Kathy MacAlister would make cocoa and toast. To drink tea, Connie had miserably discovered, made her even more sick, but cocoa and dry toast settled easily on her stomach and didn't send her, hand over mouth, to the nearest lavatory to vomit.

'Here you are, then.' Kathy smiled. 'Take it slowly, hen, and it'll stay down.' Kathy MacAlister was aunt to many, and her knowledge of pregnancy sickness had no equal. 'And don't worry. All that puking won't last much longer.'

'Thanks.' Connie took the stool beside the stove. 'Mind if I drink it here this morning.'

The galley was still a safe place; still free of the presence of the dark-haired, dark-eyed Wren. Soon, she knew, she must meet the girl who was to take her place on the launch and sleep in her bed and gossip and giggle beside the cabin fire in the long northern evenings to come. Or maybe the new girl would help them set up the table and

381

polish the glass and ask it wide-eyed questions about lovers past and lovers to come and believe every word of it; every dear, silly word.

Rising, she rinsed her plate and cup then dried them carefully.

'I'd better go. My relief just came and she'll need my bedspace. Got to empty my things out, I suppose. Bye, Kathy. Thanks for the toast.'

'Lord! Why did You make us women so stupid?' Leading Cook MacAlister demanded as she slammed on the lid of the one-gallon teapot. 'And why did You ever create men?' A world without them – just imagine! No deceit, no trouble, no wars. 'Or why, Lord, come to think of it, did You not give the wombs to men? Now that *would* have been something!'

Smiling serenely at the thought, she flung open the galley serving hatch.

'Standeasy!' she yelled. 'Come and get it!'

Megan Cadwallader was comfortably established in cabin 10 by the time starboard watch came ashore, and Connie had carried her kit downstairs to cabin 3 and made up the spare bottom bunk there.

'Hullo!' Lilith Penrose held out her hand. Word of the new arrival had reached her and a greeting was ready on her lips as she opened the door.

'Hi!' The pyjama-clad figure rose from the bed, the black eyes smiled back into Lilith's. 'You'll be Fenny and Lilith. I'm Megan Cadwallader, from *Hornet*.'

'Megan – er?' Fenny's nose wrinkled. 'You'd better spell it.'

Laughing, Megan obliged. 'Accent on the *walla*. Best get it right. It's Welsh, see? Cadwallader once was the name of princes. Proud as the Glendowers, our lot were.

But it's a mouthful, mind, and most people call me Megan Cad.'

Lilith looked again into the warm, bright face and liked what she saw. A true woman of Wales. One of the little dark people; a Celt through and through, and possessed, she shouldn't wonder, of Celtish second sight, if ever her origins surfaced. One of her own, Lilith decided, and if they must part with Connie, then Megan Cadwallader, it seemed, would fit in very nicely. Very nicely indeed.

It was the night of another Wrennery dance, an occasion which, Chief Wren Pillmoor sighed, came around with irritating regularity and was entered into with enthusiasm by all save herself. The dance was a nuisance, an upset. She resented the disruption to her orderly routine, disliked intensely the bother of clearing the mess hall, the carrying out of furniture and the noise that got louder as the dancing got rowdier. But the monthly dance was an established event which would have evoked resentment had she tried to stop it, though she had often thought with a secret, cunning longing of what might be achieved should she misplace the gramophone handle or lose the records or the rare-as-gold-dust gramophone needles. Mutiny, she shouldn't wonder, and forty-odd mutinous Wren ratings were something to be reckoned with.

No, she sighed, she would endure it as she always did, and when it was over and the stables and the wood shed and the boilerhouse all thoroughly searched, she would lock both doors and the pantry window too, and creep gratefully to her bed. And thank the good Lord fervently that she had survived yet another shindig.

'It'll be smashin',' Vi beamed, 'not being duty steward tonight. Make a nice change, bein' able to have a dance or two.'

383

'You like dancing, don't you?' Carefully Jane removed the kirby grips from her pin-curled hair.

'Love it. Gerry an' me danced a lot when he was ashore. Always went to the tea dances. Gerry'd go all poshed up in his best suit and his white silk scarf and I'd get out me Sunday frock and me silver sandals and off we'd go. Very refined, them tea dances was, an' the MC in patent leather shoes and white gloves. Spoke lovely, he did. And the sandwiches and sponge cake on little china plates and the tea in china cups. Ar,' she smiled fondly, 'wonder if them days'll ever come back again.'

Of course they would, Lucinda brooded. How could dancing ever go out of fashion? And when the war was over, they would all wear ball gowns again and forget the hops, where everyone had been friendly and the band played off key and the little man at the door stamped the back of your hand with a purple pass-out. And Mike, my darling, where are you? Please write to me? Don't let it be over between us?

'My mother and father,' said Jane, 'still talk about the grand ball at Fenton Bishop Hall. I don't remember it, but it was the talk of the Riding, it seems. It was the coming of age of Sir William's only son, and all the estate was there, and the village, and half the county and his wife. Marquees, fairy lights and an orchestra; unforgettable, my mother said. But you'll have been to loads of balls like that, Lucinda.'

'A few.' Lucinda frowned. Always with Charlie and always with Mama or Nanny in attendance. Chaperoning, really, though it was never admitted as such, and always in the big car, perched on the back seat, her skirts carefully arranged to avoid creasing. Unbelievably unreal, those balls, and everyone eyeing everyone else and nobody really enjoying the dancing, which was a great pity.

'A few,' she said again, 'and boring old affairs most of them were.'

She'd rather go to the dance hall at Craigiebur, with Mike; rather dance to that hotchpotch band and no one counting, eyebrows raised, how many times they had danced together or remarking, scandalized, how intimately he held her.

And where are you now, Mike? Is there someone else? Was there always someone else, and did you remember her, suddenly, as soon as we said goodbye after Eaton Square? Was I just another notch on your bedpost – the classy dame who was altogether too easy? Remember her, Mike? Lucy, who'll hear nightingales whenever she thinks about you, even when you've long forgotten her?

'Boring,' she said fiercely.

'That Tom of yours is a good dancer,' Vi remarked obliquely, eager to foster the relationship. 'You'll be all right for a partner tonight, Jane.'

'Yes, he's good. But I'd like it,' Jane wrinkled her nose, 'if he were just that little bit taller.'

'Oh, you would, eh? Well, some folks,' Vi snorted, 'aren't never satisfied! Who'd you want then, girl? Fred Astaire?'

Lucinda applied lipstick with concentrated care, poking out what remained with the end of a matchstick, smoothing it on with the tip of her little finger. Mike had been a good dancer, and tall and good to be close to. And the dance tonight would be hell because every sentimental tune would be one they had danced to together and every heart-rending lyric would be one he'd whispered in her ear. And who, Mike, will you be dancing with tonight?

'Well, that does it!' she gasped. 'That's the very last of my lipstick. Now what will I do?'

'You can borrow mine, queen, till you can get another. The chemist should be about due another quota. We just might be lucky if we can hit on a queue. How about going into Craigiebur tomorrow after watch, and see if we can find one.' Vi buttoned her jacket and carefully straightened her tie. 'And shake a leg, the pair of you, or the floor'll be too crowded to dance on.'

Smiling fondly, she shepherded her ewe lambs before her. Do them both good, a bit of dancing would. And make them forget their fellers for a couple of hours, with a bit of luck. 'Come on, then. Chop, chop!'

The dance got off to a good start, with Connie Dean, her smile defiant and brave, doing gramophone duty, Kathy MacAlister presiding over sandwiches and rock buns and Chief Wren Pillmoor watching the stair bottom through the open door of the regulating office – and heaven help the sailor who as much as placed a foot on it!

Vi was taken on the floor by a tall seaman she recognized as part of starboard watch pier patrol; Lucinda danced every dance, eyes too bright, smile too fixed, and Jane and Tom Tavey carried mugs of tea to the common room and sat out the interval in easy chairs of soft green leather, taken, so the buzz had it, from the first-class lounge of the SS *Mauretania* after the liner had been converted to serve the war years as a troopship and no longer had use for such finery.

'Getting hot in there.' Tom smiled. 'Worse than ever, now, when sundown comes at six and windows are blacked out early. Had a letter from Dan today. Seems all's well at home. Corn harvest stacked and ready for threshing after Christmas, and the sugarbeet and potatoes all up. Wanted to know when I'd be going on leave.'

'And when will you be, Tom?' Jane took the cigarette he offered, placing her hand on his to steady the match.

'Reckon I might just be lucky and make it for Christmas.' He smiled into her eyes before blowing out

386

the flame. 'Only got deep dives to do, then *Viper*'ll have finished working up. The buzz is that they'll send us on leave before we go operational. Be nice, if they did.

'Oh, you should spend a Christmas in Devon, Jane, at Brockhole. It's a lovely old farmhouse when the greenery is brought in and a big holly branch is all tinselled up and standing in the ingle. And Uncle Jack's special Christmas brew scrumpy flowing – jars and jars of it. You'd love it, straight up, you would.'

'Maybe I would, at that.' Better than being at Dormer Cottage for Christmas, with her mother weighing up every word she said and watching every move she made. And talking about how good Colin was and the extra pint or two he slipped them, now that milk had been rationed, and how hard he worked, poor boy, producing food for the war effort – and hadn't he grown up into a good-looking young man? Brockhole, Ardneavie House, even, would be better than that.

'Tell me about Devon,' she murmured, blowing out smoke, watching it rise and disappear.

'Devon? Best county there is.' He laughed. 'And Abbots Dart, where I come from, is a tight little place. And it's beautiful, Jane, summer or winter. Brockhole has thick walls and a good thatch, and one of the fireplaces is so big you could burn a tree trunk in it. Lovely for sitting round in winter, that fire is. You can draw the curtains and shut out the world – old Hitler included.'

'And in summer, Tom?'

'Ah, now, summer. Heaven in summer, that's what, and so hidden away you'd never find it unless you'd been born there. And lanes full of flowers and so narrow that two carts can't pass in them. Beautiful, Jane. And peaceful. I miss it.'

'Sorry you left it, Tom Tavey?' she teased. The dancing

had started again and they were alone in the common room. 'Sorry you joined?'

'Not really, my lovely. Someone had to put his spoke in for that little old Abbots Dart.' He took her mug and placed it with his own on the table beside them. 'Come outside, Jane. I want to kiss you, and it wouldn't do at all in here, would it?'

'All right.' She smiled. 'But only if you promise to behave. And you still haven't told me about tomorrow and what you'll be doing.' She placed her arm in his and they pulled aside the blackout curtain that covered the door and slipped out, into the darkness.

'Where is it to be, Jane? Stable or boilerhouse?'

'Where do you think?'

The boilerhouse was dry and warm, and Tom struck a match and held it high.

'No one here.' He drew her to him, tilting her chin, covering her mouth with his own.

Jane closed her eyes. Tom's kisses were firm and warm and undemanding. Tom knew the way things were; he wouldn't push it too far.

'Tell me about tomorrow,' she murmured, her lips touching the small pulse that beat in his neck.

'I didn't come here to talk shop, my lovely.'

'I'm not your lovely, Tom, and I really want to know about deep dives. Tell me.'

'Well.' He sighed loudly. 'We go up to the Gareloch, *Lothian* escorting, I think it'll be, and we'll do three dives. It's not so much the diving as the drill. It's getting the men off the upper casing pretty smartly and securing the hatch. Learning how it's done. It's got to be second nature when there might be a Jerry coming at you out of the sun.'

'But why the Gareloch, Tom? Why not at sea?' She was part of a submarine flotilla now, anxious to learn all she could, even though just to think of lying fathoms down on the seabed made her shiver with unease.

'Because the Gareloch's good and deep and a whole lot safer.'

'Diving's dangerous, though, isn't it?'

'Maybe. But it's better than sitting on the top, getting shot at or dive-bombed. But we didn't come here to talk about *Viper*.' He cupped her face in his broad, strong hands and kissed her gently. 'We came here to talk about you and me.'

'We came here because you wanted to kiss me.' She laughed, her voice teasing his seriousness.

'We came to be on our own for a while – and for me to ask you to come to Devon with me. You'll be due leave again about the same time as I get mine. Come with me to Brockhole and meet Dan and the uncles and aunts.'

'Tom! I couldn't!' She felt her cheeks blaze as she pulled away from his arms. 'If I went on leave with you it'd be like – well, like admitting there was something between us.'

'And there isn't?'

'No, Tom. Nothing serious, anyway. There can't be. We're good friends and I like you a lot but – '

'But you're still carrying the torch for a man who let you down, is that it?'

'*Tom* . . .' she warned.

'A man you once said was dead. And dead he might well be, as far as you're concerned, Jane Kendal. He's married and his wife's having a baby! For God's sake forget him. Let him go. He doesn't deserve you!'

'And you do, I suppose?' Her voice shook with sudden anger. 'You think that because I've lost Rob I'm going to fall into the arms of the first man who asks me. Well, I'm not! You knew the way things were when we started going out, and nothing's changed, Tom. Nothing!'

She pushed away the hand that still held her, then groped in the darkness for the door.

'Jane! Listen!' He caught her arm again, and because she knew the strength of him she didn't struggle. 'Jane, love, I'm sorry. All right, so I rushed it a bit, but don't go off like that. Kiss and make up?'

'No, Tom. And I – I think it's best I don't see you again. You're like the rest of them – out for what you can get!'

'That's not true! I want to marry you, and I'll wait till I do, if that's the way you say it's got to be.'

'Sorry.' Not when she ached, still, for Rob. Not until she had forgotten him, until she could think about him, and about Phemie too, and not feel pain inside her. 'I told you. I warned you.'

'Yes, you did. But it's not so long ago you asked me if I wanted to sleep with you, remember? I should have had you then, Jane, because, God knows, I wanted to!' He searched for her mouth and his kiss was hard with anger. 'I still want you, and I'll not let you go without a fight!'

His arms tightened around her and she felt his mouth on hers again. Passively she endured the pain of his lips, standing unresponsive in his arms, hardening her mouth so that he stood back from her, relaxing his hold a little.

'Hell, Jane, but you know how to get a bloke going, don't you? A tease, that's all you are! You lead me on and then, when you've had enough, you say, "That's it, Tavey! No more!" What the hell do you think I'm made of? But it's only a game to you, isn't it?'

'A game?' She stood with her hand on the door handle, speaking to the outline silhouetted dimly against the dull red glow of the boiler grille. 'I don't know, Tom. I only know I'm not ready yet for another big passion. Sorry, but that's the way it is. And – and I really don't think we should see each other again, not unless – '

'Not unless I play the game by your rules, is that it? What do you take me for, then? A bloody pansy?'

'I'm going, Tom.' She wrenched open the door and the cold air hit her burning cheeks with a sobering slap. 'I'm sorry, truly I am.'

'No!' He took her hand in his. 'Darling, I'm sorry. Let's start again. Friends, uh?'

'Friends?' She pulled her arm away. 'We can't be. It's over, Tom. It's got to be. Just leave me alone, will you!'

'Leave you alone to waste yourself on a man who isn't fit to black your boots? Grow up, Jane!'

'I meant it!' What right had he to criticize Rob? She'd told him all along, hadn't she, the way things were? 'And I don't want to see you again. Ever!'

She felt with her foot for the brick-paved path, stumbling a little, blinking her eyes rapidly in the shifting darkness.

'I'll see you!' he called. 'When I get back, we'll talk. And I'm not giving up. I'll have you, Jane, so help me. I *will*.'

'Oh, go to hell!' She ran towards the sound of the dancing and the rhythmic beat of feet on floor. 'Damn well go to hell, Tom Tavey!'

And damn you too, Rob MacDonald, for making me love you so much – and take care, my darling. Wherever you are, take care. And come home. Come home, Rob, as you promised . . .

'Where's Lucinda, then?' Vi demanded as they carried plates of Spam fritters, boiled potatoes and beans in bright red sauce to the table.

'Went straight into Craigiebur. Said she wanted to see if she could get hold of a lipstick.'

'But why didn't she wait for us? And why did she go off

and miss her lunch? She's usually ravenous after early watch and it's bread-and-butter pudding today.'

Vi was clearly perplexed. It took a great deal to keep Lucinda from her food. The poor kid must be taking Mike Farrow's disappearance hard.

'Haven't a clue.' Jane shrugged. 'I got the impression, though, that she'd rather go alone.'

'Ar, well. Up to her, I reckon, but if the chemist in the High Street has got his quota in, I wouldn't mind tryin' for a pot of cream. We can catch the two o'clock transport if we shift ourselves. Won't take me five minutes to get changed. How about it, Jane?'

'What you mean is that you're worried about Lucinda and you think we should try to find her.'

'Well, yes – and a pot of vanishing cream,' Vi prevaricated. 'And I *am* worried about Bainbridge. She doesn't say a lot – it's not her way.' Lucinda wouldn't weep or show her feelings in public; she was one of the stiff-upper-lip lot who didn't. But the kid was weeping inside; great, tearing sobs that nobody would know about. 'But she had it bad over Mike Farrow; worse than we thought and it's up to us to – '

'Vi! There's nothing we can do! Nothing, except be there when she needs us. And maybe Mike can't get in touch. Maybe they've sent him to some place he can't write from; somewhere dead secret.'

'Then why didn't he give her a hint the last time he phoned her? Lucinda's no fool. She'd not have said anything. But it's been a long time since then, and though I don't like to say it – '

'All right, then. *Don't* say it, Vi. Let's not give up. Not yet. It's not just weeks but *months* since I last saw Rob, but I haven't given up hope of hearing he's safe, and I will, I know it. I *know* he's alive, somewhere.'

'And married, queen,' Vi reminded her gently. 'You've got to remember – '

'I know. It's something I'm hardly likely to forget. But I'm sure, deep down inside me, that one day I shall see Rob again.'

'With *her*, Jane. With a wife and kid in tow!'

'Okay. Maybe that's the way it'll be, Vi. But just as long as he's alive . . .'

'Y'know, I never realized before how much you loved that bloke.' Vi shook her head in disbelief. 'Oh, damn this bloody war!' Impatiently she pushed aside her plate. 'I'm not hungry now. I'll just nip upstairs and get out of this overall. Won't be long.'

It wasn't like Lucinda to go wandering off alone, Vi thought. And it certainly wasn't like her to miss her food. Not that they were interfering, but best they should find her. All for one, wasn't it . . . ?

They did not find Lucinda. Though the queue for cosmetics at the High Street chemist had been and gone, there was no sign of her.

'She'll be all right,' Jane said doubtfully. 'Probably on her way back to Ardneavie now, and wondering where we are.'

'Ar,' Vi agreed. 'After all, Lucinda's a big girl now. And it's her birthday, soon. We mustn't forget.' In just a few days, if Vi remembered rightly, Lucinda would be twenty. 'We'll have to try to make it special.'

'We'll think of something.' Jane nodded. 'But let's get back to quarters.' There was nothing to keep them in Craigiebur. The afternoon was cold and damp, and window-shopping was not a lot of fun without clothing coupons. 'If we hurry, we might be back in time for standeasy.' And with luck, Lucinda would be there, demanding to know where they had been and hurrying them into the mess for mugs of strong, sweet tea and slices of bread and jam. With luck.

Lucinda stood at the little piece of land that jutted into the waters of the river Clyde: the quiet place, where the trees had screened out the war. Last time they sat here, the earth had been gentle, still, with the warmth of August, and the sun had made patterns on the water.

Just a little while they'd been together, and she had demanded to know why Mike had come all this way, just to be with her for half an hour, and he'd said he'd have come for half a minute.

I love you, remember, he'd told her.

And now Mike had left her. They'd been lovers, heard nightingales, yet he was gone. And summer had gone too, and taken their love with it.

What did I do, Mike? she asked silently. Where did I go wrong? Wasn't I good to make love to? Darling, I knew there'd been others before me, but I was so sure it was me you loved, really loved. And will you go back to Eaton Square with someone else, Mike, and will you tell her that only tonight, only *now*, matters?

She leaned against the silver trunk of a birch, leafless now, and gazed at the winter water and shivered.

It was good, Mike, and I won't forget you. And I'll always remember that our love was a bonus; that we might never have met if Molly's injection hadn't landed her in sick bay, or if Nick had turned up. And I shall always wonder what our baby would have been like if we'd made one that night in Eaton Square.

Impatiently she blinked the tears from her eyes. She hadn't come here to weep, just to say goodbye to Mike and accept, finally, that it was over. Just to say that it had been great, that small, sweet incident.

Oh, Jane had begged her to have faith. Jane's love for

Rob still blazed from her eyes and pinked her cheeks and made her completely beautiful but she, Lucinda, was made of sterner stuff. She, like all the other Bainbridges, was a realist.

'You don't,' Jane had said, 'stop loving a man as easily as that,' and she wouldn't, Lucinda acknowledged. She would always love Mike Farrow, but she must remember what had happened to Connie and Jane – and now to herself – and chalk it up to experience.

'Goodbye, Michael Johnson Farrow,' she whispered. The sky was darkening now, and the waters beyond were grey and uncaring. 'Take care of yourself, wherever you are, and think of me sometimes.'

She closed her eyes and wished him well. She would never come to this place again. Not ever. To come here alone would not be possible.

Abruptly she turned; then, head high, she walked away from the little strip of land the war seemed not to have touched.

A parrot called Mavis, indeed.

Vi was reading out the war news from yesterday's paper when Lucinda opened the door of cabin 9.

'You're back then, queen. Where've you been? We went to Craigiebur but we didn't see you. Manage to get a lipstick, did you? They'd all gone by the time we got there.'

'Yes, I got one, Vi.'

'Good. So where were you?' Vi demanded bluntly. 'Where've you been all afternoon?'

'Oh, just walking and thinking. And laying a ghost, Vi. Saying goodbye.'

Her eyes glinted with unshed tears, and no matter how hard she tried, she couldn't shape her lips into a smile. 'It's all right,' she whispered, 'truly it is. And I think there's time before supper to write a letter. One I should have written ages ago.'

Jane lifted her eyes to Vi's. *To Charlie?* they demanded.

'Can't you write it later?' Vi asked.

'It's almost time for supper,' Jane added uneasily.

'Yes, but it won't take long and it's something I've got to do *now*,' Lucinda insisted. 'You two go on down, uh?'

'All right. No hurry, queen. Think I'll just do the blackout first.'

Vi walked to the window and looked out over the sullen waters of Loch Ardneavie and the ripple of red thrown down by the last rays of a sinking sun. And she watched as a sleek, slim escort vessel moved slowly to the mouth of the loch and the boom nets parted to let it through. In its wake slipped a submarine, black against the red water.

'It's *Viper* and *Lothian*,' Vi said, 'goin' out.'

'Yes,' Jane murmured, joining her. 'Deep dives, they're doing. In the Gareloch.' She hadn't meant it, really she hadn't, when she'd told Tom to go to hell – and when he came back she would tell him so and ask him to forgive her and to give her time.

'Ar, well. Take care, then.' Vi lifted her hand and signed the air with a cross of blessing, then pulled the curtains across the window and switched on the light. 'Don't take all night, queen.' She addressed the remark to the back of Lucinda's downward-bent head. 'Remember you missed your lunch, and it smells like liver and onions for supper.'

'I'll be down, Vi,' Lucinda said softly. 'This won't take long.'

'To Charlie?' Vi asked, mentally crossing her fingers.

'To Charlie.' Lucinda nodded.

'Seemed urgent.' Vi sighed as she and Jane walked slowly downstairs to the mess hall. 'Ar, well, I suppose it had to happen.'

'Suppose it had,' Jane whispered, tight-lipped. 'But she'll never forget Mike, you know. Not if she lives to be a hundred and one. She'll never forget him. I know she won't.'

17

'What's new?' Lucinda Bainbridge rolled up her sleeves then adjusted her headset. 'War over yet?'

'Nah. Everything's close up, though,' yawned the male telegraphist who had sat out the morning watch. '*Lothian* might come up a couple of times but *Viper* isn't due to transmit till ten hundred hours.' The telegraphist was eager to hand over the watch, find a space in which to sling his hammock, and sleep. 'You know *Viper*'s call sign?'

Lucinda nodded. She knew all the flotilla call signs now. Submarines on exercise no longer terrified her. 'Thanks.' She smiled. 'See you.'

'Nasty snappy wind outside,' she remarked, accepting the cigarette Lofty offered. She didn't really want it. They all smoked too much, truth known, but smoking soothed twanging nerves or relieved boredom, and this would be a boring watch. Her set was on local wavelength and there would be little traffic this forenoon. She adjusted the dials carefully, repeating call signs in her mind. *Omega*'s was GXU3; *Lothian*'s KBA, and that of the submarine TSX. At exactly ten o'clock the letters GXU3 V TSX – *Omega* from *Viper* – would ping out in her headset and they would know that the first of the practice dives had gone well. Not, of course, that anyone but *Viper*'s skipper and *Omega*'s top brass was supposed to know where the submarine and escort were and what they were doing, but most of them did. Right now, Lucinda thought, *Viper* was submerged somewhere in the Gareloch, and at ten o'clock would surface and begin its transmission.

The CCO messenger tapped her shoulder then placed a mug of tea beside her. Lofty lifted his mug and mouthed 'Cheers', as he always did, and Lucinda knew that if she eased her headset from her ears she would hear Chief Wetherby complaining that the tea was like maiden's water, as *he* always did, and when would somebody learn to make a decent brew? Yes, a boring watch today.

GXU3 V KBA. *Lothian*, thank heaven, was alive and transmitting.

Lucinda took down the signal. It was in coded groups of figures and very short. She tapped out a receipt, tore the sheet from the message pad and held it high.

'Ta,' said the CCO messenger, plucking it from her fingers, taking it to Jock and Jane for decoding, as always.

Boring, boring, boring, Lucinda sighed, and an hour to go before *Viper* came up on her wavelength.

She began to think about Mike, then shut him from her mind and thought about Charlie instead – and the letter she had posted to him that morning. Then she thought about Lady Mead and the warm kitchen at the Dower House and the broth pan that would bubble on the stove top from October to March.

GXU3 V TAP. A signal in plain language. Motor launch 515 was requesting permission to pass the boom-defence vessels and anchor in the loch.

Lucinda acknowledged and passed on the signal. A small boat seeking the shelter of Loch Ardneavie meant that the wind was getting stronger.

Could bombers and fighters take off in windy conditions? She knew little about aircraft. And where was Mike, now that he'd gone back to flying? The north, the south or maybe Lincolnshire, even? *Take care, Mike Farrow*.

Impatiently she moved the dials on her set, searching

the airwaves, but all was quiet. Nine minutes still to tick slowly away before ten o'clock.

She checked her pencil points and placed a carbon sheet in her message pad. Dials spot-on. *Viper*'s sparker would be ready with his message. He'd transmit almost as soon as the submarine broke surface, which should be just about now. Two more minutes before ten o'clock.

Viper did not transmit at ten hundred hours. Lucinda frowned, glancing up at the bulkhead clock then down at her wrist-watch. She moved the dials minutely clockwise then anti-clockwise. Oh, damn, damn, *damn*! Surely she hadn't missed the start of it! She didn't want to have to request a repeat transmission. Chief Wetherby would blow his top in words of one syllable, and many of them quite unrepeatable.

She waited, ears straining. One more minute, that's all she would give *Viper*. She focused her eyes on the bulkhead clock and the thin red second hand, counting out each jerked-off second, then running her tongue round lips gone suddenly dry, she called, 'Chief! *Viper* hasn't come up yet. They're five minutes overdue!'

With a sharp, 'What's that, eh?' Walter Wetherby was beside her. He didn't ask her if she had missed it. Bainbridge didn't miss transmissions. Frowning, he turned to Lofty.

'Change over to local wavelength, Bates. Listen out with Bainbridge, will you, for *Viper*?'

Lofty's eyes slid sideways. 'What's going on?' they asked.

'Don't know.' Lucinda's shoulders shrugged a reply.

The boredom, if it ever existed, was gone. Even the bulkhead clock picked up the changed mood and ticked away seconds with amazing speed.

'Nothing?' Walter Wetherby asked, as the minute hand

moved decisively to ten past the hour, to ten minutes overdue.

'Nothing,' they told him.

'Right!' Chief Telegraphist Wetherby straightened his back, then lifted the telephone that connected the CCO to the signal bosun's cabin.

'Sir? Chief Wetherby here. *Viper* hasn't transmitted. She's ten minutes over. Aye-aye, sir.' He slammed down the phone and taking a pencil wrote down a message.

'For *Lothian*, chop chop,' he rapped.

'In code?' Jock hesitated.

'In code, and get a move on!'

Within the two minutes the signal was at Lucinda's fingertips, pulsating over the air. She didn't know what she was sending, but Jane did. It was short and terse. '*Lothian* from *Omega*. Request *Viper*'s position.' That's all it had been.

'What's going on, Jock?' Jane whispered.

'Seems that *Viper* should have transmitted at ten, and they haven't. That's all I know.'

'And that's serious?'

'It could be, Jane.'

'Because they haven't surfaced – is that it?'

'That's it.' He looked into the frightened eyes and remembered that she was going out with Tom Tavey. 'But anything could have happened. No need to fash yourself yet. Probably nothing wrong.'

But something *was* wrong, Jane thought, fighting the panic inside her, or why was the signal bosun here, trousers and sweater over his pyjamas, when he'd just done the night watch and was entitled to his sleep? Why was he here, unshaven, ringing the staff office, worry lining his already tired face?

She looked through the open door to where Lucinda

401

sat, to the bent fair head and the hand that wrote steadily and to the chief who stood beside her.

'This signal's from *Lothian*.' Lucinda frowned. 'And it's not in code.'

With no more emotion than a sudden tightening of his mouth, the elderly telegraphist read the message on Lucinda's pad.

Omega *from* Lothian. Viper *failed to surface at 1000 hrs. Marker buoy in position. Request instructions*.

Without speaking, he tore off the message and handed it to the signal bosun. It was out of his hands now, and he wasn't sorry. Walter Wetherby was not a religious man – thirty years of compulsory churchgoing in the Navy had seen to that – but he lifted his eyes to the deckhead in silent supplication: *Get those poor sods to the top, eh*?

The signal bosun tucked his pyjama jacket into his trouser tops and straightened his sweater, as if conceding there would be no more sleep today. His mouth tasted foul and he called for a mug of tea.

In *Omega*'s staff office, the senior duty officer made a priority telephone call to the Admiralty. That faceless lot had probably never heard of His Majesty's submarine *Viper*, he considered, but they had to be told; told that the newest addition to the 15th Flotilla lay helpless on the bottom of the Gareloch, that a marker buoy was in position above it, and that *Omega*'s top brass were already preparing to sail to the Gareloch on the Dutch frigate *Jan Mayen*.

In the communications office, starboard watch waited tensely, only half aware, still, of the plight of the V-class submarine. All they could be sure of was the dry-mouthed gratitude that caused them to thank their God that they were here, in a hot, tension-filled office on the depot ship *Omega*, and not in the cold, uncertain deeps of a Scottish loch.

It had set out to be a boring watch, thought the Wren telegraphist who, little more than an hour ago, had first raised the alarm. Would to heaven it were still so.

In the small, stuffy room off the main body of the communications office, Molly Malone read the message that tapped out on her teleprinter.

'Jaysus!' She tore it off then hurried to the signal bosun with the strip of paper.

'From the Admiralty, sir.'

The signal bosun read it, shook his head, then passed the piece of paper to the chief.

'And that,' Walter Wetherby jerked, 'is just about all we need.' Picking up the signal-deck telephone, he tapped the rest impatiently. 'He's not answering, sir. Probably can't hear, in this wind.' He turned to the messenger. 'Get up top and tell the signalman there's a gale imminent. Force eight. And shift yourself, son!'

The messenger slammed on his cap, opened the bulk-head door and went head-down into the tearing wind. Hand on head, he climbed the narrow flight of steps to the signal deck, where the duty signalman read the flashing light from the frigate that headed into the heaving waters of the loch.

The flashing light stopped, the signalman clicked out an acknowledgement then turned to the messenger at his side.

'Trouble?' he demanded.

'Nah. Only a gale force eight, imminent.'

'*Imminent*?' The fresh wind had become a fury, with the coming of a watery daybreak. No need for the warning, the signalman considered, but now, since it was official, he'd best go through the drill. Tearing off the rain-spattered signal, he slammed it into the messenger's hand.

'Here. Take this down below, and in case they can't

read it, tell 'em it says *Jan Mayen* under way 1115 hours, okay? Can't say I envy the poor buggers, though, going to sea in this lot.' It comforted him that there were others in a worse position than himself.

'Me neither.' The messenger made a sucking noise through his teeth. 'But it'll be on account of the panic, won't it?'

'What panic?' The signalman was clearly perplexed. They'd piped 'Up Spirits' over the Tannoy at eleven o'clock as usual, and the rum rations had been collected. But then, he reflected morosely, the rum ration was sacrosanct and they'd pipe 'Up Spirits' if the ship was sinking beneath them. 'What panic?' he demanded again. 'Where?'

'Don't know, exactly. But they're rushing around like blue-arsed flies down below. Something to do with one of the submarines, I reckon.' He tucked the signal into his tunic, watching with interest as the signalman took a pennant from the locker nearby and attached it to the mainmast halyard with frozen, fumbling fingers.

'There you are, then. Gale flag flying. And tell that lot below that I haven't had any standeasy yet,' he called to the messenger's fast disappearing back. 'You tell 'em, eh?'

He hunched his shoulders against the storm, wiping his rain-lashed face with a wet woollen glove. What wouldn't he give right now for a gulp or two of his rum ration, but not one of the miserable so-and-so's down there in the warmth would think to bring it up to him. Not in this weather, they wouldn't.

He thought briefly about the submarine and wondered which one it was and what the panic was about. But they told you nothing. Careless talk, he supposed. Best keep mum.

He shrugged away his curiosity. Submariners knew what

they were doing. Nobody made them volunteer, and they got extra pay for it, didn't they?

The gale flag snapped above his head and he cupped his numbed fingers and blew through them.

'Roll on my leave,' he muttered, and the wind took his words and flung them away. 'And sod this bloody war, an' all . . .'

'And what's to do with you two?' Vi demanded as Jane and Lucinda dripped water on to the polished floor. 'Look as if you've lost a shillin' and found a meg.'

'What's to do?' Jane grated. 'Listen! We've just been tossed and turned – '

'And drenched and nearly drowned – '

'Whilst some we could mention stayed warm and dry in the Wrennery, drinking tea and oh, God.' Jane's face crumpled and she held her hands to her eyes, fighting back tears. 'It's *Viper*, Vi. They're in terrible trouble. They did their first dive but they didn't surface and it's more than four hours since . . .'

'Still down? That doesn't sound too good.'

'Afraid not.' Lucinda nodded. 'God knows what's really happening. No one seems to want to admit to anything, yet signals are flying around like nobody's business and everyone's at panic stations. All we really know is that *Viper*'s in trouble. Or was, when the watch changed.'

'And this gale isn't helping,' Jane choked. 'Oh, Jock's been saying they'll be all right. He went on and on about the escape hatch and how they'd all make it up to the surface soon. So why haven't they? Coders see most of the signals, and no one has got out yet, or I'd know it. It's horrible, Vi. Just think: trapped down there. And how long is the air going to last? They say that divers are on their way to the Gareloch, but they won't be able to go down. Not in this gale!'

405

'Hey! Stop that noise!' Vi placed her hands firmly on Jane's shoulders. 'Four hours – it's nothing. Them submarines can stay down for ages. They'll be all right, queen, just you see if they aren't. So get them wet clothes off, the pair of you, and we'll see if there's room for them near the fire next door. Mother of God! Bet them three's soaked to the skin, out all morning on that launch in this weather.' She walked to the window, gazing out at the greyness, at the launch that headed back to *Omega* on its last run, watching apprehensively as it rose then smacked down into the wave troughs, making heavy going against the gale that slammed and screamed across the loch. How any woman in her right mind could endure such discomfort and danger for King and Country and fourteen shillings a week, she'd never understand. 'Don't you worry none,' she comforted. 'Them lads in *Viper*'ll be all right. They're just waitin' for this gale to blow itself out, and then up they'll all come, cheeky as a boatload of monkeys. Bet you anything you like, they will.'

'You think so?' Jane's face was pale and drawn. 'You really think so?'

'Course I do, queen. Now get them wet things off, like I told you, and let's all go downstairs for a cup of tea. A good hot cup is what you both need, and a good hot cup is what you'll have – all right?'

'Oh, Vi,' Jane whispered, her voice on the edge of tears. 'I do love you. Whatever would we do without you?'

What indeed, Vi sighed, her cheeks flushing. Kids, that's all they were, God love 'em, trying to make the best of a war that was none of their doing and giving it the best years of their young lives, an' all. And she loved them, too; loved them fiercely and protectively, and Lord help anybody who hurt them.

'She's right, Vi.' Lucinda smiled fondly.

'Ar, shurrup!' Vi choked, flinging open the door.

Anybody, she vowed. *Anybody at all!*

Jane was waiting beside the door, anxious for news, when port watch came off duty. She heard them running up the lane, and they burst into Ardneavie House, stamping and shaking themselves and grumbling about the weather and the crew of the launch that brought them ashore.

'Terrible, it was! Thought we'd capsize!'

'And those seamen aren't a patch on Lilith's lot! Took them three runs to get us alongside the jetty! Thought we'd had it!'

'I'm sick of this gale, and I'm *soaked*!'

'Aren't we all, chum? Where's standeasy?'

They looked, Jane thought, like a straggle of very wet penguins as they made for the galley and cocoa and hot toast.

'Did you hear anything?' she asked Molly's opposite number. 'Anything about *Viper*?'

'We-ell, you know how they are, playing it close to the chest. They tell us as little as they can.'

'I know, and it's so stupid. We all pass signals and code and decode signals, yet we're not supposed to know anything.'

'Well, there *is* a war on, Kendal; these things aren't supposed to be talked about. Chances are that none of it will ever make the newspapers. Bet the censors blue-pencil the lot.' She shrugged. 'But I did hear that one diver went down. He was soon up again – trouble with his airline or something – but he thinks they're all right down there.'

'How did he know?' Eagerly Jane latched on to the comforting news. 'How could he tell?'

'Seems he tapped on the hull and they tapped back. So they're alive and kicking, aren't they?'

'Oh, that's great!' Relief pulsated through her. 'Just great.'

'And there's one bit more. When the gale dies down, I think they're going to try to get *Viper* up. There's something they call camels on their way there from Garvie. No, not *animals*! Seems that these particular camels are to do with buoyancy. They'll be attached to *Viper* to float it to the surface – well, I *think* that's what will happen.'

Jane took the stairs two at a time. It was going to be all right! She'd thought the fuddy-duddy top brass were doing nothing at all to help *Viper*, but they were! She burst into the cabin, relief spilling out of her.

'Listen! Good news! A diver got down to *Viper* and they're fine. And lifting equipment is on its way. Only let this gale stop and they'll have them up in no time! There's toast and cocoa downstairs, and suddenly I'm ravenous. Come on! Let's all have a mug of kye!'

'You think more of Tom Tavey than you'll admit, don't you?' Vi demanded of Jane as they got into bed.

'Yes – oh, I don't know. I like him a lot, I suppose, but he isn't Rob. Rob was my first love and my last love – my *always* love too, I suppose. But Tom and I had a terrible row the night before he sailed, and one thing led to another, and I ended up telling him to go to hell . . .'

'That's a dreadful thing to say to anybody,' Vi admonished, putting on her Nanny face, 'especially to a bloke what's goin' to sea! Don't wonder you're relieved they're all right.'

'I am, Vi, and I'll say I'm sorry when I see him again.'

'But will you *be* sorry,' Vi pressed, 'or will it just be your conscience saying it for you.'

'I'll be sorry,' Jane said contritely. 'But Tom's getting serious about me and I'm not ready for anything like that yet – try to understand, Vi.'

'I do understand – only, be fair with him, eh? Don't lead him on. You can't do that to a bloke. It's trouble, queen. You should know that.'

'I know it – I'll try to remember it in future, I promise. And Vi, if you're having a word with the Lord tonight, will you see if something can be done about that gale? Once it's calm again, they'll be able to use the escape hatch – and picking them up when they've made it to the top will be a piece of cake for *Lothian*.'

A piece of cake, was it? Lucinda frowned, when cabin 9 was dark and still and the creaking of Jane's bedsprings had stopped. So *Viper* was only waiting for the gale to blow itself out, then they'd all come bobbing to the surface like corks in a bucket?

But it had been relatively calm when *Viper* made that dive; the gale had come suddenly and later. *Viper*'s skipper would have been ignorant of conditions above, wouldn't he, and the escape drill would have started almost at once. Or *should* have.

So why hadn't it? she wondered uneasily. Why had the crew not obeyed the blind survival instinct that should have sent them all to the surface long before now? What had gone wrong in the Gareloch? Why had no one tried to get out?

And now, she fretted, it was already long past midnight and in just a few hours they would be back on board *Omega* again. Soon, maybe, they would know the best – or the worst – of it, and until then she must try not to worry. She must close her eyes and shut down her thoughts, and sleep.

But she did not sleep, because something was inexplicably wrong, and she was afraid.

* * *

409

Sometime in the early morning, the ferocity of the wind abated as suddenly as it had begun. Ears straining, Lucinda threw back her bedclothes, walked quietly to the window and looked out into the stillness. Out in the loch she could see the dim riding-light on *Omega*'s mainmast and another, not so highly placed, a distance away. Just the two lights, which meant that *Lothian* and *Jan Mayen* were still in the Gareloch and, of the escort frigates, only *Capricious* remained.

Carefully, she eased down the window. Only the splash of breaking wavelets disturbed the quiet of the night. They sounded clear and close, as if the tide was at full flow, and she wondered if it would affect the helpless submarine in any way.

She sighed, wishing she understood the mysteries of the seas and oceans, and felt more at ease with them. Lilith said she should, for her birth sign Scorpio had its element in water.

She shivered and returned to the warmth of her bed, remembering that in just two days she would be twenty. She had almost forgotten her birthday, and now it seemed wrong to want to celebrate it. She wished she had Vi's faith and could pray as fervently as Vi did.

She closed her eyes and thumped her pillow, then burying her face in it she whispered, 'I'm so unsure and mixed up and miserable, God, and for the life of me I don't know why . . .'

It was almost a prayer. It was certainly fervent.

'It's gone,' Jane exulted as they walked down the lane. 'The wind has dropped.'

They trod carefully in the blackout, kicking through piles of rustling, windblown leaves, walking slowly, wishing the morning were not so dark.

410

'It'll be all right now for *Viper*. I wonder what news there'll be when we get on board.'

'Good, I hope.' Lucinda turned up the collar of her raincoat. Her head ached and she was tired. She had slept only briefly, to be awakened, startled, by the harsh jangling of the alarm. Reluctantly, longing to sleep again, she had left her bed. Now, deep inside her, was an unwillingness to take up her watch, and she wished with all her heart she knew why.

They were adjusting to the darkness now, and they walked more quickly, eyes fixed on the green light of the approaching launch.

How, Lucinda demanded silently, could life go on so relentlessly when thirty-nine men lay trapped and help-less? Yet when they reached *Omega* they would salute the quarterdeck as they always did, and she would take over her watch then drink the cup of tea that would be placed at her right hand; and even though the air around her vibrated with tension, they would still pipe 'Up Spirits' at eleven hundred hours, and the tide would have reached its lowest ebb and nothing would have changed. It was unreal, somehow. Cruel, almost.

'Any news, Lofty?' Lucinda offered her cigarette packet to the telegraphist at her side.

'Nothing at all.' He shrugged, striking a match. 'Jock and Jane'll get all the buzzes before we do. Bet those poor sods down there'd give anything for a smoke. They'll be fed up, sucking lollies.'

Lollies – boiled sweets, really – were issued in large tins and given to submariners to help alleviate the longing to smoke when their submarine was submerged. She glanced down at the ship's Woodbine burning in the tin lid beside her mug, and felt guilty.

411

'Heard anything, Jock?' Jane asked, confident the news would be good.

'Never a word, hen, but you know what they say about no news.'

'I do, and it's going to be all right, I know it. I expect the lifting gear will be there by now, and the divers should be able to get down to them, shouldn't they, now that it's calm again?'

'Aye.' Jock Menzies thumbed through the signal log. 'Doesn't appear to have been a great lot of traffic in the night.' He wondered if that was a good omen or a bad. He'd better be careful what he said. The lassie'd be worried about young Tavey. It wasn't for him to tell her he'd heard that *Viper* lay unevenly on the loch bed, listing heavily to port, which might explain why no one had come to the surface by way of the escape hatch. And it could be just a buzz, so best say nothing.

He wished, afterwards, that he'd told her, prepared her in some small way for what was to follow. But there had been no escaping it. As the groups of figures in the signal they were decoding became words, he had realized the futility of trying to protect her. There was a war on, after all, and wars were no respecters of wee lassies.

Jane said nothing as the words unfolded. Only the draining of colour from her face and the disbelief in her eyes betrayed her thoughts.

Omega *from* Jan Mayen. *Divers report no response from* Viper. *Am returning to base.*

The skipper and the top brass were leaving the Gareloch. You didn't have to be good at reading between lines, she thought, despairingly, to know what that meant.

'Don't worry, hen. Maybe they've got their heads down on *Viper*. Maybe they didn't hear the divers . . .'

She nodded. Jock was usually right.

'How long,' she forced herself to ask, 'will the air down there last?'

'Och, days and days, I imagine, if they don't move about too much. They'll be on the surface again long before that happens.'

'Yes.' Of course they would. Even now, divers could be attaching the lifting gear to *Viper*'s hull. They'd get them to the surface. They *would*.

Port watch brought the news ashore that night. *Jan Mayen* had returned to the flotilla. *Lothian* remained on station still, and the barges carrying the lifting gear and the tug with the divers on board. But the submarine lay in deep and muddy waters and it could be days before a lift was possible, or so the buzz had it, and by then . . .

Yet no one seemed to know what had gone wrong; what had happened to prevent the submarine blowing its ballast tanks and rising to the surface of the Gareloch. Had sea water seeped into the batteries to produce the deadly and dreaded chlorine gas? Had they hit an uncharted rock? A leaking torpedo tube? Speculation ran high. One thing only was certain. Someone, said the lower-deck lawyers triumphantly, would get his backside kicked for this little lot, and serve the bastard right. Not, they proclaimed, that any of it would get past the censor. The loss of the submarine – if lost it was – would never be allowed to make headlines in the daily papers; the Ministry of Information would put a stop to that. Only the next of kin would be told. Eventually. Killed on active service, it would be, and that would be the end of it. If *Viper* really was lost, of course, because in spite of all the secrecy and rumours, there was always hope.

But hope came cheaply, in wartime.

'What am I to do, Vi?' Jane's face was ashen, her eyes wide with apprehension. 'Port watch are back and the news is dreadful. Not one of *Viper*'s crew have got to the surface.' Her voice rose shrilly. 'And they say it could be ages before they get *Viper* to the top because it's lying awkwardly, or something.'

'Now stop your worrying,' Vi retorted with an easiness she was far from feeling. 'Who told you all this?'

'Does it matter? There's no smoke without fire, is there? Something went wrong with that dive, and by the time they get the submarine to the top it'll be too late!'

'Who said it would be too late?' Lucinda demanded. 'Molly's oppo, was it? You know what a blabbermouth she is.'

'No. Molly's oppo wouldn't speak to me. She avoided me, in fact.'

'Now listen, queen. Talk costs nothin' and talk's all it is. Putting two and two together and making it into twenty-two, that's what they're doin'.'

'No. There's no hope. They're all dead. I know it. My dad once said that in his war they sent men over the top as if they were cattle, and this lot is no better. Nobody seems to care.'

She began to sob, and Vi laid an arm around the shaking shoulders and drew her down to the bed.

'Ssh, now. Don't take on so.'

'Don't shush me, Vi McKeown!' She jumped to her feet, eyes wild. 'Say something constructive for a change! Oh, I'm not like your lot. I can't go to Confession! I've got to live with what I've done, haven't I?'

Lucinda looked on, shocked and silent, as Vi asked quietly, 'Live with what, Jane?'

'With my bloody conscience, that's what!'

'Now see here – '

'No, *you* see, Vi. I told Tom to go to hell, didn't I? They were the last words I spoke to him. He loved me. How do you think he felt about it, down there? And how

414

do you think I feel about it now?' She was bordering on hysteria, her voice harsh, her face an ugly red. 'Tom's dead, and I wished him in hell! How would you like to live with that?'

Lucinda dropped her eyes to the fingers that twisted in her lap, staying deliberately, steadfastly apart because she had known all along, hadn't she? Last night, lying there unsleeping, she'd been sure that something was wrong. It frightened her even to think of it.

'So what do you want me to say, girl? What can I do that's goin' to help?' Vi whispered.

'Do? Say? You could show a little sympathy. You could say you understand and that Tom will forgive me. I want absolution, Vi. I *need* it.'

'Jane love, you know I can't give you that.'

'Not if I'm sorry? Not if I'd give anything not to have said what I did?'

'Listen, queen – what's said is said. We can't ever take it back. We've all got to live with what we've done – yes, Cath'licks, too. We don't always get what we want or even what we need. Life's like that and you'll have to accept it. An' you've got to grow up, Jane, and – '

'Oh, shut up! *Shut up!*' Her face was ugly with rage, her breath came in short, choking gasps. 'You make me sick with your platitudes, Vi McKeown. *Sick!*'

'*Right!*' It was all the Liverpool woman needed, all she could take. Grasping the near-hysterical girl by the shoulders, she shook her violently then flung her roughly to the bed.

'Stop it, Jane! Stop it *now*, 'cos if you don't I'll land you such a belt round the ear-'ole you'll wonder what's hit you!' She held her hand threateningly high. 'I mean it. Your screamin' hysterics don't cut any ice with me!' she hissed, eyes narrow with anger.

'I – I . . .' Jane fought for breath and her eyes met Vi's.

'I said I meant it,' Vi repeated. Then softly, indulgently almost, she whispered, 'I do, queen, so don't push me.'

'I'm sorry! Oh, I'm sorry!' Jane was in Vi's arms in an instant. 'I shouldn't have said what I did. I'm nothing but a spoiled brat.'

'No, you're not. You're an only chick and it isn't all your fault. But the time has come for you to start growin' up – all right?'

'All right.' Jane sniffed loudly, sucking in deep, shuddering breaths, wiping her eyes with the back of her hand.

'Fine. Glad we've got that straight.' Vi took a handkerchief from her pocket and offered it, smiling gently. 'Now then, Lucinda, nip downstairs and get us some tea – if port watch has left any – and you, Jane, blow your nose and wash your face and let's be hearin' no more of your nonsense!'

'Do you think Tom won't ever come back?' Jane asked when they were alone. 'Don't you think they could've made a terrible mistake? Maybe tomorrow they'll get *Viper* to the surface, and there they'll be, safe as houses. Miracles *can* happen, can't they? It isn't impossible.'

'Miracles? Yes, they happen. Sometimes. But they take longer than the impossible, kid. A whole lot longer. So we'll have to hope and pray he'll be all right – that they'll all be all right. And before Lucinda comes back, did you remember it's her birthday tomorrow?' It was time to change the subject.

'Yes, but I couldn't find anything in the shops – not even a decent tablet of soap.'

'Never mind. We'll all have a run ashore tomorrow night. And don't say you can't. Bein' miserable and makin' other people miserable won't help any of them poor lads. And it's got to be tomorrow night because we go on late duty after that – all right?'

'All right. We'll make it a good birthday for her. And

I'm sorry, truly I am, for what I said and the way I acted. I won't do it again.'

'All right, then. And I won't belt yer ear-'ole.' Vi grinned. 'And for God's sake get that face washed. You look shockin'!'

They tried, next morning, not to talk about the stricken submarine or think about how it was, down there. Signals passing between *Lothian* and *Omega* confirmed that divers were working on the loch bottom and that no contact had been made with *Viper*; there was no answer to their tapping.

But that, some said, was how it was, in wartime. There was good luck and bad luck; lucky ships and unlucky ships; and HM Submarine *Viper* had been unlucky, it would seem. You didn't argue with Fate.

Sorry, Tom. Jane sent her thoughts to flower-filled Devon lanes; lanes so narrow that two carts couldn't pass, and to the Christmas holly branch they would stand in the ingle at Brockhole. And those who sat beside the fireplace big enough to take a tree trunk, would raise glasses of Uncle Jack's cider and speak Tom's name with love and praise. *I am sorry, so very sorry, but I can't mourn. I can only despise myself for what I did to you and said to you, and that's punishment enough. I should have realized what it's like. I've been hurt, too. But I'll carry my bad conscience with me for as long as it takes, Tom, and I'll remember you always.*

'There'll be loads of cards waiting for you,' Jane said as they hurried up the jetty, their sad watch over. 'And parcels, maybe.'

'Parcels?' Lucinda shook her head. 'The parents are inclined to give money – less trouble – and Charlie always gave perfume and chocolate peppermint creams.' Charlie liked chocolate peppermint creams. 'But when did you last see a box of chocolates in the shops? And as for perfume – well, it just doesn't exist.'

'We'll have a run ashore tonight, though,' Jane insisted.

'We will, Kendal dear. We'll go to the canteen for pie and beans then we'll all get merry.'

'On beer?'

'Well, maybe we'll find a pub with some gin under the counter. I feel like getting high, old love. A few gin and limes might be just what we all need to stop us thinking.'

Vi was waiting at the door, the birthday mail in her hand. 'Hurry up, queen. Get them opened. And there's a parcel for you, too.' Her cheeks were flushed, her eyes danced with excitement. 'All soft and squashy; I've been feeling it.'

'Y'know,' Lucinda smiled, 'this is just as it was at school. We're going to have a super day, aren't we?'

'We are,' Vi exulted. 'The best day ever, if you did but know it. Chop chop, then. Get on with it.'

Lucinda scanned the writing on the envelopes. One from Pa, one from Goddy and, oh dear, one from Charlie. This would be the reply to her last letter, and she didn't want to read it. Not today. Hastily she pushed it into her pocket.

The parcel came from Nanny: a navy-blue scarf, hand knitted, and the reminder to wear it constantly, now that winter was here.

'Dear Nanny,' Lucinda sighed. 'So much effort gone into it and she must have spent her own coupons, getting the wool.'

From her godfather there was a saucy birthday card and from her parents a five-pound note and the request, in the Earl's handwriting, to take her little friends for a meal.

'A fiver!' Lucinda whooped. 'We can drink Craigiebur dry on that!'

'Why,' asked Vi obliquely as they arranged the cards on Lucinda's locker, 'are you so determined to get tight, queen? Is it because of what happened in the Gareloch or is it because you'd have liked to hear from Mike today?'

'I – I . . .' Lucinda looked away, her cheeks red. 'Something of each, I suppose.'

'Well, them poor lads is in God's hands now, it seems.' Hastily, Vi crossed herself. 'But since this is a special day, I kept this one back till the end.' She drew her hand from the pocket of her overall with a flourish. 'This is the one you've been waitin' for. Funny it should arrive today, innit?'

'Oh, God! From Mike? It's not from Mike!'

'Oh? Well, it's got *Passed by Censor* on the front, and the sender's name on the back is M. J. Farrow.'

'*Mike!*' Lucinda snatched the envelope, tearing it open with fingers that shook. 'Oh, Mike, Mike . . .'

There was a small, happy silence. Lucinda's cheeks flushed pink; tears shone in her eyes.

'You read it.' She pushed the single sheet of paper into Vi's hand. 'Read it out loud so I can hear the words and know I'm not dreaming it.'

'If you're sure? I mean – '

'Please, Vi.'

'Well, then, it says, "Somewhere in transit" at the top, then it says – '

'Go on.'

'It says: *My own love. This troopship is putting into port for supplies and water, so there's a chance that mail just might get ashore, for posting. So this is to say I'm sorry it wasn't possible to tell you when last we spoke that I was going back to flying duties, overseas. When we shall meet again, my lovely Lucy, I don't know. I only know I love you. For the time being, our one night is all we'll have to hold on to, but we will be together one day, I swear it. Please wait for me, my darling. I love you, love you, love you.* And it ends: *Always, Mike.*' Vi sighed deeply. 'Ar,' she breathed, her eyes misty.

'It's true, then?' Lucinda whispered, hugging herself tightly against the sudden, exquisite trembling of her limbs, closing her eyes because any second now she was going to let go and cry and cry and cry. 'That letter – it *was* from Mike.'

'It was. On his way overseas,' Jane said softly. 'And he loves you. Four times, he loves you.'

'Oh, Lordy.' Lucinda sniffed loudly. 'And I thought I'd lost him. I'd accepted it, said goodbye to him, inside me. I never once thought, though, he'd have been posted abroad.'

'I told you to have faith, didn't I? I said you should never give up hope.'

'You did, Kendal dear, yet I – '

'You thought he'd chucked you, didn't you?' Vi accused. 'And you went and wrote to Charlie, didn't you?'

'Yes, I did.' Lucinda's eyes dropped to the envelope in her hand.

'And you told him you'd marry him, didn't you, so where are we now, eh?'

'Well, Vi McKeown, I'll tell you.' A sudden smile lifted Lucinda's lips, her cheeks dimpled. 'Yes, I did think I'd lost Mike and yes, I did write to Charlie. I finally did it! I told him I *wouldn't* marry him!'

'You did *what*? You mean you didn't – '

'Didn't agree to a wedding on the rebound? Oh, *no*. And I'm so happy! I know I've no right to be, not after *Viper* and what happened to Rob, but forgive me, please, because I am and I can't help it.'

'Then be happy, love, and enjoy it, because Vi and I are happy, too. And this will be a birthday to remember, won't it, Vi?'

'Ar,' Vi choked. 'Oh, ar . . .' It was all she was able to say.

18

Lucinda closed the cabin door, leaning against it for support, eyes closed dramatically.

'What's to do, queen? Was that Charlie on the phone, then, or your mam?'

'Who do you think?'

'Ar.' Vi had long been expecting a blast from the Countess. There were few secrets now in cabin 9. Charlie's last letter, received on Lucinda's birthday, had been a furious condemnation of the Women's Royal Naval Service, which, he declared, had been the ruination of her. Nothing and no one had been spared, and he'd ended by demanding to know when her next leave was due, insisting they be married then.

Lucinda had replied the next day, with a carefully worded letter telling him she would never change her mind and that leave, as he should well know, was never due but a *privilege* and she had no idea at all when she would be granted hers.

'So please, Charlie, don't make any plans which include me,' she had finished. The letter was a masterpiece she had been well pleased with and so firm, so brusque, almost, that she had relented and added, 'With best wishes. Take care,' and posted it immediately lest the flush of heady defiance should desert her. And that, Lucinda considered, should have been the end of it, but she had not reckoned with her mother.

'Oh, my Lord.' Vi frowned.

'Exactly. I should have known she'd not take it lying down, but I won. Or at least I *think* I did.'

'Good for you.' Jane was well acquainted with the tribulations of an only child. 'Y'know, we can be called up, bombed, shot at and damn near drowned for two bob a day, yet still our parents think they can tell us who to marry. Well, until we're twenty-one, that is.'

'What exactly did your mam say, queen?'

'She was *livid*. I'd expected it to be Charlie on the phone, saying he'd got the letter I sent him – maybe even saying he accepted it – but when I realized it was Mama, it threw me. Well, for a while it did. Then I told her about Mike. I even told her he'd picked me up, and she made very peculiar noises and put the phone down. That was all there was to it.'

In reality, it had been a harrowing experience from start to finish.

'Lucinda?' The voice had been waspish.

'Mama! I thought it was Charlie.'

'Well, it isn't, and I wouldn't be surprised if the poor boy never rings you again. Just what is the meaning of the letter you sent him? Have you taken leave of your senses?'

'Oh, *that* letter. But that one was ages ago . . .'

'I don't care when it was. Charles has only now told me.'

The Countess paused for effect and Lucinda clearly heard the tapping of her fingernails on the desk top. Mama always tapped when she was angry.

'Are you there, child?'

'Yes. I'm still here.'

'Then what have you to say? How dare you hold me up to ridicule? I mean, how am I to tell my friends there isn't going to be a wedding?'

'It shouldn't be too hard, Mama. Tell them that Charlie and I have decided it's best we don't marry. I'm sure no one will think anything at all about it. Weddings get called off all the time, now.'

She closed her eyes, taking a deep, calming breath. Please, she thought despairingly, don't go on and on, Mama. I won't marry Charlie. I *won't.*

'Not a Bainbridge wedding,' the Countess hissed. 'And I shall arrange for you to be married on your very next leave,' she finished triumphantly.

'Very well. You may make whatever plans you please.' *Oh, Mike, my darling, how I need you now.* 'But just one thing. Don't include me in them, because I won't be there. I – I'm in love with someone else you see, and – '

'In *love*? What on earth difference is *love* supposed to make?' The voice rose to shrieking pitch. 'In love with whom? Do I know him?'

'I very much doubt it. He's American and he's – '

'An *American*?' The shudder in the voice was unmistakable. 'Where on earth did you find an American?'

'At the end of Craigiebur Pier, actually. And I didn't find him, really. I picked him up, I suppose. Or maybe he picked me up. I'm not quite sure.'

There was a small, dramatic silence, broken by a vaporous sigh. Then softly, too softly, the Countess said, 'I see. Now it all begins to make sense. That time you stayed out all night. In Maida Vale, you said. With your friend from Brighton, you said. Are you pregnant, Lucinda?'

'Sadly I am not, Mama, so will you please stop upsetting yourself and accept that I will not marry Charlie? *Please*, Mama.'

There was no reply. Only a strange, gurgling sound before the line went dead.

Lucinda shrugged, then carefully replaced the receiver. It could be the fault of the war. Telephone lines went dead all the time, now. Or it could be, she realized wonderingly, that she had challenged her mother, and won!

She had taken the stairs two at a time, rushing away with all possible haste from a malevolent instrument that might ring again; back to the safety of cabin 9.

'But I think I won, Vi. I really think I did.' Weak with emotion, she collapsed on her bed.

'Good for you, queen.'

'She'll ring back. You don't know my mother. She never gives up. She'll ring again.'

'Not tonight, she won't.' Jane smiled. 'It'll take her hours to get another call through. Forget it.'

'Jane's right. Let's all go next door, eh? Let's have our standeasy by the fire and get ourselves thawed out. It's freezin' in here.'

Cabin 10 was even cosier and warmer than the common room, where the only other fire was allowed, even though most times it smelled of drying clothes and shoes.

'Fine by me, Vi. Tell them that Lucinda and I will bring the drinks up. And bread and jam, too. Won't be long.'

Another drama over, Vi thought thankfully as the pair chattered their way downstairs. But she'd have given anything to have heard that conversation and seen the vexation on the old girl's face.

'Atta girl, Lucinda,' she whispered proudly. 'You're learnin', queen. By the heck, you're learnin'.'

Had the world been at peace that night, bonfires would have blazed high into the night sky and rockets and Roman candles and Catherine wheels shone with a brief, glittering beauty. But this November night, only the hastily doused flaming of a match broke the absolute darkness. Guy Fawkes and all his trappings were banned for the duration.

And on this November night, curtains were drawn not only for the blackout that demanded it, but gratefully against the dark and damp and shifting mists outside. In

424

cabin 10, a wood fire burned in the iron grate, and the boat's-crew Wrens toasted their shins around it and dried their clothes above it. They smiled when Vi came in to share it.

'Find yourself a pew.'

'Ta.' She sat on the floor at Connie's side. 'Jane and Lucinda are bringin' the supper up. God, I hate November.'

'November is the month of the dead.' Lilith laid a log on the fire. 'I'm always glad when it's over.'

Everyone nodded agreement, though no one spoke. It was pleasant to sit in the fireglow; peaceful, too, for those who lived on the top floor were inclined to keep themselves to themselves in winter, and guard their fire jealously.

'I'm getting stiff. Think I'll go down and see if I can find a piece of toast.' Connie rose awkwardly to her feet. 'Won't be long.'

'Did you know,' Lilith demanded when the door had closed, 'that Connie has to leave before very much longer? She'll be starting her seventh month soon, and Sister wants her in the home, she says, where there's a midwife and doctor on hand. Con's still being sick and she's so thin and gaunt-looking.'

'Poor kid. How she exists on what she's able to keep down is a mystery.'

'Well, Sister reckons she should have more care than she's getting here, and I'm inclined to agree with her.'

'Life's unfair, innit? Y'know, the more I think about that Johnny, the more I don't like him,' Vi brooded. 'Ar, hey, wouldn't it be smashin' if a dirty great stoker was to give 'im a good battering?'

'Never mind about the stoker. Leave Johnny Jones to me,' Lilith said softly, 'because I swear that if anything

425

happens to Connie, that man's going to wish he'd never drawn breath.'

'So what'll you do? Ill-wish him?' Fenny demanded, only half in jest.

Lilith shrugged. 'I've ill-wished before. Only once. But if I have to, I'll do it again. Come to think of it, November's a good month for ill-wishing . . .'

'Sorry I spoke.' A feeling of fear shivered through Vi and left her strangely uneasy. But then, Lilith and her peculiar religion always did, even though, in spite of herself, Vi was drawn to the woman with the deep, dark eyes; eyes that could see into your soul – if you were daft enough to let them.

Supper arrived on two trays. Large cups of ship's cocoa and a plate piled high with bread and jam. Fresh white bread, of a kind denied to civilians, spread with jam of an unnatural red. (*Mixed fruit*, the label on the seven-pound tin ambiguously declared.)

'My, but it was cold today.' Fenny Cole licked sticky fingers and rearranged the canvas pumps laid to dry in the hearth. 'I'm sure it's freezing tonight, and you know what they say about a frost before St Martin's Day, don't you?'

They didn't. They weren't sure, even, when St Martin's Day fell.

'Is it important, Cole?'

'Of course it is. If there's a hard frost before the eleventh, it's going to be a wet and stormy winter rather than a dry one,' Fenny announced. 'Well, that's what my grandpa always says.'

'Never heard that one.' Vi frowned. 'Only know the one about Candlemas. That's in February, though. A fair Candlemas means more winter to come – according to old Ma Norris, God rest her.'

Jane shifted uneasily. Was it really less than a year since she and Rob met? Last Candlemas the air had been harsh with frost and the bombers at the aerodrome grounded. That night, she had fallen in love. Instantly, and for ever.

'I heard they're just about ready to try to get *Viper* to the top,' she murmured. 'Just a buzz, though. The CCO messenger started it, I think. Said he heard them talking in the staff office.'

She desperately wanted *Viper* to be brought to the surface. She wanted Tom and the rest of the crew to rest decently and with dignity and not be left there for ever in a soulless steel coffin.

She stared with troubled eyes into the darting flames. First Rob, now Tom. But she was a chop-girl, wasn't she, and bad luck to men; there was no denying it. There'd been a chop-girl at Fenton Bishop aerodrome: a WAAF who'd driven the aircrews to their bombers before they set out on raids. And every crew she drove got the chop, eventually, and in the end they'd all refused to let her anywhere near them.

They'd sent her away, that chop-girl, after the third crew; sent her to another aerodrome, and her bad luck with her, Rob had said. And now she, Jane Kendal, had become a chop-girl.

The door opened. Awkwardly, clumsily, Connie returned to her corner.Now, she always spent her nights in her old cabin, each of them the more precious because soon she would have to leave Ardneavie House and go to strangers to have her baby.

'Are you all right?' Lucinda smiled. She worried about Connie and her little unwanted child. She who was so completely happy, so loved, cared deeply that a friend would soon be so very alone and lonely. But then no one, Lucinda thought, had the right to be as happy as she was, this dark November night. It made her a little afraid just to think of it.

'Did you see the dawn break this morning,' she

demanded. 'The sky was wild, vermilion almost, and the clouds purple. So dramatic, with the hills black against it. Frightening, but beautiful.'

'Beautiful, my foot! A sky like that usually brings bad weather with it,' Lilith snorted.

'Heard on the news that the temperature in Moscow is eighty degrees *below*. Can't be right – can it?' Megan Cadwallader asked.

'Could be. Wasn't it the terrible cold there that put paid to Napoleon when he tried it on?' Jane's spirits lifted hopefully.

'You mean 'im what said "Not tonight, Josephine"?' Vi demanded.

'*'im*.' Lucinda nodded. 'Wouldn't it be marvellous if the same thing happened to Hitler?'

They all agreed it would, but beleaguered Moscow and Leningrad seemed a long way away this dark, brooding night, when firelight lit their faces and the stone walls of Ardneavie House circled them protectively.

'Serve 'im right if it did,' Vi said comfortably. 'Shouldn't have gone there, should he?'

Firelight and friends, and the war banished – until the morning. But it would be waiting there, long before daylight, when alarms would jangle them all awake.

So let it wait. ─

A great deal happened on the fourteenth day of that grey, cold November. It began as a dead, dull morning, then came sadly alive when Chief Telegraphist Walter Wetherby stormed, grey-faced and shaken, into the CCO.

'They've done it! Those buggers have got the *Ark*!'

'You're joking!' No one believed it. They wouldn't. *Ark Royal* sunk? Never! The *Ark* was like the *Queen Mary* and the *Queen Elizabeth*. Unsinkable. Jerry would never get the old *Ark*.

428

'Forget it, Chief. Just a buzz. They've sent *Ark Royal* to the bottom more times than you've had hot dinners,' they said.

Nasty little Goebbels, his propaganda as evil as his face, had claimed the aircraft carrier destroyed many times.

'We have sunk the *Ark Royal*!' he proclaimed. He'd proclaimed it so often it was becoming a joke.

Until this morning. Until Walter Wetherby finally accepted that the carrier on which he had spent many years as a young leading telegraphist was gone; sunk off Gibraltar by the submarine U.81. You didn't believe the propaganda and lies the Nazis put out, but when it came on one of your own news broadcasts, then it was fact. *Ark*, it seemed, had gone down slowly, reluctantly. Two-thirds of her crew were saved before the old ship finally keeled over and died. Died like a thoroughbred.

God, but this was going to be one of those days and no, he *didn't* want a mug of tea. On this day, Chief Walter Wetherby was a sad and embittered man. Oh, you expected to lose ships, he fretted; it was part and parcel of war. But lose the *Ark*? He'd have staked his pension, should he live to spend it, that they'd never have done for the *Ark Royal*. Bastards, the lot of them, and as if that weren't enough, he thought morosely, *Viper* was coming home today. Or her crew was. Bad luck, that submarine would be now. There'd been a Jonah on *Viper*. Someone in that crew had brought the ill luck with him, and that boat would always be unlucky now.

The news had arrived a couple of days ago. At last the submarine had been brought to the surface, lashed between a couple of sturdy Admiralty tugs, then berthed at Helensport.

Now, Chief Wetherby realized, chin on hand, there'd be bigwigs from the Admiralty swarming all over the flotilla, poking in their noses where they weren't wanted,

429

upsetting routine. They'd be trying to find the cause of the accident; trying, if they could, to find a scapegoat.

Not that the likes of chief petty officers who were the backbone of the Royal Navy would ever be told what had really happened in the Gareloch. That lot in London were a law unto themselves, could get away with murder, if they set their minds to it. But *Ark Royal* gone . . . ?

'Chief.' He turned to find Jane Kendal standing beside him.

'What is it, girl?' Damnit, was there no peace for anyone?

'It's – well, I've heard there's going to be a service for *Viper* this afternoon.'

'Well, what about it, Kendal?'

'I've heard all the divisions will be sending people, so can I go with the Wrens, please?'

'Is it important? And who'll stand in for you if I let you go?'

'Jock says he'll manage, Chief. And it won't be for long.'

'Oh, well.' Walter Wetherby looked again at the sad-faced girl and remembered she'd been seeing one of *Viper*'s crew. A bit of a kid who'd already lost one boyfriend, if the buzz was to be believed.

'You'll have to behave yourself on the quarterdeck – you know that?'

'If you mean am I going to break down and cry – no, Chief, I'm not.'

'All right then, Kendal. I suppose I shall have to say yes,' he said grudgingly, though he'd intended letting her go, all along.

'Thanks, Chief. Thanks a lot. And – ' She hesitated.

'*Now* what?'

'What will happen to *Viper*?' She had to know. She didn't want to see that submarine again. Just to think of it ever tying up alongside *Omega* made her feel uneasy. 'Will they send it to the breaker's yard?'

'Oh, no. Shouldn't think so. A brand new boat, *Viper* was. Reckon they'll tow it back to the builders for repair and refitting. And like as not they'll give it a new name; another V-name.'

'But it won't come back here, to the 15th?'

'Should bloody well hope not, Kendal. Renamed ships are always bad luck, and *Viper* was bad luck enough, without that. There'll be no submariners wanting to sail on *that* boat now; not a boat as jinxed as that one's going to be.'

Mentally, he crossed his fingers. Sailors were the most superstitious of mortals; it was part of their lives. And Chief Wetherby was more superstitious than most.

'Well, cut along, then. There's a war on – or hasn't anybody told you yet?' he growled, returning to his brooding. And damn this war and damn and blast those Krauts on the U.81. He glanced up at the bulkhead clock. It was just coming up to tot-time.

'Be back in about ten minutes,' he called to the leading hand of the watch.

'Right, Chief.' And let's hope, he thought fervently, that the old boy would be in a better mood, once he'd got his rum inside him. 'And roll on my leave,' he muttered when Walter Wetherby was out of sight. 'Roll on my flaming seven, that's all . . .'

That afternoon, on the quarterdeck of HMS *Omega*, they laid thirty-nine coffins in precise rows, then draped each one with a Union flag. At 1500 hours, beneath a drab, unhappy sky, a memorial service for the submarine's crew was held, attended by men from each division in the flotilla, and a scattering of Wrens. Without speaking, Jane took her place beside Third Officer St John, Chief Wren Pillmoor and Miriam, the quiet, grey-haired gardener.

Omega's captain led the singing of 'Eternal Father', the sailors' hymn that begged indulgence for those in peril on the sea. And the assembly sang it not only for the thirty-nine, but for themselves; a prayer in hand for tomorrow, or next week or next year, perhaps.

Jane stood very still, staring ahead at the stern ensign, the tears in her throat a hard, cold knot. She held them in check, because tears wouldn't bring Tom back nor the words she had said to him and, anyway, no one wept on the quarterdeck. Later, maybe, but never here.

The ship's bugler stepped forward and moistening his lips played 'Sunset', its notes clear and poignant, a last goodbye. Then the padre held his hand high over the coffins, murmured a blessing, and the brief, sad service was over. The divisions came to attention, turned right, and thankfully marched away.

Jane said her own silent farewell. She did not know where on the quarterdeck Tom lay. She only knew that when she went ashore at the end of her watch the coffins would be gone, the flags folded. Some of *Viper*'s crew were to be laid in a communal grave beside the little kirk at the head of the loch; others would go home to their families. She hoped Tom was going home; back to Dan and Uncle Jack and the aunts. Back to Brockhole and Abbots Dart and the red earth of Devon. It would be some small comfort to her conscience if he could be there, for Christmas.

She turned briefly as she left the quarterdeck. 'Goodbye, Tom,' she whispered from the deeps of her heart. 'I'm sorry. I'm so very sorry.'

Jock asked her, when she took her place at his side again, if she was all right, and she told him she was.

'I'm okay, Jock. Just give me a little time. I'll get myself straightened out by tomorrow.'

When tomorrow came, that was. And maybe, in wartime, it was best that it never should.

'Are you all right?' Lucinda asked her that night.

'Fine, love. Just fine.' She was glad it was all over. This afternoon, on the quarterdeck, she had held her feelings tightly to her, letting the searing pain of remorse tear at her without mercy. It had been a part of her growing up; a part, she hoped, of her absolution. 'But I'll be glad when this day is over.'

Tomorrow, she would weep for Tom.

A new day came, sharp with frost, a pale sun reminding them that yesterday was gone. Later that day, Lucinda received a letter from Mike: a blue, square-folded sheet with *By Air Mail* in the top left-hand corner and *Passed by Censor* rubber-stamped on the back.

'Well, come on, then.' Vi beamed. 'Let's be knowing.'

Lucinda looked up, eyes shining, cheeks pink. 'Well – I – '

'Not what he *says*, scone-head. Where he *is*.'

'Burma, would you believe. RAF Rangoon.' Lucinda shook her head in bewilderment. 'Imagine. It's half a world away.'

'Ar, yes, but he's safe,' Vi reminded her soberly. 'He's like Gerry – well out of it. There's no fightin' in Burma – well, none to worry about. Better be there than flying them fighter sweeps over France every day, just askin' for trouble.'

'I know. And I'm not complaining – not really. But I feel so guilty, though. Nobody's got a right to be this happy, have they?'

They knew what she was thinking: that yesterday had been an awful day and tomorrow Connie was leaving for the home for unmarried mothers and no one, really, should be happy today.

Lucinda hugged herself tightly, a sigh of contentment escaping her, eyes searching for Jane's. *Forgive me*, they begged. *Forgive me this happiness*. And Jane smiled back, her eyes saying, *My turn next* . . . and everything was almost all right.

'We'll all have to be there in the mornin' for Connie,' Vi said. 'We'll have to wish her luck and promise to write to her.'

'We will.' Jane smiled.

Lucinda nodded. 'And we *will* keep in touch. It's terrible that her family have thrown her out, and it'll be up to us to let her know she's not completely alone.'

'It's that baby I'm worried about,' Vi mourned. 'Poor unwanted little scrap.'

Lucinda wrote Mike's new address on the two letters she had written in readiness for this moment. Tomorrow, when Connie had gone, she would write another. And she would tell him how much she loved him and how cold it was, Somewhere in Scotland, and how she missed him. He'd want to hear, too, about the new-style hats they would all soon be wearing, and that she had finally written to Charlie. But mostly she would write, 'I love you, miss you, love you, want you,' because that, she was sure, was what a man so far away would really want to know.

Shivering with cold, she snapped off the light, whispered 'Good-night' to Vi and Jane, and burrowed contentedly into her blankets. But sleep came reluctantly and she lay wide-eyed, heart bumping. It was, she supposed, because of all the lovely, intimate things Mike had written and the way he longed for her and begged her never to stop loving him. She had never felt close to any man, until Mike. It was a new and delightful feeling, this belonging. But mostly, she had to admit, it was the nightingales keeping her awake, singing so rapturously, filling the entire room with their honey-dripped notes.

'Hush,' she whispered indulgently, pulling her knees to her chin, hugging her happiness to her. 'Be quiet, or you'll have the entire house awake.'

She closed her eyes tightly and thought about Connie and the submariners from *Viper*. I'm so lucky, she thought. *Thank you for Mike, God. And let Jane be happy again, soon.*

Wren Connie Dean waited on the steps of Ardneavie House, her kit beside her. Soon, the transport that would take her in to Craigiebur and the early ferry would come, and she tried not to look towards the loch; tried not to see *Omega* and the submarines and the escort vessels tied up to their buoys. She had tried to hate Johnny, but she could not; rather she had despised herself for her own stupidity.

'Thanks, Lilith,' she said to the woman at her side. 'Thanks for not saying I told you so.'

'That's all right, kid.' Lilith laid an arm around the drooping shoulders, wanting to help, knowing she could not. 'Think nothing of it.'

'You'll keep in touch, won't you, Dean?' Fenny sniffed.

'Yes, Con.' Kathy MacAlister pushed a sprig of white heather into her hand. 'Be lucky, hen. Let us know how things go; we'll need to know.'

'I will. You've all been great and I won't forget you, honest I won't.'

She stood there, a dumpy, dejected figure, wearing a steward's overall beneath her loosely belted raincoat, her eyes swollen and red. She had wept a great deal lately.

'Here's the transport,' she whispered. 'I'd better go. And don't any of you come down into Craigiebur with me, please. No more goodbyes.'

'If you're sure.' Lilith frowned. 'We'd all planned – '

'No. Thanks all the same. And anyway, it might make you late on watch.'

Now the time had come, she wanted to go; leave Ardneavie without ever looking back. She walked down the path to where the truck waited.

Jane and Lucinda picked up her cases. They really should go with her, Lucinda knew. Carrying all that kit couldn't be good for her.

They stood at the gate, watching as she climbed clumsily up to sit beside the driver. Words didn't seem to count for much now; being there was really what mattered, and sending their love to her in great, warm waves.

The driver gave a toot of goodbye and they all called 'see you' and 'cheerio' and 'so long'. Not goodbye, though. You never said goodbye, in wartime.

Oh, Con, Lucinda thought. I'm so sorry; sorry you are leaving, sorry about Johnny, sorry I'm so happy.

'Ta-ra, queen,' Vi called. 'Take care.'

'Poor Connie,' Megan Cadwallader murmured. 'She looks so unhappy.'

'Good luck, Con.' They waved as the transport drove away, smiles fixed on their lips.

'Hell,' Kathy MacAlister choked. 'I'm going to miss that girl.'

'Aren't we all?' Lucinda retorted, tight-lipped. 'Oh, it isn't fair.'

'Sometimes,' Lilith said, 'I hate men.'

'I hate *randy* men,' Megan qualified.

'Is there a difference?'

'I wouldn't care,' Jane frowned as the truck rounded the bend and disappeared, 'but Johnny has got away with it, hasn't he?'

'I know. Wish the big beefy crusher from port watch pier patrol would give him a good hiding.' Fenny could think of no other man more deserving of such attention. 'I'd stand there and cheer.'

But Lilith said nothing, for weren't there more ways than one to skin a cat? For the moment she must bide her time, but let harm come to Connie or her baby, then nothing would help Johnny Jones. Nothing at all.

'I need a cup of tea,' was all she said, but they knew it was what she hadn't said that mattered. Penrose was like that.

'Well, that's it.' Pat Pillmoor turned from the window. 'That's Dean gone, poor girl.'

'It's for the best. Sister was worried about her, you know, especially these last two weeks,' Suzie St John said softly. 'I don't know what it was, exactly – Sister wouldn't have told me had I asked – but I got the impression she'd be glad to have Dean off her hands.'

'Wish it hadn't happened though, Ma'am. Makes me feel I should have done more to stop it.'

'How could you, Pat? We can only warn them, you and I, and do our best if things go wrong. I shall worry about Dean, though, until I know it's all over and they're both all right. There's something about the poor child that has me worried. It's almost as if she's stopped caring. We must keep in touch. She mustn't feel deserted.'

'Don't think the girls'll let that happen, Ma'am. They've all been pretty marvellous about it. Look, you couldn't squeeze that teapot, could you? I really could do with a cup of tea.'

She sighed deeply. Who'd be a chiefie with a hostel of women to look after? she asked herself yet again. Just who, but a fool?

'You can't tell with men, can you?' Vi frowned as they settled themselves in the common-room window, eyes

437

fixed on the hills that circled the loch, trying to separate the varying shades of grey. 'When you decide which bloke you want and play hard to get till he pops the question, I mean. It's a terrible gamble, innit? Me and Gerry were lucky, but imagine landing yourself with someone like that Johnny? Wonder if his wife knows about his goings-on?'

'To be hoped she doesn't, poor soul. But she'd have him just the same, I suppose. When I realized that Mike'd had other affairs, it didn't make a scrap of difference.' Lucinda shrugged. 'And I'll bet anything you like that once Connie is out of the home and back in uniform again, she'll wonder if this corner or the next will be the one she'll turn and see Johnny Jones walking towards her.'

'Oh, ar. She had it bad for that little toe rag.' Vi scowled. 'And she'll never forget him, no matter what he's done to her.'

'You're right, both of you. I shall never forget Rob and I know that one day I'll see him again. Every new moon and every first star I wish on, it's always to see Rob.' Jane sighed. 'Sometimes it's turning a corner; sometimes it's at the stile at Tingle's Wood. Other times I'm picking up the phone and he's there, on the other end. But whenever and wherever we meet, he'll say, "Hullo, Jenny." Just "Hullo, Jenny", the way only he can say it.

'And don't tell me I'm being stupid, because I'm not. I know I'll see him again. Apart from anything else, I made a bargain with God. "Let me see Rob again, just for half a minute," I asked Him, "and you can have the rest of my life."'

'Kendal dear, you *mustn't*. You can't do things like that. It's asking for trouble, isn't it, Vi?'

'Ar – don't think so. And her faith in the Lord would do one of my lot justice.' Vi gazed up at a seagull drifting on a current of air, so beautiful, so graceful that you had to believe in miracles. But it was only hovering there until some sailor on *Omega* emptied a gash bucket over the side, then down that bird would go, screaming and shrieking, scavenging among the waste. Exactly the same as Liverpool seagulls, really, only cleaner. 'But God isn't open to bargaining, not really, on account of it all bein' written down, see.'

'No, I don't see. Tell us.'

'Well, it's only me own way of thinkin'; a kind of – ' She paused, searching for the word.

'Philosophy?'

'Ar, that's it. Philosophy. Not that Father O'Flaherty would go along with it, but I think it's all settled for us the minute we're born. It's written in our book, see.'

'Our book of life, you mean? Something like "This girl will have fair, curly hair and a bossy mama and marry an American from New England"?'

'Somethin' like that. I think the bloke who was on duty when I was born took a quick look down and said, "That one can have big feet and be good at scrubbin'. And we'll not let her have no kids, neither."'

'Oh, Vi, you're such an old love,' Jane laughed, gathering up the empty teacups. 'And I suppose it was written in my log book that I'd have red hair and a temper to go with it and that on the second day of February 1941, at about half-past eight in the evening, a sergeant-pilot would say to me, "I shall call you Jenny".' And he would promise always to love her, and she him. Were all their sweet promises written in her book and in Rob's book too? 'Wish I could turn the page and see when I'll meet him again, and where.'

'Oh no, Jane. That's against the rules. You'll have to wait and see; we all have to.' Vi rose to her feet, relieved that life seemed to be returning to normal again. 'And you two had better shift yourselves and get ready for work. Your shoes are goin' to need a good brushing. The backs of your heels were shockin', Lucinda, when you came off watch last night. And have either of you thought about getting stuck in for your leave, eh? Won't be long now, will it? Suppose it'll be up to me to see Chiefie for our chits. Y'know, sometimes I wonder just what I'm to do with the pair of you.'

She glowered at them with mock severity, her voice indulgent; terrible trials though they were, they made her war bearable. And for the life of her, Vi McKeown had no idea what she would do without them.

'Well, come on, then. Chop chop. There's a war on, you know.'

That morning in December should have been like any other winter morning, memorable only because the leave they had applied for had been granted, and all that remained for the three should have been to collect leave passes, travel warrants and ration cards from the out-tray in the regulating office.

But the morning of the eighth day of December was not like any other morning, for the news broadcast had been so breathtaking, so unbelievable, that Vi could only fling open the cabin door and gasp, 'On the wireless! The American fleet in the Pacific destroyed, and God knows how many dead!' She gasped for breath, shaking her head, collapsing on to the bed. 'Them Japs, that's what!'

'Are you sure?' Lucinda's face drained of colour. 'The Japanese? They're not at war – why should they do that? You must've got it wrong, Vi.'

'I haven't, y'know! Heard it with me own ears, didn't I? On the eight o'clock news.' She flung on her greatcoat and reached for her hat. 'I'm goin' for a paper. You two go downstairs and see what else you can find out.'

She was gone before they could question her further, running through the garden and up and over the brae to Ardneavie village. Today, she couldn't wait for Ma'am's discarded newspaper. Today, she must read one *now*!

She was lucky. There had been a demand for newspapers, but a few still remained on the counter of the little shop. Vi paid her penny and picked up a *Daily Mail*. It was stamped *Last Edition* and, though it consisted of four pages only, it told Vi all she needed to know.

JAPAN DECLARES WAR ON BRITAIN AND AMERICA, the headlines screamed. HEAVY BOMBING, HUNDREDS DEAD.

'Mother of God! The cheek of the little sods!'

The majority of starboard watch ate breakfast in the mess that morning, so great was their shock. Not for them the plates of bread and jam carried stealthily upstairs and eaten cosily in cabins. Apprehension drew them all together and they spoke in hushed and worried tones.

'All the American Pacific fleet – just *gone*?'

'But you can't do that, can you – bomb somebody else's ships without declaring war on them first?'

'They just did it, chum!'

'*Where* did it happen? Pearl Harbor? Never heard of it.'

'Well, you have now!'

Pearl Harbor. In the United States of America the name became an instant obscenity, the attack on their ships an outrage, an insult to national pride. Pearl Harbor? In the small, bomb-happy islands of Britain, men and women said it first with bewilderment then with reluctant hope. America would enter the war, now. They'd been teetering on the edge for months, hadn't they; shipping war supplies to Britain, escorting convoys and sabre-rattling in the North Atlantic. But now they would join the fight. They were a proud lot, those Yanks. Nobody kicked them in the backside and got away with it, and thank the Lord they'd be on our side!

'Seems the whole world is at war now,' Lilith observed. 'It's madness.'

'Listen, everybody, and I'll tell you what it says.' Vi spread her newspaper on the table. It read like a catalogue of betrayals. The Japanese planes, almost two hundred of them, had flown in without warning; one half attacking nearby airfields, the others, the torpedo bombers, raining down havoc on the peacefully anchored ships.

'More than two thousand killed and nineteen ships gone, it says. Well, I reckon we're goin' to have to declare war on them now. Flamin' Norah! Where's it goin' to end?'

Where indeed? And when? In two years, four years, or never?

'God knows.' Fenny sighed. 'We'll all be old and past it before this lot is over, now.' All their green years, all their good years, wasted.

'Ar, hey, cheer up. We're not doin' so bad, are we? The Army's got through to them lads in Tobruk, and they're giving Rommel a bit of his own back in the desert. And Hitler isn't gettin' it all his own way in Russia, is he? Said he'd be in Moscow for Christmas, and where is he, then? Bogged down in the cold and snow, that's where.'

'But all those men killed, without the chance to fight back,' Molly said. 'That attack was planned. It had to be.'

'Ar. Y'know, they're funny little fellers, them Japs,' Vi pronounced. 'They all wear glasses, don't they? Bet half of them can't see to shoot straight.'

'Seems they saw all right yesterday morning, and –'

'Vi! That map!' For the first time Lucinda spoke. She had tried not to look at it, but the map on the front page of the newspaper laid out a whole new theatre of war, impossible to ignore. 'Burma!' Her finger stabbed down on the country bordered by China and Siam, and already, the paper said, the Japanese had bombed Shanghai and Hong Kong and marched their soldiers into Siam.

'Rangoon. Where Mike is. And we thought he was safe.' Her face was white, her eyes wide with fear. 'I was too happy, wasn't I, Vi?'

'Now see here, queen. Rangoon is a long way from – '

She stopped, eyes on the door and Megan Cadwallader, who banged a fist on the nearest tabletop and shouted, 'Listen, everybody! It's a special bulletin!'

Reaching up, she switched on the speaker extension, and the bland, impersonal voice of the announcer filled the suddenly quiet room.

'It has just been announced . . .'

Announced that the United States of America had declared war on the Japanese nation, and that Great Britain and all her Dominions had done the same.

It was official now. The world *had* gone mad, and Mike was half a lifetime away, in the thick of the madness.

They bought saccharin-sweet tea from the trolley lady on the station and lit cigarettes. Two hours to wait before Vi's train left Glasgow; longer than that for Lucinda and Jane. If their trains ran to time, that was, which they probably wouldn't. It would be late evening, Lucinda realized, before she reached King's Cross.

'Doesn't seem long since our last leave, does it?' she murmured.

'No. And I'll bet you anything you like that someone says, "Goodness me. On leave again, Jane?"'

'Or, "Hullo, Vi. Nice to see you. When are you goin' back?" They always ask you when you're goin' back.' Vi grinned. 'Be nice, though.'

'Nice,' Jane said. 'Nobody giving me any orders . . .'

443

Only her mother. 'Jane, dear, aren't you going to give Colin a ring?' or 'Well, I do think you should have made the effort to get up for early Communion this morning . . .' No use saying she was lined up and marched to church every Sunday she wasn't on watch.

She wished her mother would stop clucking and realize she'd be nineteen on Christmas Eve and was fighting a war, which was more than Colin was doing. 'Though I suppose my mother will want to know why I'm not having my leave at Christmas, but I'd honestly rather have Christmas at Ardneavie House, wouldn't you, Lucinda?'

'Me? Oh, right now I'd rather have Christmas anywhere than Bruton Street. As a matter of fact, I'll be glad when this leave is over.'

It wasn't going to be easy, facing Mama and Charlie. Mama would either be icy and aloof or she'd go on and on about it. Lucinda didn't know whether she preferred icy aloofness or a tirade of accusations. There wasn't much to choose between either. And Charlie would be all sweet reason until he realized she meant what she had said about not marrying him. He'd shout and sulk, then, and accuse her of being selfish and stupid and tell her not to come crying to him and begging forgiveness when her American went off with a chorus girl. She knew exactly how it would be. Charlie hadn't changed. He'd always ranted and sulked when he couldn't get his own way, even as a little boy. She'd been stupid not to have thought of it, till now.

'Well, stick to your guns, queen. Don't let them get you down,' Vi murmured. 'And there's always somebody worse off than we are, don't forget.'

There was Gerry, for a start. Vi had thought a lot about Gerry lately, worrying whether he was getting enough to eat and if he was managing to keep warm. Winters were colder in Austria, weren't they? She hoped he was still working on the farm. At least it would help pass the days.

She wondered if Gerry knew about what the Japanese had done at Pearl Harbor, or that they'd sunk the battleships *Prince of Wales* and *Repulse* off the coast of Malaya. And would the prison guards have taunted them all with the news that Italy and Germany had declared war on America and America had declared war on them?

'Why the sigh, old dear?' Lucinda asked.

'Oh, I was thinkin' about Gerry and if he's getting enough food, though there isn't a lot I can do about it if he isn't.'

'I know how you feel. I keep thinking about Mike and what the future holds.'

'Future?' Jane's laugh was bleak. 'Nobody's got a future in wartime. War is a day-to-day business. If we let ourselves think about it too much, we'd all go quietly mad.'

'So don't think about it, queen. It isn't worth it. Like I said, it's all written down in our book, and nothing's goin' to change that. And things are goin' to start getting better soon. Well, they can't get much worse, can they?' Vi glanced down at her watch. Ages and ages to wait yet.

'Anybody fancy another cup of tea?'

19

December, for the Allies, was not a good month – as far as battles won went. In Russia, encircling armies prepared to sit out a long, bitter siege of Leningrad and Moscow, whilst their U-boat packs picked off ship after ship – like shooting rats in a barrel, they said – from convoys struggling to reach Murmansk with supplies of war. And in the Mediterranean, Italian warships and German dive bombers mauled merchantmen carrying desperately needed supplies to brave, bomb-battered little Malta. And as if that were not more than enough, the armies of the God-Emperor swarmed unchecked over the Far East, and the British garrison at Hong Kong prepared to fight to the last man against Japanese hordes drunk with success.

But in spite of all the bad news, or perhaps because of it, the Wrens at Ardneavie House were determined to have a good Christmas, and it fell to starboard watch to decorate quarters and help with the extra chores that Christmas brought with it.

In the galley, Kathy MacAlister sighed, remembering when Christmas cakes were heavy with fruit and nuts and drenched in brandy. Now, she gazed sadly at the last of her candied peel hoard and wondered where all the currants and sultanas and raisins had gone as she chopped up dried apricots and prunes and hoped no one would notice. Stout and black treacle replaced brandy, and the marzipan that would cover the cake was a mixture of soya, dried egg and almond essence.

On the credit side, though, the victualling officer had

promised a piece of pork and two large chickens, and hinted there might even be a plum pudding of sorts.

One thing, though, could not be denied. Obesity was becoming a thing of the past; the strict rationing of food had seen to that. Now, people grew their own vegetables – Digging for Victory, it was called – and took to keeping rabbits and backyard hens to eke out meat and egg allocations, for what could a person living alone do with one-and-tuppenceworth of meat and two not very fresh eggs?

Not that the British were starving, exactly. Bread, made with nasty brown flour that everyone abhorred, was still unrationed, and sausages and offal. A housewife would queue for half an hour without complaint for two sausages and four ounces of liver, and longer still for fish and chips – when the fryer could get fish, and if his allowance of cooking fat had not run out. And should fish and fat come together simultaneously, news went round like wildfire that the chip shop was frying tonight, and the queue would start long before opening time. Fish and chips had become a real treat, carried home in triumph, well salted and vinegared and wrapped round with newspaper.

Kathy sighed again and fell to dreaming of tinned peaches, thick with syrup, large dollops of butter-grilled steak and sherry trifles piled with cream, and wondered, drooling, if she would live long enough ever to taste such wanton pleasures again.

'I think,' said the leading Wren who worked in the paymaster's office, 'that this year we should make a special effort with decorations,' and the unofficial meeting in the common room murmured its assent.

The days of paperchains and streamers were long forgotten, for paper was a munition of war now. But Miriam offered to bring in ivy trails and said she had covered the variegated holly bush with a net to keep the birds away from the berries, and with luck, the potted tawny chrysan-themum would be ready for carrying in – if she could keep it free of frost until Christmas Eve, when she was sure it would be in flower.

'I could only get one Christmas tree this year,' she told them, 'and *Omega* wants it. They'll be lashing it to the mainmast, I think, but I could cut a piece from the spruce in the garden and stick it in a plantpot, and if we dotted it with wisps of cotton wool – '

'And anything glittery we can find – '

'And if anyone has anything wrapped in silver paper – '

A spruce branch, they all agreed, could be dressed to resemble the real thing and would smell like the real thing, too.

'Wish we could get some balloons; lots of them, all colours and shapes and sizes, hung in bunches . . .'

'Idiot! Where on earth are we to get balloons?'

Where, indeed? Latex was already in short supply and used only for things essential to the war effort, and now that the Japanese army seemed set on occupying every rubber-producing country, frivolities like coloured bal-loons were unpatriotic and unnecessary and forbidden for the duration.

'I know,' a Welsh voice offered shyly. 'Well, not balloons *exactly*.' Megan stopped, red-faced.

'Go on,' ordered Leading Wren Paymaster. 'Quiet, everybody. Megan Cad knows where we can get balloons.'

'No, I didn't say that. It's just that – well, my sister's a nurse, see, and the young doctors at the hospital – well, they blow things up, for a bit of fun, sort of . . .'

'*Things*? What things?'

'You *know* . . .'

They didn't know, they said.

'Yes, you do. *Those* things.'

There was a small, baffled silence, then,

'French letters, that's what she's on about!'

'Oh, packets of three, she means!'

'Condoms! But of *course*! Just the job, they'd be, but where on earth are we to get them? We can't just walk into the chemist's and ask for them – can we?'

They couldn't, Megan agreed sadly, which was a great pity, for fully inflated, her sister had assured her, they could reach the unbelievable length of eighteen inches and shone something lovely; every bit as good as balloons.

'I know where we can get some,' Lilith said softly. 'You know the stairway that leads from the torpedo passage to the quarterdeck? Well, every night one of the sick-bay attendants leaves a cap at the bottom, full of them. They're for the men going ashore to help themselves to, if they want them.'

'So?'

'So why don't we go to the quarterdeck by way of the torpedo passage! If each of us took one, we'd be able to make quite a good show, wouldn't we?'

The idea was voted outrageous and brilliantly ingenious and that someone had better tell port watch to do the same. Discreetly, of course, when no one was looking, though surely there was nothing in King's Regulations that forbade contraceptives to Wrens, too? And no one would miss the odd one or two, would they?

'Eighteen inches long, did you say?'

'*Cor*!'

'Hey! Hang on a minute. Has anybody thought what Chiefie's going to say?'

'Chiefie won't know a thing about it till they're hung up. And she'll see the funny side of it. Patsy Pill's all right. It's only a giggle for Christmas, after all.'

'That's settled, then,' Leading Wren Paymaster pronounced. 'And have them here by Christmas Eve and bring plenty of puff with you – okay?'

As they said, it was only a laugh, and anything that eased the tension of this damn-awful war was welcome, wasn't it? And it *was* a damn-awful war because no one, now, could see the end to it. *The duration* had at last been defined. Since Pearl Harbor, it seemed, the duration meant for ever.

A Christmas moon shone brightly, making a mockery of the blackout, lighting the frost-tipped trees till they sparkled like diamonds. In the common room at Ardneavie House, holly and ivy swathed the walls; and in the bay window that overlooked the loch, the tree stood bravely. Not a traditional peacetime tree, not a tree thick with baubles, glittering magnificently, but a fir branch, hung with coloured paper and cotton wool and dusted with flour. Quite the best tree they had ever seen.

Jane brushed up leaves and fir needles and straying wisps of cotton wool, thinking how strange was this, her nineteenth birthday, spent in another country and shared with forty-odd women. Christmas cards and birthday cards had already arrived, but she had placed them in her locker, together with two parcels from Fenton Bishop, determined not to open either until her watch was over, tomorrow.

This birthday was not like birthdays past; not like the times when the world was sane and the postman rang the front-door bell and demanded to know where the birthday girl was. Ten today, was she? Gracious! It didn't seem any time at all since she was in her pram!

'A penny for them, *cariad*,' Megan offered.

'I was only thinking how it was when I was little – birthdays, I mean.'

'Hard luck,' Lucinda sympathized, 'being born on Christmas Eve.'

'Yes, I suppose it was. But it wasn't like a birthday

because it got mixed up with Christmas, just like now. So I'd have my party in June instead, and we'd have a tea in the garden, or maybe take a picnic down to the river. It's a lovely, slow-flowing river; very shallow in summer, with lots of big flat stones, and we'd paddle and catch minnows.' It had been fun, then. She had been wholly her parents' daughter; indulged, spoiled, even. 'They were lovely days, when I was little . . .'

'What happened to change it all, queen?'

'I grew up, I suppose, and they didn't like it.' She swept the greenery on to the shovel then threw it on the fire, and it jumped and hissed and crackled briefly, and was gone. 'Well, that's the decorations finished.'

Almost finished. It still remained for the balloons to be blown up and tied into bunches. They lay now at the back of the cutlery drawer, where they had been placed, one by one, as each watch came ashore. Some had been filched nervously with a stealthy glance left and right; some had been taken with studied nonchalance; some had been grabbed as if they were red-hot by a furiously blushing Wren and slipped hastily into her pocket, where she prayed it wouldn't burn a hole. But the collection from the upturned cap at the foot of the torpedo-passage stairs had, all things considered, reached a gratifying total, and all that now remained was to hang the plunder, with the ivy trails, in each corner of the room.

'Thirty-five,' counted Leading Wren Paymaster. 'Well done, girls. Now let's get them blown up!'

It developed into a hilarious romp, punctuated by giggles, unladylike remarks and shrieks of delight when the occasional one that escaped before it was knotted flew screeching around the room.

'Don't they look good?'

They gazed at their handiwork in all its shining beauty: four bunches, and magnificent to behold.

'Beautiful,' Fenny breathed. 'Why ever didn't we think of those things before? You're a genius, Cad. Just wait till Chiefie sees what we've done. She'll be – '

She stopped, the sudden silence causing her to follow the direction of the wide, startled eyes. To Chief Wren Pillmoor; a red-faced, furious Chief Wren Pillmoor.

'Chiefie – will – be – *what*?'

'Er – pleased.'

'With the decorations, she means, Chief.'

'And you've got to admit they look lovely.'

'*Lovely*?' Pat Pillmoor's eyelashes flew upward, her eyes swivelled dramatically from corner to corner of the room. 'And where did you get *those*?'

'What do you mean, Chief?'

'You know damn well what I mean. *Those*!'

'We collected them, sort of . . .'

'Shine lovely, don't they?'

'Nearly killed us, blowing that lot up!'

'But worth it, Chief . . .'

'Now listen to me, and listen good! I shall give you all the benefit of the doubt and take it you didn't know what you were doing.' Pat Pillmoor paused for effect, looking at each Wren in turn. 'But if those things aren't down by – '

'Hullo, girls! Oh, how nice you've made it all look.' In the doorway, smiling, stood Third Officer St John, her eyes ranging the room appreciatively. 'And you've even got balloons! Wherever did you find them? Such a pity they can't make them coloured, but there *is* a war on, I suppose. Well, don't forget to hang up your stockings, will you, and Chief,' she said quietly, turning to leave, 'can you spare me a minute, please? In the wardroom.'

'Of course, Ma'am.' Chief Wren waited until her superior was out of earshot, then furiously she hissed,

'Get those things down. *Now*! And thank your lucky stars that Ma'am didn't know what the wretched things are!'

'But Chief, it's only a skylark!'

'And it *is* Christmas!'

'I don't care what it is! If anybody from *Omega* sees that little lot, we'll all be in the rattle!'

'Ar, Chiefie. Just let's keep them till tomorrow.'

'*Please.*'

'Oh, all right, then. But you take them down first thing on Boxing Day – understood?'

'Understood, Chief.'

'Thanks a lot, Chief!'

'And if they're still there when I do rounds,' she ground, 'there'll be no New Year's Eve dance, and that's a promise!'

Shaking with vexation, she climbed the stairs, feet slamming, hands to cheeks. Fiends, they were! Bloody little fiends, the lot of them! Drive a woman to drink, or worse!

'Dear Lord.' She gazed pleadingly heavenward. 'If there *is* another life on earth, and if we *are* allowed back for a second chance, don't send me back as a Chiefie. Let me be a – a *cat*. Let me be a big, evil tomcat that catches birds and chews them up and spits out the feathers. And let me live in a place, Lord, where there'll be a plentiful supply of wrens to chew up and spit out. *Please.*'

'Come in,' called Suzie St John, in answer to the knock.

'Ma'am?'

'Ah, Pat. At ease, dear.' She held up a sherry bottle. 'The victualling officer allowed me one extra, for Christmas. Fancy a glass?'

'There is nothing I'd like better.' Chief Pillmoor sank gratefully into an armchair. 'Nothing at all!'

'Tell me. The common-room decorations? Where on earth did the girls get the – the *balloons*?'

'Ma'am, I – I – ' She addressed her reply to the back of the officer busy at the drinks table. 'I really don't know.'

'They look quite – well, sort of *effective*, don't they?'

Effective? Pat Pillmoor looked at the reflection in the mirror opposite and her cheeks blanched at what she saw. Suzie St John was smiling as she pulled the cork and poured the drinks. Smiling almost wickedly, it would be safe to say.

'I say, Pat, I hope there won't be a population explosion in Craigiebur, next month!'

She turned, the smile gone, her face a mask of innocence, and handing a glass to an open-mouthed, disbelieving Chief Wren, she said, 'Cheers, my dear. And a very happy Christmas.' Then the smile returned and she murmured, 'Don't be an old spoilsport, Pat. After all, it *is* Christmas!'

'Yes, Ma'am.' Christmas? Yes, she supposed it was, and if you couldn't beat them, Pat Pillmoor sighed silently, you could always join them! Taking a satisfying sip, she returned the smile.

'Cheers!' She laughed, raising her glass. 'And a very happy Christmas to you, too!'

Chief Wren Pillmoor sat at her desk in the regulating office, wondering what the telephone call from the mother-and-baby home could be about. The caller had identified herself as the assistant matron and asked to speak to Miss St John. But Ma'am had gone on leave only yesterday, she was obliged to tell her.

'But if I can help at all,' she offered, 'I'll be only too glad.' And she had asked if the purpose of the call concerned Connie Dean, but the nurse said she'd rather not talk on the phone and would explain when she arrived.

Pat Pillmoor frowned. She hoped nothing was seriously wrong. The nurse had said she was calling first at a

Craigiebur address, so the visit was probably a courtesy call, to report on Dean's progress.

She flipped over her calendar to the twenty-eighth. Festivities almost over, thank heaven. It had been a hectic Christmas Day, with starboard watch coming ashore an hour earlier and port watch being allowed to report for duty an hour later so that, for the only day in the year, both watches could eat together.

The war, of course, didn't stop for Christmas, though it did seem to slip into a slightly lower gear; a happening which had, in all probability, been taken into consideration when the two-hour overlap was granted.

Christmas dinner at Ardneavie House had been eaten true to naval tradition, with officers and non-commissioned officers waiting at table on the lower ranks and putting up with traditional remarks about lousy service and enduring the traditional singing of 'Why are we waiting?' to the tune of 'Oh come, all ye faithful', of course, and with a deafening accompaniment of spoons on plates. But it had been a good-humoured affair. Pat Pillmoor smiled. It always was. And the Ministry of Information had not spoiled the day, either. For once, they seemed to have been mindful of the feelings of others and held back the bad news even longer than usual, delaying for two days the announcement that the garrison at Hong Kong had finally surrendered to the Japanese army on Christmas Day, which seemed to make it worse.

The loss of Hong Kong was a profound shock. How, demanded the man in the street, had it happened? Why had we lost it, and whose fault had it been? True, Hong Kong was a long way away; many weren't sure, exactly, where it was. But it was *ours*, wasn't it, and those cheeky little Nips had no right at all to it!

Hong Kong, Chief Pillmoor mused. One of the jewels in our crown of Empire, so people said. Where next, then? But think of a name; think of a country, any country, and it was at war, or threatened by war, or overrun by war. The entire world was being drawn into the turmoil, she brooded, and her hopes that it could all be over before her son would be called to register for military service faded a little more with each news bulletin.

'There's a lady askin' for you.' Vi poked her head round the door. 'And will I bring you a pot of tea?'

'Thanks, McKeown. Ask her to come in, will you?'

'An' where will I put the parcels? She's brought four with her. Big ones.'

'Parcels?' Pat Pillmoor frowned. 'Oh, bring them in here out of the way, will you? And ask MacAlister if she can spare some sugar.'

The assistant matron was slim and young and pretty.

'Thank you for seeing me.' She held out her hand. 'I had business in Craigiebur and thought it best I call on you.' She looked down at the floor. 'And I did try to keep it until after Christmas.'

Then raising her eyes to those of the older woman, 'It's sad news I'm afraid, Mrs Pillmoor,' she whispered. 'Connie Dean died on Christmas Eve.'

'*Died*? God, *no*!' Dean, dead? She couldn't be!

'I'm sorry. So very sorry.' Her voice was gentle. 'But she was already a very sick girl when she came to the home.'

'I realize that, Matron. But *dead*?' Why was she shaking so? 'What went wrong?'

'Connie started in labour eight weeks prematurely. Nothing unusual in that; seven-month babies happen all the time and have an excellent chance. But Connie's baby was already dead when she came to us, you see.'

'I don't understand.' She felt very sick and suddenly very tired. 'Can you tell me about it?'

456

'I don't see why not. Connie had already started to haemorrhage when she came to us. We examined her at once; that's when we realized her baby was dead.'

'Lord, what a mess! And what a stupid waste. Mother *and* child. How was it for her?'

'I don't know. She said very little. She was all shut up inside herself from the moment she arrived, but that isn't unusual, in the circumstances. I'm afraid her labour was a difficult one, though she took it well . . .'

'Poor Dean. I could almost wish it had happened here. At least she wouldn't have been amongst strangers,' Chief murmured sadly. 'Nothing against the home,' she hastened to add, 'but all her friends were here, you see.'

'Oh, Mrs Pillmoor, never wish that. Have you ever seen a woman die of a septic abortion?'

'A what? You can't mean she . . . ?'

'Tried to get rid of the baby? Yes, I'm afraid she did. She wouldn't tell us where she went, though we were pretty sure she'd have gone to Garvie. We've long suspected someone there, but none of the women who've been to her will ever say anything. They're too afraid.'

'God, *why* didn't I do more?' Despairingly the Chief shook her head. 'We failed her dreadfully, didn't we?'

'You mustn't think that. If anyone let her down it was the man who fathered the child – and her parents, too – if we are to blame anyone, that is.' She nodded towards the large paper-wrapped parcels. 'I'd already packed her things in her cases, but her father said he'd take them – the cases, I mean.'

'Her *father*?' So he'd relented! 'Oh, I'm so glad her parents saw reason. At least she wasn't alone.'

'I'm sorry, but Connie *was* alone. Just Matron and I there. Her father came – afterwards. For – for – ' She

457

stopped, her mouth tight with distaste. 'For her body, he said. He came in the hearse with an undertaker.'

Pat Pillmoor swallowed hard on the revulsion that rose in her throat. 'I can't believe it! How could he?' Her face flushed red with anger. 'The sanctimonious old swine! Did you know that he'd finished with her – told her to stay away with her shame? What kind of father is that, Matron?'

'An extremely unnatural one, I'd say. He insisted on going through all her things, would you believe? He wanted nothing to do with her uniform – with anything remotely connected with the Wrens, he said. He took her toilet things and her Bible and her dressing gown, but he left photographs behind. You'd think he'd have wanted those, wouldn't you? Then he said he'd take the cases as they weren't Navy property, and that was it. I was very glad when he'd gone.'

Pat Pillmoor took a cigarette from the packet on her desk then pushed it to the woman who sat opposite.

'I wonder, Matron, why he took Connie home. Could he, perhaps, have been sorry for making her suffer so?'

'He might have been, but I don't think he was. There was nothing remotely resembling sorrow about him.'

'Then that's a pity. A good attack of conscience might have done him the world of good.'

'Think so? Well, do you know what I think?' The younger woman's mouth turned derisively down. 'I think he'll have given her a proud funeral by now, and before long she'll have a magnificent headstone. I can just see it. *Constance Irene Dean WRNS. Died on active service 24.12.1941*, and he'll even have *RIP* put on it and think he's done her proud. And no one in that village will know the truth of how she died – that's what *I* think!'

'He didn't mention the baby, then?'

458

'Not a word, but we told him, for all that. It was a boy; a lovely little boy. They could have had a grandson.'

'And you're sure – about the way she died, I mean?' Chief could still not accept that a young life could end so dreadfully.

'Yes. She had a massive haemorrhage immediately the baby was born. It's often the way with abortions like that. I'd like to get my hands on the woman who did it; see her put behind bars for a very long time.'

'I couldn't agree more.' Chief rose unsteadily to her feet and, opening the door, picked up the tray Vi had left there. 'Have you time for a cup?' Her hand shook as she poured. 'I can arrange transport down to the ferry for you, if you'd like.'

'That is very kind, Mrs Pillmoor.' She opened her handbag and took out a brown envelope. 'These are the photographs I told you about. Perhaps some of Connie's friends would like to have them. And there are some of a man, too.'

'Thanks, Matron. And thank you for all you both did for the poor kid. My, but it's still a man's world, isn't it?'

'It surely is,' sighed the small, pretty woman. 'A man's world indeed. In my present employment it's brought home to me almost every day of the week.'

How long she sat there Pat Pillmoor had no idea. She felt very sick, still; the more so because soon the girls must be told and it was something she had no wish to do. Not just yet. Not until the anger that screamed inside her had eased; not until the bitterness she felt towards the men who caused it had lessened. Because the blame lay squarely on the two men who should have cared most: her lover and her father.

'Finished with the tray, Chief?' Vi hesitated in the

doorway. 'And is there anythin' else you want before I go off duty?'

'Nothing, thanks, McKeown. But when you go upstairs, pop next door, will you, and tell Penrose I'd like a word with her – if she's ashore yet, that is.'

'She is, Chief. Starboard watch came in ten minutes ago. Didn't you know?'

She gathered up the cups, glancing sideways at the pale face and an ashtray filled with half-smoked cigarettes.

'Anythin' wrong, Chief?' Vi was genuinely concerned. Patsy Pill looked shocking and she hadn't heard starboard watch come ashore, either. 'Got a bad head, have you?'

'No. I'll be all right, thanks all the same. Just find Penrose for me – okay?'

Vi lost no time. She slammed the tray on the galley hatch then took the stairs at speed.

'Hey, Lilith! Patsy Pill wants you. *Now*. And something's the matter; something dead serious,' she gasped, 'because Chiefie's been crying. I'll swear she has . . .'

They waited, cabin doors open, for Lilith's step on the stairs. No one spoke; no one wondered out loud what it was about. They knew, deep down, that it concerned Connie, or why had there been a visitor from the mother-and-baby home? They knew that's where she'd come from, because Vi had opened the door to her. And Patsy had been weeping, Vi said, and Chief Wrens didn't weep; that's why they were Chief Wrens.

They were impatient for Lilith's return, though when she came, when they saw her white, drawn face, they wished they had not been.

'It's Connie, innit?' Vi asked bluntly.

'Yes. Look – come in here, all of you.' She indicated the door of the boat's-crew cabin. 'Anybody got a cigarette?'

So it *was* serious. It had to be. Penrose rarely smoked.

Megan offered her packet. Lucinda delved into her pocket, then flicked her lighter, eyes fixed on Lilith's face.

'There's no other way of telling you, I suppose.' Gravely Lilith regarded the end of the cigarette, watching the thin trail of smoke that dipped and looped at the behest of her shaking fingers. 'Connie died on Christmas Eve.'

There. She'd said it, and nothing that came after could be half as awful. She looked round the room at stunned, disbelieving faces, wondering who would be first to break the silence. 'She wasn't well, you know. She didn't have much of a chance.'

'Chance? Don't give me that, Penrose! I've seen sicker women than her come through it all right, and a fine healthy baby to show for it!' Vi stopped, realization blanching her cheeks. 'Ar, hey, Lilith. What about the little one?'

'They lost the baby, too. A little boy . . .'

Fenny covered her face with her hands and began to weep softly.

'Are you sure?' Megan asked gravely. 'You *are* sure?'

'Someone from the home brought her clothes back; it's true.'

'But it's ridiculous!' Lucinda cried. 'Women don't die in childbirth now – well, not often. Oh, Penrose, she didn't . . . ?' She shook her head, ashamed of her thoughts.

'Didn't do away with herself? No.' She shrugged. 'Though, in a roundabout way, maybe she did.' She crushed the cigarette out savagely, rubbing it into the ashtray. 'Now listen – I'll tell you something, though if any of you ever breathes a word of it, you'll be in big trouble. Right?'

'We won't, Lilith.'

'Not a word . . .'

'Specially if it's about Connie.'

'Okay, then. But first, do any of you know if she ever went AWOL? Not for long; maybe only a day, even? Did any of you miss her at all?'

'No. Why should we?'

'Adrift, you mean? Well, she might have been, without our knowing it. She did move down to cabin 3, after all.'

'What's all this leadin' up to?' Vi demanded.

'Well, it seems that she – she went to Garvie.'

'And?' Vi shrugged. 'What's so special about Garvie?'

'Well, according to the matron from the home, Connie admitted going there. Before she left Ardneavie, it was. She went to an an . . .' Her eyes sought Vi's, pleading for help.

'She went to one of them women,' Vi supplied harshly. 'The poor little beggar went to a back-street biddy, didn't she?'

'She wouldn't!' Jane protested. 'She'd never harm the baby. She loved Johnny!'

'Maybe she did,' Lilith acknowledged, her mouth hard with distaste, 'but that's exactly what happened. Christ! What a way to die. What a damn-awful way to die!'

'Did she – was it bad for her?' Lucinda's eyes were bright with tears. 'I mean, did they say?'

'She had a difficult labour, I believe, but they said she'd been a little brick. And if you mean did she know she was going to die, then no, she didn't. She had two midwives with her, but there was nothing they could do. A haemorrhage, it seems.'

'Because of what that dirty bitch in Garvie did?'

'Maybe. I don't know.' Lilith blew her nose loudly. Sometimes, she thought bitterly, this war was altogether too much. Sometimes, she wished she could run away and hide until it was all over. 'Now don't forget what I told you. Connie died in labour and her little boy was stillborn, and that's all any of you know.'

'Poor kid,' Vi choked. 'Poor, lonely kid.'

'Yes, I suppose at the end she was. But if it's any comfort to you, her father was – well, Matron told Chiefie that Dean has been buried at home.' No need to repeat Chiefie's bitter outburst of condemnation; no need to tell them how it had really been. 'And he left these behind.' She held up the brown envelope. 'He thought that maybe Connie's friends would like to have one.'

That was kind of him, they said, though they'd always remember Dean, photographs or not.

'Have what you want.' Lilith laid the envelope on her bed. 'I've already taken one.' Her lips moved into a smile; a bitter, vengeful smile. One of Connie, that was; two of *him*. She would need a likeness of Johnny Jones, maybe. When she had thought it all out; when finally she knew there could be no other way. Then the photographs of Johnny, of smiling, arrogant Johnny, would be essential to the way it must be.

They lay in bed, the cabin 9 Wrens, talking about what Lilith had told them.

'Y'know,' Lucinda whispered, 'I've been worrying myself sick about Mike, wondering how it is with him, afraid to listen to the wireless in case the news isn't good. I worry because the Japs seem to be getting nearer and nearer to Burma. I'd thought he was safe, well out of the fighting, till Pearl Harbor happened. But I bet Connie wishes she could have my worries, poor love. There's hope for me, isn't there? Mike loves me and he *will* be all right, but it's over for Connie – so final.'

'I know what you mean,' Jane said, out of the darkness. 'I can't get to sleep for thinking about her, and – '

'We know, queen. We can hear yer bed creakin'.'

' – and all the time I should be thinking how lucky I was that Rob didn't land me in it. He could have done, yet he cared enough to think of me.'

'I hate that Johnny,' Vi snorted. 'The mucky little toe rag.'

'You don't hate him as much as Lilith does. She hasn't cried for Connie like the rest of us, but did either of you see her face when she came back from Patsy Pill's? Did you see her eyes? It was frightening, such hatred.'

'I know. She was too controlled. But I'll tell you both something for nothing. I wouldn't be in Johnny Jones' shoes; not for anything, I wouldn't. He's got Lilith to reckon with now.'

'So what's she goin' to do about it?' Vi demanded. 'Creep up behind him in the blackout and push him over the end of the jetty? What *can* she do? What can anybody do? He's got away with it, that's what. He needs a good battering, and that'd be too good for him!'

'He'll get worse than that, if what I believe about Lilith is true,' Jane insisted. 'She's going to get even with him, I know it.'

'You mean she'll use her – her *powers* on him?' Lucinda's voice held doubt. 'Oh, Kendal dear, do you honestly believe she can?'

'I don't know what I think. I only know that Connie's dead, and if you don't mind, I don't want to talk about it any more. I'm angry about it and hurt, and if we don't all shut up, we'll be weeping again.'

'You're right, queen. It's time we piped down, the lot of us.' Vi still had her prayers to say. Prayers for Gerry and merchant seamen everywhere; prayers for Mike and Rob and Jane, and for Lucinda, poor kid, who was worrying herself sick and trying not to show it. But mostly she must pray for Connie tonight, and that little baby of hers. Mind, the baby would be all right. He'd have gone

464

straight to heaven, but poor Connie's soul would need a bit of a hand on account of what she'd done, wouldn't it?

She thumped her pillow and closed her eyes. Mother of God, she'd be at it till morning. She sighed deeply and crossed herself devoutly.

Hail Mary, full of Grace . . .

Lilith came face to face with Johnny Jones early next morning, as if the Fates had arranged it. He was there, in charge of a party of seamen repairing the planking of the jetty. He stood relaxed, smoking, cigarette hidden in the cup of his hand, and there was nowhere, she thought with satisfaction, he could go to avoid her.

'Wait here,' she said to Megan and Fenny. 'Don't tie up. This won't take long.'

He could almost have been expecting her. Deliberately he turned his back at her approach then ignored her when she said, 'I want a word with you, Johnny.' She stood very still, waiting.

'Oh? And who are you, then?' He half turned, his eyes distant.

'You know damn well who I am. Connie Dean was my stoker.'

'Was she now?' He made to walk away, but Lilith took his arm and held it tightly.

'Either you talk to me here and now or I'll shout out my business so loud that the whole flotilla's going to hear it.'

'All right, then.' He looked at her as if she were a nuisance; a speck on the lapel of his best jacket. 'And make it quick. Some of us have work to do, Leading Wren.'

She looked at him without speaking, then let go his arm. Oh, he was good-looking, all right – no blame attached to Dean in that direction; but good-looking only

465

if you liked your man pretty, with a sensuous mouth. And he shaved his eyebrows above his nose, she shouldn't wonder, and his teeth were nicotine-stained. And that full, sensuous mouth was weak and now, on the defensive as he was, it fell petulantly at the corners. His eyes were still arrogant, though, and uncaring.

'Connie's dead, did you know? And your son, too.' She flung it at him without warning but he took it without any outward tremor of remorse.

'Yes, I'd heard. News gets around. But it wasn't mine, that kid.'

'It was yours,' she said flatly. Christ, how she loathed him. 'Your child, Johnny. Stillborn. Don't you feel anything?'

'Why should I?' He looked away from the searing hatred in the deep, dark eyes. 'And I did what I could for her. I don't suppose she told you that. All right, so I'm married. She knew it all along.'

'*I* knew it. The whole flotilla knew it, but Connie didn't,' Lilith flung. 'When she asked you, you told her you weren't, and she believed you. You didn't give a damn, did you?'

'I did! When she came crying to me I said I'd help her.'

'Help her? You went out of your way to avoid the poor kid. You couldn't have cared less, you randy little bastard!'

'Now see here!' His face flushed red, his eyes narrowed. 'Just watch your lip, or I'll have you in the rattle so fast you'll wonder what hit you!'

'Don't pull rank on me, Johnny. It won't work.' Defiance sparked from her eyes, and contempt and revulsion. 'Go ahead. Put me on a charge, if you want. I'd like that!'

'Now listen to me! I did what I could. I gave her money, told her where to go.'

'You – you . . .' She closed her eyes, clenching her fists

466

into balls, wanting to slam them into his face. 'You gave her money to get rid of that child?'

'Yes, I did. And if she'd gone to that woman like I said, well, things would have been all right, wouldn't they? So don't go blaming me, Miss High and Mighty!'

'But she *did* go to the dirty slut! That's why she's dead!'

'Well, now. Hard luck.' He shrugged and walked away, and Lilith let him go. She was incapable of speech; incapable of anything but loathing and detestation.

So that was it. She'd given him a chance, hoped he would show regret and remorse for what he'd done, and an iota of pity, perhaps, for Connie Dean. But he had not. He'd condemned himself, and there was nothing, now, she could do about it.

So be it. Johnny Jones had had his fun and now he would pay for it. The rules she lived by demanded that he should.

Karma. Take what you will; take it, and pay. Connie had paid. Now it was *his* turn.

20

A new year; a time for new beginnings, new hopes and new hats. No one had believed it about the hats when the buzz first started, six months back. The old-style, schoolgirl-type, fuddy-duddy hats were there to stay, they had thought. New-style hats? It would take years for the Admiralty to accept the fact that something different in women's headgear was called for, *yearned* for, in fact. Wrens might – if they were lucky, they sighed – get them in time for the victory parade in five, ten, *fifteen* years' time; but the Admiralty diehards had reckoned without the women who were now a part of their ordered, unchanging existence, and new hats for Wrens became a reality. After only three years, they were here, being tried on, tipped and tilted, gazed at, sighed over and arranged on heads in accordance with instructions – it hadn't found its way into King's Regulations yet – worn down on the forehead, an inch above the eyebrows, with the chinstrap tucked inside the said hat and only pulled down when the gale flag flew at the mainmast. The new hats were a cross between a matelot's cap and a flat beret; pert and slightly saucy and unbelievably attractive. Nelson, said an old hand, would be turning in his grave at the sight of them women in their daft caps. Nothing wrong with the old ones; nothing at all . . .

'It's a pity,' Vi frowned, snapping off the cotton, 'that we can only have *HMS* on our cap bands. Be nice, wouldn't it, if we could have *Omega* on them as well, like they used to have.'

'Ah, but we can't advertise ships' names, can we? No use telling spies the whereabouts of the Fleet, is it? I mean, if *Omega* cap bands suddenly appeared in Plymouth, they'd immediately wonder what was happening to the 15th Flotilla, wouldn't they?'

'So would we all.' Lucinda grinned, admiring the bow she had arranged to the left of the gold-lettered *HMS* and pleased that her sixpence sat so beautifully in the centre of it, for it was accepted it was no easy task to arrange a sixpenny piece in the knot of the bow.

She placed the cap – it must surely be called a cap now – on her head, tilted it forward to the correct angle, then shifted it slightly so that the *HMS* lay immediately above the bridge of her nose. 'Not bad,' she murmured, 'though it's going to be an absolute swine keeping them on in a force-eight.'

'That's what yer chinstrap's for, thick-'ed,' Vi growled, not at all sure that these cheeky new caps were suited to a woman in her twenty-seventh year, and a woman with a funny nose, at that. 'Though I must admit yours looks smashin' on you, Lucinda.' But then, with those lovely blonde curls of hers, Bainbridge could wear a dustbin lid and get away with it.

'I wonder,' Jane murmured, 'what went on in high places. I mean, it isn't just the caps, is it?'

Indeed it was not. Now, declared the latest Admiralty Fleet Order, respirators need not always be carried and, most amazing of all, civilian clothing could be worn by WRNS personnel when off duty in quarters or for sporting pursuits – though sporting pursuits, Chief Pillmoor, quickly stressed, did not include skylarking at the dance hall in Craigiebur or anything else in the nature of liberty-taking they could think up, so they'd better not push their luck, any of them! Sporting pursuits were to be defined as games, cycling and walking, and only then if they didn't cycle or walk in the direction of Craigiebur to play their games!

'It's going to be great, isn't it, being able to get out of uniform when we get ashore.' Jane thought of the grey pin-striped trousers in her wardrobe at home, frowned upon by her father as 'fast' and completely unladylike and as bad, almost, as red nails. He'd only agreed to let her wear her trousers when the vicar's niece walked the length of the village in a similar pair. 'Next time I'm on leave I'll bring back a skirt and trousers and a blouse and jumper. And walking shoes, of course.'

Vi sighed deeply. She had no civilian clothes at all, except those she'd had on when the bomb crashed down on Lyra Street. Pity she'd been set on wearing a tight slim-fitting skirt that night and her smart high-heeled shoes. She should have worn her sensible everyday shoes for the shelter and packed her smart new pair in the carrier bag, but there'd only been room for the Cape Town goblets – and they'd been more precious than a shopful of shoes. They still were. And it was, after all, the story of her life. Even as a kid, if she'd dropped her butty on the floor it had landed jam side down.

'I think,' Jane pronounced, 'that Kathy MacAlister is right. These caps look just that little bit – well – *flat*.'

'So what can we do about that?'

'We can pad them. Kathy did hers with rolled-up newspaper; it makes all the difference.'

It just might, at that, and since there was nothing in King's Regulations to forbid it, they were busy rolling and padding and preening when Megan and Fenny walked into cabin 9.

'Mind if we come in for a while?' Megan asked.

'Lilith's turfed us out, you see.' Fenny looked anxious.

470

'Why, queen? Lilith not well, or something?' Vi made for the door. 'Better take a look – '

'No! Don't go in there, Vi!' Hurriedly Megan barred her way. 'She wants to – well, we're to leave her alone for half an hour.'

'Oh, ar. So what's goin' on, then?'

'Is she in communication with the spirits?' Lucinda grinned.

'No!' said Fenny.

'Yes!' Megan frowned. 'Well – sort of.'

'Now see 'ere.' Vi's Catholic hackles were rising fast. 'If she's started her messin' about again . . .'

'She hasn't, and, anyway, Lilith doesn't mess,' Megan retorted.

'She has. Don't lie, Cad.' Fenny's eyes betrayed her anxiety. 'Lilith's got the black candles out!'

'And what the 'ell is she doin' with *black* candles?'

'Don't you know, Vi? She's – '

'Shut up, Cole. It's none of your business. If Lilith chooses to – ' Megan stopped, mouth pursed.

'If Lilith chooses to *what*?' Vi demanded, hands on hips. 'If that woman's up to something, I want to know – all right?'

'Well, if you'll not tell anyone; I mean, if Patsy got to know there'd be – '

'Lilith's doing a – a – '

'She's doing a ritual,' Megan supplied reluctantly.

'A *what*? Magic, you mean?' Jane's nose wrinkled in disbelief.

'Sort of. It won't take too long.' Megan was obviously ill at ease. And clearly, Vi decided, she was keeping something back.

'Now see here, Cad. If Penrose is muckin' about in there, I want to know. *All* of it! What do you mean – *ritual*? Is she going into a trance, or something?'

471

'Look, Vi, leave it. Okay? You wouldn't understand. I don't, not really, and –'

'And it isn't any of our business,' Megan finished, flatly.

'Well, I'm makin' it my business,' Vi snapped, addressing herself to Fenny, who was clearly the weakest link. 'Penrose is up to her tricks, isn't she, and you're goin' to tell me.'

'Well, it's Johnny Jones. Lilith says it's time.'

'Time to do it. The dark of the moon, see,' Megan offered reluctantly. 'That's when – when it's best.'

'Mother of God! Best for *what*?'

'For rituals. For ill-wishing.'

'Flamin' Norah! Is that all!' Vi's relief was evident. 'She's havin' a go at Johnny Jones, is she? Well, the best of British to her if she thinks a few words of ooky-spooky'll do any good!'

'No, Vi. I don't think Lilith is joking.' Jane's voice was little more than a whisper. 'The dark of the moon – the few days before a new moon appears – well, that's when witches do their magic, don't they?'

'Oh, ar! So that's it! It was Penrose I saw, was it, zooming down the loch on her broomstick with a destroyer escort!'

'Don't, Vi,' Megan hissed. 'Don't ridicule what you don't understand.'

'And you do, I suppose? You believe in witches, Cad, and broomsticks and eye of a newt and all that?'

'I believe that Lilith believes in them. I'm a Celt. At least I *understand*.'

'You mean, you actually believe in witches, Cadwallader dear?' Lucinda's eyes were bright with mischief. 'In the middle of the twentieth century, you believe in spells and curses?'

'Yes.' The reply was basic, and final.

'And ill-wishing? Oh, surely not?'

472

Unspeaking, defiant, Megan met Lucinda's bright blue gaze.

'Lilith *can* ill-wish,' Fenny said softly. 'She's done it before. Only once, she said, but sadly it worked . . .'

'*Sadly?*' There was a pricking at the back of Vi's nose. 'Now see here, you two. I want to know what's been goin' on next door. The truth. I mean it!'

'All right, then, but if you ever breathe a word – well, Lilith *is* a witch.'

'A *white* one,' Megan added hastily.

'They come in colours?' Lucinda asked in amazement.

'There are two paths: left and right. There's black and there's white. The blacks are – well, they belong to the devil, I *think.*'

'Saints preserve us!' Hurriedly Vi crossed herself. 'You mean, Penrose is *serious* about it?'

'Yes. It's her religion. I thought you knew.'

'You mean, she worships – '

'She believes in Our Lord. She's a *white*, I told you. But she believes in the old religion, too; the religion that's a mixing of Christianity and the old ways. When the Christians came to Britain, they did it gently. Conversions weren't easy. Oh, human sacrifices were stopped at once because Jesus was sacrifice enough, but pagan feast days were replaced by Christian feast days – saints' days and the blessing of wells – and Christianity won, in the end. But in some parts the old religion never quite died . . .' Megan stopped, breathless, embarrassed.

'You believe it, Cad, don't you?'

'Yes. And I accept it, though I'm Chapel, myself. But Lilith is deadly serious. And she's good.'

'She's ill-wishing Johnny Jones,' Vi gasped, 'and she's *good*?'

'Johnny deserves it. He asked for it,' Fenny said quietly.

'And Lilith doesn't make a habit of it. She wouldn't do

it if there was any other way. Johnny's got to pay for what he did to Connie. The laws of Karma say so.'

'So Johnny's due for a plague of boils and bad luck and –'

'Oh, no, Vi. More than that.' Fenny's face was solemn, her voice resigned. 'Lilith is using the black candles, you see. And she somehow got hold of a photo of Johnny. It's all she needs.'

'Needs for what?'

'Listen, all of you; listen, then forget,' Megan urged. 'Johnny's in trouble. You'd better pray for him, Vi, if your charity extends to shits and adulterers. I don't know a lot about Lilith's beliefs or her religion, but one thing I'm sure of. Black candles are *death* candles . . .'

They tried hard not to talk about it after Fenny and Megan had gone; tried not to notice the smell of snuffed candles that drifted on to the landing outside. They talked about the nine o'clock news instead and the government decree that no more gold jewellery was to be allowed. Gold, too, it seemed, had become a munition of war and now only wedding rings could be made – nine-carat ones at that, their retail price fixed at one guinea.

'But nobody wears nine-carat weddin' rings!' Vi regarded her pure-gold band with pride. 'I'll bet you anything you like they'd turn your finger green.'

'Well, we'll all have to, now. Or buy a better one second-hand.' Jane shrugged. 'Though I suppose anything like that will just disappear now, under the counter.'

'Couldn't care less. I'd marry Mike with a curtain ring.' Lucinda sighed.

'Yes, you would, an' all,' Vi acknowledged. 'But it's not on, is it, expectin' a woman to be married with a cheap ring?' Liverpool women always insisted on a good, solid ring. 'I wonder what them lot in London'll think up next.'

'If Lilith follows the right path – if she's a good witch, as Megan Cad says – then why did she ill-wish Johnny Jones?' Lucinda demanded, completely out of the blue.

'I don't think it's something she'd do willingly,' Jane answered.

'Then why do it?' Vi reasoned. 'And I thought we'd agreed not to talk about it. Megan said we'd got to forget it, didn't she?'

'So we'll forget it! Let's talk about Americans.'

'Let's!' Lucinda laughed. 'Let's talk about *my* American!'

'I wonder if they'll come here, now that they're in the war.' Deliberately Vi skirted round the subject. There had been no letters from Mike for a long time and Lucinda was worried sick, underneath. 'We could do with a few, couldn't we?'

'We could. But they've got their own war to fight now, haven't they?' Jane offered morosely. 'In the last war, my dad said, they made a lot of difference. But the Japanese are swarming all over the Pacific and – ' She stopped, embarrassed, knowing she had said exactly what Lucinda didn't want to hear. 'Sorry, love. It's my big mouth. It says things before my brain has time to catch up with it.'

'Don't worry, Kendal dear. I'll get a letter soon. And Mike *will* be all right. I love him so much he's got to be.'

'Of course he will. Both your fellers are goin' to be fine,' Vi pronounced, 'and my Gerry, too. And we're all alive and kicking, aren't we?'

'Yes. Not like poor Connie.'

They were back to it again; back to Johnny and Lilith and black candles. Vi sighed. And what the hell, anyway? They were all aching to talk about it.

'I think I agree with Bainbridge,' Vi resumed. 'If Lilith is good, why did she ill-wish Johnny Jones?'

'I don't think she had a lot of choice,' Jane answered. 'After all, she *is* serious about her beliefs. She wouldn't do it lightly and, anyway, it probably won't work.'

'But it *might*,' Lucinda insisted. 'I didn't say anything at the time, but I had a good old natter with Lilith a while back. It was when I thought Mike had ditched me and I asked her if she'd have a session with the wine glass for me.'

'And?' Vi prodded.

'Well, she said I wasn't a very good subject. Some people just aren't, she said. But we talked about things – you know, about Lilith's ways – and I got to understanding them a little better, and liked her better, too.'

'But we've always liked her.'

'You know what I mean! I got the impression that Lilith and her kind are leftovers, sort of, from a long time ago. The way they act, the way they believe – their strange powers, even – must be born with them. They know no other way; they don't feel in any way different, and their mucking about, as you call it, Vi, doesn't really hurt anyone, so where is the harm in her?'

'She's trying to harm Johnny Jones,' Jane reasoned.

'Ar, well, there's somethin' I didn't tell you two, an' all.' Vi regarded her fingertips in detail. 'Lilith told me, nearly a week ago. She talked to Johnny, she said, and it was him gave Connie the money to go to that woman in Garvie. And he didn't give a damn about it, either.'

'So it was all down to Johnny in the end,' Jane said soberly.

'Yes, it was, when you think about it. Johnny killed Connie. Not by making love to her, not by getting her pregnant. He killed her with that money.' Lucinda choked. 'And it seems he didn't care either, so what

476

choice did Lilith have? Come to think of it, I'd ill-wish the little sod myself, if I knew how!'

'Me, too. Being lovers was one thing,' Jane continued. 'Connie knew what she was doing. But giving her money for *that*! And his own kid, too! He doesn't deserve any sympathy at all. Not that there's anything Lilith can really do about him, more's the pity.'

'Well, it's a funny business an' no mistake.' Vi sighed. 'And it's time for lights out, so who's first for the bathroom?'

A real funny business, she thought restlessly, when the only sound to disturb the night was the creaking of Jane's bedsprings and the odd little sigh Lucinda gave when she turned over.

Vi finished her prayers then lay in the darkness, counting her blessings as she always did. She hadn't prayed for Johnny, as Megan had suggested. Johnny wasn't worth it, and besides, it was all a load of old codswallop. Raising spirits; ill-wishing, indeed. Whatever next?

Yet though she didn't believe one word of it, Vi fell asleep that night, tightly clutching her rosary. Just to be on the safe side.

They came, as war-weary Britain hoped they would. The first American soldiers – they called them GIs – landed in the north of Ireland on a Sunday at the end of January. They had come, they said, to help the Limeys finish off the Krauts before they got around to sorting out the Japs. And more quickly followed. They poured ashore at Greenock and Liverpool, seeing for the first time the land their founding fathers had left so many years before; seeing for the first time the devastation of cities, rubble-piled streets and alleys, and the quiet acceptance of a people who had stood alone against Hitler.

They were fit and brash and well-fed, those young

Americans, and unbowed; eager for the fight, still raging inside against the treachery that had been Pearl Harbor.

Those who sailed up the river Mersey and came ashore in Liverpool marched with a swagger through the bomb-shattered city. They marched in peculiar steel helmets, rifles over shoulders. Their uniforms, thought men who stood to watch their passing, were smart and of high quality. Ordinary soldiers, they were, dressed like officers. And the military policemen they brought with them were big fellows who wore white helmets, gloves and gaiters and yelled, 'At the double, man!' and 'Move, soldier, *move*!'

The Government-Issue men marched down Lime Street, glancing right and left, answering reluctant smiles with beaming grins, thinking it a pity that Limey girls must be treated as a guy would wish his own sister to be treated, remembering what had been dinned into them on the troopship coming over.

The British are hungry, they were told, their houses cold. If asked to a British home, don't eat their food, soldier; it is severely rationed. Do *not* call the British Limeys. But stranger still, hardest of all to comprehend, would be the British cops; 'bobbies' they were called, and would you believe it, those cops didn't carry a gun! Not even in wartime!

The street kids of Liverpool, though, quickly assessed the situation. Long before the chanting, stamping columns of men reached the waiting trains in Lime Street station, the first contacts had been made and established.

'Hey, Yank, I've gorra big sister at 'ome! Smashin', she is!'

'Yer not goin' to like it 'ere, Yank. The beer's warm an' it'll make yer sick!'

And the warm-hearted GIs who liked kids gave out candies and Hershey bars and packets and packets of strangely flavoured chewing gum to children who quickly learned to like GIs, and of those first encounters was born the phrase that would grow to be almost as famous as the V-sign: *Got any gum, chum?*

Limey kids welcomed their American allies with heart-warming fervour. It was an encouraging start, thought the Americans, and it was not to be long before their sisters followed suit.

'Our Mary says,' said Vi, without looking up from the letter she was reading, 'that there's a lot of American soldiers come to Liverpool. They've billeted them at Aintree, on the Grand National course. Fancy that, eh?'

'I've been wondering,' said Jane, whose letter from Fenton Bishop had been quickly read, 'if Mike will join the American Air Force, now that his lot are in the war.'

'I don't know what will happen.' Lucinda had not received a letter from anyone. 'Mike thought that by taking the King's shilling, so to speak, he could have forfeited his US citizenship. It might be he'd have to get that back before he could transfer to an American unit. But I'll tell you both something for nothing! Once this war is over and I've got him safely back, if that crazy guy so much as joins the Band of Hope he'll have me to reckon with.' She laughed. It was an uncertain laugh, though, because she was blinking away the tears that came so readily to her eyes every time the mail was slotted into the letter board. 'It's been three weeks since I've had a letter, you know.'

'We know it is, queen, but he'll be all right. You'll get ten letters, all at once. It's the way it is with mail from abroad.'

'Mike's all right,' Jane said firmly. 'I know he is; just as I know that Rob is going to make it.'

'Bless you both.' Lucinda blew her nose loudly. 'What would I do without you?'

'Sometimes I wonder, girl. Sometimes I wonder.' Vi shook her head dolefully. 'Now, are you both going to get a move on? It's nearly time for Chiefie's rounds, and this cabin's a tip!'

Of course she wondered; she wondered all the time. What she would do without *them*, that was.

February came, bitterly cold, with a harsh wind blowing from the north. A snow wind, thought Lucinda, breathing on the window pane, rubbing away the frosted fern patterns, looking out at a sullen Loch Ardneavie and the black, forbidding hills.

Cabin 9 was almost unbearably cold now, and when not on watch their time was spent in the warmth of the boat's-crew cabin next door, huddled round the driftwood fire. No one begrudged Lilith's crew this comfort when most days now they spent soaked with spray, hands in wet woollen gloves, almost too numb with cold to pull on a rope or wield a boathook.

'It looks awful out there.' Lucinda shivered. 'Everything is white with frost.' There was no colour; just greys and black and white. The blue skies of summer, the sunlight that had bounced off the water in dazzles of gold, were only a memory.

Jane closed her eyes to recall another such winter, a year ago exactly. Candlemas, and the bombers standing frostbound, their guns removed, with a stamping sentry blowing through fingers numb with cold, hearing faintly the sounds of the aircrew mess dance, wondering if they knew in that hot, crowded room that the poor bastards guarding their planes outside were slowly freezing to death.

The aircrews had neither known nor cared; they'd just

480

been grateful for runways pitted with frozen snow. Tonight, they would drink warm beer and laugh and dance and know that when morning came they would still be alive.

That night she had met Rob and fallen wholly in love. He hadn't been married to Phemie then, but it had been she, Jane, who had made all the running.

'Will I see you again?' she had asked him. 'Can we meet again tomorrow?' And he'd told her that tomorrow they might all be flying if a thaw came overnight. So she had prayed that it wouldn't and waited for him, shaking with cold in the dark of Yeoman's Lane. That night he had come, but how many times since had she stood there in vain?

One year, since last Candlemas. A whole year of loving him and losing him and refusing to believe they would never meet again.

'Come on, you two! Get a move on! I'm gasping for a mug of tea!'

Breakfasts were no longer carried up the back stairs. The warmth from the galley that percolated through to the mess hall was too precious to waste. Now, they ate downstairs, and this morning, with luck, it would be hot porridge and scrambled dried eggs. And mugs of scalding tea they could wrap their fingers around.

'Never mind.' Lucinda smiled. 'It'll soon be spring; we'll be going on leave again in a month.' She thought with longing of the warm kitchen at Lady Mead dower house and hot-water bottles in her bed and plates of home-made soup so hot it scalded her tongue. Nanny had been right to warn about winters in Scotland and the need to wear her warm knickers. 'I just might,' she said, as they clattered down the uncarpeted stairs, 'split my leave between Lincolnshire and London. The railways let you

481

break your journey, don't they, and I could pick up some civvy togs whilst I'm about it.'

There were plenty of clothes packed in trunks and stored away, both at Lady Mead and at Bruton Street; some of them her own but most belonging to her mother – many unworn and too precious, now, to be given to charity or jumble sales, the Countess stated selfishly.

'Well, it won't take me long to go through my wardrobe.' Vi grinned, sipping gratefully at her tea. Chiefie would take one look at her straight skirt and patent leather shoes and up would go the eyelashes and that would be it, for there was no sport on earth which demanded the wearing of hobble skirts and three-inch heels, and she wished once again that she had been wearing her flat, sensible shoes and something more in keeping, the night the bomb had blown her home away. It wasn't clever to be wise after the event, and the good Lord hadn't given her the gift of hindsight at birth, she sighed; only the promise of big feet.

'Poor old Vi,' Lucinda sympathized, scraping clean her porridge plate. 'I say – ' She stopped, spoon poised, as the idea was born. 'Why don't I sort you out some clothes when I'm getting my own together! You're just about Mama's build, and some of those things are brand new. My mother used to buy clothes when she was bored and often never wore them. Would you mind awfully, Vi?'

'Mind?' Of course she wouldn't mind, though there was something Bainbridge had overlooked, bless her. 'I don't suppose there'll be many big shoes in them cases, though?'

'Oh, Lord. I'd forgotten shoes. Mama takes a five, like me, and you're an – '

'An *eight*, queen.'

'Oh dear. It would appear we do have a problem.'

'We haven't, you know.' Jane chuckled. 'Well, not if those clothes aren't going to be missed.'

'Of course they won't be missed. Mama doesn't know for certain what she's got – well, apart from her furs, of course, and she keeps them with her.'

'Then why don't you take a few and give them to someone in exchange for five coupons? Then Vi could buy a pair of shoes.'

'Brilliant!' Lucinda beamed. 'Who can we offer them to?'

'We–ell, our Mary is short of a good warm coat. I know that. She's got to give most of her own coupons to them kids, they grow so fast,' Vi offered. 'She can't afford sixteen coupons for a coat, apart from the money, but I'm sure she could manage five. But isn't it against the law, trading coupons like that?'

'So who's going to tell?'

'Well, Mary won't, that's for sure.' And it wasn't as if, they reasoned, swopping coupons for a coat was illegal, exactly. It all boiled down, really, to conscience. True, all illicit dealings in rationed commodities came under the heading of black market and if discovered carried a heavy fine or even imprisonment, but consciences only shied away from those things brought to Britain by sea, like petrol or butter and sugar, which involved risking the lives of the seamen who brought them here; few people would have anything to do with *that* side of the black market.

But unwanted clothing, bought even before the war began, seemed harmless enough, Lucinda reasoned. They had not been brought here in convoy, nor had they risked the life of a single seaman.

'Well, our Mary'd be real chuffed,' Vi conceded, 'but what about your mam, Lucinda? What's she goin' to say when she finds one of her coats gone missing?'

'Mama's hardly likely to go to Lady Mead, is she, rummaging through trunks? And if she does, then I shall tell her I gave them to the WVS for the bombed-outs. She couldn't object to that, could she?' She could, of course. She most certainly would, even though she had no use for them herself; but no one would take a scrap of notice of her grumblings. 'So is that a deal, Vi? If I make it worth Mary's while – a coat, say, and a few warm things – do you think she'd mind giving five coupons in exchange?'

'*Mind?*' Mary Reilly would be tickled pink. 'Course she won't mind.'

'And you won't, either?'

'Nar.' Vi shrugged. 'Not me!'

'That's settled, then.' Lucinda sighed, delighted by the absolute brilliance of her idea and a valid excuse to see Nanny and Lady Mead again after almost two years.

'Hey, you lot! The post's arrived!' came the call, which caused an instant emptying of the mess hall. All letters were precious; those from husbands and lovers were without price.

Lucinda walked reluctantly to the letter board, unwilling to experience yet again the bleakness of disappointment, the apprehensive drying of her mouth.

Then she saw the pale blue of the airmail lettercards and Bainbridge, L.V., written on them, and she snatched them eagerly. Four letters. All from Mike. Quickly she checked the numbers written on the backs: 6, 7, 9 and 11, which meant that two were adrift still, and even these she held safely in her hands were probably a month old. But *four* letters! Instantly it was a wonderful day, her disquiet banished; banished for a little while, at least, for the nagging apprehension about the relentless advance of the Japanese army was never far from her mind. Kuala Lumpur in Malaya had been occupied, the Ministry of Information admitted only last week, but it had been shrugged away by the British public. It would be all right, said the man in the street. No panic. Singapore was still holding out, wasn't it?

Singapore. Now *that* was where the Japs would get their comeuppance, most people thought. Singapore, now that they were aware of its existence, was an impregnable fortress, it seemed; something those Nips would discover before so very long. At Singapore their advance would be halted at last, for the island bristled with guns and men and could hold out for ever, just as Malta was doing, and Tobruk.

That was why, Lucinda often sighed, no one here seemed to care overmuch about the war in the Far East. Names like Siam and Malaya and Burma were still exotic places on a faraway map and the Japanese more to be ridiculed than feared. Even music-hall comedians now included a slant-eyed idiot they had named Hari Kari in their repertoire of jokes. They poked fun at him; mocked his pidgin English. Just objects of derision, those little yellow men. Monkey men. You laughed at the funny little fellows, unless, of course, someone you loved till it hurt was out there fighting them.

But this morning, she would not worry. This marvellous morning there had been four letters from Mike.

Vi smiled at the sight of Lucinda's blissful face. Vi understood the unspoken anxiety that had already begun to cloud Lucinda's eyes and lessen the brilliance of that lovely smile. And it made her all the more thankful, she thought rebelliously, that Gerry was safely out of it all. Stood to reason, didn't it, with that great German battleship *Tirpitz* skulking in the fjords along the Norwegian coast then slinking out to savage our often helpless convoys. Vi admitted that she was downright happy her man was no longer at sea, especially now that our ships were being called upon to make the hazardous voyage to Archangel and Murmansk in Arctic Russia. The Murmansk run, it was called now; a suicidal journey north, where U-boat packs waited like lip-licking cats for a convoy of sparrows. On the Murmansk run in winter, a torpedoed seaman had no chance of being picked up as Gerry had been. In winter, in those vicious seas, the end was quick. No man survived such unbelievable cold for long. Ten minutes in the water, and it was all over.

Vi closed her eyes and thanked yet again the German submariner who had plucked her man from an April Atlantic. There were still some good Germans left, she supposed. Maybe not all of them were Nazis.

'Loves yer still, does he, queen?'

'He loves me.' Lucinda smiled, the dimples back. 'And he's fine. Just fine.'

Mike was going to be all right. Mike was a survivor. And the Japs were nowhere near Burma; of course he'd be all right.

It happened on a Sunday – the fifteenth day of February, to be exact – and the voice of the announcer, unusually grave, read out the news that the garrison at Singapore had surrendered.

Surrendered? *Our* Singapore? But they'd said it never could, never would, protested a stunned Britain.

All those men. All those heavy guns that should have made mincemeat of any Jap ship that sailed within their range.

The man in the street was stunned, insulted, outraged. There must be a mistake, of course. Somebody, somewhere, had got it wrong, because if they hadn't, somebody, somewhere, had a lot to answer for. Not the poor devils who'd done their best out there, of course; not the nine thousand who had died and the eighty thousand more taken prisoner. Taken prisoner, would you credit it, by them, the monkey men! It made your British blood boil. It made you angry, and suddenly afraid.

All wireless sets were tuned that night to the Home

Service and the broadcast the Prime Minister was to make to the nation. They'd get the truth of it from him. Churchill never lied to them. After Dunkirk he'd promised them blood, toil, tears and sweat, and by God, they were getting it. And he'd said this war would be a long and bitter struggle, and it was beginning to look as if he'd been right. And tonight, in his growling, bulldog voice, he'd tell them what had really happened at Singapore.

Jane and Lucinda were not on watch that evening and they sat with Vi in the common room, the wireless tuned to the Home Service, waiting for a broadcast they would rather not hear.

The loss of Singapore was fact. Two things, it seemed, had contributed to its downfall. An acute shortage of water and the fact that the enemy had invaded not by sea, as had been expected, but from the north, landwards from the Malayan Peninsula.

The cunning little sods, gasped an unbelieving nation, had crept in by the back door, and the sad fact, Mr Churchill admitted, was that Singapore's big guns had been pointed immovably seawards.

But it had happened before, accused the man in the street, to the Maginot Line; to that impregnable ring of men and guns and concrete, built by the French to ensure that not one German jackboot should touch the soil of France.

So Hitler's armies had marched round it, simple as that, and occupied Holland and Belgium without so much as a by-your-leave. Now it had happened again, this time to us. Would the idiot Blimps in London never learn?

Winston Churchill hurled the bad news at a shocked nation without mercy. It was his way; without fear or favour or excuse. That was why he held the nation's trust. Singapore, he told them, had fallen, and the Mediterranean Sea was now virtually closed to the ships of the

Allies. The only ones to brave the Mediterranean would be in heavily guarded convoys of supplies and ammunition for defiant Malta, or what remained of Malta after air raids that even the British Isles had not experienced. Convoys would still battle through to that brave little spot in a hostile sea, he pledged, even if only one ship limped into Valletta Harbour.

On the *good* side, Mr Churchill reminded them, America was now our ally and the Russians were holding back Hitler. German troops had not taken Moscow and Leningrad by Christmas, as Hitler boasted they would, and his troops were suffering horribly in the vicious cold of a Russian winter.

'Here is the moment,' the Prime Minister concluded phlegmatically, 'to display the calm and poise combined with grim determination which not so very long ago brought us out of the very jaws of death. Let us,' he urged, 'move forward steadfastly together into the storm and through the storm . . .'

So that was it; the unvarnished truth. Winston had said it was so, and Winston didn't lie. And follow him into the storm and through the storm they would, because there was no other way. With the old warhorse in command, they would be all right. Things weren't so bad, now that they knew the worst. Things could only get better. One day.

Britain sighed, and dials moved as one to tune in to the Forces' wavelength and Tommy Handley and his ITMA gang. Tommy would make them laugh, wouldn't he? And laughter seemed all that was left now, for the war in the Far East had moved suddenly nearer to home and brought with it fear and bewilderment.

White-faced, eyes round with apprehension, Lucinda said, 'I think I'll go upstairs and wash my hair – okay?'

She didn't really want to wash her hair. She wanted to be alone to hug her fears to her and read Mike's letters again. And pray as she had never prayed before.

Take care, Mike. Wherever you are, my love, take care.

21

Chief Wren Pillmoor drew aside the regulating office blackout and gazed with relief at the world outside. Snow, frozen solid for the past two weeks, had melted overnight, almost, in an unexpected wind from the south. The outlook was drab and drenched, but paths and roads were clear at last and her lips traced a small, satisfied smile.

'Good! Now we can get some in!'

Because of the harsh weather there had been no squad drills for almost the entire month of February; that could now be remedied. A few brisk marching sessions would do that lazy lot a world of good; let them know they hadn't got away with it, as they were beginning to believe. With a distinctly malevolent smile, Pat Pillmoor wrote down *Squad drills daily until the end of Feb*, then pinned it to the noticeboard.

In a dripping garden, Miriam greeted the thaw with pure pleasure, gently moving aside dead leaves beneath the beech hedge, smiling to discover clumps of snowdrops, brave and beautiful.

'Hullo, little things,' she whispered, pleased to see them and the green-ruffed aconites growing beside them. Winter was surely almost over. Soon she could start digging and planting again. Singing happily, she pushed open the door of the potting shed.

Wren Lucinda Bainbridge too was happy, for on that late February morning, more letters from Mike had arrived; the one numbered 12, and with it the two she had missed. Now, it would seem, she had them all safely.

Her cheeks flamed as she read them. Mike's letters

were passionate and filled with love and longing. Mike cared nothing for any censor who might read what he had written, a censor who searched each line for the careless phrase or hidden innuendo that could betray secrets to an enemy only too eager to intercept mail. Mike Farrow wrote without inhibition of his need for her, his love clear and unashamed.

Lucinda smiled at Jane across the breakfast table and tucked the letters into her paybook pocket.

'It's a whole lot warmer this morning,' she remarked, though greatcoats and scarves were still rig of the day and cabins uncomfortably cold. 'Two days more and we'll be into March.' She ate her breakfast with pleasure. Funny how the arrival of letters from Burma made tinned tomatoes on toast taste like ham and eggs and mushrooms served from a silver dish.

'Soon be time for us to put in our leave applications,' Jane, who liked going home really, but was never over-sad to return to Ardneavie House, reminded her. 'Leave seems to have come round quickly, this time.'

'Our Mary,' said Vi over the top of the letter she was reading, 'says her coal ration for February ran out and she had to spend the best part of a day trying to find something to burn. Got a sack of logs and a gallon of paraffin for the oil stove, though, so at least them kids'll be warm till the coalman's due again.' Mary would be glad to get the winter coat Lucinda had promised, and Vi's warm heart embraced all civilians, most of whom had spent an uncomfortable winter in poorly heated homes. 'She'll be thankful the snow has gone.' Queueing for food and fuel couldn't have been a lot of fun in a coat long past its best. She hoped, when it arrived, that the coat would have a thick, warm lining and a collar of softest fur.

Poor, lovely Lucinda, Vi sighed silently. How long before she heard the news? On late watch, Jane and

Lucinda had slept in, but Vi had heard the early-morning bulletin and her blood ran cold.

'Units of the Japanese army,' read the announcer gravely, 'are now only fifty miles from the outskirts of Rangoon.'

Only fifty miles from Mike's fighter squadron. Mother of God, was there no stopping them!

'Come on, you two. That cabin's got to be cleaned real well this mornin' and all your rubbish put away for Captain's rounds.'

That morning, at eleven hundred hours, was the commanding officer's monthly inspection of WRNS quarters, which necessitated the stowing away of everything movable and the dusting and polishing of everything which was not. A morning spent cleaning the cabin, Vi decided, would at least keep the pair of them away from news and newspapers for a little while longer.

'And I want them bedspreads the right end up and towels folded properly,' Vi warned. 'You know how Chiefie goes on if the Captain finds anything wrong.'

Fifty miles from Rangoon, and what Lucinda would do when she heard about it just didn't bear thinking about. The way things were, those letters she'd had this morning could be the last she would get for a long time to come, Vi realized, anger surging through her. Oh, damn this war! Sod and flaming *damn* it!

'Well, come on then, and get stuck in!' she snapped. 'What are the pair of you waitin' for? Pancake Tuesday, or somethin'?'

Starboard watch felt the change in the weather the instant they stepped on to the jetty. It was noticeably warmer; the breeze that made wavelets on the surface of the loch was almost gentle on their faces after the harsh gales of winter.

'Oh, damn it! Gold braid ahead.' Molly Malone sighed because there could be no avoiding the approaching officer. On a jetty barely ten feet wide, there were no shop windows they could turn to and gaze into until he had passed; the saluting of officers, of some officers at least, was a fact of life the lower decks resented. There were some, of course, whose rank they acknowledged gladly. The navigating officer was one such man. 'Navvy', an ex-Merchant Navy officer, treated all Wrens with an old-fashioned courtesy that could only be a leftover from his cruise-ship days. Or perhaps it was simply that he was a gentleman, someone had suggested.

So they saluted the navigating officer without rancour, and Commander Bill Brian, in direct command of sub-mariners, because he was a seasoned old seadog and man enough not to resent the presence of women on HM ships. And they saluted the surgeon commander and the surgeon lieutenant because they were decent types, and the dental surgeon, too. And Miss St John they saluted with a smile, because Suzie was a sweetie. But the officer who approached them now was a two-ringer Wavy-Navy hos-tilities-only man who liked to be saluted and expected to be saluted.

'You take it, Bainbridge,' Molly murmured, and Lucin-da's right arm jerked upward, her fingers horizontally touching her cap at her eyebrow, her elbow at shoulder level.

Molly and Jane, backs ramrod-straight, gave a smart eyes-right, then walked on the required two paces, gazing to front again as Lucinda's arm snapped down to her side.

'And the same to you, sir,' Molly murmured, comfort-ably out of earshot.

Her remark was the only redress they had. If they didn't say the words, they thought them, most times – though why they allowed saluting to get them ruffled not one of them knew. Saluting was a fact; the way it had always been. In Nelson's day a rating tipped his forelock to his betters, so it followed, didn't it, that if it was good enough for Nelson . . .

Lucinda took the bad news from the Far East very well. She had learned of the Japanese advance on board *Omega*, and apart from the brief panic that widened her eyes and paled her cheeks, she had said little about it.

'He'll be all right,' Jane whispered as the launch carrying them ashore at watch-end headed towards the dim blue jetty light. 'I *know* he will.'

'Bless you, Kendal dear. And – and fifty miles is a long way, isn't it?'

'One heck of a long way.' In the darkness, Jane reached for the hand of her friend and held it tightly. 'Try not to worry, old love. Mike's been in worse trouble than this, remember.'

'Of course he has.' Lucinda was glad of the blackout. It enabled her to wipe away an escaping tear and take in deep gulps of cold night air to help calm the fear that screamed through her like a pain.

God, I'll do *anything*, she prayed silently. Only take care of him. *Please*.

Vi was hovering at the front door as starboard watch chattered in, and a look at Lucinda's face told her all she needed to know.

'Are you all right then, queen?'

'I'm fine, Vi. Just fine.'

'Good. They've just called late standeasy, so you'd both better come and get a cup of somethin' hot inside you.'

'No, thanks. Think I'll just pop upstairs,' Lucinda told her. 'Not very hungry, old dear.'

'Hey! A cup of somethin' hot, I said,' Vi repeated belligerently, 'or you'll be tossin' and turnin' all night.'

There were times, she thought grimly, when she had to put her foot down, and this was one of them – though nothing anyone could say or do would be of any comfort at all. Still, if Bainbridge was going to toss and turn all night, she might as well do it with a slice of bread and jam inside her, and a mug of hot tea.

'Come on,' she said with a brightness she did not feel. 'Just for once, queen, you'll do exactly what you're told!'

'We'd better,' Vi reminded them sternly next morning, 'get our squad drill over and done with.'

They had done only one of the two compulsory monthly drills; there was always a rush to complete the quota as the end of each month approached.

'I don't know why we should have to,' Jane grumbled. 'Lord knows, we did enough marching at the training depot to last us for the duration. And it isn't as if we march anywhere, now. We aren't infantrymen.'

'But, Kendal dear, we had to learn the discipline of squad drill when we first joined up because it was a part of the order of things, of the *procedure*,' Lucinda pointed out.

Vi studied her friend's face closely. Of Lucinda's fears there was no outward sign, but then no one *would* know anything was wrong; not even if her heart were breaking.

'I know exactly what you mean. Like, "Aye-aye; here comes another intake of darling ewe-lambs. Let's get stuck in and show them who's boss," kind of thing?'

'That's it. After all, it's an accepted fact that if they can't break you in heart and mind in the first two weeks, then you're okay. Remember how it was? Everything at the double, almost, and then, when we were all fit to drop, another hour of squad drill or marching.'

'But we were rookies then. We don't need it here, so why this twice-a-month thing?' Jane persisted.

'To keep us on our toes, that's why,' Vi pronounced, 'and anyway, the War Weapons Weeks are goin' to be starting again when the better weather comes. You know Ma'am likes us to put on a bit of a show for Craigiebur's do.'

War Weapons Weeks. They were held in every hamlet, town and city to collect money for the war effort. Not money given in charity; that would have been asking altogether too much of the war-weary public. War Weapons money was put into savings or War Bonds with the understanding that it would remain untouched, if it were at all possible, for the duration of hostilities. Money was raised in this way for many things. A large city, during its week, would pledge its population to save enough money to 'buy' a destroyer, and a thermometer-like indicator outside some prominent building would show how well and how generously the week was going. And when the target was reached – as it always was – the top of the indicator would display a large Army boot aiming a well-deserved kick at Hitler's backside.

For its last War Weapons Week, Fenton Bishop had chosen a ship's lifeboat for its target, Jane recalled, though her father had grumbled at the meanness of the village, tiny though it was, and said they could have bought two, at least. Hadn't Dunsley, very little bigger, bought a field gun, and Norton – a rich village with a reputed millionaire living there – had saved enough during their week to buy a Churchill tank.

Such fund-raisings made a welcome break from the monotony of war. They developed an air of carnival, with parades and garden fêtes and dances. Children bought sixpenny savings stamps to stick on their cards, and women whose purses had never been fatter bought bonds and savings certificates against a time when spending would no longer be a sin. Money saved now would one

496

day buy rugs and linoleum and sofas and pots and pans; yes, and wallpaper, too. How they ached for wallpaper.

'I'll go and put our names down for tomorrow mornin', then. That okay with you two?'

'Suppose it'll have to be.' Lucinda sighed. 'Or Patsy'll be on the warpath.'

'Next month, we'll do our drills early on,' Jane muttered, and Lucinda nodded agreement, though they knew it would be a last-minute rush again, as it always was.

'And collect our application-for-leave chits whilst you're about it, there's a love.'

'I'll fill them in for you, if you want. I'll do you a flippin' song and dance if you ask me nicely,' Vi flung as she slammed the cabin door behind her. Saucy young beggars! But life would be very dull without them. Oh, ar. Very dull indeed.

Almost every Wren rating who was not on duty gathered in the stableyard for squad drill.

'All right, girls. Settle down!' Deftly Chief Pillmoor arranged the company into ranks of four. 'And I want to see some good, smart marching this morning, so the sooner we get it right the sooner we'll all be back in quarters – okay?'

The day was too cold for the fancy stuff, she concluded; much too cold for forming two-deep ranks or forming fours and right-wheeling and left-wheeling. Today was just right for a brisk march.

Chief Pillmoor considered her newly set hair and decided against the lochside road. Up the sheltered brae and through the village would be the better route this morning. Then a couple of miles to where the road dwindled into a lane at the edge of the moor, perhaps, and a couple of miles back would see them home in time for the midday meal.

'Squa-a-aad, atten . . . *shun*! Squa-a-aad, right turn! By the left – quick – march!'

They moved off, arms swinging, skirts the required length from the ground. Wrens came in all heights; that could not be avoided, but a proper skirt-length could and was insisted upon – for nothing, Pat Pillmoor declared, made a squad look more ragged than ranks of undulating hems.

So belts had been slackened and skirts pulled down a little or up a little, and Ardneavie's chiefie was gratified that her charges appeared to be learning, at last, that there were two ways of doing things. *Her* way, or the wrong way.

'Chins in! Arms up!'

The squad settled down to an even rhythm, arms swinging up to shoulder level. Fingers clenched, thumbs jutting, they took the left-hand side of the road, knowing they looked good. They were used, now, to marching in public and gone was the embarrassment they first felt when bystanders stood curiously to watch them pass. When they were clear of the village, someone, doubtless, would begin to whistle softly and others would hum, but in full view of the population of Ardneavie, they knew better than to give of anything but their best.

Jane glanced sideways at Lucinda. Outwardly, her friend was calm; only the tension at her mouth and the miles-away look in her eyes betrayed her feelings.

I know what it's like, Lucinda love, she thought. *I truly do*.

Dear, sweet heaven, why did wars allow men and women to fall in love so easily, then part them so readily? Why was life lived so keenly now? Why were joys so joyous and miseries so abysmally miserable? Why couldn't life be normal and even-tempered as it once had been?

'Squa-a-aad . . .' came the warning command.

They were approaching the Ardneavie bus stop and Jane squinted ahead to the RAF officer who waited there.

'Squa-a-aad, eyes right!'

Pat Pillmoor lifted her hand in salute as every other head turned in acknowledgement. The officer returned the salute, his eyes bright with mischief. He was young, Jane thought, the wings on his tunic so obviously new. Probably just out of flying training and on seven days' posting leave.

A kid, thought Vi. A kid no older than Bainbridge and Kendal. A bit of a lad in command of a bloody great bomber.

A bomber pilot, Lucinda decided, who wore his tunic buttoned up and not as fighter pilots did, as Mike did, with the top button unfastened. *Mike, where are you? Take care. Please, please take care.*

From the rear of the squad came a long-drawn-out wolf whistle and the young pilot received it with a wink.

'Squa-a-aad! Eyes front!' came the command as the salute ended. Heads turned as one. Wolf whistle apart, the chief was pleased with her squad.

They marched on, feet slamming, hips swaying, leaving the village behind. Tentatively, the whistling began. 'Colonel Bogey', of course. It had to be that perennial favourite, that most popular of marching tunes, so delightful to parody. Those who could not whistle took up the melody, humming it softly.

They moved in perfect time, like a well-kept engine, to the road-end ahead. Chief Pillmoor slowed her pace and stepped to the side of the squad, her eyes sweeping the precise, well-ordered ranks, gratified that this morning they were doing it her way.

'Hitler,' came the melodious whisper, 'has only – *sniff, sniff, sniff.*'

'No singing in the ranks!' Chief Pillmoor warned. She might have known it. Too good to last!

The feet tramped on, the whistling began again softly. Then, as one, the singing started, a mischievous challenging of authority.

> Hitler has only got one ball,
> Goering's are very, very small,
> Himmler's are very sim'ler,
> And Doctor Goebbels has no –

'QUIET!' To a woman, they sensed the anger in the Chief Wren's command. The chanting stopped at once.

'Squa-a-aad . . . *halt*!'

Left, right. Two steps more, and the marching feet came to an efficient stop.

'Squa-a-aad . . . right *turn*!'

They swivelled on heel and toe to face her, waiting for the next command, but it was not given. She did not order 'at ease', but left them feet hard together, arms at sides, shoulders taut. Nor did she speak, but walked the length of the column, head tilted slightly as if she were counting. Then she turned and retraced her steps.

'Twenty-eight,' she hissed. 'On return to quarters I shall require twenty-eight names to be left at the regulating office, and each of those twenty-eight ratings will forfeit her late passes for a week. Is that understood?'

'Oh, Chiefie!'

'Why?'

'What did we do?'

'Chief!'

The protest rose in volume.

'*Quiet!* Will forfeit her late passes for the next *two* weeks!'

The silence was immediate and stunned.

'The next *two* weeks,' the Chief Wren repeated, 'and

500

then she will perhaps understand that singing in the ranks is *not on*, and singing dirty little ditties about the lack of masculinity of certain persons is most certainly *not on*. It is very unladylike,' she said primly. 'And dead common, too!' she snarled, as an afterthought.

Slowly she traversed the ranks again, glaring at each in turn from slit-narrow eyes.

'Right, then. If that is understood, we'll finish the drill,' she said softly; much, much too softly. 'Squa-a-aad, left turn!' she almost whispered.

They reached Ardneavie House tired and foot-weary. Two miles more had been added to their march, making them so late returning there was hardly time to eat their midday meal. Chastened, they ran down the jetty to the waiting launch.

'Chiefie's a bitch!'

'She's a monster!'

'And an old cow!'

'I mean, does it matter? I don't give a damn about Hitler! I don't care if he's got *three*!'

'I care about my late pass, though! I've got a date tonight.'

'Patsy Pill's a *miserable* old cow!'

It would be a long time before starboard watch derided Hitler and his cronies in song – within Chief Pillmoor's hearing!

'What was the commotion at the regulating office?' enquired Third Officer St John of her Chief Wren.

'A matter of late passes, Ma'am, and singing in the ranks. A – a *disorderly* song, Ma'am.'

'Oh dear. And which song was it?'

'You might well ask, Ma'am.'

'I see. The "Colonel Bogey" song.' Suzie St John

smiled. 'You know, I often wonder if Hitler really does have only one – '

'Miss St John!' Chief Pillmoor's eyes flew wide with shock. 'I really don't think – '

'Or would you suppose it's something invented as, say, the ultimate insult?' the officer continued, unabashed.

The chief's mouth gaped open.

'Mind, rumour has it that Dr Goebbels has none at all, which is probably why he's such an odious little man! Ah well, we shall never know, Pat, and I don't suppose it's really all that important.'

'*Ma'am!*' It *was* important. When a squad of thirty Wrens sang about it in public then it damn well was important! And now, if you please, Miss St John was at it!

'Oh dear. I've shocked you, Pat. How about a glass of sherry before lunch?'

'Thanks.' Chief Pillmoor removed her hat and gloves then sank uneasily into a chair.

'You mustn't be upset by my – er – directness, Chief. Sometimes I'm inclined to forget my medical background, you see.' Smiling apologetically she turned, glass in hand. 'Just managed a couple. Ah well, that's the last of the ration until next month! Yes, dear,' she continued mildly, 'perhaps I should have mentioned that my father is a doctor in general practice, my mother a one-time ward sister at Guy's and my younger brother has just qualified. He hopes, eventually, to be an anaesthetist. Now, perhaps, you'll understand why the mention of certain male attributes – or *lack* of them – doesn't upset me at all. I grew up with them, you might say.'

'And I thought . . .' Pat Pillmoor recalled the Christmas condoms then laughed out loud. 'I'm afraid I always thought you were – well, a little unworldly, Ma'am.'

'Did you? Well, perhaps I do give that impression

sometimes, but don't tell the girls. They think I'm a pushover, you see. And Pat – the late passes. You've stopped them, I take it?'

'Yes. For two weeks.'

'Hmm. *Two* weeks, Chief?'

'I can't back down, Ma'am – can I?'

'The girls would love you if you did.' Suzie St John smiled sweetly. '*One* week, perhaps?'

Pat Pillmoor gazed unspeaking at her superior. Unworldly? Suzie St John had more cunning than a pack of monkeys.

'You know, Pat, girls have a lot more – well, *knowledge*, these days. They must have, especially in the women's forces. It's awful to remember the innocence of some girls I came across in training depot.' The officer frowned. 'One girl there thought that if a man kissed her and put his tongue in her mouth, she'd get pregnant. Another didn't know what a Lesbian was. Girls have to know things, these days. It must have been a terrible decision for someone to make – the compulsory drafting of women into the forces, I mean – if they ever stopped to think of the implications. Imagine – girls from sheltered homes, pitch-forked into *this*? You and I, Chief, have a great responsibility.'

'You're right, Ma'am.' Of course girls knew things now that not so very long ago no nicely brought up young lady would even have heard of. And if they didn't know, it was essential they be told about the rights and wrongs. But in wartime, right seemed so right, and wrong – well, with tomorrow so uncertain, who could blame anyone, man or woman, if wrong didn't seem so *very* wrong? 'Maybe one week's stoppage would be enough, all things considered.'

'If you think so, Pat. It's entirely your decision.' Diplomatically Suzie St John handed the kudos to her Chief Wren. 'Oh, and I've signed the three leave applications

503

for cabin 9. If you're going on board *Omega* to see the victualling officer this afternoon, perhaps you'd be a dear and leave them with the paymaster?'

'Cabin 9.' The chief frowned. 'Thick as thieves, those three. Hardly ever apart. Talking about Lesbians – you wouldn't suppose, I mean, well, *would* you?'

'No. I wouldn't. Nothing there,' the officer said firmly. 'It's merely the case of a woman who was a homeless widow – or thought she was a widow – and a couple of young girls, each of them an only child, I understand, in need of a bit of attention. McKeown's the motherly sort – and quite a few years older. Nothing more to it than that.'

'You're right, of course. Sad about Kendal, wasn't it? Learning her boyfriend was dead then taking up with a submariner from *Viper*. Makes me glad I'm not so young, any more.'

'Well, there's always hope. Look what happened to McKeown. Oh, but I enjoyed it, that morning, giving her such wonderful news. Made me feel like God, for a little while. McKeown's a good steward and I like her. She makes me laugh. Salt of the earth, that one. But tell me, Chief, about Bainbridge.'

'What about Bainbridge? Seems to be doing all right. The assessment I had from her divisional officer for her record sheet was good.'

'I'm not talking about her work, Chief. . .'

'Ah, yes. The good-looking American? Rumour had it that she fell pretty badly for him. But he's overseas now, I heard.'

'Ah.' The sigh was one of relief. 'Not that I'm prying, but I do like to keep tabs on things, if I can. As I said, we do have a responsibility, you and I, and I did understand that Bainbridge was already engaged. Still, we can't live their lives entirely for them, can we?'

'We can't, Ma'am.' Thank God!

504

'Oh dear, Chief. Won't life be dull when this war is over.'

'Dull, Ma'am? Yes.' And peaceful. And bloody marvellous!

Pat Pillmoor rose reluctantly to her feet and gathered up the applications. Lucky dogs to be going on leave, she sighed. Seven days away from women, she thought longingly; seven days at her mother's home, away from uniforms and war.

Suddenly, the hard-headed Chief Wren had an over-whelming longing to be there, in Shropshire. To be a mother for seven days; to be with Peter, her son.

22

'Thanks, chum.'

Lucinda jumped down from the cab of the Army lorry, gave the driver a thumbs-up salute, then stood quite still, eyes closed, holding back the moment when she would open them to see the rooftops of Lady Mead rising unevenly above the treetops. Lady Mead, unchanged and unchanging, always there though she had not seen it in more than two years. It beckoned her now like a light on a storm-lashed night, its arms ready to reach out and clasp her to its rose-brick breast. It had been her childhood; now it was her refuge. Now she needed it as she had never needed it before because she was still reeling from the shock of the newspaper headlines, and home was the place to be when your world had stopped turning and you were afraid and in need of comfort.

She crossed the road and stood at the fence, looking out across the deer park. This was the view she liked best, remembered most often; the view of the very old part of the house built in stone and Elizabethan brick, where the Bainbridges had lived before they became powerful and rich; before her distant forebears had even dreamed of an earldom. Lady Meadow Place it was called then, and Elizabeth Tudor had probably never even heard of it, let alone slept there.

Frowning, she picked up her respirator and case and set off diagonally in the direction of the Dower House. She wasn't at all sure if she was allowed to be here now, but the Air Force would soon warn her off, she supposed, if she wasn't.

It was a little after Peterborough when she'd found out; just before the train clattered over the points then swayed on towards Grantham and Lincoln, that the corporal had opened his newspaper.

RANGOON FALLS TO JAPS. The headlines stood out two feet tall; there was no missing them.

For a moment she refused to believe it. She closed her eyes then opened them again, but nothing was different. It was there, stark black on white. Rangoon had fallen and RAF Rangoon too, she thought bleakly.

Her stomach contracted into a tight, hard ball. Her mouth went dry then filled with spittle. She was going to be sick; here, in this dirty, crowded compartment, where a dozen people were squeezed into seating for eight. She would be sick here and now, were the floor not littered with respirators and kitbags and cases and brown paper carriers.

She stumbled through the compartment door then stood in the corridor, arms clasped tightly over her stomach, whispering, 'No, no, *no*!'

Mercifully she was not sick; the smoke-tainted coal-scented air that whipped cold through the open window saw to that. Reaching for the hand rail, she clung to it desperately, steadying her shaking legs, bracing herself against the rocking of the train.

'Are you all right?'

Lucinda blinked her eyes into focus; saw breeches and knee-length stockings and a bright green pullover.

'You look terrible. Trains make you sick, do they?'

The landgirl's face was warm with concern; a hand reached out for Lucinda's and held it tightly.

'I – no. Thanks all the same.' Brown eyes, soft and caring, held hers. 'It's just that – well – Rangoon, I mean. The paper in there . . .'

'Ah. Just seen it, then? Heard it on the early news

myself, just before I left home. It's a right bastard, ain't it? You got someone there, dear?'

'My boyfriend. He's in the Air Force.' Her voice sounded strange; as if she were speaking into a dome that took her words and threw them back distorted at her disbelieving ears. 'At RAF Rangoon.'

'Aircrew, is he?'

'Yes. Flies a Spit.'

'Well, let's hope he got the hell out of it before they got there. Makes you wonder, don't it, when we're going to win something.'

'Gets you a bit browned off,' Lucinda managed to say. She was feeling less dizzy now, though she still clutched the work-roughened hand. 'It – it was seeing it like that, you see. Those headlines just came out and hit me for six.'

'Well, you sit down on my case, dear, and next time we stop, I'll nip off and get you a cup of tea. There's always a WVS trolley at Grantham.'

Lucinda had bought a newspaper at Lincoln station, but it did nothing to calm her fears. The headlines were the same, almost, as those she had seen on the train, and when she had read it and read between the lines too, searching for just one grain of comfort, nothing had changed. It was a repeat of a Ministry of Information handout; Rangoon had fallen and fierce fighting continued to the north of the city. And God alone knew what it was really like out there; how many men had been taken prisoner – if the Japs took prisoners, that was – and how many had died. And not one word about RAF Rangoon.

The screaming, raging panic she had felt on the train gave way then to a dull, throbbing pain, though her legs were steadier. She closed her eyes and sent another thank you to the landgirl who had helped her: wrapped her

508

fingers round a hot cup of tea and demanded that she drink it down.

That was one of the few good things about this sick-making war, Lucinda conceded as she made for the gate that opened on to the drying green. People were kind now, because this was everybody's war and strangers cared; strangers you met in canteens, in the street, in the blackout, even. You met and smiled and touched and cared. Then passed on, each to his own.

She bore left at the damson hedge, skirting the estate yard and the high walls of the kitchen garden, turning her back on the house now, and the outer yard where once the head keeper kept snares and traps and ferret hutches; where dog houses stood in a long straight row of six, enclosed in iron railings.

No keeper there now; no dogs.

They had taken the front gates from the Dower House, and the railings too. Taken them without so much as a by-your-leave, to melt down into iron for the war effort. Yet the old place was still there as she remembered it, like a piece broken off from the big house and set down in half an acre of trees. The old dowager had moved there immediately Pa and Mama were married, Nanny once said; glad to be out of the damp, echoing Lady Mead and its cold stone-flagged passages. And now Nanny lived there in a part of it, guardian of Bainbridge treasures and heirlooms and a string of Bainbridge portraits reaching back to that very first earl and his sheep-faced, prolific wife.

They'd all been prolific, the Bainbridge women. Except Mama. One had reared four sons and four daughters and outlived her earl to marry again and go on producing a lesser line.

She wondered if Charlie's wife would give him a lot of children or merely the required two sons, and felt dismay surge through her. Not at Charlie marrying someone else, but dismay to think of the wife who would come here with him. But she, Lucinda, had made her choice. That night at Eaton Square, she had finally surrendered Lady Mead to a faceless woman and given all her love to Mike.

Mike. How could she forget, even for a second, that Mike was in a faraway city which two days ago had been occupied by the enemy! How had it been? Another Hong Kong? Had they taken it by stealth, marching in in straight, orderly ranks – or had they taken it by fury? Had their bombers blasted it into submission and had Mike's squadron flown sortie after sortie until they could fly no more? Had it been another Spitfire summer for the Rangoon fighter pilots?

Swallowing hard on tears that stuck in her throat, she began to run; like a frightened, bewildered animal she made blindly for shelter and comfort and home.

Nanny Bainbridge had not changed. She still wore her grey dress and white apron, and her breasts were still soft and large and comfortable to cry on. Gathered into an unspeaking embrace, Lucinda gave way to her grief. It was all right, now. She was back and she could weep, because she was a little girl again and little girls were allowed to weep.

'Oh, it's been so long!'

'There, there, there. Hush that noise at once,' the grey-haired woman clucked indulgently, offering an immaculate white handkerchief. 'I wasn't expecting you until tomorrow. How did you get here?'

'I hitched a lift outside the station.' She dabbed her tears and blew her nose obediently.

'Is that wise, dear?'

'Oh, yes. Everybody hitch-hikes, now. Someone always stops for you, if you're in uniform.' The fears that thrashed inside her were quietening now and her heart thudded less loudly. 'I came early because Bruton Street is empty. Mama is visiting in Dorset – I think she'd forgotten I'd be coming – and Pa seems busier than ever with his Home-Guarding.' She trailed into the kitchen, placing her case tidily behind the door, hanging her respirator on a peg.

The kitchen was just as she had pictured it in her fond imaginings: the row of pans, shelved above the Aga; the wooden plate rack over the sinkstone; the soup pan on the hotplate. And because this was a living room now, a large table set around with chairs, and two well-cushioned rockers either side of the stove.

'And Captain Charles? Did you see him?'

'No. Pa said he's away on a course. The house seemed dead. I went to the theatre last night, just for something to do. Saw *Blithe Spirit*, but it was all over by half-past eight . . .'

She had walked back to Bruton Street afterwards; walked back in the half-light through a waiting, watching London; taking the long way round through Berkeley Square. And she had stood there alone, gazing at the bare branches of the plane trees, wondering where the nightingales were, sending her love to Mike in great, warm waves. Last night, she hadn't known about Rangoon. No one had.

'It's lovely and warm in here. Would there be a cup of tea, Nanny? I've brought you a seven-day ration card. Tomorrow I'll bike down to the village and spend it.'

'Soap,' said Nanny, reaching for the teapot. 'Would you have believed it? Of all things, *soap*.'

Soap meant cleanliness, which was next only to godliness, and *They* had no call to ration soap! And a niggardly four ounces a week, at that. How was a body to manage? She believed implicitly in King, Country and Empire, and would defend them with her last breath, but the rationing of soap last month had tried her patience sorely.

'I've got a couple of coupons I don't want,' Lucinda offered. 'You're welcome, if you want them.'

Soap rationing had hardly caused comment at Ard-neavie House. When rationing had begun, soap coupons for personal use were issued at each pay parade, the only problem being that of finding a shop with a decent tablet of toilet soap to sell.

'Can you spare them?' Her eyes showed her pleasure. 'A bar of White Windsor would be most acceptable, if you could manage to get one.'

'I'll try. And how about my meat ration? What shall I buy? What does one get a lot of for one-and-tuppence?'

'I think shin beef goes the farthest. And maybe when you go to the butcher's, it might be a good idea if you were to wear your uniform, Lucinda, and ask him if he's got any sausages.' Sausages were still off ration, but harder than ever to come by. 'He'll not refuse sausages to a member of the Forces,' she added complacently.

'You crafty old thing!' Lucinda laughed out loud, and the sound of it shocked her. She had wanted, since this morning on the train, never to laugh again or smile again until Mike was safely home, but it had just slipped out. Maybe, though, laughter was necessary, just to survive. And laughter was better than tears. 'But I suppose it's hard, making ends meet on one ration book?'

'I manage.' Nanny poured tea into china cups. 'You can, you know, if you put your mind to it. And your Pa has still got Lady Mead land, and the Home Farm. The Air Force didn't take them over. Johnson is still farm manager, and he lets me have one or two things. Some-times he'll give me a rabbit, and at pig-killing time he sent some liver. I told him you'd be coming on leave and he promised me a few fresh eggs and a pint or two extra of milk. I think he might have left them in the washhouse at the back – quietly, you know . . .' She tapped her nose significantly and nodded her head.

'Why, Nanny! You're in the black market, you old fraud!'

'Indeed I am *not*! I wouldn't touch sugar, Lucinda, nor any of *those* things!'

No, Lucinda was sure she wouldn't. People were often hungry now, yet most would refuse even a few ounces of tea or sugar or anything imported.

'I know you wouldn't,' she said warmly. 'But we aren't having a very good war, are we?' She wanted desperately to talk about Rangoon. She wanted especially to tell Nanny about Mike; make her understand. Charlie didn't write now – she couldn't blame him for that – and after two acid telephone calls and a letter calling her ungrateful and uncaring, there had been little contact with her mother since the dropping of her bombshell. Now it seemed as if they were waiting for her to finish her fling and creep back to the fold, begging Charlie's forgiveness. 'We don't seem to be winning much.'

'Oh, I don't know, dear,' came the placid reply. 'The Russians are doing very well. They're used to the cold, aren't they? This last winter has been on their side. Not that I agree with the Bolsheviks and what they did to their Czar, but they *are* our allies now, I suppose. And one of our convoys got through to Malta, which was one in the eye for Mussolini. But tell me, how was London?'

'Oh, battered and bruised and dusty and dirty, but surviving. And more theatres have reopened, since the bombing eased off a bit – but that isn't what you meant, is it, Nanny?'

'Well, Lucinda, I did have a very strange letter from your mama, but perhaps she got it wrong.'

513

'About Charlie and me, you mean? No, she didn't. We aren't engaged any more. It wouldn't have worked.'

'I got this jumper for sixpence at the Red Cross jumble sale.' Nanny picked up a bundle of red knitting, changing the subject so firmly that it was almost like a slap. 'Would you believe it?' She held up the offending garment. 'Body too short, sleeves too long. Knitted for a baby chimpanzee, I shouldn't wonder. It hasn't been worn, either, and four coupons at least wasted. So I unpicked the seams and now I'm pulling it out and winding it into balls. There'll be at least eight ounces, when I'm done. I think I shall knit something for one of the Farley children. You remember Farley, Lucinda?'

'The estate carpenter who went missing at Dunkirk?' Missing, as Gerry had been; like Rob and now perhaps Mike. A knife turned inside her and the pain was real. 'Nanny, about Charlie and me. I want – '

'Still missing. The Army has given her a war-widow's pension, but she won't have it that he's not coming back. Oh, she tries, poor girl, and she's still in an estate cottage. Your pa said she was to stay there, but it's a shame. She's a young woman, and people say she'll marry again one day when she's over it. But who, will you tell me, is going to take on the rearing of four children not his own?'

'Nanny, please let me talk to you. You only know what Mama has told you. Charlie and I – '

'More tea?' Nanny held up the brown earthenware pot, her lips pursed into a tight bud of obstinacy, her face arranging itself into its subject-closed expression. 'Or would you like to go upstairs and unpack your case? Perhaps I should sponge and press your uniform; it's looking a little creased from the train.'

Lucinda rose obediently to her feet, carrying her cup and saucer to the sink. It wasn't any use. Nanny didn't want to know and, anyway, she'd have to be on Mama's side, wouldn't she? So what hope was there of telling her about Mike and how much she loved him; how she'd loved him right from the start. And she needed so much to talk about him; to tell someone how afraid she was and glean a little comfort and gain a little hope, perhaps, in the telling.

'The little dressing room, is it?' She paused at the door, her eyes begging indulgence, but the older woman only nodded and carried on with her pulling out and winding.

'Nanny, where is my school trunk?'

A rare blaze of defiance took Lucinda. She would *not* be sent upstairs like a naughty child. She was twenty, now, and she'd been in the Wrens a year. Nursery discipline no longer applied!

'It's up at the house, dear, in the basement with all the other cases. They let us keep a few rooms down there, you remember, for storage.'

'And my civvy clothes? What happened to them?'

'The clothes you left at Lady Mead are upstairs in the dressing room. I've kept them all well aired. Why do you ask?'

'I want to take some of them with me. There wasn't anything suitable at Bruton Street. All town clothes, really. And I want to look out a warm coat for Mary.'

'Mary?'

'Vi's sister. Mary has two young children who won't stop growing, so they take all her clothing coupons. We've got it all worked out.' She explained about the five coupons so necessary for Vi's shoes, and Mary's need of a warm coat. 'So you see,' she finished, 'it seems very wrong that there are masses of clothes lying around here, doing nothing. And no one will miss the odd coat – will she?'

'I don't suppose she will, dear, but if you are going to have theft on your conscience, make it worth while. Look for the cabin trunk marked *Wanted on Voyage*. You'll easily recognize it; it's got *Queen Mary* labels on it. There's some good stuff in that particular trunk. I know. I had a look, you see – to make sure the moths hadn't got in.'

'Moths. Of course. But how do I get into the house?'

'You go to the front door and ask the duty corporal for Group Captain Wilson. He's a very nice gentleman – he and I often have a chat. Tell him who you are and he'll let you in.'

'No trouble?' Nanny, it seemed, knew the drill. Nanny was not only keeping an eye on family belongings stored at the Dower House but was, it seemed, making sorties to Lady Mead, too. 'I'll get in all right?'

'No trouble, dear. Remember me kindly to the group captain, and whilst you're up there, have a rummage around and see if there's anything suitable for duffel-coat linings, will you? *Small* duffel coats. I managed to – er – come by a grey RAF blanket, and grey blankets are ideal for duffel coats and cost no coupons, either. I'm making them for the two eldest Farleys. They're both at school now and in desperate need of something warm.'

'And how did you get hold of an RAF blanket?' Lucinda teased.

'It's a long story, dear.' She was still intent on her winding. 'I'll tell you, perhaps, when you're twenty-one.'

'You're turning into a spiv, Nanny.'

'Aren't we all, dear? Aren't we all?' Her reply was complacent and unrepentant. 'It's a matter of survival, you see, and the two Farleys do need coats. Now run upstairs and take off your uniform. Supper's in half an hour. Soup and Woolton pie and a surprise for pudding. And there's enough hot water for a six-inch bath.'

Nanny sighed contentment. Her child was home. With problems in need of sorting, unfortunately, but home. It was a comfortable feeling.

She regarded the product of her pernickety labours. Eight balls of coupon-free red wool, set in a precise row on the table top. *Coupon-free.* That was a comfortable feeling, too.

Lucinda came downstairs to supper in a pleated skirt and a Viyella blouse. The bathwater had been hot, and even though she kept to the statutory six inches, it had been soft as rainwater. And the towels had smelled of lavender, as they always did. These few days in Lincolnshire should have been special and good, but now there was this terrible fear inside her and a barely suppressed panic that would rise up and engulf her, were she to let it. She wanted to listen to the six o'clock news, yet knew she dared not. But then again, if she did not hear it she might miss something of great importance; perhaps even that the newspapers had got it horribly wrong and that Rangoon was still in British hands – and the RAF was having great success against the Japanese fighters and not one of our pilots lost or missing.

She might, of course; but things didn't happen like that any more and, anyway, Nanny had decided for her.

'There you are, dear. We'll not tune in to the six o'clock news. Let's wait until nine, shall we?'

So they said grace, drank soup such as only Nanny could make, then divided the pie equally between them.

Lucinda gazed at it thoughtfully. A Woolton pie was an interesting experience. It contained anything and everything but meat or cheese, a mixing of vegetables, seasoned with herbs and moistened with left-over gravy. An end-of-the-week concoction, when the meat ration was used up and there had been no luck in the fish queue.

'The pie crust, you will notice, is almost white,' Nanny remarked with a certain degree of smugness. Nanny did not like the wartime national wholemeal flour. No one

517

did. It was coarse and dirty-looking, and goodness only knew what it did to a body's insides. The British liked their flour fine and white, and the only way to achieve it was to sieve out the nasty brown bits; through an old silk stocking had proved the most efficient way. Sieving was a long, laborious job, but worth it for a near-white pie crust. 'We are turning into a nation of improvisers and scavengers, and the strange thing is that the more one is able to make do, the better one is supposed to feel. But I for one,' she continued bleakly, 'can't wait to get back to days of good red meat in plenty and cream on Sundays!'

The surprise pudding was by way of a farewell. 'The last of my rice, Lucinda; the very last ounce. I think I must have known you'd be here for supper when I put it in the oven.' She sighed loudly. 'Now heaven only knows when we'll be able to buy any more, with the Japanese taking over all the rice-growing countries.' Rice pudding had been a regular part of pre-war nursery meals. It was inconceivable to contemplate an England without rice. 'But they're a strange race. Not European, you see . . .'

'Nanny, did you know about Rangoon?' Now was the time to tell her about Mike; now, whilst she was aggrieved about the rice, perhaps she would listen and maybe understand. 'Did you hear?'

'I did. On the early news, this morning. Burma seems a long way away, but they'll have to be stopped, those Japs, or where next? India?'

'Mike's in Rangoon, Nanny.'

'Mike? Do I – '

'Of course you know him, but you're like Mama. You think that if you ignore him he'll fade away! But he won't, because I won't let him! I love him, and – '

'Lucinda, I cannot tolerate outbursts at the supper table!'

'Then damn it, when will we – '

'Nor swearing.'

'*Please?*' But it was useless, wasn't it? Lucinda Bainbridge had offended against the rule by which her kind of people lived: Do what you like, dear, but don't rock the boat. She should have had a raging affair with Mike then returned demurely to marry Charlie, in white! 'But I'm wasting my time, aren't I? You, of all people, I thought might understand. But if you can't understand, Nanny, can't you listen? Even if you don't know what loving someone is like – loving him till you'd die for him, I mean – couldn't you just let me talk about him?'

The poised rice-pudding spoon hit the table with a clatter and the lined face blanched. Then she drew a deep breath and fixed her gaze on the window and out and away a million miles beyond it.

'Don't I?' she choked. 'What makes you so sure? What makes you think that before I became Nanny Bainbridge I wasn't a living, breathing person? Couldn't I, perhaps, have once been in love? Oh, you silly, self-centred little girl!'

'I'm sorry. Were you? I mean – I didn't mean to – I'm sorry,' she said again, deflated.

'Yes, I *was* in love, and yes, I accept that you didn't mean to be pert.'

There was a silence between them; a meeting of eyes and a new, strange understanding. A nanny recalling a past love; a girl stepping into womanhood.

'Tell me about him,' Lucinda said softly. 'What was he called?'

'William Jones. *William*, not Bill.'

'Go on.'

'He – he was an under-gardener at Southquays. A very good under-gardener, nearly out of his time, ready to leave the bothy and ask for a cottage of his own so he – *we* – could be married. I was nursery maid at Southquays,

519

then, for the Newsome family. Nice people. In shipping. And William and I were so in love. We were walking out publicly, going to church together. Good times, Lucinda; near-perfect, but for the war. My generation had a war, too, child; an obscene war that dirtied everything it touched. Immoral, our war was.'

'I know, darling. The war that didn't end all wars.' Lucinda reached for the hand that lay unmoving on the table top and held it tightly.

'Well, we managed to put the war behind us, William and me. "You'll not go?" I'd beg him, and he said he wouldn't. Not until the time was right. He'd go then, he said. So we had our lovely summer, and William spoke to the head gardener; there were fifteen gardeners at Southquays, would you believe? And the head gardener spoke to the master, who said that William could have a cottage of his own come Michaelmas, and we began to make our plans.'

'So what went wrong? The war, wasn't it?'

'The war. William came out of his time and agreed a rate with the head gardener, and we set our wedding for the next Easter. Only then those men came to the village; a recruiting sergeant and two lance corporals. They came on horses, dressed up to the nines, making a lot of noise, buying drinks at the pub.

'"Your country needs *you*!" the sergeant said, except it wasn't an asking – more an accusation. Young, fit men should be in the trenches, fighting the Kaiser, defending King and Country. *Tcha!* I almost shouted out that that was where *he* should be, not inveigling young men away from their sweethearts!'

'So William went?' Lucinda prompted gently, her heart aching at the wrong of it.

'He went. The time must have been right. And five others from Southquays went with him. And only two of them came back. Oh, I hated that sergeant. Flash, he was. I wished him dead for what he'd done to William and me. They said he got a shilling for every recruit. Judas money. But perhaps he hanged himself, too . . .'

Tears smarted in Lucinda's eyes. 'Don't upset yourself. I'm – I'm sorry I said what I did. Forgive me. Don't let's talk about it any more. Try to forget . . .'

'Forget? But I don't want to. The young girl I was still loves William. She always will. Most times now, though, it doesn't hurt so much, and I still hope, you know. I have silly little daydreams and all of a sudden William is there, still looking for me, twenty-five years after.'

A stupid old woman, that's what she was, she thought, but not too old, never too old, to dream.

'I waited there for William for three years after the war was over. Southquays nursery was a busy one. Time passed quickly. There was a new baby every two years, regular as clockwork, so there was little time to mourn. But he didn't come back, and I heard that a young countess was looking for a nanny, and the rest you know.'

'And when did you accept, darling? When did you finally give up hoping?'

'Never. You never give up hope – not really. But I think I accepted it when I finally saw his grave. He died – was *killed* – at the Somme. The last battle of the Somme, just a few weeks before the Armistice. You had just gone to boarding school and I was restless, so I spent all my savings and went to France.

'It was very final, seeing his name on a gravestone. Not at first, though, because even then I told myself that a lot of William Joneses must have died. But seeing his name and his number together made me accept.

'I wish he could have been laid in English earth, though some kind person had put flowers there. He'd have liked that. And there were birds singing in the trees. They gave me comfort, those birds. Ah, well. Eat up your pudding, child.'

'I want to tell you about Mike,' Lucinda whispered. 'I need to tell you. He's at Rangoon, you see . . .'

The grey head moved sharply and concern showed for an instant in the faraway eyes. Then, 'If you don't eat that pudding, I shall be obliged to serve it up at breakfast.' She smiled, like Nanny of old. 'And I can see there'll be no peace until you've told me about your young man, so finish your supper and then we'll wash the dishes and have a cup of tea afterwards. I think the rations will run to a pot.'

They sat, rocking gently, either side of the stove.

'Where shall I begin?' Lucinda asked.

'The beginning is usually the best place.'

'Well, we can never agree who picked who up, but I think it was me who – er – picked Mike up . . .'

And then she spoke of every remembered word; the way he stood a head taller when they danced; the way he smiled, just a little crookedly because of the scar. She told of New England and Grandma Farrow, who had been a governess, and Mavis the parrot. And she whispered, pink-cheeked, of her love and longing and her need of him and her fears for him.

'I love him so much, you see. There won't ever be anyone else. Don't say I'm being melodramatic, Nanny.'

'I won't, child.' There had never been anyone else for her, either.

'Mike's got to be safe. He's *got* to come back. I don't think I could go on living if he didn't.'

'You would. You'd manage. And we can hope, and wish. We can wish on new moons and first stars and loads of hay and wish your Michael safely home.'

And if wishes were horses, child, then beggars would

ride. And I would have given William two fine sons and a bonny little daughter.

'And we can pray, Lucinda. Do you still say your prayers every night?'

'Only private ones, now. Vi's very good, though. She prays for almost everyone.'

'I like the sound of your Vi. When will I meet her?'

'Soon, Nanny. Next leave, maybe, in June. And Jane, too. Can you squeeze us all in?'

'I'll do my best. You'd all be very welcome.'

'Oh, it's been so long.' Lucinda sighed. 'I didn't know till now how much I missed you. You'll be on my side, won't you? Mama still thinks I'll marry Charlie when the war is over and I come back to my senses. But I won't, and you must tell her –'

'It isn't my place to tell her ladyship anything.' The elder woman bit hard on a smile. 'Your mama is still my employer, remember. But be sure I shall understand.'

'Bless you. Don't ever leave me, Nanny. Come with Mike and me to America.'

'What? Another mouth to feed? Could you afford it?'

'I don't really know. Funny, but we never talked about money. Mike will have a job to go back to, I think, and there'll be money coming to me, when I'm twenty-one. Not a lot, but enough to buy us a little house, I suppose.'

'Well, let's cross that bridge when we come to it, shall we? And it's nearly nine o'clock. I think we should listen to the news. No use running away from it. Switch it on, will you?'

The later news bulletin brought no comfort with it. 'I think,' Nanny said wryly, 'we should have tuned in at six. That must surely have been less gloomy.'

She moved the dial to the dance music that had just begun. It would be cheerful, quicksteppy music tonight.

Dance-band leaders seemed to sense when the nation was in need of something happy, if only a happy tune. But not even music could have detracted from the sombre intonations of the announcer. Fighting had been heavy around Rangoon and now continued in the north. Casualties had been heavy on both sides, he read. And Mike was there, perhaps an injured statistic or even –

'Come and help me with the blackouts, Nanny.' Lucinda jumped to her feet, her hands restless. 'It's getting dark and I'm not sure of my way around. At Ardneavie we call it darkening ship.'

'Very well, dear. The flashlights are on the dresser.' There were two; one stuck with strips of brown paper to minimize the light, the other, for use indoors, without. 'We'll take one each. All the light bulbs in the storerooms have been taken out, but if ever you need one, Lucinda, you'll find spares in a box in the hall cupboard. But be careful of them, won't you? Light bulbs are like gold dust, now. I haven't seen one in the shops for ages.'

The Dower House had four bedrooms, two dressing rooms and a bathroom, of which two small rooms and the bathroom were used by the custodian. Those remaining were crammed from floor to ceiling with Bainbridge possessions, with only a narrow passage left free between door and window. When the high-ranking RAF officer had visited that day, telling them that the authorities would require the use of Lady Mead for the duration of hostilities and would expect it to be made available within fourteen days, he had left them in a state of shock and agitation.

'It's going to take a month to pack and catalogue and shift this lot,' the man from the removals firm had declared gloomily in the pandemonium that followed. 'Just haven't got the staff, you see. All called up.'

The task had been completed on the afternoon of the

fifteenth day, and by nightfall RAF transports were rumbling up the drive, passing the Countess in high old dudgeon, driving one of the cars to London with her furs and jewellery safely encased on the rear seat. Lady Kitty had never cared for Lady Mead, but disliked intensely being ordered out of it.

'I open the windows every day in the better weather.' Nanny swept the beam of her torch along the narrow alley for Lucinda to follow. 'And in winter I try to light a fire in each room at least once a month. The woodman lets me have logs when he can, but wood fires can be very dangerous, you know, and need a lot of watching. Last winter, a beech blew down and Johnson had it sawn up and carted away before the Air Force could get their hands on it. Beech logs are best for burning; they don't spit or crackle, you see.'

Lucinda lifted a dust sheet and recognized a gilt armchair from the salon, then bent down to read *Sèvres dessert set*, daubed in black on a tea chest.

'Hurry, child. There's all downstairs to do, yet.' Nanny closed over the window shutters and slid home the bolts. 'Careful, now. Don't bump into anything.'

'Quite a ritual, twice a day,' Lucinda remarked when the high window on the half-landing had been covered and the four downstairs rooms made secure against the night. 'They didn't leave you a lot of room, Nanny.'

'Oh, I do well enough, though it's a pity the attics can't be used.' Attics must remain empty, by Government emergency decree. 'Ah well, it makes sense, I suppose. No use having to plough through years of junk to put out a firebomb.'

So every attic in Britain had been emptied and buckets of sand and buckets of water placed inside each door, at the ready. And please God they need never be used, Nanny often pleaded silently, for the roof timbers of old

525

houses were dry and brittle and would go up like tinder. Parting with Lady Mead had been trial enough; to watch it blaze as so many other houses had blazed would be near unbearable.

'Where is the silver, Nanny? They don't expect you to be responsible for that, too?'

'Oh, no. The silver is all up at the house in the butler's pantry, locked up in the cupboards. It's as safe there as anywhere, with the Air Force to guard it.' Though what state it would be in when the black paper wrappings were eventually removed was anybody's guess. 'And having a little storage up there does give me the opportunity to get in, once in a while, and have a look around,' she added. 'Remember to keep your eyes open when you go there tomorrow; we don't want Mr Chads all over the walls or drawing pins stuck in the panelling, do we?'

Dear, loyal Nanny; grateful for a roof over her head. An underpaid, overworked drudge for Mama. But they would take her with them to Vermont, she and Mike, no matter how much another mouth to feed would cost. She must not stay here to skivvy for another Bainbridge.

'No, dearest, we don't.' Yes, indeed. Charlie's lady must look elsewhere for a nanny, when the time came.

'Goodness, is that the time? You must be tired out, child.' It was more of a statement of fact than an enquiry. Eleven o'clock was already an hour past bedtime.

Nanny unscrewed the stopper of the earthenware bed-warmer, inserted a funnel, then filled it to the brim with water from a steaming kettle.

'These warmers,' she mused, almost to herself, 'must have been in service since your grandmother's day. Goodness only knows what will happen when the rubber rings perish.'

526

Rubber. Malaya, taken by the Japanese. Were there rubber plantations in Burma, too? *Mike, where are you?*

'Ah well. We'll worry about that if it happens,' Nanny decided comfortably, screwing the stopper tight, slipping the hot, barrel-like container into an old woollen stocking, and tying it top and toe to form a carrying handle. 'Now pop this into your bed, and I'll put the milk on to boil.'

Carefully she measured out two mugs, grateful for the farm manager's bounty, wondering if she had delved too deep into the past, turned too many pages of a hitherto unopened book. But the child had been in need of comfort. You didn't rear a babe from the first hour of its life and not know that. And it had been good to talk about William.

'Drinks are ready. Don't burn your tongue, dear.'

Lucinda smiled and watched the saccharin tablets fizz to the top of her mug. Nursery bedtimes with Ovaltine and Marie biscuits, only tonight the milk had been stealthily left in an outhouse and Marie biscuits were a thing of the past.

'Clean your teeth and brush your hair, child. Fifty strokes. I'll be up by and by to tuck you in.'

Obediently Lucinda climbed the stairs, counting as she went, knowing that tonight Nanny had deliberately turned back the clock for her, wiping out the news of this awful day, making it disappear like a bad dream.

She undressed slowly in the unaccustomed privacy of the little room, folding her clothes into a neat pile on a chair, placing her shoes beneath it. Nursery habits, so easily recalled.

Throwing back the bed clothes she wriggled the stone warmer to the bottom of the bed with her toes. The sheets smelled of lavender, too. Nanny had always picked it from the hedge at the end of the knot garden, waiting exactly for the day the flower buds were about to open, hanging it in bundles to dry in the day nursery. Nanny and Lady Mead and lavender bags. Blowsy Bourbon roses on the south-wing walls; the scent of rain-soaked grass; syrup of figs every Friday night. And the smell of damp rooms when autumn came, and beech logs burning, and the Christmas tree in the hall, eight feet high. Lady Mead. Home and safety.

She closed her eyes and listened to the night sounds; the *kurr-kark* of a pheasant disturbed at its roost, the screech of a hunting owl. There were still tawny owls, then, in Little Hill Spinney.

From the distance a sharp, commanding voice told her that the guard at the main gates was being changed. Funny, that; a guard at Lady Mead, and the little gate lodge a guardroom now.

Tonight, it was all right. She was home and safe and a child again, and Nanny would be next door, if she had a bad dream. Tonight, nothing could harm her, nor Mike, but in the morning the war would be back and nothing could keep it from her, not even the great thick walls of Nanny's love.

William Jones. He'd been there all the time in a special, secret corner of Nanny's heart and she had never known it. He was still there, but the pain of him had gone and only summer-scented days at a house called Southquays remained.

And how will it be for me, if Mike doesn't come back? How will I accept the injustice of it, learn to live with the loneliness? Will I ever stand at a graveside and make that final act of surrender, give him back to a July evening of long ago?

She closed her eyes and banished a tomorrow where up in heaven the Books of Life would be opened once more, to see whose day this would be; opened as they had been

528

on the day of that last Somme battle and the name of William Jones touched by the finger of death.

And she banished the morning three days hence, when she would take the train to Manchester and from there to Glasgow, where Vi would be waiting, and Jane. And they would take the last ferry to Craigiebur and she would tell them of her fears for Mike, and they would understand.

Lucinda made her bed, tucked her folded nightgown beneath the pillow and put away yesterday's clothes, and when she pushed open the door of a gently warm kitchen, Nanny put down the paper she was reading, laid her spectacles on the table and raised her cheek to be kissed.

'Did you sleep well?'

Guiltily, Lucinda realized she had, recalling that the last thing she remembered was a feeling of sympathy for the guard who would tramp up and down in the cold at Lady Mead's gates.

It surprised her that she ate her breakfast with enjoyment. 'This isn't a shop egg,' she murmured, eyebrow raised quizzically, dipping a finger of bread into the bright yellow yolk.

'No, dear.' Neither explanation nor apology was offered for the off-ration egg. 'The hens are coming out of the moult now and starting to lay again,' was all that was offered on the subject. 'Are you going up to the house this morning?' she demanded, eyeing Lucinda's trousers and thick blue jumper.

'Yes. As soon as I'm finished. I'll take my paybook with me.'

Everyone was required to carry identification now; for civilians, a card printed with name, address and number – the number that made her feel like a felon, Nanny said; the number that must be written on all ration books and quoted on all official correspondence. Lucinda wondered how far she would get without being stopped. It would be good to go back to the old house. She wished Mike could have been with her, but Mike was –

She dug in her spoon and scraped out the last of the egg. She would *not* give in. She would be like Farley's wife and stubbornly hold out, even against officialdom. Mike would be all right. In a month, a year, two years, even, he would come back to her. Like Jane, like Mrs Farley, like a hundred thousand other women, she would wish her man safe and will him back.

There would be nowhere now, she realized, to send her letters, but she would write to Mike each day; a diary it would be, even though diaries were forbidden to all those in the armed forces. Letters to a lost lover, more like, and when he came back she would give them to him. And the first page would be written tonight.

Wednesday, 11 March 1942. Mike, my own darling, Yesterday I came home to Lady Mead . . .

Hands in pockets, just for the hell of it, Lucinda set out across the parkland. She wondered how many of the old staff were left and if she would see them. Skirting the drying green, she walked through the kitchen garden and even though it was in obvious neglect, her pleasure was intense. In the corner to her right, the one sloe bush frothed white, a sure sign that winter was in retreat, though none of the fruit trees trained round the high brick walls had blossomed yet; not even the early plum.

She walked on towards the greenhouses and cold frames and the bed where asparagus once grew. The greenhouses were empty, save for a line of Air-Force blue shirts pegged out to dry in the peach house, and dead, rotted weeds filled the cold frames.

The dovecot outside the estate yard gate was empty, too, but the estate offices were alive and from each came the tapping of typewriters and the familiar *chack-chacking* of a teleprinter.

She was enjoying this incursion; wondering how far she could get without challenge. A girl in the uniform of an aircraftwoman walked past her; a face appeared at a window, then was gone. It was as if, Lucinda frowned, she were completely invisible, an aura from the past.

The outer yard was filled with transports of all sizes parked in precise lines, and she walked through the stableyard, where cars were garaged now. Most of them were painted over in the familiar drab colours of camouflage; only one, a bright red sports car, defied convention.

Someone *must* stop her soon, she thought, leaving by the ten-feet-high wide-open gates and joining the main drive that curved round to the front steps. She knew exactly how many steps, for it was there, as a little girl, that she had learned to count from one to fifteen.

Without quite knowing why, she turned round, then realized that she had opened and closed four sets of gates, surprised that here at least they appeared to have escaped the iron collector's eye.

The airman who stood guard at the front door came to attention but did not challenge her.

'Good morning.' She smiled. 'I'd like to see Group Captain Wilson if he isn't too busy.'

'Name, ma'am?' said the airman.

'Bainbridge, L. V.' The reply came automatically. 'I – I mean Lucinda Bainbridge.' She laughed. 'I'm staying at the Dower House. I'd be very grateful if you could get a message to him.'

There was no need. A smiling group captain opened the door; the guard stamped his foot again. It seemed that her progress had been monitored from the moment she set foot on the drying green. She was glad she was not in uniform. Had she been, she would have been obliged to

531

salute him, and it was obvious from his manner that he would not have expected it.

'Lady Lucinda! Good morning!' He held out his hand, smiling broadly.

'Good morning, sir.' She returned the greeting, deferring to his rank. She liked the middle-aged, balding man at once, even though she would have preferred a less effusive welcome. 'I hope I haven't disturbed you. I wondered if I could get something from the basement? Don't want to be a nuisance, but – '

'No trouble at all,' he said, closing the doors behind them. 'I was warned you might come.'

Lucinda looked around her. To her left was the library; to her right the formal withdrawing room, doors closed.

'Feeling strange, Lady Lucinda? How long is it?'

'Two years. Everything's the same, yet different.'

'I know. Hollow and empty-sounding. The library is still a library,' he said, reading her thoughts, 'and the room opposite has been made into an office. But the dining room is still a dining room – well, mess, actually and the salon is used as an addition to it.'

'And the tapestry room?' Lucinda wanted to know. 'Oh, perhaps you don't know that room. We took the tapestries down,' she added hastily. 'They're stored down at the Dower and we're keeping our fingers crossed that they'll be all right.'

'That room is usually locked, Lady Lucinda. We keep secret and confidential files and the like in there. Apart from that, you can go anywhere you like on this floor and in the basement, though upstairs is all sleeping quarters. I'm afraid you'd see some dreadful apparitions if you strayed up there.'

'You're very kind and I do appreciate your letting me come. I only want a few civilian clothes. I'm almost sure I can lay hands on them pretty quickly.'

'Take all the time you want. No trouble. Just let someone know when you're leaving, will you? Oh, and we do use the chapel. All the time.'

He was going out of his way to be helpful and she was grateful; grateful for understanding her concern for the house and explaining the way things were; glad beyond measure that prayers were still said in the chapel.

'Could I,' she asked, 'have a quick peep in there before I go?' For no reason that she could think of, it seemed important that she should.

'Of course.' He smiled. 'I don't have to tell you where it is.'

Alone again, she stood for a moment, wanting the house to know she was back, filling her senses with the smell and the feel of it. Then quickly she crossed the hall, its marble floor covered with protecting hardboard, passed the salon doors and the entrance to the dining room, then slipped down the basement stairs, as easy and relaxed as though the years between could be counted in days and she was a little girl again, creeping down to the servants' hall to share a plate of buttered currant bread and a cup of tea from cook's brown pot.

But the servants' hall was a sergeants' mess now – it said so, on the door – and the room next to it, the butler's pantry, was double-padlocked because the silver lay there, tarnishing to black.

A smell of cooking wafted through the open kitchen doors: a mixing of new-baked bread and the savoury odour of meat and onion stew. A tall young man wearing a long white apron looked out at her passing and whistled and called, 'Hullo, darling. You looking for me?'

'Sorry.' Lucinda grinned.

'Me too,' said the cook, with a wink.

Still smiling, she opened the still-room door, glad there was a cheeky RAF cook in the kitchen, glad the group captain had thought it was important she should know about the chapel.

They had been able to bargain for the use of the lamp room, the still room and the housekeeper's sitting room, Lucinda recalled, pressing down a switch and filling the room with light.

The cabin trunk was easily recognized. Taking the bunch of small keys from her pocket, she selected the one she thought might fit and was instantly rewarded.

The contents had been carefully packed between layers of tissue paper and she removed them to reveal, almost at once, a coat which appeared to be exactly the one she sought. Of brown and green tweed, and silk-lined, its collar was thick with fur, and its matching skirt lay beneath it.

'Good,' she breathed. And hadn't Nanny wanted coat linings, and surely somewhere she would find a skirt for Vi and a blouse and cardigan, maybe?

Her search uncovered long-forgotten things. The black cocktail dress, stained by a spilled gin and orange; a pleated white dress with a sailor collar. She had been wearing it the day they learned they were at war. They'd been expecting the war for almost a year, yet its coming was met with shock and dismay. And here was the apricot satin bridesmaid's dress she had worn to Cynthia Stewart's wedding and the wreath of rosebuds, crushed flat now.

Charlie had got very drunk at the dance afterwards and, nose in air, she had completely ignored him and partnered someone else all night – which must have pleased Charlie no end, come to think of it, because tipsy or sober, Charlie hated to dance.

She spent a long time remembering, and forgot the war and the blackout and Ardneavie and Morse code pinging in her ears. She even forgot, for a little while, that Mike was missing, now.

Then through the window, although she could not see them, came the crunch of marching feet, and the war was back again. Sighing, she blew the dust from an empty case; carefully she folded into it the clothes she had chosen, repacking the trunk, replacing the layers of paper. Perhaps in June she would come here again. She hoped so, but it didn't do to make plans. One day at a time was how it must be.

She rose to her feet, unwilling to leave. From the kitchen came a gust of bawdy laughter; someone was telling a risqué joke, perhaps, or teasing an aircraftwoman and making her blush. But she had already stayed too long. This house was no longer her home; it never would be, now. When the war was over, when the Air Force gave it back, Pa's agent would take stock of things and get someone in to tidy it up and decorate the worst-used rooms, maybe. And doubtless Charlie would be with him, because one day all this would be his and the least he could do would be to care a little about his inheritance, she thought, strangely sad.

But nothing really mattered now; only that Mike should be safe. Still alive, she supposed she meant, though just to think the words sent despair tearing through her.

Brushing the dust from the knees of her trousers, she pushed the cabin trunk aside, looking at the *Queen Mary* labels, realizing that Mama had been on that wonderful maiden voyage. And now the *Mary*, as that liner was affectionately called, and the *Lizzie*, her equally loved sister ship, sailed alone across the Atlantic and the Pacific and the Indian Ocean; unescorted, scornful of submarines, setting a zig-zagging course that confounded all predators. She had seen them often in Garvie Sound, tiny with distance, taking on troops. And she always sent them her love and wished them godspeed and a safe landfall. One moment, those great ships would be there for all to see; the next, they were gone, defiantly alone. They had upped anchor and left; like saucy old tarts, two fingers cocked at U-boat commanders who ached to sink them. Yet for all that, those war-soiled, rust-caked troopships remained the queens they were and *ours*, built proudly on the Clyde. And one day they would be liners again, and maybe she and Mike would cross the Atlantic in one of them.

She left the suitcase in the alcove at the top of the basement stairs, then crossed the hall again, walking past the foot of the main staircase, past the tapestry room, the study and the snug little boudoir the Countess had claimed as her own. Milady's sulking room, the servants had called it, and in truth they hadn't been far wrong.

The ornately carved doors of the chapel were immediately beyond at the foot of four wide steps. It had been added to the east wing by the third earl whose wife, a secret Catholic, used it exclusively and often.

Gently Lucinda closed the doors behind her and, ignoring the covered family pew at the rear, walked slowly to the altar rail and sank to her knees. Interlocking her fingers, she gazed around her. Beside the font at which she had been christened stood a vase of flowering currant, forced into early blooming by the warmth indoors. At that font one May day, Goddy said, she had cried the devil out of her.

The altar glowed gold with daffodils, gathered from the orchard, no doubt, where the first to break bud could always be found.

The familiar peace of the little chapel touched her, calmed her, wrapped her round like a shawl. Here was sanctuary; here, if anywhere, prayers would be answered.

'Keep him safely,' she implored the doe-eyed Virgin on the altar triptych. 'Bring him home, and Gerry and Rob

536

and Farley.' The Virgin had lost her son; she would understand. 'And let this war soon end.'

She knelt there for a long time, unwilling to leave the safety of Lady Mead, reluctant to step forward in time again, into the real world. And when she did, she would leave behind her an anguished prayer; leave it at the feet of the doe-eyed Virgin.

At the doors, she turned, fixing the altar with anxious eyes. 'Please,' she whispered. '*Please.*'

The large parcel arrived at the little house in Ormskirk just as Vi, hands black with coal dust, poked her head round the kitchen door and wailed, 'How is it when I'm up to the elbows in muck, that me nose starts to itch?'

Mary produced a handkerchief, banished the tickle, then gasped, 'Look! Postmarked Grantham. It's come, Vi!'

'Ar.' Vi rinsed her hands in the rainwater tub beside the door. 'Told you she'd send one, didn't I? Come on then, girl; get it opened.'

Maddeningly, Mary unpicked each knot, winding the string into a skein around her fingers because even string was in short supply. Then carefully she removed the brown paper wrapping.

It had been packed in a cardboard box bearing the name of a Bond Street shop; a box, Mary vowed as she eased off the lid, that she would never throw away.

'Aaaah, look . . .' She removed the protective tissue paper and it rustled deliciously as it floated to the floor. 'Oh, my,' she sighed, shaking out the folds. 'Vi, it's beautiful.' She caressed the beige silk lining with trembling fingertips, buried her face in the sensuous fur of the collar. 'And there's a skirt to match. Heaven help us, whatever will the neighbours say when they see me in these?'

537

'They'll think you're on the game.' Vi grinned.

'Let them!' Mary eased on the coat, fastening it carefully. 'Even the buttons must've cost the earth.' She walked into the sitting room, turning this way and that before the mantelpiece mirror. 'I'll write and thank her straight away. What do I call her? Your ladyship? Lady Bainbridge?'

'Nah,' Vi murmured, her eyes on the hemline. 'Lucinda, that's who she is. Doesn't go a lot on that ladyshippin' lark. You know what, our Mary, the length's just right. That coat might have been made for you.'

'You can take the letter with you tomorrow, can't you? And there must be something I can give her, something I can do for her?'

'She wouldn't want anything – only them five coupons for me. She'd be real pleased if you wrote to her, though.' Mary was good at letter-writing. Mary had been born with more than her fair share of brains and had won a scholarship to the Catholic high school; she'd been a clerk with a monthly salary, not a wage. She'd got that job, Vi decided, because the nuns had learned her to talk proper; learned her to talk like a fruit, she supposed. Very ladylike, Mary had turned out to be. 'Lucinda'll be dead chuffed that you like the coat.'

'*Like* it?' Mary Reilly had never had such a coat. She closed her eyes blissfully and pulled the collar round her ears. 'Oh, I hope,' she whispered from the deeps of its furry softness, 'that it snows tomorrow.'

'Well then, if you've finished preenin' and paradin', maybe you could come outside and take a look at all the coal balls I've made,' Vi demanded. 'Are you sure they'll dry hard, all right?'

'They'll be fine.' Like most housewives, Mary was an authority on coal balls. 'Thanks a lot, sis. It's a dirty old job.'

A very dirty job. Before the war, no woman had thought she would find a use for a bucket of coal dust, but one part of coal dust mixed with two parts of sawdust, a few well-rotted leaves and a couple of handfuls of cement – if you'd been lucky enough to find the cement, of course – was a welcome addition to the meagre coal ration and well worth the mess and bother.

An old bucket, well holed in the bottom to allow drainage, was essential – and a stout stick for stirring. Then the unlikely mixture would be carefully dampened, formed by hand into balls and laid out to dry. Hoarded with care against a day when fuel stocks were running low, they would be placed on top of the fire to blaze as brightly as coal, almost.

Better than coal, said some, though the fine white ash they left behind them made a dusty mess if not handled with care. But coal balls, briquettes the higher-class ladies liked to call them, were there for the duration, dirty hands or no.

'There you are then,' Mary said that evening, when her children were asleep and they sat down to share a pot of tea. 'Five of the best, and no clothing coupons more willingly parted with.' She laid down the scissors, with a gaze akin to pity at the solitary coupon remaining. 'Well, that's the last one until the first of July.' She sighed. 'What can I do, will you tell me, with *one*?'

'How about some wool?' Vi suggested. 'Well, you did say you'd like to do something for Lucinda, didn't you? Not that she'd expect it, mind, but two ounces of navy-blue wool would be enough for a pair of gloves, wouldn't it?' Mary was a good knitter, always had been. Mary was good at everything; not only in producing two children, but in making sure she had one of each.

'I'll do that, if you're sure it's what she'd like.' Mary blushed with pleasure.

'Same size as you, I should think.' Vi frowned. 'And I know she'd like it.' For all she was out of the top drawer, so to speak, Lucinda was delighted almost to tears by small kindnesses. 'And Mary, when you write to her, tell her you'll remember her in your prayers, will you? She'd like that, an' all.'

She'd need them, too; need all the prayers she could collect, poor kid, if what the papers said was true.

But she would see for herself tomorrow how things were. Vi sighed. By the heck, but they were having a bad time of it, those two of hers. Still, she'd be with them again soon. Come to think of it, she could hardly wait to get back to them.

Jane and Vi were already waiting beside the bench at the top end of platform 8 when Lucinda's train pulled into the station at Glasgow. Her face was drawn, her eyes dark-circled. She ran to them, arms outstretched, and her hug of greeting was too warm, her eyes too bright. Nor did she say 'Hi!' or ask if they'd had a good leave, or even use the customary teasing phrase, *You've had it, chum*, which was what people always said when a leave was over.

'Look,' she whispered, instead. 'Can we not talk about – anything? Not just yet?' Mutely her eyes begged their understanding.

'All right, queen,' Vi said gently. 'But don't forget that we've still got each other, eh? It's still all for one . . .'

They were together again. It wouldn't free Gerry or bring Rob back or let Lucinda forget about Rangoon, but it would make it bearable.

The Garvie train had left on time, as it sometimes did, now that the bombing had lessened and the railways were

540

repairing damaged tracks and stations. Now the three friends sat in the little saloon of the Clyde ferry and shared what was left of their sandwiches.

'I've an invitation from Nanny. She'd like you both to spend your next leave with her,' Lucinda said, just as a blast from the siren told them they were approaching Craigiebur Pier. 'Sleeping might be a bit of a problem, but we'd manage. I'd like it awfully if you would.'

'I'd like it too,' Jane acknowledged, wiping crumbs from her skirt. Though she was loath to admit it, her leave had not been a success, exactly. Her mother had praised Colin from morning till night and her father's extra duties had prevented her from seeing as much of him as she would have liked. She had resented her mother's meddling, and even if she had never met Rob, Jane brooded, she wouldn't have wanted to be seen out on dates with Colin Clayton, who was, after all, a civilian – and young, fit men of twenty-two who were civilians were as bad, almost, as a conscientious objector, and nobody would be seen dead with a conchy. 'I'd like it a lot. I've had it up to here' – she placed her hand dramatically beneath her chin – 'with Fenton Bishop.'

'That's settled, then.' Vi smiled, glad that Lucinda had found her tongue and managed to string a sentence together. 'Lincolnshire it'll be then, in June.'

'And you won't mind if Nanny fusses a bit, and calls you "child"?'

Jane grimaced. 'She couldn't be worse than my mother.'

They gathered their luggage together and made for the upper deck. Craigiebur seemed more and more like home to them now, and the submarine and escort that passed them in the distance, familiar friends.

'One of our lot, going on patrol,' Vi murmured, mindful that bulkheads had ears. 'Wonder which one it is.'

'It's an S-boat, that's for sure.' Jane screwed up her eyes.

'It's *Sparta*,' Lucinda said quietly. She knew every submarine in the flotilla and where each one was. She felt responsible for them, lying miles away, yet no farther from her than the fingertips of her right hand.

The ferry came alongside smoothly, as all Clyde ferryboats did, and the gangway clattered down.

'Any more of our lot to come?' asked the driver of the Ardneavie transport.

'Didn't see anyone on the ferry.' Vi threw her case in the back then heaved herself up. She'd be glad to see Ardneavie again. Until this war was over, Ardneavie House was her home and Jane and Lucinda her family. There were worse places to be. A prisoner-of-war camp in Austria, for instance, though Gerry's last letter had been cheerful enough. But Vi had refrained from mentioning it. No one with a grain of sense in her head talked about prisoners of war to a girl whose man might even now be in the same position. If he were lucky, that was.

'Look!' Jane pointed to another submarine, smaller than *Sparta*, that lay off, waiting for the boom tugs to drag aside the steel-mesh nets that protected the mouth of Loch Ardneavie. 'There's one, waiting to come in. What is it – a U-class or one of the Vs?'

'It's a V-boat, I think, though I can't be sure in this light.' In spite of double summertime, the March night was drawing in. 'Wonder if it's – if – ' Lucinda stopped, her eyes on Jane's face.

'If it's *Viper*'s replacement?' Jane finished. 'It could be.'

Jane still thought about Tom Tavey, still regretted they had parted in anger. Truth known, she was sad that she couldn't have loved him as he'd loved and wanted her, but she would always remember him, and wonder what might have been had she never met Rob.

542

But Rob MacDonald was fact, and he was alive, too. Every instinct told her he was; every aching beat of her heart made her more and more certain.

They came to a stop in the lane outside the gates of Ardneavie House and the driver jumped out and ran to the back of the transport to let down the tailboard.

'That's it, then.' She grinned. 'You've had it, girls. Welcome back to the Bastille.'

They set down their cases inside the familiar old house, stopping only to take down the *On leave* discs that had hung beneath each of their nameplates for a week, replacing them with ones bearing the words *In quarters*.

It was Vi who first saw the letter, recognized the familiar pale blue of the air-mail lettercard. Reluctantly she handed it to Lucinda.

'One for you, queen,' she whispered, eyes sad.

'Thanks.' The letter with Mike's writing on the front bore a date two weeks old and consisted of only a few words.

Lucy, my darling, I love you, love you, love you. Wait for me. M.

'Well,' she said shakily, 'the guy still loves me.' Lips set tightly to stop their trembling, she folded the sheet of paper back into four again. It had been written in haste, she knew; a last outpouring of his love. Without thinking, she turned it over and what she saw there made her draw sharply on her breath.

Written on the reverse side was the number of the letter. It was thirteen.

On the signal deck of HMS *Omega*, Chief Telegraphist Wetherby breathed in the night air and gazed, eyes narrowed, around the loch, taking stock, making a final check.

'So that's *Sparta* under way,' he said, half to himself, watching the flashing Aldis lamp of the submarine that had just entered the loch.

'What's he making?' he demanded of the signalman at his side.

'It's in plain language, Chief.' The signalman read the message. 'He's asking permission to come alongside.'

'And who is *he*?' demanded the elderly telegraphist, a stickler, as always, for correct procedure.

'It's the *Virgil*, Chief. It'll be *Viper*'s replacement, then.'

'*Virgil*, is it?' Walter Wetherby chuckled. 'There's going to be some fun with that one, if you see what I mean.'

The signalman saw exactly, and grinned. It wouldn't be long before the new submarine was known as the *Virgin*; the only virgin, so talk would insist, in the whole of the 15th Flotilla!

Chief Wetherby blew down the voice pipe. 'Submarine *Virgil* requests permission to come alongside,' he intoned, then settled down comfortably, elbows on the guard rail, to see if the new skipper knew his stuff and how efficiently he'd bring his boat in. And then he stiffened and looked again, and frowned.

'*Virgil* my arse,' he hissed, the corners of his mouth turned down. '*Virgil*, did you say, lad? That thing out there is the *Viper*, if you ask me. I'd bet a week's tots on it!'

It was *Viper*, he was sure of it. Coffin to thirty-nine men it had been. They'd brought it to the surface too late, then sent it back to the yard that built it – and that should have been the last they saw of it. *Viper* was already bad luck, without slinking back with another name and pendant number on it; renaming the thing only added to the jinx it carried with it.

'For God's sake, whatever possessed that lot at the

Admiralty to send the bloody thing back here? Out of their tiny minds, were they?'

Jaw set tight as a trap, he turned and slammed down the ladder, pushing open the CCO door with unnecessary force. Walter Wetherby was an old sailor and superstitious as they came, and *Viper* was back with its ill luck clinging to it like a bad smell.

Viper, *Virgil*, call it what you would – it could only mean one thing. Trouble.

23

'I'm goin' downstairs now.' Vi buttoned her overall and looked meaningfully at her watch. 'You two've got five minutes.'

'Okay. We'll be down.' Jane knotted her tie and tugged it straight. This was the worst part of early watch; the five-fifteen alarm, the warmth of the bed she was reluctant to leave; then tea and toast, still only half awake. But the mornings were lighter now, the cold less intense, and soon it would be April.

In the mess, the first news bulletin of the day came over the speaker. Teapot in hand, Vi glared at it, willing it to be quiet.

The communiqué from Burma was not good. Fighting was still going on in the north, and what the hell did they mean, orderly retreat? Lucinda let go her knife with a clatter then picked it up again, resolving to go through the motions of eating.

'Chin up,' Jane urged as they walked down the jetty. 'You're not alone, love. There's plenty more like us.'

'I know, but it doesn't seem to help. What am I to do? The shaking inside me won't stop. It was fine when I was on leave; I could shut it out. But the minute I put on my uniform, the war was back and I was on my own again.'

'Didn't I just tell you you're not on your own?'

'You did. But how do you take it? Me – I could throw up every time I think about it.'

And so could I, Lucinda, even now. 'Suppose I've had time to get used to it,' she said instead, turning up the collar of her greatcoat as an unexpected coldness took her. 'That shaking inside you, that – *crawling*; I know what it's like. It was with me every time Rob was flying. The night he went missing I hated the world. I wanted to die.' Briefly she touched the arm of her friend. 'Give it time. You'll learn to live with it. I have, almost. Vi did.'

'How, for God's sake? It's the not knowing. What do I do?'

Jane glanced sideways at the distraught face. She had never seen Lucinda like this before but, so far at least, no one had had the need to – She shut down her thoughts, feeling again the pain of her father's hand on her cheek. Blocking out the memory of it, she said, 'Do? Well, first you stop bashing your head against a wall – it's marvellous, when you do – and then you get a letter off to Mike's family. When there's news about him it'll be sent to Vermont, not to you, remember. And at least you had the sense to get his address.'

'And when I've done that, then what?' Lucinda persisted.

'Then you wait and hope and pray, and you never stop loving him. Not for a minute do you stop.'

'And how long before I learn to live with it, before I accept?'

'Ah now, there you have me, because you never wholly accept it. The truth can be staring you in the face, and still you hope. And if I'm honest, I don't think I'll ever quite learn to live without Rob. It's like having a nagging tooth – bearable, if you don't dwell on it too much.'

'Hell! I'm an insensitive brat! You make me feel ashamed.' Tears so readily there of late came to her eyes and impatiently she dashed them away. 'You can't ever have Rob; there isn't a hope for the two of you, yet still you go on loving him.'

'Yes, I do. But you don't choose who you love.' Jane shrugged. 'It isn't something you can turn off, either. So

547

Rob's married? Phemie's baby will be six months old, now – I've learned to accept that, too. But one thing I'm sure of: Rob isn't dead. I'd know if he were. I think of it all the time – the day I'll meet him again, I mean. Sometime, I don't know when or where, it'll happen. That's what keeps me going; the corner I'll turn one day, to see him there.'

'Will you tell me then,' said Molly, who had followed their progress from the quarterdeck, 'what it is that's so interesting? There's the pair of you going at it like it's state secrets you're swopping.'

Jane raised an eyebrow. 'What do you think?'

'At a guess, darlin', I'd say it was fellers.'

'At a guess, you'd be right,' Jane murmured, her eyes warning off their inquisitive friend. 'What else is there to talk about?'

The central communications office had not changed in the span of a week. It still carried a stale, dusty smell; still reeked of metal polish and floor polish and well-stewed tea.

'What's new?' Lucinda adjusted her headset and settled it over her ears.

'Not a lot. *Sparta*'s out on patrol, and *Skua*.' Lofty offered his cigarette packet, as he always did. 'And the new submarine arrived last night.'

'Yes. I saw it waiting to come in.' Lucinda flicked her lighter. '*Viper*'s replacement.'

'That's the one. *Virgil*.'

'Oooh!' The old mischief showed briefly in Lucinda's eyes. 'The mind boggles!'

'Oh, aye. They'll have a bit of fun with that one – till they find out what it was. I suppose you know it's *Viper*, back again?'

'*Viper*?' At once there was a pricking at the back of Lucinda's nose. 'Was that wise of them, do you think?'

'Chiefie said much the same thing.' Lofty grinned. 'Only he didn't put it quite so delicately. The old boy's playing merry hell about it.'

'Hullo, there! Missed me?' Jane took off her jacket and draped it over the back of her chair.

'Och, here's the bane of my life back again!' Jock Menzies groaned. 'Had a good leave, hen?'

'Marvellous.' So she told lies, sometimes. 'Been busy?'

'So-so. By the way, the new one's arrived. The buzz has it they'll be doing speed trials today and target shoots tomorrow, off Ailsa Craig. They already did their deep dives down south, at *Dolphin*, it seems. But that would make sense, wouldn't it, after what happened last time.'

'Last time?' Jane inserted a carbon sheet in her message pad. 'Not quite with you, Jock.'

'Then you'll no' have heard?' Damn it! He'd been sure she'd know by now. '*Virgil*'s the new name for –'

'For *Viper*,' Jane finished dully. Oh, please, not that one back!

'Aye, and a deal of trouble it'll bring with it, I shouldn't wonder.' She'd taken it better than he'd thought and he sighed silent relief as the first signal of their watch slammed down on the desk between them. 'We're in business, lassie.'

'Fine!' Tom's boat back! *I'm sorry, so very sorry, Tom. I never meant to hurt you and I shouldn't have said what I did.* 'K-tables?' Why had she gone so cold? Why had something just crawled over her grave? Leave me be, Tom. Please go away.

The good thing about early watch was that it allowed time for shopping and evenings free for dates and dancing, and

549

the three made straight for Craigiebur, Vi's precious five coupons safe in her pocket.

'I think,' she said wearily as they paused outside the shoe shop, 'that it might be a good idea to go mad and have a meal at the British Restaurant – save us goin' back to Ardneavie, wouldn't it? Then maybe we could go to the pictures afterwards. Have we got enough, between us?'

An emptying of money belts established that they had; but first, the shoes.

'I said, didn't I, that eights were goin' to take a bit of finding.' Vi sighed as they pushed open their third and last shoe-shop door. 'Even in a place the size of Liverpool, they're hard to come by.'

Why couldn't she take a five, like most other women, or even size four, like Mary? 'Size *eight*?' a cheeky shop assistant once said. 'Ever thought of trying Cammell-Laird's, missis?'

'Size eight?' frowned the elderly assistant in the last-hope shop. 'I'm afraid there isn't a lot of call for us to stock that size.' Then miraculously he smiled. 'A walking shoe, did you say? Perhaps there *is* something.' He nodded, bending down behind the counter. 'Pre-war quality, but only a seven, I'm afraid.'

The shoe was in softest brown suede, supple enough to be bent almost double and at a greatly reduced price, the assistant told her, since there wasn't a great demand for suede these days. A good match, too, Vi thought longingly, for the pleated skirt and cardigan Lucinda had given her.

'You could try them,' Jane suggested.

'I could,' Vi mourned, fingering them lovingly. They were indeed beautiful shoes: hand stitched, with a tongue that flapped over the lace-holes. 'I suppose I could.'

The assistant eased them on with a shoe-horn then tied

550

the laces and arranged the tongues. 'There now.' He smiled, rubbing a thumb across the fronts. 'Is there room for madam's toes?'

There was room and to spare for madam's toes, and she rose to her feet and sailed back and forth along the strip of carpet especially provided for the purpose.

'*They fit,*' Vi breathed. 'They fit like slippers!' But there had to be a catch. 'How much?' she demanded warily, and when he told her she took two ten-shilling notes and the five coupons from her pocket and handed them to him with something akin to disbelief.

The shop assistant smiled, tied string around the shoe-box, made a little hoop with the ends to slip over her finger, then handed her five shillings and a penny in change.

'A pleasure.' He smiled, opening the door. The brown suede shoes had lain there for a long, long time; he was well-content to be five coupons in hand, and where had been the need, he demanded of his conscience, to tell the lady they were men's shoes?

Vi gazed at her change. 'This night out is on me,' she breathed joyfully, 'and no arguin'.'

Only a size seven. There were times, she exulted, when your cup ran over, and this was surely one of them. Cammell-Laird's shipyard, indeed!

'Sevens,' she breathed joyfully. 'Well, how about that, then?'

They ate their supper in the Spartan environs of the government-sponsored British Restaurant in Craigiebur.

'Not exactly your Adelphi Hotel,' Vi observed. The floor was bare, the table tops clothless, but the food was hot and cheap. And where else could a body eat soup, shepherd's pie and carrots, and fruit tart to follow, and

551

still have tuppence change from a shilling? And afterwards, at the picture house, after paying for seats in the ninepennies, Vi was still fourpence in hand on the shoeshop change.

Still glowing inside her, she hugged her size-seven bargain to her in the darkness, and Spencer Tracy had smiled lovingly down on her euphoria.

'That was a smashin' run ashore,' she sighed, as they undressed for bed; though she would be the first to admit that whilst Lucinda hadn't been quiet, exactly, she had lacked her usual sparkle. The darting, dazzling smile was seldom seen now, the dimples never, but that was understandable since most of her was in Burma, with Mike. Mother of God, but this was a pig of a war, she thought. It didn't do to be too happy. Them up there got narked if you did. 'Who are you writing to, queen? Mike's mam, is it?'

'No.' Lucinda looked up. 'This one's for Mike. Oh, I know I can't post it, but I write to him every day – just a few lines – and when he comes home, he can read the lot.'

'You will get in touch with Mike's folks, though?' Jane pressed. 'You said you would.'

'And I will, though I'm not at all sure what to say. I'm certain they know about me, but I'll have to be careful. After all, Mike's family might want him to marry someone else; they mightn't take very kindly to me. Mama wasn't a bit pleased, was she, when I told her about Mike?'

'Don't you want to get in touch with Vermont, then?' Vi demanded, perplexed.

'Of course I do.'

'Then get writin', queen. If I had a son and he brought home a girl like you, I'd be dead chuffed.'

A small smile touched Lucinda's lips. Of course she would write to Mike's mother. At the worst she could ignore the letter and at the best she just might be dead chuffed to receive it.

'I'll write tomorrow.'

'You know what they say about tomorrow.'

'I'll write. I promise.' She shrugged and shook her head. 'Promises. So easy, aren't they? Mike promised to take care.'

'And he will.' Jane rolled her hair into pincurls. 'Rob promised never to stop loving me and I think, somehow, that he still does, in spite of what happened. Promises can be very sweet, too.'

'Ar. I know what you mean.' Vi's eyes were tender. 'Gerry promised he'd come back to me, and when that Richie Daly told me he'd seen Gerry's ship blown out of the water, I thought that promises were easy made and just as easy broken. But he made it, didn't he? Perhaps, when he was in the water and gettin' tired and ready to jack it in, he thought about what he'd promised and it helped him hang on just a little bit longer. And Mike'll do his best to get back to you. I know he will, queen.'

'Yes, and how do you know that he isn't all right?' Jane urged. 'How do you know that when things got hot he wasn't told to get into his Spit and ordered out of there, pretty damn' quick? Don't think the worst.'

'I'm sorry, Kendal dear, but I can't be like you. You're so optimistic I'm afraid for you.'

'Then don't be, because I'll never stop hoping. And there are worse places than Burma, you know. You'd be just as worried if Mike were in Malta. They've had more bombs on them there than the whole of London. And three battered old fighters, that's all they've got. *Three*. Don't give in and don't give up. Don't ever give up!'

Lilith Penrose was not exactly surprised that the petty officer in charge of the party she was taking ashore was

Johnny Jones, or that the seamen in his charge seemed little pleased with their ultimate destination.

'Liverpool,' growled one as he threw his kitbag into the bows of the launch. 'What a lousy dump. What is there in Liverpool, eh?'

'Scousers, for a start,' said the young sailor whose Lancashire twang suggested that the port of Liverpool was nearer home than Loch Ardneavie had ever been.

'You there! Stow that kitbag properly!' Lilith ordered, establishing her authority as coxswain of the launch.

Her eyes jerked up to meet those of Johnny Jones, and she held her stare defiantly so it was he who turned his head away.

So the bastard had copped up a draft chit! A bit of real sea-time, a spell on escort duty in a force-eight would soon knock the bounce out of that one, Lilith reckoned, well content that the 15th Flotilla was seeing the back of him at last. 'Let go for'ard!' she cried.

Megan pushed with her boathook against *Lothian*'s side and the launch swung nose-out into the loch.

'Let go aft!' The seaman at the foot of the gangway coiled the stern rope and tossed it into the launch. The engine kicked and roared then settled down to a steady rhythm.

Another trip across the loch; another of many before her watch ended, but this one was more special than most. This trip, Lilith sighed, satisfied, was the seeing of Johnny Jones on his way – and more the pity he hadn't made it a long time ago.

They came gently alongside Ardneavie jetty. The engine died and Megan leaped across three feet of water to pull in on the bow rope the instant her feet touched the planking.

The seamen filed off, hauling out kitbags; Lilith secured the wheel then stepped on to the jetty.

'Well, well, well,' she murmured. 'Going somewhere, Johnny? Nowhere nice, I hope.'

He looked into her eyes again, this time recognizing the enmity that glinted there. Then he shrugged, his face a blank, remembering the last time they had spoken; on that very spot, almost. Without a word, he walked away.

'Going? To the *Malvern*, that's where,' volunteered the last-off seaman. 'Based in Gladstone friggin' dock. Big deal, eh? Ah, well, cheers, girls. Be seeing you.'

'So-long, lads. Good luck,' Fenny called as they made for the transport that awaited them at the end of the long narrow jetty.

Good luck? Lilith frowned. Those seamen would need it if they stayed with Johnny Jones. She'd put her mark on Johnny; done it with all the hate and venom she could call out of herself, then ripped his likeness into two and burned each piece in the flames of the black candles. That ill-wishing had not been easy, but she had done it, eventually; done it for the girl who left Ardneavie House with a heart that was breaking.

It'll be all right, Connie. Lilith's thoughts flew high and far. Fate would present the account, soon. Payment would be in full. There'd be no way of escaping it, for Johnny.

The end-of-March Wrennery dance was almost over when starboard watch came ashore from late duty. Couples danced the last waltz; others slipped outside to the stables, the boilerhouse, to anywhere dark and warm and private for a last goodnight. The duty steward checked the pantry-window latch, and in the galley, Kathy MacAlister prepared tea and toast for the incoming starboard watch.

'Nearly over.' Vi smiled, joining Jane and Lucinda. 'It's been a good dance, though – what I saw of it. And a parcel came for you, Kendal. I left it on your bed.'

'A parcel? Grab me some toast, Vi. I'll nip upstairs and see what it is.'

She heard the sobbing as she reached the first landing; heard it clearly through a half-open door to her left and, frowning, she listened. Someone whose date had stood her up, perhaps, or had danced too often, too close, with someone else? Or maybe it was bad news from home, or sad news? Whatever the reason, though, weeping like that could not be ignored.

'Who is it?' she asked softly, pushing the door wider. 'It's Jane. Is the blackout all right? I'm putting on the light.'

Sitting on her bed, the girl continued to weep, hands over eyes. 'I'm all right,' she choked. 'Just put the light out and go away.'

'Sorry, chum, but you're not all right.' Jane sat on the bed beside her. 'Would a cup of tea help? Kathy's just made a pot.'

The unfamiliar Wren shook her head vigorously then blew her nose loudly. 'All I want is to be left alone. You can't even have a bit of a weep in private in this place!'

'It didn't sound like a bit of a weep to me,' Jane remarked flatly. 'I heard your crying all the way down the passage. You're new, aren't you? I'm Jane Kendal from CCO starboard watch.'

'Hullo, Jane.' The slight, sandy-haired Wren let go a shuddering sob.

'Want to talk about it?' Jane offered her cigarette packet.

'No. I – I mean no thanks. And there's nothing the matter, really, just – '

'Just a bad dose of homesickness? Don't worry, we've all had it. Most of us got it over with in training depot.'

'Oh, training depot was fine.' The new girl gathered her handkerchief into a ball and clasped it tightly. 'I joined up

556

at Plymouth, you see, not so very far from home, and it wasn't till they drafted me up here, such a long way away, that it hit me. I miss my family. I want my mother.'

'How old are you?' Jane placed a caring arm round the drooping, defeated shoulders.

'I'll be eighteen in August. And the awful thing about it is that I wanted to join up. Now, I just want to go home.'

'Back to Devon?' It was easy to place her. 'Where, in Devon?'

'Oh, you won't have heard of it. You could pass through it and never notice the place. But it's home . . .'

'And does that little place have old houses with thick walls and thatched roofs? And fireplaces so big you could burn a tree trunk in them?' She closed her eyes, remembering Tom, speaking his words. 'Is it such a little village that you'd never find it unless you'd been born there and are there lanes full of flowers; lanes so narrow that two carts can't pass in them? And peaceful is it, my lovely?'

'Yes. That could be my village.' Another sniff, another shuddering sigh.

'It's Abbots Dart. Have you heard of it?'

'Course I have. Not all that far from me. You've been there, Jane?'

'No, but someone I know – someone I *knew* – lived there. He was a farmer. He loved Devon, too.'

He's there now. They sent him back to Abbots Dart in a flag-draped coffin. And I thought I could forget him, but I can't, because I told him to go to hell . . .

'Well, now. It's a small world, isn't it? Only five miles away, Abbots Dart is, though I don't know anybody from there. It's like that, with villages.'

'I know. I come from one too.' From a village where everyone knew their own and all others were foreigners. And if this war hadn't happened, she thought, a village girl like me would have known who she would marry, because with luck she might just have had a choice between two boys she grew up with.

'Then you'll know how much I'm missing home.'

'Yes, I do.' But I don't want to go back to Fenton Bishop, she realized. I've broken free, and when this war is over I don't want to live there again. I knew too much happiness there, and lost it. 'But if you won't come downstairs, how about giving your face a splash? You'll have puffy eyes in the morning if you don't. It won't be long before you'll be going on leave, and things won't seem half so bad by then. Truly they won't – so cheer up.'

'I'll try. And thanks for listening and talking to me about home. I'll be fine now.'

'Goodnight, then.' Jane turned, hand on door. 'You'll be all right soon, I promise.' Of course you will, but I won't be, she thought. I can't cry out of me what I said to Tom, where I wished him. And now *Viper* is back, to remind me. 'Sleep well.'

'And where the 'eck have you been?' Vi demanded when Jane rejoined standeasy. 'The toast's all gone and your tea's cold and –'

'There was a new girl having a little weep – but she'll be all right, now,' Jane explained. 'And if anyone is interested in my parcel, it's a box of chocolates from Australia.'

'Got relations there?' People with family overseas counted themselves the fortunate ones; the ones who received food parcels. Throughout the Dominions it was feared that people in Britain were dangerously near to starvation, and even though many of the parcels never arrived, they still felt it their duty to send what they could to the folks at home.

'Yes, my mum's sister. She sends things all the time.

There were chocolates in the last one, especially for me. We'll eat them tomorrow.'

'Eat what?' Lilith joined them, picking up the teapot. 'And I've been meaning to tell you about Johnny Jones. Did you know he'd gone? Got a draft chit to Liverpool a couple of days back. To the *Malvern*, I believe, and good riddance, say I.'

'The *Malvern*?' Vi frowned. 'I saw that one, last time I was home. A destroyer, I think it was. There's an overhead railway in Liverpool, see. Runs right through the docks from the north end to the south end. You can sit on that train and see every ship that's in port and most of those in the river, too. Smashin' if you're a German spy . . .'

'Well, Liverpool is where they've sent him. Don't suppose it'll be long before he's got his feet under somebody's table there.' Lilith sniffed. 'That one'd fill his boots wherever he went.'

'Ar, I wouldn't say that, exactly,' Vi counselled gloomily. 'The *Malvern*'s with a destroyer pack that's on convoy escort duty, see. Used to do the Atlantic run, but it's not so good for them now.'

'What do you mean?' Lilith's head shot up. 'The draft I ran ashore were going to Gladstone Dock. Was the *Malvern* there? Could you be sure?'

'It was there; I've seen that dock more times than you've had hot dinners, Penrose. Them Gladstone Dock destroyers are all on the Arctic run now. It's the best-known secret in Liverpool.'

'The Russian convoys, you mean?' Triumph flamed briefly in Lilith's eyes. 'On the Murmansk run?'

'That's where.'

'Then you could almost be sorry for him,' Jane observed. 'Did you hear about that convoy on the news yesterday? PQ13, it was; bound for Archangel . . .'

'I heard,' Lilith said soberly. 'Most of it wiped out before it got there. Well, it seems he's got landed in it, this time.'

Johnny on the Murmansk run, where even in summer the Arctic waters killed in minutes, where U-boats waited to pick off any ship they chose and a merchant ship's master counted himself lucky ever to make a safe landfall. Karma, Johnny. Kismet.

'You ill-wished Johnny Jones, didn't you?' Vi demanded bluntly. 'Doesn't it worry you, him gettin' landed with the Russian convoys?'

Lilith looked down at the mug in her hands. 'Yes, it does,' she said eventually. 'It worries me because he won't be alone. He'll carry his bad luck with him and it could rub off on others. But I'm not sorry for him. Why should I be?'

'All right – for what he did to Connie he deserves what's comin' to him. But you wished him there, Lilith; doesn't that bother you any?'

Lilith looked at the faces around her, listened to the waiting silence. 'N-no.' She hesitated. 'So I ill-wished Johnny? I wanted him to pay, but Life will decide what the payment is to be, not me. And if his death really is at my door, then hard luck, Penrose. We take what we want, do what we want and we pay. Johnny was responsible for Connie's death, that's all I know. If I did wrong, then I'll have to pay, too; and if not in this life, then it'll have to be in the next one.' She smiled briefly, sadly. 'I knew what I was doing,' she said softly. 'For Connie, you see . . .'

Later, in the too complete stillness of pretended sleep, Jane thought about the new girl and remembered Tom and the words she had flung in anger; anger because Tom was alive and Rob was gone. Would she, then, have to pay? Karma, had Lilith called it? *I'm sorry, Tom. Forgive me.*

In the throes of a misery made worse by a sleepless darkness, Lucinda thought about Mike and wondered what she had done in life to have merited a punishment such as this; what had been so wicked in her past to demand so high a price for such a brief, shining happiness. *God, whatever it was, I'm sorry.*

And Vi thought about Lilith and her funny religion and wondered how anyone could manage to live with such a burden of conscience. Trouble was, though, that Penrose had meant well, and even though Father O'Flaherty would not approve, there was nothing for it but to include the daft woman in her prayers tonight. *Sorry, Father.*

The parcel arrived for Lucinda on the first day of April. It was small and flat and carefully packed, each precise reef knot touched with sealing wax and the ends secured with the brown sticky-backed paper usually reserved for the criss-crossing of window glass.

Vi recognized the handwriting and the postmark. The navy-blue gloves had come, and she hoped the receiving of a present would bring a smile, no matter how small or brief, to Lucinda's face.

'Here y'are, queen. A pressy for you.' Vi beamed. 'Come on, then, get it opened.'

'Gloves!' Lucinda pulled them on, reading the letter folded between them. 'They're from Mary, and so beautifully knitted, too.'

'Ar.' Vi nodded, proud of her gifted sister, for Mary did everything beautifully, even to the packing of a parcel. 'An' she's got the fit just right, an' all.'

'Oh, Vi, the time she must have spent! How good of her. People are so kind it makes one want to weep.'

'Kind? Yes, queen. Reckon that's what Mary thought

when you pinched that coat for her. Works both ways, you know.' And if Mary had been true to her word, Vi knew she'd have knitted a little prayer for Lucinda into every stitch of those gloves, which might not have been such a bad idea, either, when you saw the state the kid had got herself into over her feller. Mary even prayed beautifully; always had them answered. Thick as thieves, her and St Anthony were. 'Reckon them gloves are goin' to be lucky for you, Lucinda.'

'You think so?' Her cheeks flushed as she grasped the thought to her. 'Then why don't I keep them for something special? I'll not wear them until – until Mike comes home.'

Until Mike comes home. What had she said? The happiness left her as quickly as it had come and fear took her once more, and hurt showed again in her eyes.

'But of course!' Jane was quick to home in to the sudden changing of mood. 'Your lucky gloves! Here, give one to me and let me have a wish on it.'

'No, Jane.' Lucinda hid her hands behind her back. 'My luck just ran out. I'm never going to see Mike again, I know it. It's a feeling inside me and it won't go away. I've got to make myself accept it and be – '

'Stop it, Lucinda! That's stupid talk, and you know it! Mother of God, girl, you'd try the patience of a saint!'

'Vi's right. You'll be saying next you've decided to marry Charlie after all,' Jane flung, 'and then we'll both know you're out of your tiny mind!'

Marry Charlie? Oh, no, she could never do that. Not after Mike. Not after Eaton Square and the joy of him; never, after that exquisite loving. But had that night truly happened? Had they been real, the pale green pyjamas, the rose-scented bath crystals? She had been apprehensive, suddenly, until the nightingale began to sing, and she had wanted to weep, afterwards, at the wonder of it. She wanted to weep now, for a love that was lost.

'Hey!' Fingers snapped beneath her nose. 'Wake up!'

'Sorry, Vi. I was miles away.'

'You can say that again, girl. And for Pete's sake, stop apologizin', or I'll be gettin' annoyed with you, Bainbridge!'

'Sorry,' Lucinda said again. 'But give me time. Bear with me, won't you?'

'Ar, now don't you be worryin' none, queen. Me and Jane understands. Just nip down to the galley, the both of you, and bring up the tea and toast while I make the beds. Go on! Shake yourselves, or them gannets downstairs'll have nicked all the marmalade!'

She shooed them through the door with a cheerfulness she didn't feel. This war wasn't fair on them kids; it wasn't as if our lot were getting anywhere, she brooded. Them Japs were still at it: still advancing wherever the fancy took them and sinking our ships like it was them ruled the waves. And it wasn't just our ships, either. They'd machine-gunned our lads in the water, an' all. Nasty, that was. Worse than the sharks, because sharks weren't supposed to know no better.

Vi fluffed up a pillow with unnecessary force. Oh, it was all right for Mr Churchill to say that nobody was weary of the struggle; to say that if that lot could play rough, so could we. But when, she frowned, were we going to get the chance? One victory, just *one* battle won, she sighed, would do everybody the power of good. If we could just win *something*, Vi pleaded, wouldn't it be great? How about getting through to them lads in Tobruk with a few crates of ale, or putting paid to that dratted *Tirpitz*?

'Somethin' to cheer us all up,' she whispered, her eyes

heavenwards. 'Just for once, somethin' worth listening to on the news.'

'Grab a dollop of marmalade, will you, and I'll get in the tea queue. And don't forget the knives,' Jane called, edging towards the wheezing urn.

Over the speaker extension, the voice of the news announcer droned on impartially. Okay, so we were supposed to be glad that Bomber Command were hitting hard and deep, as they put it, into enemy territory. But how many aircrews were lost last night – *really* lost – and how many of our aircraft didn't make it back to base?

'The news doesn't get any better,' Lucinda commented, reappearing at Jane's side. 'They've bombed Mandalay now. I wonder if Mike's there. I wonder if his squadron got out of Rangoon. Do you suppose he's – '

'He's *all right*,' Jane interrupted, wanting to reach up and silence the speaker or, better still, smash the thing. 'Mike promised – remember. One day it's going to come right for both of us. One day, we'll bloody well win this war, d'you hear me, Lucinda?'

They walked unspeaking up the back stairs to the cabin in the roof loft, Lucinda's mind numb with apprehension, Jane ashamed of her doubts. But oh, *when* would it be over?

Before I'm too old to care, she begged silently. Don't let them take *all* my green years, God.

'Well, what d'you know!' Vi waited eagerly for their return, the morning paper at the ready. 'Just listen to this! They've given a medal to Malta; given them the George Cross cos they've had such a rotten time of it. More than two thousand air raids it says they've had. We've got to call it Malta GC, now. Ar, that's luv'ly, innit?'

Lovely indeed. Malta GC. The man in the street liked

the sound of it, thought the decoration the best idea that lot in London had come up with since the little ships of Dunkirk. Fancy that, then, and them with only one fighter left now. Pride rose in every throat.

'They deserve it,' Lucinda said softly, remembering the London of little less than a year ago, the morning she had walked the smoke-shrouded streets to Goddy's office. 'What a wonderful idea.'

'Says here it was the King.' Vi nodded, remembering Lyra Street. 'The King told Churchill they was to have it.'

The King had been bombed, hadn't he, so he knew a bit about what it was like. But that medal wasn't just for Malta, was it? That George Cross was also for all the sailors and the merchant seamen who'd died trying to keep Malta going. Seamen like Gerry, that medal was for. It made Vi want to weep with pride. It was almost as though we'd won something at last!

From the window of cabin 9, Jane looked out across the loch to the far, bordering hills, green-tinted now with tender new growth. Spring had come reluctantly, but now the cherry tree in the garden was showing its first flowers and beneath it, bluebell leaves lay in a dark green carpet, their flower buds fat and swollen.

There would be bluebells, soon, in Tingle's Wood and forget-me-nots and tall purple foxgloves. And in the orchard at Dormer Cottage, the cuckoo-pints would be flowering and the last of the white violets in the shelter of the hedge.

But Dormer Cottage belonged to another life, another world; a place to be visited four times each year. So how could it be, then, that Yeomans Lane still led down to a steel-mesh fence, and other lovers now would meet there and love there, then part?

And why did it still hurt so, even to think of it? Why

did every heartbeat, every breath she took echo Rob's name, and why did every smallest part of her cry out for him still?

She had tried to forget him, to hate him, even, but she could not and would not. And if by some small miracle they were to meet again in Yeomans Lane, she would lift her face for his kiss as she always did and his lips would touch her eyelids, her forehead and the hollow at her throat, then whisper across her cheek to her waiting, wanting mouth.

And the small, sensuous pulses inside her would begin to beat out her need of him, and there would be no words between them as they walked into the green deeps of the wood; no asking, as he took her.

The doorlatch cracked like a pistol shot and Jane spun round, her other world lost, her dreams shattered.

'Hi!' Lucinda came to stand at her side. 'Watching them go?'

Them? Jane blinked her eyes into focus and saw for the first time the submarine and escort vessel.

'See them, Jane? *Jan Mayen* taking *Virgil* out. First patrol – wish them luck.'

Jane did, oh, she did. She wished those submariners a safe return, but *Virgil* was *Viper* still, and just to see it made pimples rise on her arms and her mouth suddenly go dry.

'They'll be back soon, flying their first Jolly Roger.' Lucinda smiled fondly. And later today, when *Jan Mayen* had taken the submarine to the safety of deep water and left it to its patrol, it could well be she who would send their first signal, then send it again later, just to be sure they'd received it. Good luck, *Virgil*. See you.

'Take care,' Jane whispered, turning abruptly from the window. Why did the sight of that submarine distress her so? Was it entirely because of Tom? Was it a part of her penance, or something more sinister; a cold, accusing finger from the past, or a warning of things to come?

'*Virgil* bothers me,' she admitted. 'When I look at it I think of slugs – black slugs – crawling on my grave . . .'

'Jane! Don't! Don't even think such a thing. Tom wouldn't harm you!'

'Who said it was anything to do with Tom?' And who gave you leave to read my thoughts, Lucinda; to say aloud what I'm afraid even to think? 'I know he wouldn't wish me harm.' So whose cold hand clutched at her entrails and why was she so very afraid? 'As a matter of fact, I was thinking of having a word with Lilith about – well, about one or two things. It's a long time since we had a bit of a giggle with the glass, isn't it?'

'Suppose it is.' Lucinda's face was grave. 'But don't you think we should try to forget that glass? It upsets Vi, and do you truly think it works? A bit of a giggle, didn't you say?'

'You could be right,' Jane agreed, 'and if we don't get going on this cabin we'll be in trouble from Vi. Come on – let's make a start on the beds.' It was all right, now. The slugs had gone. But they'd been there . . .

Vi came back with mops and dusters and letters; letters in the pocket of her overall which no one could read, she said, until the cabin had been cleaned and the floor polished.

'There's a fat one for me from Mary.' She smiled, because it meant there was one from Gerry inside it. 'And there's one each for youse two, an' all. So chop chop, eh?'

Her smile was broad and secret. Just wait till Lucinda saw the letter with the American stamp on it. From Mike's mam, that's who, though it would be too early yet for it to bring news of him – good or bad.

Poor kid. Lucinda was taking it badly; suffering inside

her, keeping that stiff upper lip on her when a damn good cry would have done her a lot more good.

'Come on, then,' she urged. 'What's the pair of you waitin' for? Want Chiefie to see all that fluff under them beds, or somethin'?'

They read their letters at standeasy.

'From Colin,' Jane said, scanning hers hastily and pushing it into her pocket. She waited expectantly for news of Gerry and wondered if the reply to Lucinda's Vermont letter would be warm and loving as she so desperately hoped.

'Gerry's fine, thanks be.' Vi beamed. 'Says I'm not to worry and to take care of myself. And he sends regards to youse two.' Eyes moist, she folded the sheet carefully. 'Now then, queen – what's Mike's mam had to say?'

'It's all right!' Lucinda's eyes were bright, her cheeks pink. 'She's got no news for me but listen to this bit . . . *I am so very happy you have written to me and of course I will send you any news of Michael the moment we get it. I realize this may never reach you, the Atlantic being a dangerous place, even for letters, so I will write again in a few days to make doubly sure you know how dearly we all keep you in our thoughts. Grandma Alice sends her love and hopes you are safe and well, as do I, my dear. I wish it with all my heart* . . . Now, isn't that sweet of her? I was so afraid she wouldn't approve of me. I'd convinced myself she wouldn't even reply.'

'And here she is instead, saying she'll write again in a couple of days, just to make sure.' Jane smiled. 'It's a good omen, isn't it, Vi?'

'It is an' all. It's goin' to be all right, queen. Me an' Jane have always said so, haven't we?'

'All right? Yes, of course,' Lucinda echoed.

So why did she feel so afraid? Why was her heart so

cold inside her and why was she so very sure that she and Mike would never see each other again?

Why did we have to meet so briefly, so passionately, my darling, and oh, thank God that we did . . .

Vi walked slowly and soundlessly up the back stairs; so soundlessly that the woman who carefully closed the door of cabin 9 behind her neither saw nor heard her.

Instinct froze Vi into stillness at the head of the staircase and she watched, breath indrawn, as Lilith Penrose disappeared into her own cabin.

Not that there was anything unusual, Vi realized, in what she had just seen. It wasn't wrong to go into the cabin next door and, finding no one there, to leave it again. But there had been a strangeness in the other woman's manner, in the way she'd walked, the too careful closing of one door and the opening of another. Penrose was up to something, wasn't she; up to her tricks again, and involving cabin 9 in it, too.

Vi pulled back her shoulders and, chin jutting, knocked loudly on the door of cabin 10.

'Was there somethin' you wanted?' she asked bluntly when it was opened to her.

'Wanted? Me? No, Vi.'

'Then what was you doin' next door? I saw you, Lilith. Creepin' out.' Vi's manner left no room for denial. 'Lookin' for me, was you?'

'Oh, I suppose you'd better come in. I didn't want anyone to know.' Quietly Lilith closed the door again. 'You'll not say anything, Vi, if I tell you?'

'It depends.' She was having no truck with goings-on.

'It's Bainbridge, you see. I want to get out the glass for her. As a matter of fact, I'd do a lot better if you were to help me, Vi.'

569

'Oh, no. Not me!' She'd landed herself with too many Hail Marys over Penrose and her religion. 'Sorry.'

'Ah well, no harm in asking. I just felt the time was right for a session; try to help the poor girl. She's looking terrible, you know. She'll make herself ill, if something isn't done.'

'Think I hadn't noticed?' Vi countered. 'Think I'm not worried sick about her?'

'Of course you are. That's why I went into your cabin. I wanted something of Lucinda's; something to help me.'

'You haven't been into her locker?' Vi's cheeks flushed with indignation. 'Now see here, Penrose, I'm not standin' for that!'

'Of course I haven't. I went for' – she held up a piece of folded notepaper – 'for *this*.' Carefully she opened it to show the pale blonde hairs that lay there. 'I took them from her comb. I need them, Vi.' She folded the paper into two again, holding it firmly between finger and thumb, away from Vi's reach. 'It's for Lucinda's own good, and tonight is when it's best I do it.'

'Now hang on a minute will you? That anchor on your arm doesn't give you the right to go pokin' and pryin' in other people's cabins.' Vi jabbed an accusing finger. And it didn't give her the right to start messing around with other people's private business, either. 'And what's so special about tonight?'

'Want a smoke?' Lilith offered her packet.

'No, ta. What I *do* want is for you to tell me what all this is about. You're not usually so cagey about it.'

'True.' Lilith lit her cigarette, inhaling deeply before she replied. 'If there's good news from the glass, something good to tell – well, that would be fine. But if there isn't, then it's best left unsaid, isn't it? Best no one else should know about tonight.'

It made sense, Vi admitted; if anything about Penrose's

goings-on made sense, that was. 'Why tonight?' she asked again.

'Because tonight is the eve of Beltane; an old festival, Vi, that once welcomed May Day and the coming of summer.'

'So it's the first of May in the mornin'? What do we do – say "white rabbits", or somethin'?'

'Beltane was an important feast. They lit huge bonfires and – '

'Well, let's hope yer funny friends don't go lighting none tonight,' Vi retorted, 'or they'll be in dead trouble.'

'There'll be no fires lit.' The reply was sharp. 'We're not entirely stupid.'

'Sorry, queen, but you know how it is, with me.' Vi shrugged. 'I know you mean well, but don't go upsettin' Bainbridge.'

'I won't, Vi. She'll hear nothing bad from me, I give you my word.'

Vi looked into the deep, dark eyes; looked long and hard and saw only compassion there.

'You'd tell me, though, if there was anything? Best I should know, Penrose.'

'I'll tell you, Vi. Good *or* bad. Fenny and Cad are going out tonight. There'll be no one else involved.'

'You're a flippin' nuisance, you and your daft religion; you know that, don't you?' Vi got up to leave.

'Yes, I know. But I mean well, and in the end that's all that matters, isn't it?'

All that mattered? Vi had to admit it probably was. At the door she paused, frowning. 'I thought you once said that Bainbridge wasn't a lot of use when it came to that glass – what's so different about her now?'

'I said that Bainbridge had no vibrations, either positive or negative, but things have changed a bit since then. She's started to live.'

571

'Live? The poor kid's worryin' herself into a decline. She's hardly eating a thing.' Not even bread-and-butter pudding, and that was serious. 'It's like she's not with us any more. She won't even let herself cry.' Vi's hackles were up, her eyes angry. 'That's living, is it?'

'You know what I mean, Vi. Since she's been here things have – well – *happened*.'

'You don't have to tell me that.' The anger was gone as quickly as it had come. 'But think on, Penrose – no messin'. And you'll let me know? Whatever it is, you'll tell me?'

'I thought you didn't believe in my religion.'

'There's good and bad in everything. It takes all sorts, dunnit' – Vi shrugged – 'to make a world. You'll tell me?'

'I'll tell you. Good *or* bad . . .'

24

Soon, Vi realized, it would be exactly one year; a year since the night she accepted that Gerry was dead; since the bomb wiped out what was left of her life – her life with Gerry. Yet now, just twelve months on, she was contented, almost; as content as she could be for her man to spend what remained of the war in a prison camp in Austria; content to scrub and clean at Ardneavie House and watch over Jane and Lucinda.

Things could be worse. Nothing lasted; not bad times, nor good. If only Lucinda could accept that and hang on and believe that Mikc Farrow would get back, somehow. Even if he didn't; even if his Book of Life had already been turned to the last page, at least Lucinda could hope for a little while longer.

Vi gave a final rub to the brass door-knocker and knob, emptying her head of such thoughts. This was a glorious morning. On mornings like this there must be nothing but hope.

The month of May had dazzled into Loch Ardneavie and instantly the bleak, bitter winter was banished and forgotten. This morning, daybreak had come with early-watch call and tonight the blackout curtains need not be drawn over windows until well past ten. Summer was coming, and with it good things. From the garden drifted the scent of wallflowers in bloom, and Vi raised her hand in greeting to Miriam, who was hoeing between the rows of newly through potatoes.

All this beauty, Vi marvelled, reluctant to go indoors.

Apple trees in blossom and tree-covered hills and the sun glinting on the loch. Such blessings to be counted.

Eyes narrowed, she paused to watch the launch that cut through the blue-grey water; Lilith's launch doing the morning mail-run from *Omega* to the escort vessels. It reminded Vi that she wanted a word with Penrose, for the woman had been avoiding her, huffing and puffing and not giving the straight answer she had promised.

Reluctantly, Vi closed the door on the delights of the morning. 'What do you mean,' she had demanded, 'nothing, *exactly*? You said you'd tell me, didn't you? Good *or* bad, you said.'

But there had been nothing to tell, Penrose insisted; nothing but a nonsense from the table top that she could make neither head nor tail of. Bainbridge had never been a good subject; the glass had never taken to her.

'You're keeping somethin' back,' Vi accused, but still she had learned nothing of the outcome of the Beltane Eve session. And for the life of her, she sighed, she didn't know why she bothered. She'd known all along it was a load of nonsense.

Yet Penrose was holding back and it made Vi all the more determined to get to the bottom of it. And she would an' all, before so very much longer. You couldn't go sneaking into cabins, taking hairs from a comb and then say nothing had happened. Penrose, Vi declared silently and grimly, hadn't heard the last of it. The truth, she had promised, and the truth Vi would have.

'This lovely evenin',' said Vi at suppertime, 'is too good to waste. How about getting ourselves togged up and goin' for a walk to the top of the loch? The view is lovely from there.' The wearing of civilian clothing after duty had still not lost its appeal; the wearing of brown suede walking shoes – size seven brown suede walking shoes – was an

574

even greater delight. 'Well, what else is there to do?' What indeed, with pay muster three days away, money pockets near-empty and walking costing nothing?

'Did you know,' Lucinda asked later as they sat on the short, springy grass at the loch head, gazing down the length of Loch Ardneavie, 'that last night one of the telegraphists tuned in on the spare set to Lord Haw-Haw?'

'Oh?' Vi's chin jutted belligerently. *That* idiot who came on the wireless every Sunday night, right after the nine o'clock news. A slight moving of the dial and there he was, pouring his hatred of the Allics over the air.

'*Germany calling. Germany calling.*' An Englishman turned traitor, and who supplied him with his information was anybody's guess. From our own daily papers, some said, even though sometimes his reporting of events in Britain beat both newspapers and the Ministry of Information to it. Spies in our midst, people said darkly; that was all it could be.

'A load of old nonsense,' Jane said, sensing dangerous ground.

'Ar. Gets on my nerves, with that stupid voice of his.' Nasal like the haw-hawing of a donkey. 'People shouldn't listen to him.'

'That's what Chief Wetherby said,' Lucinda murmured. 'Gave the telegraphist a rollicking, I believe, then wanted to know what Haw-Haw had said.'

'And?' Vi demanded.

'Seems he was going on about Burma. Said our army there would be completely wiped out and that the Government was keeping it from us. He said our troops had been trying to cross the Irrawaddy, but there'd been another Dunkirk.'

'But Dunkirk wasn't really a defeat!' Jane gasped. 'What about all the soldiers we managed to lift off the beaches?'

Yet there was some truth, she frowned, in those evil outpourings. People only listened to Haw-Haw for the laughs, they admitted guiltily, yet still they wondered, sometimes, how he managed to get it so right, so often.

'That Lord Haw-Haw's nothing but a fool,' Vi hissed. 'They should hang him when this war is over!' Hang him or shoot him, that's what. And right now, seeing the misery on Lucinda's face, she would willingly have done both. Completely unaided.

'Know what tomorrow is?' she demanded firmly, determined to have no more talk of Haw-Haw's treachery.

'No, lovey,' Jane murmured, 'but you're going to tell us, aren't you?'

'Tomorrow,' Vi pronounced, 'is the eighth of May; just a year since I volunteered. A right old paddy I was in; Lewis's bombed and me job gone and a dirty great bomb smack in the middle of number seven. And Richie Daly had just told me he'd seen Gerry's ship go down and no survivors.' She remembered the groping hands, and shuddered. 'So I went into Liverpool to the recruiting office. They only wanted stewards, which was just as well, cos housework was all I was really good at.'

'May the eighth?' Jane took up the remembering. 'That was the night I lost Rob; *first* lost him, I mean.' Because she had lost him again, and finally, to a bleached-blonde, pig-eyed woman called Phemie.

'I suppose I should remember that date, too,' Lucinda said softly. 'Mama was being awful – more than usually awful, I should say – and we'd had a dreadful set-to. So I slammed out and went to the Admiralty to see Goddy. If you think about it, I suppose I was taking the first steps towards Mike.'

Mike, Vi thought flatly. They were back to Mike again, and Rob.

'This grass feels damp,' she said, 'and it's getting cold.

576

Think we'd better be on our way. It's a fair step back to Ardneavie.' Meticulously she brushed the clinging grass from her skirt, searching her mind for something – any- thing – that would not lead back to Rob and Mike. 'Had you thought,' she asked, inspired, 'that it's less than four weeks to our next leave? Remember that first one? Seemed ages coming, yet now the time just flies past. Still want Jane and me to come to Lincolnshire, Lucinda?'

Lady Mead. Now that at least was safe ground.

Vi came face to face with Lilith in the drying room that night; face to face and completely alone.

'You've been avoidin' me, Penrose,' Vi accused, peg- ging up stockings with studied care. 'I think there's somethin' I should know, and you don't want to tell me, do you?'

'I did tell you. There's nothing,' Lilith insisted. 'A load of rubbish was all I got. All right – so there was nothing good. There was nothing bad, either. I was wrong about Bainbridge; her vibes haven't improved as I thought. I tried, Vi. I really did.'

'And that's the truth?' Vi demanded sternly. 'Nothing bad?'

'I said so, didn't I? Think I'll just have to leave it for a while.'

Firmly the door closed behind her and Vi conceded defeat. And she'd been so sure there was something other than a load of rubbish; she still was. But best leave it, she sighed. What she didn't know, she couldn't worry about.

The trouble with McKeown, Lilith thought as she made for cabin 10, was that she was far too much of a psychic for her own good.

There had been something to tell, and Vi knew it. But what kind of a friend was it who came up time after time with a name, a woman's name – and blabbed about it? Because that was exactly what had happened.

'A word,' she had whispered into the glass. 'Just one word will do; some word for Bainbridge to recognize and latch on to, with hope.'

So what did you do when all the comfort you could give was the name of another woman – Mike Farrow's other woman, perhaps? Or even his wife?

A pity when you thought about it; a very great pity, but McKeown could poke and pry from now till the crack of doom, but it would get her nowhere.

Men! thought Lilith, tight-lipped. They were all alike, it seemed.

They were laying out clothes; skirts and jackets over chairbacks, shoes on the floor beside each bed, ready for tomorrow's early call, when the door of cabin 9 opened.

'Phone call for Bainbridge,' called the duty steward.

'Damn!' Lucinda pulled on her dressing gown. 'Who on earth, and at this hour, too?'

Mama, most likely. She might have known, she supposed, that any day now her mother could be relied upon to return to the matter of the broken engagement. 'Won't be long,' she said hopefully, though Mama had no thought for phone bills once she reached full flow.

'Who do you suppose it is,' Jane demanded, 'ringing at this hour?'

'Dunno, but she'll soon tell us,' Vi said comfortably, folding back her bedspread, turning down the bedclothes. And the hour didn't have a lot to do with it, really. You took your telephone calls when you could get them and counted yourself lucky, these days, to get through at all. 'Most likely it'll be her mam. Been too quiet lately, that one has.'

They did not have long to wait.

'That was Charlie,' Lucinda said in answer to their unspoken question. 'He's coming up to Stirling in a couple of days, on a course.'

'Seems to be going on a lot of courses,' Vi observed uneasily.

'Yes, he rather does. Anyway, he wanted to meet me and asked how to get to Ardneavie from there.'

'And you told him?' Jane demanded.

'I told him, Kendal dear. After all, I haven't seen him since – well, since – '

'Since you packed him in,' Vi finished.

'Yes. So I think I owe him some kind of an explanation – eyeball to eyeball, so to speak.' Lucinda shrugged, eyes on fingertips. 'I gave him my watches for the next three weeks and the times of the ferries from Garvie. It'll be quicker for him by ferry; take all day to get here by the coast road.'

'Well, queen, I hope you know what you're doing,' Vi said gloomily. 'And I hope you realize that Charlie could be havin' another go at changing your mind for you.'

'Well, he did sound rather nice – not a bit bossy,' Lucinda conceded. 'But I won't change, Vi. I won't, you know!'

Vi did most of her constructive thinking after lights-out; after the creaking of Jane's bedsprings had ceased and the little turning-over sighs from Lucinda, and she wondered who the patron saint of love lives was; of messed-up love lives. But the best she could come up with was St Anthony, who found lost things, and St Anthony it would have to be, tonight.

And he'd better find Mike Farrow and get him back here pretty quick, she thought grimly, because that Charlie was up to his tricks again; because somehow or other he'd known just when to have another go at Lucinda.

When her defences were down; when she'd begun to think there was no hope for Mike, and nothing left to live for.

A sly one, Charlie Bainbridge was; he'd need to be watched. And, come to think of it, so would Lucinda. For her own good, of course. Very closely watched.

'So that's her gone.' From the upstairs window Vi watched the Craigiebur transport disappear down the shore road. 'That's her goin' head-on into trouble.'

'She isn't,' Jane said with certainty. 'Lucinda's learned to think for herself a bit since she left home. Charlie won't get it all his own way.'

But Vi was not so sure. Vi had met Charlie and disliked him on sight; one of those, she had been forced to admit, who thought he'd been born with the God-given right to order lesser mortals about.

'You know what's goin' to happen? Lucinda's startin' to imagine she's lost Mike, and she just might give in under pressure.'

'She won't.'

'She *might*. She just might think, "Oh, sod it!" and before you know it, Charlie and that old mam of hers'll have got their own way.'

'They won't, I tell you. Lucinda won't ever take Charlie back. She fell for Mike in a big way. Mike's the one she wants, and she'll never take second best; it isn't in her nature,' Jane said, quietly and confidently. 'She just wouldn't.'

'Want to bet?' Vi remembered the arrogance of him, the way he'd expected – *demanded* – to be deferred to. 'By the heck, Kendal, *I* wouldn't bet on it. That Charlie,' she brooded darkly, 'is up to somethin'!'

Captain Charles Bainbridge was waiting at the entrance to Craigiebur Pier, which surprised Lucinda greatly when she arrived there, because most times it was she who waited.

'Hullo! You're early!' She wondered whether to salute him, offer her hand or kiss him. She decided upon the latter, brushing his cheek with her lips, smiling up at him. 'Got here all right? No trouble?'

'Of course not. And I'm not early, Lucinda.'

'Oh dear. That means I'm late, then.' She decided against argument or apology. 'Never mind. You're looking well, Charlie. Going off on courses must suit you. You've lost weight.'

'Yes. Needed to shed a few pounds. But I came here to talk about us, Lucinda.'

'Yes, you did. Shall we walk? Or there's a tearoom in the High Street, if you'd like a cup?' The tearoom might be safer ground.

Thank you, he said, but he would not. He did not intend discussing his future – *their* future – in a seaside café.

'A walk, then? It's quite pleasant along the front.' She almost took his arm, then remembered that men and women in uniform did not link arms. Well, not in broad daylight. 'What's happening at Stirling, by the way, or can't you tell me?'

'Just some new guns – that sort of thing. Nothing really hush-hush. Well, it *is* time I got some in. Can't sit out my service at the War House.'

'No. I suppose not.' So he was being posted to an active-service regiment. Ah well. He'd had a good spell of desk duty, she supposed, then at once felt shame for her uncharitable assumption. Charlie just might have volunteered. 'Are you expecting to – '

'See here, old girl; right now it's you and me we're supposed to be talking about, if you don't mind. For a

581

start, where do we stand? I've got to admit your letter took a bit of understanding.'

'Why, Charlie?' It had been a good letter, she had thought. Straight and to the point. She had met someone else and she wanted to marry him. She had asked – humbly, almost – that Charlie accept this and remain her dear friend, if he could. She thought it a kind letter, but explicit, for all that.

'Why? Because it was always understood, Lucinda, that you and I would marry, one day. No hurry, of course, but one day . . .'

Understood? Oh, yes. From as far back as she could ever remember. Charlie and Lucinda. Lucinda and Charlie. And of course there had been no hurry. Why should there be? They weren't desperate for each other; the sight of him hadn't set her wanting him, needing him. They'd been a habit, in fact.

'Yes, understood, I suppose. Or taken for granted, perhaps,' she ventured. 'Something we drifted into, almost.' They had reached the limits of the seafront walk and automatically turned to retrace their steps. This interview, this discussion, serious though it might be, was to be taken at a slow march along Craigiebur promenade. Funny, really. 'Drifted, Charlie, if we're to be brutally honest.'

'Maybe.' He shrugged. 'But we got on all right. Did it have to be a mad, flaming passion?'

'Yes, it did. For me it did, though I didn't realize it before this.' Now was the time to make him understand what a terrible mistake they could both have made. 'Oh, Charlie dear, we grew up together. You were there, always. You spent more time at Lady Mead than you did at your own home. Your mama could never keep a nanny, and every time one left you came to us. We grew up as brother and sister, really. We had our measles together, didn't we, and chicken pox. And the first time I saw you in the bath I was absolutely intrigued and asked why I didn't have one of those things. Don't you remember?'

'No, I don't.' His face had gone very red. 'I really don't.'

'Well, I do. Nanny said it was so people would know when we were born whether we were boys or girls. And I asked – and I could only have been three or four at the time – if it mattered. And she said it would matter, one day, and when we were both older we'd understand. Even then the mystery had gone out of it, for us. Even when we were little they'd started brainwashing us. Well, Mama had, because *she'd* already decided.'

'So? Would it have been all that bad, Lucinda?'

'Yes, it would. It would have been – well – *indecent*, almost, and you know it!'

'Oh, I say! That's a bit strong!'

'No, Charlie!' She had to say it. For her future and Mike's, she had to. 'I used to think about living with you at Lady Mead and us having babies together; more Bainbridge babies to carry on the line. I accepted it, you see. Oh, we were cousins, but there were no impediments to pass on – it would have been the perfect solution. But I want my babies to be made in love, and it wouldn't have been love between you and me, would it? I used to think sometimes that perhaps a few drinks beforehand would make it more bearable. *Bearable*, Charlie. God! It should be – ' She stopped, feeling her cheeks blaze red. 'I'm sorry. I didn't mean to hurt you, truly I didn't.'

'You haven't.' He said it quietly. 'Look here, maybe we should have that cup of tea, after all.'

'Yes,' she said, shaken. She had expected trouble and so far there hadn't been any. And so far she'd done all the talking, and Charlie had let her. 'Yes. Maybe we should.'

* * *

The tearoom had once been a genteel, copper-kettle sort of place, but now it struggled to survive the strict rationing placed upon it. Now, cups and saucers no longer matched and the covered shelves which once must have shown displays of tea breads and cream cakes held only a stone jug of bluebells now, and a few ornaments.

'Hullo, my dear.' A middle-aged waitress addressed herself to Charlie, sighing because her feet ached and there were still three hours to go before closing time. 'Tea for two, will it be, and I'll see if I can do you a scone.' She always tried to do a scone for His Majesty's forces.

Charlie nodded, Lucinda smiled.

'Mind if I smoke?' Charlie offered his gold case. He'd got that, she remembered, for his twenty-first birthday, just before the war.

'Please do, but not for me, thanks.' Sometimes, he'd lit one for her, and she couldn't bear it if he did that now. 'Can you manage to get them all right? We get a ration of twenty a day on the ship. I brought a packet along, just in case.'

She laid twenty on the table and he took them, gratefully.

'That's very decent of you, old thing. Haven't managed to get round the girl in the Stirling NAAFI yet. Well, as we were saying – '

'No, as *I* was saying. Sorry if I went a bit far, but I did mean it about the brother-and-sister thing. You and me in bed wouldn't have been right – well, not to me, at least. Not after Mike.'

'Mike? That's his name?'

'Yes. I told you in the letter, didn't I? He's in the Air Force; our Air Force. One of the girls was sick and she'd fixed up a blind date. So I took it over for her – well, went along to explain to him.'

'And he was your blind date? You mean you actually –'

'No.' She smiled fondly, glad to be talking about Mike, even to Charlie. 'I thought he was, but when we got it sorted out he wasn't Molly's date. Mike had just been standing there, watching a submarine. It was more of a pick-up, when you get down to brass tacks.'

'And that was it, Lucinda? Right from the word go?'

'That was it, Charlie. It hit me. *Wham!* I didn't tell him about you because I thought I'd never see him again. But we did meet, and well – the rest you know.'

'Yes.' He shrugged. 'I suppose so. But we've got to get this thing straight. There's a war on, Lucinda. I've got to know where I stand.'

'I agree absolutely. It's got to be sorted out.'

'It has. I've got to know if it's just a flash in the pan, for you. Come to think of it, you're the loser, not me. I've always known I'd never have had a look-in if Lady Mead hadn't been a part of the package. Well, not when you got old enough to really think about it, I mean.'

'You could be right, Charlie.' Not could be. He *was* right. 'That old house was always very special to me, and I wouldn't be losing it when the time came for Pa to go. You'd be getting it, therefore so would I. Beyond that, I hardly ever thought. And when I did think about it, I'd tell myself it would be all right, in the end. But it wouldn't have been, would it?'

'No. I suppose it wouldn't. But is he worth it, then? Worth giving up Lady Mead for?'

'Worth everything.' She said it in a whisper. 'I'm sorry. Don't mean it to sound a criticism of you, but I do love him. I wish you could understand.'

'Well, maybe I just do.' Without looking at her, he stubbed out his cigarette. 'But I had to meet you, Lu, and get to the bottom of it. We'd had an understanding, you and me, and I was still willing, in spite of the letter, to give it another try. And I still will, even though – '

'Here we are, then. I managed a couple for you.' The waitress placed two hardly buttered scones on the table and one teaspoon of jam, set solitary in the centre of a dish. 'Can't always manage scones, dear. Rationing, you see . . .'

'Thanks,' Charlie said briefly.

'You're very kind. They look lovely.' Lucinda smiled, picking up the teapot, pouring out two cups. Then she smiled again. 'And you would have, Charlie – even though?' she prompted.

'Well, it's just that I – ' He stopped, watching her spread jam on his scone then place it on his plate. 'Just that – '

'Charlie! You've met someone. I know it!'

'Oh, it's something or nothing. She's a decent sort, though.'

'Hey! You can't refer to a girl as something or nothing. And we don't much like being called decent sorts, either.'

Someone else! Oh, my goodness! And yet, she thought, her elation all at once gone, he'd still have been willing to go through with their marriage, even though he really liked the girl, whoever she was.

'You know what I mean.' His eyes were fixed on his plate.

'Yes, I think I do. Tell me her name. Where did you meet her?'

'At a party, as a matter of fact. Went up to the girl and asked her to dance.'

'You mean you were actually willing to go on the dance floor?'

'Yes. Seemed the only way, at the time. Of course, I'd had a couple.' He grinned.

'Then she *must* be special!'

'More than you'd think, Lucinda. I asked her to dance and she said, "Be it on your own head, then. I've got two left feet and I'll probably cripple you for life." I couldn't believe my luck. She can't abide dancing, either. So we sat it out instead, and had a bit of a chinwag. Her name's Isobel, though they say it *Eyes*-obel, where she comes from.'

'And where is that?'

'New Zealand. Came over to see what she could do. Damn decent of her, really. Her people breed horses – bloodstock.'

He took a bite out of his scone then looked at Lucinda expectantly; almost as if he wanted her blessing.

'And is she going to suit you, this Isobel? And does she know what an old grouch you can be sometimes?' she demanded.

'Well, we've only gone out a few times; didn't want to get too fond of the wench, you see; not if – '

'Not if there was a chance I would change my mind, and you and I got together again, do you mean?'

'Not exactly.' He smiled. 'It was more Aunt Kitty. She's a bit of a martinet at times.'

'She is.' Lucinda smiled back. 'But she won't make me change my mind, so don't worry. You'll be all right. And I do wish you luck with your Isobel. I truly do, Charlie. Maybe she and I can meet, if the leaves allow.'

'I'd like that. But tell me about your airman. Not after your money, is he?'

'Money, Charlie? You above all should know we haven't got any. *Things*, yes. Money, oh no. But we didn't talk about that side of it. I think he'll have a job to go back to, so we should manage all right with the grand-parents' cash to help out – when I get it. He's American, by the way. From New England. His grandmother is

English, so that's very nice. He joined the RAF when war started.'

'And how well do you know him, Lucinda?'

'As well as I'll ever know any man, Charlie. He's in Burma, you know.' The words slipped out before she knew it. 'I-I haven't heard for quite a while.' She took a steadying breath before she was able to whisper, 'I'm so worried. I can't think about anything else.'

'That's a bad show, Lu.' He reached across the table and took her hand in his, squeezing it tightly. 'Chin up, eh? God knows, I wish him safe for you. When was it you last heard?'

'March. A letter written on the twenty-sixth of February. Three months ago. But don't say anything to anyone, huh? Nanny's the only family who knows, apart from yourself. Couldn't bear it if Mama got wind of it . . .'

'Not a word. And I honestly wish him well; you know that, don't you?'

'Yes, I do. And I'm glad we had this talk. Let me know when the wedding is.'

'Early days yet.' His face reddened again. 'But fingers crossed for me.'

'Fingers crossed.' She smiled. 'Look, there's a ferry at four. Do you want to catch it?'

'Wouldn't mind, if it's okay with you.'

'It'll be fine. I'll walk you there. By the way, does Isobel fancy being a countess, one day?'

'Don't know. Haven't told her. Why do you ask?'

'Haven't a clue, really. I suppose, though, that I want her to be good to Lady Mead.'

'Haven't told her about that, either. It's one hell of a place for anyone to take on.' He held up his hand, nodding to the waitress, and she walked slowly over and laid the bill on the table. 'And hold on, old thing. She hasn't said she'll have me yet.'

'Then ask her. She will.' Lucinda smiled, taking his hand affectionately. 'If you're always as nice to her as you've been to me today, it's a cinch she'll have you.'

Their parting kiss was warm and he held her in his arms for a little while, patting her back awkwardly, telling her it would be all right about Mike.

She stood for a long time after the ferry cast off; watched it until it was no more than a toy thing on the horizon. She was glad they had met and talked; gladder still he'd found someone.

Oh, Charlie Bainbridge, you old fraud, she thought, you can be really rather a dear, when you set your mind to it.

Slowly, she walked away, knowing she had time to wait before the next Ardneavie transport left, stopping to lean on the rusting railings and gaze out over Garvie Sound. Briefly, she considered returning to the secret place. The trees were in leaf again now, the war shut out once more from that little jut of land.

She had said goodbye to Mike there, yet not long afterwards his letter had come, telling her of his love, asking her to wait. Dared she then go there again?

No, not without him, or news of him. It would be tempting the Fates too much, pushing their luck too far, and she was too afraid to make so brave a gesture alone.

She began to walk, all the while watching the choppiness at the mouth of Loch Ardneavie as the tide turned, and the boom-net tugs rising and falling in the swell. And wasn't that a submarine, standing off, waiting entry into the loch? *Virgil*, home at last?

They'd had a long first patrol; the buzz had it that they'd gone in to Scapa and revictualled and taken on more fuel there and gone back to the fjords. Now, long before sundown, they'd come alongside *Omega* to a first-patrol welcome back, their Jolly Roger flying from the conning tower.

She was glad Jane would not be on board to see it happen. Jane had feelings about *Virgil*. Her conscience, poor love, was not so easily sorted as her own had been this afternoon. But that was Kendal's one besetting sin, Lucinda decided. All her emotions ran high. Kendal loved too well, hated too bitterly. And what other women might feel as a pang of conscience, then chalk up to experience and forget, Jane brooded over and turned into a major sin, and unforgivable, at that.

Why does she have to love you so, Rob MacDonald? And where are you? Lucinda asked silently.

And where are *you*, Mike Farrow, and why do I have to love you in just the same way?

'Now, then.' Vi's head shot up as Lucinda walked into cabin 9. 'Everything all right, was it?'

'Fine. Any reason why it shouldn't be?'

'No. But I was just thinkin' – ' She stopped, embarrassed. 'Thought maybe – '

'Thought maybe he'd huffed and puffed and demanded I marry him? Is that what you were thinking, Vi?'

'Don't know what you mean. None of my business.' Vi reddened.

'Of course it's your business, though you needn't have worried, either of you.' She smiled suddenly, brightly. 'Charlie's got a girl of his own now. One he's chosen for himself, this time, and she sounds rather nice. He just wanted me to know, that's all.'

'*All!*' Vi shrieked. 'Here's me been worryin' myself silly all afternoon, imagining the worst! Ar, queen, that's good news. Gettin' married soon, is he?'

'I rather fancy he will.' Lucinda smiled again. 'He was

awfully sweet about Mike; really wished us well. Charlie's rather a dear, actually. When he finds he doesn't have to marry me, that is.' It was a gentle, sad smile now. 'Ah, well, that's one problem solved. Now, it would seem there's only – '

'Mike will be *all right*,' Jane insisted. 'I know he will, just as I know about Rob and me. Try to believe it, Lucinda. Please try.'

'I do try, Kendal dear.' Lucinda threw her hat on to the bed, then unbuttoned her jacket. 'I try all the time.'

'Then try harder, clot! Oh, there are times I could take you and shake sense into you, so help me!'

But Vi held her peace. It was terrible seeing Bainbridge the way she was. She'd lost weight since March, that was very easy to see, and the dark circles beneath her eyes and the paleness of her cheeks made her look almost ill.

Vi understood that Jane should want to comfort her friend, but wouldn't it have been kinder to leave it, let things take their course? No use buoying her up, making it all the harder to accept if the worst really did happen. And happen it could. It was something most women learned to live with, these days.

Vi wished there was something she could do; really do. She wished with all her heart for Mike to be safe, but there was a crawling inside her whenever she thought about Lilith and that too vehement denial. Penrose was not a good liar and Penrose had been lying through her teeth when she'd said there had been nothing to tell about that Beltane Eve session.

And before long, Lucinda was going to hear what she and Jane had just heard on the last news bulletin: that units of our troops had begun to straggle across the frontier between Burma and India. Soon the fighting there would be at an end and soon they'd be taking tally of our dead and wounded and missing. For better or worse, it wouldn't be long before there could be a letter from Vermont, and that could be when Lucinda might need them as she'd never needed friends in the whole of her life. Just to think of it, to admit that such a thing could happen, made Vi feel sick inside. And very, very helpless.

'Look, why don't we all go out?' Jane suggested brightly. 'Let's walk up to the village and have a couple of drinks.'

'We couldn't go in our civvies.' Vi frowned. 'Suppin' ale isn't exactly what Chiefie calls sport.'

'So we'll sup ale in our uniforms. What do you say, Bainbridge?'

'Well, I want to write my few lines to Mike – '

'Oh, come on! Be a devil! And maybe, when we get back, you'll have something of phenomenal importance to tell him – like the landlord having some gin under the counter!'

'All right, then. And we do have to talk about leave. Nanny's going to want plenty of warning, to give her time to organize a few black-market eggs and some milk and a rabbit, perhaps. You do both still want to come?'

'You bet we do.' Vi grinned. 'Our Mary hasn't been able to get a spare bed yet; not even a second-hand one. A bit of an upset, I am, though Mary won't have it.'

'My mother won't like it.' Jane frowned. 'But it is *my* leave, after all.' And Nanny wouldn't go on and on about Colin. 'I'm all for it. Be about the eleventh of next month, won't it? Only a couple of weeks away.'

'Yes. We can talk about it at the pub.'

Lucinda wanted desperately to go home to Lady Mead, to forget the war for just a few days and pretend that none of the past year had happened; none of the bad bits, anyway. But meeting Mike and loving Mike and being loved by him – those brief, precious moments would be with her for all time and worth all the heartache in the world.

'Come on, then,' she commanded in a voice too bright, too brittle. 'What are we waiting for?'

25

Nanny Bainbridge smiled a welcome from the top step of the Dower House, her everyday grey set aside in favour of a printed cotton afternoon dress.

'Dearest!' Lucinda threw herself into the wide, welcoming arms, 'It's so good to see you again!'

'And it's good to see you, child. And how nice to meet your friends.' More hugs, more warmly kissed cheeks. 'Now tell me,' she demanded, affectionately reproving, 'who is Mrs McKeown and who is Jane?'

Lucinda made the introductions; hands were shaken formally.

'You'll be pleased to know,' said Nanny, leading the way into the kitchen, 'that I have solved the problem of sleeping. It came to me that somewhere in all those rooms of furniture I'm looking after, there must be something better than a put-u-up – and there was. It's been airing in the sun this week past – a nice single bed. I've put it in the big bedroom; Mrs McKeown can have it and you and Jane, dear, can sleep in the double. I have already moved into the dressing room. Will that suit you?'

They said it would, that they shared a room all the time.

'Good. Then take your cases upstairs and wash your hands whilst you're up there, and I'll get the meal on the table.'

'Why,' Vi wondered when they were out of earshot, 'does your nanny call me Mrs McKeown?'

'Because you're a married lady.' Lucinda laughed. 'It'll be Lucinda and Jane and *child* as far as we two are concerned, but Nanny is a stickler for doing things properly.'

'So what do I call her?'

'You'll call her Mrs West. That's her real name, Dorothy West, but she's almost always known round here as Nanny Bainbridge. Nannies often take their name from the family they're with.'

'I didn't know she was a widow.' Jane folded the towel and hung it carefully over the rail.

'That's something else. Mrs is a courtesy title. Most nannies prefer to be Mrs. It's just the way things are.'

'Hmmm.' Vi thought it a funny carry-on Lucinda's lot had, and no mistake, though she was secretly pleased, for all that, with her elevation. 'Ah well, queen, don't know what she's got in the oven, but it smells good enough to eat!'

They dined on rabbit stew – after grace had been said, and stiffly starched napkins unfolded – with oven-baked apples to follow, and for the first time in many weeks, Lucinda ate what was set before her.

They would not, Nanny pronounced, spooning custard, listen to the nine o'clock news tonight. It was bound to be depressing, she said comfortably, and it would keep until morning.

'Tonight,' she said, 'when we've finished eating, you might like to walk over to Home Farm. Johnson was sorry to have missed you last time you were here, Lucinda, so I think a call would be appreciated. And best you should thank him for you-know-what in the outhouse and tell him a little more of the same wouldn't come amiss this week. And anything else he might have,' she added, tapping her nose with her forefinger.

* * *

'Sorry about the uniforms,' Lucinda said as they walked down the narrow lane to the white-painted farm gates, 'but Nanny does so want everyone to see me in mine, bless her. We'll put them away tonight, though, and get into something cool. There are plenty of my things at the Dower, Vi. There's sure to be something you can wear. Nanny says I'm to ask the group captain tomorrow if you can have a lift into Lincoln on Sunday morning. They lay on an RAF truck, she says, for the Catholics.'

'Ar. That's good of her.' No peace for the wicked.

'I told you she'd boss us about, didn't I? And I'm to ask if Nanny and Jane and I can go to Sunday service in Lady Mead chapel.' Lucinda smiled apologetically. 'No getting out of church parade, is there? Hope you don't mind. Nanny's worse than Patsy Pill, sometimes.'

They didn't mind, they said. They were far too contented to stroll the length of the lane, hats on the backs of heads, jackets open, breathing deeply on the cool night air.

'What did Nanny mean – a little more of the same?' Jane asked, eyebrows raised. 'And what goes on in the outhouse?'

'Oh, the direst black-market dealings you've ever heard of.' Lucinda giggled. 'Actually, she was on the cadge for some extra milk and some eggs for breakfast. The Air Force left us the Home Farm, so she still gets the odd favour or two. But she'll blow her top if we call it black market. We'd better not say too much because she doesn't admit to it, really. Johnson leaves it sneakily in the outhouse and Nanny swears blind the little people bring it.'

'I'm goin' to enjoy this leave.' Vi grinned. 'I like Mrs West. Bet you wish she was your mam, Lucinda.'

'But she *is*,' Lucinda said softly. 'Right from the day I was born, I suppose I was hers. She was always there, you see, as mothers should be; always looked after me when I was ill. And it was Nanny who came in the night when I had bad dreams. I suppose that's why I feel safe, here; as if nothing bad can happen to me.'

'Good. That's better,' Jane remarked approvingly. 'And keep on feeling like that. It's the only way!'

Vi said nothing. True, Bainbridge had visibly relaxed since the moment they'd got off the train at Lincoln; but Vi had her own opinions, which were sometimes best kept to herself – though if Lucinda felt better just to be here and didn't pick at her food and push it aside, and if she didn't toss and turn all night, then she for one would be more than glad.

'Ar,' she murmured. My, but she would sleep tonight, strange bed or not. The minute her head touched the pillow.

'It's been a lovely day,' Jane whispered to Lucinda, whose head lay on the pillow next to hers in the big double bed. 'I get the feeling, you know, that this is going to be a smashing leave. Something good will happen – I'm sure of it.'

'I hope so, Kendal dear.' Things, Lucinda thought despairingly, couldn't be much worse, though here at the Dower the letter she dreaded receiving could not reach her. It would be waiting there when she got back, maybe, but here at least she was safe for a week from all bad news. 'But we'd best pipe down or we'll have Vi awake . . .'

Vi was awake. She had not fallen asleep the moment her head touched the pillow but lay there quietly thinking about Lucinda and how so many on the estate had been pleased to see her tonight; genuinely pleased. Milady, they'd called her, and it had sat well on her; Lady Lucinda, who was in her right and proper element here at

Lady Mead. My lovely Lucinda, Vi thought sadly, who is giving up all this for Mike Farrow; for a bloke who was somewhere in Burma and whose last letter had been written at the end of February. Poor, anxious Lucinda.

In the little dressing room, Nanny Bainbridge whispered her prayers then counted her blessings; not one blessing, tonight, but two. Two chicks to cluck over for a whole week and that nice, down-to-earth Mrs McKeown an added bonus.

She wondered if she should have asked for news of Lucinda's young man, then decided she had been right to say nothing. Later, perhaps, if the opportunity arose.

But it was a sad time for the young ones, she sighed. They didn't start the wars, only inherited them. Every generation the same, it would seem. She, whose joy it was to rear children, did not enjoy to see them numbered and sent off to war.

She closed her eyes and resumed the counting of her blessings, amongst which, she sternly hoped, would be the discovery of a pint or two of milk and six brown eggs in the outhouse. Left there by the fairies, of course.

'You see the house best,' Lucinda said, 'if you approach it from the deer park. Don't think we'd better go the back way through the kitchen garden and the stableyard; not three of us. The Air Force just mightn't like it.'

They turned the corner of the narrow, winding road, and Lady Mead lay before them, serene and sunlit, surrounded by trees, with roses and wisteria clinging to its walls.

'It's beautiful,' Jane breathed. 'Just as you said.'

'Ar.' Vi had seen big houses before, but she had never associated those aloof, elegant mansions with real people. Yet there below them was Lucinda's home, its windows catching the morning sun and shining it back to them in a hundred welcomes. 'Ar hey, queen, but all them windows'll take some cleanin'.'

'Don't you like it, Vi?'

'Course I like it. Terrible for you, havin' to leave a place like that.'

'They'll give it back, when the war's over.'

One day, Pa would get it back, and then it would be Uncle Guy's, and one day Charlie would live there. It would never be hers, now, Lucinda accepted. Only for a little while, perhaps, after the war.

Be good to Lady Mead, Isobel-from-New Zealand. Take care of it for me.

'Are you sure it's all right for us to be here?' Vi frowned as they reached the curve in the drive.

'Yes. The CO said it was okay – and once every three months isn't exactly making a nuisance of ourselves. And I've got to ask him about Sunday, so we might as well go down to the basement and have a root around. There's a tea chest full of shoes, if I remember rightly. There just might be something we could use.'

'It's very big,' Jane conceded. 'Did you need a lot of servants?'

'Quite a few, I suppose, but mostly estate staff. Farm workers, you know, and gardeners and a woodman. And two keepers, I think we had. Mama never rode again after the accident, so there weren't any horses, but Pa had a chauffeur – he hates driving – and Mama had her own maid.' Lucinda shrugged apologetically. 'We'll not be able to afford them again, though. It's my guess we'll have to live in just a part of it, when we get it back. If we ever come back at all, that is. I worry about it sometimes. Mama likes London, you see, and Pa prefers Scotland and Cromlech. But it isn't important, really.' Possessions, she thought, were wrong when there was a war on. Just being alive and staying alive till it was all over – now that *was* important.

'Come on.' She smiled. 'Let's go in.'

They spent what remained of the day pressing the summer dresses Lucinda insisted Vi should have, and securing buttons and letting down the hems. As for the flat leather beach sandals they had found in the tea chest – which could well have been Charlie's in his younger days and fitted Vi as if they'd come from the same last as the brown suede walking shoes – words could not describe their delight.

'We had a super time. So many memories, packed away in boxes and trunks and no, I didn't see any sign of moths,' Lucinda reported, anticipating Nanny's question. 'And your nice group captain says we'll be welcome in chapel on Sunday at ten. Vi is to wait by the Dower gate at seven thirty and the driver will stop for her. I did all you said.'

'Good.' Nanny nodded. The day had started well, with brown eggs for breakfast and two left over from the half-dozen to make a baked custard for supper tonight because, strangely, she had a spare pint of milk too. And it had continued well, because Nanny Bainbridge had young ones to fuss over, and the upset of them was welcome and their noise too, and next week this would be a silent, lonely old house again. 'I suppose you know I'll be going to the WI on Monday night? We'll have to think up something handy for supper. I can't be late; I'm the speaker, you see.'

'You, Nanny? What about?' Lucinda murmured, pins in mouth.

'About making things out of nothing, as it were.' Nanny did not wish to boast, but since the eldest Farleys had walked to school wearing their splendid – if a little on the large side – duffel coats, her advice had been sought from all quarters about the ekeing-out of clothing coupons in general and the making of school coats from blankets in particular. On Monday evening the Women's Institute would listen intently to what she had to say and pay her five shillings for her pains. For Nanny Bainbridge, it was an evening not to be missed.

'Clever old you.' Lucinda smiled. 'Fame at last.'

'Well, I'll admit I'm looking forward to it.' The reply was suitably modest. 'But I'd rather you didn't come and listen to me.' She had never spoken in public before, not even given a vote of thanks. 'It might be a bit off-putting if you were all there.'

They said they wouldn't be. They'd find something to do and she wasn't to worry. And not only would they make the supper, but they would wash up afterwards so she could keep calm and arrive unflustered at the village hall and do full justice to her undoubted knowledge.

'You'll be all right? You're sure?'

They were very sure. Just to be here, doing what they liked, more or less when they liked, was pleasure enough.

'We're sure, Nanny.'

It seemed such a pity, Vi sighed, to be putting on her uniform again, but the Air Force was giving her a lift into Lincoln to Mass and it didn't seem right for an RAF transport to have a civilian in it.

She had awakened that morning to the sound of bird-song and gone quietly to the bathroom, leaving Lucinda and Jane soundly asleep in the big double bed.

Sometimes attendance at Mass was a duty, but this morning Vi wanted to go; wanted to light candles for Gerry and Rob, and for Mike too, even though she wasn't at all sure of his religious persuasions. And she wanted to pray for the speedy ending of this war, though it was going

601

to take more than prayers to put paid to this lot. Miracles, more like, and then some.

Quietly she opened the back door; quietly she closed it behind her then walked to the gate to await the transport which would soon be passing.

She lifted her face to the morning, took in the scent of honeysuckle and lilac and new-cut hay. And she looked into a sky so blue it was unbelievable it could harbour planes with bombs in them, and fighters spitting death.

This morning, this heart-hurting exquisite June morning, she could almost find it within her to be happy.

'God,' she whispered, 'when you can make a world this beautiful, what got into you to let this war happen? Just what, eh?'

For the sake of all the Bainbridges past, Lucinda agreed to wear her uniform to chapel, and for the sake of unity on the lower decks, Jane wore hers.

It was a nice gesture, Nanny said, and one which would please the group captain, since he'd been kind enough to allow them to attend morning prayers at the house.

At the top of Lady Mead's front steps, Nanny inclined her head in that gentleman's direction, but the salutes from Jane and Lucinda were automatic and smart.

'That was extremely nice of you both.' Nanny beamed as they walked across the hall towards the tapestry room and the tiny boudoir. 'You did that very well, both of you. I'm sure the group captain appreciated it.'

'He'd have played merry old hell if we hadn't,' Lucinda remarked soberly. 'He does have rank up, you know.'

'You go first, dear.' After all, Lucinda was a Bainbridge and this, in Nanny's eyes, was still a Bainbridge house, and when they were inside the little chapel she motioned with her head to the covered family pew, curtained in faded red velvet.

Lucinda stepped inside, reached for a hassock with the toe of her shoe then knelt down, her eyes on the altar triptych.

Jane too sank to her knees, watching as Nanny, unashamedly high church, bowed her head low to the altar then entered the pew, closing the little carved door behind her.

Lucinda closed her eyes tightly, unaware that the chapel was slowly filling with RAF personnel; unaware of anything but her need to plead with the doe-eyed Virgin.

I asked you before to keep Mike safe and to let him come back to me. And I'm here again to beg you to take care of him. I love him so much, you see; so very much. Don't let anything have happened to him. Let me hear something good, soon.

God, it's Jane Kendal. Jane gazed through fan-spread fingers at the red roses in the altar vases. *Please let something happen soon, for Lucinda. I'm sorry about Tom. I'll be sorry all my life for what I said to him and I want you to forgive me. But it's Rob I love, and can I see him one day, please? Just for half a minute, as I said? Just half a minute, God, and you can have the rest of my life, if you want it.*

Nanny Bainbridge said the Lord's Prayer, then commended all she loved to the mercy of the Almighty. He knew best, after all. He alone knew how much she had loved William; how much she still loved him. And how much her ageing heart grieved for Lucinda, and for Jane, whose young man had been killed. And goodness, how hard these hassocks seemed since last she knelt here. Or were her knees getting older? A little of both, perhaps.

Vi was already back when they returned to the Dower House, dressed in one of her newly acquired frocks, her bare feet in the beach sandals.

'I found the key under the stone where you left it, Mrs West. The kettle's on the boil and the teapot's warming.' She beamed. 'My, but it's goin' to be a beautiful day.'

Nanny gazed approvingly at the tray set with cloth and china cups, and, peeling off her Sunday gloves, she smiled at the memory of the truck-load of young airmen. Boys, they'd been, hardly out of the classroom and leaning out and waving and whistling to them. Going to Lady Mead, she supposed. There seemed to be a lot of comings and goings at the big house, these days.

'Penny for them,' Lucinda teased. 'Or are they worth more?'

'A great deal more, I should say, child. I was thinking about not only how well-attended chapel was, but about the airmen we passed on the way back, and how young they were. And I was wondering why they all had white bits in their caps.'

'Flashes, Nanny,' Jane murmured. 'They wear them because they're training to be aircrew.' One of her photographs of Rob showed him wearing his white flashes – taken before he went to Canada to do his night-flying training. Rob had been so very young then. Like the boys they'd waved back to this morning. 'I think we were wolf-whistled by a truckload of sprog pilots.'

'Young monkeys.' Nanny smiled fondly. 'Though I doubt they were trainee pilots, dear. Much too young for that.'

'Old enough, Nanny; just too young to vote,' she choked. 'Funny, when you think about it.'

'I'm sorry,' the older woman said gently. 'I know I haven't said anything to any of you about – well – anything. But I do remember you all in my prayers, I promise you I do. And I *do* know what it's like to love someone very much, so don't think that old Nanny doesn't care, will you? But let's be happy today, shall we? Today is always the best day for being happy, isn't it?' Carefully she wiped away a tear. 'Now then, who's for tea?'

'I rather think,' said Lucinda as they passed the water-mill and made for the river bank, 'that Nanny would like this afternoon to herself. Tonight's her big night and I've a feeling she wants to rehearse her talk and get some examples and things together.'

True to their promises, they had prepared a salad for supper, leaving it on the slate slab in the pantry. And they would be back from their walk in good time to slice the Spam and cut the bread and see Nanny on her way to the village hall.

'Wasn't the news terrible this morning?' Jane murmured as they stopped at a shaded spot by the riverside. 'A village wiped out. Nothing left of it; no people any more; no houses, no church.' She tried to imagine standing at the crossroads at home and looking down on – nothing. No Fenton Bishop; no Dormer Cottage. Just charred ground where bulldozers had finished the job the avengers had begun.

'Lidice, you mean?' Someone from a little village in Czechoslovakia had killed Nazi Reinhard Heydrich; someone had murdered a murderer, so a village was obliterated. 'If one of our lot had killed that man, he'd have been given a medal for it,' Lucinda remarked. 'We shouldn't have listened to the news this morning. We'll try not to again; not until our leave is over.'

'There was a convoy got through to Malta, though,' Vi consoled them, chewing on a piece of grass and squinting up through the trees. 'That was worth hearin'.'

'I suppose so. The trouble is that tragedies like Lidice become just, well, history, eventually. Like the Vikings who were here.' Lucinda frowned. 'I suppose they caused a terrible upset in this village, once upon a time, but it'll all be the same, I suppose, in a thousand years.'

They lay on the grass, listening to the sound of the little river that flowed through the wood; through birch trees and beech trees and clumps of comfrey and kingcups and yellow flag irises. This was like the secret place at Craigiebur, Lucinda thought; here, too, the trees screened out the war. And she could lie for ever; lie here until she petrified and became part of it all, and in another thousand years people would wonder who she was, and no one would care.

'I wonder what they're doin' at Ardneavie,' Vi speculated, folding her cardigan and settling it beneath her head. 'Bet they wish they were here, doin' nuthin'.'

'Bet they do. I suppose port watch will have just come ashore and Lofty and Jock and Chief Wetherby will be missing us like mad.'

'They say that *Virgil* had a good patrol,' Lucinda offered, then stopped, angry that she had forgotten Jane's dislike of the submarine. 'Sorry, love,' she murmured. 'Let's not talk about the war. Let's shut it out until Wednesday.' Until Wednesday, when they would start their journey back, with stiff collars chafing, thick stockings scratching their legs again, and the train hot and crowded and late.

'Let's just lie here and think about lovers,' Jane whispered. 'Think how it will be when we see them again.' Fantasies. Daydreams. 'Let's think about a time and a place and what we'll say when we meet them. And what we'll be wearing.' On some station platform, would it be, or would the phone ring and would someone say 'Hullo, darling'? Or would she just turn a corner, as always in her imaginings, and there Rob would be? And would he say, 'Hullo, Jenny,' as if that May night had never happened, nor Phemie, nor anything?

'Ar,' said Vi. 'Good idea.'

Lucinda said nothing. Lucinda closed her eyes and Mike's lips met hers. And nightingales sang for them.

It was Vi who sat up, complaining that her bones had gone stiff, reminding them it was time to be getting back to make supper, as they had promised. And they had left the river bank behind them, and the water-mill and were almost in sight of the fence by the deer park when Vi hissed, 'Damn! I've left it in the wood! I'll have to go back.' She couldn't leave it lying there; not her beautiful brown cardigan. 'You two go on.'

'No. I'll get it, Vi. I can run faster than you,' Jane offered. 'I know where we were. Won't be long.'

She set off at once, then turned as Lucinda called, 'Kendal dear! On your way back, there's a short cut. Just as you cross to this side of the bridge. A little path that'll bring you out at the back of the stable block. Okay?'

'Right!' She set off at a run again. Vi had been asleep this afternoon, a small smile on her lips – miles away, with Gerry. Jane remembered the spot, and she soon found the trees they had lain beneath; the shapes their bodies had made in the grass.

Vi's cardigan was where she had left it, carefully folded, the indent of her head in it still.

'Good,' she grunted, glad she had found it. She would hate Vi to lose anything. Vi had so few clothes, and a cardigan – well, it was eight clothing coupons, to say the least. She turned and made her way back to the water-mill. If she ran like the wind she could be home as soon as they were.

The short cut was easy to find. It was well-trodden; used, no doubt by the airmen from the big house. She moved swiftly, the ferns and tall grasses brushing her as she passed. And there was the stable block ahead of her; just bear left towards the deer park and –

She stopped abruptly. That officer walking towards the iron gate, he could have been . . . he was the same height, had the same swinging walk. Yes, he could have been . . .

There was a tingling inside her and a strange rushing in her ears. It wasn't him, of course. It couldn't be, and yet . . .

She ran to the gate he had carefully closed behind him, her mouth dry, the tingling a shaking now she could not control. There were no sergeant's stripes on his arm and all this was a part of this afternoon's dreaming; but half a minute, they'd agreed, she and God. Just half a minute, and already he was walking away from her!

She grasped the gate top; grasped it and held it because the ground beneath her feet was rocking. She pulled her tongue round dry lips. A few more seconds, and he'd be gone and she would never know.

'Rob!' she screamed. 'Rob MacDonald!'

He heard her, and stopped. Then slowly he turned and ice-cold shock stiffened her body. She looked into his face for many seconds before he became real, before the mists cleared and he stood sharply in focus again, his head tilted.

She fixed him with her eyes, willing him not to turn and go. She held her breath, but it did nothing to still the shaking inside her or the harsh dry sobs that writhed in her throat.

Then slowly he raised his hand and her own moved in response. She watched, unbelieving, as he walked towards her. She ought to say something, but the sobs were still there and she could not. So she waited until he was within hearing distance then whispered 'Hullo.'

No sound came, just a sighing, but he must have read

the moving of her lips because he smiled a little then said, 'Jenny!'

She stood unmoving, watching his pace quicken, not believing it, counting as her half-minute slowly spent itself. Then he was standing there, so close that had she moved her hand just a little to her left, they would have touched.

Why was she spoiling this moment? Why was she wasting it? The sobs rose higher, hurting her so much she could fight them no more and the tears came; tears of shock and disbelief and pain and love. They ran unchecked down her cheeks as the world still rocked beneath her.

The gate shook as he vaulted it. She felt his arms taking her, gathering her to him, holding her close, hushing her.

She clung to him, moaning softly. It *was* him; his voice the same and the feel of him, the scent of him, the thinness of him, all unchanged. And this was Yeoman's Lane and a May evening. 'Promise,' she had begged. 'Promise always to love me.' And there had been no in-between, no parting, no Phemie, and if the dream must end, if the God she had bargained with said her seconds had run, then there was just one thing to say.

'I love you,' she whispered.

He pushed her from him a little way, feeling in his pocket, and she saw the wings on his tunic – his old wings, his first ones, a little dull against the newness of his uniform. And she held up her face as he dried her tears, closing her eyes because she loved him so much and soon it must all be over.

How did you stretch half a minute into eternity? How did you hold back time, keep this moment precious and golden for ever, even though it might only be a dream?

'It *is* you! Jenny, what are you doing here?' His face was white, his hands were shaking, too.

'I'm on leave. At the Dower House. Are you at Lady Mead?'

'Yes. Till tomorrow. I've come to collect a draft of sprog pilots.'

She gazed at him, wanting him to hold her again, needing him to kiss her as he had always done; kiss her eyes, the hollow at her throat, her mouth.

He lifted his hand and touched her cheek with his fingertips, and she turned her head quickly and her lips touched the palm of his hand and left a kiss there.

'I must go, Jenny. There's a muster at half-past four, and I'm late already. When can we meet?'

'Tonight,' she whispered. There was so much she must know; so much to tell him.

'Where? What time?'

'Here, Rob. At seven.'

A small smile moved his lips. 'At seven.'

'At least you won't be flying tonight.'

'Not tonight. Not for a year. You'll come?'

'Yes, I'll come.' She would be there. Nothing would keep her away from him; not hell nor high water nor anything on or under or above this earth. 'Yes,' she said again.

'In case you don't . . .' He cupped her face in his hands and kissed her mouth gently. 'In case you change your mind . . .'

'I won't,' she said. 'I promise.'

He turned on his heel and left her as he had so often left her. At the corner of the stable block he turned and raised his hand, then was gone.

She bent down and picked up the cardigan from the ground at her feet and buried her face in its softness.

If Vi hadn't left it behind; if she hadn't offered to go back for it; if Lucinda hadn't called to her to take the short cut, they would never have met.

*God, this is Jane Kendal, and thank you. Thank you for
everything.*

'You found it, then?' Vi smiled.

'It was there, right where you left it.' Reluctantly Jane
gave the garment into the outstretched hand.

'Hey, girl, are you all right?' Vi's right eyebrow shot
up. 'You look a bit – peculiar.'

'I'm fine. I've been running. I tried to beat you home.'

Not now. Not yet. When Nanny had gone to her
meeting, perhaps then she would tell them. When the
shaking had stopped and the thudding of her heart was
less loud in her ears. And anyway, Nanny thought Rob
was dead. Everybody did, except Lucinda and Vi. And
Tom, of course. And it wouldn't do to tell Nanny he
wasn't, and never had been, or she'd wonder why he
hadn't found her before this.

Not that it mattered, of course. Nothing mattered but
that she had turned her corner and seen him there, just as
she knew she would. And his lips had been real and warm
and gentle on hers, and tonight they would meet. Tonight,
at seven and –

'I said, supper's ready.' Vi was looking at her strangely.
'Listen, girl, are you *sure* you're all right? You've been
crying, haven't you?'

'No. Something in my eye; a little black thing,' she said
as Nanny came into the kitchen. 'It's all right now. I'll just
go and wash my hands.' And take deep, deep breaths and
splash my face with cold water and try to act as if nothing
had happened, until Nanny leaves.

And God, it's Jane Kendal. Did I say thank you? Did I?

'Right, then!' said Vi when they were alone; when Nanny
Bainbridge had left with her carrier bag of examples and
notes, her Sunday hat secured firmly with pearl-ended

pins. 'What's to do with you, Jane? And don't say nothin's the matter, because it *is*.'

Lucinda stood unspeaking and perplexed. Vi was right. Jane had hardly touched her supper and if she hadn't been so preoccupied with her talk, Nanny must surely have remarked on it.

'Somethin' happened, didn't it, when you went back for my cardi? What was it?'

'Happened,' Jane choked, turning red-cheeked to face them. 'Oh, yes, it happened as I said it would. One day I'd turn a corner, I said, and he'd be there.'

They didn't speak, Vi and Lucinda. They looked at her with disbelieving eyes, waiting, wondering.

'I told you I'd meet him again. He's here, at Lady Mead.'

'Rob? *Here?*'

Jane nodded, trying to smile. And then the sobs began again. From deep inside her they jerked up into her throat, bursting into new tears.

'Rob MacDonald *here*? Ar, girl . . .' Vi gathered the shaking body into her arms and felt warm tears on her own cheek. 'There now, it's all right. And maybe it wasn't him. Maybe – well – all that sun, eh?'

Jane shrugged away Vi's arms, dabbing her cheeks, forcing a smile. 'Sorry. Didn't mean to cry again. But it *was* Rob. He's an officer, now.'

'Did you speak to him?' Lucinda demanded, her voice uncertain. 'Did you ask where he's been? And actually here, at Lady Mead? Out of all the Air Force billets, he's got to be *here*! Today!'

'Here. And if you hadn't left that cardigan behind, Vi, I'd never have seen him. It's so frightening I can hardly bear to think about it.'

'Well, I did leave it and you did go back for it. It's

called the hand of Providence, I suppose.' Vi beamed. 'Hey, girl, smashin', innit?'

'Kendal dear, I'm so glad for you. You were so sure, always.'

'So sure.'

'Well, tell us then. What did he say?'

'Not a lot. We only had two or three minutes – I'm not sure how long. But much longer than I'd ever hoped for, though. I used to bargain with God, you know. Half a minute, I said. Just let me see him for half a minute and, oh, I wish I could stop this silly weeping.'

'But *where*?' Lucinda persisted. 'Where was it?'

'At the stableyard. He was closing the gate behind him. I stood there, not believing it, watching him walk away. And then I yelled his name and it was him. He just said, "*Jenny!*" and it was all right. But he'll tell me where he's been and how he got home. I'm seeing him tonight. At seven.'

'Don't get hurt again,' Lucinda said softly. 'Remember – '

'Remember that he's married? I'm not likely to forget that, am I? But I want to see him. I need to.'

Vi gazed with compassion at the vivid face, the pink-flushed cheeks and eyes bright with tears. There was no rhyme nor reason in it at all. Jane was in love, and common sense flew out of the window when love came in at the door. 'Of course you want to see him, queen. He owes you that,' she said gently. 'But be careful, or you're goin' to get hurt all over again. You know that, don't you?'

'Yes, Vi. I know it.'

'Well then, you'd better be gettin' yourself ready. Get on with it, then! Me and Lucinda'll see to the washing up.'

'Bless you,' Jane gasped. 'Bless you both for understanding. And just one thing. What do I tell Nanny? After all, I am a guest in her home.'

'I see what you mean.' Lucinda frowned. 'Couldn't you say you bumped into someone here you'd known at Fenton Bishop – someone you knew well and wanted to talk over old times with, to find out what's been happening to him? Well, that would be *almost* the truth. There mightn't be any need to say anything, if you're in before half-past ten. That's when she'll be back.'

'See how complicated it gets,' Vi said with mock severity, 'when you start goin' out with married men? Ar, push off and get yourself ready, or he'll think you've stood him up.'

It was, as Vi said afterwards when Jane had run from the house like a girl on her first date; when they had cleared the supper table and washed the dishes and left a tray set ready for Nanny's return and were sitting in the rocking chairs on either side of the stove and thinking about it dispassionately, not really any of their business.

'Like I said, Kendal's a big girl now. She knows the score, but I hope she realizes what she's doing, what she's lettin' herself in for again. I hope she realizes.'

The stableyard clock showed five minutes before seven o'clock when Jane reached the gate. Rob wasn't there, but it was almost always she who waited.

She checked her hair with fidgety hands, ran her tongue round carefully painted lips, then checked the clock with her wrist watch. She wondered if she should have worn her uniform; he'd never seen her in it, had he? But her uniform was a part of her new life and tonight belonged to the past. Tonight they would tie up loose ends and say all those things they should have said, and hadn't. And

614

they would part like civilized people who had once been lovers and who would always care for each other.

That, she told the stableyard clock as it jerked away another minute, was how it should be. How it *would* be depended on Rob, because she, Jane, had not changed. And could not change, and would not. She still loved him and wanted him, and the knife still turned inside her when she let herself think of Phemie, and the baby.

He came quietly from behind her so that she spun round at his cough, startled to see him.

'You came, Jenny.'

'You knew I would. Kiss me, Rob.' She closed her eyes and lifted her face to his and he kissed her eyes, her ears, the hollow at her throat; kissed the tip of her nose, as he'd always done, then trailed his lips across her cheek to her mouth.

The kiss was hard and urgent. It wiped out all the months between and they stood in Yeomans Lane again, beneath the beech tree.

'I shouldn't have done that.' Roughly, almost, he pushed her away. 'It wasn't fair.'

'I asked you to. One kiss, Rob. Surely you owe me that?'

'I owe you an explanation,' he said tersely. 'When I knew you'd been – God, I'm sorry, Jenny. It broke my mother's heart, she said, to tell you.'

'And do you think it didn't break mine, to hear it? I went AWOL to find her, did you know? But I want to know about *her*; about Phemie.'

'What do you want me to say? What can I say?'

'You can tell me all of it. *All*,' she whispered. 'I think if only for what happened between us, you should do that.'

'Is there somewhere we can go; somewhere we can talk? Not the pub, though.'

'There's the river walk. We were there this afternoon.'

615

And she'd gone back, hadn't she, for Vi's cardigan. 'It's pleasant there.'

When they came to the place where they'd lain, hands behind heads, talking, squinting up through the trees, laughing, she turned, looking back at him, shaking her head.

'What is it, Jenny?'

'I-I don't know. It's just that – well, I can't believe any of this; not any of it. I'm trying to be cool about it, and calm, but I can't. And I can't believe that yesterday we were probably both in the same house, and I didn't know it. We came up to Lady Mead to chapel – why didn't bells ring?'

'I don't know, and I don't know what to think, either. All this takes a bit of getting used to.'

'Used to? God! I keep wanting to touch you, Rob; make sure you're real.'

'I'm real enough. We both are.' Hesitantly he took her hand and they began to walk again, slowly; not speaking.

'How did you get out of Europe?' she said, when the silence became unbearable. 'France, was it?'

'No. My crew bailed out over France, though, when we got hit. They all made it. In a POW camp now, but they're whole and they'll live. I kept on. The plane was playing up, losing height, damn near out of control, but I managed to get my 'chute on, and get out.' The words came in a rush of relief. 'Hell, I was scared, but I made it – a soft landing in the sea. I put my feet down and I was standing in two feet of water and I thought, just how lucky could I get?'

'And what about the plane, Rob?' The Halifax bomber she'd blessed on its way that May night; watched until the twilight took it. 'It went down in the sea?'

'Yes. Only seconds after I jumped I saw the old girl fall

like a stone and blow up. But all I could think was that I'd made it back; bloody well made it! And then I heard the men and the rifle bolts clicking and I couldn't say a word. I just stood there in the darkness, thinking I'd had it. Then one of them said, "Get the bastard!" Said it in English, Jenny, and I yelled, "No! For God's sake, no!" and he said, "Hold it. He's one of ours." Not England, Jenny. Not home. I'd landed a bit short. Jersey, would you believe?'

'And I was so sure you'd be somewhere in France.'

'Near as damn it, I suppose, the Channel Islands. Anyway, they got rid of my 'chute and took me to a house and dried me out. Later, they moved me to Alderney on a fishing boat and hid me there. There wasn't much on Alderney. Only camps for political prisoners, I think they were. The Resistance brought me food as often as they could. I managed. I slept in the roof space of a derelict cottage. I'd hear our lot flying over, most nights, but time dragged. I was alive, though. That was all that mattered, and suddenly I stopped being afraid. Somehow, I knew that if the Germans didn't find me and I got back to Blighty, I'd be all right. With luck it'd be me flying over that cottage and some other poor sod, hiding out up there.'

'And they got you out? Did it feel good?'

'No. Not if you thought of the risks the Resistance were taking. I just felt thankful. Look, Jenny, I shouldn't be talking about it. When I got back I was debriefed and they told me to say nothing that might land those men in any more danger than they were already in. It's prison camps, maybe the gas chamber, for those men, if they're caught. Another man was taken off at the same time as I was. I wasn't allowed to speak to him; he was either one of theirs they'd had to get out in a hurry, or an agent, so forget what I've told you. Some day I'll be able to tell you

617

all about it. I did try to thank them for what they'd done for me, but they told me to get flying again and drop some more bombs on the bastards.'

'Some day, Rob? Will there be a *some day* for us?'

'Don't, Jenny. Let me tell it to you my way.'

'Okay. So you made it back and you finished your tour of ops,' she said tritely.

'Yes. I made it to my thirtieth. When I got back, I picked up a crew that was short of a pilot. No bother, really.'

'You make it sound easy.' Short of a pilot? A pilot who had been killed, didn't he mean? 'Did you ever think about me?'

'All the time. They didn't send me back to Fenton Bishop. I went to Norfolk, after I'd been through the debriefing and kitting-out routine. But I always thought about you, especially at take-off.'

He quickened his step, walking a little ahead of her on the narrow path as if her nearness distracted him, and she reached out for his hand because she couldn't bear them to be apart; couldn't bear not to touch him.

'Rob,' she whispered, 'just for tonight can we pretend? Can we pretend things are as they used to be? Don't shut me out.'

'I'm sorry. Suppose I'm still as shocked as you are.' His mouth was hard with tension. 'But there are things to be said. You've got to hear them.'

Yes – things. *Phemie*.

The knife turned again inside her, even though they were together, touching and loving. Because they *were* loving. It sparked from him to her like an electric current and danced in the air around them.

'All right. Say them.' *But don't think anything will stop me loving you.* 'Tell me.'

They walked on, eyes lowered because the path was

618

narrow and pitted in parts, and tussocky, like Tingle's Wood.

'Before I went back to flying again, they gave me a week's leave. I got home just ten days after you'd been there, Jenny, and a week after I joined the new squadron in Norfolk, Phemie had her baby.'

'*Her* baby? Yours and hers, surely?' She had to say it. Not to hurt him, but to hurt herself.

'No, Jenny. Not mine.' He said it quietly, pausing to give emphasis to his words.

'Good God, Rob! Why not yours? You married her, didn't you?'

'Aye, I did. What the hell? I thought. It was short odds I'd ever make the end of the war. Some pilots cop it on their first operational flight. I'd done six ops already; nine was the considered average. *Nine*, Jenny. I'd only three to go, then I was living on luck. She said the baby was mine. I'd been with her all night.'

'She was two months on, I believe? A Hogmanay baby, your mother said. Drunk, were you?'

'Drunk? Oh yes. I'd just got back from Canada, my wings up, and the reality of what I'd come back to hit me bang between the eyes. From then on I'd be on operational flying; it scared the hell out of me. My brothers both got a seventy-two-hour leave pass. I hadn't seen them for over a year and we went out that night and tried to drink Glasgow dry.

'The pubs always seem to have something in reserve for Hogmanay, more's the pity. "See you at the Cross at midnight," they said, in case we got separated. Glasgow Cross, Jenny, where we'd always seen the new year in. There was a clock there, and bells to ring it in, you see.

'But bells aren't allowed any more, and a clock face you couldn't see was no' a lot of use, so revellers had taken to seeing in the new year away over at George Square, only I didn't know it then.

'When I got to the Cross it was practically deserted. A guy with a bottle gave me a swig from it, then left me sitting on the pavement. It was Phemie who found me and took me to her room. I woke up next morning stark naked in her bed. Somehow, she'd undressed me; said she had brothers of her own and I wasn't to worry about it. I didn't think anything had happened but my head was banging too much for me to care.

'My mother gave me a row for being out all night, then gave one to my brothers for getting me tight, but apart from that – well, I forgot that Hogmanay. I was posted to Fenton Bishop, and the rest you know.'

'Yes. We met, then you went back to Glasgow and married Phemie, a shotgun in your back. Then you came back to Fenton Bishop, and made love to me.'

She closed her eyes, wishing she could take back the words. Why was she hurting him so, because she was. He'd flinched as if her words had been blows.

'Yes, I did. I loved you right from the first night we met, and after the wedding I felt cheated – trapped. I wanted you and I knew you wanted me too.'

'So straight from your honeymoon bed you came to me, Rob?'

'No! There was no honeymoon. I was cold sober, that day. I wished Phemie well, then slept at home. And she did nothing to stop me.'

'So there was just the once, between you?'

'No. Not even the once. Drunk as I was, I'd have known if we'd been together.'

'Yet you married her, believing that?' She tried to keep her voice even, to hide the bewilderment, the disbelief. 'You married Phemie, knowing how much I loved you?'

'You were a child, Jenny. You were eighteen – a minor.

Would your parents have given their permission for you to marry me? You know what they thought about aircrew. It seemed there was no future for you and me – me, especially. How were we to wait three years till you were of age? And did I have three years left? Sorry, sweetheart, but that was the way it seemed to me, so I did what they call the decent thing by Phemie.'

'Permission?' she choked. 'Yet I was sent to a country where a girl of eighteen is a woman and needs no permission to marry. Three weeks, that's all it needed, and I'd be domiciled in your country then, Rob, and could marry under your laws. And you did love me, didn't you? It was me you loved?'

'Loved? Love? I did. I do. I always will!' He stopped, biting off the words, hands on her shoulders as if he wanted to shake sense into her. 'What do I have to say, to do, to prove it?'

'You could have written; just a line, letting me know you were safe.'

'Oh no. I'd done you enough harm; my mother made that quite clear. She told me to leave you alone, that you were a whole lot too good for me, and it hurt. It bloody well hurt, because what she said was true.'

'So? Phemie had her baby and you finished your tour of ops and got some rank up,' she said, suddenly unable to think straight. 'What now, Rob?'

'Now I'm instructing for a year. I'm away with a load of trainee pilots, somewhere overseas, for their night-flying.'

'And you're going tomorrow?'

'We'll be leaving here tomorrow morning, early. What happens then, where we'll end up and how, I don't know. But after tonight . . .' His hands were on her shoulders still, his mouth only a kiss away. 'After tonight, it's goodbye again, Jenny.'

'It doesn't have to be that way, Rob. Not if you don't want it.'

'You know I don't!'

'So do we have a choice?'

'I told you Phemie's baby wasn't mine. That's the choice you have, Jenny. *Your* choice: to believe me or not to believe me. It's up to you.' Naked with pleading, his eyes looked into hers.

She held his gaze steadily, remembering the misery of the past year, the longing, just to see him. Yet now they were together, and all the festering pain and all the reproaches and doubts seethed and writhed inside her like snakes in a pit. And why, when she loved him so? When she always had and always would?

'Then I choose to believe you,' she whispered.

'Why? Tell me why.'

'Because I love you. Isn't that reason enough?'

He gathered her to him then, and she felt the tension leave him. And he cupped her face in his hands and kissed her, gently, as he'd kissed her at the stableyard gate.

'Then will I tell you something, now,' he said softly. 'Phemie had her baby at the end of July; full term, the midwife told my mother. A *full-term* boy.'

'Look, I know I'm missing something, but – '

'A child born full term in July is conceived in October, Jenny. In October I was in Canada. Phemie was looking for a man – any man – to father her baby on. She was already two months pregnant when she found one – drunk in the blackout at Glasgow Cross.'

'And because of that, Rob, I've lost you.' Pain took her again and twisted her insides in cold, cruel hands. 'You married her of your own free will, your mother said, in your own church. And there's no divorce for a Catholic, is there?'

'No divorce, Jenny. But Phemie admitted what she'd

done; even agreed our marriage was never consummated. So no divorce was needed; just an annulment. Under civil law the marriage is already over, but it'll take a while longer for the church to undo it. But I'll get an annulment, there's nothing so certain, within the year.'

Bells should have rung then, and lights – blinding lights – flashed in front of her eyes and the world should have stopped its spinning. Or Rob should have vanished from before her as if he'd never been, and Vi should have been telling them that it was time to go back and make the supper. Vi, putting on her brown cardigan.

But nothing happened. Only the river, going on its way, uncaring; only a quiet so complete that perhaps time had stood still. And words in her head; free, free, *free*. And laughing and crying and searching, eyes closed, with her lips for his.

'Say it. Tell me again,' she choked. 'Say *"I'm not married!"*'

The world was rocking beneath her feet again and she clung to him, shaking. It wasn't true. It couldn't be.

'I'm not married. I never really was.'

Not married. She reached for his lips again, holding his head in her hands, her heart thudding with indescribable joy.

'Look at me, darling.' He tilted her chin with a gentle finger. 'Is it all right, then? Will you marry me? I'll be a year away, but when I come back, will you? Please.'

Bells rang, then; a hundred thousand bells. And lights flashed and the world stopped its spinning just long enough for her to say, 'I'll marry you, Rob MacDonald. With all my love and for all my life, I'll marry you.'

She shook her head, gazing around her, bemused, printing a picture of this evening in her mind; a June picture, green with young summer, and flower-scented. And she would carry it always to keep him near her when she was alone, and she would feed on these few shining hours until he was with her again. He was hers, and nothing could part them now.

'Do you realize, my darling,' she whispered a long time after, 'that if it hadn't been for a cardigan, an ordinary brown cardigan, I'd have lost you?'

And he smiled and said, 'Is that a fact, now?' then kissed her again.

Only seconds before Nanny Bainbridge sailed in through the front door, Jane slipped in through the back.

Lucinda, measuring milk into a pan, looked up and smiled. Vi, rocking in the chair, raised an enquiring eyebrow.

'Oh, but you'll never guess, either of you!' Arms hugged tightly around herself, Jane paced the length of the kitchen, and back. 'Never in a million years will you guess!'

'So tell us, queen.' If she needed to, that was. If her star-shining eyes, her smile, the air of delight that wrapped her round didn't spin their own love story. Whatever had happened tonight had been worth the price. 'You know you're burstin' to.'

'My dears!' Nanny appeared at the kitchen door, hat slightly askew, gloves in hand. 'Such an evening, you'd never believe it! Such interest in all I had to say. Most kind. I thought I'd never get away. And I've been asked to give my talk again, over at Caseby. Is that the Ovaltine, child?' She sank into a chair, overcome. 'Just what I need after all the excitement.'

'Fame at last. What did I tell you?' Lucinda smiled, her eyes still on Jane.

'Yes, and fortune, too. There was even a hint that I might hold afternoon classes on a regular basis for young mothers; a sort of make-do-and-mend thing. Think of it!

I'd be helping with the war effort in a roundabout way. And it's all because of the Farleys' duffel coats!'

'Tell you later,' Jane mouthed. Nanny's evening of triumph must be savoured and shared and exclaimed upon. Only then would she tell them her wonderful news. For more than a year she had longed for this; another hour was nothing.

And all because of the Farleys' duffel coats, Nanny? she said silently. Oh, but I know a better one than that. About a brown cardigan . . .

'*Now* will you tell us, Kendal dear?' Lucinda gasped as they closed the bedroom door behind them. 'For nearly two hours you've kept us waiting. What happened? Something wonderful, wasn't it?'

'Something *unbelievable*! Just think – this morning he was on the run in France, I thought, and all I wanted was to know he'd get home safely. Yet just half a day later – well, all *this*!' She began to wind the alarm clock, but her hands were shaking too much and she handed it to Lucinda. 'Here, you set it. For half-past six. Rob's leaving at seven in the morning and I want to see him again – just a glimpse as he goes past.'

'Jane! Are – you – going – to – TELL – us?' Vi hissed. 'Or must we shake it out of you?'

'All right! All right! To put you out of your misery, Rob *isn't* married. He's getting an annulment and he'll be free by the time he gets back to the UK in a year.'

'Not married?' Lucinda gasped. 'But I thought it was all signed and sealed?'

'Yes, I know.' She shook her head impatiently. 'There *was* a wedding, but Phemie tried to pull a fast one – '

'Ar. The old, old story.' Vi nodded, sagely. 'That baby wasn't Rob's?'

'That's right. But shall I tell you about it from the

beginning? It's all so marvellous that I don't want to go to sleep. I never want this day to end.'

'Right from the beginning,' Lucinda said fondly, placing the clock at Jane's side and switching off the bedside light. 'Every word.'

Gladly she told them. Every wonderful, unbelievable word of it, right from the start. And Vi sent up a little prayer to St Anthony for finding Rob and getting him to Lady Mead. Must've taken quite a bit of doing, that must.

Lucinda hugged herself tightly, excitement and hope churning inside her, for hadn't Jane insisted all along that they must hope? Hadn't she always said it would come right – for *both* of them?

Please, *please*, let it be my turn next, she pleaded silently.

Nanny Bainbridge heard the whispering and murmuring from across the passage, but she didn't mind. Young things on leave, and enjoying themselves. And she would only have them for two days more; just two days, then her brood would be gone.

But it wouldn't seem so lonely without them, now. Not when she'd found herself so suddenly in demand. Goodness gracious, there wasn't going to be a minute to spare.

She turned her pillow over and sighed. My, but it had been a wonderful day; simply wonderful.

Jane waited near the main gates, standing just a little way away because of the sentry who stood there. She was early, but then she always was.

What a day yesterday had been, and why, when she awoke that morning, hadn't she known? But it *had* happened, and in her pocket were Rob's wings, to remind her.

'My first wings, Jenny.' So precious, a pilot's first wings. 'I want you to have them. I got my batman to take them

626

off my tunic and sew up another pair,' he'd told her last night as they parted. 'Sounds grand, doesn't it – my batman? I suppose I'll get used to it. Keep them to remember me by. I'll send you a ring, if I can get one, wherever it is I'm going.'

'And you'll write, Rob?'

'Every day. I promise.'

'Promise to take care and never to stop loving me.'

'I promise, Jenny.'

Their lovely promises again, their sweet, sweet promises. Outside Nanny's back door, they had renewed them. And oh, she mustn't be so happy. She really mustn't.

She knew he was coming when the sentry began to push open the gates, and she ran to stand where Rob could see her; where she hoped Rob could see her as the transport drove slowly through.

He was there, sitting at the front beside a WAAF driver, and he lifted his hand and smiled, surprised, as they passed.

Then the truck slammed to a stop and the cab door opened and she was in his arms, their lips meeting. And because she had not expected this, because a glimpse of him and a wave and a smile would have been enough, their kiss was something she would always remember. With the sentry standing there, smirking, and the sprog pilots in the back clapping and cheering and wolf-whistling.

'I love you, Jenny. Take care, my darling. Promise.'

'I promise. And you, Rob. Come home safely to me.'

'I will. God, how I love you.'

Then he turned and ran back, and the cab door slammed and they were all away. She waved to the sprog pilots, and wished them luck. They'd be all right, with Rob. Rob would teach them care and caution and how to get through a whole tour of ops. *Take care, all of you.*

She smiled at the sentry, who was closing the gates again, though she couldn't see him properly through the tears.

God, it's Jane Kendal. No more happiness for me, please. Let Lucinda have some, soon. It's Lucinda's turn, now.'

The train was hot and crowded, as they had known it would be, and their stiff collars chafed their necks and thick black stockings scratched their legs. But it had been a good leave; the best ever. One day, they would do it again. One day, they would all go back to Lady Mead, they said.

And tomorrow, sitting on their beds in cabin 9, they would each write a thank-you letter to Nanny. When they had done their watches; when they had settled in and their war had caught up with them.

'Egg sandwiches,' Lucinda said, opening the packet Nanny had packed for the journey. 'Johnson's fairies have been at it again!'

'Ar,' said Vi, folding the newspaper she had been reading and passing it back to the ATS girl she had borrowed it from. 'And Joe Stalin's at it, an' all. Screamin' for a second front; wanting our lot to make a landing in Europe, somewhere, to take the pressure off Moscow.'

A second front, she thought, biting into her sandwich. And how the heck were we to manage that, with Rommel's lot closing in on Tobruk? Tobruk, which had held out for months and months, now looked as if it was going to fall. Flamin' Norah, they were going to kick us out of Egypt now, and Stalin wanted a second front!

'I don't know what they've been doin' while we've been on leave.' She frowned. 'But it looks as if they've got themselves into a bit of a mess without us. Ar well, we'll soon be back now.'

In less than an hour they would be in Glasgow, Jane realized, in the city she and Rob would live in, one day.

'Soon be back.' She smiled. 'We've had it, till September. But oh, wasn't Lady Mead marvellous!'

Marvellous, they agreed. Just marvellous.

26

'Nothin's changed,' said Vi as the ferry gangway slammed down on Craigiebur Pier. 'I wonder why we always expect it will have.'

'The cabbages have grown,' Jane remarked, casting a country-woman's eye over the vegetable-filled seafront flower beds, thinking how pleasant this small promenade must once have been, with carefully painted railings and beds bright with flowers. But paint was in short supply and not to be wasted on railings – the few railings that had escaped the iron collector – and the growing of garden flowers almost a sin, now.

Nor, when they got there, had Ardneavie House changed. The brass-edged doorstep, the knocker and door handle still gleamed without her ministrations, Vi acknowledged grudgingly, and the unclaimed letters waited in the rack, as they always did. Ah well, best get it over with.

'One for me.' Vi noted the Ormskirk postmark, felt with fingertips for what it might contain. 'One for Jane, and here you are, queen.' She handed the narrow envelope to Lucinda, checking the name and address of the sender, neatly written on the reverse; the address in Vermont, United States of America; the name, Josephine Farrow. Vi had thought there would be one from Mike's mother. 'Get it opened, then.'

'I'll read it upstairs.' Lucinda snatched up her case and respirator, running ahead of them.

'Leave her.' Vi adjusted the discs on the In/Out board.

'I'll let the regulating office know we're back. There's nothing we can do and, anyway, it'll be all right.'

'All right? What makes you so sure?'

'Ar. It's such a lovely evenin', innit? Not an evenin' for bad news.'

Which was a load of old nonsense, Vi realized. Bad news could come with equal ease when roses filled the air with the sweetest of scents and laburnums hung yellow with tassels. Bad news didn't hold back for a November day, then creep in out of a dripping grey fog. Men died in the sunlight, too.

'It's all right.' Lucinda smiled shakily when they opened the door of cabin 9. 'No good news, but no bad. And I'm an idiot, aren't I? I could hardly open the envelope, my hands were shaking so.'

'Listen, love – remember what I said,' Jane urged. 'It's your turn next. It *is*.'

'I know. I keep hoping, Kendal dear. I truly do. But I'm getting to accept that I'd settle for Mike being a prisoner, now. At least he'd be alive. Well, Gerry's all right, isn't he, Vi? Sometimes you say you're glad he's not at sea any more.'

'Sometimes I do, queen.' At least Gerry McKeown would never do the Murmansk run. 'And no news is good news, innit, so let's get unpacked and our beds made up. At least somebody's thought to bring up our clean sheets.'

The seven days in Lincolnshire had been kind to Lucinda. She had begun to eat again, had laughed and seemed happy, and her smile found the dimples in her cheeks once more. But already the haunted look was back in her eyes, Vi noticed, and now they would once more scan the letter board with unease and reflect anxiety at each news bulletin. And as for Mike being a prisoner of war, well, the Japs weren't all that keen to take prisoners, so talk had it, and those they had taken could count on a

631

lean time, it would seem. Stood to reason, because the Japanese weren't like us, were they? Come to think of it, they weren't like the Germans, either.

'Let's be gettin' on with it, then. Soon be time for standeasy.'

It did not take long for Jane's news to run the length and depth of Ardneavie House. Good news was always snatched upon eagerly; news such as Kendal had for the telling blazed like wildfire.

'Isn't it just great, Pat?' Suzie St John smiled. 'Kendal's boyfriend alive and well! It doesn't do to give up hope, you see.'

'They're engaged now, so the buzz has it.' Chief Pillmoor collected buzzes. It was the only way she could keep one jump ahead. 'Just turned up out of nowhere when she was on leave, I believe. I don't suppose we'll get a lot of sense out of her for a day or two. Don't think she's altogether with us, yet. Seems he was got out of wherever it was by the Resistance, but she won't say a lot about it – and I suppose she's right.'

'Quite right. Nor must we ask. He's back and well, and that's all that matters. I suppose,' the officer chuckled, 'it won't be too long now before she puts in a request for marriage leave. Er – tea, Pat?'

'Please.' Chief Pillmoor settled herself comfortably for their evening chat. 'Though I don't think there'll be a wedding yet. Seems he's been sent overseas again, but even that hasn't wiped the smile off Kendal's face,' she said, remembering a long-ago defaulter's parade and the misery etched deeply in every feature. 'But it's nice to hear good news, isn't it?' Because there was enough bad news about, Lord only knew. More than enough of it.

* * *

The last thing in Wren Kendal's mind that night was bad news. Her world was perfect, complete in every way. She and Rob were together again, together for all time, and in little more than a year they would be married. Yet she still had to remind herself it had happened; still needed the reassurance of those wings. They lay, now, beside a pile of neatly ironed handkerchiefs in the drawer of her locker, and all she had to do was open that drawer just a couple of inches and they would be there to say, 'It happened, Jenny. It happened.' Rob's first wings; his sprog wings. They'd been with him a long time; on thirty bombing raids; in hiding in a derelict cottage on Alderney. They'd been with him on his new officer's tunic, the afternoon he had walked across the stableyard at Lady Mead, and now they were hers.

'Are we going downstairs for standeasy,' she asked, 'or shall I bring it up?'

'Let's have it up here. The loch is so beautiful in the sunset. And look at those ships, so stark against the sky. What a pity we aren't allowed to take photographs.' Even supposing they'd had a camera, Lucinda sighed, and a film to put in it. 'Come and look, both of you. There's *Jan Mayen* taking three of them out; a T-boat and an S-boat,' she said, proud of her knowledge of *Omega's* submarines, 'and the other one can only be *Virgil*. Come and wish them luck.'

Luck? *Virgil* would need more than luck to wipe out the taint of the Gareloch, Jane thought uneasily. She wished that submarine had never come back; wished she could be free of the memories it had brought with it.

I'm sorry, Tom; sorry for this sudden happiness. She wanted him to understand, to know that she and Rob were together again. She needed him to wish her well, to let her go. *I love Rob so much; I couldn't have loved anyone else. You were my friend, Tom – my very good friend – and I'll never forget you and how you helped me when I needed a shoulder to cry on. But it's Rob I love. It always was.*

She turned from the window impatiently, walking swiftly to her locker, pulling open the drawer. Rob's wings were there to watch over her. Nothing could harm her.

'Going down to the galley,' she called. 'Won't be long.'

They said they'd been half expecting it, that one day it just might happen, but when they listened to the news on that evening in late June, they hadn't thought it would come quite so soon, or so viciously.

The mention of the convoy number caused an immediate, listening silence in the mess; a careful laying-down of knives and forks. The letters PQ preceded every Russian-bound convoy number; everyone knew what Peter Queenie implied, and every ear strained to catch every unwanted word.

Twenty-four ships sunk! *Twenty-four* out of thirty-five ships just gone, sunk without trace!

'Jeez . . .' Vi hissed through her teeth. How many widows, now? How many more kids growing up without a da?

A May evening came back to her. '*He didn't suffer none, Vi.*'

No, Richie Daly, only them that get the letters suffer; the letters with a signature you can't read. Was the little that got through to Murmansk worth all those letters?

'. . . *and of these, two were naval destroyers, His Majesty's Ships* Tamerlane *and* Malvern. *It is feared there is little hope of survivors, and the next of kin have been informed . . .*'

Mother of God, the *Malvern*!

'Hell, Penrose, you couldn't wait, could you? Heard that, did you – the *Malvern*. And twenty-odd others.'

'Sssh, Vi. Not here,' Fenny whispered. 'Calm down.'

'Calm down? Just like that, eh? You said he'd take his ill luck with him, didn't you, Penrose? Are you satisfied now?'

'Vi, love – *please*,' Jane urged, taking her arm, pushing back her chair. 'Come on – we've finished. Let's get out of here.'

'And it isn't just the *Malvern*, is it? What about all them merchant ships, eh? God, but I hope Penrose can live with that conscience of hers!' Vi exploded when Lucinda closed the door of cabin 9 firmly behind them. 'Now just listen here, you two; if you ever go muckin' about again with that glass next door, I'll – I'll – '

'Tell me, Vi. You'll what?'

Lilith stood there, door in hand, her face pale and grave.

'I'll bloody well scratch your face, lady, that's what!' Vi spat. 'Feels good, does it, to know you can do things like that?'

'Vi – all of you – the *Malvern* would have been sunk whether Johnny Jones was on it or not,' Lilith said quietly. 'My ill wishes only took him there. Only *his* death is on my conscience, and for that I'll pay, if I have to.

'Oh, it's fine for you, Vi. You go neatly to your Confession, accept your penance and that's it. But I can't do that. Karma decides how I shall pay and when, and I accept that. And I *must* accept that maybe my payment will have to be made in another life. Who's to say I won't be given the body of a man, of a seaman, next time around? Or who's to say that in a past life, I didn't have a daughter who had a faithless lover?

'No – you do it your way, Vi.' She smiled sadly, her eyes far away. 'And I'll do it mine. Only time will tell which one of us is right, though I doubt either you or I will be here to say "I told you so." And at least Connie understands,' she said, as she closed the door behind her. And Connie and her little stillborn baby were all that mattered.

That beautiful summer month was not all bad news. On the fourteenth of July, Rob's first letter arrived in an envelope bearing the words *Passed by Censor* and a Rhodesian stamp.

'*Rhodesia!*' Jane cried. Rob was in Africa, where it was safe – except for Egypt and Libya in the very north.

She opened his letter again as they sat on the launch, heading for *Omega* and late watch; read each word over and over.

He loved her. He would go into Salisbury as soon as he could, he wrote, and buy her a ring. The shops in Bulawayo and Salisbury still had rings to sell.

'I must tell him when I next write,' Jane murmured half to herself as she folded the letter, 'not to send a ring.'

A ring would have been lovely, of course, but she already had Rob's wings, and the farthing he'd given her, hanging on the chain round her neck with the confirmation cross and the clumsy red disc with her name, number and religion stamped on it. A ring could get lost; ships carrying mailbags in their holds were sunk all the time and few packets came by air – only the little four-folded letter-cards. No, he must not risk sending a ring she knew he couldn't really afford, and she would tell him so when she wrote back tonight. They were together again, and in love, and in a little more than a year they would be married. It would make better sense if he were to buy a wedding ring out there and bring it back with him.

Oh, but it was good to make plans again, to be released from her limbo, to be living once more, and loving. She almost said as much, then bit off the words.

Lucinda couldn't make plans; Lucinda was still in her

own private purgatory. Twenty weeks, now, since there had been news of Mike; nearly five months. Poor, unhappy Lucinda.

But Vi had waited that long, hadn't she, and she herself had endured far longer. Yet Gerry had come back from the dead, and Lucinda must not give up hope. There had been no telegram to Vermont, no letter. Not yet. She reached for Lucinda's hand and squeezed it tightly. 'Your turn next,' she whispered. 'And don't you ever forget it.'

And Lucinda smiled briefly then rose to her feet, because the launch had come alongside *Omega*, and Lilith was giving the order to carry on aboard.

Another day to be lived through, to be accepted and endured, Lucinda thought wearily. Feet slamming as always up the gangway steps, the automatic salute at the top of them.

Then smiling at Lofty, asking what was new; lighting the cigarette he always offered. After that, headphones on, all other sound shut out. And signals pinging in her ears, *dit-da, dit-da, dit-da*. On and on. Thank heaven there were three boats out on patrol and another on exercises. Best to be busy, to have no time left for thought.

But how much longer? And how much more could she take? How long before the dots and the dashes she gathered in out of the air ceased to become clear and concise letters and figures? How long until she lost control and they were no more than one long scream in her head?

'You'll do the next transmission, Bainbridge, at fourteen hundred hours – all right? Know the wavelength?'

She said she did. Chief Wetherby placed signals at her left and she moved them a little aside because soon someone would bring the tea, would tap her shoulder and place it at her left hand, as always.

Signals in code, always figures. *Taureg* and *Virgil* and

Sparta – good old *Sparta* – at sea, and another submarine doing speed trials off Arrochar. *They* couldn't crack up and neither could she.

She glanced up at the brassbound bulkhead clock. Two minutes to transmission. Another watch, another day. Day one hundred and six.

Not all of July was bad news; just most of it. First, there had been the announcement of sweet rationing, which was bad news to all because people who had so far never indulged their sweet tooth now hunted the shops for humbugs, mints and acid drops to help quell the longing for the cigarettes they couldn't buy.

Two ounces of sweets a week, the ration was to be; two miserable ounces. It wasn't worth bothering with, said the man in the street. And what about the nippers, eh? How would they manage? Sweeties were a part of growing up, and now even the kids would suffer. It was coming to something, wasn't it, when they had to cut down on sugar to that extent. True, sugar was now produced from home-grown beet, though most of it was still imported. But it was a sign of the times, wasn't it, when people's pear drops and humbugs and peppermints had to be rationed. It only remained, said the man in the street, panic rising just to think of it, for that lot in London to cut the sugar allowance to the breweries, deplete still further the already depleted beer stocks, and that would be it! Rioting in the streets there'd be then, and mutiny and unconditional surrender to the Germans, who brewed better beer than we did, anyway.

'Ar, listen to this!' Vi smiled up from the letter she was reading. 'Our Mary says that young Paul has offered to do a deal with her. Says he'll swop his soap ration for his mam's sweetie ration. His contribution to the war effort, he says. Mary says he got a clip round the ear for his

638

cheek. I suppose they'll give us a sweet ration,' she mused. 'Suppose they'll give us sweetie coupons, along with our soap coupons, at pay muster. Think I'll let them two kids in Ormskirk have mine. *My* contribution to the war effort, eh?'

But just imagine, two ounces on each ration book. Half a dozen caramels, and that was it. Hard luck on the kids. And when he'd said his bit about the rationing of his humbugs, the man in the street directed his indignation to Tobruk, and the running of the war.

Tobruk ought never to have fallen to the Germans. Our troops, and the Australians too, had seemed set to hold out for as long as it took. And now Rommel had overrun it and was thundering on towards Alexandria and Cairo. They were like the Japs, it appeared. Unstoppable. Siam and Burma and Pearl Harbor were a long way off. But Egypt was altogether another matter, and that lot in London must explain themselves.

Hong Kong wouldn't fall, they said, nor Crete nor Singapore, but what had happened? Now we'd gone and lost Tobruk, and where next, eh? If Rommel kicked our backsides out of Egypt, what would happen to Malta? Malta next, would it be, then Gibraltar?

The man in the street had endured the rationing of his food, his clothing and footwear and the virtual disappearance of his smokes. He'd accepted separation from his near and dear ones or worked without complaint in factories and shipyards till he was almost too weary to stand, and he couldn't buy a nip of whisky or rum with his extra earnings because spirits had all disappeared under the counter. And his beer, the man in the street mourned, was becoming weaker and weaker and hardly worth walking to the pub to drink. All that he'd endured, but the fall of Tobruk was the last straw, almost, and that lot in London must give an account of themselves – and would, soon, because somebody in Parliament had tabled a motion of no-confidence in Churchill, and there'd be high old jinks down there before long.

Mind, it wasn't Winston's fault. The old lad was doing his best. All he needed was a victory; one real victory. Something to be proud of and pleased about; something to turn the two-finger V-sign right round to mean altogether something else when applied in Hitler's direction. One victory, that was all.

'The way they're carrying on,' Jane said indignantly, 'you'd think the Air Force was doing nothing! But what about those air raids, the thousand-bomber raids!'

Now *that* must have been something. Not twelve aircraft taking off, but a hundred times that number, almost, and most of them Halifaxes and Lancasters. What a sight it must have been; what a roar of defiance from four thousand Merlin engines.

It had taken one small bomb to wipe out four houses in Vi's street and now a thousand times that amount had been dropped on Cologne in one night. Then again on Essen, and now a third massive air raid, this time on Bremen, home of the U-boat. A flash in the pan, were people saying? It couldn't be.

But for all that, she was glad Rob was in Rhodesia — even flying with sprog pilots was a whole lot safer than crowding the skies over the Fatherland. For a whole year, Rob would be safe. For more than that, she could not ask; for longer than that, when wars were lived from day to day, she dared not even contemplate. She and Rob had each other again; her happiness was golden. She wanted to take the world in her arms and share it with them; with Lucinda especially, whose heart was slowly breaking.

'I think,' she said to Vi, 'that tomorrow we'll all go into Craigiebur and see what we can find in the shops.' The chemist must be due his quota of cosmetics any day now;

perhaps they could find a queue to join, and chance their luck. 'I'm in dire need of a lipstick.'

'I could do with a pot of vanishin' cream myself,' Vi agreed, going on to recount the article she had read in *Woman's Own* about using liquid paraffin for face-cleansing instead of cold cream, and that the minutest amount of castor oil applied to the eyelashes was nearly as good as mascara and made the lashes longer and stronger. And the article had gone on to warn of the dangers of using black shoe-polish as a substitute for mascara and painted a dire picture of its consequences.

'I read somewhere that Vaseline is good for dry skins,' Jane added, 'but where can anyone find Vaseline?'

Where could they find most of the things they had once taken for granted, when most shops displayed a notice regretting they were unable to supply vacuum flasks, saccharin tablets, lipsticks, rouge, vanishing cream, razor blades and Nivea cream, whilst others announced that there was a waiting list for prams, teats for feeding bottles, fireguards and baby baths.

'Lucinda said she needed a new toothbrush,' Jane said thoughtfully, 'so I think we should all get the next transport. Even if we don't come back with anything, it might keep her mind off things for a couple of hours, don't you think?'

Jane's happiness was such, now, that she could not bear to see her friend so downcast. Jane's happiness glowed around her and shone from her eyes and her so-ready smile. As Vi once predicted, Jane had become beautiful, almost overnight. Would that just a little of the stardust could touch her friend.

Lucinda was lucky. She was able to buy a toothbrush and a tube of toothpaste, and though Vi had missed the vanishing-cream allocation by two days, she was well satisfied with a tub of rouge and a tablet of Vinolia soap.

641

And afterwards they ate jam and bread at the British Restaurant and drank cups of tea, and talked about the goings-on of Mary Reilly's small family and the letter Jane had received from Rob's mother: a kind, generous letter that left no doubt of her joy that she and Rob were together again. Mrs MacDonald suggested Jane should talk to a Catholic priest, in order to understand the implications of marrying someone of that faith; once she had received her instruction, there would be nothing to delay their wedding, should the Air Force decide to send Rob home sooner than he thought.

'Ar, you'd better let me arrange it with the padre in Craigiebur,' Vi offered. 'He'll not try to convert you, nor nothin'; just have a few chats – and make sure you understand that our lot'll get the kids,' she grinned.

'Rob's mum is a dear.' Jane smiled. 'She says I must visit her as often as I've a mind to. Everything's just perfect, isn't it? You don't think I'm too happy, Vi?'

'Nah.' Vi dismissed the notion with scorn. 'We all of us get what we deserve, and I don't care who says different. You and Rob deserve some happiness, after what that Phemie did – and so do you, Lucinda,' she added. 'Your turn'll come. It *will*, I know it.'

'There was a phone call for you,' the duty steward told Lucinda when the three returned to Ardneavie House.

'Me? Who was it?' Lucinda frowned. Please, not Mama. 'Did she leave a message?'

'It was a *he*. Chiefie knows about it. It was Chiefie took it.'

Lucinda tapped on the door of the regulating office. 'The phone call, Chief?'

'Ah, yes, Bainbridge. Can't tell you a lot. I asked him to leave a message, but the line was dreadful.'

'He'll ring again, I suppose.' Lucinda shrugged.

'He never said. Just asked which watch you were on – at least I *think* he did; I could hardly hear him. I told him you'd be starting a week of lates tomorrow.'

'Thanks, Chief. Not to worry.' He'd probably call back, if the telephonists at the War Office could get through again.

'Who was it?' Vi demanded without preamble.

'Charlie, I think.'

'Ar hey; not him again!' Vi had not entirely dismissed Charles Bainbridge from Lucinda's life.

'Most probably wanting me to be the first to congratulate him.' Lucinda's lips tilted briefly upward. 'Maybe he's popped the question to Isobel. I'd be really glad, you know, if he had.'

And so would she, Vi thought. If the girl accepted him, that was. And there was no accounting for taste. 'Would you be glad about her gettin' Lady Mead?'

'Not glad, *exactly*, Vi. But I want Mike, so Lady Mead doesn't come into it now.'

'You're right, girl. What's an 'ouse, anyway? Only bricks and mortar. Look what happened to mine, and it wasn't the end of the world. Let's get ourselves tidied up for supper. Smells like liver and onions,' she predicted, nose twitching. And on liver-and-onions-day there was usually bread-and-butter pudding. Not that it would interest Bainbridge. Nothing interested her any more. It was terrible to see her going farther and farther away from them. It worried Vi. It worried her a lot.

The House of Commons gave a massive vote of confidence to Winston Churchill; an overwhelming vote of confidence, said the man in the street, when you considered that in the end only twenty-five had dissented.

The man in the street was relieved. He wouldn't have liked Winston to think the motion of no-confidence was against him personally. They liked the old boy; enjoyed his arrogant defiance of Hitler and Tojo, his scathing disdain of Mussolini. Churchill was the man for the job, the British population declared, and instantly forgave him his seemingly inexhaustible supply of cigars.

But the little rumpus at Westminster would shake that lot up a bit, for all that. Maybe now, said the man in the street hopefully, they'd be getting that victory – that one victory they so desperately needed – just that little bit sooner.

'We'll have to remember,' said Jane, 'that today is the last day in July and tomorrow morning we must all say "White rabbits" and make a wish.'

'That's a load of old nonsense, and you know it,' said Vi scornfully. 'White rabbits never did nothin' for nobody, except for that bloke who wrote *Alice in Wonderland*.'

'Doesn't hurt to wish,' Jane insisted. 'And you never know.'

No, you never knew, Lucinda thought, buttoning her shirt. She wished on everything, now: new moons, loads of hay – there'd been quite a few loads of hay around, lately – first swallows and first stars. She wished on anything and everything just for Mike to be safe, so it couldn't do any harm to cross her fingers the moment she awoke tomorrow, whisper 'White rabbits' and add yet another wish.

'Might as well try it.' She shrugged, searching her locker top. 'And who shifted my collar studs when she dusted?' she wailed.

'Nobody shifted nothin'. They're where you left them, queen, on the window sill. I keep tellin' you to put them –'

'Phone call for Bainbridge.' The door opened without

644

ceremony. 'Hurry up. It's from a call box,' said the breathless duty steward.

'Damn!' They might have waited till she'd finished dressing. But she hurried down the back stairs, because that was the quickest way, and you never knew, did you?

'Bainbridge,' she said, picking up the receiver. 'Wren Bainbridge,' she said uneasily into the silence. 'Who is it?'

'Lucy, honey?'

Lucy? Nobody called her Lucy. Only – oh, God! This was it. She was cracking up. She *was*. 'Who's that?' Her voice came faintly and she coughed to clear her throat. 'Who *is* it?'

'It's me, darling. Remember me? Mike Farrow.'

'No!' she shrieked. 'Mike! Where've you been, for God's sake?'

'Rangoon. Thought you knew.'

This was not true. It was Mike's voice, but it wasn't, couldn't be, Mike. Somebody was playing a joke, a nasty, peevish little joke – and that wasn't fair, because for one sweet, unbelievable second it *had* been him.

'It isn't you! It can't be. Where are you?'

'Where am I? Let's see now. How if you put the phone down, Lucy, and – '

'No! I don't want to!'

'Put the phone down,' the voice insisted, 'then open the front door. Put it down. *Now*.'

'Mike!' He couldn't do this! He mustn't! 'Mike, don't go!'

The receiver purred in her ear. This wasn't true. He'd phoned. Mike had phoned, then told her to go to the front door. My God! Was he really outside?

Slamming down the receiver, she flung open the door and stood there, shaking. And he wasn't here!

The phone box, that's where! She ran down the path

and across the road, looking neither right nor left, wrenching open the door even although she could already see there was no one inside.

Wildly she stared around her. He wasn't here, nor standing beside the front door nor beside the gate. He wasn't anywhere. No one was here, only Miriam standing at the hedge with a pair of shears in her hand; Miriam smiling at her, sharing the joke.

'Looking for someone, Lucinda?' she asked.

'Miriam, did you see – ' She stopped, her eyes following the pointing finger.

'You *did* see. Was someone in the phone box?'

Miriam laughed. 'Try the wild garden.'

'Mike!' Calling his name, she began to run. 'Mike, darling!'

He was standing there, beneath the silver birch trees, his respirator and cap on the ground beside him; standing there with a world of love in his eyes and a smile on his lips; standing there as if nothing had happened and Rangoon had never been nor the months of torment nor –

'Honey, it's all right. It's me – bad penny.'

She threw herself into the waiting arms then, pulling him close to her, her lips searching for his. All right, so it wasn't true, so she'd really blown it, but oh, this kiss was good and his lips tasted like Mike's lips. Pulling away a little, she looked up into his eyes: Mike's eyes. Wonderingly her fingers touched his cheek, gentled their way down the scar that lay white against his tan. She'd done that before, hadn't she: traced the line of it then laid her fingertips against his lips, to be kissed. And if she did that now, if he kissed the tips of her fingers, as Mike, the *real* Mike, did, she would know, wouldn't she? Know he was safe and here in her arms.

She lifted her hand again, her eyes on his. Slowly,

gently she drew her fingertips down his cheek then laid them to his lips. Slowly, gently, he kissed them then took her hand in his and kissed each fingertip separately, sensuously. It was Mike! It *was*!

'Why didn't you write?' She was crying now; big tears, warm against his hand.

'I did. All the time, on my way back.'

'They didn't get here. You could have phoned – sent a telegram.'

'I rang you a couple of days ago and you weren't there. So I decided to stop wasting time trying to get through, and surprise you.'

'It was you! That call was from *you*!'

'Of course it was from me. Who did you think it was – Charlie?'

'I did, actually.' Oh, dear lovely God, don't let this madness end.

'That guy still sniffing around, is he?'

'No, darling. He's got another girl now. Oh, Mike, tell me! Tell me it's you and that you love me and that you'll never leave me again. Pinch me. Bite me.'

'It's me, Mike Farrow. And I love you, Lucy Bain-bridge.' He ran his fingers through her hair; through the soft baby curls he'd thought about so often during those weeks on the run and dreamed about when he'd slept in swampy dugouts.

He cupped her face in his hands and kissed her again. He'd dreamed about that kiss too, and how it would be when he got back to her. Because he *was* getting back. Somehow, come hell or high water or the frightening, fetid wastes of Burmese jungle, he was getting back to her.

'How did you make it, Mike?'

'Oh, it's a long story, darling.' A long, weary, some-times nightmare story, and best forgotten. 'The bastard

Japs got our Spits. Shot 'em up, then bombed the landing strip. So we were told to get out, to make our way north the best way we could. The trucks soon ran out of petrol, so we set fire to them then teamed up with an Indian regiment. They gave us rifles and ammo – dead men's rifles, they were – and we went along with them. But it's over, honey. I'm back and I love you.'

'And I love you, Mike. When did you get back? How?'

'Three days ago. I made it into India – to Chittagong – then they just shunted us all over the place; anywhere there was an empty place in trucks, planes or jeeps. I ended up in Cape Town and caught up with a troopship. The *New Amsterdam*. Berthed at Rosyth.'

'Rosyth? So near?'

'Yup. That's where I tried to call you from. Since then I've been in London, getting kitted out again and seeing a lawyer to get a few things sorted. And I called at our embassy to see if they could get news through to my folks, some way. They said they would, but I sent a cable, just to make sure.'

'I'm glad your family will know, by now. I've been writing.'

'You have, Lucy? Bet Mom was real glad to have your letters.'

'She was.' Lucinda smiled. 'And your grandma sent love and your sister wrote to me, too. But what else were you doing in London, Mike? Nearly three days – three days wasted.'

'Not wasted, exactly. I had to go to the Air Ministry and find out what they intended doing with me. After all, I have lost two of their fighters. And there were other things to be done. I didn't waste my time entirely. And it took me a day to get up here; your railways sure haven't improved since last I used them.'

'So how much leave did they give you? How long can you stay, Mike?'

'I've got four days, if you can count today.'

'Only *three* days more!' she cried, dismayed.

'Afraid so.'

'Oh, Mike, why didn't you think to send me a telegram?'

'I did. At the same time I cabled Mom.'

'I haven't had it yet.'

'Did you expect to?' he asked, severely. 'Don't you know there's a war on?'

They began to laugh then, and it eased away the tension and stopped her tears.

'Darling,' she whispered, dabbing her eyes, her nose. 'Why didn't you come to me at once? All that time wasted . . .'

'Because, my love' – he bent to kiss her again – 'I was dashing all over London getting this, as well.' He dipped into his pocket and brought out a folded piece of paper, holding it between his first and second fingers. '*This*. Read it.'

She frowned. 'What is it?'

'I hope it's all okay.' He grinned. 'Y'know, it's amazing what I didn't know about you. I managed to tell them the place of your birth – it *was* Lincolnshire, wasn't it? And I said your old man was a landowner because I didn't know what his gainful employment was, but I had to think real hard about your date of birth; not the date, exactly, but the year. I had to do a quick calculation to work it out.'

'Work *what* out?'

'All the things they needed to know for the licence. That's what this is, sweetheart. A special licence. We can be married today, tomorrow . . .'

'*Married!*' It wasn't true. It wasn't! 'Darling, I'm not twenty-one yet.'

649

'I know, but I told them the wedding would be in Scotland and they said it would be all right.'

'Of course!' Scottish laws were different. Sensible. A woman didn't need to be twenty-one, here. '*Married*, you said?'

'Yes, Lucy. Will you? I know I should have done it better, but I figure we just don't have time for the moon and June and moonlight and roses bit. Will you, darling? Tomorrow, at ten?'

'At ten.' The shaking had started again. 'You've got it all worked out, then?'

'Sure have. Saw the minister this morning, soon as I got off the ferry. Poor guy was halfway through his porridge, but we got it sorted. Will you? Will you marry me?'

'Yes, I'll marry you. Do you know how much I love you?'

He kissed her then; kissed her long and hard, holding her close so she knew his need of her. The trees made a canopy above them, and somewhere close by a bee buzzed, while thinly across the loch came the keen wail of a bosun's pipe.

But nightingales sang in the evening, didn't they? Later, there'd be nightingales. She closed her eyes and pulled his head down. Perhaps all this *was* happening.

'Sweetheart.' He drew away a little. 'There's just one thing more. Best I tell you.'

'Okay,' she murmured, eyes closed. 'You've got a wife in the US of A.'

'Oh, sure. And another in Rangoon. Be serious, woman. This is you and me we're talking about. Last night, before I got the train, I went to Bruton Street.'

'You did *what*!' Her eyes opened wide. 'Now why did you do that? *Why*?'

'Because I intended marrying their daughter just as

650

soon as I could. Only right they should know about it, honey.'

'Mike, you absolute idiot!' she chided fondly. 'What did they say?'

'Not they. Just your mother. Your father was out, she said, but she did ask me in. The – er – interview took place in the hall, at the foot of the stairs.'

'And you got the worst of it?' Lucinda frowned. 'Poor darling.'

'Nope. Guess it was a draw, kind of. She was a bit icy; very much on her dignity. Said the Earl was not available, but that she could speak for him, and under no circumstances would he – or she, for that matter – give permission for us to be married. So I didn't bother telling her it didn't matter, anyway, with you domiciled in Scotland. I rather got the impression she thought I was after your money.'

'Mike – I'm so sorry. I'm afraid Mama can be a little – well, direct. Don't worry, though. I'm a big disappointment to her. I don't think she likes me very much.'

'Lucy, honey, I'm not after your money – you know that, don't you?'

'Yes, I do, and I'm glad, because I don't have any, you see – not until I'm twenty-one, and then only just about enough to buy us a little place somewhere. You'll have a job to go back to, won't you, Mike?'

He smiled. 'I will. That I guarantee.'

'Then we'll be fine, won't we?'

'Just fine.'

'Oh, Mike,' she sighed, nestling closer again, laying her cheek against his. 'Is this really happening? I *am* awake, aren't I? It *is* you? I'm not dreaming this?'

'No, my lovely love. Forget Burma, forget everything. Just think about tomorrow at ten at the church in Craigiebur.' He looked down at his wrist. 'And shouldn't you be on watch soon? And come to think of it, I'd like to get a couple of hours' sleep. I travelled up here overnight, standing in the corridor. Do you suppose that gorgeous brunette over there would give me a lift into Craigiebur?' He nodded, laughing, in the direction of the Wren driver who leaned, arms folded, against the cab of her truck. 'I've got to see the minister again, tell him that ten o'clock's okay; that the lady said yes. Oh, and we'll need two witnesses – can do, honey?'

'Jane and Vi. I'll fix it. When will I see you again? I must see you. I'll be ashore at half-past eleven tonight. Can you make it? I can't go until morning without seeing you again. Please, Mike.'

'I'll be there,' he said. 'Round the back. And remember to fix the pantry window.'

'I suppose I must go.' She sighed. 'I'll have to see Chiefie about leave and I'll have to make it all right with my divisional officer on the ship. But they hardly ever refuse marriage leave, so I should get it okay.'

'What if they say no?' he teased, kissing her gently.

'I'll go AWOL. And Mike – watch it with the gorgeous brunette driver. For one thing, you're almost a married man, and for another, her boyfriend's a Commando, and nasty with it. Give me another kiss, uh, then shove me in the direction of the Wrennery, will you.'

He kissed her, then twined his fingers in hers and tucked her arm in his, and they walked together down the garden path, past rows of lettuces and cabbages; past the greenhouse, where tomatoes hung in heavy green trusses. And she called to Miriam, who was pulling radishes, then ran to her, hugging her close, whispering 'He's back, Miriam! He's back!'

And the woman whose lover had not come back from a different war hugged her tightly, eyes moist, and said she was very, very glad.

'See you tonight, Lucy.'

'Tonight, Mike. When I come ashore. And – take care.'

She watched as he walked to the transport, watched the driver salute him, smiling, then open the truck door for him.

'Michael Johnson Farrow,' Lucinda whispered, the words leaving her lips like a benediction. 'Just how am I going to get through the next ten hours without you?'

She turned, remembering suddenly, and took the stairs in leaps of two.

'Vi!' she gasped, slamming open the cabin door. 'Jane! Listen! He's – '

'Now see here, queen.' Vi's face was grave. 'There's somethin' just came for you, an' it's probably nothin' at all to worry about, but if you like, I'll open it for you.' She held out the small yellow envelope. 'Now sit down, eh? Telegrams aren't always bad news.'

Silently Jane stood by, eyes apprehensive.

'Shall I open it, pet, and get it over with?'

'No, it's all right. I'll do it.' Airily, Lucinda took the envelope, slitting it, lips twitching, with her thumb. Slowly she withdrew the sheet, then her face dimpled into a smile, into that old, darting, lip-tilted smile, and she began to laugh.

'Sorry, both of you, but it's all right. I know about it. Mike sent it yesterday. Here – read it!'

'Mike? *Mike?*' Vi unfolded the piece of paper. '*Safe and well,*' she read out loud. '*See you soon. I love you. Mike.* He's all right! And me and Jane have been havin' kittens, wondering what was in that thing! But how did you know it was from him?'

'Because he just told me. That phone call – it was him.' She beckoned them to the window. 'He rang me from the call box across the road. He's there' – she pointed – 'in front of the transport. Look! See for yourselves! It's Mike,

653

safe and well, as he said. And now I've got to put on my collar and tie and go and ask Chiefie for a seventy-two-hour pass. We're getting married,' she cried, 'and, oh, Vi, *where* are my collar studs?'

'Come here, girl. Let me give you a hand. You're shakin' like a leaf. Married, did you say?' Vi folded the stiff white collar then attached it to the back of Lucinda's shirt-neck. '*Married?*'

'Yes. Tomorrow at ten. You're both to come.' She eased in her tie then adjusted it carefully before making the knot. 'I know it sounds crazy, and it is. Mike comes back after all this time so it's virtually, "Hullo, darling, how was Rangoon? Yes, of course I'll marry you. Goodbye. See you tonight!" and I go on board on watch as if nothing had happened. My world turns upside down; all I want is to be with him, touch him, make sure he's real, yet I go on watch as if the war would stop if I didn't. What's this war doing to us?'

'Now calm down, queen. It's doin' what wars always do. It's expectin' us to do what they tell us to do, *when* they tell us to do it. That's the way it is. Anyway, you'll not object, will you, when they sign your pass. The war does things like that, too – gives a girl leave to marry her feller.'

'But that's just it, Vi. They *give us leave*! As if they owned us.'

'They *do* own us, pet. For the duration, they do.' Vi smiled her lopsided smile. 'So can you take a deep breath, eh? And can you shurrup for long enough for us to say how smashin' it is to have Mike back?'

'Well, I *did* tell you.' Jane smiled smugly. 'I told you it'd be your turn soon.' Impulsively she gathered Lucinda to her, kissing her cheek, hugging her. 'And we'll be there, if you want us.'

'Want you? If you don't both come, it's not on,' Lucinda warned, laughing.

'Ar, queen, but it's good to see you happy again,' Vi choked, eyes misty. 'Who'd have thought it, eh? Who'd have thought when we got up this mornin' that all this would happen?'

'I don't know,' Lucinda murmured, bemused. 'You know, it's only now starting to get through to me. Mike *is* back, isn't he? You saw him, didn't you, in the transport? And that telegram *did* come from him, didn't it?'

'If his name's Mike and he loves you, yes, it was from him. Now can we have a bit of organization in this cabin? And Jane, will you take that girl to the regulatin' office and see she fills in that leave chit properly? And I'll get down to the mess and fetch three plates for us – okay? And be sharp about it, will you? You're due at the end of the jetty in less than half an hour.'

'I don't want any food, Vi, thanks all the same,' Lucinda called over her shoulder. 'I couldn't eat a thing!'

'Couldn't you, my girl?' Vi muttered. 'We'll see about that!'

A bit of law and order, that's what this cabin wanted; and a bit of law and order it would get, she vowed, folding towels, placing shoes two by two beneath bedside chairs. But just think of it. Mike back home, and him and Lucinda getting married!

There were days, she thought, closing the cabin door behind her, that she would never forget – and this day would be one of them. But that was the way things were, she supposed, when there was a war on. Everything happened so suddenly, always. It wasn't only the bad news that travelled fast; now the good news was coming in, too. Three lots of good luck they'd had in cabin 9: Gerry, then Rob, and now Mike. It made you wonder, just a bit, if they hadn't had too much.

But ar, what the heck? Those two deserved a bit of luck, didn't they? They'd be all right – both of them.

'And by the way,' she whispered to the door marked nine, 'did any of us say "White rabbits", this morning?'

'I don't understand it.' Lilith Penrose frowned as she waited at the end of the jetty for the arrival of her launch. 'Between you and me, and that's *strictly* between you and me,' she said sternly to Fenny and Megan, 'I did a session with the glass and board for Lucinda when she was so down in the dumps, and could I get any sense out of it? Could I heck! And it should have worked. I even got some of her hairs to help it along because I really thought her vibes were beginning to improve. I asked the glass to give me a message for her – *anything*. "Just one word," I said, "to give Lucinda comfort; one word she'll recognize, to hang on to . . ."'

'You didn't tell us about it,' Fenny complained. 'Why not?'

'Because if it went wrong – if things looked bad, I mean – it was better that only I should know. And Vi, too. Well, she caught me taking hairs from Lucinda's comb. But nothing happened – well, nothing I could tell Bainbridge or Vi. I just kept getting a name – the same name over and over again – and I couldn't let on about that, could I?'

'Why not? It could have been a name that might've meant something to her.'

'It might.' Lilith shrugged. 'But I wasn't risking it. Lucinda was miserable enough without me adding to it. I couldn't – '

'Hi! We made it!' Red-faced and breathless, Jane and Lucinda joined the little group. 'And what couldn't you risk Lucinda hearing about?' Jane demanded. 'Come on, Penrose – we heard it. Well, enough to make us curious.'

656

'No! I-I – ' Cheeks red, Lilith tried to dismiss the careless remark. 'It was nothing – really nothing.'

'So why are you looking so embarrassed?' Lucinda teased. 'Come on, Penrose. There isn't a word you can say this morning that would upset me. Not one single word.'

'Well, it was just that I had a go with the glass on your behalf, Bainbridge,' she muttered, eyes down. 'And it came up with a load of rubbish, that was all.'

'So why should a load of rubbish make me more miserable than I was?' Lucinda insisted. 'You can't not tell me, now.'

'It was only a name, Lucinda; a name that kept coming up, that's all. It wouldn't have meant anything to you, and to be quite honest – '

'*Go on.*'

'Well, if you must know, I'd got it into my head it was a name connected with your American – maybe someone close to him, if you see what I mean?'

'You mean, it could have been another woman in Mike's life?' Lucinda laughed with delight. 'His *wife*, maybe?'

'Now see here, I was only thinking about you. There was nothing mischievous in what I did. You were looking so miserable and lost.'

'I know, Lilith. You wanted to help and I appreciate it, I truly do. And Mike isn't married. I've been writing to his family for ages, so I'm sure of it. But you've got to tell me the name of the mystery woman. Whatever it is, I promise it couldn't make one iota of difference to me.'

'I tried, Lucinda, several times. Just a word, I asked the glass, that maybe you could recognize – give you comfort – and every time it came up; the same name.'

'Then tell us,' Jane demanded. 'Just *say* it.'

'Go on,' Lucinda urged. 'See if it would have helped.'

'Well, it was – look here, Bainbridge, would the name *Mavis* mean anything to you? Do you know her?'

'That's what the glass spelled out? Mavis?' Lucinda demanded. 'You're sure?'

'Afraid so,' Lilith choked. 'Every time. It was most insistent. Sorry if I stumbled on to something I shouldn't have.'

'Oh, Lilith, don't be sorry – well, only be sorry you didn't tell me sooner. You see, it *would* have helped; it would have helped more than you know!'

'She's real, then?'

'I'll say she's real! And Mike thinks the world of her.' Lucinda chuckled. 'Mavis is a parrot, Lilith, and only I could have known that. Mavis is Mike's Aunt Addy's parrot!'

It was a funny old world, Lilith Penrose decided, as she stood, wheel in hands, at the stern of the launch heading across the loch to HMS *Lothian*. She'd been right, after all. Bainbridge's vibrations really were improving and that one word *had* meant something.

But who'd have thought it? A pesky parrot! It took all sorts to make a world, she supposed, but a parrot called *Mavis*?

'I'm gettin' too old,' Vi wailed, 'for all these shocks. First you, Jane, and now Lucinda. I can't keep up with your goings-on.' She held out her hand, finger jabbing at her watch. 'And where the 'ell is she?'

'You know where she is. Round the back, with Mike. Don't worry, Vi. She'll be all right. She *is* going to marry the bloke tomorrow, you know.'

'Yes, I *do* know. It's nearly midnight – nearly tomorrow already! And you know it's bad luck to see your bride-groom on your weddin' day – till you meet him at the church, that is.'

'She'll be in. Stop panicking and get into bed.' Jane continued the laborious winding of her hair into pin-curls. 'We've got to be up bright and early in the morning, remember.'

'I'm not likely to forget it,' Vi remarked, tight-lipped. 'And I'm goin' downstairs to see where she is. Are you sure that pantry window's all right?'

'Sure I'm sure. I checked it myself. And I told the duty Wren Lucinda was still out. It'll be all right – oh, talk to yourself, Kendal,' she grinned to Vi's fast disappearing, indignant back.

Vi met Lucinda on the landing, cap in hand, jacket open, shirt buttons undone. Her cheeks were very pink, her eyes bright.

'And where the 'ell have you been and what have you been up to?' Vi demanded, following her up the stairs. 'Comin' in in that state, all unbuttoned! And did you remember to fasten the pantry window?'

'To answer your questions in strict numerical order, I've been round the back with Mike.' Lucinda smiled, dimples dancing. 'And we've just had a lovely snogging session, and if I hadn't counted up to ten and thought about you, Vi dear, I'd have stayed out all night. And yes, I fastened the pantry window *and* I put the light bulb back in *and* I saw to the blackout and Vi, dear, bossy Vi, I do love you.' She whirled her friend around the cabin. 'I love the whole world, and tomorrow I'm getting married!'

'Today, you mean,' Jane corrected her. 'It's tomorrow *now*. And for goodness' sake get yourself into bed, will you, or nobody'll be going anywhere tomorrow, except to defaulter's!'

'And how,' Vi demanded, ever practical, 'is Mike goin' to get back to Craigiebur at this hour of the night? He'll be shattered in the mornin'.'

'No he won't. He fixed it with the pier patrol lads while he was waiting for me to come ashore. They're going to give him a lift in their truck when they do the last run into Craigiebur. He'll be fine.'

She slumped down on her bed, eyes closed, arms hugging herself round, thinking about Mike and the joy of his coming; thinking that tomorrow – *today* – today, in little more than ten hours' time, she and Mike would be married. She and Mike were the lucky ones, and they'd have three days together, really together, and that was as far ahead as she could think. That, and how very much she loved him.

27

'Now then, Lucinda, you've got to do it properly; you've got to do it like always – something old, something new,' Vi fussed.

'Yes, and you'd better get a move on,' Jane urged. 'We've got to be on the nine-thirty transport, don't forget.'

'As if I could,' Lucinda murmured. This was her wedding day, after all, though she wished she didn't feel quite so – *peculiar*.

'Did you feel the way I look, Vi?' Lucinda gazed thoughtfully into the mirror. 'On your wedding morning, I mean.'

'Pale and interestin' and just a little bit sick? Yes, I did, queen. Most brides do. Only natural, innit?'

'You should have eaten some breakfast,' Jane scolded. 'There'll be dreadful noises in the church and it'll be your tummy rumbling.'

'I'm all right, Kendal dear. As Vi says, just a little bit sick. Nerves, or something.'

'Nerves – yes.' Vi frowned. 'Doubts – *no* – so don't be coming it, queen, or you're goin' to spoil it for yerself, and you don't want that, do you?'

'No, Vi. Only it's all so different – well, different from the way one thinks it will be . . .'

'And how would it have been?' Jane asked softly.

'Oh, you know. Some big do – most probably at Lady Mead; marquees on the lawn and Nanny fussing and a lovely white dress and veil. And loads and loads of bridesmaids – tiny tots with pink sashes – and pageboys in satin breeches . . .'

'Oh, ar.' Vi nodded. 'Go on, then.' Best she should get it out of her system. 'And what else?'

'And a glamorous trousseau – hand-stitched silk, you know, and a honeymoon in Venice.'

'And Charlie?' Vi suggested, eyebrows raised.

'Yes, Charlie. And instead it's Mike and just the three of us and Wren-issue pyjamas and a seventy-two-hour pass. And I want you to know that I'm very, very happy and I wouldn't want it any other way.'

'Good.' Vi beamed. 'That's settled, then. No regrets?'

'No regrets. None at all.'

'Right! So you've got your case packed?'

'Yes. Sponge bag and a clean shirt and collar and a change of underwear and one civvy dress and shoes. Oh, boy, some trousseau, eh?'

'Could be worse,' Jane commented. 'Now then, what about that something old?'

'My uniform? My shoes – okay?'

'Well, they'll do, I suppose. Now what've we got that's new, queen?'

'My gloves. Mary's gloves. You said they'd bring me luck, Jane. I put them away; said I wouldn't wear them until Mike came home. Oh, Vi, Jane.' Lucinda covered her face with hands that shook, wiping away sudden tears, taking in great gulps of air because she didn't want to make a mess of her face; not today. 'I'm sorry. Too stupid, but I'm so happy, you see.'

'I know the feelin', queen, and Jane's goin' down to the galley for a strong cup of tea for you and a fresh slice of toast, aren't you, Jane? Tell Kathy that Lucinda's in need of it – all right? And did you remember to pack some clean handkerchiefs?' she asked in her Nanny Bainbridge voice.

662

'Yes, Vi, I did, though I won't be needing them. No more tears.' She sniffed. 'I promise.'

'Good.' Relieved the drama was over, Vi returned to fundamentals. 'Well, that's something old and something new – something blue, we want now.'

'Well, there's – there's my blackouts. Does navy-blue count?'

'*Blackouts*? Lucinda Bainbridge, you are not walkin' down the aisle in them shockin' navy-blue knickers. Mother of God, yer honeymoon'll be over before it's begun if Mike claps eyes on you in them things! Haven't you any decent civvy knickers?'

'Well, there *is* something, if I can find them . . .' Lucinda rummaged in her locker drawer then drew out the garment triumphantly. 'There's these – okay?'

She held up a pair of palest blue, bias-cut, lace-trimmed knickers with a pearl-button fastening at the waist. She'd bought them in Paris, she recalled, the year she left school – not so very long ago, really.

'Now that's a bit better,' Vi approved. 'A bit more sinful, like. So how about something borrowed?'

'Borrowed? Haven't a clue, Vi.' Lucinda ran cold water into the basin then splashed her face vigorously. 'But we'll think of something, between us. And here's Jane, and suddenly I do feel like something to eat. You're so good, both of you, putting up with my nerves.'

'We wouldn't have missed your wedding-day nerves for anything,' Jane told her, 'so eat up that toast, whilst it's hot. I hope you've noticed there's butter on it. And has anybody spared a thought for Mike, will you tell me? Do you suppose he's all of a dither, just like you, Lucinda?'

'Bet he's cut himself shaving,' Vi offered.

'Or was last seen boarding the first ferry out,' Lucinda gasped, eyes wide. 'Lordy. What if he doesn't turn up?'

'What if purple pigs start flyin' past that window?' Vi

clucked impatiently. 'Come on, now; what can we think of that's borrowed? Surely we can come up with something.'

'You can borrow my best tie, Lucinda.'

'Nah. Ties don't count.' Vi had the family tiara in mind, or a beautiful old veil, at the very least.

They thought hard and long but in vain, which was a pity, Vi thought, though if people would get married by special licence, and nowadays a great many people were getting married by special licence, there wasn't always time to go round borrowing things. A very great pity, come to think of it, because she would have liked Lucinda to have done things the traditional way, even at such short notice.

'Something borrowed?' she fretted. 'Ar, well, I suppose we can't have it all ways.' And it *was* getting very close to half-past nine.

The brunette driver ignored the usual transport stop and drove them to the church gates, helping them down, calling good luck to Lucinda.

'Is that him?' Vi whispered, eyes lighting on the tall, disturbingly handsome pilot who stood at the church steps with the minister. 'Do we salute him?'

'No!' Lucinda lifted her cheek for Mike's kiss, relieved beyond measure he had come, wondering why she'd thought, even for a moment, that he would not. 'Hullo,' she whispered, feeling stupidly shy.

'I'm Alexander McArdle.' The minister smiled and held out his hand. 'And the registrar is already inside. Now you're not to worry, lassie. There hasn't been time for a rehearsal or even a chat between us, but we'll manage just fine.'

'Thank you. Thank you very much.' Lucinda felt a little better, though she wished the peculiar feeling in her legs would go and that her mouth could be just a little less dry. Running her tongue round her lips, she introduced Vi and Jane, realizing that though they knew so much about Mike they had never actually met.

'You all right, Lucy?' Mike asked softly.

'I'm fine. Just a little nervous.'

'Me too.' More than a little nervous. Come to think of it, he hadn't felt this nervous since the day the fighter came out of the sun at him and he'd pressed the eject button. 'No regrets, though?'

She shook her head, smiling. And, oh, Mike, she thought, I do so love you and want to be with you for ever. And if I could have a wedding-day wish, I'd wish for you to come through this war safely and for you and me to grow old together. Very old, my love . . .

'We're ready then?' the minister asked.

They all nodded, unspeaking, and Vi gazed at the tall, well-built Scot with the thinning hair and the kindly smile. He reminded her a little of Father O'Flaherty – on one of Father O'Flaherty's better days, that was – and she wondered what that hidebound old priest would say if he discovered her participation in a Protestant wedding. He wouldn't approve, of course, but what he didn't know need never worry him; and this was Lucinda's wedding day, and not even a reprimand from the Holy Ghost would have kept her away.

'Fine,' said the minister heartily. 'Now, it's almost time. If the bridegroom would like to go into church, then the bride and her ladies can follow at ten, perhaps. I mind fine there isn't a best man, but he's only a traditional figure, really, though useful for the safe-keeping of the ring, I'll own, so if you'd all like to – '

He stopped, his eyes on the stricken face of the groom. The Reverend Alexander McArdle recognized that look; knew exactly what the young man was going to say.

'The ring, Lucy! I didn't get a ring!' Mike turned agonized eyes on the minister. 'Just didn't think, sir. It was all go . . .'

The minister's kindly smile did not waver. He'd done a lot of marryings, and this was not the first anxious bridegroom who had forgotten, or misplaced, or even nervously dropped the ring and watched, horrified, as it disappeared into the depths of the heating system.

'Not to worry. I keep an emergency ring at the manse. I'll give the registrar a call, and he'll be away over and get it for us.'

'No! There's no need!' Pulling off her glove, Vi removed the heavy gold band from her finger. Since Gerry put it there it had hardly left her hand, but Lucinda wasn't going to be married with any old ring. 'Use mine, queen. Something borrowed, eh?'

'Lucy, darling. I'm sorry. What can I say?' Mike choked, red-faced.

'It doesn't matter. It doesn't matter at all.' Nothing mattered. All she wanted was to marry Mike. Now. She leaned towards him, lips close to his ear. 'Now put it safely in your pocket and' – she lowered her voice to the softest of whispers – 'and I love you.'

She smiled as he left her, shaking still, but very sure that their marriage was right and good. This was the day she had longed for and prayed for and wished for and had sometimes doubted she would ever see. But that day had come, and very soon now she would be Mike's wife.

The fingers of the clock on the squat church tower showed one minute before ten o'clock. In one minute she would open the door and join Mike in the church. It was to prove the longest minute of her life.

'Right, then,' Vi whispered. 'Deep breath. Head up, queen.'

Gently Jane pushed open the door.

The inside of the church was small, devoid of echoing heights, its walls white-painted. It smelled, like most churches, of musty books and dusty hassocks and dampness. But on the simple altar stood a vase of roses, buds unfurling, the dew still on them; picked that morning for a bride.

Lucinda stood very still and a blur of navy and white loomed at her from the back rows of the church.

'Ar,' Vi whispered. 'Look who's here.'

The minister raised his head and nodded. Mike turned, watching her walk slowly to him.

Then she was at his side and he smiled down at her; a smile that told her it was all right; that it would be all right for as long as they both should live.

This was it, then. Lucinda wished the shaking would stop. She looked ahead, fixing her gaze on the pink and white and red rosebuds standing in a slant of sunlight. One simple vase on a simple altar. No massed banks of flowers; no choirboys; no little bridesmaids with pink sashes; no fine gowns or wedding hats. Just her and Mike; Mike, with Vi's wedding ring in his pocket.

This was the way she wanted it. Turning, she smiled up into his eyes.

Fifteen hazy minutes later, in the little church dedicated to St Munn and in accordance with the rites of the kirk, Squadron Leader Michael Johnson Farrow and Wren telegraphist Lucinda Veronica Bainbridge became man and wife. And in the vestry, when she had signed away her old name and signed her new one for the first time, she took off the ring with which she had been married, laid it tenderly to her lips, then gave it back.

'Thanks,' she said softly. 'I couldn't have borrowed anything more precious.' Then she walked up the aisle, her hand in Mike's, with Jane and Vi walking behind, like bridesmaids.

At the door, she paused, surprised, then smiled happily at the guard of honour lining the church path. All of starboard watch standing there, smiling back, wishing her well. Lilith and Fenny and Megan Cad, lanyards gleaming white; Molly Malone, who'd been the start of it all, and Kathy and Miriam and the clerks from the paymaster's office. And Chiefie too, smiling broadly, wishing them happiness, shaking Mike's hand.

'It couldn't have been a lovelier wedding,' Lucinda sighed as they answered the calls of 'Good luck, Bainbridge!' And 'All the best!' and 'Don't forget, now. We'll be expecting a signal from you indicating course, position and speed, at midnight!' Smiling, she watched as Chief Pillmoor formed them into a squad, then marched them off to the waiting transport. 'Even,' she murmured impishly, 'if I'd had a ring.'

'Lucy, what can I say? All I could think about was getting that licence pretty damn quick and you and me getting married. We'll go now and buy one. Where do we find a jeweller's?'

'In the High Street, but he only opens one day a week, now. He's got hardly anything to sell, you see. Gets his wedding rings in quotas, once in a blue moon. Shouldn't wonder if he doesn't have a waiting list months long.' She laughed. 'Mike, a ring doesn't matter. We'll find one, somewhere, some day.'

She picked up the case she had left in the church porch and he took it from her. 'Can we walk a little way?' she asked. 'I want to get it all straight in my mind. It was all a little vague in the church, you see. I seem to remember seeing all the girls sitting there when I walked in. I hadn't expected them to come and it rather threw me. So kind. All I really do remember is feeling relieved that Vi's ring fitted, and that you didn't drop it. We are married, aren't we, Mike? It did happen?'

'It happened, honey, and I have the piece of paper that proves it, in my pocket. I do love you; you know that, don't you, Lucy? You won't ever doubt it, will you?'

'I won't. Never again.'

'Okay then, Lucy Farrow.' He smiled down at her. 'Let's go, shall we? For better or for worse, world, here we come!'

By mutual, unspoken consent they walked to the pier; to the place they had met. It seemed right that they should.

'I know the exact spot.' He moved her a few feet to her right. 'Just here, it was. I'd been watching you waiting there, and thinking what a jerk some guy was to keep a girl like you hanging about. And then you came up to me, blushing like crazy, and you said – '

'You remember, Mike? You actually remember what we said?'

'Every word of it.' He'd said the words over and over in his mind when things had got bad in Burma. They'd been like a prayer, almost. 'You walked up to me, and you said, "Excuse me, sir. Are you Nick?" It was a quarter after eight, exactly. "Nick," you said, "who's meeting Molly at half-past seven?"'

'Yes! Then you said if you were you were unforgivably late, and that you sure wished you were Nick.' Lucinda laughed. 'Well, all I can say is that I'll be grateful to my last breath for the injection that put Molly into sick bay – and to Nick, for not turning up.'

'I was in love with you then, Lucy.'

'You were? Right from the start?'

'Yup. And the next night, when we'd been to the dance, I wrote my grandma and sent her a snap of the girl I was going to marry.'

'Just a year ago, Mike.'

'A year and a month.'

They leaned, arms folded on the rails, shoulders touching, gazing across Garvie Sound. To their left the boom-defence tugs rode gently at anchor and above them seagulls wheeled and dived, keen-eyed for scraps.

'This is a lovely way to spend a honeymoon,' Mike said softly. 'Just you and me, for three whole days. Where shall we go now?'

'To my secret place.' To where trees screened out the war and sunlight patterned the thick, lush grass. Last time, she had gone there alone because she thought he had left her; now she must go back, exorcize a sad-eyed ghost, tell her it was all right.

They sat beneath the trees on the little jut of land; sat there for a long time, thinking, remembering, kissing gently because they were a little bemused, still, at the newness of it all, and a little unbelieving it had come so right for them.

'It was all so hazy in the church,' she murmured, 'and the service was strange to me, but one thing I do remember is the way your hands shook when you put the ring on.'

'I know. Guess I've never been so scared in all my life. You were shaking a bit, too. And you said, "I, Lucy Veronica Bainbridge," then you took a deep breath and closed your eyes and said, "Lucinda Veronica." I married you both. Lady Lucinda and my own Lucy.'

'It was lovely of the girls to come, wasn't it? I don't ever want to leave Ardneavie, Mike; not until it's over. I want to stay with Vi and Jane. Cabin 9 is lucky for us.'

'I like your friends, Lucy. Think we should've taken them out for a meal?'

'We couldn't have. They're all due on watch' – she looked down at her wrist – 'just about now. I'll make it

670

up to them, have a party when – ' *When you've gone back, my darling.* She couldn't say the words. 'I'll throw a party, later. We'll have to let your family know about this morning, and Mama.' Better do it soon; better get Mama over with.

'I've done it already – cabled my folks, I mean.'

'A bit premature, weren't you? Didn't you once think I mightn't turn up?'

'Not once. Not for a second.'

'You're arrogant,' she murmured, taking his hand, kissing it gently. 'And I love you.'

'I love you, too. You hungry, by the way?'

'Not especially.'

He rose to his feet, giving her his hand, pulling her to him. 'Where shall we go now?' She read the asking in his eyes, and was glad.

'Have you booked us in somewhere?'

'Sure, honey. Same place I always stayed. Same room.'

'Good.' She lifted her face, eyes closed, for his kiss. 'Then where do you think we should go now?' she whispered. 'Wherever do you think, husband?'

When they lay together afterwards, bodies warm and moist and spent from loving, when the afternoon sun made patterns through curtains drawn against the world, he lifted her unadorned left hand, kissing each fingertip.

'You must have a ring, Lucy.'

'It's all right,' she murmured, her lips against the hollow at his throat. '*I* know I'm married.'

'Sure. It's all the other guys I want should know it.'

'Y'know, darling.' She gave a little laugh. 'Once, when Vi and Jane and I were talking about wedding rings – it was when you were in Burma, and I'd no idea what had happened to you – I said I couldn't care less whether

671

wedding rings were twenty-two-carat or nine-carat. I said I'd marry you with a curtain ring.'

'Guess I can do a bit better than that.' He eased his arm from beneath her shoulders, then drew the ring from his little finger. 'This was Grandma Alice's signet ring.' He held it between first finger and thumb. 'Her parents, my English great-grandparents, gave it to her when she left home for America. See, darling, you can still pick out the initials – A.J. She gave it to me for luck when I joined the Air Force. Think it'll do, until I can manage to get one for you?'

'Mike! It's just perfect.' She held out her hand and he slipped the ring on to her wedding finger. 'And it fits. Thank you, my love. I wouldn't want any other.'

'Good.' He leaned over her, loving her, wanting her again. 'Grandma will be pleased when I tell her. But I'll send you a set – a matching set – before long. Back home, they're often sold in pairs; engagement and wedding rings together.'

'This one will do nicely, thanks all the same.' She held up her hand, loving her ring; loving it the more because of the intimacy of its giving. And it would never leave her hand, matching set or no.

'What did you mean – matching sets back home? *Send*, Mike? Darling, there's something you ought to tell me, isn't there?'

'Ssssh, now.' He drew her close again, feeling the sudden tensing of her body, cursing his carelessness. He could have done it more gently; he should have.

'Look, sweetheart, you'll have to know, but I didn't want it to be today. After this, there'll be no more leave for a while. I'm moving on. I know when, and where.'

'When?' she demanded, stiff-lipped.

'Thursday or Friday, it'll be. We'll be flying out. To Washington.'

'*Your* Washington?' She sat bolt upright. 'You're going home? Why?'

'Guess they've gotten sick of me pranging their fighters.' He smiled, wanting her to smile with him. But she didn't, so he pulled her close again, kissing the rounds of her shoulders, needing her against him once more. 'No, it's this war we're both in; your lot, and mine, now. The Brits are sending a kind of cross-section liaison staff – Army, Navy and Air Force – to America. Guess they thought I was a natural for the job – me knowing the language, understanding the natives, sort of.'

'It'll be more of an office job then? But that's wonderful, Mike; you'll be safe, there. I won't have to worry about you.'

'Safe? Hell, darling, I didn't get myself into this war to fly a goddamn desk! I'm a pilot, and a good one too. You think I'm pleased about this posting, uh?'

No, he couldn't be. And nor could she, she admitted. But in Washington he'd be safe; as Gerry was safe in Austria, and Rob out of it, too, in Rhodesia.

'Mike Farrow, you've done your bit – *more* than your bit. You've had three years of it and you've been lucky. And I don't care if you're pleased or not; *I* am. I won't have to worry about you every time I hear a news bulletin, and just think – you'll be near your family. It's ages since you saw them; think how happy Grandma Alice is going to be when you turn up on her doorstep. Darling, if you've got to go somewhere, Washington's the best place to be.'

'Okay. So they're sending me back to where it's safe, and I'm leaving my girl, my *wife*, damn it, back here in the firing line. How d'you reckon that makes a guy feel?'

'I could always volunteer for overseas service and get near you.'

'Oh, sure. And if I know the powers that be, they'll ask you where you'd like to go then send you to Australia!'

He wrapped her in his arms, pulling her close, kissing her ear, feeling the tremor that ran through her.

'Mike,' she whispered, eyes closed. 'You know what that does to me.'

'Lucy – what say we go dancing, tonight?'

'No!' she gasped. 'Not with most of port watch there. Sorry, darling, but we can turn on the wireless when the late-night music comes on and dance here, as we did at Eaton Square. Remember Eaton Square?'

'I remember, you wanton hussy.'

He kissed her ear again, and this time she did not demur.

'Lucinda'll be back soon. Poor kid. Three days isn't long, is it?' Vi had missed her; they both had. 'And if I know that one, she'll be scramblin' in, last minute, through the pantry window – like the Bainbridge of old.'

'*Farrow*,' Jane corrected. 'Wonder what she's doing now.'

'Jane! For shame!' Vi gasped, though she was smiling inside as she said it, and hoping Lucinda *was*.

The Admiral, who worked in a small, dark room at the Admiralty, replaced his telephone receiver as if it were too hot to hold and decided not to phone his friend Kitty Bainbridge for a long, long time.

'My word, Leading Wren,' he remarked to the writer who placed tea and a chocolate biscuit at his right hand, 'but that was a broadside, if you like!' And all because he had asked, innocently enough, about the health and happiness of his goddaughter Lucinda; a perfectly reasonable request, considering he was extremely fond of the pretty young thing. And for his pains, he'd received an ear-blasting the likes of which he hadn't experienced since his days as a midshipman.

'What do you mean – how is your favourite Wren? You haven't heard, then?'

And Kitty had told him, from start to finish and in the most clipped of phrases, how this fortune-hunting American disguised in the uniform of an RAF officer had called at Bruton Street and announced – *announced*, mark you – his intention to marry their daughter.

And now, would you believe, the ungrateful wretch had telephoned her from somewhere in Scotland to say she was married – and *legally* married, at that – to this American, who was going to get the shock of his life when he realized her expectations were scant and her fortune not a fraction of what he imagined.

And what was more, if a stupid, senile admiral had done his duty by his goddaughter and had not connived at her entry into the Wrens, such a catastrophe would never have occurred!

'Oh, dear, sir. Never mind. Eat your biscuit.'

'I wouldn't care,' he sighed, biting into the chocolate biscuit his leading Wren always managed to supply at standeasy – a rarity her young man at the American Embassy seemed able to obtain with amazing ease. 'I wouldn't care at all if I hadn't acted with the best intentions. Lucinda's mama can be trying at times, you know. Kitty Bainbridge is a very bossy woman, Leading Wren.'

'Sir, would this American be the one who joined our air force at the outbreak of hostilities and got himself wounded and a couple of medals and – '

'Sounds very much like him, poor boy. Why do you ask?' The Admiral moistened the end of his forefinger and collected chocolate-covered crumbs from his plate. 'Heard any buzzes that I haven't?'

'No, sir, but I did see last night's newspaper. Just a few lines, but the Press thought it worthy of mention, it would

675

seem. Something about the American air ace from the well-known New England family and his marriage in Scotland, two days ago, to the Lady Lucinda Bainbridge. So I mentioned it to my friend from the embassy; we were out at the pictures last night, and he said he knew of the guy – er, knew of the officer we're talking about.'

'And, Leading Wren?'

'Well, it would appear that this American's family is just about as well known as the Fords and the Rockefellers – in the USA, that is. The Farrows have a finger into just about everything; real estate, construction, oil, shipbuilding and now munitions. I believe they've got an old matriarch of an English mother and grandmother to thank for it. Or so my friend at the embassy said.'

'So you wouldn't say, Leading Wren, that this American from New England is after my goddaughter's fortune?'

'No, sir. Quite the reverse, I should think.'

'And he's rich?'

'Well, according to my friend at the embassy, he came into a multi-million bequest the minute the midwife smacked his bottom, so to speak.'

'Ha!' The Admiral's face glowed with pleasure, his eyes danced with mischief. 'Got you, Kitty my girl.' Picking up the receiver he began to dial the number of the Bruton Street house. 'Rich, did your friend at the embassy say?'

'Filthy rich, were his exact words; *filthy* rich, sir.'

'Did anyone ever tell you, Leading Wren,' asked the Admiral, his face alight with pure delight, 'what a very good girl you are?'

'Often, sir. It's why I never have any fun. Well, I'm going off watch now. Don't stay too long on the phone,' she cautioned holding back a smile. 'Remember there's a war on.'

* * *

676

Wren Lucinda Farrow, née Bainbridge, and her husband of three days and two nights stood at the open window of their bedroom and looked out over Garvie Sound.

'Our last night, Mike,' she whispered.

'Our last night for a while,' he corrected. 'Did I tell you lately that I love you?'

'You did, but tell me again. It's my favourite cliché.'

They stood unspeaking for a long time, arms entwined, bodies close, watching a half-sun sink into purple waters, watching a ship of war, black against a vermilion sky, gliding on silk-smooth waters to a rendezvous unknown.

'It's like a painting, isn't it? Not a sound; hardly a movement.'

Only a lone seagull, drifting on a current of air, called plaintively into the sunset. It could almost, Lucinda mused, be a nightingale.

She turned in her husband's arms, closing her eyes, searching with her mouth for his.

'Come to bed,' she murmured.

28

August, and high summer blazing. Swallows feeding nestlings and strawberries hiding red beneath big green leaves. And wild, white roses in the hedgerows, and foxgloves, and the last of the honeysuckle, fragrant on the night air. It was possible, sometimes, to shut out their war; a war, which apart from the bombing of Germany, was going little better. But they, the three who slept in the low-ceilinged room at the top of a house that once belonged to a shipyard owner, had found a contentment they would never have thought possible at that first meeting on platform 8.

'Just think,' Vi murmured, half to herself. 'Gerry's fine. Got a suntan, he says, and he never had that before; not shovellin' coal, he didn't. And Mike's been to see his mam and Rob's had a seventy-two-hour leave pass to Salisbury.'

'And it's pay muster tomorrow,' Jane sighed blissfully, squinting into a sky empty of clouds, 'and here we are, lying in the sun, and not a man between the three of us.'

'But they're all right,' Vi said hastily. 'They're all three safe. We've got to be thankful for that.' And they were; they knew they'd had more than their fair share of luck lately. 'Things have turned out pretty good for us.'

Lucinda remained silent, eyes closed against the sunlight. Vi was right. So much to be glad about: a near-perfect world for them all, but for the war – and *Sparta*. They had waited, on the depot ship *Omega*; waited and worried and swept the air waves, but now it was official. His Majesty's Submarine *Sparta* was overdue from patrol and presumed lost at sea. Official, though the loss had not yet been reported in the newspapers nor read out on the news. And Lucinda remembered the time she had first realized that *Viper* was in trouble and a time, later, when they had come to accept that the V-boat would never surface again – at least, not under its own power or with a living crew. And now it was *Sparta*, lost somewhere off the north of Norway. It had hurt her more than she would have thought.

What had happened to the telegraphist who had sent that first transmission; that first, frightening signal to come at her from nowhere, which she had written down figure by shaky figure on that first, frightening watch? *Sparta*, pendant number P268, call sign Charlie Able Easy, was never coming back to Loch Ardneavie. Sorry, lads. So very sorry . . .

'You're quiet, Lucinda. In Washington?' Jane enquired. Thinking of a city, was she? A safe place where there was no blackout, and things to buy in the shops. A place where there was no chance of a sudden, wailing siren, and bombs. 'Thinking about Mike?'

'I was thinking about *Sparta*, if you must know. Always had a soft spot for the old boat. Terrible, isn't it?'

'A swine,' Jane said flatly, recalling *Viper*, and thirty-nine coffins on *Omega*'s quarterdeck. Recalling Tom, too.

'Shockin',' Vi brooded, 'but that's war, innit? You never know the day. Tomorrow it might be my turn, or yours; that's the way life is. Don't take on, queen. Can't do nothin' for them lads now.'

'No. It could even have been one of our men, yet the world would have gone about its business, as always.' The business of killing or being killed.

But life was cheap in wartime. Young life, mostly; fresh-faced young men who'd hardly had the chance to know anything but war, and learning the hard way to survive for just that little bit longer.

'I know, girl, but don't spoil this smashin' night, eh? Think about them poor townies who'd give a lot to be layin' here, with us. And think about all them poor Wrens and WAAFS and ATS girls who've got lousy drafts and lousy billets and might be spendin' the night in a shelter somewhere. And the poor old civvies, an' all.' The civvies were getting the worst of it, and nothing would convince Vi otherwise. 'And there's somethin' else we ought to think about. We never had that run ashore for my birthday, did we?' So much had been happening, the day Vi McKeown began her twenty-eighth year. 'How about me treating us all to pie and beans in the canteen and a seat in the ninepennies; have a bit of a celebration, like? Better late than never.'

'Lovely, Vi, and thanks a lot.' Lucinda accepted promptly. 'It's payday, pies and pictures tomorrow, then? Seems ages since we saw a newsreel. There might even be something worth watching.'

About Bomber Command's onslaught on German factories and war installations, it would likely be; and Fighter Command's daylight sweeps over Europe, shooting up troop trains and gun emplacements and convoys of lorries.

And the Russians, still holding off the Germans, and a new general gone to Egypt to take command of our scattered army. But there'd be no real victories yet on the cinema newsreels; just the war dragging on and the end of it nowhere in sight.

'Rob said something peculiar in his letter today,' Jane said as they walked back to Ardneavie House. 'Said that if I ever get a letter or anything with his handwriting on it *and* a UK stamp, I'm not to have a sudden rush of blood to the head and imagine he's home. He'll just be getting one over on the censor, he says, whatever that could mean. And how *that* particular letter got past the censor,' she puzzled, 'I just don't know. But it's queer, isn't it?'

A letter, written in Rhodesia yet bearing a UK stamp and postmark. Yes, they agreed; decidedly peculiar.

'Ar, well. Let's be getting a move on,' Vi urged. 'I'm dyin' for a mug of tea.'

In mid-August, when poppies flamed in fields of ripe corn and farmers the length and breadth of Britain were grateful that the extra hour of daylight enabled them to continue cutting wheat and barley and oats until late into the evenings, one word filled the minds of every man, woman and child and made the man in the street demand to know just what was going on.

Dieppe. It stood large in the headlines and was repeated again and again in news bulletins. Dieppe? Just across the English Channel, almost opposite Hastings, wasn't it?

School atlases were opened to establish where exactly the raid on the mainland of Europe had been; that assault by Canadians, British, Americans and Frenchmen on the coast of France.

An invasion attempt that had failed, exulted the Germans; a combined-operations raid to destroy a radio-location station and its surrounding anti-aircraft batteries as well as an emplacement of long-range guns and an ammunition dump, declared the Allies.

A rehearsal for the second front that Stalin still demanded? asked the man in the street, wondering if all the dead, wounded and missing and more than a hundred of our aircraft lost had been worth it. What was going on? And what had that raid achieved?

And, if that were not enough, the announcement came of the death of a royal duke: Princess Marina's airman husband, brother of the King, killed in a flying accident in the highlands of Scotland.

It seemed that this war was no respecter of persons,

said the man in the street. Death's finger was impartial when it turned the pages of the Book of Life.

Jane leaned against the rail of the signal deck, looking out over the loch, realizing that the submarine making slowly into view was the *Virgil* and that *Omega*'s company, gathering on the well deck below, had been briefed, just as she had, about its spectacular patrol and the welcome it was soon to receive. Caps off, caps in the air, and three cheers for *Virgil*. But she wouldn't linger to watch its coming alongside. She was here to deliver a message and to snatch a moment in the fresh air; she had no wish to see *Virgil*, *Viper* – call it what you would – or read the Jolly Roger it would impudently fly. A Jolly Roger was no novelty now, though she had found it hard to believe the first she had ever seen, flying from *Taureg*'s conning tower. Three torpedoes for three ships sunk; the man who stood at her side had explained the symbols to her. And there'd been a dagger there for a special operation – an agent landed in Europe, had it been? – and a gunnery action, too. All those things were there on *Taureg*'s Jolly Roger the day she met a spare-crew submariner called Tom Tavey.

He'd called her Jenny. 'Penny for them, Jenny,' he'd said, and angrily she told him that her name was Jane and he was not to call her Jenny.

She turned, shrugging away the memory, to return to the coding office. *Virgil* had done well, was fast gaining the reputation of a successful killer submarine, the deaths of the thirty-nine vindicated, some would have it. Yet still it did not free her conscience of Tom, who lay in a Devon churchyard; Tom, who had loved and wanted her. Her goodbye to him had been a curse, almost, and the words would always be with her.

Last Sunday, she had gone to Mass with Vi, had sat

there watching, not taking part, for the service was unfamiliar and the words strange. But she had knelt, that morning, and prayed in her own way for Rob and for Tom, and that all *Viper*'s crew should be at peace. But they couldn't be, because *Viper* was back again in Loch Ardneavie with another name and another number, and each patrol so successful because *Virgil* had two crews, now; one living and one dead.

Leave me be, Tom, she pleaded silently. Go away from here, from this loch, from the submarine that once was *Viper*. Go back to Devon and take my guilt with you. Go home to the narrow lanes and the farmhouses with thick walls, to the hidden-away villages. Leave my conscience alone, Tom.

The days were crisper now, the morning grass heavy with dew. And the swallows had flown; had they gone to Africa, or Asia or the Mediterranean? What clever little birds to know nothing of this war; to know nothing of the monotony of early watches and late watches and being back in quarters by 2030 hours unless by permission. And going on leave every thirteen weeks, fare paid, with a leave pass and a card for one week's civilian rations.

But this war wasn't really monotonous, Lucinda amended mentally. There had been good times and bad times; times of despair and of joy, and would be so again. The real root of her unrest, she knew, was loving someone so much that it hurt, and marrying him and being with him, being wonderfully with him, for just three days. Then being parted and standing there, watching him go whilst every nerve and sinew and drop of your blood, every smallest part of your being cried silently for him to stay.

And through all that, you smiled; you smiled and held up your hand in farewell and whispered, 'See you,' or

'Come back soon,' or sometimes, stupidly, 'Be good!' But you never said goodbye. Not ever. And when you'd whispered, 'Take care,' when he was gone, you wept. Only when he was gone did you weep.

Three days. Three nights. The total of their marriage, and wanting him so much that now it was the bane of her life; wanting him wantonly and without shame and hating a war that had given him to her then snatched him back after only three days and three nights.

And when would this waiting end? When would this war end, and how many of their precious nights would it steal from them? The news this morning had been disturbing. There had been mentions in the newspapers about it from time to time, questions asked in Parliament, but now it seemed it was fact, read out on the official news bulletins and sickeningly real.

Death camps; killing camps. Human beings acting like animals; human beings being treated like animals. Men and women and children, even, being herded into gas chambers. Mostly Jews, but anyone the Nazi regime hated or feared.

It couldn't be true. They'd got it wrong on the news. They must have. Either that or the world was going mad, said the man in the street.

So the man in the street closed his mind to the concentration camps, not daring to believe their existence, and thought instead about the Russians, who weren't doing too badly. At least they were holding the Germans; not flinging them back as they ought to be, but pinning them down, killing them. And all the while Comrade Stalin demanding more munitions from the Allies, as if we hadn't lost enough men and ships already, getting guns and tanks to them.

And the man in the street was sceptical about the new general who'd gone to Egypt to take charge, because there'd been more commanders-in-chief in the Middle East than Churchill had had cigars. Montgomery, wasn't this latest one called?

Well, they'd give him a chance; it was the least they could do. But when push came to shove, said the man in the street, the war was still not going the way he wanted it to go; the way it should be going. When would they hear something on the wireless worth listening to – apart from Tommy Handley and Geraldo? When would we win this war and get fathers back home where they ought to be and women back in kitchens again and pints in plenty and good red meat and fags on the shelves, as many as you cared to buy?

When, demanded the man in the street more reasonably, were we going to win something? Anything. Anything at all.

The package Rob had hinted about in August arrived in early September, and because it had been registered, Jane was called to the regulating office to sign for it. Posted in Tewkesbury, bearing a United Kingdom stamp and addressed in a strange hand. But before she reached cabin 9 she had removed the envelope inside it – an envelope which *did* bear Rob's handwriting – and even as she slit it open and pulled aside the cotton-wool and carefully unfolded the tissue paper in which it was wrapped, Jane knew what Rob had sent. She had told him not to, but here it was, lying in her hand, the ring she had longed to wear.

'Ar, lovely, innit?' Vi sighed. 'What's them blue stones called?'

'Sapphires.' Lucinda took the ring carefully, closing her eyes, wishing.

'He says be sure and look inside it,' Jane whispered, reading Rob's letter. Then taking back the ring, she carried it to the window, blinking back tears, that she might read the minute inscription. J & R. 2.2.41.

'Put it on, then,' Vi urged. 'Make it official, girl. And make a wish, while you're doin' it.' Vi had never had an engagement ring, but she had great faith in engagement-ring wishes.

Jane held up her left hand. 'It's beautiful, isn't it? It came with a trainee pilot who's got night-blindness and has to remuster, Rob says. That was what he meant – I see it, now. I suppose they do that – wait until someone is sent home then give him things to post here. Less risk of them being lost at sea.'

'Well go on, then. Out into the garden with you, and have your little weep. You know you're burstin' to,' Vi ordered, shooing Jane out then closing the cabin door. 'I suppose you and me will have to get stuck in and clean this cabin, queen. There'll be no more sense out of that one for the rest of the day. By the way, couldn't Mike do something like that? Couldn't he buy you a weddin' ring and smuggle it in?' Such smugglings were considered legitimate by members of HM forces. Getting one up on those faceless, soulless creatures, the censors; getting one over on mean-eyed Customs and Excise men, was fair game.

'I like the one I've got,' Lucinda said defensively. Her ring was precious and unique and no amount of money could buy it.

'Ar. Perhaps Mike's better saving his cash, queen. You'll be surprised the things you'll need when you set up house, and the price things are goin' to be when this war's over. Best he should hold on to his money, eh?'

'Best he should,' Lucinda said uncomfortably, wondering when she should tell them about Mike; tell them the way it really was. Maybe when she knew for sure; when she had talked to Mike's London solicitor and the banker

686

who had written asking if she'd be kind enough to call in next time she had leave and discuss the account her husband had opened in her name. So very rich, yet never a word until their last night. 'Best he should,' she said again.

When she had been on leave, when she really knew, she would tell them. In just two more weeks they would all be going. Not long, now. And Pa and Mama to face. Oh, Lordy.

'Good, isn't it,' said Lilith at standeasy, 'to see Jane so happy?'

'Smashin'.' Vi nodded, watching as Jane displayed her ring to oh's and ah's of admiration. 'She's a different girl from the one who came back from AWOL, isn't she? Loves the whole world, she does – except that sometimes, just sometimes, she gets that look in her eyes.'

'*Look?*'

'Yes. It's that *Virgil*. Never should have been sent back here. Jane doesn't say a lot, but I know it's got her bothered. It reminds her of Tom, I think. Remember Tom – the Janner who was real gone on her? Well, she once said to me that sometimes she feels she's got no right to be so happy, no right to have got Rob back.'

'In heaven's name, why?' Lilith demanded. 'The kid had it rough for a long time; surely she deserves – ' She stopped, frowning. 'Are you sure it's because of Tom she gets these feelings?'

'Think so.' Vi shrugged. 'They had words, see, that last time they were together; before *Viper* went to the Gareloch. She told him to go to hell; she was angry at the time, and meant it. Now she thinks she shouldn't have said it – especially in view of what happened.'

'And she wants Tom's forgiveness – is that it?'

'I don't know.' Vi lifted her shoulders. 'And maybe it

isn't anything to worry about, really. Like I said, it's just sometimes it seems to come over her . . .'

'Well, *I* know,' Lilith said, tight-lipped. 'You see, I get the feeling too. Every time I go near the *Virgil* my flesh crawls. And Tom Tavey was nothing to me, Vi. It isn't Tom she should be worrying about. He loved her; he probably still does. Love doesn't end with death. No, Tom isn't the cause of the upset, I'm certain. It's that damned submarine. It's evil. There's evil in it and around it; I'm as certain as I can be. And it's likely Jane senses the evil too. That's what's really bothering her, though she thinks it's what she said to Tom. I'll have a word with her if I can, before she goes on leave. And I'll do a ritual, for Tom, though I feel sure he's at peace.'

She rinsed her cup at the sink then set it to dry, frowning. No, the apprehension she felt – that Jane felt too – was nothing to do with any one of the thirty-nine men who had died in the Gareloch.

The evil was here, *now*, in and all around the submarine *Virgil*. It was very, very real, and not only Jane had cause to fear it.

Lucinda rang the doorbell of the tall, narrow house in Bruton Street and was surprised to have the door opened almost at once.

'Lucinda. Not on leave *again*?' demanded the Countess of Donnington from the depths of a towel. 'You're always on leave.'

'Mama, it's six months since last you saw me.' Lucinda kissed the offered cheek, determined not to apologize for anything.

'Ah, well, you'd better come in now that you're here. I'm washing my hair. Simply dreadful, trying to find a hairdresser who isn't booked up weeks ahead!'

'Never mind. Give me five minutes to get organized,

then I'll wind it into pin-curls for you. You've got some grips? I *can* have my old room, I suppose?' she asked.

'If you're staying.'

'I'm staying, Mama. You and I have things to discuss.'

'We have indeed, child. I suppose you know the whole of London is talking about you, sneaking off like that? Is this so-called marriage legal in England?'

'Not so-called, Mama. Our wedding is fact. We were married in a proper church by a proper vicar – *ministers*, in Scotland – and there's nothing anyone can do about it. I was living in Scotland at the time and was entitled to be married under Scottish law.'

'I suppose you'll want a cup of tea? You'd better come down to the kitchen. The stove's been lit.' Kitty Bainbridge was adept at subject-changing. 'If you could put the kettle on whilst I root out some pins and things?'

Lucinda had made a pot of tea and arranged cups and saucers on a tray by the time her mother appeared with grips, hairpins, towels and a bottle of Amami setting lotion.

'You'd better leave the pot for a while to brew.' Lucinda seated her mother on a chair beside the stove and towelled her hair vigorously. 'I didn't use a lot of tea, so it'll be a little weak yet. Now about my being on leave again, Mama. We work very hard in the Wrens, you know, and deserve some time off, once in a while. We work seven days a week with hardly ever a make-do-and-mend – '

'A make and *what*, child?'

'A make-do-and-mend. And please stop calling me *child*. A make-and-mend was a privilege given to the lower decks in Nelson's time to clean and mend their kit,' she replied crisply, determined to retain her undoubted advantage. 'We still get the odd one or two – if we're lucky.'

'But my dear, Nelson is *dead* . . .'

689

'Not in the 15th Flotilla he isn't, Mama. Now if you'll just hold still while I make a parting. Left side, is it?'

'I suppose you know that Charles is seeing another girl?'

'Yes, and I'm very glad. Isobel. She sounds very nice. Charlie told me about her when we met. I'm very pleased for them both,' she said firmly.

'You went to Lady Mead, I believe. How was everything? I suppose the place is wrecked beyond redemption?'

'No. Actually, it seems well cared for. The CO is a very nice man. I met him. He let me in whenever I asked him and we all went to Sunday service in the chapel.'

'And the Dower House?'

'Everything's safe. Nanny's well, too,' Lucinda added, tongue in cheek. 'But you really want to talk about Mike, don't you, Mama?'

'I suppose I do. Why didn't you tell me you were marrying money?'

'You didn't ask, and anyway, I hardly knew anything about Mike when I married him.'

'Then more fool you! Ouch! You're pulling my hair!'

'*Anything* about him except that I loved him very much,' Lucinda continued belligerently. 'I only knew he had three days' leave before he was sent overseas again and I was prepared to settle for that. I didn't know about the money, though I suppose I should have suspected,' she mused, 'that time I saw Eaton Square.'

'He's got a house in Eaton Square?' The Countess jumped visibly.

'No. Only an apartment – a flat – and I rather think it belongs to the firm.'

'So how did you finally find out about the Farrow fortune?'

'Quite by accident.' Lucinda speared a round, flat coil

690

of hair with pins. 'It came up in conversation, sort of, in bed. Pillow talk, I suppose it was.'

'There is no need to get down to' – the Countess shifted uncomfortably – 'to banalities, child.'

'Being in bed with Mike is not at all banal, Mama – do let's get that straight, shall we?'

'Why? Are you pregnant? Was that the reason for the hasty marriage?'

'No, I am not pregnant, more's the pity. But the money, Mama. We were talking, you see, and I sort of mentioned about the grandparents' bequests, and I asked Mike if I'd get a marriage allowance from the Air Force. He said he supposed I would but that I wasn't to worry about money. That's when it all came out. I was quite shocked.'

She had asked him, then, why he hadn't told her before this, that he could have said *something*. 'All that money, I mean,' she'd whispered incredulously, and he'd told her the omission had been deliberate on his part. 'Y'see, honey, I've always had money – ever since I can remember – so it got to be important, right from the start, that people liked me for *me*, not because I was a rich kid.'

'His grandmother is English.' Lucinda pulled herself back from that last night together. 'She married a building worker and it seemed it wasn't long before they were doing well. Mike never knew his grandfather, but even so he was left money by him; quite a lot, though the money isn't important, Mama. For Mike to survive the war *is*. But you met him. He came especially to talk to you and Pa about our getting married. Didn't you like him?'

'He's handsome, I'll grant you that,' Kitty Bainbridge conceded. 'But we didn't have a lot to say to each other.'

'No. You hadn't realized his suitability as a husband, then.'

'He didn't say I was a little abrupt – did he?' The Countess's face reddened.

691

'As a matter of fact he didn't, but I'm sure you were.'

'Lucinda – why are you talking to me like this?' She twisted round in her chair, her eyes accusing. 'Pa and I only wanted what was best for you. How could we know you'd run away to the Wrens and come back married to an American businessman?'

'Now look here, Mama! Mike is my husband now and I think you should at least try to accept it, and accept him, too. And if you're going to be disagreeable about it I shall pick up my case and spend my leave at Eaton Square!'

Eaton Square? And she could, too! The realization made her feel a little dizzy; that, and the fact that for the first time in her life she had challenged Mama to verbal conflict and appeared to be winning.

'Lucinda! My hair! You can't go off and leave it half done! I've got to get it dried. I'm on duty tonight!'

'*Duty?*' Lucinda stopped, mid-curl. 'You've taken up war work?'

'Of course. Hasn't everyone? There *is* a war on, you know.'

'And what,' Lucinda demanded, wide-eyed, 'are you doing?'

'I'm with the WVS. I drive for them. And when I'm on late turn I sometimes go down into the underground with a trolley for the bombed-outs. They're very appreciative, those people . . .'

Mama distributing tea and comforts to the tube-dwellers? Mama donning a uniform and helping, actually acknowledging after three years of it, that there really was a war going on outside her front door?

'But whatever made you do it. I thought you didn't agree with the war.'

'No more do I, but there comes a time when one simply must do one's bit.'

'I see. Then I'm very pleased for you.' Lucinda smiled

692

because she knew the reason behind the sudden rush of patriotism. Mama's age-group would be coming up, soon, for registration. She would have to go to the nearest Ministry of Labour office and queue up like everyone else and be officially registered for work of national importance. All women had to, now. From eighteen to fifty, no one was exempt save women with children under fourteen.

So Mama had beaten them to it and chosen her own particular brand of war work rather than be directed to work in a munitions factory, or as a clippie on the buses, or deliver letters twice a day.

'Very pleased,' Lucinda repeated. Oh, but they said Winston Churchill was a wily old fox, but when it came to craft and cunning, Kitty Bainbridge could give him a head start and leave him standing. 'And I think the tea will be ready now.' There really wasn't much else to say.

Later that evening, Lucinda went to Eaton Square. Not to sleep; just to look at everything again, and bring Mike a little closer.

'Good evening, milady.' The janitor seemed pleased to see her, handing over the key with a smile. 'We hoped you might come.'

'I won't be staying. Just here to – to collect something.'

To have a look, really. To make sure it had been real, that pink and white bathroom and the big double bed. To look again at where they'd first been lovers and remember how she had stood there, embarrassed, in the pyjama jacket with the too-long sleeves.

Not a lot had changed, though there was an air of loneliness about the place, as if it wanted them back.

'I want him back too,' she whispered into the emptiness. She wanted him so much; needed his hands to touch her body, every smallest part of it; wanted his mouth on hers, his tongue probing.

In the bedroom and for no reason at all, she pulled back the bed cover, and her heart gave a leap of joy because they were there, neatly folded on the pillow: Mike's pale green pyjamas.

She snatched them to her, holding them to her cheek, then rolling them tightly, she pushed them into her handbag.

The pink and white bathroom was still the same; waiting, like the rest of the rooms. Fluffy towels still lay in neat piles, the bottle of Chanel perfume was still there, unopened.

Impulsively Lucinda reached for it. It wasn't doing a lot of good, sitting beside the mirror looking decorative, and Mama hadn't had a decent bottle of scent, she said, since Dunkirk.

A peace offering, perhaps? Well, why not?

Jane had been home several hours before her new ring was remarked upon, and even then it was by her father.

For the first time in many months she had been pleased to come home to Dormer Cottage, free for the first time from the misery of Rob's loss. And she had endured a rapturous, face-licking welcome from Missy and a kiss from her mother, whose reproachful look made it plain she should not have spent her last leave in Lincolnshire.

But she had refused to let anything spoil her complete and shining happiness, and had hurried upstairs to the attic bedroom and taken Rob's picture from beneath the lining paper in her underwear drawer and placed it beside her bed.

Her ring had been ignored throughout supper, even though she was still unused to its being there; still did things with her left hand instead of her right. It was not until she stood with her father at the gate of Ten-acre Pasture, which was a pasture no longer, watching the uppings and downings of the tractor that ploughed in the last of summer's stubble, that acknowledgement came.

'Mother wondered about your ring, lass,' Richard Kendal said. 'It isn't an engagement ring?'

'It is, Dad, and you both know it is,' Jane said softly, her eyes not leaving the earth that reared up then fell like a wave at the blade of the plough. 'Rob sent it from Rhodesia a couple of weeks ago. Don't spoil it for me. Please.'

'Rob? He's the pilot, isn't he? We thought – ' He stopped, embarrassed.

'You thought he was dead, that it was over, didn't you? Well, *I* never did. He's overseas for a year, training pilots, and when he comes back we want to be married. And you might as well know, Dad, that he's a Catholic and I shall marry him in a Catholic church.' She took a deep, calming breath, glad it was all in the open. Then, calmer, she added, 'That's the worst of it as far as you and Mum are concerned, and the best of it is that I got him back and I love him very much – and if only you'd give him a chance you'd both come to care for him too.'

Richard Kendal fished in his pocket for his tobacco and pipe and made a great play of filling and lighting it. Then he whistled to Missy, who was nosing the hedgerow, tail wagging.

'Come on, girl. Good bitch, then. Come here!' he called, and Jane knew they would never accept Rob, let alone make him welcome in their home or try to like him.

Anger rose in her throat at the injustice of it, and for a moment she wanted to reason with him, beg his support against her mother's stubbornness. Because it was her mother, really, who clung to her as if she were a child still; her mother who clucked like a too-old hen with its

695

one chick. Then she looked down at her ring and remembered that Rob had chosen it and had the Candlemas date engraved inside it. And she recalled his letters and all the lovely, intimate things he had written as he counted off another day towards his homecoming. And she vowed that when they were married they would have several children – three, at least – so that not all their hopes and love and ambitions should be centred on one unfortunate young being. And more important than that, they would be *young* parents.

'Come on, Dad,' she said gently. 'It's getting cold and you look tired out.'

And because she didn't storm or sob or throw a tantrum as once she might have done, because there was a sureness about her smile and in the softness of her voice, he knew they had lost her, this child who had come to them in their middle years. She was a woman now, and that woman was in love. It seemed there was nothing they could do.

On the last evening of her leave, Jane went to Yeomans Lane, walking to the beech tree, climbing the stile into Tingle's Wood. The fingers of the clock on St Crispin's tower pointed to seven; it was right that they should, even though Rob would not come.

The incredible happiness inside her glowed like a flame; she had not thought such a feeling could be possible, yet it wrapped her round like a cobweb-soft shawl, shone like sudden sunlight on a November day, made her think of new-born lambs, the call of the first cuckoo, the scent of orange blossom.

'God,' she whispered, lifting her face to the September sky. 'God, it's Jane Kendal, and thank you for my happiness. Thank you.'

She walked on to the perimeter fence, shaking it,

searching for the break through which Rob had pushed. It was still there. They hadn't found it and repaired it.

Ahead, she could see the hangar roofs and to her right the black and green and khaki control tower, and she wondered if crews were being briefed and their WAAF drivers waiting beside the trucks that would take them to their bombers.

Tonight, nerves might be stretched, mouths dry. Tonight, young men with old men's eyes might take their aircraft slowly around the perimeter track then wait for the green light that would flash them on their way. Then they would send their clumsy, heavily laden craft hurtling down the runway, sweating, urging, wrestling them into the air. If they were flying, tonight.

She turned, calling to Missy, marvelling that this was the first time she had come here with a heart that was easy.

'Come on, girl. Let's go home.'

She heard the first cough and splutter of an aircraft engine as she climbed the stile and stood, legs straddled, to listen as it became a throb then swelled to a roar and was joined by more and more engines, until the air shook and shivered with their noise and vibrations.

They were running the engines of the Halifax bombers, warming them up in a full-throated crescendo. They were flying, tonight. They were operational tonight at Fenton Bishop, and Rob was safe in Rhodesia with his sprog pilots.

'Missy!' She began to run, past the beech tree, up the lane, not stopping until she reached Dormer Cottage.

'I'm back,' she called, taking the stairs two by two, the bitch at her heels. Flinging open the windows, she settled herself on the window seat, Missy beside her.

'They're going tonight, girl,' she whispered, clutching the labrador to her. 'We'll sit here and see them off, eh?'

She sat there, silently, to wait and watch and wish them all well. She would keep vigil until the bombers became airborne and their clumsiness had turned to grace as they headed up and out into the lonely sky. And she would bless each one on its way, and her love and caring would go with them.

Soon, now, they would start. Soon she would see the first distant green light then count each flash. Twelve, would there be, like the last time she counted? And in less than half an hour they would have screamed down the runway and shuddered over the rooftops of the village.

'Take care,' she would whisper. 'Come home safely.'

Tonight, there was no fear inside her, no cold hand clutching her heart; just a good wish for youths who were old enough to fly and to kill yet too young to count themselves men. The first green light flashed distantly, and she began to count.

Downstairs, Richard Kendal sat beside the kitchen fire and took comfort from the words of his wife.

'You're worrying over nothing, love. That ring on her finger means not a thing. She's a child, still. She won't be twenty till Christmas, let alone twenty-one. She can't marry him yet, so stop your fretting, Richard, and call her downstairs from that window, because that's where she'll be, the silly young thing.'

Marry that pilot? Oh, *no*!

Vi sat on the front seat of the bus, on her way to the presbytery, and thought of the pleasure on her sister's face when she had greeted her.

'Vi, girl! It's so long since we've seen you!'

She was grateful for Mary and that Mary's children were hers for the sharing. She smiled at the recall of delighted young faces, eyes alight at the chocolate bars she had brought them. They had talked late into the night, she and her sister.

'Ar, girl, if you was to see that great big house Lucinda once lived in; dozens and dozens of rooms – even had their own chapel. And Nanny Bainbridge so nice and polite to me . . .'

And she had narrated, word for dramatic word, the tale of Jane's meeting with Rob, and they had tut-tutted together over Phemie's shameful behaviour, and had the time of their lives, gossiping away the events of six months apart.

Vi left the bus at the first of the Scotland Road stops then walked the short distance to Lyra Street. To pass the mound that had once been her home – hers and Gerry's – no longer bothered her, even though now it seemed to have become a dumping ground for rubbish. Now she could tell herself calmly that life did not revolve around houses and possessions. It was people who mattered, and keeping alive and hanging on to the end of the war.

'Well, now, if it isn't Violet Theresa! Come along in, girl. My, but the sight of you is welcome.' Father O'Flaherty beamed. 'No need to ask if you're well.'

'I'm fine, Father. And how's yourself, then? Busy are you? Keepin' going?'

'Just about, Theresa. And busy? I tell you, girl, that I wouldn't know what to do without the Sisters, and that's the trut' of it.'

'Ar.' Vi nodded. 'Busy.' Yes, he would be. There'd be a lot more goings-on and sinning for him to cope with, these days. Stood to reason, with a war on.

'Will you come in, now? Mrs O'Keefe's away again to Bootle to their Bridie's. Another baby on the way, it seems, and herself there by the minutes. Will you tell me, Theresa, what it is gets into a sane and sensible housekeeper the minute she becomes a grandmother?'

'Ah, now, there you have me, Father.' A grandmother was something she would never be. 'But I'll not keep you. Just thought I'd call and tell you about it all.'

'You'll not mind the kitchen, Theresa?' The priest set the kettle to boil. 'You'll be taking a cup of tea with me? And what have you got, then, to tell me?'

'Well, Father.' Vi hung her cap on the back of the chair and unfastened her jacket. 'You'll remember I told you about the shockin' mess them friends of mine had got themselves into with their love lives, an' all that?'

She dipped into her pocket and brought out her cigarette packet, offering it to the priest, passing her matches so he might light it himself.

'I remember. Lit candles, we did.' He inhaled deeply, blissfully, on a Capstan full-strength.

'Well, it's sorted itself out. Lucinda married her man.'

'The right man, was it?'

'The *right* man, Father. And Jane – well, you'll never believe this . . .'

And she went on to recount the miraculous meeting and explain away the good Catholic marriage that hadn't been a marriage at all. And Phemie, of course, and Phemie's baby.

'There now. The poor man,' the priest clucked. 'The deviosity of some women! Make you shudder, so it would. But didn't you tell me your friend was not of the faith?'

'Ar. Jane's a Protestant.'

'And will there be complications, do you think?'

'Nah. She's taking instruction for when Rob comes back. And she's been with me to Mass, though she didn't understand one blind word of it. But she knows the kids'll have to be Cath'licks, so it'll be all right. All she wants is to marry Rob. She wouldn't care what he was.'

'There's no hope of a conversion, is there?'

'Don't know. She might; she might not. But the weddin'

700

will be in Rob's own church, in Scotland,' she offered, reassuringly. 'Well, it'll have to be. She couldn't get married in England till she's twenty-one – her mam and da wouldn't buy it – and she won't be twenty till Christmas, so she doesn't have a lot of choice. But everything's going well for Jane and Lucinda – both of them happy, now.'

'The power of prayer, Theresa; the power of prayer. And how's your Gerald getting along?'

'He's fine, Father, and the better for being away from them Russian convoys. I sometimes wonder if he'll ever go back to sea again, once this lot's over.'

'Time will tell, child. Our Lord knows best. And how's Mary Reilly, then?'

'She's well, and her man won't have to go into the Army just yet, so she's not lettin' herself worry about it till it happens. Ah, well, I'll be goin'. Just wanted you to know everything had turned out all right. And by the way, Father, are you still havin' trouble with your ciggies?'

'I am, Theresa. And some days it's down to three. To be sure, I don't know what the world is coming to. I tried to give them up for Lent, but I was giving terrible harsh penances and snapping and snarling something awful. Only lasted four days. I'm weak, child.'

'Then it's a good job I thought to save you a few out of my ration, isn't it?' Vi rummaged in her shoulder bag and brought out three packets. 'Here y'are, Father.'

'Theresa – what can I say? You're a kind and thoughtful girl, so you are.' The tired old eyes misted over.

'Now I don't have to remind you, Father, that them ciggies are for HM ships only. I'm not supposed to give 'em to civilians, you know that, don't you? So smoke them private, like.'

'I will, child. I will.' He'd lock himself in the lavatory and smoke them there, so he would, and not even that

701

sharp-nosed Mrs O'Keefe would get so much as a whiff of one of them.

'Well, I'll be off.' Vi buttoned her jacket and arranged her cap. 'Goin' back to Ardneavie on Thursday, so ta-ra, Father. Take care now.'

'And you, Theresa. God bless you and yours.'

Vi waited, thinking, at the tram stop. Maybe a quick trip down to the Pier Head to have a look at that mucky old river and see if the liver birds were still perched there?

She liked riding on the rocking, swaying trams rattling along like war chariots and everything getting out of their way. She was glad she'd made the effort to see the old priest. He'd been made up with them few ciggies, God love the old devil. And she'd been glad to come to Liverpool on leave, to feel the sense of homecoming the minute she set foot on the platform at Lime Street station; glad to hear the familiar Scouse twang, and see them all at Ormskirk.

But she'd be glad to be going back to Ardneavie; to Jane and Lucinda and Lilith's lot and Patsy Pill.

She had missed them; missed them more than she'd ever thought possible, especially them terrible two in cabin 9. One for all and all for one, eh?

The tram clanked to a halt. The conductor called, 'Pier 'ead. Come along then, girl. We haven't got all day!'

Missed them both, she had. More than she cared to admit.

29

'The old ones used to say,' remarked Lilith, observing the brambles that hung in ripe purple sprays on the stableyard hedge, 'that it was unlucky to pick those berries after Michaelmas Day.'

'And why was that, *cariad*?'

'It would seem, Megan, that they believed Lucifer fell out of heaven into a bramble bush on St Michael's Day, so he spat on it and cursed it.'

'So would you,' Jane grimaced, remembering her own youthful encounter with a bramble bush.

'Merely a point of interest.' Lilith shrugged. 'And don't pile any more in that basket, Fenny, or it'll be too heavy to carry upstairs.'

The boat's-crew Wrens and the Wrens in cabin 9 were sawing the wood gathered through summer and splitting it into logs. Now, the days were shortening and mornings held a hint of autumn and the top-floor Wrens were making ready again for the cold dark days of a northern winter.

'Won't be long before we'll be lighting our fire,' Lilith observed when she and Jane were alone. 'It was a good summer, wasn't it?'

'Perfect,' Jane sighed, 'in every way.'

'I'm glad things turned out so well, Kendal. It's good to see you so happy,' Lilith said softly. 'Don't let anything spoil it for you.'

'Spoil it?' Jane frowned, eyes questioning.

'You know what I mean. I've been wanting the chance

703

to get you alone since before you went on leave. Don't worry about – well, about anything, uh?'

'Worry?' Jane saw only concern in the deep, dark eyes.

'Worry about Tom. Vi says she thinks you do, sometimes.'

'Vi's an old fusspot, but yes, Lilith, I do have feelings, sometimes.' Useless, she realized, trying to hide anything from a woman whose eyes could look into your soul.

'Then don't – at least not where Tom Tavey is concerned. Vi told me Tom cared a lot about you.'

'You and Vi *have* been busy.' Jane made to walk away.

'Listen, love. Hear me out. We only want you to be happy with Rob,' Lilith pleaded softly. 'You worry about what you said to Tom, don't you?'

'Yes, I do.' Once released, the words spilled out unchecked. 'It was bitchy of me and I'm sorry about it. I'd give anything never to have said what I did. Sometimes – just sometimes – I think I'm too happy and that I've no right to be. Whenever I see *Virgil* I think I'll have to pay for it.'

'Who's to tell?' Lilith's voice was tinged with sadness. 'We don't any of us know what's to come for us. Stands to reason, doesn't it? But it isn't Tom you have to fear – please believe me, Jane. If he loved you, and I believe he did, he'll be glad, now, for you. If you want to find the cause of it all, I think you should look no further than *Virgil*.'

'*Viper*, don't you mean?' Jane demanded.

'*Virgil*,' Lilith repeated firmly, 'though there's *Viper*'s ill luck clinging to it like a bad smell, as far as I'm concerned.'

'You feel it too?'

'Not half! Me and anyone else with an iota of sensitivity in them. *Virgil*'s a renamed boat, and that in itself is enough to put a jinx on it, apart from what happened in

704

the Gareloch. But my teeth water whenever I'm near the thing. I sense it, too, so don't think what you feel is anything to do with Tom. Your uneasiness is none of Tom's doing; *Virgil* is the cause of it, and there's nothing directed at you any more than at the rest of us. So stop worrying, that's an order, and quiet, they're coming back.'

They came chattering across the yard; Megan and Fenny carrying empty log baskets, Vi and Lucinda following close behind.

'Standeasy.' Vi set down the tray she carried. 'Thought we'd have it out here. There won't be many more good afternoons left.'

'Scones?' Jane's eyes alighted on the plate. 'At standeasy? MacAlister had a funny turn, or something?'

'Maybe she had a bit left over from the rations, more like,' Vi retorted, 'and thought she'd give us all a treat. Be grateful for small mercies, girl.'

And they were, all of them, as they sat on the pump trough for afternoon break. Ahead, the loch was greying into autumn, and around them the full-gloried bloom of Miriam's garden was coming to an end, the trees turning to red and gold. But this was a good day, a special day, Jane mused. A day to be tucked deep inside her and brought out and lived again when she was old and in need of memories.

Brightly, gratefully, she sent her smile to Lilith. 'Thanks,' it said. 'Thanks a lot.'

'There's something I must tell you both,' Lucinda said as they polished the cabin floor one late-watch morning in early October. 'Something I've been trying to get around to for a while now.'

'You're havin' a baby!' Vi cried. 'Ar, queen . . .'

'No, Vi. Sorry.' Lucinda sat back on her heels. 'I should have told you straight away, I suppose, but I put it off till

705

I'd been on leave and seen those men in London. It was such a shock, you see, I can hardly believe it, even now.'

'Believe *what*?' Jane demanded. 'And what's so awful that it's taken you this long to tell us?'

The floor-cleaning had stopped. Whatever it was, Lucinda's news seemed nothing if not dramatic. If ever she got around to telling them.

'Go on, queen.'

'We-e-ll, we were in bed, Mike and me, just talking and – '

'Ha!'

'Honestly. Talking about how it would be after the war, you know; castles in Spain, day-dreams, I suppose. And then we got around to money – well, *I* did. I knew I'd get a wife's allowance from the RAF and I *did* want to talk about our saving as much as we could, and things like that. Anyway, Mike told me, then; straight out of the blue. Said we were wasting time talking about ways and means and I wasn't to worry because he'd got enough money for us both. I couldn't believe it.

'"Have you, Mike?" I asked him. "Enough to get us a house and the things we'll need?" and he said sure, any house I wanted. So I made him tell me how much, and I wish now that I hadn't.'

She got off the floor, then sat down heavily on her bed, spreading her hands in a helpless, appealing gesture.

'Why not?' Jane demanded. 'What's so terrible about Mike having a bit in the bank? I'd like to think that Rob had, but buying my ring probably cleaned him out, poor love.'

'A bit? Listen – Mike's *rich*,' Lucinda choked. 'The day he was born he was worth three million – imagine that! Money left in trust by his grandpa Farrow, who'd not long died.'

'Mother of God! Three million quid! That's – that's *sinful*.'

'Dollars, Vi. Not pounds.'

'Even so.' Jane's jaw sagged. 'Shocked? So would I be.'

As if the floor were suddenly not the proper place to be, Jane rose to her feet then stared down, perplexed, at Lucinda.

'And that was when he was born, Jane. Now he's worth – well, he doesn't know, exactly. But it's a whole heap more, in spite of the Wall Street crash. They survived that, all right. They're in construction and engineering and oil and property – just the family. Nobody else. And now I'm family, it seems, and when I went to see Mike's solicitor in London he told me that I've got shares in Farrow's, too. Seems Mike arranged it when he got back from Burma – transferred some of his own stock to me. In anticipation of marriage, I think the legal phrase is. And he opened a bank account for me, too.'

'And you never said,' Vi breathed, amazed. 'All that money out of the blue, and you didn't say a word.'

'I know, and I'm sorry. And the longer I put it off, the harder it got. And I didn't tell you because I wanted to get it all straight in my mind, when I was in London. Mike seemed so casual about it, you see. It's taken a lot of getting used to. I'm still a bit cock-eyed about it. As I said – a shock.'

'But why, girl?' demanded Vi, who couldn't think of anything less shocking than being told by Gerry that he wasn't short of a pound or two. 'You've always been well-heeled, haven't you?'

'But that's just it, Vi; I haven't. Nor has Pa, really. Oh, I suppose if you take the price of land per acre and multiply it by several thousand it does add up to quite a lot; and if you add to that the houses and everything in them, I suppose you could call it being well-heeled. But

707

not if you can't realize on any of it – and we can't, except in very exceptional circumstances. Just try paying the heating bill with a few acres of arable land or a square inch of a Gainsborough! We've only got *things*, Vi, and things to be passed on, at that. Pa gave me an allowance when I left school, but it wasn't a lot, and for anything else I had to rely on handouts from Mama or borrow from Charlie.'

'Ar, I wasn't bein' funny.' Vi sighed. 'You know I wasn't. And I'll admit it would shock me if I was suddenly rich. Even hearin' about you has made me go funny inside.'

'It must have, Vi, and I'm sorry if I sound ungrateful, because I'm not. I used to think it would be marvellous when I was of age and getting the grandparents' money, but that's a drop in the ocean compared to what Mike gave me – a marriage settlement, he said I'd better call it. Gracious! I'm still, well – '

'Shocked?' Vi supplied.

'Yes.' Lucinda was feeling a little better. 'But don't say anything about what I've told you in quarters, will you? Wouldn't want it shouted around. It makes me think about something Mike said, and it makes good sense. Said it was best people didn't know you were well-off, and then you could be sure they liked you for yourself. So keep it under your hat, won't you.'

They said they would, that it was forgotten already, though both knew it wouldn't be forgotten for a long, long time. Such earth-shattering news was like winning the Irish Sweepstake ten times over, and then some. No wonder Lucinda had been knocked sideways; no wonder she was still apprehensive about it. But they wouldn't say one word about it ever again, honest to God they wouldn't.

'Good.' Lucinda smiled, relief relaxing her face. 'Now

we can talk about something else? Shall I tell you what Mike said in his letter this morning? The silly man said he was so browned off with his being there and my being here that he's going to try to get a posting back to England. So I shall write back and tell him not to dare. I wouldn't want him flying again.'

'Maybe not.' Vi frowned. 'But you can understand Mike worryin'. Gerry worries about the bombing here because it's still bad, isn't it? We're safer at Ardneavie, all ringed round by hills and ack-ack batteries and barrage balloons; but with all those hit-and-run raids by the Luftwaffe, we're dead lucky they haven't had a go at us. What about Canterbury, eh? All them people killed and injured! And why Canterbury? What's there that's so important?'

'They had a go at York last year, remember?' Jane added. 'And there's nothing there, either, except all the lovely old buildings and the Minster.'

'So you can't blame Mike for worrying, can you, girl?'

'I suppose not. But I don't want him back here, because he'd go operational straight away. I'd rather he was safe, even if it means waiting years till I see him again.'

'Hmm. Our trouble is that we want it all ways, don't we?' Jane brooded. 'We don't know how well-off we are, up here. Just think of being in Stalingrad! What about those pictures in the papers yesterday? Not how many houses destroyed, but how many left standing! Just ruin and desolation. We'd know about it, if we were there.'

'Just imagine fighting street by street and house by house in London or York.'

'Or Liverpool!'

'Yes. And the dead just lying there, frozen stiff. It's awful. And women fighting beside the men . . .'

'It could have been us,' Jane said soberly. 'Hitler could have just as easily invaded us. I'll bet if he'd known how very little we had left after Dunkirk he would have, too. Think what it would have been like.'

'Now that's enough!' Vi picked up her polishing cloth. 'I'm not havin' no more of that talk here, so let's get this floor finished, eh? No more of your nonsense. We're goin' to win this war – all right?'

Yes, they said. Of course we were. But *when*?

'Did you know,' Jane murmured thoughtfully, 'that Stalingrad was once called Tsaritsyn? Don't you think it's a much nicer name?'

'Tcha!' Vi snorted. As if it mattered. 'And by the way, Lucinda, how did Mike manage to get all them shares and all that money out of America when there's a war on?'

'I'm not really sure.' Oh dear, they were back to the money again. 'I gather the share transfer was *on paper*, I think they call it. I don't actually get them in my hands.'

'And the money in your bank?' Vi needed to know because she was still trying to make sense of those first three million dollars and having great difficulty arranging so many noughts.

'The bank account was easier. Farrow's have a UK subsidiary, so it was fairly simple, I think, though I haven't touched any of it yet. But don't let's talk about it. If it's been a shock to you, how do you think I felt when Mike told me?'

'Could have been very off-putting, queen.' Vi grinned.

'It was, for a while. Mike began to wish he'd never told me.' Lucinda grinned impishly back. 'But it was all right, in the end.' Then her face became sad and her eyes lost their laughter. 'It isn't right, though, is it? All our own bombed-outs, and those poor women in Stalingrad, and the winter coming on. I feel guilty about the money, somehow.'

'I know just how you feel,' Vi said softly, eyes looking out over the loch to a pile of rubble in a Liverpool backstreet. 'It's a funny old war and you never know the day it's going to be your own turn. But there's nothin' we can do about it – not a blind thing – so let's get this dratted cabin finished before Patsy Pill gives us the short end of her tongue.'

But all that money, right out of nowhere? It would take Lucinda a bit of getting used to. Come to think of it, it was going to take them all a bit of getting used to. Very peculiar stuff, money was.

It would be more to the point, Vi considered as she dressed to go on watch, if they could be told a little bit more about what was happening in Egypt and Libya. They'd gone to sleep, she shouldn't wonder, at the Ministry of Information, for all the news they gave out these days. Mind, she conceded, they did have a point. There were a lot of things couldn't be broadcast over the wireless or written in the newspapers; the weather forecast, for one. Wouldn't do to let the German air force know there was going to be good clear night skies over England. But them faceless little men had no right to hold back news just because it might be of help to the enemy. The enemy probably knew already. They only had to ask that Lord Haw-Haw, who seemed to know the lot. And to add injury to insult, there had been the matter of the bathwater. No news blackout in *that* quarter.

'Well, if that isn't the bleedin' end,' Vi had exploded from the depths of the *Sunday Pictorial*. 'Just listen to this! Do this and don't do that, and now what do you think? That lot in London says we've got to cut down some more on the bathwater. Five inches it's got to be now; *five* inches, not six! We'll save thousands of tons of coal a year, would you believe, if we lower the water-level in our baths by one inch! Now I wonder which clever-clogs at the ministry worked that one out? Five inches isn't goin' to be a lot of good. Even when it was six, it didn't cover your bum!'

'You know, whenever I run a bath,' Jane grinned, 'I always expect a little man to pop up out of nowhere – you know, a dear little fellow with glasses on the end of his nose and pin-striped trousers and a stiff collar – and take out his ruler and measure the depth of the water!'

'Ssssh!' Lucinda whispered dramatically, eyes swivelling to right and left. 'Careless talk, Kendal dear. Keep your voice down, or that ear in the wall will hear you; and before we know what's happening, they'll be conscripting little pin-striped men and sending them out with their rulers, spying.'

They began to giggle hysterically, and it was good to hear them laugh, Vi thought fondly. Laughter was better than thinking about the war and the blackout and winter coming on, and worrying about an inch less of bathwater and how things were going in Egypt; and Malta, bombed almost out of existence, now. And it was a whole lot better than tears.

Winter waited just beyond the hills; hills that had thrown off their summer greens and stood grey now, and distant. Soon, greatcoats and warm woolly scarves would be rig of the day again, and early watch would go on board *Omega* in the gloom of a blackout not lifted until six in the morning.

Already the fire burned in the boat's-crew cabin and the last of autumn's leaves hung dead on the trees, waiting for the next wind that blew from the north-east to whip them off and away.

The loch reflected the grey of the early November sky as starboard watch ran the length of the wind-lashed jetty and arrived breathless in quarters to hot standeasy tea and new-baked bread and jam.

'Letters for both of you. Came second post. One for you, Lucinda, and two for Jane.' Vi smiled, handing them over. 'Cor! Love's young dream. An' before you get openin' them, Lilith says if we want to share their fire tonight, we're welcome.'

Of course they would sit around the fire in the cabin next door and warm their pyjamas beside it and gossip and grumble and maybe, Jane thought, slitting open the first of her letters from Rhodesia, they might even have a session with the wine glass tonight. Only for fun, of course, for she and Lucinda were sure in their love, now, and only if Vi wanted to. But Megan was having problems with her boyfriend which needed sorting out, and three extra forefingers on the upturned glass would be of help.

My sweet Jenny, she read, and at once it was a May evening and Rob was with her, his mouth on hers. And every smallest part of her eager, wanting body beat out for him as they clasped hands and walked into the thick green deeps of Tingle's Wood. Scarcely five months since he had gone; five lifetimes. How was she to last out the remainder of this year away, endure the months until he came home?

I miss you, my darling girl. I want you . . .

Seven months was nothing! They would fly past, and even if they didn't, if they crawled with sickening slowness, what were seven months out of a lifetime of loving?

Close your eyes, Jenny, as you always did. Lift your face and I'll kiss you . . .

She closed her mind against a small voice that whispered, 'Think, now. You might never have gone back that afternoon for Vi's cardigan.' But she had gone back; it was meant to be. She closed her eyes and lifted her face and Rob's lips were gentle on her own.

J & R. 2.2.41. Jenny and Rob, for ever.

* * *

713

'I think,' said Lilith, 'that since this is the month of the dead we might try something with the glass tonight.'

She looked directly at Jane, silently asking her support. Lilith believed it was time for Tom Tavey's spirit to be allowed to rest; time for Jane truly to accept he meant her no harm.

'Month of the dead?' Lucinda's nose wrinkled. 'Why should November be called that?'

'Because that's what it is; what it always has been. It's the Celtic *Samain*, dedicated to those gone. In old times, you know, bonfires were lit so the sun would return and November was the month when ghosts roamed free in the still nights; roamed in the mist and fog, unseen.'

'So you're thinking we might get in touch with someone who's passed over?' Fenny asked. 'I thought you didn't agree with that, Penrose? Let them rest, you always said.'

'Did I? Well, maybe I did. Perhaps we should leave them to their wanderings.'

'Well, you can count me out till I've got my kit together. I'm a bra and one stocking short. I suppose none of you lot have seen them, cos I'll be in dead trouble at kit inspection,' Megan wailed, 'if I don't find the thieving so-and-so who took them!'

'You're always losing things, Cad,' Fenny flung, derisively. 'Have you tried Patsy's lost-property box? That's where they'll be.'

'They're not, because I've already been. I got one stocking out of it, that's all. There's always a run on lost property before kit inspection, you should know that. I'm still a stocking short, and where my bra is . . .'

'Never mind, Cad. Let's have another look in the drying room.' Lucinda smiled. She still glowed warm from reading Mike's letter. Loving and being loved made her want to help the whole world – after she had got over the screaming want for him his letters always aroused in her.

'I'm sure we can find another stocking somewhere, and if we can't find your bra you can borrow one of mine to wear tomorrow; a civvy one I've got with me. Patsy will only want to see two sets of underwear, remember. We *are* allowed one set on, you know.'

Tomorrow morning, before starboard watch left for early duty, they would lay kits on beds and bunks, ready for Chief Pillmoor's scrutiny; and an amazing assortment of underwear would take the place of garments missing and an amazing number of brassieres and blackouts and vests would find their way back to the drying room, afterwards, to be retrieved by legitimate owners – most without name-tapes, of course – when the inspection was over and done with for another month.

'By the way.' Lucinda paused in the doorway. 'In her last letter, my mother-in-law' – how she liked to say those words – 'said there was a parcel of goodies on its way over, so fingers crossed, everybody, that it gets here safely. If it does, we'll all share it.'

'A changed girl,' Lilith said. 'Bainbridge – er – *Farrow* has got one heck of a good aura, now. Remember when she came? Not a spark of life in her, vibes-wise. But she'll do, now. And if we're going to have a session, somebody had better bring in the table while I warm the glass and polish it. As a matter of fact' – she dropped her voice to a whisper – 'Megan has asked me to do something about her boyfriend. Seems he's cooling off a bit and she wants to know what's going on. We could do a sitting for her.'

'Don't see why not,' Vi agreed without too much reluctance. Keeping tabs on an erring lover was a whole lot safer than messing about with the roaming dead outside. And it *was* only a bit of a lark. 'I'm game, if everyone else is.'

She rose to bring in the table that stood on the landing outside, and everyone drew closer to the fire as the door opened, letting in a blast of cold air. She had given that table an extra polish only that morning, Vi remembered; as if she had known they would use it tonight. And best go along with Penrose's funny little whims; after all, it was her fire they were keeping warm beside and a whole lot better than sharing the fire in the common room with the noisy remainder of starboard watch. 'Give me the numbers and letters and I'll put them out for you,' she offered, clearing a space in the centre of the room.

'Mix them up well,' Lilith murmured, breathing into the wine glass, then polishing it gently with a handkerchief. 'Y'know, I feel as if something wonderful is going to happen. I can feel it inside me; restless and churning, sort of.'

'It'll be the liver and onions.' Vi sniffed. 'Does the same for me, too.'

'No! Not *that* kind of feeling. This is good and – and *special*.'

'Something to do with the glass?' Jane asked. 'Good responses, tonight?'

'I don't know, Kendal. I don't know at all. I'm only sure that there's an excitement inside me and I don't know why. And where,' she fretted, 'have those two got to?'

She was soon to know. Almost at once the cabin door slammed open and Megan, waving a stocking, and Lucinda, civilian brassiere in her hand, came panting in from two flights of stairs taken at speed.

'Gracious! One of the November dead after you?' Fenny teased.

'Just wait!' Megan gasped, breathing deeply. 'Just wait till I tell you!'

'You'll never believe it. On the wireless!' Lucinda added. 'Amazing, wasn't it, Cad?'

'Amazing. That old announcer actually came to life. All excited, he was, when he said it. Not like they usually are

– you know how they always read the news all solemn, like, with a voice like – '

'An undertaker,' Lucinda supplied. 'Well, this one didn't! Not tonight. He was really excited.'

'Announcers on the wireless *never* get excited,' said Lilith scathingly. Imagine Alvar Lidell or Stuart Hibberd getting excited!

'All right then, *merchi*, if that's how you feel, *don't* believe us.' Megan shrugged. 'So why is there going to be a special news broadcast, then? Because that's what he was getting excited about.'

'There is.' Lucinda nodded. 'We heard it. The announcer interrupted the programme. Said that listeners shouldn't switch off after the last broadcast because there'd be the best news for years on the wireless at midnight. Honestly! I heard it, too.'

'Midnight? We'll have to listen, then.'

'How can we?' Vi demanded. 'It's lights-out at half-past eleven; how are we goin' to manage it?'

'But that's just it – we *can*,' Megan rushed on. 'Chiefie says that anyone who wants can stay up for it. She says she's going to. Everybody's going to. It's bound to be something good.'

'Right, then. We'll all go down, eh?' Lilith's churning increased. 'I said something was going to happen, didn't I, Vi?'

'What do you suppose it is?' Jane whispered. 'Do you suppose they've got rid of Hitler?'

'Ha! More likely to be an extra ounce of butter on the ration, or five more clothing coupons.'

'It won't,' Lilith asserted. 'It'll be better than that, I know it.'

'Then why don't we ask the glass?' Lucinda gasped. 'Let's ask it what this wonderful news is all about.'

717

'Right, then! Let's get on with it! Get the chairs round and close the door, Fenny. Make sure it's all right.'

Chairs were pulled to the table; Fenny placed the door wedge in position then made it fast with her toe.

'Okay, Cadwallader, since it was you brought the news up, maybe you should ask it the question.' Lilith set great store by Megan's Celtic origins. 'Just ask it what we're going to hear.'

Cheeks flushed, eyes too bright, they settled themselves at the table. At a nod from Lilith, Megan picked up the glass and, cupping it in hands that shook, she whispered, 'Glass, tell me please about tonight. Tell me if it's good. *Please*. Tell us all.'

Carefully, the stem held gently between forefinger and thumb, she placed the glass, rim down, in the centre of the table.

Fingers reached out; eyes willed it to move. Lilith whispered, 'Tell us. Tell us,' as the glass took off; took off and skittered this way and that, circling, zigging, zagging, stopping, starting. Then it slid to the figure four and began a series of anti-clockwise turns around the table.

'Damn!' Lilith hissed. 'Widdershins! It's useless when it starts going the wrong way round. We'll have to try again. Think it'll have to be me, this time.'

Picking up the wayward glass, she polished it again, then cupping it as Megan had done, she warmed it with her breath, softly repeating the question.

And again the glass misbehaved. Again it skittered and slid and refused completely to do their bidding.

'What's the matter with the daft thing?' Vi demanded.

'I don't know. One of us isn't concentrating.' Lilith frowned. 'Or are we just too excited? The glass can't cope with excitement, so if you all feel the way I do, I think we should give it a rest, for tonight.'

'Pity,' sighed Megan, who had really wanted to sort out her perfidious lover. 'But you're right, Penrose.'

'Okay. So if you've got all your kit seen to, Cad, I think we should go down for standeasy then get ourselves undressed and our curlers in. I don't think the Axis will have surrendered, and news or no news, we'll still have to be up with the lark for earlies.'

'That's what we all like about you, Penrose,' Fenny commented. 'You're such a raving optimist.'

But they agreed, grudgingly, that probably she was right, and letters and numbers and wine glass were gathered up and the table returned to its place outside.

'Come on then, you two.' Vi collected pyjamas from the fireguard. 'See you all downstairs, then, though I can't imagine what all the fuss and bother's about.'

Even so, her heart was bumping; just as it used to when she was a kid and she awoke too early on Christmas morning. There had never been the doll or the enormous tin of toffees or the pale pink slippers she had so desperately wished for. Only disappointment. Would tonight, at midnight, be the same?

They were all there: starboard watch in dressing gowns and curlers; port watch not long ashore from *Omega*, drinking kye, wondering, waiting.

Vi smiled at Jane and Lucinda, then looked again at the common-room clock. One minute to go. One minute to midnight – 2359 hours on Wednesday, the fourth day of November, her mind supplied; a time and a day to note and remember?

Immediately inside the door sat Third Officer St John and Chief Wren Pillmoor. Most times, the common room accommodated half the Ardneavie House Wrens at one time; tonight, both watches came together for the first time since Christmas Day dinner, squashed into chairs, sitting on chair arms, on stools, on the floor beside an already dead fire.

'Quiet!' Pat Pillmoor called as the pips began, and then the announcer – and yes, he really wasn't speaking in his solemn undertaker's voice – saying that this was the BBC Home service, saying 'Good evening, everyone,' and then, oh, and then his wonderful, wonderful news.

'*Here is a special joint communiqué issued from British Headquarters in Cairo.*

'*The Axis forces in the Western Desert, after twelve days and nights of ceaseless attacks by our land and air forces, are now in full retreat.*

'*Their disordered columns are being relentlessly attacked by our land forces and by the Allied Air Force by day and night.*

'*This far, we have captured over 9,000 prisoners and destroyed more than 250 tanks and at least 270 guns. In the course of these operations our air forces, whose losses have been light, have destroyed and damaged in air combat, over 300 aircraft and destroyed, or put out of action, a like number on the ground.*

'*At sea, our naval and air forces have sunk 50,000 tons, and damaged as much again, of shipping carrying enemy supplies to North Africa. The Eighth Army continues to advance . . .*'

For a moment, for just one unbelieving, uncomprehending moment, there was complete silence, then,

'Yaaah *hoo*!' yelled the first to find her voice, and,

'Did you hear that?'

'Nine thousand prisoners! A rout, that's what!'

'Good old Desert Rats!'

'Good old Monty! He did it!'

Chairs scattered. There was hugging, jumping, laughing.

Molly Malone, in pyjamas and curling rags, jumped atop the table and began to sing.

We're gonna hang out the washing
On the Siegfried Line . . .

and it was taken up by all the Ardneavie Wrens and sung with gusto and delight and just a little disbelief.

Have you any dirty washing, mother dear?
We're gonna hang out the washing on the Siegfried Line
Cos the washing day is here . . .

The Siegfried Line. Nazi Germany's gun-bristled wall of defence. No Britisher had sung that song since Dunkirk, when, bloodied and bewildered, our army had been plucked from the beaches of France by the skin of its teeth and the aid of many miracles. The Dunkirk evacuation had knocked the bounce out of the British and, chastened, they had ceased to chant that taunting song.

But now we had won something! 'We'll be back!' we'd said after Dunkirk, and now it looked as if we would be.

We're gonna hang out the washing
On the Siegfried Line
If the Siegfried Line's
Still there!

'Quiet, you lot!' Pat Pillmoor yelled.

'Leave them,' urged a smiling Suzie St John. 'I think you and I should have a tiny glass of victory sherry, eh?'

'We've won something!' They'd bloody well won something!

The jubilation continued. They conga'd, chanting, round the common room and out past the regulating office and round the mess and back again, still singing and stamping and laughing and whooping. We had won a battle, a *big* battle, and we were going to win this war! Our Eighth Army, our long-suffering Desert Rats, were sweeping on victorious, just as the Japanese army had swept through the Far East, and Hitler's armies had swept arrogantly across Europe and into Russia.

Well, it was *our* turn, now; the taste for winning was on our lips and *we* were sweeping through North Africa, and nobody, but nobody, was going to sweep us back!

The announcer was still speaking; saying that films of our great victory would be shown on cinema newsreels on Monday next.

What a night that would be! What a sight! Monty in his black Tank Regiment beret, or would it be his famous Anzac hat? And Rommel, proud Rommel, routed, and nine thousand prisoners marching to captivity, hands clasped behind heads.

There would be queues at the picture houses on Monday night; queues to see what the man in the street had been waiting to see, had needed to see, since Dunkirk.

There was a tiny light at the end of the long, dark and often frightening tunnel; a light so small it was no more than a pin-prick. But it *was* there. Things were looking up at last. Victory, total and unconditional victory, was a long way away – but we had won a battle and, damn it, we were going to win a war!

The man in the street was cock-a-hoop. This would show them, those Axis buggers. He'd known it all along, of course. There'd never been a doubt, really, in the mind of the man in the street. He'd known who was going to win.

Mind, it had been dicey, at times, and the going tough, but our lads had done it!

Winston Churchill was jubilant when, not long afterwards, he addressed a gathering in the City of London.

This was not the end, he warned; it was not even the beginning of the end, but it was, he said, his face alight with pride and not a little relief, the end of the beginning.

Good old Winnie, said the man in the street. He'd never lied to them. He'd laid it straight on the line, always; the blood, toil, tears and sweat.

But now he'd tell of victories, of battle after battle won. The British were fighting mad again, so watch your backside, Hitler!

On Sunday, the fifteenth day of a November no longer grey and gloomy, the church bells were rung for the first time since the victorious defeat at Dunkirk had silenced them. Thereafter, the sound of church bells could have meant only that our country was being invaded, and the man in the street hoped and prayed they would never be heard.

But on this wonderful Sunday, every bell in every steeple and tower rang and clanged and rocked and called out with joy for a victory in a desert in Africa; a clamour of gladness, a peal of thanksgiving.

And on that Sunday evening, that marvellous, unbelievable, bell-crazy Sunday evening, the man in the street, when he had listened smugly to the nine o'clock news, turned the dial of his wireless set just a fraction and sat back complacently to listen to Lord Haw-Haw's account of the victory in Egypt.

The man in the street was bitterly disappointed. In vain he listened, waited, adjusted his dials, but on that joyful Sunday, Lord Haw-Haw's wavelength was empty of words, as silent as a tomb.

Lord Haw-Haw, it seemed, had nothing to say. That night, Germany was *not* calling.

30

Things, Vi considered as she polished the regulating office floor, were beginning to look up. Polishing was a tedious occupation which gave the mind free range for thought, and since she polished windows and baths and floors with daily regularity, she had ample time for the counting of blessings, for putting her immediate world to rights and for generally mulling over what she had avidly read in Ma'am's discarded newspapers.

Things were getting better. It had started with the victory at El Alamein and the heady ringing of the church bells; and the bells were rung again not long after, on Christmas Day. Not for another battle won, but because it was Christmas and to remind people the tide was running our way again.

That winning in Egypt had been the start of it all, just about the time of Lucinda's twenty-first birthday. And *that* had been a bit of a do, if you like, with food parcels from Vermont carefully hoarded for the big day; chocolate biscuits, tins of peaches, tins of cream, and a rich fruit cake, vacuum-packed in a fancy tin, would you believe?

Starboard watch had high old jinks that night, with big eats, and champagne, sent up by Lucinda's da, though how it ever arrived without getting smashed to smithereens, Vi could not imagine. Put down the day she was born, Lucinda said; twenty-one bottles, though the Earl had only parted with six, the crafty old devil.

But it had been some party – Vi smiled down at her

724

hazy image on the brown linoleum – and the first time she had tasted champagne, come to think of it. It hadn't sent bubbles up her nose like it did in films she had seen, but it made her feel very happy.

And not long after, it was Jane's turn. Twenty years old and out of her teens, thank heaven, she said, though having a birthday on Christmas Eve was never the same as having one on an ordinary day. But Jane had had a birthday letter from Margaret MacDonald, which tickled the kid pink; getting on smashing now, them two.

Mind, it didn't do to let things go to your head. Vi frowned. There had been more air raids, with London copping the worst of them. Made you wonder just how many bombers and bombs Hitler still had up his sleeve, especially since Leningrad.

Leningrad. That had been another victory for Mr Churchill to crow about on the wireless. A city relieved after more than a year on starvation rations. People had been real glad about that. And then Stalingrad, soon after, and the Russians bursting out, mad for revenge. It had made good listening on the news broadcasts, though how they had decently buried their dead was a mystery, Vi's Catholic soul mourned, when the ground was frozen so hard that neither side could get a spade into it.

But wars were nasty, dirty things, no matter who was winning. And Hitler's lot were losing now; nothing was more certain – though Vi hoped they wouldn't turn nasty about it and take it out on the poor prisoners of war.

Take care, Gerry lad. Look after yourself. She sent her thoughts to the man she loved and who loved her. Because he did. He wrote it now in every letter.

'If you've finished your little reverie, McKeown, perhaps you could remove that look from your face and get on with the floor. I'd very much like my office back, if you don't mind.'

725

'Finished, Chief. Just goin'.'

Vi got to her feet, not best pleased with Chiefie's acid tongue. She had been enjoying that little daydream, and there was still the news about the bomb on Hitler's personal plane to mull over. An *alleged* bomb, the news announcer had said, that didn't go off. Pity, that. Seemed that quite a few Germans didn't like Hitler, either. Vi hoped they wouldn't find the people who'd put it there; hoped there would be no reprisals. Anyone who killed *that* man deserved canonization, not hanging.

And now, she thought as she continued her polishing in the mess, the winter was almost over, thanks be. It had been a particularly vicious one at Ardneavie, with cabins freezingly cold and more than one Wren sleeping with a Balaclava helmet over her curlers. But March was coming to an end and summer was ahead to look forward to – and even more victories and battles won to make them all glad, she shouldn't wonder.

'Well, what d'you know?' said Lucinda over the letter she was reading. 'Charlie's got engaged. Sweet of him to write, wasn't it? Finally popped the question to his Isobel, though I think there'll be complications. Seems she doesn't want to live in England; well, you can't blame her, can you?' Europe wasn't the best of places to be at the moment, though she hoped Isobel would give it a try, for Charlie's sake. And for Lady Mead's sake too, she thought, all at once realizing the implications of such a decision. Isobel was becoming homesick, though that was to be understood. New Zealand was a long way away, and this was Britain's war, after all. Decent of her to come over, really.

'Did you hear,' Jane asked as they cleared the tables after supper, 'about those barge things that came into the loch today?'

They said they hadn't. *Barge things*?

'Yes. I saw them when I went up top to the signalman. He told me they were to do with the second front, so it seems there *is* going to be one. It isn't just talk.'

'There'll have to be,' Fenny observed gloomily. 'We'll have to get back on the continent if there's to be an end to this war.'

An end to it? Lucinda sighed. She was missing Mike; wanting him so much. Sometimes in her bleaker moments she longed desperately for his return, second front or no, but she soon dismissed such thoughts from her mind; though once she had almost taken leave of her senses and wished they'd never had those three days.

But the wish was short-lived, for those few sweet days could be conjured up at will and lived again, and every whispered love word, every kiss and touch and, oh, *everything*, was heartbreakingly exquisite to recall. And she must never wish away those three days when they might be all she would ever have of him.

'If you really want to know what those *barge things* were,' Lilith supplied, 'I got a good look at them – had a signal to deliver to one of them – so I had a chat with one of the crew. They're called landing craft and they *are* for the second front. And there'll be a whole lot more of them coming in and out of the loch before very much longer. Those you saw today, Kendal, were for tanks, and they were going to McKinley's Yard, for degaussing.'

'Sounds disgusting.'

'Well, it isn't,' Lilith countered. 'It's something they do to them to stop magnetic mines exploding when they pass over them. Clever stuff, you know. They're dead serious about this second front. There'll be one, all right, so don't let anybody tell you otherwise.'

So the second front everybody kept going on about, the landing in Europe Stalin constantly demanded of his allies, was beginning to be fact, Jane thought bleakly. And how many pilots – experienced pilots – would be needed, when it happened?

'Stay where you are, Mike,' Lucinda thought, fear tearing through her. 'Don't try to get back here. I want you so much that sometimes I don't know how I'm going to bear it. But I want it all ways, my darling. I want you with me, making love; I want to be a proper wife. But I want you to stay in Washington, too, away from flying and second fronts.'

But why should she be feeling so miserable, so tense and angry today? Probably her period due again, she supposed. And *that* was something else. Why hadn't they made a baby together? Heaven only knew, they should have.

She took a deep, calming breath. She wasn't alone feeling like this; wasn't the only woman who ached for her man in the dark, empty hours of endless, lonely nights. Because wars weren't just about killing and staying alive and making sure your side won. Wars were about separations and loving someone and not being able to reach out and touch him and tell him so.

'I feel like going out tonight and getting as high as a kite,' she ground. 'Anybody game?'

Not very long after that, when harmony was restored all round in cabin 9 and April hardly a week gone, Jane put down Rob's latest letter and murmured, 'Lucinda – how long did it take Mike to get back home?'

'From Burma? I'm not quite sure. About seven weeks, I think, once he'd got into India. Why?' She looked with concern at her friend's face, which had suddenly gone pale. 'Kendal dear, what is it?'

'But Burma is much farther away, isn't it?' Jane persisted. 'And things weren't good for us then in North

728

Africa and we couldn't use the Suez Canal. Ships had to sail all the way round the tip of Africa, then. It should be different now, with the fighting almost over in Egypt.'

'What's the girl goin' on about?' Vi laid aside her newspaper. 'Just what has he said in that letter?'

'When I write to Rob it takes a little over two weeks for him to get it, doesn't it?' Jane begged the question. 'By airmail, of course. But Rob has just written that I'm not to send any more letters. Says he'll probably manage to get a couple more off to me, but then that'll be it.'

'Well? Go on, queen?'

'So don't you see, both of you? If I'm not to write to Rob any more, it must mean he'll be leaving Rhodesia within a couple of weeks,' she gasped, sitting down heavily on her bed, eyes round with suppressed excitement. 'It looks as if he'll be on his way home before very long. He can't say so outright or the censor would have it out of his letter like a shot. But I hadn't thought it would be so soon. Seems Rob could be home by the end of May. He could be *home*!'

She jumped to her feet, arms clasped tightly, walking to the window, turning, walking back. 'Home,' she whispered, 'and I didn't dare hope until at least July.'

'Since when did the Air Force – or any of *that* lot, for that matter – ever do anything the way we think they should do it? Ar, Jane, I'm chuffed for you. I'm made up, honest I am. But don't get too excited. Just wait a bit, till the letters stop arrivin', and then you'll really know.'

'It's wonderful, Kendal dear. I'm so happy for you. Your turn, now.'

'I know, and, oh, isn't it a lovely world!' Jane swept her arms wide, her face alive with joy. 'Will you both just look at that lovely world out there!'

'We just did, queen. It's pourin' down.'

'Oh, Vi, Lucinda – I'm a selfish brat, aren't I? And I

729

shouldn't talk like this, with Mike and Gerry so far away. But I can't help it, truly I can't.'

Lucinda smiled. 'We know you can't, old love. And it's our turn, now, to dance at *your* wedding. Come to think of it, why should you be the only one of us to be footloose? One for all and all for one, remember?'

'I remember,' Jane whispered, her voice thick with near-tears. 'I remember the night we said it. Glasgow Central station, two years ago. My, but we've come a long way since then. And aren't we just the luckiest Musketeers ever? Aren't we?'

They said they were, and they did a little dance around the cabin; and Jane sent a smile and her love to Tom, and hoped he would know she was so very, very happy. Tom understood. It was all right, now.

'I didn't think it was possible,' she murmured, 'for life to be so good. I feel as if I'm going to explode and go up in a puff of smoke any minute.'

'Oh no you're not, Kendal. You're goin' to get stuck in and get this cabin cleaned with the both of us, that's what!'

'And who says so?' she challenged, laughing.

'*I* say so, because I'm the oldest and the biggest and the bossiest.' Vi grinned, hands on hips. 'And then the pair of you will put on your sou'westers and get yourselves on watch. There's a war on out there – or had you forgotten?'

Jane wiped away her happy tears. But then, she was always happy, now; so happy it just wasn't true. And if she hadn't been sent to *Omega* and met Lucinda that night on the station, and if they hadn't missed two trains and become friends, and if they hadn't all gone to Lady Mead – oh, such a little word, *if*.

God, it's Jane Kendal. She closed her eyes. *Let Rob have a safe journey home.*

* * *

April was a good month, with little to mar the contentment of the Wrens who slept in cabin 9, that luckiest of cabins. True, *Sparta*'s replacement joined the flotilla, to set Lucinda thinking sadly and fondly of that first watch when she had been so afraid; a sprog telegraphist who had still to learn that in wartime ships not in home waters do *not* transmit; and who had still to prove herself a good telegraphist. After that, there had always been an especially warm feeling inside her for *Sparta*; for the submarine that helped her break her duck.

Now *Sparta* was gone and HM Submarine *Sereus* come to take its place; *Sereus*, pendant number P289, she noted as the S-boat came slowly to *Omega*'s port side, her skipper and number one at the conning tower, her crew, in new white sweaters, lining the fore and after casing.

Good luck, *Sereus*; so long, *Sparta*. Hail and farewell. And this is a pig of a war.

'The new boys are looking very smart,' Jane observed. 'Hope they do all right. But you wouldn't get me inside one of those things for a big clock, as Vi would say.'

She was happier now about Tom, and grateful to Lilith for relieving her conscience of such a burden. Tom was at peace; she accepted that now. But *Virgil* still gave her feelings of foreboding, if she let it. Lilith was right: *Virgil* spelled ill luck for someone, even though every patrol it made was a good one; every torpedo that ran from it a killer.

'Come on,' she said. 'Can't stand here watching the new boat, or Chiefie'll give us a blast for being late.' And come to think of it, she pondered, hanging up her cap and draping her jacket on the chair back, wasn't there a strong buzz that *Virgil* might go foreign; might join the submarine flotilla in the Mediterranean? Not so long ago, *Thunderbolt* had been lost out there; might not *Virgil* leave to take its place – and take its ill luck with it?

She smiled at Jock as she took her place beside him. And Jock smiled back and thought how good it was to see the lassie so pleased with herself these days, and so bonny with it, too.

'And how's wee Jane, if I needed to ask?' he enquired paternally.

And then, when May came to Loch Ardneavie with a flourish of blossom and suddenly blue skies, there was the intriguing business of the nylon stockings.

Nylon? She *had* got it right? Lucinda frowned. They came in an envelope tucked inside yet another food parcel from her concerned mother-in-law, with Mike's handwriting on it, which meant he must have been home in Vermont at the time the parcel was packed.

Try these for size, Lucy darling.

'Nylons?' Lucinda held them up against the window light, wondering at their fragility. 'Mrs Farrow says they're all the rage in the States; says they're made from glass.'

Glass? 'Goodness, aren't they fine!'

'Amazin',' Vi agreed. So fine they even moved in the slight current of air from the open window. 'They'll ladder first time on, I shouldn't wonder.'

'They're supposed to be quite tough,' Lucinda murmured. 'They'll outlast silk, my mother-in-law says, and if I like them she'll smuggle me another pair in.'

Mike's lovely mother was kind and indulgent and so afraid her son's wife would waste away for want of sustenance if she didn't keep the food parcels coming.

But as for the stockings – well, would anything ever take the place of fully fashioned silk?

There was a great feeling of elation the evening of the news broadcast about the breaching of the Moehne and Eder dams, deep in Germany. Another victory for the

732

Allies, Britain exulted when first the news was released. But when the man in the street read the morning papers on that mid-May Tuesday, he was not so sure.

'Hey, listen.' Vi frowned from behind her newspaper. 'This is a queer carry-on, innit? Says here there was nineteen bombers took off – Lancasters – and only ten got back.'

Sixty-three men killed, Jane calculated automatically. Sixty-three letters to next of kin, praising, regretting . . .

'And have you ever heard of a *bouncing* bomb?' Lucinda demanded, peering over Vi's shoulder. 'A bomb that bounced over the water till it hit the dam walls?'

'Gerraway,' said Vi, obliquely.

'Read it, then. In heaven's name, what was the point of it? A suicide raid, if ever there was one.'

'The buzz has it,' Jane offered, 'that the squadron that flew it is based at Scampton, but the Air Ministry isn't saying it out loud – fear of reprisal raids, I suppose.'

'But Scampton's not all that far from home,' Lucinda gasped.

'Well, there you are, queen. You never know the day, do you?' There was a nasty taste in Vi's mouth. There shouldn't have been, because two great dams breached and three hundred and fifty million tons of water roaring out in two great torrents should have been good, especially if you remembered that from those dams came water and power for the war factories of the Ruhr.

'Mother of God, they must've been mad, sending them crews out like that,' she said, her voice hard with disbelief, trying not to remember Mam's bitter outburst about Da's war; about the faceless ones who sent men over the top at the wave of a hand and about life being cheap; less than the price of a gas mask.

'Getting our own back is one thing,' Lucinda murmured, homing in on Vi's thoughts with frightening accuracy, 'but that raid was altogether something else. How many children died in those floods – kids, sleeping peacefully?'

The man in the street said very little about the results of the raid. The bravery of the aircrews was beyond question; they all deserved the Victoria Cross, but although the man in the street knew what the receiving end of an air raid was like, he felt a grudging sympathy, sometimes, for the women and children who were being bombed almost out of existence in parts of Hitler's Germany.

'Yes, and people like Ma Norris,' Vi said, thinking much the same. Poor, simple Ma Norris at number five, who'd thought she was safer beneath the kitchen table; safer, that was, from the telegrams that kept coming from the Somme.

'Rob will be on his way back now,' Jane remarked. Back to action again, to another tour of ops. God, she must have been mad to want him home.

'It was their lot started it,' muttered the man in the street. 'Hitler wanted this war. He's to blame,' they said, when Halifaxes and Lancasters and the great American Flying Fortresses took off night after night after night. 'See how *they* like a bit of their own back.' Yet the man in the street was beginning to long, now, for the whole damn war to be over and done with. And forgotten.

'Shall we go out?' Vi asked. 'Somehow I feel like walking. Anybody coming?'

Walking till her feet hurt. It wouldn't help the war; wouldn't bring Gerry back any sooner or stop the killing, but if she turned her back on Loch Ardneavie and walked towards the hills and the trees, walked along the newly green lane that narrowed into a track, she might forget the war for a little while. And tomorrow she would feel better; tomorrow, they all would. It was the way things always were, when there was a war on.

* * *

It was a busy time for starboard watch, next day. *Skua* and *Tarquin* and *Virgil* went out on patrol again, and *Sereus*, the new one, started its working up with speed trials off Arrochar. And Jane ticked off another day, another few hundred sea miles that must surely be bringing Rob nearer home, and wondered how it would be, when he got back.

A phone call like Lucinda's, perhaps? A letter, or a telegram? Or would the duty steward bang on the door of cabin 9, calling, 'There's a pilot downstairs, asking for Jenny Kendal . . .' Lovely, lovely daydreams.

'You'll no' have heard, lately?' asked Jock, who was usually informed of the arrival of letters from Rhodesia.

'No. Nothing for three weeks. He *must* be on his way home, now.'

By the end of the month, she hoped. Not later, please. Not when she would be on leave in mid-June. My, but that would be a laugh: Rob thinking she was at Ardneavie, and she not daring to leave the phone at Dormer Cottage.

'Fingers crossed, lassie.'

She smiled and nodded. Dear, sweet heaven, but this waiting for Rob was murder. And marvellous. And, oh, how she loved him.

A little before the end of May, as starboard watch came up the lane in a twilight touching on darkness, the door of Ardneavie House slammed open and the duty Wren called, 'Phone call, long distance, for Kendal!'

'Rob!' It *must* be! Breathless from surprise and delight, Jane snatched up the receiver. 'Rob? Rob, it *is* you?'

'It's me, sweetheart. I'm back!'

'Where are you?' Let him be outside, as Mike was. 'Darling, I can hardly hear you!'

'I'm at St Athan. And I'm fine. In case we're cut off, I love you. Did you hear me, Jenny?'

'Yes, and I love you too!' The incoming watch was straggling in, chattering, banging doors, but she didn't care. 'I love you,' she shouted again. Damn this line! 'When will you be home?'

'Tomorrow. I'm leaving now. Can you get some leave?'

'*Your time is up, caller.*' The long-distance operator interrupting, reminding them their minutes had run, not even asking if they wanted more time. '*Your time is up,*' she said again, but she gave them a little longer. Just seconds enough for Rob to say, 'I'll ring again. Soon. I love you.' And for Jane to cry, 'I'll fix the leave. I love you too!'

The line went dead. Just a purring in her ear. But Rob was back and on his way home. Tenderly, almost, she placed the receiver on its rest, then turned to smile tremulously at Vi and Lucinda waiting close by.

'Did you hear that? Did you?' she exulted. 'He's on his way!'

'We heard. It was me answered the phone.' Vi grinned. 'And you were dead lucky, girl. Most of them three minutes was wasted gettin' you up the lane!'

'It doesn't matter.' It *didn't* matter. He was back. And he loved her, and tomorrow or the next day they'd be together again. 'Oh, Vi, Lucinda,' she choked, then straightway burst into tears.

'Kendal dear, it's all right. Don't cry.' Lucinda gathered her close, hushing her. 'Don't cry. Please don't cry.'

'I'm not. Not really. It's just that I'm so happy. All of a sudden, it's just too much.'

'Okay. So take a deep breath and dry your eyes,' Vi admonished, 'then we'll get ourselves a cup of tea.' Nothing wrong with Kendal that a cup of strong, sweet tea wouldn't set to rights, Vi thought, as they went into the mess, though those dratted bedsprings of hers would

736

be at it all night long, like as not. 'Now, where is he and when is he comin' home?'

'In Wales, somewhere, but he said he was leaving, so he's probably on his way home now. How long will it take, do you think?'

'Dunno. Overnight trains seem to make better time. I think he'll have made it before you go on watch. And you'd better catch Chiefie now and ask her about leave,' Vi chivvied, ever practical. 'You're entitled, you know, you bein' engaged official.'

'We can ask her when she does last rounds.' Lucinda jammed a slice of bread. 'She's probably in the wardroom with Ma'am now. And Jane, I'm so glad for you. You above all deserve this.'

'Thanks, Lu. Is there any bread left? I'm shaking so much I can't hold this cup! Is it wrong to be this happy? Is it?'

'*No!*' Lucinda smiled.

'No, it isn't, queen, and listen, everybody!' Vi held up her hand for attention. 'Kendal's feller is home! How about that, then?'

She smiled across at Jane, because wasn't good news the better for sharing, and starboard watch deserved to hear the good bits since they'd all been so smashin' to Kendal right through the bad. And didn't she look marvellous? Cheeks flushed, smile all brilliant and wobbly, eyes shining and her eyelashes still spiky from crying. Kendal, Vi thought darkly, was enough to make a saint sick. Kendal was the only woman she knew who could come out of a bout of weeping looking beautiful.

My, but that one had been a trial, at times. Lucinda's controlled emotions were not for Jane. Oh, dear me, no. That one's pain hurt more, her setbacks bordered on misery, her joys were near-uncontrollable. And Vi loved her deeply. She loved them both. Between them, they had made her life bearable.

'Well, come on then. Let's be havin' you,' she fretted. 'Chiefie's goin' to be yelling for lights out soon, and us still down here, supping tea!'

'I won't sleep,' Jane choked, pulling loose her tie, placing her collar studs by force of habit in the little glass pot in the top drawer of her locker, next to Rob's wings. 'I won't. And what if Chiefie says I can't have leave? I'll have to go AWOL, I suppose.'

'Oh no you won't! We're not goin' through *that* carry-on again.' Vi put on her no-nonsense face. 'They'll let you go, queen – even if it's only one sleeping-out pass. And that's Chiefie next door, so you can ask her yourself.'

When Chief Wren Pillmoor had admonished cabin 9 for its light, she listened sympathetically to Jane's anxious enquiry.

'When is your fiancé due home, Kendal?'

'Some time tomorrow, Chief. I don't know for how long, though. We hardly had a minute on the phone. But there'll be a lot to be done.'

'They're planning gettin' married,' Vi supplied. 'Mixed, see, so they'll have to talk to the priest and all that.'

'I don't think you need worry.' Pat Pillmoor remembered a face ravaged with misery and pain, and her lips moved into a smile. 'Think we can fix up a pass – *this* time. See me in the morning, first thing, Kendal. I'll get Ma'am to sign it, and then you can take it on board with you and get the okay from your divisional officer. And get this blasted light out, or nobody'll be going *anywhere*!'

'Ar, she's not a bad old stick,' Vi smiled when the door had closed behind the Chief Wren. And the Chief Wren leaned against the door and swept her eyelashes upward in a gesture of resignation. Those Wrens of hers and their

738

love lives! Keeping up with forty of them, keeping just one jump ahead of them, was giving her grey hairs. And not only their love lives. What about their fiendish behaviour at the dances every month, and the way they all closed ranks and ganged up on her, especially over that pantry window and the boilerhouse key! A shower of evil-minded, devilish tormentors, the lot of them!

Yet she was smiling as she unlocked the regulating-office filing cabinet and took out an application-for-leave form, placing it on her desk. If anyone deserved a seventy-two-hour-compassionate, young Kendal did.

After a restless night and a morning spent hovering within sound of the telephone, Rob's call came only minutes before starboard watch left for late duty.

'Jenny?'

'Darling! You made it! I can hear you fine this time. Where are you?'

'I'm a wee bit nearer. Glasgow. Just arrived. Tell me.'

'I love you, love you – and listen! My leave's okay. Just got to get the div. to sign it – but he will. I've got three days.'

'Only got four myself. Got to go south again and get crewed up, then they'll give me some more.'

'Rob, can we talk? Have we time?'

'Of course. I've got loads of change. Why?'

'Nothing, really. Only if we're going to get cut off . . .'

'We're not, just yet. And I love you. Jenny – are we going to talk about a wedding?'

'Yes, Rob. *Yes*.'

'You'll need to see the priest. Sorry, darling, but – '

'It's all right. I've been seeing Vi's chaplain. All taken care of.'

'Can it be soon, Jenny? We've wasted so much time.'

'As soon as we can make it, Rob. Idiot! D'you think I don't feel the same?'

'Hell, sweetheart, we nearly didn't make it, did we?'

'Lady Mead, you mean? It was never in doubt, my love. Lady Mead wasn't a coincidence. It was *meant* to be. And I love you, did I tell you?'

'When will you be here?' His voice was low, indulgent.

'I'm going on watch soon. I won't be able to get the last ferry tonight, but I'll be on the first one out in the morning. Can you meet me? I'll make Glasgow just before noon, with luck. Platform 8, Rob.'

'I'll be there. Hang on a minute . . .'

A coin fell with a ping.

'Jenny?'

'Still here, darling. And don't put any more money in. I'll have to go. Tell me you love me.'

'I love you, Jenny Kendal. I've loved you from the minute I saw you. I was scared witless you were meeting some other fellow.'

'It was me who asked you for a date afterwards, though. I'd no shame, had I?'

'No shame at all. I do love you. I always will.'

'Always? Promise?'

'I promise. Gladly.'

'And I'll love you, Rob, for the rest of my life. Only you. And if you don't hang up, I'll be weeping again.'

'All right. See you. And Jenny – take care.'

'I will. See you.'

She stood there for a long time afterwards, arms clasped tightly round herself, eyes closed, loving him, wanting him, not knowing how she would get through the watch ahead of her, how she would endure one more night without seeing him, touching him; without closing her eyes and lifting her mouth for his kiss.

God, this is Jane Kendal. Thank you.

* * *

740

She had been right, Jane conceded. It was being a long-drawn-out watch with few signals for decoding except those which were routinely boring – apart from two from *Virgil* requesting permission to break off patrol; requesting permission to enter the loch. A generator fault that could not be repaired at sea.

Virgil, Viper, she thought, concentrating hard on subtractions she would normally have done automatically. But it was all right, now. Lilith had known it all along, hadn't she?

'*Jane*.' Jock's impatience jerked her back to the groups of figures in front of her. 'Och, for all the use you've been to me this watch, you'd better have been in Glasgow, so you would.'

But he said it as he would have said it to his daughter, because he cared for young Kendal and was glad she'd soon be with her man.

She had only slept in fits and starts that night and spent most of it sending her love to Rob and thinking about Rob and reaching out with her heart for him. Yet tomorrow had come, reluctantly; refusing to be hurried. And, no thanks, she didn't want any breakfast. She really hadn't the time.

'There's all the time in the world, queen. It's seven o'clock and the transport doesn't leave for another half-hour, and you'll get something to eat inside you – if I hold your nose and force it in,' Vi threatened.

'Do I look all right? Is my hair all right?'

'Your hair is beautiful, and you know it is. Just do as Vi says, Kendal dear, and go downstairs and get some toast. If it's a bit choppy on the ferry, you'll be glad you did.'

Jane smiled, absently. 'I wonder if he'll be wearing

uniform or civvies when he meets me. I've only ever seen him in uniform, you know.'

'What are you expecting, girl? A kilt and sporran?'

'His uniform, I should think,' Lucinda decided. 'I don't suppose his civilian things will fit him now. I know Charlie's wouldn't.'

'Do you think the train will be on time?' Jane fretted.

'Don't see why not. It's only from Garvie to Glasgow.'

'Hope Rob remembered the platform number.'

'God give me patience!' Vi's eyes swept upward. 'Listen, queen, Rob's just come back from Rhodesia; Rob can find his way to Germany and back in the dark. He did it a lot of times. Surely he can find where the Garvie ferry train comes in?'

'Sorry, both. I'm being a nuisance, aren't I?'

'No, Kendal dear, you're not.' Lucinda smiled. 'Not so very long ago we'd both of us have given anything to see you this happy. We are rather fond of you, you know.'

'Yes, you would. I know you would,' Jane whispered, the silly, happy tears there again. 'Y'know, I don't have a sister, but if I did she'd be just like you two. You've both been such loves.'

'Now don't be startin' your weepin' again,' Vi warned. 'Just get yourself to Glasgow and get that wedding date fixed – all right? Tell Rob that me an' Lucinda will want an invite.'

'I will. Look – I'd better be going. It's nearly twenty past, and I don't want her leaving without me.'

'She won't. The driver knows about you. Everybody does. Now be off with you, girl. And have a good time, don't forget.'

'Got everything? Undies? Clean shirt and collars?'

'I have. All packed.' Jane picked up her case and raincoat.

742

At the door she paused, then turned. 'Thanks, both of you,' she whispered. 'Thanks for – well, for *everything*.'

'Out!' Lucinda ordered. 'This minute! You've got a heavy date, remember.'

'Ar,' Vi sniffed. 'God love her, eh?' She blew her nose loudly and took the back of a hand across her eyes. 'Beautiful, didn't she look?'

'Just beautiful, though it'll be murder when she gets back. *Rob, Rob, Rob*.' Lucinda laughed. 'Well, at least she made her bed before she went. But then, she was awake before six.'

'Awake? She never went to sleep. Them bedsprings was creakin' all night. Ar, well, let's get this cabin cleaned, eh? Let's get back to normal.'

'She's made it.' Lucinda smiled from the window. 'She was in such a state I half expected her to go walking down the jetty.'

Vi nodded. 'An' the transport's just turnin' round. One more minute, then she'll be on her way. Now then, how about gettin' these beds – '

It hit them. A crashing, roaring, house-shaking explosion. It hit them out of nowhere, and they jumped back from the window, startled by the suddenness and the flash and the high-pitched crack of shattering glass.

'*Jee – sus!*' Vi hissed. 'What was *that*?'

Eyes wide, shaking her head free of the fearful noise, Lucinda took a hesitant step back to the window.

Then something hit her. A fist. Hard in her abdomen. '*God! Vi . . .*'

Smoke, they saw. Smoke, and earth flung against the shattered window glass that clung in slivers to the criss-crossed brown paper. And a hole. A hole so big it would have hidden a bus. A hole where Jane had been standing, and the transport lying on its side at the top of the jetty.

'*Jane!*' Vi wrenched open the door. 'Get her inside!'

The same stench. The stench of destruction. Like it had been in Lyra Street. A bomb, and no bloody siren!

'Wait, Vi! Wait!'

Together they hurtled down the stairs and out into the lane; into the flying dust and the smoke. Everywhere there was movement.

The planing dinghy, bouncing shorewards; the launch, wallowing in its wake. And Sister from sick bay three houses down, running, skirts flying.

'*Jane!*' Vi screamed. '*Jane!*'

People running, still. And noise. Every bosun's pipe on every ship wailing, and an air-raid warden, steel helmet askew, and Chiefie wrenching open the door of the transport, calling, 'Here, Sister! Over here!'

'Where's Jane?' Lucinda choked. 'For God's sake, where is she?'

The boat's-crew Wrens were there now, pulling sweaters over bell-bottoms, asking what it had been. And Suzie St John in dressing gown and slippers, hair trailing down her back.

'Vi!' It was Miriam, way down the lane. Miriam on her knees, calling, waving. 'She's here! Jane's here!'

'God!' Vi hissed. 'All that way! And she's all right?'

'Out cold, that's all,' Miriam answered, eyes glazed with shock. 'What was it? Not a bomb. Couldn't have been a bomb. A mine, do you think? A mine washed up, was it?'

'Don't know.'

They were running up the jetty now; running with stretchers, and the Surgeon-Lieutenant sprinting ahead of them, jacket open, bag in hand.

'Get him over here,' Vi ground. 'Get him here.'

They were opening doors, now, the people who lived at the loch edge, looking up at roofs, treading carefully over shattered window glass and broken tiles, asking what had happened, drawn in bewilderment to the great, gaping hole.

'Over here, sir,' Vi urged, and the medical officer dropped on his knees at Jane's side, reaching for her wrist.

'She was waitin' for the transport,' Vi said. 'Right up there. Blast, that's what. Blew her clean down here. What did it, sir?'

He took the face in his hands, searching for a pulse at her throat.

Blast, yet not a mark on her. You wouldn't believe it. Standin' there, she'd been, yet not so much as a mark.

Jane, it was, lying there, so still. Jane, eyes wide, cap lying beside her, hair shining. *It's all right, queen. Yer hair's lovely.* Jane, white-faced, blood at the corner of her mouth; blood, trickling slowly to her jawbone then falling in droplets on to the stiff, stark whiteness of her collar.

The doctor placed fingertips on her eyelids, closing them gently. Then he reached for the raincoat that lay beside the cap and drew it over her. Right over her face and the blood that still trickled from the corner of her mouth. Covering her.

'*Jane!*' Vi screamed. An animal cry of pain and grief and outrage.

She snatched back the coat. She wasn't having that! Not covering her face.

With her handkerchief she began to wipe away the blood; gently like wiping the face of a new-born child. 'Jane, girl . . .'

'Chief Wren!' the doctor called.

Pat Pillmoor looked up from the stretcher on which they had laid the injured driver, then rising stiffly from her knees, she walked reluctantly to where the doctor stood.

He said nothing, inclining his head instead at the supine

body and then to the woman who wiped the still, white face, whispering softly, incoherently.

'McKeown! Go inside! Leave her!'

'Chief. Where's Lucinda, Chief?'

'She's over by the wall. Go to her.' Lucinda, bending over, hands across her abdomen, retching, spewing. 'Look after her, McKeown.'

'Ar.' Vi rose to her feet, swaying. 'It's all right.' She walked to where Lucinda stood. Funny the way her legs were shaking; funny about her feet. Drunk, she was. 'Ar, Lucinda.'

She placed an arm tightly round the waist of her friend then laid a hand on her forehead, pushing her head down. 'All right, girl. Let it come. You're all right now. You're all right.'

'So sorry.' Lucinda pulled a shirt-sleeve across her mouth. 'Made a mess. So sorry.' She swallowed hard then dabbed at her eyes. 'Jane? How is she?'

'The MO's with her, and Chiefie. They're takin her to – to the hospital.'

'What was it, Vi?'

'Dunno, pet. Come on inside, eh?'

'A bomb?'

'A mine, Miriam thinks. A mine, broke free and washed up. Come inside. You're cold, girl, and shakin'.'

'There was blood on Jane's face, Vi. Why was there blood?'

'Come inside, queen. A cup of tea, eh?'

They stood on the signal deck, eyes straining shorewards.

'What the hell was it, sir?' asked Chief Wetherby of the signal bosun.

'God knows, Chief.' He handed the binoculars to the man at his side. 'Here, you take a look. Something's going on. Can't have been a bomb.'

746

'There's one hell of a mess outside the Wrennery. And that's the ambulance on the shore road, going like hell.'

'Sir.' The duty signalman coughed and stood, arms at sides, uneasy, knowing they wouldn't believe him. 'Sir, I saw it.'

'Saw what, lad?'

'Saw the thing running. Just stood and watched it. Missed us for'ard by feet, it did, then straight on . . .'

'*What* missed us?'

'A torpedo, sir. That's what did that lot ashore. A bloody torpedo!'

'Talk sense, man,' rapped the bosun. 'There's no way a – ' He paused, pulling his tongue round his lips, looking questioningly at Walter Wetherby.

'From over there, Chief.' The signalman turned, pointing to the submarine tied up at the buoy. 'From the V-boat that came in last night. *Virgil*, Chief. Came from *Virgil*, it did.'

The signal bosun closed his eyes and pulled his fingers through his hair. 'You'd swear to that, lad?'

'Swear, sir? Yes, sir.'

'Get 'em on the blower, Chief. Get hold of the staff office. I'd better tell them, see what they make of it.'

God Almighty, but somebody was in for a rollicking, if it was a torpedo; somebody was going to cop one up if it was one of ours.

'Can I have a word, Chief?'

'Come in, McKeown. Shut the door.' Pat Pillmoor pushed her cigarette packet across the desk, but Vi shook her head. 'How are you feeling now?'

'Awful, Chief. She was goin' to him, you know. Happy, she was. That's why I'm here. Somebody'll have to tell him, tell Rob. And her mam and dad as well.'

'Miss St John has already been on to the local police;

they said they'd get in touch with the vicar at Fenton Bishop.'

'Jane's dad *is* the local police, Chief.'

'The York police, McKeown. There's a letter on its way, but Ma'am wanted to break it gently and for her parents to tell us – '

'What they want doin'?' Vi supplied, tight-lipped. 'But what about Rob MacDonald? It was him she loved, and he'll be waiting there.'

'Where?' Christ, this was a disgusting business. 'How can I get hold of him?'

'Well, her train – he was meeting it. Platform 8 at 12 o'clock, at Glasgow Central, Chief. I think he'll be in uniform. Flying Officer MacDonald. He's got a right to be told.'

'All right, McKeown. I'll get in touch with the RTO's office there. Anything else I can do, if they miss him?'

'His mam isn't on the phone, but the Glasgow police could find where she lives. Mrs Margaret MacDonald. It's in a block near McFadden's bread shop, Maryhill way. There's a coder in the CCO; Jock Menzies; he'll know better where it is. But Jane would want Rob to know; before her mam and dad, she'd want Rob told.'

Vi closed her eyes and clenched hard on her teeth. No tears. Not here.

'All right. I'll do that. Cut along now,' Pat Pillmoor said gently.

'Chief?' Vi stood her ground. 'When?'

'Tomorrow, McKeown. She'll be going home tomorrow.'

'And the – the funeral?'

'I don't know about that yet. We'll make sure there are flowers, though.'

'Me and Farrow want to take our own. We want to go.'

'*Go?* All the way to Yorkshire? You can't do that,

748

McKeown. You wouldn't be given leave. Neither of you is next of kin. It wouldn't be any use asking.'

Not next of kin? Her and Lucinda, not next of kin? Them that had been together all this time and shared everything? They must be mad!

'Chief,' Vi said quietly. 'Me and Lucinda's goin'.'

'*No!* Don't even try it, McKeown. That's a warning *and* an order. Rules are rules. No compassionate leave.'

Vi stared defiantly, unspeaking. She was good at dumb insolence.

'Did you hear me? Don't try it, either of you, or I'll have you picked up the minute you set foot on the graigiebur Pier, so help me.' She closed her eyes and shook her head wearily. 'Look, I'm sorry. I know how you both feel and how close you all were, but King's Regulations state only next of kin or immediate relatives, and you and Farrow are neither. Don't push it, McKeown. Please.'

'Can I go now, Chief? You'll remember Rob, won't you?'

'I will. I'll get word to him, somehow. And *you* remember, won't you? I'm sorry, but – '

'Chief, if Rob MacDonald rings, will you speak to him? We couldn't, Lucinda and me – just couldn't.'

'I'll speak to him.' All part of being a Chiefie, dammit.

'Thanks.' In the doorway, Vi turned. 'Her things? Her personal things. Will I pack them?'

'Could you, McKeown? I'd appreciate it if you would.'

'I'll do that.' It would be near-unbearable, but she'd do it. There were things that weren't getting sent back to her mam and dad; all her letters, the little precious things. Rob's first wings. 'I'll see to it.'

'They aren't goin' to buy it, Lucinda.' Vi sat down heavily on the bed. 'They'll not let us go. King's Regulations. We don't qualify, not being next of kin or anything. It's a bugger, innit?'

'Shall we just skip? I'll pay the fares. We could change into our civvies in the toilets on the pier.'

'Chiefie said she'd have us picked up if our feet so much as touched Craigiebur Pier. And even if we made it on to the ferry, they'd have us at Garvie. With hair like yours, queen, the crushers would see us coming a mile off. I shouldn't have asked her. We should just have gone, and sod 'em.'

'What are we going to do without her, Vi? I just sat on her bed and the springs creaked.' Her mouth trembled ominously.

'I know. That bloody bed used to get on my nerves; now I wouldn't care if it kept me awake all night, every night. Not if she could be back, I wouldn't.'

'There'll be somebody else in it soon. Her relief. Just like it was when Megan Cad came. Only it'll be worse for us, having somebody else in her bed.'

'What are we goin' to do, queen?'

'God knows.'

'Got any money, Lucinda?'

'Plenty. Why?'

'I feel like goin' out and getting mad fightin' drunk, only it wouldn't be right, would it?'

'No, it wouldn't. And anyway, you can't get drunk when you're miserable. It wouldn't work. Only make us sick.'

'I want to cry, queen, only I can't.'

She wanted to weep as she had wept the night Richie Daly came; the night she threw the sepia vase. Great, tearing sobs they'd been, and her on her knees on the floor, beating it with her fists. That's the way she wanted to cry now.

'Me, too. I want Mike. I want him to hold me and tell me it'll be all right. I need someone's arms.'

'There's only mine.' Vi sat down on the bed beside her friend, then gathering her close she laid a cheek on her hair, on the baby-soft, white-blonde hair. 'Only mine, Lucinda. 'Fraid they're goin' to have to do.'

After a long time, after a lot of tears, they found the courage, between them, to pack Jane's case.

Chief Wren Pillmoor walked into the wardroom without knocking and took a chair without being invited.

'Better news from the hospital, Ma'am. She's comfortable.'

'Thank heaven for that.' At least the driver would be all right. 'It's hardly believable, is it? A torpedo, I mean. And one of our own. Makes you wonder about that submarine, doesn't it? First the trouble in Gareloch and now this. If one was inclined to superstition . . .'

'How could it have happened, Ma'am? And think what it *might* have hit. I mean, if they go shooting off – '

'Not shooting off, Pat; not exactly. It *was* an accident, though between these four walls I'd have called it down-right carelessness. It seems that when a submarine comes back from patrol there's a routine of checking, and a part of it is blowing the torpedo tubes, whatever that means. Some officer from *Omega* does it, and always has, without incident, until today.'

'So why now, Ma'am? Why this?'

'Well, it seems *Virgil* had to abandon patrol because of engine trouble and lines must have got a bit crossed. Someone must have forgotten to mention they were still carrying one unfired torpedo.'

'And everyone will be blaming everyone else, and meantime, Jane Kendal is dead. Will there be a court martial, Ma'am?'

'I should damn well hope so! Somebody, somewhere, should feel the backlash of this one!' St John's anger, though rarely shown, was very real. 'It'll never make the papers, of course. Killed on active service, they'll tell her parents. And she was on her way to meet her boyfriend, wasn't she?'

'Yes. To arrange their wedding. Her parents are going to take it badly. She's an only child.'

'And McKeown and Farrow?'

'What do you expect? We'll have to talk about cabin 9 soon. Tomorrow, maybe?' Reluctantly she got to her feet. 'I'll have to go. I want to get the downstairs windows, at least, boarded up, and there's a hole in the roof. It isn't likely to rain tonight, but I'd like to make sure the working party puts a tarpaulin over it.'

'Thanks, Pat. You know, I'm grateful for all you've done today,' the officer said softly. 'Pop in later, if you can.'

'I will, Ma'am. If I can.'

'So it was *Virgil*, then?' Buzzes had been two a penny, but now the cause of the tragedy seemed certain.

Lucinda and Vi sat disconsolate in the boat's-crew cabin, trying bitterly to find a scapegoat.

'*Viper!*' Lucinda ground. 'She was always afraid of that submarine. And why it ever came back here, I'll never know.'

'She knew,' Lilith mourned softly. 'She always knew. I told her not to worry, that Tom Tavey would never wish her harm, but it was *Viper* took her, in the end. Forty lives that submarine has had. I hope it goes to the bottom on the very next patrol.'

'Don't, Lilith.' Fenny shifted uneasily. 'There's been enough bad luck already. Don't ill-wish.'

'Ill-wish? I'll tell you something for nothing, Cole; somebody's got to pay for this one.'

'So leave them to God, eh? Leave them to karma. Don't interfere, *cariad*,' Megan begged. 'This one's best left alone.'

'The hell it is! I lit the candles for Johnny Jones and I'll light them again if – '

'Oh, stop it, will you! For God's sake, stop it!' Lucinda cried, white-faced. 'Light all the candles you want, Penrose! Curse and ill-wish till you're blue in the face if it pleases you, but nothing's going to bring Jane back, is it? And candles won't help her parents, nor Rob. What about Rob, then? Never mind your stupid damn religion! I'm sick of this day, and you know what you can do with your bloody cant!'

Eyes wild, she flung across the room, and the door shook with the force of her anger as it slammed shut behind her. Down the stairs, out, through the door, past the great, yawning hole – ringed round now with posts and wire – past the place where *she* had been.

On, feet slamming, and on, and damn this war for hanging a disc around your neck and turning you into a number, a statistic.

Shaking uncontrollably, she walked uncaring, knowing she was not wearing her cap – so let them do her for being improperly dressed! And came at last to the secret place, to the little jut of land where not so long ago she had sat, strangely shy, with Mike. And they had kissed gently and the trees screened out their war that day. Their wedding day.

Sick and spent, she sank to the ground. The grass was cold with the coming of evening, but she didn't care.

Mike, I want you so. I need you, my darling. Just to have you hold me and your lips near mine, telling me it's all right, that I'll awaken soon and find it happened to

*someone else, in some other place. I'm so alone. I hurt so.
Why aren't you here, Mike?*

A little before midnight she pushed tentatively on the
pantry window and found it had been left unbolted.
Wearily she eased herself up and over the sill. She felt
drained of tears, mentally neutered. It would be a long
time before she would forget this day, or forgive it.

Carefully she slid home the bolt, then closing the door
behind her she kicked off her shoes and walked slowly up
the stairs.

Chief Pillmoor was waiting on the first landing; waiting
there as if she had known the exact minute.

'Downstairs, Farrow,' she hissed, 'to the regulating
office. *Now*. And put your shoes on!'

Unspeaking, they walked down the stairs. Quietly the
Chief Wren closed the door, then banging the desk top
with a fist hard with tension she demanded, 'And where
the hell have you been? When did you go out?' Oh, she'd
known all along, hadn't she, about the bathroom lark, but
tonight she had been too weary to check. 'Why didn't you
tell someone?'

'So I'm an hour and twenty minutes adrift, Chief, and
no late pass! So I'm in the rattle!'

'Now listen to me, Farrow – '

'No, Chief, *you* listen. Listen, then tell it to the bastards
who let that torpedo go today! Tell them to go to hell,
Chief. Tell them that from me, will you? From me and
Kendal. So I'm eighty minutes adrift? Shocking, isn't it?
I've been walking, if you want to know; walking and
weeping and trying to make sense of it all! And I almost –
almost – went to the hospital and asked them to let me
see her, but I couldn't do it. Because I've had it. Up to
here, I've had it!' Dramatically she swept her hand
beneath her chin; beneath a face hard with misery. 'So

754

please excuse me, now. I've walked to Craigiebur and back and I'm very, very tired. And don't worry. I bolted the pantry window!'

Quietly she turned; too quietly she closed the door of the regulating office behind her. She would be sorry about this in the morning. You didn't talk to a Chiefie like that and get away with it. But tonight, with minutes still to run of this terrible day, she was glad for what she'd said. She was *bloody* glad.

Vi was waiting when she opened the door of cabin 9.

'You're back, girl,' she said gently. 'You had me worried. I left the pantry window open for you – told Chiefie you were in the bathroom when she did last rounds.'

'And I told Chiefie what she could do with her King's bloody Regulations when she caught me on the landing!'

'Ar hey, so we're both in trouble, then. Mother of God, but this has been a pig of a day. What are we goin' to do without her, eh? How will we ever get over it?'

31

'So that's it, then. Can't say I'm not relieved it's over.'
Taking off hat and gloves, Chief Wren Pillmoor sank
wearily into a wardroom chair. 'Two, in less than two
years: Dean and Kendal, and little more than kids, either
of them,' she said, tight-lipped. 'Must be a terrible thing,
looking forward to your daughter's leave next week, then
having her come home like – like *that*.'

'Leave, Chief! Farrow and McKeown are due theirs
next week, too.' Talk about anything, the officer thought;
talk about ships, shoes, sealing wax and, yes, talk about
leave, too. Talk about anything but the hospital mortuary
they had just left. She, a doctor's daughter, yet this
afternoon had clawed at her heart. She was thankful the
last two days were behind her. She wouldn't want to live
through either again. 'It isn't going to work, you know.
Not now – their staying on in cabin 9, I mean.'

'No, it isn't.' Pat Pillmoor lit a cigarette then regarded
it with distaste. She didn't really want the thing but,
God, how she needed it. There were things about this
war made you want to jack the whole lot in, she thought
bitterly; watching the coffin of a young Wren being
carried on to the ferry, for one, and knowing that when
it reached Garvie a young pilot would be waiting at the
quayside. Viciously she crushed out the cigarette. 'It
isn't. Right from the start they've been close, Ma'am.
Even that morning they got here, McKeown had them
under her wing like a broody hen. I suppose we couldn't
split them up, the two of them – put each in a different
cabin?'

756

'We could, but I don't think it would work. If there's to be a split it must be more than that. It's time for them both to move on, Chief. Separately.'

Draft them to some other base; the ultimate solution. 'With respect, Ma'am, isn't that a bit like cheating?'

'Yes, I think perhaps it is, but can you come up with anything better?'

The officer smiled as she recognized the knock on the door and called 'Come' because she knew it was a tea-tray, and a cup of tea was what she wanted – *needed* – at this moment.

'I've put on an extra cup,' Vi said, her eyes on Suzie St John.

'That was thoughtful of you, McKeown.' The officer's voice was gentle. 'And we took your flowers . . .'

So Jane was gone, really gone from them, now. Vi stood there clutching the tray, knuckles white. Then setting it on the table she said, 'Will there be anything else, Ma'am?'

'Thank you, no. That will be all, McKeown.'

That will be all. So what else was there to say, damn it?

'Farrow is officer material, you know.' Pat Pillmoor picked up the teapot. 'It's time she had a commission.'

'Yes, but does she *want* one?'

'That'll be up to her – and if she passes the initial board. It's my guess she'll soon let them know at Greenwich whether she does or not. She went out last night, by the way. Came in very late, then gave *me* the length of her tongue.'

'Insubordination, Chief?'

'*Gross* insubordination, but you couldn't blame her. I don't intend taking it any further. Had to admire the girl, really. Didn't think she had it in her.'

'Is she back on watch today?'

'Yes. She's got things under control now. Yesterday was a different matter, but best she should get back to it again. McKeown too.'

'McKeown? She's a good steward, you know. Don't you think it's about time she was made up to Leading Wren?'

'But that would mean we'd lose her.' McKeown was a damn nice person, too. 'Do we want that?'

'Being moved to some other base always follows promotion, and we can't deny her promotion just because we'd prefer to have her stay here.'

'You're right, Ma'am. Put their leave forward a week, will we, then send them on from there? Best they don't come back here, isn't it?'

'Best they don't. All right, Pat. I'll see to it. I think they'll agree with me, at *Omega*.' Eyes closed, she took a sip of tea. 'The sooner it's done, the better.'

When she came ashore after late watch, Lucinda knocked on the regulating office door, then stepped hesitantly inside.

'Well, close the door, Farrow, and make it quick!'

'I'm here about last night, Chief, to apologize. What I said was unforgivable and I regret it. I'm very sorry. Not for *saying* it,' she added hastily, 'but sorry I took it out on you.'

'So was I. You made quite an impression.' Pat Pillmoor looked up, with a crooked smile. 'Though it bordered on gross insubordination, I hope you realize. But I'd have done the same, in your shoes. Cut along now. You're not in the rattle – *this* time.'

'Thanks, Chief. Thanks a lot.' She stood there, eyes troubled. 'Jane? Has – has she . . . ?'

'This afternoon,' Pat Pillmoor said softly. 'We took the

flowers, and yours and McKeown's too. Now go and get some standeasy.'

'Yes. Yes, I will. Goodnight, Chief.'

'Well, that's it then, queen. You an officer and me a Leading Wren. Flamin' Norah!'

The news had been unexpected. Even yet, it would take a bit of getting used to.

'Yes. Only I don't want a commission. I wouldn't even consider going down for an interview if it wasn't a means of getting away from here. Because there's no way I want to stay with *Omega* without you, Vi. I'll miss you like hell, as it is. And you know why they're doing it, don't you? It's to split us up. That's all it is.'

She walked to the window and looked out. The glass had been replaced now, the roof repaired, and a working party was busy where the great, yawning hole had been at the edge of the loch.

'But well meant, Lucinda. Ma'am knows what a bugger it's goin' to be in this cabin without *her*.'

'And what a bugger it would be for the coder who takes her place. I couldn't bear to have anyone else in Kendal's bed.'

They hadn't touched her bed, yet; hadn't stripped off the sheets or folded the blankets.

'Sendin' us on leave a week early, eh? Well, the sooner we're away, the better. Tell you what, girl. How about me being your steward, eh?'

'I haven't got my tricorn hat yet. And I won't take any old commission, Vi. If they won't give me something in wireless, then it's not on. I'm a good sparker; as good as any man. Wish they'd made me up to Leading Wren, like you. I'd far rather have had my hook.'

'So try telling them that and you'll get a flea in yer ear. It'll be funny, won't it, us goin' on leave then not coming back here; not meetin' up at Glasgow,' Vi said softly, sadly.

'Don't, Vi. Part of me wants to stay, but I know it's best we go. Jane would always have been with us, had we stayed. She once told me, y'know, she asked God to let her see Rob again; just *see* him. For half a minute. And for that, she said, He could have the rest of her life if He wanted it.'

'Don't talk like that, girl. Don't take on. And anyway, you can't make bargains with God. What happened to Jane was none of His doing. It was that bloody Book of Life. They opened it that day and someone had written her name on a torpedo . . .'

'Leaving isn't going to be easy, though.' Lucinda turned from the window then walked the length of the cabin, arms folded. 'There'll be everybody to say goodbye to: Chief Wetherby, Lofty and Jock. Jock's cut up about Jane, you know.'

'Ar. And there'll be Molly and Miriam and Kathy. And Patsy Pill, and Ma'am. And what about next door? I'll miss that Lilith and her goings-on. Mother of God, girl, I wish I'd never come here.'

'I don't, Vi.' Lucinda dropped to her knees, elbows resting on the bed beside her friend. 'I wouldn't have missed one second of it: good bits, bad bits, nor you and Jane. Knowing what I know now, I'd still want these two years again.'

She closed her eyes against the ever-threatening tears. She wanted Mike. Just to be with him, hands clasped. Just to have him hold her close, tell her that one day the pain would lessen.

'I wonder how Rob is,' she whispered. 'They told him, didn't they, at the station?'

'Chiefie said they did. I don't know if he's phoned here, though, but they wouldn't tell us, anyway.'

'I looked in Jane's address book, Vi, when we were packing her things. Mrs MacDonald's address was there. I wrote it down.'

'We'll have to send Rob his letters back, and his wings. And we'll have to tell him how happy she was, won't we?'

'We will, love. We will.'

They threw their kit in the back of the Craigiebur transport then took their places beside the driver. A new driver; not the one who gave Mike a lift the morning of the telephone call, Lucinda thought, her heart beating dully, painfully. Mike's gorgeous brunette was in hospital, but alive. The lucky one.

'Don't look back, queen.' Sailors didn't look back, nor Wrens, either. Not even so much as a glance at *Omega*, nor the loch shimmering in the June heat. And certainly not up at the window of cabin 9, because you never knew, did you, who might be standing there; whose sad-eyed wraith might be looking down. 'Chin up, girl – not the end of the world.'

'No, Vi. Not the end.'

Not quite the end because there was worse to come. The Garvie ferry, for one, and trying not to look back at Craigiebur Pier and the little jut of land not far from it where summer trees screened out your war.

'We'll be all right.' Vi reached for the hand of her friend and held it tightly. They wanted to go; they wanted to stay. They wanted it never to have happened; they wanted to put back the clock and live it all again; to begin once more at the RTO's office and the leading hand – him with the hook – being snotty, then pies and beans and getting lost in the blackout. 'We'll get over it. Nothing lasts . . .'

* * *

They stood on the station at Glasgow amid a litter of kit. They stood and wondered why they were here; wished they were not.

Vi looked again at her left sleeve and the new royal-blue anchor: her *hook*, the badge of her new rank. There had been a lot of sewing on to do: hooks on overalls, on jacket-sleeves, on her greatcoat. Seven shillings a week extra pay and a couple more late passes, that was all. Yet once, not so long ago, she had thought a Leading Wren was the be-all and end-all of the Women's Royal Naval Service.

'I wonder,' she said, trying to smile, 'if we could find that canteen again?'

'I doubt it, and anyway, it wouldn't be the same.'

The cheery lady in the flowered pinafore, pies and beans in tomato sauce and the airman in the corner, writing letters.

'No, queen. Not the same.' Never the same.

'I shall spend this leave at Eaton Square. It's different at home now. Mama and Pa always out.' Lucinda shrugged. And at Eaton Square she would be nearer to Mike; she could sleep on his side of the bed, the pale green pyjamas clutched tightly to her.

They had refused Mike's request for a transfer back to England. She was glad, really, though he would ask again – nothing was more certain – when he got the letter telling him about Jane.

'I'm glad the goodbyes are over. There'll be someone else in cabin 9 before the week is out. Before long they'll have forgotten us.'

'Ar. It's like that, innit, when there's a war on.'

Unlike Lucinda, Vi already knew her ultimate destination. Report to the offices of Flag Officer in Charge, HMS *Eaglet*, Liverpool. Bloody amazing. Number 44455, Leading Wren McKeown, V.T., was going on draft to

Liverpool, to a Wrennery in one of the big houses in Sefton Park. She and Gerry had often gone there in the old days. Lovely, it had been there, and that great big glasshouse full of palms and orchids and tropical plants; and the big tall trees and sweeps of grass – just like being in the country.

There'd be damn all to see there, now. The grass ploughed up, like as not, and the bombing would have put paid to the glasshouse. But her new quarters wouldn't be all that far from where her sister lived. If ever she got a make-and-mend, Vi realized, she'd be able to make it to Ormskirk for a few hours.

'Had you thought, Lucinda, that when you get your commission, you'll – '

'*If* I get a commission . . .'

'*If* you get a commission you'll have a bit more clout, like. Ever thought you could ask them to draft you to Washington?'

They had walked back to the seat at the top end of platform 8, again. Half an hour still to run before the London train left; where better, then, to spend it?

Lucinda pushed her cap to the back of her head and unfastened her jacket. Hell, but it was hot! Just as it had been that day, two years ago, when first they sat here.

'Want one?' She took out her cigarette case and lighter. Smoking outdoors in uniform was not permitted, but who the hell cared?

'Ta. Had you, Lucinda? Thought about Washington, I mean.'

'Yes, I have, but it wouldn't be on. "Where's your husband, Farrow? Washington?" Then guess who'd get a draft chit to Aden or Sydney or Gibraltar? Honestly, Vi, did you *really* want to be drafted to Liverpool?'

Gloomily Vi drew on her cigarette. Liverpool, even

though it was her own very dear city, was a bit of a come-down after Loch Ardneavie. 'No, I didn't,' she admitted.

'Well, there you are, then. That's why they're sending you there. I told you about the girl in training depot, didn't I? She had a pig of a father, it seemed, and she volunteered before her age-group was due for call-up, just to get away from him. She lived in Dover, and guess where they sent her?'

'Ar, Dover. They would, wouldn't they? You've got my address, queen, and Mary's? You'll write?'

'You know I will. And as soon as I know where I'm going to end up, I'll let you know at once. We mustn't lose touch, Vi. We won't, will we?'

'No, girl. We'll keep in touch. I'll write all the time, I promise.'

Promises. They'd write, of course. But then the letters would get fewer and fewer, and before long it would only be birthday cards and Christmas cards, and by the time the war was over they'd both have forgotten cabin 9 and Ardneavie House and the 15th Flotilla. It was the way things were. Wartime friendships were like holiday romances, really.

'You'll remember me to Nanny when you write? It was smashin' at Lady Mead, wasn't it?' She stopped, angry for talking about Lady Mead, because Lady Mead was laughter and fun and being shut away from the war for six days. And Jane had found Rob again there, so she shouldn't have mentioned it. Not yet.

'I'll give Nanny your love. She'll be very pleased to hear about your hook, Vi.'

'Ar.'

They were making small talk, filling in minutes that crawled into hours; wanting to be away, wanting to stay; to stay on Glasgow Central station with time standing still, waiting for the York train to arrive, and Jane stepping off it.

'You ought to be making your way, queen – try to get yourself a seat.'

'Yes,' Lucinda whispered.

The tears came, then; tears she had been fighting since she got out of bed this morning and realized that this was the last day in cabin 9; tears because Jane wasn't coming, and soon she and Vi would part and they'd never see each other again; tears because Mike was in Washington and she was, oh, so *very* weary of this war.

'Come on then, girl.' Vi picked up a suitcase. 'I'll give you a hand.'

'What about your own kit?'

'Ar, sod it. Leave it.'

They stood at the barrier, looking at the London platform. So much to say, so very hard to say it.

'Well, then, Lucinda . . .'

'Oh, Vi!' Reaching out, Lucinda hugged her close. 'Take care, old love. Don't forget me.'

'I won't. And be careful, eh?' She nodded in the direction of the train. 'Ta-ra, then. Off you go.'

She picked up Lucinda's respirator and hung it on her shoulder, then folded greatcoat and raincoat lengthwise and placed them one over each arm. She didn't speak as Lucinda picked up her cases. Even as she walked away, head high, back ramrod-straight in spite of her load, Vi did not speak.

Lucinda walked slowly, tears running down her cheeks, and she left them unwiped and unchecked because she was so miserable and, anyway, her hands were full.

Then, even though Vi had said she must never do it, she turned, scanning the length of the platform, but Vi was lost amongst the pushing, hurrying crowd.

'See you, Vi,' she whispered. 'And goodbye, Jane. Goodbye, Kendal dear . . .'

The aloneness hit Vi like a blow as she looked around the familiar railway station. Everything was the same, yet everything had changed now. But couples would still meet here and part here; people would laugh and weep as they had done since the start of this war, nearly four years ago. And the few dim lights would be blue-painted until it all ended and the single bulb in the left-luggage office shaded with the same brown paper. And there it was, in the far corner, the Naval RTO's office.

Vi smiled briefly. Would little Hitler still be there – him with the hook? Well, she had a hook of her own, now, so how about paying him a visit?

An imp of mischief stirred briefly inside her, then was gone. That leading hand would have left long ago, and if she thought to find two lost young kids there, kids with still-fluffy uniforms and too-long skirts – well, they were gone, too.

One for all and all for one it had been, yet now she was on her own again. They would never meet again, but it had been good. She wouldn't have missed any of it; the conga chains, fingers on a glass, the hissing, spitting fire in cabin 10, the pantry window. Yet what was she to do now? There was still half an hour before the Liverpool train came in, and God alone knew how long before it left.

Slowly she walked back to the bench at the end of platform 8; back to where she had left her kit. Strange that the wooden seat should still be there beside the barrier; that the Garvie ferry train would leave in just a few more minutes and she would not be on it. None of them would. Never again.

She picked up her case and kitbag and respirator and

walked away, to the platform from which the Liverpool train would leave. Funny how big and empty this station could be. Odd that a place so full of comings and goings and people and noise could be so lonely.

She looked around her for the last time. Come to think of it, this was exactly how it had started, just two years ago. This was where she came in, she supposed. Funny, that was.

'Ta-ra, well,' she said again.

32

1946

Vi sat primly, handbag on knee, ankles crossed, looking out at a country at peace; at a whole world at peace. Just six years after it all started, and she was a civilian again – and Gerry was home and there was so much, so very much, to be glad about.

The train slowed, hooting, then rumbled over a level crossing. Through the window, at a meeting of two roads, workmen were replacing a signpost. Soon, everyone would know where they were again and how many miles to such and such a place, and in which direction. Five years ago they had taken down all the signposts. No use telling Hitler's lot where they were, when the invasion came; no use letting those paratroopers dressed as nuns know they were only ten miles from London, or Birmingham, or Glasgow.

Glasgow. Central station and platform 8. And going on leave and coming back from leave and saying goodbye there. Well, it was all over, now. The Americans had dropped two bombs – two very frightening bombs – and that had been the end of it. *Kaput!* or whatever the Japanese word for surrender was. That war they all thought would drag on and on in the Far East had ended three months after Victory in Europe Day. My, but they'd been lucky. The whole world had been lucky, except the poor beggars who'd copped the two bombs up.

She looked again at her watch. Train journeys were still slow, though now the British public had ceased to be asked if their journey was really necessary. It was all right to travel, now that most of the servicemen and women had been sent home. She had found a seat without bother at Lime Street station; a corner seat was best, Gerry had said, placing her case on the rack opposite, where she could keep an eye on it.

'Now you're all right, girl? Got enough in your purse, have you?'

'I won't need money, Gerry. I'm bein' met.'

'Just in case, though.'

'I've got money, lad. Now stop your fussin' and get yourself back home. Don't hang around here.' She still didn't like being waved off, though she liked to be met. 'I'll let you know what time the train's gettin' in on Monday. And don't be late at our Mary's, mind.' Gerry would be having his suppers at Mary's house whilst she was away. Wouldn't do to be late for a meal when her sister took such pains over the cooking of it.

'I won't, girl. Now you'll be all right on your own? Know which stop to get off at?'

'I do, lad. I do.'

Oh, Gerry McKeown, you daft ha'porth, she'd thought. I've been travellin' the length and breadth of the country on my own for the last five years!

'Well, ta-ra, girl. Have a good time. Give them my regards, eh? Say sorry I couldn't come but – '

'Pressure of work.' Vi had nodded solemnly. 'They'll understand.'

'That's right.' His face had brightened and he'd bent down to kiss her cheek. 'Well, I'll be on my way, then. See you, girl.'

'See you. If you shift yourself you'll just catch the Ormskirk bus. Ta-ra, well.'

Her eyes misted over just to think of the day he'd come back, two weeks before the end of the war in Europe.

Thinner, but straighter and fitter, and finished with shovellin'. No more sea-time, he had said, God love him.

Vi checked her watch yet again. They weren't making bad time; shouldn't be all that late arriving. But things were improving all round, now. Mind, there was food rationing still, and terrible shortages of everything. Stupid of them to have imagined that one week after it was all over the shops would be bustin' at the seams with curtain material and wallpaper and rugs and armchairs, and clothes off the ration and butter and joints of beef for the asking. Things wouldn't be back to normal for a long time, but at least the killing was over and the lights on again, so nothing else mattered, really. Not if you'd got your man back, it didn't.

And the trains were cleaner than they'd been for ages. Still shabby from six years of war, but clean, and water in the toilets again. There had never been water during the war, but it wouldn't have made a lot of difference since the toilets were always packed out with kitbags and cases; so full, the doors wouldn't close.

And there was something else she'd noticed. Porters were back on the station platforms again. Porters willing to carry cases and help you on to trains and help you off. No more pushing and shoving and heaving, now. Ar, yes. Things were on the mend. Slowly, mind, but getting better bit by bit.

The sound of the train changed. The noise of the wheels took on a lower pitch and streets and rows of little houses were slipping past the compartment window. Another few minutes and she would be there.

She reached for her coat, shrugging into it, bracing herself against the seat as the train braked sharply then ran on. Excitement surged inside her as she fastened buttons with unsteady fingers, then reached for her case. She sat down again as the train pulled slowly into the station and jerked to a stop with a grinding of brakes and a final hiss of steam.

She wasn't in any hurry. Just a few seconds to sit still and savour the moment. After all, it had been a long time . . .

Then, smiling, she walked the length of the corridor, stepping carefully down on to the platform, looking left and right, wondering if they were here yet.

And then she saw her. She'd have known that hair anywhere. Those pale-blonde, baby-soft curls, and still cut short to her head.

'*Looo-cinda!*'

'Vi!' They hugged and laughed and kissed, and the years between had never been. 'Vi! You haven't changed a bit.'

'Neither have you, queen. Just the same, 'cept – ' She stopped, frowning. The girl was putting on weight, a bit. *Weight?* Vi held her at arm's length, taking in the thickening at her waist, the rounding of her abdomen. 'You're not, girl? You *are*! Lucinda! How far gone are you? Half-way?'

'I thought you'd never notice! I'm nearly six months, actually. I kept it as a surprise.'

'Ar, queen, I'm made up for you. I'm dead chuffed.' Ar, Lucinda pregnant at last!

Mike stood there, smiling. Over Lucinda's shoulder, Vi gave him a wink of congratulation. 'Mike, lad, it seems that long since I saw you! The weddin', wasn't it?'

'The wedding, Vi.' He kissed her cheek. 'And you'll be pleased to see I got the girl respectably and properly fixed up before we made that baby.'

He held up a little finger to show Alice Farrow's signet ring, back where it once had been, then reached for Lucinda's left hand. 'She got her wedding ring, in the end.'

771

'And about time, too,' Vi said scathingly, then hugged her friend again because it was three years since they parted and there was so much more to say than letters or telephone calls could ever have done.

'The car's in the parking lot.' Mike picked up Vi's case. 'Guess the pair of you are going to be talking into the small hours. Nanny's looking forward to seeing you, Vi.'

'Ar.' Vi choked, hands to her burning cheeks. It was all too much. Not just seeing Lucinda and Mike and Nanny; not just them being together again after so long; not even the baby. It was just, well – *everything* . . .

'You'll be sad, queen,' Vi murmured as they drew out of the station, 'at Lady Mead having to be sold.'

'Yes. It was tragic, Uncle Guy going so soon after Pa; though I suppose if we could choose, it's the way we'd all want to do it – to slip away quietly in our sleep. And Uncle Guy never wanted the bother of the title or the estate, anyway. But for Pa to have Home-Guarded his little patch right through the war, then to be killed by almost the last flying bomb on London was awful. Well, he died in his uniform and that's what he'd have wanted, poor old love. Trouble is, there are two lots of death duties for Charlie to find, and there's nothing for it but to sell up and pay up.'

'How did the Air Force leave the place?' Deftly, Vi changed the subject. Lucinda was getting upset and there would be time enough for upset tomorrow. 'Did they do much damage?'

'What! With Nanny keeping tabs on them? No. They were very good, really. And they got out pretty quickly, once the war was over. The Ministry of Works did essential repairs. They put the roof right, for a start. Y'know, I'll bet anything you like Pa was looking down and laughing like a drain at that. Used to say Lady Mead's roof was in such a bad state that the repairs would bankrupt him, after the war.'

'And Charlie's the Earl, now? What's he got to say about this sellin'-up business?'

'Relieved, now that he's used to the idea. He's going to settle in New Zealand – though he won't be here for the sale. Isobel's second is nearly due, so Charlie wouldn't leave her. And Mama's staying with friends in Ireland and refuses to come near, though Charlie's trying hard to keep Bruton Street, so she'll be able to stay on there, I shouldn't wonder.

'That was why we came over for the sale. A sort of last fling before I get too big to go anywhere – and for someone to be here to say goodbye to the old place, I suppose.

'Oh, and did you know that Nanny is coming back with us?' she rushed on. 'She's so thrilled to be nannying again, though I'm not pushing the little thing into the nursery the minute it's born. I want a hand in the bringing-up of *my* children.'

'*Children*, she says.' Mike opened the car door. 'And I've still not gotten over the morning-sickness drama of this one yet.'

'Well, Grandma Alice is delighted. Says she aims to stay alive to hold her first great-grandchild.'

'Grandma's having a field day with Lucy's title, the old snob.' Mike grinned. 'There's Lucy trying hard to be *Mrs* Farrow and the old girl insisting she's still a lady.'

Vi smiled. 'You'll always be Bainbridge, L. V., to me, girl.'

'Yes, and the best telegraphist in the Flotilla!'

'You were, queen.'

'And no one, darling, to touch you when it came to climbing through very small windows.' Teasing her, Mike

773

placed his hands on her abdomen. 'Bet you couldn't do it now!'

'Oh, Vi, isn't this nice,' Lucinda sighed, 'us all being together again; well, *almost* . . .'

'Nice.' Vi nodded, complacently. 'I'm that pleased to see you, and there's so much to catch up on.'

'Yes – so we won't think about tomorrow until tomorrow comes.'

Tomorrow. Losing Lady Mead would be hard, Lucinda realized, because tomorrow she would *really* be losing it – not giving it over to Isobel. After tomorrow there'd be no more Bainbridges there. A pity, because one way or another they'd been around for almost five hundred years.

'Oh, just remembered!' The smile was back. 'I've brought you some nylons, Vi.'

Mike Farrow looked back at the face of his wife; his adored, adorable Lucy. It was still hard to take it in that, given their fair share of luck, they would grow old together.

'Have I the right to be this contented, Vi?' he asked softly as Lucinda ran ahead of them to the front door of the Dower House.

'Nobody has a *right* to anything, Mike.' Vi smiled her broad, knowing smile. 'But if it comes your way, then enjoy it – that's what I say.'

'My word, Mrs West,' Vi remarked when Lucinda had been sent upstairs for her afternoon rest and Mike gone off to Lady Mead, 'this house is so empty now, that it rattles. Nearly as empty as ours.'

'Ah, that's because all the furniture has gone, you see. The sale was last week. I watched them carry it all out and set it up in the big house, every piece with a little number stuck on it, and I remembered the days we all worked so hard to bring it here and somehow fit it in.

Lucinda not long out of school, and the war just a year old. But tell me about your new home,' she urged. 'You must have been very relieved to find somewhere to live.'

'Relieved? Divine Providence, that's what. Half of Liverpool knocked down in the bombing, and there we both were, jammed in at our Mary's, when Father O'Flaherty called with a job on a plate for Gerry – and a job with a house to it.

'Sister Annunciata – she was one of the parish nuns, if you remember, at St Joseph's – was goin' to be headmistress at a Cath'lick school not very far from where our Mary lives, and they were looking for a caretaker with experience of boilers – the old boiler bein' past its best – and someone who could see to the gardens.

'So Father O'Flaherty said he knew just the man for the job; said Gerry had experience with boilers and was a keen gardener, too. God forgive the old rogue; Gerry had never planted nothin' more than a rose bush, though nobody could say he wasn't good at shovellin' coal into boilers. And him bein' a prisoner of war counted in his favour, so the job was his – *and* the house.'

She thought back to the neglected little house and its overgrown garden, remembering that she had loved it at once.

'Mind, it's only a diddy house, Mrs West. There's a small front parlour, but a real big living-kitchen, nearly as big as this one, and two bedrooms. And a bathroom. Gerry was always desperate for a bathroom. He managed to get hold of a couple of tins of paint, so it was the bathroom that got decorated first. Cream and green he's done it. Beautiful, it is.'

'And how did you manage for furniture? Such a worry, and still none in the shops.'

'Ar, well, there were the dockets the bombed-outs could apply for so we got ours, though they only allowed

775

us enough to buy lino for two floors and curtains for two windows – and a bed, and chest of drawers, and a table to eat off. Oh, it's empty all right, but it's ours – mine and Gerry's – and we're together again, and soon he'll be planting me a rose bush. It's all I ever wanted, and there's not many get all they've ever wanted, is there?'

'Very few. I think,' said Nanny comfortably, 'that this calls for a cup of tea, Mrs McKeown. Lucinda brought such a lot of food over with her – even fancy biscuits, though I must learn to call them cookies, once I'm living there. Now, you tell me about your Gerald, will you, whilst I put the kettle on. It must have been a wonderful moment when you first saw him after all that time.'

'Well, it's funny, but it happened awkward, like, and not a bit like I'd imagined it would. I was stationed in Liverpool then; not very far from where my sister lives. And there was a phone call for me – it was Mary, saying there'd been a telegram for me and she'd opened it. Gerry was on his way – just before VE Day, it was. But I didn't know which train he'd be on – the soft ha'porth hadn't thought to tell me the time – so I got a seventy-two-hour pass and sat it out at Mary's house. And he just walked up her path, large as life. Held out his arms, he did, and hugged me. We stood there for ages, just holding each other, and then he said, "Hullo, girl. All right, then?" Eh, I don't know. Talk about romantic!'

'But he was back, and well?' Nanny prompted.

'Oh, ar. They hadn't been treated badly – not in *his* camp, anyway. And he used to get sent out to work on a farm – a "trusty", like. The prison guards used to drop him off in the morning then collect him at nights. The farmer gave him what food he could, though things got bad for them when the war started to go our way. But he always gave Gerry potatoes or bread, and every day a cup of milk. I think it was workin' on that farm that saved his sanity. And Gerda.'

'Gerda?' Nanny looked up from the biscuits she was arranging.

'The farmer's daughter. Only four when he first went there, but he loved that little thing, him not havin' any kids of his own, and she was fond of him, too. Followed him everywhere. But he never said anythin' in his letters about the food the farmer gave him, nor Gerda. Wouldn't have done, he said. They'd maybe have stopped him working there if they'd known he'd liked it so much. They censored everything going out and every letter coming in, too. But me and Gerry were the lucky ones. I still think about Jane, Mrs West. Never had a fair crack of the whip, that kid didn't.'

'Jane.' Nanny sighed. 'Poor, pretty Jane. Lucinda told me about it when she visited to show me her officer's uniform. Such a terrible, terrible tragedy. That poor young man . . .'

'Ar. Lucinda and me still write to Rob – just sometimes, to make sure he's all right. For Jane's sake, I suppose we do it. I think he'll emigrate. It was on his mind, last time I heard from him. He was on leave when Jane was killed – went to her funeral he told me. Not with the family, or anything. Just stood there, in the graveyard. Tore my heart out, that letter did. Lucinda and me tried to get leave to go, but it wasn't on. Ar, it was a nasty old war, at times. I'm glad it's over, Mrs West, but I'm glad I had a hand in it, too. I'll always be glad about that . . .'

Later that evening, Vi and Mike walked over to the big, empty house.

'Strange to think that Lucy was born in a place like this. Things must have been very different in those days, Vi.'

'They were.' Carefully Vi negotiated the unlit basement

stairs. 'Coal was one and sixpence a bag and you could get enough steak for a shillin' to feed a family of four; if you had a shillin' to spare, that was. Servants came cheap, too. A young girl straight out of school got bed and board and five bob a week.'

'Say, that's a real shocker!'

'Nah, not really. If a girl got with a good family – one like Lucinda's – she counted herself lucky. Probably never eaten so well in her life. And a bed all to herself for the first time, most likely – not sharing one with her sisters. The Bainbridges would've been all right to work for, except that I've got a feeling that Lucinda's mam could be a bit moody, sometimes. But she didn't like Lady Mead so she wasn't there a lot to bother them. Lucinda loved the place, though; nearly married Charlie to get it. She's goin' to be real cut up tomorrow. She won't show it, Mike, but it'll go deep. I know her. Her lot don't show their feelings – not in public – but losing this old house is goin' to hurt.'

'Yup. But I'll be around, Vi, and so will you, and Lucy is never down for long.' Mike smiled. 'What say we go and take a look upstairs? I'd like to see the nursery again. Tell me, why did they always stick nurseries out of the way, at the top of the house, usually?'

'Dunno.' Not having had experience of nurseries, Vi declined to comment.

'And I want to take a look at the south wing again. That south wing doesn't seem to fit, somehow.'

'No. Lucinda said it was built on after, same as the chapel at the far end. All the south-wing rooms get the sun. It's her favourite part.'

'I know. That's why I want to see it. By the way, did you know that Cousin Charlie managed to wangle a few of the family portraits for himself? And he's given us a wedding present, too: a portrait of the very first Lady

778

Lucinda, done by Reynolds in 1763, and there's one heck of a resemblance. It's uncanny: same colouring, same eyes. We're going to keep it, yet I know it would have brought a fair amount for Charlie at auction. Our London office is getting an export licence so we can take it back with us.'

'Going back on the *Mauretania*, aren't you, Mike? Bet it's smashin', travelling in luxury again.'

'An experience I looked forward to for six years, and better for Lucy than flying, though flying's going to be the thing before very long. But we ought to be getting back. Lucy's tired – it's been a big day for her and I don't want she should come looking for us.'

'Don't worry.' Vi closed the door of the summer room behind her, thankful she didn't have to find linoleum for a floor *that* size, nor curtains for all those windows. 'Nanny'll have got the Ovaltine made. She'll have her bundled up to bed if she thinks she needs it.'

'Guess she will, at that. Say,' Mike's face broke into a smile and Vi knew then what had caused Lucinda's bemusement that night she had first climbed in through the pantry window. 'Do you suppose that when Nanny's got our sprog to fuss over, she'll stop calling Lucy *child*?'

'Dunno, Mike. But remember she loves her. Lucinda's closer to her than ever she was to her real mam or her da, for that matter. Nanny was her mother – and Nanny's so chuffed at being wanted; having a nursery again and a baby in it.'

'You're right. Thanks, Vi, for reminding me.'

They walked back quickly, Vi hugging herself against a September night turned not exactly cold but hinting, for all that, at autumn.

'I'm glad the estate isn't goin' to be split up,' Vi commented. 'It wouldn't be right to sell it off in job lots, would it?'

'No. I don't know if it'll be a help or a hindrance, though. The tenants are all protected, and the tenant farmers. The place'll have to be properly run, if it's to pay its way. Say, will you look at the ironwork in those gates!'

They were walking into the stableyard and across it to the small gate at which Jane and Rob had met.

'Yes. Lucky all that beautiful work didn't get melted down. Sinful, that was, taking people's gates and railings without a by-your-leave. That dratted old war.'

'It's *over*, Vi,' Mike said softly.

'Yes.' She closed the gate behind them, her hand lingering on it. 'Yes, it's over, thanks be.'

The morning of the sale was crisp and bright, with an early mist that cleared quickly at the breaking-through of the sun.

Lucinda slipped out of bed, then walked softly downstairs to the warmth of the kitchen.

She needed tea. Funny how tea had made her very sick for the first few weeks of her pregnancy, yet now it was fine again. Everything was fine – or would be, once today was over. And at least Nanny was going back with her. Nanny knew how much she cared for Lady Mead and would understand if sometimes she needed to talk about it.

She set the kettle to boil, then sat rocking gently, hands on her abdomen as her embryo child kicked sharply.

'Hey! Stop it!' she whispered indulgently. She liked being pregnant. She wanted to get really big so everyone would have to notice and know that she and Mike had made a child together. And they would have more. Several, she shouldn't wonder, when making them was such an unbelievable delight.

She smiled at the first puff of steam from the kettle spout. She still wondered, at times, about all that money.

Sometimes she was glad about it; sometimes she was sad – ashamed they should have so much. This morning she was glad, because she knew it would take care of Vi and Gerry's passage over for the christening, at Easter, most probably. Because Vi *must* be godmother; Lucinda had set her heart on it.

The kettle lid began to heave gently and she took down the brown teapot. She would keep herself in hand today. There would be no need for side glances from Nanny. She wouldn't let it hurt her when they started haggling over Lady Mead, because she was so lucky. She had Mike and the baby and Mike's lovely family, and friends like Vi. She had so much, and nothing mattered, really, except the man she loved and the child she carried. Nothing.

The sale of the Lady Mead estate – by direction of the twelfth earl of Donnington, stated the particulars-of-sale brochure – would be held at Lady Mead in the salon on Saturday the fourteenth day of September 1946 at 1.30 P.M.

The day began early, with the arrival of the caterers and the small van carrying the men who checked the guy ropes of the marquee, tightening them, securing the pegs with mallets.

The auctioneer and his staff followed not long afterwards, and the placing of pointing arrows and the arranging of folding chairs into precise rows began.

In the village inn that stood close beside the water-mill, the landlord had also been up early, checking beer pumps, counting glasses, carrying in more chairs, for this would be a big day, hereabouts. A sad one, true, but trade was trade and he had a living to make. Such a sale was rare and not to be missed, and not one in a hundred of those who attended would be in any way interested in the purchase of so large an estate. Just there for the occasion, they'd be.

From a village close by came a farmer's wife, once head parlourmaid at Lady Mead. Hers was a sentimental coming, a last look around the house she had worked in and learned the ways of her betters in, and the homemaking skills that had made her a desirable match for a man who appreciated a good table and a well-run farmhouse.

And there was a man in his middle years; one with the hands of a gardener, who had come to see how the old place had made out since he had scrubbed plantpots in ice-cold water in his apprentice days here. He'd helped in the planting of that beech hedge, too. A fine, secure hedge it had turned out to be, though it needed attention now, he noticed, frowning. Grown too leggy, but that was the fault of the war. Be as right as ninepence in a couple of years – with a bit of expert pruning.

They came in scores; some to gloat at the selling of the estate, others sad that the Bainbridges should come to this. They came to wonder who would buy and how much he would pay. Other people's money still fascinated those who had none, or said they had none.

At the Dower House they ate a midday meal of salad and tinned meat and fruit, brought over in a trunk by Lucinda – enough food to last out the duration of their stay.

'I'm not very hungry.' Lucinda pushed lettuce from one side of her plate to the other. 'I want this to be over, really, yet I don't want it to start. I wonder who'll buy it.'

'A guy with at least four hundred thousand pounds, because that's what the auctioneers are banking on it bringing in, I believe.'

'Mother of God, who's got that kind of money to give for an 'ouse?' Vi gasped.

'The newly rich, perhaps.' Nanny shrugged. 'There are

some, you know. Some profited from the war.' But she for one would not be there to see the vultures picking over the carcass. Nanny Bainbridge would not knit beside the guillotine.

'Nanny – can I go, now? Can we leave the washing-up to you? It's turned one o'clock and I want to be away. Now. Are you coming, Mike?' she demanded fretfully.

'I'll be there later, honey. Got to wait for that London call. Just take it slowly. I'll follow you up.' He looked anxiously towards Vi. *Stay with her*, his eyes asked.

'Right, then.' Vi pushed back her chair. 'You and me will amble up there, queen – see what's doin'.'

'Try not to be long, Mike.'

'I won't. Just give me another few minutes. And take it easy.'

'I will. And I'm not acting up, truly. Just, well, a little sad.'

'I know, sweetheart.' He took her chin in his hand, tilting it gently, kissing her mouth. 'I know, Lucy.'

Vi and Lucinda walked the back way to Lady Mead, skirting the outbuildings, coming in from the deer park, climbing the broad front steps. There were still fifteen; Lucinda still counted.

The entrance hall was full of noise and there was a great deal of mud on the marble floor, though it wasn't her worry now, Lucinda thought. People stood about, talking, unwilling just yet to enter the salon, looking around them at who were locals and who were incomers; wondering if one of those strangers had half a million pounds tucked away, because that was what local gossip had it the place might fetch. If the Earl was lucky.

A woman and child sat on the bottom stair, arms tucked round knees, listening to the echoes. Lucinda had watched the child trying the door handles and was glad that most rooms appeared to be locked.

'When I was little I used to have my birthday parties in the salon,' she whispered confidingly. 'A lovely big room, for parties.'

And nannies and governesses sitting round, watching, and frilly party frocks and pretty pumps and someone always sick. And Mama never there. Never, ever there. And why she was remembering pre-boarding school birthdays she had no idea, because it had all happened so long ago – to a different child in a different world.

'Think we should go in?' Vi asked. She wanted to get Lucinda settled on an aisle seat, just in case. 'They're due to start in a few minutes.'

'There are still people in the marquee, I can hear them. But maybe they don't intend coming to the sale; maybe they're just here for a look.'

'It's a free country, queen. You pays your money and you takes your choice.'

'Yes, and you gawp – or most of them do. That's what they're here for, Vi. A *gawp*. It's so sad.'

There was a long table in the salon window. At the centre of it sat the auctioneer. He had a lot of papers in front of him, and a gavel; a brass gavel, Lucinda noticed, not one of wood. It was very beautiful, really: perfectly proportioned, with a long, slender handle. But it *was* a gavel. It would bang down on the table with every bit as much finality when he said '*Sold to* . . .'

'There's a couple of seats at the front,' Vi whispered. 'On the left. Come on, they'll do.' Just what she wanted. Two seats with an uninterrupted passage to the door, in case Lucinda wanted to be sick, or anything.

'Who are all them people?' Vi nodded towards the table. They looked like a jury.

'Oh, there'll be the auctioneer, and I think the blonde

girl must be his assistant. And there's Pa's agent and solicitor – I mean *Charlie's* agent and solicitor – and who the other three are, I don't know.'

She picked up the particulars-of-sale brochure and fanned through it. There was a plan of the entire estate at the back of it. She would keep this brochure. A reminder, kind of . . .

The auctioneer rose to his feet. He didn't speak at once; just stood there to stop the talking and the shuffling. He had a nice face, really, Lucinda considered. Nice and open, and his glasses suited him.

He smiled, completely at ease. Vi watched, fascinated, one eye on the table, one eye on Lucinda, which took a bit of doing, come to think of it. Then he looked at his wrist watch, wished them all a good afternoon and lifted his copy of the ornately produced particulars-of-sale brochure.

'Gentlemen. You will already be familiar, I am sure, with the details of the Lady Mead estate sale, but if any of you would like me to refresh his memory and remind you that this is a most elegant property and one which I am instructed to offer initially as a whole. Your particulars-of-sale brochure contains details of tenanted properties, their tenants and incomings, and two cottages – Tilly Cottage, marked number seven on your plan, and Pump House Cottage, number eleven – have vacant possession. I have recently been advised that the Dower House, marked number three in the bottom left-hand corner, will very shortly be vacated.'

There was a crackling and straightening of plans, a low murmur of curiosity.

The auctioneer held up his brochure, allowing time for the folding and tucking away of plans; for settling down. He seemed very sure of himself, of a good sale, Lucinda thought, as he asked the assembly if they had any questions.

It seemed they did not. Those who were there for the occasion said nothing; those who were there to bid said nothing. No interested party wished to reveal his identity; his bids would be made by the slightest of nods or the merest moving of the brochure in his hand. And the auctioneer would know when that interest was past. Wide-eyed, Lucinda watched, her eyes not leaving his face.

'Very well, then. Gentlemen, where will you start me? Can I say four hundred thousand pounds?'

There was a murmuring; almost a gasp. Nearly half a million? But it was only a come-on, wasn't it? *Half a million?*

There was a pause, an indrawing of breath. Eyes were lowered to hands. From the back of the room came a movement. The auctioneer raised his head.

'Two hundred thousand,' came the call.

'Two hundred thousand pounds? I am bid two hundred thousand pounds.'

The auctioneer looked slowly from right to left, inviting the second bid; his assistant looked apprehensively at the pregnant young woman two rows back, then looked enquiringly at the woman at her side.

Vi saw the look. Lucinda's face had gone very white, her eyes were closed.

'Are you all right, Lady Lucinda?' The assistant moved quickly to her side. 'A drink of water?'

'No. Thank you, no.' She rose unsteadily to her feet.

Her chair grated on the floor so that it sounded like a thunderclap. Vi rose with her.

'Thanks,' she mouthed. 'I'll see to her.'

Heads turned as they walked out. Quietly Vi closed the salon door, then taking Lucinda's arm in hers, walked her firmly to the open door and the sweep of stone steps.

786

'Want to sit down for a minute, queen?'

'No, Vi. Too stupid of me, really. Such a fuss . . .'

'Come on, girl. Deep breaths. We'll not go back in there, eh?'

'It was when he asked for four hundred thousand and the bid of two hundred thousand came back. Derisive, it sounded, though I know they always start high, just to jolt someone into making a start. But suddenly, Vi, I didn't want to listen. Could we walk a little way?'

'If you're sure you're all right, girl. Not goin' to pass out on me?'

'No, Vi dear. It was only my pride taking a bit of a bashing. I wanted us – well, Charlie and Isobel, to keep it.'

They walked down the steps, through the formal garden, then on, past the sweep of lawn where the marquee stood, through the archway into the walled kitchen garden.

'There were usually about a dozen dogs in those.' Lucinda nodded as they passed the dog houses. 'Sometimes they'd set up such a howling.'

'Ar. They would.' Vi pushed open the high, ornate stableyard gates; gates wide enough, she supposed, to have allowed a coach and horses through.

'We'll go back by the short cut, shall we?'

They made for the little gate; the one that opened on to the estate yard; the gate at which Jane and Rob once stood.

'I told you, didn't I, that Mike and I are building a house – that it'll be ready, just about, by the time we get back.'

'Yes, queen. You did say.'

'And the baby will be born there, and I'll be with Mike's lovely family and have Nanny there, too. I'll have just about everything any woman could ever want.'

787

'Sounds a fair description to me,' Vi admitted.

'Then why am I feeling like this? Will you tell me why, right now, I'm feeling so bloody awful? Why am I making such a fuss, Vi, over a pile of bricks and mortar, when Jane is dead?'

'Didn't know you was makin' a fuss, girl.'

'I am, and you know I am. I'm churning and shaking inside me.'

'Well, stop it this minute.' Vi put on her Nanny Bainbridge look. 'Churnin' and shakin' isn't doin' that little baby any good!'

'I know that. But just think – whoever buys this place won't even know that this gate is special. And what's worse, I don't suppose they'd care much, if they did. God! They could have ten Lady Meads if Jane could be here now.'

'Ar, and my little 'ouse thrown in, an' all. But we're both feelin' this way because we haven't been here since – well, you know. We've both been wantin' to and we've neither of us done it, till now – come to Jane's gate, I mean . . .'

It was easier, now, to talk about her.

'You know that this is going to be a Christmas baby? Everybody's hoping for the twenty-fifth, but I'd like it to be on Christmas Eve.'

'*Her* birthday.'

'Yes. I won't forget her. I'm glad we're both here, talking about her; it's a help. But losing Jane was like losing my sister.'

'Yes, I know. I lost her, too. But now we can say goodbye to her decent, like, and she'll know we won't forget her.'

They stood, one either side of the little gate, remembering.

'Sometimes, Vi, when I'm living in America, it's going

to come over me, you know. There'll be things I shall want to remember about my other life – my *English* life. There'll be Lady Mead, and Berkeley Square, and Ardneavie.'

'And cabin 9, and Lilith's lot, next door.'

'And the Wrennery dances and squad drills and kit inspections and Lofty and Patsy Pill.'

'And runs ashore into Craigiebur and the three of us goin' through our money belts to see if we'd got enough between us for three halves of ale.'

'Yes. The *three* of us. You and Jane and me. Wren telegraphist Bainbridge, L. V.'

'You got to be an officer, though.'

'Yes, but it was best at *Omega*. They were good days, Vi. Already we're beginning to forget the bad bits and only remember what we want to.'

'One for all and all for one, queen. She'll never leave us.'

'And we don't want her to.'

Lucinda's hand rested on the gate top as if she reached out to touch their friend; Vi laid her own gently upon it, to complete the chain.

'I'm glad we had that photo taken together. Remember the day? Mother of God, we looked right Charlies in them first hats – beggin' Charlie's pardon, of course.'

'You're going to be godmother to the baby, aren't you, Vi? I've thought about it. How about an Easter christening? Gerry could get away, surely – school holidays, I mean?'

'I'd be pleased and proud, queen – if you want a Cath'lick godmother, that is, but – '

'The money?'

'Yes, Lucinda. It would cost the earth.'

'After what we've just said, Vi McKeown! One for all and all for one, then you immediately get stuffy over two sailing tickets. Can't they be my present to you and Gerry? You wouldn't say no – not to *me*?'

'I can't say it wouldn't be nice.' Vi wavered. 'And come to think of it, Gerry has shovelled his way across that Atlantic more times than you and me have had hot dinners, girl. Might be a real treat for him to cross it in style.'

'Then you'll think about it, Vi?'

'I'll think about it.'

'Seriously?'

'*Very* seriously.'

'Good. Then we'll take it as read – or should it be *said*?' The tension had left Lucinda now. The colour was back in her cheeks, and when she smiled, the dimples were back, too. 'I needed to come here, though, just to talk to you about her. And Vi, when I'm over there and I think about Lady Mead and the drying green and the deer park and the roses on the south-wing wall, I shall think about this little gate too. Jane's gate.'

'So will I, queen. So will I.'

'I suppose we'd better go back, hadn't we?' Lucinda smiled. 'Mike will be there looking for me and they'll have told him I left, all upset. Come on, Vi. Hurry, there's an old love.'

'When we get back, they'll have sold it, most likely,' Vi cautioned.

'Yes, Vi. I know.' Then she turned, and looked back. 'Goodbye, Kendal dear . . .'

When they got back to the house it seemed as if everyone was looking for her. The auctioneer smiled broadly, as if he were very pleased with the afternoon's work, then said 'Ah' when he saw her.

'I was wondering about you,' said the auctioneer's

pretty, blue-eyed assistant. 'Are you all right now? Rather stuffy in here, wasn't it?'

'Yes it was, rather, and thank you for being so kind.' Lucinda smiled.

And there was Mike, hurrying to her side, his face a mixing of worry and relief.

'There you are! I've been looking for you. They told me you'd gone out, unwell.'

'No, darling.' How good it was to see him. An hour apart was too long. 'It just got a bit warm in there, that was all, and Sprog got restless . . .'

'You're sure, Lucy? You're all right?'

'Fine. Who bought it?'

'A guy called Capaldi.'

'A – a *foreigner*, Mike?'

Not an Italian. Vi frowned. Not when we'd just been fighting them!

'Depends by what you mean by foreigner, honey.'

'I think she means the name sounds – well, a bit *Italian*,' Vi supplied.

'Yes. Reckon it does, at that. But I didn't get here till it was all over, and I'd sure like to know what he gave for it.'

'Mike – I don't think – well, quite frankly, *I* wouldn't ask him,' Lucinda retorted primly. 'Mightn't it be better if you were to ask the auctioneer?'

'Vi.' Mike sighed. 'Will you ask my wife to stop pouting and come over with me and meet Benny Capaldi? And could you tell her, while you're about it, that he's a third-generation American and he fought on *our* side in the US Army Air Corps?'

'Did you hear that, queen?'

'I did, thanks. It would seem, Vi, that an American has bought Lady Mead.'

'Sure does. Come along over and say hullo.' Mike

791

linked his arm in hers and they walked towards the dark-haired, dark-eyed man who was speaking to the auctioneer's assistant.

'Hi there, Benny. Come and say hullo to my wife.'

'Hi, sir! Afternoon, Lady Lucinda. Nice to meet you.' He nodded, eyeing Lucinda gravely.

'So – *you* tell her,' Mike said.

'You mean she doesn't know?'

'Not only does she not know, but she thinks you're a foreigner, and that our lot were fighting your lot, not so very long ago!'

'*Mike!*' Lucinda's cheeks went very red, but the third-generation American with the Italian name threw back his head and laughed.

'You mean she doesn't know I was bidding for Farrow's?'

'I – er – didn't mention it, just in case you didn't get it. How much, by the way?'

'Well, that's it, you see. Had to go a bit higher . . .'

'How much higher, Benny?'

'Went up to five-fifty thousand. I had to, sir. Last thing Mrs Alice said to me was, "Now look here, Ben. See that boy doesn't come back without that house. Her ladyship's real fond of the old place and I want she should have it." What's a guy to do? I know you said half a million sterling, but put yourself in my shoes. What was I to do, will you tell me?'

You didn't cross Mrs Alice. You didn't give her back-chat, either. Benny Capaldi would rather have flown with a Zero on his tail than take on Alice Farrow.

'Not a lot, I guess. When the Brits gang up on us, there isn't an awful lot any of us can do.'

They had paid over the odds, Mike calculated, which really meant, he supposed, that he needn't feel so badly about accepting the Reynolds portrait. There were two sides to every question, after all.

He was smiling, now, and looking at Lucinda as if the sun shone out of her eyes, Vi thought. Real lovely it was, the way he looked at her.

'Mike, will you tell me – *please*.'

'Tell you?'

'That you've bought Lady Mead, because you have, haven't you? '

'Hey! Hold on, there! *Farrow's* has bought it, not me. And I'll tell you something else, Lucy. Lady Mead has got to start paying its way now – that right, Benny? Benny's our chief accountant, did I tell you?'

'Sure has to,' said the man who all at once had Lucinda Farrow's complete trust and affection.

'But *why*? Why should you – Farrow's – want this house?'

'Because Europe is going to be one heck of a big market before so very much longer: rebuilding, motorways – you name it, it'll all be happening. And Farrow's want their fair share of it, so Farrow's need headquarters – a head office, kind of, in Europe. One in Lincolnshire will do every bit as well as one in London or Lucerne or Lisbon.'

'Oh, Vi.' Lucinda laughed. 'Did you hear that? Did you? It's *ours*.'

'It belongs to the *firm*; to Mom and Dad and Alicia and me and Grandma Alice – though I guess a bit of it is yours, too.'

'Then can my bit be a couple of rooms in the south wing? Can it, Mike?'

'I thought we'd get around to that.' He was looking at her, Vi thought, as if she could have the whole house if she wanted it, and the sun and the moon and the stars thrown in. Just as Gerry would give them to her; just as he would plant her a rose bush – a whole field of rose bushes, if she asked him. 'As a matter of fact, Vi and I had a look at it again last night. Those four rooms could be made into a decent little apartment, I guess – and easily separated from the rest of the house.'

'So that's why you spent so much time poking around up there? And it's *five* rooms, darling. You forgot the attic.'

'Five, then – but the rest of the estate is business premises, okay? *Strictly* business, Lucy.'

'Of course. Y'know, I've just thought – we're all standing in my living room, aren't we? And the ante-room will make a nice little kitchen, and – '

'Vi, I've got business with Benny, here. Take my wife back to the Dower, will you? And before you even *ask* it, Lucy, the Dower is already spoken for!'

'I think, queen,' said Vi as they took back the news to Nanny Bainbridge, 'you ought to get your feet up as soon as we get back. You've got yourself far too excited and – '

'Vi! Dear, nice, bossy Vi – pipe down! And I am not spending a minute, not one single minute of this lovely day with my feet up, let alone an hour. And do hurry, there's an old love.'

When the auctioneer had gone, and the caterers, and all the visitors, and the men who had erected the marquee were busily taking it down, Lucinda and her husband walked in hand across the deer park, to stand for a while at the little gate at the end of the stableyard.

Eyes raised to his, eyes that loved him, wanted him, she traced the outline of his face with her fingertips, then laid them to his lips to be kissed.

'I love you, Mike Farrow,' she said huskily. 'Did you know there are nightingales in the wood behind Priest-house Cottage?'

'No, darling.' He kissed each fingertip. 'You never said.'

'I've only just remembered.' Her voice betrayed the need in her.

'Lucy Farrow.' He gathered her to him. 'Do you remember when *I* first wanted to make love to *you*?'

'Yes, I do. In the wild garden, behind Ardneavie House.'

'And do you remember that you said, "No, Mike! Not at half-past ten in the morning!"'

'I remember it. But you've got to admit I've come a long way since then,' she murmured, lips on his. 'Let's slip out tonight, Mike, and listen to the nightingales.'

'What if there aren't any?'

'It won't matter,' she said softly. 'It won't matter at all.'

Nothing had changed; but then, nothing ever changed in little out-of-the-way villages like Fenton Bishop. No spew of post-war houses in places where fields had been; just a general tidying-up. No more brown paper strips on windows; and gardens were planted with flowers again and the outsides of most of the cottages newly decorated, as if everyone had been waiting for paint to come back into the shops, then furiously covered over the drabness and neglect of war.

Nothing else had changed in Fenton Bishop, save that the Air Force had gone and the aerodrome was given back to farming again. Nothing else, except that coloured lights burned over the bar counter in the pub, visible through the window. And later tonight, there would be lights everywhere, shining from windows and through glass doors; people were still reluctant to draw curtains, especially after dusk. It was an unconscious act of defiance; a cockahoop V-sign to all the ARP wardens who had yelled '*Get that light out!*' for six years.

He wouldn't see the lights of Fenton Bishop. He'd be long gone by lighting-up time. The last bus to York was at eight o'clock and he must be on it.

The hands on the clock face at St Crispin's church pointed to twenty five minutes to seven. That, too, had been newly painted; bright gold numerals on shiny black.

He walked past the vicarage and two cottages with open front doors. In each garden a man was digging and each glanced up and nodded as he passed. Insular people, these Yorkshire folk. They didn't ever say much. Not two words where one would suffice. They would note, though, that he was a stranger and follow his progress past the policeman's house, their eyes on his back all the way past Tenacre Pasture, wondering what his business was in Yeomans Lane. Then they would resume their digging, because whatever it was, it was nothing to do with them.

He breathed deeply on the early-evening air as if he were breathing in words once spoken; words that drifted, still, on this September night.

The sky was still blue, the sun reluctant to start its setting, and on his right hand, apples hung ripe on the trees and late roses glowed pink in the hedge, the hedge of Dormer Cottage, where once she had lived. And he could see the windows that jutted from the high roof; the windows that gave the house its name.

It had to be tonight, this final goodbye, this parting of the ways. Now it was three years on; three years since they'd told him she wouldn't be on the train that was soon to pull into platform 8.

He hadn't believed them, the Naval policemen. He'd stood there at the barrier so that none should pass through it without his close scrutiny. And he had waited for the next Garvie Ferry train, and checked it too, before he picked up the phone and asked for the Ardneavie number, a little before five o'clock. Three years ago, that had been.

He climbed the stile into Tingle's Wood. Wild mallow bloomed there and cow parsley stirred in the breeze in a dance of white lace. The path through the wood was still well-trodden. Lovers still came here and held aside the low boughs of the trees to melt into the green-cool undergrowth.

He stopped at the high steel-mesh fence, surprised it should still be there. On either side of the runway, the stubble of summer's harvest waited for the plough, though the perimeter track was still there, growing weeds. Before long, it would be entirely grass-covered and no one would know exactly where it had been, except in a dry, hot summer when it would yellow quickly.

'Well, now, just look,' they would say. 'You can see where that old track used to be.' The track S-Sugar had lumbered round seventeen times before seventeen take-offs.

He pulled aside the wire-mesh fence – strange he should remember exactly where the break was – and squeezed through as she had done the night of that last op. Sitting on the grass, his back against a concrete post with rusting bolts, he lit a cigarette, wanting to light one for her, too.

Just three years, Jenny, since it happened. I couldn't believe you'd left me; couldn't believe they could take away a love like ours. Not after all we'd said; not after all the promises. So many of them made by so many lovers during those no-tomorrow years. All the sweet promises, made only to be broken.

She was beautiful, his Jenny; more beautiful still, that day at the old house in Lincolnshire. He'd only been there for a day and a night, so he found it hard to remember its name. But he remembered that she had called his name; remembered turning to see her standing there.

He had never seen her in uniform, come to think of it. Only in the photograph she had sent to Rhodesia and on the one her friends sent him later of the three of them together.

We keep in touch, Jenny. Your friends were kind, when it happened; sent my letters back and my wings and your spare set of collar studs in a little glass pot. I don't know why they sent the collar studs, but I'm glad they did.

I'll let them have my address, when I get there. I'm leaving, Jenny. That's why I'm here, to tell you, and to say goodbye. Going to Australia to try my luck there with a pilot from down under. Pooling our gratuities and all we've got besides; trying our hand at bush-flying.

I'll be sailing next week from Tilbury; might never be back . . .

He crushed out the cigarette in the grass. That was the trouble with a lot of them now, especially the single ones. They'd lived life dangerously and to the limit; lived on tightly drawn nerves and wild, relaxing parties. Civvy street had taken a bit of getting used to, and not being the glamour boys any longer; going back to offices and shops; to building sites and factory benches. 'Wouldn't join a Christmas Club after this lot,' they said. 'They've had me, next time.'

But they had missed flying and the life that had been ordered and orderly and chaotic and frightening.

It's getting better, Jenny. At first when I lost you there was this great tearing rage inside me, but the bitterness has gone and there is only sadness there – and wanting you, still.

It was going to be for ever, you and me, but it was only an interlude; the whole war was an interlude.

But I'll never forget you, my lovely girl. No matter what happens, I'll never forget . . .

He reached for another cigarette, placing it between his lips, watching the match burn down to his fingertips.

The aerodrome was dying slowly, now. A lot of the

prefabricated buildings had gone – easily dismantled and carted away. The big hangar was still there, doors wide open, and the control tower, its khaki and black and olive-green camouflage faded with a year of peace so that it blended in now, better than it had ever done.

No more taxi-ing round the perimeter track to take-off; no more waiting, dry-mouthed, for its green flashing light commanding *Go*! or the blessed red Very flare that aborted the whole damn show.

And no more meetings at the stile beneath the beech tree.

The church clock struck seven. He hadn't heard it before. Clocks weren't allowed to chime, then, nor church bells to ring. But there was no longer a war on and now this clock would chime away the hours and the days and the weeks and she would always be there, always young, always his. And if he ever came back here, she would be waiting.

We were almost there, Jenny. An earlier ferry, a later ferry, and we'd have made it . . .

He looked again at his watch, then rose to his feet. She wasn't coming and he had to go.

He pulled aside the steel-mesh fence and pushed through. The leaves were dark and dry now and ready to fall, the air sharp with a hint of autumn. There would be Michaelmas and Yuletide and Candlemas and Lammas; season by season and year by year, and still she wouldn't come.

He climbed the stile, hand on the beech tree, then walked up the lane, past the house she had lived in and the men, still digging. Past the pub, open now, and the vicarage.

He knew exactly where she was. He had stood there, apart and unseen, anger and grief tearing him in two. It was a kind little corner, bounded on two sides by a hawthorn hedge, red now with berries.

She was there with the two WAAFS, the two aircraft-women killed in the hit-and-run raid just a week after he'd come to Fenton Bishop.

There was a stone at her head now; the same simple grave-marker given to all servicemen and women the world over. Chiselled at the top was the crest of the Women's Royal Naval Service – an anchor and a crown entwined. And perched atop the anchor, a tiny bird with a tip-tilted tail. And beneath the crest, so that a stranger might know her:

JANE KENDAL WRNS

24.12.1923–30.5.1943.

DIED ON ACTIVE SERVICE

I have to go, Jenny. Goodbye, my lovely love. I won't forget you. I promise.

He turned then, and walked away from her. He did not look back.